PROMISE of BLOOD

THE POWDER MAGE TRILOGY:

BOOK I

BRIAN McCLELLAN

www.orbitbooks.net

ORBIT

First published in Great Britain in 2013 by Orbit
This paperback edition published in 2014 by Orbit

Maps by Isaac Stewart

A CIP catalogue record for this book
is available from the British Library.

ISBN 978-0-356-50200-7

Printed and bound in Great Britain by
Clays Ltd, St Ives plc

Papers used by Orbit are from well-managed forests
and other responsible sources.

Orbit
An imprint of
Little, Brown Book Group
100 Victoria Embankment
London EC4Y 0DY

An Hachette UK Company
www.hachette.co.uk

www.orbitbooks.net

By Brian McClellan

The Powder Mage trilogy

Promise of Blood

The Crimson Campaign

For Dad

For never being hesitant that I'd make it this far.

Even when you should have been.

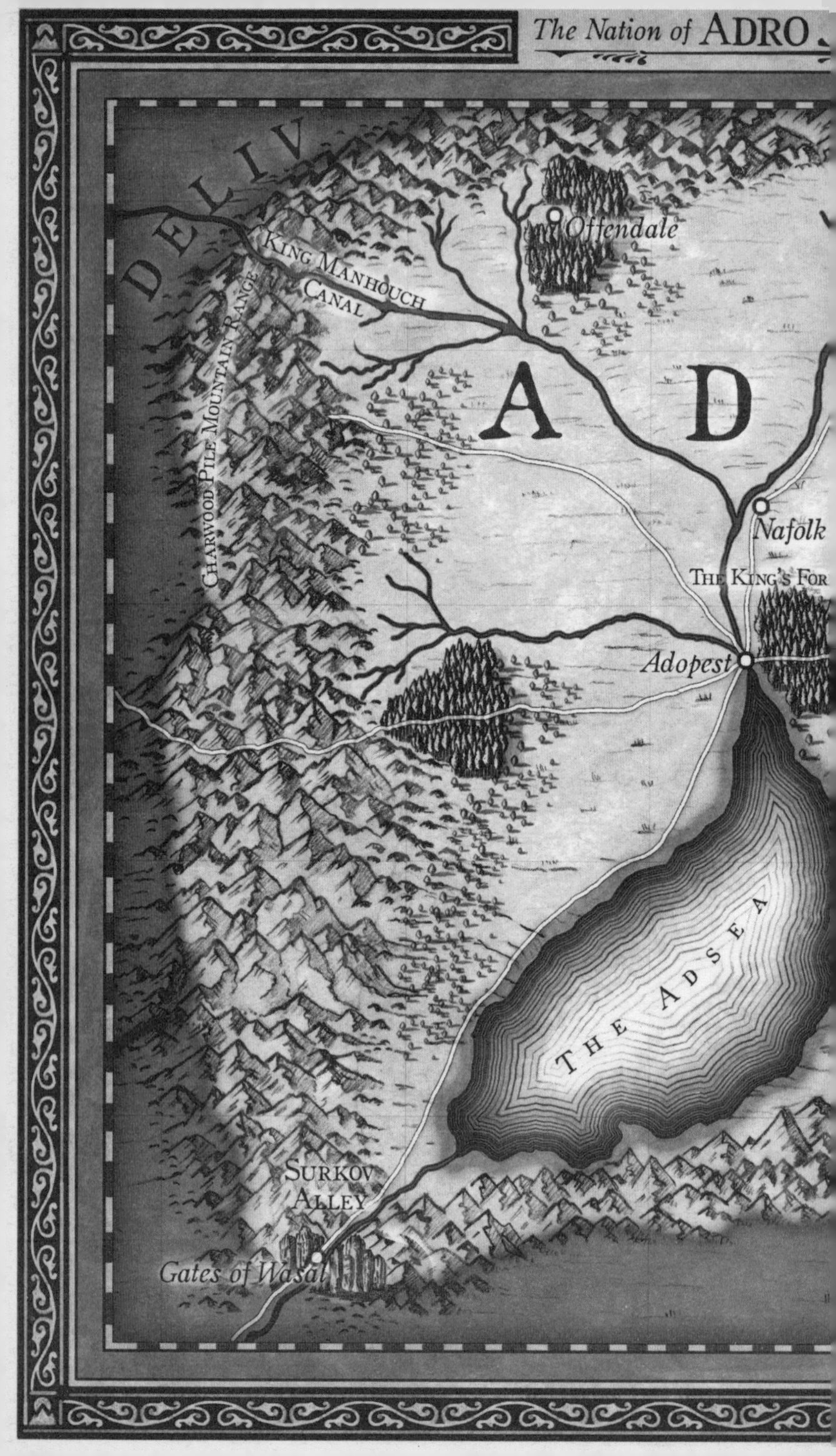
The Nation of ADRO
DELIV
King Manhouch Canal
Charwood Pile Mountain Range
Offendale
A D
Nafolk
The King's For
Adopest
The Adsea
Surkov Alley
Gates of Wasal

& Neighboring Countries
Kresim Kurga
Shouldercrown
South Pike
Mountain
Scale in Miles
0
50
100
2012

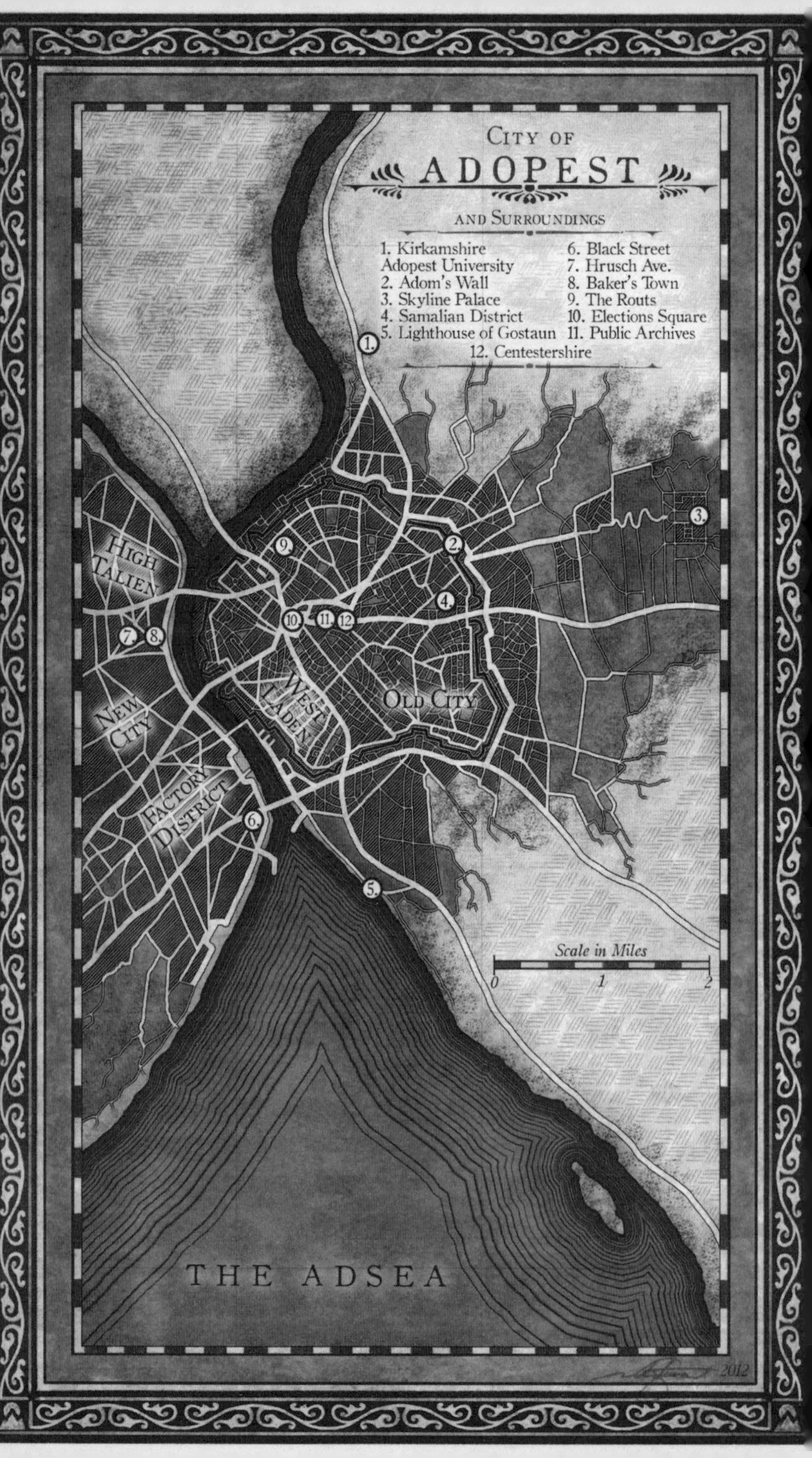
City of
Adopest
and Surroundings
1. Kirkamshire Adopest University
2. Adom's Wall
3. Skyline Palace
4. Samalian District
5. Lighthouse of Gostaun
6. Black Street
7. Hrusch Ave.
8. Baker's Town
9. The Routs
10. Elections Square
11. Public Archives
12. Centestershire
High Talien
New City
Factory District
West Laden
Old City
Scale in Miles
0
1
2
The Adsea
2012

SHOULDERCROWN FORTRESS
AND
THE KRESIM CALDERA
KRESIM CALDERA
Kresim Lake
KRESIM KURGA
Kresimir's Palace
Novi's Perch
Shouldercrown
Mopenhague
To Adopest
Scale in Miles
0
5
10
2012

CHAPTER 1

Adamat wore his coat tight, top buttons fastened against a wet night air that seemed to want to drown him. He tugged at his sleeves, trying to coax more length, and picked at the front of the jacket where it was too close by far around the waist. It'd been half a decade since he'd even seen this jacket, but when summons came from the king at this hour, there was no time to get his good one from the tailor. Yet this summer coat provided no defense against the chill snaking through the carriage window.

The morning was not far off but dawn would have a hard time scattering the fog. Adamat could feel it. It was humid even for early spring in Adopest, and chillier than Novi's frozen toes. The soothsayers in Noman's Alley said it was a bad omen. Yet who listened to soothsayers these days? Adamat reasoned it would give him a cold and wondered why he had been summoned out on a pit-made night like this.

The carriage approached the front gate of Skyline and moved on without a stop. Adamat clutched at his pantlegs and peered out the window. The guards were not at their posts. Odder still, as they continued along the wide path amid the fountains, there were no lights. Skyline had so many lanterns, it could be seen all the way from the city even on the cloudiest night. Tonight the gardens were dark.

Adamat was fine with this. Manhouch used enough of their taxes for his personal amusement. Adamat stared out into the gardens at the black maws where the hedge mazes began and imagined shapes flitting back and forth in the lawn. What was…ah, just a sculpture. Adamat sat back, took a deep breath. He could hear his heart beating, thumping, frightened, his stomach tightening. Perhaps they *should* light the garden lanterns…

A little part of him, the part that had once been a police inspector, prowling nights such as these for the thieves and pickpockets in dark alleys, laughed out from inside. *Still your heart, old man*, he said to himself. *You were once the eyes staring back from the darkness.*

The carriage jerked to a stop. Adamat waited for the coachman to open the door. He might have waited all night. The driver rapped on the roof. "You're here," a gruff voice said.

Rude.

Adamat stepped from the coach, just having time to snatch his hat and cane before the driver flicked the reins and was off, clattering into the night. Adamat uttered a quiet curse after the man and turned around, looking up at Skyline.

The nobility called Skyline Palace "the Jewel of Adro." It rested on a high hill east of Adopest so that the sun rose above it every morning. One particularly bold newspaper had compared it to a starving pauper wearing a diamond ring. It was an apt comparison in these lean times. A king's pride doesn't fill the people's bellies.

He was at the main entrance. By day, it was a grand avenue of marbled walks and fountains, all leading to a pair of giant, silver-plated doors, themselves dwarfed by the sheer façade of the biggest single building in Adro. Adamat listened for the soft footfalls of patrolling Hielmen. It was said the king's personal guard were everywhere in these gardens, watching every secluded corner, muskets always loaded, bayonets fixed, their gray-and-white sashes somber among the green-and-gold splendor. But there were no footfalls, nor were the fountains running. He'd heard once that the fountains only stopped for the death of the king. Surely he'd not have been summoned here if Manhouch were dead. He smoothed the front of his jacket. Here, next to the building, a few of the lanterns were lit.

A figure emerged from the darkness. Adamat tightened his grip on his cane, ready to draw the hidden sword inside at a moment's notice.

It was a man in uniform, but little could be discerned in such ill light. He held a rifle or a musket, trained loosely on Adamat, and wore a flat-topped forage cap with a stiff visor. Only one thing could be certain... he was not a Hielman. Their tall, plumed hats were easy to recognize, and they never went without them.

"You're alone?" a voice asked.

"Yes," Adamat said. He held up both hands and turned around.

"All right. Come on."

The soldier edged forward and yanked on one of the mighty silver doors. It rolled outward slowly, ponderously, despite the man putting his weight into it. Adamat moved closer and examined the soldier's jacket. It was dark blue with silver braiding. Adran military. In theory, the military reported to the king. In practice, one man held their leash: Field Marshal Tamas.

"Step back, friend," the soldier said. There was a note of impatience in his voice, some unseen stress—but that could have been the weight of the door. Adamat did as he was told, only coming forward again to slip through the entrance when the soldier gestured.

"Go ahead," the soldier directed. "Take a right at the diadem and head through the Diamond Hall. Keep walking until you find yourself in the Answering Room." The door inched shut behind him and closed with a muffled thump.

Adamat was alone in the palace vestibule. Adran military, he mused. Why would a soldier be here, on the grounds, without any sign of the Hielmen? The most frightening answer sprang to mind first. A power struggle. Had the military been called in to deal with a rebellion? There were a number of powerful factions within Adro: the Wings of Adom mercenaries, the royal cabal, the Mountainwatch, and the great noble families. Any one of them could have been giving Manhouch trouble. None of it made sense, though. If there had been a power struggle, the palace grounds would be a battlefield, or destroyed outright by the royal cabal.

Adamat passed the diadem—a giant facsimile of the Adran crown—and noted it was in as bad taste as rumor had it. He entered the Diamond Hall, where the walls and floor were of scarlet, accented in gold leaf, and thousands of tiny gems, which gave the room its name, glittered from the ceiling in the light of a single lit candelabra. The tiny flames of the candelabra flickered as if in the wind, and the room was cold.

Adamat's sense of unease deepened as he neared the far end of the gallery. Not a sign of life, and the only sound came from his own echoing footfalls on the marble floor. A window had been shattered, explaining the chill. The result of one of the king's famous temper tantrums? Or something else? He could hear his heart beating in his ears. There. Behind a curtain, a pair of boots? Adamat passed his hand before his eyes. A trick of the light. He stepped over to reassure himself and pulled back the curtain.

A body lay in the shadows. Adamat bent over it, touched the skin. It was warm, but the man was most certainly dead. He wore gray pants with a white stripe down the side and a matching jacket.

A tall hat with a white plume lay on the floor some ways away. A Hielman. The shadows played on a young, clean-shaven face, peaceful except for a single hole in the side of his skull and the dark, wet stain on the floor.

He'd been right. A struggle of some kind. Had the Hielmen rebelled, and the military been brought in to deal with them? Again, it didn't make any sense. The Hielmen were fanatically loyal to the king, and any matters within Skyline Palace would have been dealt with by the royal cabal.

Adamat cursed silently. Every question compounded itself. He suspected he'd find some answers soon enough.

Adamat left the body behind the curtain. He lifted his cane and twisted, bared a few inches of steel, and approached a tall doorway flanked by two hooded, scepter-wielding sculptures. He paused between the ancient statues and took a deep breath, letting his eyes wander over a set of arcane script scrawled into the portal. He entered.

The Answering Room made the Hall of Diamonds look small. A pair of staircases, one to either side of him and each as wide across as three coaches, led to a high gallery that ran the length of the room on both sides. Few outside the king and his cabal of Privileged sorcerers ever entered this room.

In the center of the room was a single chair, on a dais a handbreadth off the floor, facing a collection of knee pillows, where the cabal acknowledged their liege. The room was well lit, though from no discernible source of light.

A man sat on the stairs to Adamat's right. He was older than Adamat, just into his sixtieth year with silver hair and a neatly trimmed mustache that still retained a hint of black. He had a strong but not overly large jaw and his cheekbones were well defined. His skin was darkened by the sun, and there were deep lines at the corners of his mouth and eyes. He wore a dark-blue soldier's uniform with a silver representation of a powder keg pinned above the heart and nine gold service stripes sewn on the right breast, one for every five years in the Adran military. His uniform lacked an officer's epaulettes, but the weary experience in the man's brown eyes left no question that he'd led armies on the battlefield. There was a single pistol, hammer cocked, on the stair next to him. He leaned on a sheathed small sword and watched as a stream of blood slowly trickled down each step, a dark line on the yellow-and-white marble.

"Field Marshal Tamas," Adamat said. He sheathed his cane sword and twisted until it clicked shut.

The man looked up. "I don't believe we've ever met."

"We have," Adamat said. "Fourteen years ago. A charity ball thrown by Lord Aumen."

"I have a terrible time with faces," the field marshal said. "I apologize."

Adamat couldn't take his eyes off the rivulet of blood. "Sir. I was summoned here. I wasn't told by whom, or for what reason."

"Yes," Tamas said. "I summoned you. On the recommendation of one of my Marked. Cenka. He said you served together on the police force in the twelfth district."

Adamat pictured Cenka in his mind. He was a short man with an unruly beard and a penchant for wines and fine food. He'd seen him last seven years ago. "I didn't know he was a powder mage."

"We try to find anyone with an affinity for it as soon as possible," Tamas said, "but Cenka was a late bloomer. In any case"—he waved a hand—"we've come upon a problem."

Adamat blinked. "You... want my help?"

The field marshal raised an eyebrow. "Is that such an unusual request? You were once a fine police investigator, a good servant of Adro, and Cenka tells me that you have a perfect memory."

"Still, sir."

"Eh?"

"I'm still an investigator. Not with the police, sir, but I still take jobs."

"Excellent. Then it's not so odd for me to seek your services?"

"Well, no," Adamat said, "but sir, this is Skyline Palace. There's a dead Hielman in the Diamond Hall and..." He pointed at the stream of blood on the stairs. "Where's the king?"

Tamas tilted his head to the side. "He's locked himself in the chapel."

"You've staged a coup," Adamat said. He caught a glimpse of movement with the corner of his eye, saw a soldier appear at the top of the stairs. The man was a Deliv, a dark-skinned northerner. He wore the same uniform as Tamas, with eight golden stripes on the right breast. The left breast of his uniform displayed a silver powder keg, the sign of a Marked. Another powder mage.

"We have a lot of bodies to move," the Deliv said.

Tamas gave his subordinate a glance. "I know, Sabon."

"Who's this?" Sabon asked.

"The inspector that Cenka requested."

"I don't like him being here," Sabon said. "It could compromise everything."

"Cenka trusted him."

"You've staged a coup," Adamat said again with certainty.

"I'll help with the bodies in a moment," Tamas said. "I'm old, I need some rest now and then." The Deliv gave a sharp nod and disappeared.

"Sir!" Adamat said. "What have you done?" He tightened his grip on his cane sword.

Tamas pursed his lips. "Some say the Adran royal cabal had the most powerful Privileged sorcerers in all the Nine Nations, second only to Kez," he said quietly. "Yet I've just slaughtered every one of them. Do you think I'd have trouble with an old inspector and his cane sword?"

Adamat loosened his grip. He felt ill. "I suppose not."

"Cenka led me to believe that you were pragmatic. If that is the case, I would like to employ your services. If not, I'll kill you now and look for a solution elsewhere."

"You've staged a coup," Adamat said again.

Tamas sighed. "Must we keep coming back to that? Is it so shocking? Tell me, can you think of any fewer than a dozen factions within Adro with reason to dethrone the king?"

"I didn't think any of them had the skill," Adamat said. "Or the daring." His eyes returned to the blood on the stairs, before his mind traveled to his wife and children, asleep in their beds. He looked at the field marshal. His hair was tousled; there were drops of blood on his jacket—a lot, now that he thought to look. Tamas might as well have been sprayed with it. There were dark circles under his eyes and a weariness that spoke of more than just age.

"I will not agree to a job blindly," Adamat said. "Tell me what you want."

"We killed them in their sleep," Tamas said without preamble. "There's no easy way to kill a Privileged, but that's the best. A mistake was made and we had a fight on our hands." Tamas looked pained for a moment, and Adamat suspected that the fight had not gone as well as Tamas would have liked. "We prevailed. Yet upon the lips of the dying was one phrase."

Adamat waited.

" 'You can't break Kresimir's Promise,' " Tamas said. "That's what the dying sorcerers said to me. Does it mean anything to you?"

Adamat smoothed the front of his coat and sought to recall old memories. "No. 'Kresimir's Promise'... 'Break'... 'Broken'... Wait—'Kresimir's Broken Promise.' " He looked up. "It was the name of a street gang. Twenty... twenty-two years ago. Cenka couldn't remember that?"

Tamas continued. "Cenka thought it sounded familiar. He was certain you'd remember it."

"I don't forget things," Adamat said. "Kresimir's Broken Promise was a street gang with forty-three members. They were all young, some of them no more than children, the oldest not yet twenty. We were trying to round up some of the leaders to put a stop to a string of thefts. They were an odd lot—they broke into churches and robbed priests."

"What happened to them?"

Adamat couldn't help but look at the blood on the stairs. "One day they disappeared, every one of them—including our informants. We found the whole lot a few days later, forty-three bodies jammed into a drain culvert like pickled pigs' feet. They'd been massacred by powerful sorceries, with excessive brutality. The marks of the king's royal cabal. The investigation ended there." Adamat suppressed a shiver. He'd not once seen a thing like that, not before or since. He'd witnessed executions and riots and murder scenes that filled him with less dread.

The Deliv soldier appeared again at the top of the stairs. "We need you," he said to Tamas.

"Find out why these mages would utter those words with their final breath," Tamas said. "It may be connected to your street gang. Maybe not. Either way, find me an answer. I don't like the riddles of the dead." He got to his feet quickly, moving like a man twenty years younger, and jogged up the stairs after the Deliv. His boot splashed in the blood, leaving behind red prints. "Also," he called over his shoulder, "keep silent about what you have seen here until the execution. It will begin at noon."

"But..." Adamat said. "Where do I start? Can I speak with Cenka?"

Tamas paused near the top of the stairs and turned. "If you can speak with the dead, you're welcome to."

Adamat ground his teeth. "How did they say the words?" he said. "Was it a command, or a statement, or...?"

Tamas frowned. "An entreaty. As if the blood draining from their bodies was not their primary concern. I must go now."

"One more thing," Adamat said.

Tamas looked to be near the end of his patience.

"If I'm to help you, tell me why all of this?" He gestured to the blood on the stairs.

"I have things that require my attention," Tamas warned.

Adamat felt his jaw tighten. "Did you do this for power?"

"I did this for me," Tamas said. "And I did this for Adro. So that Manhouch wouldn't sign us all into slavery to the Kez with the Accords. I did it because those grumbling students of philosophy at the university only play at rebellion. The age of kings is dead, Adamat, and I have killed it."

Adamat examined Tamas's face. The Accords was a treaty to be signed with the king of Kez that would absolve all Adran debt but impose strict tax and regulation on Adro, making it little more than a Kez vassal. The field marshal had been outspoken about the Accords. But then, that was expected. The Kez had executed Tamas's late wife.

"It is," Adamat said.

"Then get me some bloody answers." The field marshal whirled and disappeared into the hallway above.

Adamat remembered the bodies of that street gang as they were being pulled from the drain in the wet and mud, remembered the horror etched upon their dead faces. *The answers may very well be bloody.*

CHAPTER

2

"Lajos is dying," Sabon said.

Tamas entered the apartments of the Privileged who'd been Zakary the Beadle. He swept through the salon and entered the bedchamber—a room bigger than most merchants' houses. The walls were indigo and covered with colorful paintings that displayed various Beadles in the history of Adro's royal cabal. Doors led off to auxiliary rooms, such as the privy and Beadle's kitchens. The door to the Beadle's private brothel had been ripped apart, splinters no bigger than a finger scattered across the room.

The Beadle's bed had been stripped of sheets, the Beadle's body tossed aside for a wounded powder mage.

"How do you feel?" Tamas said.

Lajos managed a weak cough. Marked were tougher than most, and with the gunpowder Lajos had ingested, now coursing through his blood, he would feel little pain. It was little consolation as Tamas gazed on his friend. Half of Lajos's right arm was gone—lengthwise—and a hole the size of a melon had been torn through his abdomen. It was a miracle he'd lived this long. They'd given him half a horn's worth of powder. That alone should have killed him.

"I've felt better," Lajos said. He coughed again, blood leaking from the corner of his mouth.

Tamas drew his handkerchief and dabbed the blood away. "It won't be much longer," he said.

"I know," Lajos said.

Tamas squeezed his friend's hand.

Lajos mouthed the words, "Thank you."

Tamas took a deep breath. It was suddenly hard to see. He blinked his eyes clear. Lajos's breathing came to a rasping stop. Tamas made to pull his hand away when Lajos gripped it suddenly. Lajos's eyes opened.

"It's all right, my friend," Lajos said. "You've done what needed to be done. Have peace." His eyes focused elsewhere and then stilled. He was dead.

Tamas closed his friend's eyes with the tips of his fingers and turned to Sabon. The Deliv stood on the other side of the room, examining what was left of the door to the harem where it hung on the frame by one hinge. Tamas joined him and looked inside. The women had been corralled away an hour ago by his soldiers, taken to some other part of the palace with the rest of the Privilegeds' whores.

"The fury of a woman," Sabon murmured.

"Indeed," Tamas said.

"There's no way we could have planned for this."

"Tell that to them," Tamas said. He jerked his head at the row of four bodies on the floor, and the fifth that would soon be joining them. Five powder mages. Five friends. All because of one Privileged that had been unaccounted for. Tamas had just put a bullet in the Beadle's head—a man who he'd shaken hands with and spoken to on a regular basis. Tamas's Marked stood around him, ready in case the old man had some fight in him. They were not ready for the other Privileged, the one hiding in the brothel. She'd sliced through that door like a guillotine blade through a melon, Privileged's gloves on her hands, fingers dancing as her sorcery tore Tamas's powder mages to shreds.

A powder mage could float a bullet over a mile and hit the bull's-eye every time. He could angle a bullet around corners with the power of his mind, and ingest black powder to make himself stronger and faster than other men. But he could do little to contest Privileged sorcery at close range.

Tamas, Sabon, and Lajos had been the only men with time to react, and they'd barely fought her off. She'd fled, echoes of sorcerous destruction following her through the palace as she went—probably nothing more than a show to keep them from following. Her parting shot had been Lajos's mortal wound, but it had been randomly flung. It very well could have been Sabon, or even Tamas himself, who'd died there on the bed a moment ago. The thought chilled Tamas's blood.

Tamas looked away from the door. "We'll have to follow her. Find her and kill her. She's dangerous on the loose."

"A job for the magebreaker?" Sabon said. "I wondered why you've kept him around."

"A contingency I didn't want to use," Tamas said. "I wish I had a mage to send with him."

"His partner is a Privileged," Sabon said. "A magebreaker and a Privileged should be more than a match for a single cabal Privileged." He gestured at the wrecked door.

"I don't like to fight fair when it comes to the royal cabal," Tamas said. "And remember, there's a difference between a member of the royal cabal and a hired thug."

"Who was she?" Sabon asked. There was a note in his voice, perhaps reproach.

"I have no idea," Tamas snapped. "I knew every one of the king's cabal. I've met them, dined with them. She was a stranger."

Sabon took Tamas's anger without comment. "A spy for another cabal?"

"Not likely. The brothel girls are all checked. She didn't look like a whore. She was strong, weathered. The Beadle's lover, maybe. I've never seen her before in my life."

"Could the Beadle have been training someone in secret?"

"Apprentices are never secret," Tamas said. "Privileged are too suspicious to allow that."

"Their suspicions are often well founded," Sabon said. "There has to be a reason for her presence."

"I know. We'll deal with her in good time."

"If the others had been here..." Sabon said.

"More of us would be dead," Tamas said. He counted the bodies again, as if there might be fewer this time. Five. Out of seventeen of his mages. "We split into two groups for precisely this reason." He turned away from the bodies. "Any word from Taniel?"

"He's in the city," Sabon said.

"Perfect. I'll send him with the magebreaker."

"Are you sure?" Sabon said. "He just got back from Fatrasta. He needs time to rest, to see his fiancée..."

"Is Vlora with him?"

Sabon shrugged.

"Let's hope she gets here soon. Our work is not yet done." He raised a hand to forestall protests. "And Taniel can rest when the coup's over."

"What must be done will be done," Sabon said quietly.

They both fell silent, regarding their fallen comrades. Moments passed before Tamas saw a smile spread on Sabon's wrinkled black face. The Deliv was tired and haggard, but with a hint of restrained joy. "We succeeded."

Tamas eyed the bodies of his friends—his soldiers—again. "Yes," he said. "We did." He forced himself to look away.

A painting stood in the corner, a monstrosity with a gilded frame on a silver tripod befitting a herald of the royal cabal. Tamas studied the painting briefly. It showed Zakary in his prime as a strong young man with broad shoulders and a stern frown.

A far cry from the old, bent body in the corner. The bullet had entered his brain in such a way as to kill him instantly, yet his lifeless throat had gasped the same words as the others: "You can't break Kresimir's Promise."

Cenka was white as a mummer's painted face after the first of the Privileged cried out as they died. He'd demanded that Tamas summon Adamat here, to the heart of their crime. Tamas hoped that Cenka was wrong. He hoped that the investigator found nothing.

Tamas left the cabal's wing of the palace, Sabon following close behind.

"I'll need a new bodyguard," Tamas said as they walked. It pained him to speak of it, with Lajos's body still cooling.

"A Marked?" Sabon asked.

"I can't spare one. Not now."

"I've had my eye on a Knacked," Sabon said. "A man named Olem."

"He's a soldier?" Tamas asked. He thought he knew the name. He held his hand just slightly below his eyes. "About this tall? Sandy hair?"

"Yes."

"What's his Knack?"

"He doesn't need sleep. Ever."

"That's useful," Tamas said.

"Quite. He has a strong third eye as well, so he can watch for Privileged. I'll have him briefed and by your side for the execution."

A Knacked wouldn't be as useful as a powder mage. Knacked were more common, and their abilities were more like a talent than a sorcerous power. But if he could use his third eye to see sorcery, he would be of some benefit.

Tamas approached the barred doors of the chapel. A pair of Tamas's soldiers emerged from the shadows by the wall, muskets at the ready. Tamas nodded to them and gestured at the door.

One of the soldiers removed a long knife from his belt and slid it between the doors to the chapels. "He flipped the Diocel's latch," said the soldier fiddling with the knife, "but he didn't even bother to stack anything in front of the door. Not very enterprising, if you ask me." He flipped up the lock and he and his companion pushed the doors open.

The chapel was large, as were all the rooms in the palace. Unlike the rest of the palace, however, it had been spared the seasonal remodeling customary of the king's whims and remained close to what it must have looked like two hundred years ago. The ceiling was vaulted impossibly high, with boxes for the royalty and high nobles set about halfway up the walls in between columns as wide across as an oxcart. The floor was tiled in marble designed in intricate mosaics of various shapes and sizes, while the ceiling contained paneled depictions of the saints as they founded the Nine Nations under the god Kresimir's fatherly gaze.

Two altars sat at the front of the chapel, raised slightly above the benches, next to a pulpit of blackwood. The first altar, smaller, closer to the people, was dedicated to Adro's founding saint, Adom. The second, larger altar, sided by marble and covered with satin, was dedicated to Kresimir. Beside this altar huddled Manhouch XII, sovereign of Adro, and his wife Natalija, Duchess of Tarony. Natalija stared behind and above the altar, her lips moving in silent prayer to Kresimir's Rope. Manhouch was pale, his eyes red, lips drawn to a thin line. He spoke in a desperate whisper to the Diocel. He stopped as Tamas approached.

"Wait," the Diocel called, one hand rising as the king jogged down the steps from the altar and stormed toward Tamas with purpose. The Diocel's old face was fraught, his robes wrinkled from a hasty rush to the chapel.

Tamas watched Manhouch march toward him. He noted the one hand held behind his back, the fury of emotions playing across Manhouch's aristocratic young face. Manhouch looked barely seventeen thanks to the high sorceries of his royal cabal, though in reality he was well into his thirties. It was supposed to reflect the monarchy's agelessness, but Tamas had always found it hard to take such a young-looking man seriously. Tamas stopped and regarded the king, watched him falter before coming closer.

Five paces away, Manhouch revealed his pistol. It came up swiftly. His aim was sure at that range—after all, Tamas himself had taught the king to shoot. It was an unfortunate reflection on his detachment from the world, however, that Manhouch attempted it at all. He pulled the trigger.

Tamas reached out mentally and absorbed the power of the powder blast. He felt the energy course through him, warming his body like a sip of fine spirits. He redirected the power of the blast harmlessly into the floor, cracking a marble tile beneath the king. Manhouch danced away from the cracked tile. The ball rolled from the barrel of his pistol and clattered to the ground, stopping by Tamas's feet.

Tamas stepped forward, taking the pistol from the king by the barrel. He barely felt it burn his hand.

"How dare you," Manhouch said. His face was powdered, his cheeks blushed. His silk bedclothes were rumpled, soaked with sweat. "We trusted you to protect us." He trembled slightly.

Tamas looked past Manhouch to the Diocel still beside the altar. The old priest leaned against the wall, his tall, embroidered hat of office balanced precariously on his head. "I suppose," Tamas said, shaking the pistol, "he got this from you?"

"It wasn't meant for that," the Diocel wheezed. He stuck his chin up. "It was meant for the king. So he can take his life honorably and not be struck down by a godless traitor."

Tamas sent forth his senses, looking for more powder charges, but there were none. "You only brought one pistol, with one bullet," Tamas said. "It would have been kinder to bring two." He glanced at the queen, still directing her prayers toward Kresimir's Rope.

"You wouldn't..." the Diocel said.

"He won't!" Manhouch spoke over him. "He won't kill us. He can't. We are God's chosen." He took a deep, shaky breath.

Tamas felt a ripple of pity for the king. He knew Manhouch was older than he looked, but in reality he was nothing more than a child. It wasn't all his fault. Greedy councillors, idiot tutors, indulgent sorcerers. There were any number of reasons he'd been a bad—no, terrible—king. He was, however, king. Tamas squashed the pity. Manhouch would face the consequences.

"Manhouch the Twelfth," Tamas said, "you are under arrest for the utmost neglect of your people. You will be tried for treason, fraud, and murder through starvation."

"A trial?" Manhouch whispered.

"Your trial is now," Tamas said. "I am your judge and jury. You have been found guilty before the people and before Kresimir."

"Don't pretend to speak in God's name!" the Diocel said. "Manhouch is our king! Sanctioned by Kresimir!"

Tamas laughed mirthlessly. "You're quick enough to invoke Kresimir when it suits you. Is he on your mind when you've got a concubine wrapped in your silk sheets or when you eat a meal of delicacies that would have fed fifty peasants? Your place is not at the right hand of God, Diocel. The Church has sanctioned this coup."

The Diocel's eyes grew large. "I would have known."

"Do the arch-diocels tell you everything? I thought not."

Manhouch gathered his strength and matched Tamas's gaze. "You have no evidence! No witnesses! This is not a trial."

Tamas flung his hand out to the side. "My evidence is out there! The people are unemployed and starving. Your nobles whore and hunt and fill their plates with meat and their glasses with wine while the common man starves in the gutter. Witnesses? You plan on signing the entire country over to the Kez next week with the Accords. You would make us all vassals to a foreign power simply to dissolve your debt."

"Baseless claims, spoken by a traitor," Manhouch whispered weakly.

Tamas shook his head. "You will be executed at noon along with your councillors, your queen, and many hundreds of your relatives."

"My cabal will destroy you!"

"They've already been executed."

The king paled further and began to shake violently, collapsing to the floor. The Diocel slowly made his way forward. Tamas looked down on Manhouch for a moment and pushed aside the unbidden image of a young prince, perhaps six or seven, bouncing on his knee.

The Diocel reached Manhouch's side and knelt. He looked up at Tamas. "Is this because of your wife?"

Yes. Tamas said aloud, "No. It's because Manhouch has proved that the lives of an entire nation shouldn't be subject to the whims of a single inbred fool."

"You would dethrone a God-sanctioned ruler and become a tyrant, and still claim to love Adro?" the Diocel said.

Tamas glanced at Manhouch. "God no longer sanctions this. If you weren't so blinded by your gold-lined robes and young concubines, you'd see it is so. Manhouch deserves the pit for his neglect of Adro."

"You'll surely see him there," the Diocel said.

"I don't doubt it, Diocel. I'm sure the company will be anything but dull." Tamas dropped the empty pistol at Manhouch's feet. "You have until noon to make your peace with God."

CHAPTER

3

Taniel paused on the top step of the House of Nobles. The building was dark and silent as a graveyard this hour of the morning. There were soldiers stationed at intervals on the steps, at the street, and at every door. He recognized Field Marshal Tamas's men in their dark-blue jackets. Many of them knew him by sight. Those who didn't saw the silver powder keg pinned to his buckskin jacket. One of them raised a hand in greeting. Taniel returned the gesture and then produced a snuffbox and sprinkled a line of black powder on the back of his hand. He snorted it.

The powder made him feel vibrant, animated. It sharpened his senses and his mind. It made his heart beat faster and soothed frayed nerves. For a Marked, powder was life.

Taniel felt a tap on his shoulder and turned. His companion stood a full head shorter than he, and her body was as slight as a youth's. She wore a full-length travel duster that filled her out only a little and kept her warm, and a wide-brimmed hat that concealed most of her features. An early spring chill filled the air, and Ka-poel came from a much warmer place than this.

She pointed up at the building above them quizzically, revealing a small, freckled hand. Taniel had to remind himself that she'd never seen a building like the House of Nobles. Six stories high and as wide as a battlefield, the center of the Adran government was big enough to house the offices of every noble and their staff.

"We're here." Taniel's voice seemed unusually stark in the quiet of the early hour. "This is where his soldiers said to go. He doesn't have an office here. Did it happen tonight? I could have picked a better time..." He trailed off.

He was prattling on to a mute, betraying his nervousness. Tamas would be livid when he heard about Vlora. Of course, it would be Taniel's fault. Taniel noticed he still held the snuffbox. His hands were trembling. He tapped out another dark line on the back of his thumb. He snorted the powder and tilted his head back as his heart pumped faster. Lines in the darkness grew sharper, sounds louder, and he sighed at the comfort the powder trance gave him. He held up a hand to the light of the streetlamp. It no longer shook.

"Pole," he said, addressing the girl. "I haven't seen Tamas in some time. He's a hard man to all but a close few. Sabon. Lajos. Those are his friends. I am just another soldier." Green eyes regarded him from beneath the wide-brimmed hat. "Understand?" he said.

Ka-poel nodded briefly.

"Here," Taniel said. He reached into the front of his jacket and removed his sketchbook. It was a worn book, ragged from use and travels, bound in faded calfskin. He flipped through the pages until he found a likeness of Field Marshal Tamas and handed it to Ka-poel. The sketch was in charcoal and smudged from wear, but the field marshal's severe face was hard to mistake. Ka-poel studied the drawing for a moment before handing the book back.

Taniel pushed open one of the giant doors and headed into the grand hall. The place was pitch-black but for one pool of light near a staircase to Taniel's left. A single lantern hung on the wall, and beneath it dozed a weary form in a servant's chair.

"I see Tamas has moved up in the world."

Taniel listened to his own voice echo in the grand hall and was satisfied to see Sabon jump from his chair. Lines stood out on Sabon's dark face, details Taniel could only see because of the powder trance. Sabon looked to have aged ten years in the mere two it had been since they'd last met.

"I don't like it," Taniel added, swinging his rifle and knapsack from his shoulder and onto the plush red carpet. He bent to rub feeling into his legs after twenty hours in a coach. "Too cold in the winter, too lonely in the summer. And space like this just invites houseguests."

Sabon chuckled as he came over. He clasped Taniel's hand and pulled him into an embrace. "How is Fatrasta?"

"Officially? Still at war with the Kez," Taniel said. "Unofficially, the Kez have sued for peace and all but a few regiments have returned to the Nine. Fatrasta has won their independence."

"You kill a Kez Privileged or two for me?" Sabon said.

Taniel lifted his rifle to the light. Sabon ran his finger along the row of notches in the stock and whistled appreciatively. "Even a few Wardens," Taniel said.

"Those are hard to kill," Sabon said.

Taniel nodded. "Took more than one bullet for the Wardens."

"Taniel Two-Shot," Sabon said. "You've been the talk of the Nine for a year. The royal cabal has been scared stiff. Wanted Manhouch to recall you. Marked killing Privileged, even Kez Privileged, is a bad precedent."

"Too late, I assume?" Taniel said, glancing around the dark grand hall. Else he wouldn't be here. If all went as planned, Tamas had slaughtered the royal cabal and captured Manhouch.

"It was done a few hours ago," Sabon said.

Taniel thought he saw a hardness to the old soldier's eyes. "Things didn't go well?"

"We lost five men." Sabon rattled off a list of names.

"May they rest with Kresimir." Even as he said it, the prayer sounded hollow in Taniel's ears. He winced. "And Tamas?"

Sabon sighed. "He is...tired. Toppling Manhouch is only the first step. We still have the execution, a new government to establish, the Kez to deal with, starvation, the poor. The list goes on."

"Does he foresee problems with the people?"

"Tamas foresees just about everything. There will be royalists. It would be stupid to think there won't, in a city of a million people. We just don't know how many or how organized they'll be. Tamas needs you; you and Vlora both. She didn't come with you?" Taniel glanced toward Ka-poel. She was the only other person in the hall. She'd left Taniel's gear in a pile on the floor and was making a slow round of the place, gazing up at paintings that could barely be seen in the dim light. Her rucksack was slung over one shoulder.

Taniel felt his jaw clench. "No."

Sabon drifted a step back and jerked his head toward Ka-poel.

"My servant," Taniel said. "A Dynize."

"A savage, eh?" Sabon mused. "Did the Dynize Empire finally open their borders? That's big news."

"No," Taniel said. "Some of the Dynize tribes live in western Fatrasta."

"Doesn't look more than a boy."

"Careful who you call a boy," Taniel said. "She can be a bit prickly about that."

"A girl, then," Sabon said, giving Taniel a wry glance. "Can she be trusted?"

"I've saved her life more times than she has mine," Taniel said. "Savages take that sort of thing very seriously."

"Not so savage," Sabon murmured. "Tamas will want to know why Vlora's not here."

"Let me handle that." Tamas would ask about Vlora before he even asked about Fatrasta. Taniel knew he'd be a fool to imagine two years would have changed much. Two years. Pit. Had it been that long? Two years ago Taniel had gone abroad for what would have been a short tour of the Kez colony of Fatrasta. Time to "cool his head," Tamas had said. Taniel arrived a week before they declared their independence from Kez and he'd been forced to pick sides.

Sabon gave a curt nod. "I'll take you to him, then."

Sabon lifted the lantern from its hook while Taniel gathered his things. Ka-poel drifted a few steps behind them as they traveled the dark corridors. The House of Nobles was eerie and huge. Thick carpet muffled their footsteps, so they trod almost like ghosts. Taniel didn't like the silence. It reminded him too much of the forest when there were enemies on the prowl. They rounded a corner, and there was light coming from a room at the end of the hallway. Voices, too, and they were raised in anger.

Taniel paused in the doorway of a well-lit sitting room—the antechamber of some noble's office. Inside, two men faced each other before an overlarge fireplace. They stood not a foot apart, fists clenched, on the edge of blows. A third man, a bodyguard, with more presence than most and the battered features of a boxer, stood off to the side, looking perplexed, wondering if he should step in.

"You knew!" the smaller man was saying. His face was red, and he stood on his toes to try to match the other's height. He pushed a pair of spectacles up his nose, only to have them slide down again. "Tell me true, have you planned this all along? Did you know you'd move up the schedule?"

Taniel watched Field Marshal Tamas raise his hands before him, palms outward. "Of course I didn't know," he said. "I'm going to explain it all in the morning."

"At the execution! What kind of a coup..." The little man noticed Taniel and trailed off. "Get out," he said. "This is a private conversation."

Taniel removed his hat and leaned against the doorframe, fanning himself casually. "But it was just getting interesting," he said.

"Who is this boy?" the little man demanded of Tamas.

Boy? Taniel glanced at the field marshal. Tamas couldn't have expected him this very night, but he didn't show a bit of surprise. Tamas wasn't one to betray his emotions. Taniel sometimes wondered if Tamas had any emotions.

Tamas let out a sigh. "Taniel, it's good to see you."

Was it? Tamas looked anything but happy. His hair had thinned in the last two years, and his mustache had more gray than black now. Tamas was getting old. Taniel nodded slowly to the field marshal.

"Forgive me," Tamas said after a brief pause. "Taniel, this is Ondraus the Reeve. Ondraus, this is Marked Taniel, one of my mages."

"This is no place for a boy." Ondraus caught sight of Ka-poel hovering behind Taniel. He squinted. "...And a savage," he finished. He squinted again, as if unsure of what he saw the first time. He muttered something under his breath.

Tamas introduced Taniel as a powder mage. Was that all he was to the field marshal? Just another soldier?

Tamas opened his mouth, but Taniel spoke first.

"Sir," he said. "I'm a captain in the Fatrastan army, a Marked in service to Adro, and I know all about the coup. I can kill a pair of Privileged at over a mile with one shot and have done so on several occasions. I'm hardly a boy."

Ondraus sniffed. "Ah, yes, Tamas. So this is your famous son."

Taniel played at his teeth with his tongue and watched his father. *So I am, aren't I? It's good of you to remind him, Ondraus. He tends to forget.*

"Taniel has a right to be here," Tamas said.

Ondraus examined Taniel for a moment. His anger was slowly replaced by a look of calculation. He took a deep breath. "I want promises," he said to Tamas. The emotion had gone from his voice. It was all business, and there was a note of danger there far more frightening than his former fury. "The others will be as angry as I, but if you let me get my hands on the royal ledgers before the execution, I'll give you my support."

"How kind," Tamas said dryly. "You're the king's reeve. You already have the royal ledgers."

"No," Ondraus said as if explaining something to a child. "I'm the city reeve. I want Manhouch's *private* accounting. He's been spending like an expensive whore at the jeweler's for ten years, and I intend to balance the books."

"We agreed to open his coffers to the poor."

"After I balance the books."

Tamas considered this for a moment. "Done. You have until the execution. At noon."

"Right." Ondraus crossed the room, leaning heavily on a cane. He gestured the big man to follow him. They both pushed past Taniel and moved down the dark hall, their footsteps echoing on marble.

"Without so much as a 'by your leave,'" Taniel said.

"The world is nothing more than figures and arithmetic to Ondraus," Tamas said with a dismissive gesture. He motioned Taniel into the room and stepped forward. They shook hands. Taniel searched his father's eyes, wondered if he should pull him into a hug like he might with comrades long absent. Tamas was frowning at the wall, his mind on something else, and Taniel let the thought go.

"Where is Vlora?" Tamas asked, looking curiously at Ka-poel. "Didn't you visit her in Jileman on the way here?"

"She's taking another coach," Taniel said. He tried to keep his tone neutral. First thing Tamas asked. Of course.

"Sit down," Tamas said. "There is so much to talk about. Let's begin with this. Who is she?"

Ka-poel had set Taniel's knapsack and rifle in the corner and was examining the room and the curtains with some interest. Her time in the cities of the Nine had been hurried, as she and Taniel had taken coach after coach, sleeping as they traveled, to arrive in Adopest.

"Her name is Ka-poel," Taniel said. "She's a Dynize, from a tribe in western Fatrasta. Pole," Taniel instructed, "remove your hat." He gave his father an apologetic smile. "I'm still teaching her Adran manners. Their ways are very different from ours."

"The Dynize Empire has opened their borders?" Tamas seemed skeptical.

"A number of natives in the Fatrastan Wilds share blood with the Dynize, but the strait between Dynize and Fatrasta keeps them from suffering their cousins' isolationism."

"Does Dynize concern the Fatrastan generals?"

"Concern? The mere thought gives them heartburn. But the Dynize civil war has shown no signs of stopping. They won't turn their eyes outward for some time."

"And the Kez?" Tamas asked.

"When I left, they were already making overtures of peace."

"That's a pity. I'd hoped Fatrasta would keep them occupied for some time yet." Tamas gave Taniel a look up and down. "I see you're still wearing frontier clothing."

"And what's wrong with that? I spent all my money on passage home." Taniel tugged on the front of his buckskin jacket. "These are the best clothes on the frontier. Warm, durable. I forgot how bloody cold Adro can be. I'm glad I have them."

"I see." Tamas stepped over to Ka-poel and gave her a look-over. She held her hat in both hands and boldly returned Tamas's gaze. Her hair was fire red, and her light skin was covered in ashen freckles—an oddity unseen in the Nine. Her features were small, petite. Not at all the image of a big, savage warrior that most of the Nine had of the Dynize.

"Fascinating," Tamas said. "How did you come across her?"

"She was the scout for our regiment," Taniel said. "Helped us track Kez Privileged through the Fatrastan Wilds. She became my spotter, and I saved her life a few times. She hasn't left my side since."

"She speaks Adran?"

"She's a mute. She understands it, though."

Tamas leaned forward, looking into Ka-poel's eyes. He examined her cheeks and ears as well, as one might a prize horse. Taniel wondered if Tamas would check the teeth next. Ka-poel would bite him for that. Taniel almost hoped he did.

Taniel said, "She's a sorcerer, a Bone-eye. The Dynize version of a Privileged, though their magic is somewhat different, from what I gather."

"Savage sorcerers," Tamas said. "I've heard something about them. She's very small. How old is she?"

"Fourteen years," Taniel said. "I think. They're a small-statured people, but demons on the battlefield. Not bad with a rifle either. Ah," he said as he suddenly remembered. "I wanted to show you something."

He pointed to his rifle. Ka-poel undid the knot holding his satchel to it and brought it to him. Taniel grinned and held the rifle out to his father.

"Is this . . . ? Is this the rifle you used for that shot?" Tamas asked.

"Sure is."

Tamas took the rifle by the barrel, flipped it up, and sighted. "Awfully long. Good weight. Rifled bore and a covered pan on the flintlock. Beautiful craftsmanship."

"Take a look at the name under the barrel."

"A Hrusch. Very nice."

"Not just the design," Taniel said. "Made by the man himself. I spent a month with him in Fatrasta. He'd been working on it for quite some time, made it a gift to me."

Tamas's eyes widened. "Genuine? I've not seen better-made rifles. We bought rights to the patent a year ago and have been churning them out for the army, but I've only seen one made by the man himself."

Taniel felt warmth at his father's wonder. Finally something new. Something Tamas might be proud of. "The Kez tried to buy the patent too," Taniel said.

"Really? Even though they were at war with Fatrasta?"

"Of course. The Hrusch rifle kicked their asses on the frontier. Hardly a misfire, even in the worst of weather. Hrusch wouldn't sell it to them, not for a chest of gold and an earldom. And Kez gunsmiths can't replicate his work."

"No one can, not unless they've been trained by the man himself." Tamas examined the rifle closely for several minutes before handing it back.

"You like it?" Taniel said.

"Remarkable." His interest seemed to wane suddenly, his attention becoming distant.

Taniel hesitated. "Then you'll like this." He held out a hand to Ka-poel. She brought him a wooden case, a little longer than a man's forearm and made of polished mahogany.

"A gift," Taniel said.

Tamas set the case on a table and flipped open the top. "Incredible," he breathed.

"Saw-handled dueling pistols," Taniel said. "Made by Hrusch's oldest son—who they say is a better gunsmith than his father. Refined flintlock with a rainproof pan and a roller bearing on the steel spring. A smoothbore, but more accurate than most." Taniel felt the warmth return as his father's face lit up.

Tamas lifted one of the matched pair of pistols and ran his fingers up and down the octagonal barrel. Ivory inlay caught the lamplight, the polish on it shining beautifully. "These are incredible. I'll have to provoke an insult, just so I can use them."

Taniel chuckled. That sounded like something Tamas would do.

"These are... wonderful," Tamas said.

Taniel thought he saw something glisten in his father's eyes. Was he proud? Grateful? No, he decided, Tamas doesn't know the meaning of those words.

"I wish we had more time to talk," Tamas said.

"On to business?" Of course. No time for chatting. No time to catch up with a long-absent son.

"Unfortunately," Tamas said, either missing or ignoring the sarcasm. "Sabon," he called. The Deliv appeared in the doorway. "Bring in the mercenaries." Sabon disappeared again. "Now, where is Vlora? We need you both. Did Sabon tell you about our losses?"

"Sabon told me. Sad news. I imagine Vlora will be along eventually," he said with a shrug. "I didn't exactly talk to her."

Tamas scowled. "I thought—"

"I found her in another man's bed," Taniel said, feeling a jolt of satisfaction at the shock on Tamas's face. The shock turned to anger, then grief.

"Why? When? For how long?" The words tumbled from Tamas, a moment of true confusion that Taniel wondered if any had ever seen in Tamas, or would again.

Taniel leaned on his rifle and fought back a sneer. Why should Tamas care? It wasn't *his* fiancée. "For several months, from the gossip. The man was paid to seduce her. Some nobleman's son, in it for the thrill and the money."

"Paid?" Tamas asked, his eyes narrowing.

"A scheme," Taniel said. "Petty revenge. No doubt hatched by a wealthy nobleman." Taniel hadn't taken the time to find out who the culprit was, but he had little uncertainty. The nobility hated Tamas. He was common-born and had used his influence with the king to prevent the wealthy from purchasing commissions in the army. Only the capable rose in the ranks. It flew in the face of tradition, but also made the Adran army one of the best in the Nine. The nobility feared Tamas too much to attack him directly, but they'd strike him any way they could, even through his son.

Tamas's teeth clenched in a snarl. "I've arrested half the nobility this very night. They face the guillotine with their king. I'll find out who paid, and then..."

Taniel suddenly felt tired. Years fighting a war that wasn't his, followed by months of cramped traveling, only to come home to betrayal and a coup. His anger had been sapped. He thumbed a line of black powder onto his hand and snorted it. "The guillotine is enough. Save your men." *Save your anger, though Kresimir knows you have enough of it. No pity, though. None for your son, the betrayed.*

Tamas rubbed his eyes. "I should have had her watched."

"She's free to do what she wants," Taniel said. It came out as a snarl.

"The wedding?"

"I nailed her ring to the bastard bedding her. They'll have had to cut him off his own sword."

Sabon reentered the room. He was followed by a pair of disreputable-looking characters wearing the clothes of people who slept in the saddle, or on a barroom bench. One was a man, tall and lanky with a hairline that touched the back of his head, though he couldn't have been older than thirty. He wore a belt that covered his entire stomach, carried four swords and three pistols of different sizes and shapes, and he wore the gloves of a Privileged—though instead of white with colored runes, the gloves were navy blue with gold runes. The man was a magebreaker: a Privileged who'd given up his natural-born sorcery to nullify magic at will.

The other was a woman. She looked to be in her late thirties and wore riding pants and a jacket. She would have been beautiful but for the old scar that lifted the corner of her lip and traveled all the way to her temple. She, too, wore the gloves of a Privileged, which allowed her to touch the Else. Hers were white with blood-red runes. Taniel wondered why she wasn't in a cabal. He could sense she was strong enough even without opening his third eye.

Mercenaries, Tamas had said. These two had a look. A Privileged and a magebreaker together were a dangerous combination. They were used to hunt Knacked, Marked, and Privileged. Taniel wondered which his father had in mind.

"A Privileged escaped our cull at Skyline," Tamas said. "Not one of the royal cabal, but powerful nonetheless. I want you three"—a glance at Ka-poel—"four to track her down and kill her."

Tamas settled into the role of a man used to briefing his soldiers, and Taniel realized his homecoming amounted to little more than a briefing and an assignment. Off hunting another Privileged. He glanced at the two mercenaries. They had a competent look to them. Taniel had had less to work with in Fatrasta. This Privileged they meant to hunt had killed five seasoned powder mages in half a breath. She'd be dangerous, and Taniel had never hunted in a city before. He decided the challenge would keep his mind off... things.

Taniel lifted his snuffbox once more and tapped out a line on the back of his hand, ignoring his father's disapproving look.

Nila paused for a moment to watch the fire burn beneath the big iron pot suspended in the fireplace. She rubbed her chapped hands together and warmed them over the flames. The water would boil soon, and she'd finish washing the laundry for everyone in the townhouse. There was a small pile of dirty laundry stacked by the pantry, but most of the family's clothes, as well as the servants' livery, had been soaking in the large vats of warm water and lye soap since last evening. They would need to be boiled, rinsed, and then hung out to dry, but first she needed to iron the duke's dress uniform. He had a meeting with the king at ten. That was still hours away, but all of it, the washing, rinsing, and ironing, had to be done before the cooks got up to make breakfast.

The door to the washroom opened and a boy of five came into the kitchen rubbing the sleep from his eyes.

"Can't sleep, young master?" Nila asked.

"No," he said. The only child of Duke Eldaminse, Jakob was very sickly. He had blond hair and a pale face with narrow cheeks. He was small for his age, but bright, and friendlier to the help than a duke's son ought to be. Nila had been thirteen and an apprentice laundress for the Eldaminse when he was born. From the time he could walk he'd taken a liking to her, much to the chagrin of his mother and governess.

"Have a seat here," Nila said, rearranging a clean, dry blanket near the fire for Jakob. "Only for a couple of minutes, then you need to go back to bed before Ganny awakes."

He settled onto the blanket and watched her heat the irons on the stove and lay out his father's clothes. His eyes soon began to droop and he settled onto his side.

Nila dragged a large washbasin over beside the iron pot. She was just about to pour in the water when the door opened again.

"Nila!" Ganny stood in the doorway, hands on her hips. She was twenty-six, and severe beyond her age; well suited to be the governess of a ducal heir. She wore her cocoa-colored hair up in a tight bun behind her head. Even in her nightclothes, Ganny seemed more proper than Nila with her plain dress and unruly auburn curls.

Nila put a finger to her lips.

"You know he's not supposed to be in here," Ganny said, lowering her voice.

"What should I do? Say no?"

"Of course!"

"Leave him be, he's finally asleep."

"He'll catch a cold down here."

"He's right next to the fire," Nila said.

"If the duchess finds him here, she'll be furious!" Ganny shook her finger at Nila. "I won't stick up for you when she turns you out on the street."

"And when have you ever stuck up for me?"

Ganny's lips took on a hard line. "I'll recommend your dismissal to the duchess tonight. You're nothing but a bad influence on Jakob."

"I will..." Nila took one look at the sleeping boy and closed her mouth. She had no family, no connections. The duchess already disliked her. Duke Eldaminse had a habit of bedding the help, and he'd been looking at her more often lately. Nila didn't need any trouble with Ganny, even if she was a bully. "I'm sorry, Ganny," Nila said. "I'll get him back to bed now. Do you have any clothes I can get the stains out of for you?"

"That's a better attitude," Ganny said. "Now..."

She was interrupted by a hammering on the front door, loud enough to be heard all the way at the back of the townhouse.

"Who is that at this early hour?" Ganny pulled her nightclothes tightly around her and headed into the hallway. "They'll wake up the lord and lady!"

Nila put her hands on her hips and looked at Jakob. "You'll get me in trouble, young master."

His eyes fluttered open. "Sorry," he said.

She knelt down beside him. "It's all right, go back to sleep. Let me carry you to bed."

She'd just lifted him up when she heard the scream from the front of the house. Shouts followed and then the hammering footsteps running up the stairs in the main hallway. She heard angry male voices that didn't belong to any of the house staff.

"What is that?" Jakob asked.

She set him on his feet so that he couldn't feel her hands shaking. "Quickly," she said. "In the washtub."

Jakob's bottom lip trembled. "Why, what's happening?"

"Hide!"

He climbed into the washtub. She dumped the dirty laundry on top of him and stacked it high and then hurried into the hallway.

She ran right into a soldier. The man shoved her back into the kitchen. He was soon joined by two other men, then another holding Ganny by the back of the neck. He shoved Ganny to the floor. The governess's eyes were full of fear mingled with indignation.

"These two will do," one of the soldiers said. He wore the dark blue of the Adran army, with two golden service stripes on his chest and a silver medal that indicated he'd served the crown overseas. He began to loosen his belt and stepped toward Nila.

Nila grabbed the hot iron from the stove and hit him hard across the face. He went down, to the shouts of his comrades.

Someone grabbed her arms, another her legs.

"Feisty," one said.

"That will leave a mark," said another.

"What is the meaning of this!" Ganny had finally gotten to her feet. "Do you know whose house this is?"

"Shut up." The soldier Nila had hit climbed to his feet, a swollen burn covering half of his face. He punched Ganny hard in the stomach. "We'll get to you soon enough." He turned to Nila.

Nila struggled against hands too strong for her. She turned to the washbasin, hoping Jakob would not see this, and closed her eyes to wait for the blow.

"Heathlo!" a voice barked.

She opened her eyes again when the hands that held her suddenly let up.

"What the pit you doing, soldier?" The man who spoke wore the same uniform as the others, only set apart by a gold triangle pinned to his silver lapel. He had sandy hair and a neatly trimmed beard. A cigarette hung out of the corner of his mouth. Nila had never seen a soldier with a beard before.

"Just having some fun, Sergeant." Heathlo gave Nila a menacing glare and turned toward the sergeant.

"Fun? No fun for us, soldier. This is the army. You heard the field marshal's orders."

"But, Sergeant..."

The sergeant leaned over and picked up the iron from where it lay on the floor. He looked at the bottom, then at the burn on the soldier's face. "You want me to give you a matching one on the other side?"

Heathlo's eyes hardened. "This bitch struck me."

"I'll hit you somewhere prettier than your face next time I see you try to rape an Adran citizen." The sergeant pointed his cigarette at Heathlo. "This isn't Gurla."

"I'll report this to the captain, sir," Heathlo sneered.

The sergeant shrugged.

"Heathlo," one of the other soldiers said. "Don't push him. Sorry, Sergeant, he's new to the company and all."

"Keep him in line," the sergeant said. "He's new, but I expect better from you two." He helped Ganny to her feet, then touched his finger to his forehead toward Nila. "Ma'am. We're looking for Duke Eldaminse's son."

Ganny looked at Nila. Nila could tell she was terrified. "He was with you," the governess said.

Nila forced herself to look into the sergeant's blue eyes. "I just carried him up to bed."

"Go on," the sergeant said to his soldiers. "Find him." They left the room quickly. He remained and gave a slow look around the kitchen. "He's not in his bed."

"He has a habit of wandering," Nila said. "I just put him to bed, but I'm sure he was scared by the noise. What is happening?" This was no accident. Those soldiers knew exactly whose house this was. The sergeant had mentioned a field marshal. Adro only had one man of that rank: Field Marshal Tamas.

"Duke Eldaminse and his family are under arrest for treason," the sergeant said.

Ganny blanched and looked as if she might faint.

Nila felt her stomach tighten. Treason. Accusations like that would see the whole staff put to the question. There was no escape. She'd heard a story once of an archduke, the Iron King's own cousin, who plotted against the throne. His family and every member of his staff had been sent to the guillotine.

"You're free to go," the sergeant said. "We're only here for the duke and his family." He stepped toward the washbasin, frowning. "You'll want to find new employment. In fact, if you can, you should leave the city for at least a few days." He put the cigarette between his lips and lifted a pair of trousers from the top of the washbasin.

"Olem!"

The sergeant turned his head as another soldier entered the room.

"They find the boy?" Olem said, the washbasin forgotten.

"No, but a summons came for you. From the field marshal."

"For me?" Olem sounded doubtful.

"Report to Commander Sabon immediately."

"All right," Olem said. He crushed his cigarette out on the kitchen table. "Keep an eye on Heathlo. Don't let him rough up any of the women. If you have to give the boys an armful of loot to keep 'em occupied, do it."

"But our orders—"

"The boys will break some of our orders one way or another. I'd rather they break the ones that won't see them hanged."

"Right."

Olem took one last look around the kitchen. "Get any valuables you have here and leave," he said. "The duke won't be coming back for anything, either..." He touched his forehead toward Ganny and Nila before leaving.

So take what you want. Nila finished the sentence in her head.

Ganny gave Nila one quick look before she ran into the hallway. Nila could hear her feet on the servants' stairs a moment later.

Nila fished the butler's key from its hiding place above the mantel and unlocked the silverware cabinet. Nothing she had hidden under her mattress upstairs was worth a fraction of the silver she now piled into a burlap bag.

She waited until she couldn't hear any of the soldiers in the hallway and pulled Jakob from the washbasin. She helped him pull his nightclothes over his head and handed him a pair of dirty trousers and a shirt from one of the serving boys. They'd be too big, but they'd do.

"What are we doing?" he asked.

"Taking you someplace safe."

"What about Miss Ganny?"

"I think she's gone for good," Nila said.

"Mother and father?"

"I don't know," Nila said. "They'll want you to come with me, I think." She took a handful of cool ashes from the corner of the fireplace and mixed them in her palm with water. "Hold still," she said, smearing the ashes in his hair and on his face. She took his hand, and with a sack full of pilfered silver over her shoulder, Nila headed out the back entrance.

Two soldiers watched the alley behind the townhouse. Nila walked toward them, head down.

"You there," one of the men said. "Whose child is this?"

"Mine," Nila said.

The soldier lifted Jakob's chin. "Doesn't look like a duke's son."

"Should we hold him till we find the boy?" the other said.

"Sergeant Olem said we could go," Nila said.

"Fine," the soldier said. "Off with you, then. We've a busy night."

CHAPTER

4

Adamat took a carriage straight home from Skyline, driven by one of Tamas's soldiers. It was a long journey, accompanied only by his worries and self-doubts as the driver navigated the quiet night streets of Adro. Adamat silently wished they could go faster. It didn't help. The eastern sky had begun to lighten when he leapt from the carriage and pushed through the old gate and past his small garden to his front door. He fumbled with his keys, dropping them once, before he stopped to take a deep breath.

He'd seen worse than this, he told himself. It would be no worse than the riots in Oktersehn. He jammed the key in the lock and twisted, the rusted metal squeaking as he half pushed, half kicked the door open.

He took the stairs two at a time to the second floor and thumped each door as he ran down the hallway. He reached his own room and threw open the door.

"Faye," he said.

His wife lifted her head from the pillow and regarded him by the light of a low-burning lamp. The shadows moved across her face, darkened by a halo of black, curly hair. "What hour is it?" she asked.

"Sometime after five o'clock," Adamat said. He turned the lamp up and threw the covers back. "Get up. You're going to the house in Offendale."

Faye clutched the covers to her chest. "What's gotten into you? What house in Offendale?"

"The one we bought when I first entered the force. In case there was ever danger to you and the children."

Faye sat up. "I thought we sold that house. I...Adamat. What has happened?" A note of worry entered her voice. "Is this about the Lourent family? Or a new case?"

The Lourent family had hired him to look into the checkered past of their youngest daughter's suitor. The whole affair had ended badly when he was forced to expose the man as a fraud.

"No, not the Lourent case. Bigger than that." Adamat turned at soft footfalls in the hall. "Astrit," he said softly. His youngest daughter held a frayed, stuffed dog under one arm. She wore her nightgown and an old pair of Faye's slippers that were several sizes too big, and in the dim light she looked like a miniature version of her mother. She tilted her head quizzically. Adamat said, "Go get your travel coat, darling. You're going on a trip."

"Do I have to wear a dress?" she asked.

Adamat forced a smile. "No, love, just a travel coat over your nightgown. You're leaving very soon. Don't forget your shoes."

She smiled at him and turned, skipping down the hallway, the old stuffed dog dangling from one hand. Her older siblings gave her odd looks as they began to emerge from their rooms.

"Josep," Adamat said to his oldest son. "Get your brothers and sisters ready to go. Quickly. Get them all to pack a bag for a few weeks."

The boy was a serious youth, just past his sixteenth year and on holiday from school. He rubbed nervously at the ring on his finger; it had been a gift from Adamat's father before the old man passed, and the boy was seldom without it. Josep waited a moment for an explanation. When none was forthcoming, he nodded before herding his siblings back to their rooms.

Good lad. Adamat turned back to Faye, who was now sitting up in bed. She ran a hand through her hair, pulling at tangles.

"You'd better have a good explanation," she said. "What has happened? Is there danger to the children? To you? Is this about some new job you've taken? I told you to stop snooping after noblemen's wives and going on about other people's business."

Adamat closed his eyes. "I'm an investigator, my dear. Other people's business *is* my business. There will be riots. I want you and the children out of the city within the hour. Just a precaution, of course."

"Why will there be riots?"

Damned woman. What he'd give for an obedient wife. "There has been a coup. Manhouch will face the guillotine at noon."

He had the brief satisfaction of watching her jaw drop. Then she was on her feet, headed toward the closet. Adamat watched her for a moment. Her body was more angular than it had once been; sharp elbows and wrinkled skin in place of soft curves and a gentle, lovely plumpness. The years since his retirement from the force had taken their toll on her, and she was not as beautiful as in her youth. Adamat pictured himself. He was no one to judge. Short, balding, his round face grown leaner over the years, his mustache and beard thinner. He wasn't exactly as young as he used to be. Still... he bit his lower lip as he watched Faye, entertaining actions that would need to wait some time.

She turned, saw him watching her. "You're coming with us, aren't you?" she said.

"No."

She paused. "Why not?"

He should lie. Tell her he had previous commitments. "I've become . . . involved."

"Oh no. Adamat, what the pit did you do?"

He stifled a smile. He loved it when she swore. "Not like that. No. Tonight's summons. Field Marshal Tamas has a task for me."

She scowled. "Only *he'd* have the rocks to pull down a king. Well, stop grinning and summon a carriage and help the children with their shoes." She made a brushing motion with her hand. "Go on!"

Twenty minutes later, Adamat watched as his family piled into a pair of carriages. He paid the drivers and stood for a moment with his wife. "If the riots seem to be moving toward you, don't hesitate to take the children to Deliv. I'll come find you when things have settled down."

Faye's face—usually harsh, firmly disapproving—was suddenly soft. She was young again in his eyes, a worried girl waiting for her lover to walk the midnight roads. She leaned forward and kissed him tenderly on the lips. "What should I tell the children?"

"Don't lie to them," Adamat said. "They're old enough."

"They'll worry. Especially Astrit."

"Of course," Adamat said.

Faye sniffed. "I haven't been to Offendale since we went on holiday after Astrit was born. Is the house there in good order?"

"It'll be small," Adamat said. "Cozy. But safe. Do you remember our code phrases? The post office is in the next town. I'll send a letter to Saddie asking her to bring you the mail."

"Is all that necessary?" Faye asked. "I thought it was just riots."

"Field Marshal Tamas is a dangerous man," Adamat said. "I don't . . ." He paused. "Just as a precaution. Humor me."

Faye said, "Of course. Take care of yourself." Adamat returned his wife's kiss, then leaned in the window of each carriage in turn, giving every one of the nine children a kiss, two for each of the twins. He stopped at Astrit and knelt down on the floor of the carriage to look her in the eye. "You'll be away for a couple of weeks. The city is going to be a bit rough."

"Why aren't you coming?" she asked.

"I've got to help make it safer." He thought of Kresimir's Broken Promise. The words made him shiver.

"Are you cold?" Astrit asked.

He brushed a finger across her cheek. "Yes," he said. "It's very chilly. I'd better go in before I catch cold. Have a safe trip!"

He closed the carriage door and stood in the street, watching them trundle off until they turned a corner. He would miss Faye for many reasons. When it came to his investigations, she was more than a wife to him. She was a partner. She had a vast network of friends and acquaintances and knew how to coerce gossip to find out information that even he could not turn up.

He headed back to the house, stopping for a moment only as he saw a movement in a doorway across the street. A young man in a long, stiff coat emerged from the shadows and headed off in the opposite direction from the carriages. He spared one glance for Adamat and doubled his step.

Adamat watched the young man go, making sure the stranger felt his gaze. One of Palagyi's goons, no doubt. Adamat would hear from him shortly. Adamat returned to the house, locking the door behind him, and went immediately to the study. He dug through his desk drawers until he found a stack of stationery.

The sun had finally touched his study window, looking in over the houses and the distant mountains, when Adamat finished addressing letters. His hand ached from writing, and his candle had burned to a nub. He yawned, letting his mind wander for a moment, when the faint scratching sound of metal on metal caught his ear.

Adamat pushed the whole stack of letters into a desk drawer and locked it. He picked up his cane and twisted until it clicked, then walked through the house, listening for the sound. He reached a rear door, small and old, that led to an overgrown trellis in what amounted to their garden between their house and the one behind it. The garden could be reached from the house itself or from a small corridor that ran between two houses, which contained a locked gate.

Adamat jerked the door open, cane in hand. Three men stared back at him. Two of them wore the faded coats and simple brimmed hats of street workers. The one's knees and shirtsleeves were stained black—likely from shoveling coal into a furnace—and the second, the lockpick, wore clothes much too big for him, the common practice of a street thief who wanted to secret a number of things about his person. The third man was richly dressed, a gray overcoat over a sharp black waistcoat, and had shoes shined well enough that one could check one's teeth in them.

The lockpick gaped up at Adamat from his knees.

"You're making enough noise, you might as well have knocked on the front door," Adamat said. He sighed and lowered his cane and spoke to the best-dressed of the three. "What do you want, Palagyi?"

Palagyi seemed surprised to see him here. He pushed at a pair of round spectacles that rested more on his chubby cheeks than on his thin nose. The man was an oddity, with a body that would seem more at home in a circus than anywhere else. He had a round belly that hung far over his belt, but his arms and legs were no thicker than a sapling. It made him look like an oversized cannonball with sticks for arms.

He was a longtime street thug who had just enough ruthlessness to rise to legitimate businesses and not quite enough intelligence to leave his dark life behind him. Aptly suited as a banker. Adamat cataloged his criminal record in his mind in an instant.

"Word had it that you'd skipped town," Palagyi said.

"You mean the word of that inbred you've had skulking around my house for the last couple of weeks?"

"I have a reason to keep my eye on you." He seemed annoyed that Adamat was actually still there.

Adamat gave a long-suffering sigh and watched Palagyi grind his teeth. Palagyi hated when he wasn't taken seriously. He'd changed little since he was just a half-drunk loan shark. "I've got two months until my debt is due."

"There is absolutely no way you're going to gather seventy thousand krana in two months. So when I hear your family is skipping town in the middle of the night, I think perhaps you've decided to take the coward's way and run for it."

"Careful who you call a coward," Adamat said. He reversed his grip on his cane.

Palagyi flinched. "I took my last beating from you long ago," he said, "and you're no longer protected by the police. You're just one of us now, an ordinary gutter rat. You shouldn't have taken out a loan with me." He laughed. It was a tinny sound that grated on Adamat's nerves.

It was Adamat's turn to grind his teeth. He'd not taken out a loan from Palagyi, but from a bank belonging to a friend. That friend proved a bad one when he sold the loan to Palagyi for nearly one hundred and fifty percent of its worth. Palagyi had promptly tripled the interest and sat back and waited for Adamat's new publishing business to fail. Which it had.

Palagyi wiped a tear of mirth from his eye and snorted. "When I learn that one of my biggest private loans has sent his family out of town just two months before his loan is due, I check on it personally."

"And try to break into his house?" Adamat said. "You can't clean me out and throw us onto the street until after I've defaulted."

"Perhaps I got greedy." Palagyi smiled thinly. "Now, I'm going to need to know where your family is so that I can check in on them."

Adamat spoke through clenched teeth. "They're at my cousin's. East of Nafolk. Check all you want."

"Good. I will." Palagyi turned to go, when he stopped suddenly. "What's your girl's name? The youngest one. I think I'll have some of my boys bring her back, just in case you try to slip onto one of those new steamers and make for Fatrasta."

Palagyi had just enough time to flinch before Adamat's cane cracked over his shoulder. Palagyi cried out and stumbled into the garden. The coal shoveler punched Adamat in the belly.

Adamat doubled over from pain. He'd not expected the man to hit so fast or so hard. He nearly dropped his cane, and it was all he could do to remain standing.

"I'll have the police on you!" Palagyi wailed.

"Try it," Adamat wheezed. "I still have friends there. They'll laugh you into the street." He regained his composure and pulled himself up enough to slam the door. "Come back in two months!" He locked the door and slid the deadbolt.

Adamat held his stomach and staggered back to his office. He'd have indigestion from that blow for a week. He hoped he wasn't bleeding.

Adamat spent a few minutes recovering before he gathered his letters and set out into the streets. He could feel tension growing around him. He wanted to attribute it to the coming conflict that he knew would happen—the revolution that would sweep the city when Manhouch was declared dead, and the chaos that would follow. Adamat prayed that Tamas would keep it in check. A task that might very well prove impossible. But no, the tension was likely just Adamat's growing headache and the pain in the pit of his stomach.

Not far from the postmaster's, Adamat stopped on a street corner to catch his breath. His stride had been unconsciously hurried, his breathing hard, a worried sense of danger lurking in the back of his mind.

A newsie lad, no more than ten, sprinted into view. He stopped on the corner next to Adamat and took mighty gasps before throwing his head back and shouting:

"Manhouch has fallen! The king has fallen! Manhouch faces the guillotine at noon!" Then the boy was gone, onto the next corner.

Adamat snapped himself out of a stunned silence and turned to watch others do the same. He *knew* that Manhouch had fallen. He'd seen the blood of the royal cabal on Tamas's jacket. Yet hearing it spoken aloud on a public street made his hands tremble. The king had fallen. Change had been forced on the country, and the people would be forced to choose how they'd react.

The initial shock of the news passed. Confusion set in as pedestrians changed their plans midstride. A carriage turned around abruptly in the street. The driver didn't see the small girl selling flowers. Adamat rushed out, grabbed her by the arm, and pulled her away before the horses could trample her. Her flowers spilled into the street. One man shoved another in a sudden, hurried dash across the street and was in turn shoved to the ground. A fistfight began, only to be quickly put down by a truncheon-wielding police officer.

Adamat helped the girl pick up her flowers before she ran off. He sighed. *It's begun.* He put his head down and pushed on toward the postmaster's.

CHAPTER 5

Tamas stood on a balcony six floors above the enormous city square called the King's Garden, his face in the wind, watching the crowds gather. His two hounds slept at his feet, unaware of the importance of this day. He wore his freshly pressed dress uniform; dark blue with gold epaulettes on each shoulder, and gold buttons—each of them a small powder keg. The lapel, collar cuffs, and wings of his uniform were of red velvet, his belt of black leather. He wore his medals at the insistence of his aides: gold, silver, and violet stars of various shapes and sizes awarded to him by half a dozen Gurlish shahs and kings of the Nine. He held his bicorne hat under one arm.

The sun was just barely above the rooftops of Adopest, yet he guessed there were already fifteen thousand people below watching as crews constructed a line of guillotines. It was said the Garden could contain four hundred thousand, half the population of Adopest.

They would find out today.

His gaze fell across the Garden to the tower that rose like a thorn against the morning sky. Sabletooth had been built by Manhouch's father, the Iron King, as a prison for his most dangerous enemies, and as a warning to all the rest. It had taken almost half of his sixty-year reign to build and its color had given the Iron King his nickname. It was three times the height of any building in Adopest, an ugly thing, a nail of basalt that looked like it had been ripped from the pages of a legend from before the Time of Kresimir.

At the moment Sabletooth was full to capacity with nearly six hundred nobles and many of their wives and oldest sons, as well as another five hundred courtiers and royal dignitaries that couldn't be trusted on their own. When Tamas closed his eyes, he thought he could hear wails of anguish, and he wondered if it was his imagination. The nobility knew what was coming to them. They had for a century.

Tamas turned away from his view of the city when the door behind him clicked. A soldier stepped out onto the balcony. His solid blue uniform with a silver collar matched Tamas's, with a gold sergeant's triangle pinned to the lapel, and stripes of service above his breast to indicate ten years. The man looked to be in his midthirties. He wore a finely trimmed brown beard, though military regulation forbade it, and his hair was cut short above his ears. Tamas gave the man a nod.

"Olem, sir. Reporting."

"Thank you, Olem," Tamas said. "You're aware of the duties I need you to perform?"

"Bodyguard," Olem said, "and manservant, errand boy. Anything the field marshal bloody well pleases. No disrespect meant, sir."

"I take it those were Sabon's words?"

"Yes, sir."

Tamas suppressed a smile. He could like this man. Too free with his tongue, perhaps.

A thin ribbon of smoke rose from behind Olem.

"Soldier, is your back on fire?"

"No, sir," Olem said.

"The smoke?"

"My cigarette, sir."

"Cigarette?"

"All the latest fashion. Tobacco as fine as snuff, sir, and half the price. All the way from Fatrasta. I roll them myself."

"You sound like an advertisement." Tamas felt annoyance creeping on.

"My cousin sells tobacco, sir."

"Why are you hiding it behind your back?"

Olem shrugged. "You're a teetotaler, sir, and it's well known among the men you won't abide smoking either."

"Then why are you hiding it behind your back?"

"Waiting for you to turn around so I can have a hit, sir."

At least he was honest. "I had a sergeant flogged once for smoking in my tent. Why do you think I'll treat you any differently?" That had been twenty-five years ago, and Tamas had almost lost his rank for it.

"Because you want me to watch your back, sir," Olem said. "It goes to logic that you won't hand out a beating to the man you expect to keep you alive."

"I see," Tamas said. Olem hadn't even cracked a smile. Tamas decided he did like the man. Against his better judgment.

They examined each other for a moment. Tamas couldn't help but watch the ribbon of smoke rising from behind Olem. The smell reached him then. It wasn't terribly unpleasant, less pungent than most cigars, but not as pleasant as pipe tobacco. There was even a minty tinge to it.

"Do I have the job, sir?" Olem asked.

"You really don't need sleep?"

Olem tapped the middle of his forehead. "I have the Knack, sir. Runs in the family. My father could smell a liar from a mile away. My cousin can eat more food than a hundred men, or none at all for weeks. My particular Knack? I don't need sleep. I even have the third sight, so you know it's the real thing."

Men with a Knack were considered the least powerful among those with sorcerous ability. It usually manifested itself as one very strong and particular talent, though some were quite powerful. There were plenty of men who claimed to have a Knack. Only those with a third eye—the ability to see sorcery and those who wield it—were truly Knacked.

"Why haven't you been swept up as a bodyguard before?"

"Sir?"

"With a talent like that you could be running security for some duke in Kez and making more money than a dozen soldiers. Or perhaps serving overseas with the Wings of Adom."

"Ah," Olem said. "I get seasick."

"That's it?"

"Bodyguards to the rich need to be able to sail with them. I'm useless on a boat."

"So you'll watch my back as long as I don't go sailing?"

"Pretty much, sir."

Tamas watched the man for another few moments. Among the troops, Olem was well known and well liked—he could shoot, box, ride, and play cards and billiards. He was an everyman as far as soldiers were concerned.

"You've one mark on your record," Tamas said. "You once punched a na-baron in the face. Broke his jaw. Tell me about that."

Olem grimaced. "Officially, sir, I was pushing him out of the way of a runaway carriage. Saved his life. Half my company saw it."

"With your fist?"

"Aye."

"And unofficially?"

"The man was a git. He shot my dog because it startled his horse."

"And if I ever have cause to shoot your dog?"

"I'll punch you in the face."

"Fair enough. You have the job."

"Oh, good." Olem looked relieved. He removed his hands from behind his back and immediately stuck the cigarette in his mouth and pulled hard. Smoke blew out his nose. "It would have gone out soon."

"Ah. I'm going to regret this, aren't I?"

"Of course not, sir. Someone's here."

Tamas caught sight of movement just inside. "It's time." He stepped toward the balcony door and paused. The hounds rose from their sleep and crowded around Tamas's legs. He gave Olem a look.

"Sir?"

"You're also supposed to get the door for me."

"Right. Sorry, sir. This might take me a while to get used to."

"Me too," Tamas said.

Olem held the door for Tamas. The hounds hurried in ahead of him, noses to the floor. The room was near-silent despite the growing volume of voices in the Garden. Running on days without sleep, Tamas found the silence soothing.

He was in a grand office, if a room so big could be called that. Most houses could fit inside. It had been the king's, a quiet place for him to study or review decisions by the House of Nobles. Like everything else that required a hair of a brain or a single krana's care for how the country was run, the room had remained vacant for the entirety of Manhouch's reign—though Tamas had it on good authority that Manhouch lent it to his favorite mistress last year, before his advisers found out.

Ricard Tumblar stood over a table of refreshments, picking through a stack of sugar cakes for the best ones. He was a handsome man despite his receding hairline, with short brown hair and full features, and lines in the corners of his mouth from smiling too much. He wore a costly suit made out of some animal hair from eastern Gurla, and his beard was worn long in Fatrastan style. A hat and cane of equally eclectic and expensive taste rested by the door.

Ricard controlled Adopest's only workers' union and of all of

Tamas's council of coconspirators; he was the only one that could provide pleasant company for longer than a few minutes. Hrusch and Pitlaugh sniffed at him till he gave them each a sugar cake. The dogs took their prizes and retreated to the window divan.

Tamas sighed. He hated it when people fed them. They wouldn't shit right for a week.

"Help yourself," Tamas said.

Ricard grinned at him. "Thank you, I will." He popped a sugar cake in his mouth and spoke around a mouthful. "You did it, old boy. I couldn't believe it, but you did it."

"Not quite," Tamas said. "The executions must be carried out, the city brought to order; there will be riots and royalists, and I still have the Kez to deal with."

"And a country to run," Ricard added.

"Lucky for me, I'll leave that to the council."

Ricard rolled his eyes. "Lucky you indeed. I dread working with the rest of them. We need your balancing hand to keep us from each other's throats."

"I agree," Ondraus said.

The reeve entered the room at a slow walk, cane in one hand, a thick ledger under the other arm. He crossed the room and tossed the ledger down on the king's desk, then dropped down in the chair behind it. Tamas stifled a protest.

Ondraus opened the book. Tamas would have sworn dust rose from the thing. He stepped closer. It was an ancient tome, with gold-thread lettering stitched onto the front—a word in Old Deliv. Something about money, Tamas guessed. The pages themselves seemed almost black. Closer inspection revealed tiny writing—letters and numbers boxed off, written so densely as to require a looking glass to see the actual figures.

"The king's treasury is empty," Ondraus announced. He produced a looking glass from his pocket and set it on the page, peering through it as he perused a few numbers at random.

Ricard inhaled sharply, choking on a sugar cake.

Tamas stared at the reeve. "How?"

"I haven't seen this thing since the Iron King died," Ondraus said, gesturing at the tome. "It records every transaction made in the name of the crown for the last hundred years, to the krana. It's been in the hands of Manhouch's personal accountants since he took the throne. They kept solid records; that's the best I can say for them. According to this, there's not a krana in the king's treasury."

Tamas made a fist to stop his hands from shaking. How would he pay his soldiers? How would he feed the poor and bankroll the police forces? Tamas needed hundreds of millions—he'd hoped for at least tens.

"Taxes," Ondraus said, closing the ledger with a thump. "We'll have to raise taxes first thing."

"No," Tamas said. "You know that's not an option. If we replace Manhouch with even higher taxes, stricter control, then it'll be our heads in a basket within a year."

"Why should we raise the taxes?" Arch-Diocel Charlemund swept into the room, long, purple robes of office trailing behind him. He was a tall man, strong and athletic, who'd not lost the power of his youth in middle age like most men. He had a square face and evenly set brown eyes, his cheeks clean-shaven. He was swathed in fine furs and silk, with a round, gilded hat upon his head. There were rings on his fingers with enough gold and precious stones to buy a dozen mansions. But that wasn't uncommon for an arch-diocel of the Kresim Church.

"I see you brought the whole wardrobe," Ricard said.

Tamas inclined his head. "Charlemund," he said.

The arch-diocel sniffed. "I'm a man of the Rope," he said. "I have a title you may use, though it weighs upon me to inflict it."

"Your Eminence!" Ricard mimed removing a hat from his head and bowed low to the ground.

"I wouldn't expect a man like you to understand," the arch-diocel said to Ricard. "I'd call you out, but you're too much of a coward to duel."

"I have men to do that for me," Ricard said. There was the slightest fear in his eye. The arch-diocel had been the finest swordsman in all the Nine before his appointment to the Rope and he was still known to call men out on occasion and—priest or not—gut them mercilessly.

"Property," Tamas said to the reeve. "We own half of Adro now, what with every nobleman and his heir about to find himself tasting the guillotine's edge. Ondraus, I expect you'll take great delight in this: Dissolve the property. Slowly, but fast enough to fund all the projects we've discussed. Sell it outside the country if need be, but get us some damned money."

"There were plans for that property," the arch-diocel said.

"Yes, and—"

"What is being done with the property?"

Tamas sighed. Lady Winceslav entered the room in a gown that could easily compete with the arch-diocel's robes for whose used the greater amount of cloth and jewels in the tailoring. She was a woman of about fifty years with high cheekbones and a slim waist, diamonds in her earrings. She owned the Wings of Adom, the most prestigious mercenary force in the world, and was a native Adran. Her forces had been quietly pulled out of foreign postings and recalled to Adro over the last few months in preparation for the coup, and Tamas knew he'd need them desperately in the time to come.

Close behind her followed a big, bald man in a one-piece robe: the Proprietor's eunuch. Finally, Prime Lektor—Vice-Chancellor of Adopest University—came in behind them. He was easily as old as the reeve and weighed ten stone more. He staggered over to a chair.

All six of Tamas's coconspirators had arrived: five men and a woman who had helped him plan Manhouch's downfall and who would now determine the future of Adro.

"By the pit, Tamas," the vice-chancellor said, wiping the sweat from his forehead. A purple birthmark spidered across the lower left side of his face, touching his lips and one eye. He wore a beard, but no hair would grow on the birthmark, giving the old scholar a particularly barbaric appearance. "You had to choose the top floor? You're going to regret it in a few years when your bones start to weary."

"Lady," Tamas said, nodding to Lady Winceslav, then to the vice-chancellor and to the eunuch. "Prime. Eunuch. Thank you for coming."

The eunuch slid over to the corner and glanced out a window. He moved like an eel and smelled like southern spices, but the Proprietor, the strongest figure in Adopest's criminal element, never attended these meetings personally—he sent his nameless lieutenant instead. "We had little choice," the eunuch said. His voice was soft, like a child speaking in church. "You moved up the timeline."

"There's more," Charlemund said. His voice thundered unnecessarily. "He's trying to claim the property we've confiscated from the nobility."

Tamas held his hands up to calm a sudden clamor of voices. He glared at the arch-diocel. "We're not here to carve up Adro," he snapped. "We're here to give it back to the people. The king's treasury is empty. If we're to keep any semblance of control over the nation in the next few years, we desperately need the money. Your mercenaries will have land, Lady, and Ricard your union will have its grants. Everyone will get a cut."

"Fifteen percent for the Church," the arch-diocel demanded quietly, studying his nails.

"Go to the pit," Ricard snapped.

"I'll send you there," the arch-diocel said, stepping toward Ricard. A hand went into his robes. Ricard scrambled backward.

"Charlemund!" Tamas said.

The arch-diocel stopped, turned to Tamas. "The Church will collect its normal fifteen-percent tithe. This was the price of our support."

"The price?" Tamas said. "I thought this coup was sanctioned by the Church because Manhouch was letting his people starve. Or was it because Manhouch was taxing the Church in order to pay for his palace of concubines? I don't remember which. The Church will get five percent and be happy with it."

The arch-diocel took a step toward Tamas. "How dare you."

Tamas matched the step. His hand twitched toward the small sword at his hip. "Call me out," Tamas said. "I'll make it interesting and not choose pistols."

The arch-diocel hesitated. A smirk stirred at the corner of his lips. "If I were to remove you, this nation would collapse into chaos and anarchy," he said. "My first charge is toward my God. My second charge is to my country. I will speak to my fellow arch-diocels and see what I can do." He removed his hands from the robe, spreading them in a gesture of peace.

Tamas gave Charlemund an insincere smile. "Thank you." He rested his hand on the hilt of his sword.

The eunuch spoke up. "If there isn't any money in the king's treasury, what has Manhouch been spending?"

"The Church's money," the arch-diocel grunted.

"Some of it," Ondraus corrected. "He's taken out enormous amounts of credit with a number of banks all across the Nine. The crown owes the Kez government nearly a hundred million krana."

Ricard gave a low whistle.

Tamas turned to the reeve. "The crown is about to drop into a basket. Once you've started to dissolve the nobility's property, begin to pay back the domestic banks. If there's any money to be found, pay off our allies next."

"It's mostly to Kez," Ondraus said with a shrug.

"Good. Let them rot."

He turned at the sound of laughter. The eunuch was still by the window. He'd fetched himself a glass of chilled water and was now staring into the bottom. "Your personal vendetta against the Kez is going to see us all on the wrong side of a headsman's blade," the eunuch said.

"It's not personal," Tamas snapped. But he knew he wasn't fooling anyone. They all knew about his wife. All the Nine knew. That didn't stop him from denying it. "That debt explains why Manhouch was so eager to sign over Adro to the Kez." He paused. "Have any of you actually read the Accords?"

"They were meant to curtail the unions," Ricard said.

"And outlaw the Wings of Adom," Lady Winceslav added.

"Have any of you read the parts of the Accords that didn't have something to do directly with yourselves?"

Sitting toward the back of the room, the vice-chancellor raised his hand. Everyone else avoided Tamas's gaze.

"They would have destroyed Adro as we know it," Tamas said. "We would have been slaves to the Kez in all but name. The people are starving, the nation suffers under Manhouch and would suffer more under the Kez. *That* is why we send Manhouch to the guillotine." Not because the Kez did the same to Tamas's wife and Manhouch let it happen without protestation.

"Are you going to say anything?" Lady Winceslav spoke up suddenly.

"To whom?" Tamas said.

"To the crowd. You need to speak to the people. Their monarch is about to be beheaded. They will be leaderless. They need to know they have someone to direct them, to get them through the times ahead."

Through the almost inevitable war with Kez, she meant. "No," Tamas said. "I'll say nothing today. Besides, I'm not stepping in for the king. The six of you are. I'm here to protect the country and keep the peace while you create a government with the interests of the people in mind."

"It would be wise to say something," the vice-chancellor said, his birthmark shifting strangely as he spoke. "To keep the peace."

Tamas took them all in with his gaze. "The people want blood right now, not words. They've wanted it for years. I've felt it. You've felt it. That's why we came together to pull Manhouch from his throne. I'm going to give them blood. A lot of it. So much it will sicken them, choke them. Then my soldiers will funnel them toward the Samalian District, where they can loot the nobility's houses and rape their daughters and kill their younger sons. I intend to let them choke on their madness. In two days' time I will stifle the riots. Proclamations will be made. My soldiers will put down the rioters with one hand and give food and clothing to the poor with the other, and I *will* restore order."

The six members of his council stared back at him silently. Lady Winceslav had paled, and Ricard joined the eunuch in a study of the bottom of his glass. Tamas would let them think on that. Let them consider what he would do to protect his country, to see that justice is done and order restored.

"You are a dangerous man," the arch-diocel observed.

"You speak as if you can control a mob," the eunuch said. There was disdain in his voice.

"Mobs can't be controlled," Tamas said. "But they can be unleashed. I'm willing to accept the consequences. If you must object, then do so now, but I tell you: These people need blood."

The rest of them remained silent. After a few moments Tamas continued. "We've many other things to discuss."

Tamas took a seat in the corner and did more watching than talking as his coconspirators argued over the details of the coming months. Governors had to be appointed, laws rewritten, workers paid. They had a long, hard road ahead of them. He gave a low whistle, summoning the dogs, then rested a hand on each of their heads as he listened.

Tamas raised his head when the door to the balcony opened and he suddenly realized he'd been dozing.

"Sir," Olem said. "It's time."

Tamas stood up, shaking the sleep from his head. He went to the door, holding it open for Lady Winceslav. "My lady."

The group filed out onto the balcony. Tamas looked out over the Garden and the sight took his breath away. Not a single cobblestone could be seen between the pack of bodies below. People stood shoulder to shoulder, the murmur of voices sounding like the lap of waves on the beach. The crowd filled the King's Garden to excess and poured out into the five connecting streets. There was no end to the throng for as far as the eye could see.

"Sir," Olem said.

Tamas forced himself to look away from the crowd. He prided himself on being a man who felt little fear, but the size of such a throng made him feel small. He wondered briefly if he was mad. No one could control that writhing mass. The looks on the faces of his companions assured him that they shared his awe—even dry, annoyed Ondraus was speechless.

Tamas adjusted his hat to block out the noonday sun and ran a hand across his cheek. He realized he hadn't shaved in two days and the stubble was thick on his jaw. Hardly appropriate for a field marshal in a dress uniform.

The sound below them had sunk to a barely audible whisper. He turned and felt a surge of his heart when he realized that every face was directed at him.

"Never have I seen a crowd so large. An audience so willing," Tamas murmured. "Is everything ready?" he said to Olem.

"Yes, sir."

Tamas scanned the rooftops of the surrounding buildings. His powder mages and his best marksmen lined those rooftops, rifles sighted into the crowd. Tamas tried to picture the face of the Privileged who'd ripped apart his mages the night before. Weathered, older, with gray in her hair. Wrinkles in the corner of her eyes, and a robe that smelled of dust. He wondered if she'd show here in a bid to rescue the king. Up at Skyline Palace, visible on the horizon to the east, Taniel and the mercenaries were picking up her trail.

Tamas glanced at his companions on the balcony and wondered

what they'd say if they knew they were bait for a Privileged. He could sense that Olem's third eye was open and examining the crowd.

"Give the signal," Tamas said.

Olem lifted a pair of red signal flags. He waved them twice.

The gates to Sabletooth opened with a grinding shriek heard for half a mile around. The crowd turned away from Tamas, bodies twisting in giant waves as their attention was fixed to the opposite side of the King's Garden. Tamas leaned forward, heart ringing like a hammer in his chest.

Mounted soldiers poured through the gates of Sabletooth. They pushed their way through the crowd. Tamas could make out Sabon's shiny black pate at the head of the column, shouting directions. The crowd was forced back and a cordon opened. A simple prison wagon followed them out.

The crowd roared as with one voice and surged forward. For a moment Tamas feared that Sabon and his men would be pulled down. Would the king even reach the guillotine?

The soldiers pushed the crowd back. They inched across the square, soldiers fighting the mob the entire time. The king's cart came to rest before the guillotines, right below Tamas's balcony. Soldiers stretched out behind the wagon, forcing the cordon to remain open like a giant snake through the multitudes. Tamas swallowed a lump. Between the two rows of soldiers was a string of over a thousand people, legs connected by chains. The string led all the way back to Sabletooth. They were nobles and their oldest sons, plus many of their wives. Their rumpled finery meant nothing in the jaws of the mob as spittle and spoiled food flew past Tamas's soldiers.

"The headman's going to retire after this one," Olem said.

The sight both made Tamas's heart soar and sickened him, all at once. This was the culmination of decades of planning. He trembled in excitement and shook with self-doubt. If there was one action he'd be remembered for in the histories, this would be it.

There was a commotion down Queen Floun Avenue to Tamas's right. His heart jumped into this throat. "Rifle," he ordered.

Olem handed Tamas a rifle.

"Spare charge."

Tamas took the spare powder charge and broke it between his fingers. He touched the black powder to his tongue and felt an instant sizzle there. He shuddered and clutched at the railing as the world warped in his sight. He squeezed his eyes closed, and when he opened them, everything was in sharp focus. He could pick out individual hairs on the heads six floors below, and he could see half a mile down Queen Floun Avenue as if he was standing there himself.

"Dragoons," he said. "A whole company."

The dragoons wore the decorated uniforms of the king's Hielmen and pushed forward upon mighty warhorses. They shoved through the crowd as if it was an empty street, stampeding over women and children without a glance back. Swords were drawn, pistols out as they thundered forward.

Olem lifted the signal flag in one hand without being prompted. He twirled it over his head, then leveled it horizontally down Queen Floun Avenue. Tamas could see black-coated men, mere dots in the crowds, begin to head in that direction. They were big, surly men from the famed Mountainwatch, brought in just to work the crowds. The riflemen on the buildings above Queen Floun Avenue shifted to look down upon the dragoons. Tamas spared a glance at Olem: Sabon had briefed him well. Professional, unblinking, even when the Hielmen threatened the very heart of their plans.

"Don't fire until my signal," Tamas said. Olem's flag jolted out the order.

The dragoons slowed as they reached the King's Garden. The crowds were too thick even for their hundred-and-forty-stone animals. More bodies disappeared beneath their horses as there was no place to flee. People turned toward the dragoons.

The Hielmen's horses came to a complete stop. Where else could they go? Climb upon the very heads of the mob? The Hielmen frantically urged their mounts forward as wails went up behind them, friends and families screaming in anger, trying desperately to help their wounded.

The first Hielman was pulled off his mount and disappeared beneath the surface of the crowd. Hands reached for the others, who began swinging their sabers in panic. A pistol shot went off, and the crowd responded as one: with a roar of fury.

One Hielman lasted for several minutes, forcing his mount in a circle, hooves thrashing, sword swinging to hold off the crowds, before he joined his comrades, pulled down and gone. Tamas heard a gasp of disbelief. Lady Winceslav fainted. A head rose above the crowd. It still wore a Hielman's tall, plumed hat, but it most definitely lacked a body. It trailed blood and tissue as it was passed from hand to hand. Other heads soon joined it.

Tamas forced himself to watch. This was all his doing. For Adro. For the people.

For Erika.

"A bad way to go, sir," Olem said. He took a drag of his cigarette, watching the crowd with Tamas when even Charlemund had turned away.

"Aye," Tamas said.

The king and queen were led onto the guillotine platform. There were six guillotines, lined up and ready, operators waiting at attention. Manhouch and his wife stood before the crowd, pelted by rotten food. Tamas blinked as a chunk of bloody meat slapped the queen in the face, leaving red smeared on her alabaster skin and her cream nightgown. She fainted, falling to the floor of the platform. Manhouch didn't seem to notice.

Tamas glanced back toward the Hielmen's heads. They were making their way through the crowd, closer to the guillotine.

The king stared up at Tamas, then fumbled in his pocket, removing a soiled piece of paper. He cleared his throat and started to speak, though Tamas doubted anyone but the headsman could hear his words. The noise grew as Manhouch tried to yell his speech, until he finally fell silent, chin falling as he gave up. The headsman pulled on Manhouch's chains. Frozen, the king did not move until the headsman cuffed him on the back of the neck and dragged him to the guillotine.

It was a small blessing for them both, Tamas decided, that they were unconscious when the blade fell.

Manhouch's head dropped into a basket below the machine, and a fountain of blood sprayed the closest onlookers, even though an area of ten paces had been cleared for that purpose. The queen was loaded into the next machine as workers began to reset the first. Her head fell, a tumble of blond curls.

"This will take all day," Ricard murmured.

"Yes," Tamas said. "And tomorrow, too. I told you I'll give the people enough blood for them to choke on." He looked down on the crimson pool gathering underneath the guillotine, spreading out under the nervous feet of the nearest men and women. "It'll soak the King's Garden and stain the stones to rust."

Tamas scanned the crowd one more time and stepped away from the balcony. The Privileged hadn't come. It left another enemy out there unaccounted for. No, he corrected himself. Not unaccounted for. Taniel would find her. "The riots will start when people begin to get hungry," he announced to no one in particular. "We'll impose curfew tomorrow. Until then, I suggest you all stay off the street."

CHAPTER

6

Adamat hired a carriage to take him to Adopest University. It should not have been a long trip, but it seemed that the entire population of Adopest was heading toward the middle of the city, while the university was located on the outskirts. By the time they reached Kirkamshire, the tide of humanity had turned to a trickle. The university town was eerily quiet.

They'd all gone to see the execution. Tamas must have sent his fastest riders to the outskirts of the city to give everyone the chance to come see Manhouch's death. A risky move. The people would welcome it. Adamat welcomed it. He only hoped that they hadn't traded an idiot for a tyrant.

A distant buzz caught his ear as he walked the deserted university grounds. Adamat imagined it to be the roar of a million voices as the people watched the king's death. Looting would start soon, when people trickled away from the execution and realized everyone had left their doors unlocked, their shops untended. The riots would follow as brother turned against brother. Kresimir willing, he'd be back home before then.

He passed between the solarium and the library, his footsteps echoing in the empty courtyard, and up the steps of the main administration building. The mighty oak doors, banded with iron, were unlocked. Inside he passed by many office doors. He paused at a painting of the current vice-chancellor. Prime Lektor had been ugly, even in his youth, with a purple birthmark obstructing a third of his face. It was said he was an unrivaled scholar. Adamat continued on past the vice-chancellor's office to the next door down.

It was a small door, propped open with a wedge of wood, and it could very well have been a janitor's closet for all its bareness. From the hall Adamat could hear the scratching of an old-fashioned quill.

Adamat knocked twice on the open door. A young-looking man sat behind a plain desk in the corner of a cramped room. One might expect clutter in the office of the assistant to the vice-chancellor, but every scrap of paper, every book and scroll, was in its place and every surface dusted daily. Adamat smiled. Some things never changed.

"Adamat," Uskan said. He set his pen in its holder and blew on the ink before setting the paper to one side. "A pleasant surprise."

"I'm glad you're here, Uskan," Adamat said, "and not watching the execution."

A shadow flickered across Uskan's face as he rounded his desk and came forward to clasp Adamat's hand. "One of my understudies has a very creative pen. I told her to write down everything for posterity." Uskan made a disgusted face. "I have work to do. What need do I have for bloody spectacle?"

Adamat examined Uskan. His friend did indeed look young, far younger than forty-five years. He had the pinched face of a man who squints a lot, reading by too little light. "It's the spectacle of the century," Adamat said.

"Of the millennia," Uskan said. He returned to his desk and

offered Adamat the only other chair in the room. "Never in the history of the Nine, since their founding by Kresimir and his brothers, has a king been dethroned. Not once. I don't even... I don't even know what to say." He brushed the worried look from his face like a mote of unwanted dust. "How is Faye?"

"Out of town with the children, thankfully."

"A stroke of luck."

"Yes."

Uskan perked up. "How's the printing press working? I've been knee-deep in work for so long I haven't even thought to send you a letter. Must be exciting to see it work. The first steam-powered press in all of Adro!"

"You hadn't heard?" Adamat grimaced.

Uskan shook his head.

"It exploded."

Uskan's mouth fell open. "No."

"Killed an apprentice and destroyed half the building. I'd stepped out for a cup of tea and when I came back..." Adamat mimicked an explosion with his hands. "No more Adamat and Friends Publishing."

"Surely you were insured."

"Of course. They refused to pay. I sued for damages. They found it cheaper to bribe the magistrate than to cover all my expenses."

Uskan's mouth kept working silently. "I can't believe it. That had all the makings of fame and fortune. You'd be a wealthy man now if that had succeeded. Why, I've just read in the papers that eleven bookstores have opened in Adopest alone in the last six months. Reading is becoming very fashionable. Poetry, novels, history. The industry is booming!"

"Don't rub it in."

Uskan cringed. "Adamat. I'm so sorry."

Adamat waved a hand. "Things happen. It was nearly a year ago. Besides, I'm not here to talk about my troubles. I'm working."

"An investigation? At least you have that to fall back on."

"Yes."

"Anything I can do to help," Uskan said.

"I hope it won't be a bother. I need to know about something called 'Kresimir's Broken Promise,' or 'Kresimir's Promise.' "

Uskan leaned back and frowned at the ceiling. "It sounds..." he said after a few moments. "Something on the edge of my memory. But I do not recall. Not everyone has your gift." He stood up. "Let's go look."

They left the administration building and crossed to the library. Someone had thought to lock the ancient doors of the big building, but Uskan had his keys.

The vestibule was little more than a place to hang coats and wipe your shoes. Beyond that was one wide, open room with three tiered levels. Staircases and ladders seemed to be everywhere, with tables for research haphazardly placed at the end of bookshelves or beneath windows.

"I hope you have some idea of where to start," Adamat said. It was easy to forget how big the library really was—Adamat hadn't been there for decades. "Else this will take all day."

Uskan headed confidently to their right and up the nearest flight of stairs. "I think I do," he said. "Though it might take a while. We've had some major additions to our collection lately and I've not spent as much time in the library as I want. Still, can't complain about new books. The industry is booming, but books are still expensive." He glanced at Adamat. "A steam-powered printing press would have begun to change that."

Adamat rolled his eyes. Uskan meant well, but he spoke as if the explosion had been Adamat's fault.

Uskan counted rows of shelves before turning down one with purpose. He grabbed a sliding ladder and pushed it along in front of him. His voice echoed in the empty space above them. "It used to be Jileman University got all the good library grants. In fact, the Public Archives in Adopest is twice the size of our collection. Why didn't you go there first?"

Adamat paused to run his fingers along a leather book spine. He liked libraries. They were dry and dusty, with the smell of papers, the smell he associated most with knowledge. To an inspector, knowledge was paramount. "Because the city center is a zoo right now. Execution, remember?"

Uskan turned to blink at him. "Oh, right." He resumed pushing the ladder. "If we don't have luck here, go to the Archives. They're quite well organized. Some very talented librarians down there. Cross-reference 'theology' and 'history.' At least, that's where I'm going to look first." Uskan halted the rolling ladder and climbed up it. The heavy iron rattled as he climbed, and Adamat put a hand out to steady it.

"I try not to reference theology at all."

Uskan's dry chuckle drifted down from ten feet up. "Who does these days?" A pause. "Now, that's strange."

"What?"

The ladder rattled as Uskan came back down. "The books are missing. Someone must have checked them out. Only faculty are allowed to take books out of the library, and our school of theology is in shambles right now. It consists of three brothers who spend half the year on sabbatical in warmer climate. Hardly anyone studies theology anymore. It's all about mathematics and science. Kresimir, our physics and chemistry departments have quadrupled in size since I started here." He glanced back up the ladder to the empty spots on the bookshelf. "I distinctly remember... no matter, let's look somewhere else."

Adamat followed his friend up to the third floor. The books he thought to find there were also missing. They looked in two more places before Uskan leaned against a bookshelf and wiped his brow. "Someone must be doing a theology dissertation," he said. "Damned theology students always take the books. We don't get many these days, but when we do, they think they own the place because their grandfathers gave this grant or that back in the day."

Adamat wondered how much to tell him about his investigation.

The words had little danger on their own, but Adamat wanted as few people as possible to know the nature of his investigation. No sense risking being branded a traitor before Tamas was in full power.

"Do you have any books from the Bleakening? I've heard there is an abundance of writing on Kresimir from that time."

"Where did you hear that?"

"A newspaper I read in early spring, three years ago."

"Bah, the newspapers will print any rubbish. It was a very religious time, certainly, but the Bleakening was a dark ages bereft of knowledge. Kresimir and his siblings had disappeared. The new monarchies were locked in a struggle with the Predeii—an ancient caste of powerful Privileged. Not much of anything survives from that period. The vice-chancellor once told me that if we had half the knowledge about sorcery and science that we did during Kresimir's Time—most of which was lost during the Bleakening—we'd be living in a golden age for noble and peasant alike."

"Well, try referencing theology, history, and sorcery."

"I'll make a librarian of you yet," Uskan said.

"What do you know about sorcery?" Adamat asked.

"Sorcerous philosophy is a bit of a hobby of mine, though I have no talent for sorcery myself. My grandfather was a Privileged. A healer, actually." Uskan paused here and gave Adamat an expectant look.

"Yes?" Adamat prompted.

Uskan scowled. "A healer. They're the rarest of Privileged. Even schoolboys with an introductory class on sorcery know that. It's said the human body is so complex that only one of every hundred Privileged has more than the most rudimentary healing capabilities."

"Rare, then?"

"Very rare, Adamat. Lord, with your penchant for details one would think you'd know about this sort of thing. Don't you know anything about sorcery?"

"Not really," Adamat admitted. He lived in a world of city streets, citizens, and criminals. He didn't have time for sorcery and frankly, it was a foreign thing. He came across the odd Knack here and there, but stronger stuff was the realm of the cabals, and an inspector had no business with any of that. What he knew came from a few hours of schooling when he was a boy.

"You're a Knacked," Uskan said, "so you have the third eye, correct?"

"Yes, but I'm not sure what that has to do with anything..."

"So you can see the auras of all things when you open your sight and look into what Privileged call the Else?"

Nowadays Adamat rarely opened his third eye. It was an uncomfortable feeling at best, but he remembered the glow that surrounded everything in that sight, as if the world had been painted in vibrant pastels. "Yes."

"A Privileged manipulates the Else," Uskan said. "Each of a Privileged's fingers is attached to one of the elements: Fire, Earth, Water, Air, and Aether."

"But fire isn't an element," Adamat said. "It's the result of combustion."

Uskan sniffed. "Bear with me. This explanation is recognized as imperfect in the light of discoveries of the last hundred years, but it's the best we have. Now, each finger corresponds to an element and to a Privileged's strength with that element, the thumb being the strongest digit. A Privileged uses his strong hand—most often his right—to call upon the auras of that which he wants to manipulate in the Else. He uses his off hand to direct those auras once they have been pulled into our world."

"So how does a powder mage's magic work?"

"Bugger if I know. Privileged hate powder mages, and the cabals have always discouraged a study of them."

"Why such a strong hate?" Adamat had heard most Privileged were allergic to gunpowder.

"Fear," Uskan said. "Most Privileged's spells have a range of less than a half mile. Powder mages can shoot from over twice that.

The cabals have never liked being at a disadvantage. I've also been told that whereas all things, living or dead or elemental, have auras in the Else, gunpowder does not, and that makes Privileged nervous. Ah, here we are."

Uskan paused in front of a bookcase. He ran his finger along several spines before taking them out and piling them into Adamat's arms. Dust rose as the books thumped against each other. "Only one missing," Uskan said. "I know just where it is, too. The vice-chancellor's office."

"Can we get it?"

"The vice-chancellor is away, summoned to Adopest early this morning with some urgency. I don't have a key to his office. We'll have to wait until he gets back."

They retired to one of the tables with their stacks of books and set to their research. Adamat sat down and flipped open the first book. He frowned. "Uskan?"

"Hmm?" Uskan looked over. He leapt to his feet and rounded the table, moving faster than Adamat had ever seen him. "What is this? Who the pit did this?"

The first several pages of the book had been removed, and dozens after that had whole sections of the text blacked out, as if someone had dipped their finger in ink and smudged it along the page. Uskan mopped at his forehead with a handkerchief and began pacing behind Adamat.

"These books are invaluable," he said. "Who would do such a thing?"

Adamat leaned forward and squinted at the ripped line of the paper. He judged the book in his hands. It was made with vellum, thicker than today's paper and four times as tough. The ripped edge was slightly blackened.

"A Privileged," Adamat said.

"How can you tell?"

Adamat pointed to the ripped edge. "Do you know of anything

besides sorcery that could make a burn like that without damaging the rest of the book?"

Uskan resumed pacing. "A Privileged! Kresimir damn them. They should know the value of books!"

"I think they do," Adamat said. "Else they would have burned the whole thing. Let's take a look at the rest here." He reached for the next book, and then the next. Of the eleven they'd removed from the shelf, seven had passages smudged or had pages ripped out. By the time they finished the stack, Uskan was fuming.

"Wait till the vice-chancellor finds out! He'll head straight down to Skyline and beat those Privileged senseless, he'll—"

"Tamas has executed the entire cabal."

Uskan froze. His nostrils flared in and out, his lips bunched in a fierce frown. "I suppose there will be no redress for this, then."

Adamat shook his head. "Let's take a look at what we have."

They spent some time with the books and they found eight different places where smudged writing could have been references to Kresimir's Promise. Yet the passages were indecipherable.

"That last book," Adamat said. "The one in the vice-chancellor's office...?"

"Yes," Uskan said absently, scratching his head. "'*In Service of the King.*' It outlines the duties of the royal cabals in their protection of the kings of the Nine. A very famous work."

Adamat smoothed the front of his coat. "Let's see if he left his door unlocked."

Uskan returned the books and chased Adamat out into the courtyard of the library. "He won't have left it unlocked," he said. "Let's just wait until he gets back. The vice-chancellor is a private sort of man."

"I'm on an investigation," Adamat said as he entered the main administration building.

"That doesn't mean you have the right to look through other people's studies," Uskan said. "Besides, the door will be locked."

He smiled triumphantly at Adamat when the doorknob rattled but did not turn in Adamat's hand.

"No matter," Adamat said. He crouched down and removed the tiny set of lockpicks he kept in one boot. Uskan's eyes grew wide.

"What? No, you can't do that!"

"When did you say the vice-chancellor will be back?"

"Not until late," Uskan said. "I..." He realized his mistake at once as Adamat began fiddling with the lock. Uskan huffed and slumped against the wall. "I should have told you, 'Any minute,'" he muttered.

"You're a terrible liar," Adamat said.

"Yes, I am. And I won't be able to lie to the vice-chancellor when he asks if someone's been in his office."

"Come, now. He won't know."

"Of course he will, how can..."

The lock clicked and Adamat pushed the door open gently. The office inside was more representative of what one might expect from a university type. Books and papers were everywhere. There were plates of half-eaten food on chairs, tables, even the floor. The entire room was walled by bookshelves twice as tall as a man, and those were overflowing, sagging with the weight of too many books stacked haphazardly upon each other.

"Don't move anything," Uskan said. "He knows exactly where he left every item. He'll know if..." Uskan fell silent at a look from Adamat. "Here, let me find the book," he said sullenly.

Adamat stayed at the edge of the paper-and-ink jungle that was the vice-chancellor's office while Uskan looked for the missing book with the natural grace of a secretary. Papers were lifted, plates and books shifted, but everything was returned to its exact place.

Adamat stood on his toes and surveyed the room. "Is this it?" Adamat asked, pointing to the center of the vice-chancellor's desk.

Uskan pulled his head out from beneath the vice-chancellor's chair. "Oh. Yes."

Adamat stepped gingerly through the room. He lifted the book carefully and began to leaf through it. Uskan came up beside him.

"No damaged pages," Adamat reported. He scanned the pages, flipping through, looking for just two words to stand out. He found his prize in the book's afterword, on the last page.

Adamat read aloud: "And they will guard Kresimir's Promise with their lives, for if it is broken, all the Nine might perish." He scanned the page, and then the page after, and then the page before. There were no other references. He scowled at the pages. "This doesn't make sense."

Uskan's finger stabbed the middle of the book, right at the spine.

"What?"

"More pages missing," Uskan said. "Half the afterword." His voice trembled with rage.

Adamat looked closer. Sure enough, the pages had been torn clean from the book. The binding was different on this volume, making it difficult to tell that the pages were missing at all. He sighed. "Where can I find another copy of this book?"

Uskan shook his head. "Maybe the Public Archives. I think Nopeth University has a copy, too."

"I'm not sitting in a coach for the better part of a month just to 'maybe' find a book at Nopeth University," Adamat said. He snapped the book shut and returned it to the vice-chancellor's desk. "I'll have to check the Public Archives."

"The riots," Uskan protested as Adamat made his way to the door.

Adamat paused.

"They'll have it locked up," Uskan said. "The Archives contain tax records, family histories, even safe-deposit boxes. They have guards, Adamat."

That was only a problem if they caught him. "Thanks for your help," Adamat said. "Let me know if you find anything else."

CHAPTER

7

Taniel eyed the mob moving systematically down the street and wondered if they'd give him much trouble. The city was in chaos; wagons overturned, buildings set ablaze, bodies left in the street to fall victim to looters and worse. The smoke hanging like a curtain over the city seemed as if it would never blow away.

Taniel flipped through his sketchbook randomly. The pages fell open to a portrait of Vlora. He paused there for just a moment before he gripped the spine of the book in one hand and tore the page out. He crumpled it up and threw it to the street. He stared at the jagged rip in his book and instantly regretted damaging it. He didn't have money for a new sketchbook. He'd sold everything of value in order to buy a diamond ring in Fatrasta. That damned diamond ring he'd left nailed to a fop in Jileman. He could still see the blood spreading from the man's shoulder, crimson dripping from the ring he'd slid on the man's sword before he shoved it in.

Taniel should have kept the ring. He could have pawned it. He forced a lump down in his throat. He regretted not saying something—anything—to Vlora as she stood in the bedroom door, sheets clutched to her chest.

He checked the time on a nearby clock tower. Four hours until his father's soldiers would begin to reassert order. Any of the mob left out after midnight would have to deal with Field Marshal Tamas's men. The soldiers might have a hard time of it. There were a lot of desperate people in Adopest these days.

"What do you think of these mercenaries?" Taniel asked. He bent over and picked up the rumpled sketch of Vlora and smoothed it on his leg, then folded it and tucked it into his sketchbook.

Ka-poel shrugged. She watched the approaching mob. They were led by a big man, a farmer with worn, old overalls and a make-shift truncheon. Probably moved to the city to work in a factory but couldn't join the union. He saw Taniel and Ka-poel standing in the doorway of a closed shop and turned toward them, raising his truncheon. More victims to be had.

Taniel ran a finger along the fringe of his buckskin jacket and touched the butt of a pistol at his hip. "You don't want any trouble here, friend," he said. Ka-poel's hands tightened into little fists.

The farmer's eyes fell to the silver powder keg pin on Taniel's chest. He came up short and said something to the man behind him. They turned away suddenly. The rest followed, dark looks for Taniel, but none of them willing to get mixed up with a powder mage.

Taniel breathed a sigh of relief. "Those two hired thugs have been gone a long time."

Julene, the Privileged mercenary, and Gothen, the magebreaker, had left to follow the Privileged's trail almost an hour ago. She was close, they'd said, and they'd scout her out, then come back for Taniel and Ka-poel. Taniel was beginning to think they'd been abandoned.

Ka-poel jerked her thumb at her own chest and then shaded her eyes, thrusting her head out as if looking for something.

Taniel nodded. "Yeah, I know you can find her," he said, "but I'll let these mercs do the groundwork. That's all they're gonna be good for any—"

Taniel's head cracked against the stone of the building at his back, his ears pounding from the sudden explosion. Ka-poel rocked into him and he caught her before she could fall. He steadied her on her feet and shook his head to dispel the ringing in his ears.

He'd been half a mile from a munitions dump once when the powder caught fire. This had felt like that kind of explosion, but his Marked senses told him it wasn't powder. It was sorcery.

A gout of flame shot into the air not two city blocks from them. As quickly as it was there, it was gone, and Taniel heard screams. He checked on Ka-poel. Her eyes were wide, but she seemed unhurt. "Come on," he said, and broke into a run.

He ran past the mob, all scattered on the cobbles like so many children's toys knocked down by an angry fist, and turned the corner to head toward the explosion. He thumped into someone and was thrown off his feet. He hit the ground and immediately pushed himself up, sparing barely a glance for the person he'd run into.

He was two steps into running again when what he'd seen caught up with him: an older woman with gray hair, a plain brown jacket and skirt, and Privileged's gloves.

Taniel whirled, drawing his pistol.

"Stop!" he shouted.

Ka-poel careened around the corner, directly into his line of fire. He lowered his pistol and ran toward her. Over her small shoulder he watched the Privileged turn. Her fingers danced, and Taniel felt the heat of a flame as the Privileged touched the Else.

Taniel grabbed Ka-poel and flung them both toward the ground. A fireball the size of his fist tore past his face, hot enough to curl his hair. He lifted his pistol and sighted, feeling the calm of the powder trance take him as he concentrated on the aim, the powder, and his target. He pulled the trigger.

The bullet would have hit the woman's heart had she not stumbled at that moment. Instead it took her in the shoulder. She twitched with the impact and snarled at him.

Taniel looked around. He needed someplace to take cover and reload. An old brick warehouse twenty paces away would do. "Time to go," Taniel said to Ka-poel. He jerked her to her feet and ran for the warehouse.

Out of the corner of his eye he watched the Privileged's fingers dance. It was a fascinating thing, watching a Privileged touch the Else—if that Privileged wasn't trying to kill you. With their mastery of the elements a skilled Privileged could throw a fireball or call lightning.

Taniel felt the ground shudder. They got behind cover of the warehouse, but the building rumbled. He felt the scream wrench itself from his throat in anticipation of the powers that would tear through the building and destroy them.

The building cracked, jerked, but it didn't explode. Smoke billowed from sudden cracks in the mortar. An audible *wump* split the air. Then everything was still. They were alive. Something had stopped whatever sorcery the Privileged had been about to throw at them.

Taniel glanced at Ka-poel. He felt a shaky breath escape him. "Was that you?"

Ka-poel gave him an unreadable look. She pointed.

"After her. Right. Come on."

He sprinted out into the street, switching his spent pistol for a loaded one. He paused a moment when he saw Julene and Gothen running toward them.

Julene looked like a keg of powder had exploded in her face. Her hair was scorched, her clothes blackened. Even Gothen had a wild look in his eyes and black marks on his shirt, and sorcery wasn't supposed to be able to touch him. The sword in his hand was missing a foot of blade.

"What the pit did you two do?" Taniel said. "You were supposed to come back and get me before going after her."

"We don't need a damned Marked getting in our way," Julene replied with a rude gesture.

"She shouldn't have known we were there," Gothen said. He gave Taniel a sheepish look. "But she did."

"And she did that?" Taniel pointed at Gothen's broken blade.

Gothen frowned. "Oh, for pit's sake." He threw the half sword on the ground.

"We stand here talking and we'll lose her," Taniel said. "Now, Julene, try to flank her, I'll—"

"I don't take orders from you," Julene said, leaning forward. "I'll go straight down her throat." She tugged at her gloves and took off running down the street.

"Damn it!" Taniel slapped Gothen's shoulder. "You're with me."

They headed down a side street, then onto the next main thoroughfare, running parallel to Julene.

"What the pit happened?" Taniel asked.

"We found her in an astronomer's shop," Gothen said between gasps as he ran, swords, buckles, and pistols rattling. "We circled the place, checked all exits, and laid our trap. We were just getting ready to go in after her when the whole front of the building blew off. Julene barely shielded herself. I could feel the heat of the explosion! That's not supposed to happen. I should be able to nullify any aura she can summon from the Else. No fire, no heat, no energy from it should reach me, but it did."

"So she's powerful."

"Very," Gothen said.

Taniel saw Julene sprint past an alleyway the next street over. He came up short and took a deep breath, motioning for Gothen to stop. Something was wrong. He turned around.

"Ka-poel?"

She'd stopped in the mouth of the alley. She put a finger to her lips, her eyes half-lidded. She pointed down the alley.

Taniel gestured for Gothen to go first. He would void any traps or sorcery flung at them. Taniel lifted his pistol, keeping it aimed just over Gothen's shoulder. The alley was filled with debris—trash, mud, and shit; a few half-rotted kegs. Nothing big enough for a person to hide behind. It was well lit by the noonday sun.

"There!" Gothen surged forward, and Taniel caught a movement in the alley up ahead. He blinked, trying to see clearly. It was as if light were turning in on itself, making a slight shadow where a person could hide.

Then the Privileged appeared. Her hands twitched and she leveled them at Gothen. Gothen braced himself.

The air shimmered, distorted by a furnace of impending sorcery. Gothen yelled, the veins on his neck standing out. Taniel fired.

The bullet glanced off her skin as if it were metal, ricocheting harmlessly down the alley. The Privileged threw her hands out. Gothen tumbled backward and fell to the ground.

There were handholds built into the brick side of the building for roof access. The Privileged climbed them with the ease and speed of someone far younger, and was over the roof two stories up before Taniel could reload one of his pistols. He took a snort of powder and climbed up after her.

"Don't lose her!" Taniel shouted back to Gothen. Ka-poel raced back out into the main street to track the Privileged's progress.

Taniel made it to the roof and swung up over. The Privileged leapt to the next roof over and spun, throwing a fireball. The powder trance burned through Taniel. He could *see* the auras of her sorcery, could *feel* the path the fireball would take. He ducked and rolled, then came back to his feet. She fled, clattering and sliding across the clay-tiled roof.

Taniel cleared the next gap easily. He lost sight of the Privileged with the slant of the roof, then found her again as she crested the next roof over. He fired off a shot.

He hit her once again, but once again she didn't go down. It had been a square shot, right to the spine. She should have been dead, or at the very least wounded and bleeding. She hardly stumbled.

Taniel snarled. He put away his pistols and swung his rifle into his hand. He fixed his bayonet. He'd do this the hard way.

A powder mage in a full trance could run down a horse. He was within feet of her in two more buildings. She leapt between roofs. Her toe barely caught the lip of the next. She slipped and fell, grabbing the tiles.

Taniel cleared the roof with space to spare. He skidded to a stop and turned, ready to put his bayonet through her eye. She let go of the roof and fell to the street below.

Taniel swore. He hesitated only a moment before jumping after her. Even in the height of a powder trance his knees ached and his body shivered when he hit the ground. He landed in a crouch next to the Privileged, who was already on her feet. He reacted on instinct, thrusting his bayonet. He felt it slide home.

The woman slumped above him, her gloved hand a mere foot from his head. She had the face of an aging woman who'd once been very beautiful, her skin now lined and weathered, crow's-feet in the corners of her eyes. She let out a gasp, then jerked herself off the end of Taniel's bayonet.

"You've no idea what's going on, boy." Her voice was a deadly whisper.

Taniel heard the jingle of Gothen's weapons as the magebreaker ran up beside him, his pistol leveled.

Taniel felt the earth rumble.

"Get down!" Gothen leapt between Taniel and the Privileged.

The ground splintered and cracked and fell out from under them. Taniel's whole body screamed at the pressure released. He felt as if he'd been jammed into the bottom of a cannon and used as fuel for an explosion. His ears popped, he felt dizzy. His head pounded.

Masonry rained down all around them.

When the dust began to clear, Taniel saw Gothen still crouching over him, his face in a grimace. The magebreaker opened one eye. His lips moved, but Taniel couldn't hear a thing. The whole world wavered. Taniel got to his feet and looked around. Ka-poel approached him through the haze. Julene was not far behind. The buildings on either side of him were completely gone, leveled to their foundations, damp basements filled with rubble and hovering curtains of dust. There were smears of blood and bits of flesh in the debris. There had been people in those buildings—people who hadn't had a magebreaker standing between them and the explosion.

Taniel drew a shaky breath.

Julene marched straight up to Taniel and knocked him off his trembling legs with a shove. Ka-poel slid in between them, her silent glare driving Julene back a step. It was several moments before Taniel could hear well enough to know what Julene was shouting.

"... let her go! You let her get away! You bloody fool!"

Taniel climbed to his feet. He gently pushed Ka-poel out of the way by the shoulder.

Julene stepped forward and punched him full in the face. His head jerked back. He reacted without thinking, grabbing her next blow out of the air and twisting her hand. He slapped her. "Back the pit off." Taniel turned and spit blood. "She's dead. There's no way anyone could have lived through that."

"She's not dead." Julene's cheeks were flushed, but she made no move to continue the fight. "I can still feel her. She got away."

"I ran her through with three spans of steel! She wasn't walking away from that."

"You think steel can hurt her? You think it can really hurt her? You don't know shit."

Taniel took a deep, calming breath, then a snort of powder. "Ka-poel," he said. "Is she still alive?"

Ka-poel hefted the end of Taniel's rifle in her small hands and drew her finger through the blood along the bayonet's edge. She smeared it between her fingers. After a moment she nodded.

"Can you track her?"

Ka-poel nodded again.

Julene scoffed. "I can't even track her," she said. "She's covered her trail. Even wounded she's far more powerful than you can know. This damned girl can't find her."

"Pole?"

Ka-poel snorted and turned away. She paused a few moments to get her bearings, then pointed.

"We have a heading," Taniel said. "Get yourself under control and watch how a real tracker does it." He gestured to Ka-poel. "Lead on."

Taniel shaded his eyes from rain and looked up at Julene. She stood above him, arms folded, a belligerent smile twisting the scar on her face. "It's been two days," she said. "Admit your pet savage can't track this bitch and we'll get out of this rain and tell Tamas there's a problem."

"Giving up so easily, eh?" Taniel kept his hand in the gutter and tried not to think about the substance squelching between his fingers. Storm drains collected everything, from human waste to dead animals and whatever garbage and mud piled up in the streets. During a storm like this, all of it was swept down into the large sewers beneath the city. This drain was clogged, leaving Taniel up to his shoulder in rainwater and filth, and he was enjoying it just about as much as he was enjoying Julene's constant badgering. "You know Tamas won't pay you until the job's done, don't you?" he reminded her.

"We'll find her," Julene said. "Just not today. Not in this rain. *She* caused this storm. I can feel it. The auras swirl, summoned from the Else. It muddies her trail too much, but once the rain has cleared up, *I'll* find her trail again."

"Ka-poel already has her trail." Taniel stretched a little farther, his cheek touching the squalid puddle he lay in. He felt something hard, wrapped his hand around it, and pulled it out.

"She's been scraping her fingernails between street cobbles and having you dig in every ditch between here and . . . what the pit is that?"

Taniel climbed to his feet. The glob of gray mud in his hand looked like the scrapings from a hundred boots. His stomach crawled at the smell of it and he held it at arm's length. The whole mass clung to a long piece of wood. With a squelching, sucking sound the puddle at his feet slowly began to drain.

"Broken cane, I think," Taniel said.

Ka-poel came over to examine the stinking mud. She poked it with one finger, her head held up and away, scrutinizing the whole mass down the bridge of her nose. Her fingers darted in suddenly, then came out, pinched together.

Julene leaned forward. "What's that?" She shook her head. "Nothing. Stupid girl."

Taniel washed his arm in the cleanest puddle he could find, then took his shirt and buckskin coat from Gothen. To Julene, "You need sharper eyes. It's a hair. The Privileged's hair."

"That's impossible. To find a single hair from the Privileged in all this muck. Even if it did belong to her, what can your savage do with it?"

Taniel shrugged. "Find her."

Ka-poel walked away and opened her satchel. She worked with her back to them for a few moments. When she turned around, she straightened her satchel on her shoulder and gave a brisk nod. She tapped herself in the middle of the chest and then made a grasping motion.

Taniel grinned as he buttoned up his shirt. "We have her."

They flagged down a hackney cab. Ka-poel sat up with the driver to direct him, and Taniel, Julene, and Gothen climbed inside. Julene made a disgusted sound a moment after the door closed.

"You smell like filth," she said. "I'd rather be in the rain than in here with you. I'll be on the footboard." She swung back outside. A moment passed, and then the carriage jerked forward.

"Ka-poel can track the Privileged with a hair?" Gothen asked after they'd been moving for several minutes, his knees knocking uncomfortably close to Taniel's.

"Hard to do it with one hair," Taniel said. "Helps if there's more. The blood from my bayonet, a discarded nail in the street—this Privileged bites her nails—an eyelash. One bit leads to the next. The more she has, the easier it is to track. If we want to sneak up on this Privileged, we need a precise location."

Taniel opened his sketchbook and flipped through it, pausing briefly on the sketch of Vlora tucked between two pages, before moving on to a half-finished drawing of the Privileged. He was sketching from memory, but he'd been the only one of the four of them to get a good look at her. Gothen scanned the drawing for a few moments. When he finished, Taniel snapped the book shut, returning it to his jacket.

"How does Ka-poel's sorcery work?" Gothen asked.

"No idea," Taniel said. "I've never seen her do magic. Not what we think of as magic, anyway. No fingers twitching, no summoning elemental auras." He'd long ago stopped trying to figure out her sorcery.

Gothen cleared his throat after a minute. He didn't look at

Taniel directly, but a sly smile crossed his face. "Julene and I, we have a bet."

Taniel tapped out a line of powder on the back of his hand and snorted it. "What's that?"

"Julene thinks you're bedding the savage. I say you aren't."

"Not exactly the bet of a gentleman," Taniel said.

"We're all soldiers here," Gothen said. His grin widened.

"How much was the wager?"

"A hundred krana."

"So much for women's intuition. Tell her she owes you a hundred."

"Thought so," Gothen said. "Men are so much easier to read than women. You look at her—the savage—like that once in a while, but even then it's only a hint of longing, not the look of a lover."

Taniel scowled at the magebreaker and shifted in his seat, not sure how to respond. In an officers' setting he'd call a man out for that. Here, though . . . well, like Gothen said, they were both soldiers.

"She's nothing more than a kid," Taniel said. "Besides, the whole time I've known Ka-poel, I've been engaged to another woman."

"Ah. Congratulations."

"The engagement is off."

"Your pardon," Gothen said, looking away.

Taniel tapped out another line on the back of his hand. He waved his snuffbox in the air dismissively. "Think nothing of it." He snorted the black powder and took a deep breath, then leaned his head against the side of the carriage. He listened to the patter of rain on the rooftop, to the clatter of the horse's hooves and the wheels on the cobbles. So many noises that could drown out his thoughts.

Where was Vlora, he wondered, at this moment? Perhaps just arriving in Adopest. Maybe already here and gone, sent off on assignment by Tamas. He'd forced the question out of his mind every silent moment since he'd nailed that fop to the wall, wriggling on his own sword like a pinned butterfly. What had gone wrong? He'd made a mistake, going off to Fatrasta like he did. Getting tangled up in a war just to impress Tamas. He'd left her alone for too long. The man who'd bedded her was a professional philanderer. It wasn't her fault.

He made a fist, reeled in his anger. Was he mad because he loved Vlora? Or was he mad because another man had sullied his woman? Had Vlora truly been *his* woman? Taniel couldn't remember a time at which he *wasn't* going to marry Vlora. Tamas had thrust them together in every possible situation. She was a gifted powder mage, and chances were their children would be gifted as well. Tamas had encouraged them to be together for years. If anything, Vlora was more Tamas's future daughter-in-law than she was ever Taniel's future wife. He swallowed that thought, and with it the satisfaction with Tamas's disappointment. Now Taniel didn't have to marry at all if he didn't want—or he'd find a wife of his own, not some prearranged powder-mage bride. Maybe Ka-poel. Taniel chuckled aloud, ignoring Gothen's curious glance. Tamas would be absolutely livid if Taniel married a foreign savage. His amusement died down, and he resisted the urge to open his sketchbook and look at Vlora's drawing.

"Awfully nice part of town," Gothen said, pulling Taniel from his thoughts. The magebreaker held back the curtain just enough to see outside. A moment later the carriage jostled to a stop. Taniel opened the door.

They were in the Samalian District. Thick smoke hung over the entire city, mixing with the light rain and stinging Taniel's eyes. The place was silent—the mob had been quelled two days prior and in their wake had left little of what had once been rows of stately manors. Smoldering ruins and gutted houses were all that remained.

Except this one. The townhouse was three stories tall, and made of ancient gray stone. It had been modeled after castles of old with parapets and walks. The walls were blackened from the fires raging around, but the building itself seemed undamaged. It was easy to see why.

The parapets were manned by soldiers. Cobbles had been torn up from the street and made into a waist-high wall in front of the main entrance. More soldiers squatted behind that, their muskets at the ready, watching Taniel's carriage with outright hostility.

Taniel swung out of the carriage. Julene was already on the ground, pulling on her gloves. Ka-poel climbed down from beside the driver.

"Whose house is this?" Taniel asked the driver.

The man scratched his chin. "General Westeven's."

A squad of soldiers issued from the townhouse and headed straight toward them. Taniel felt his gut wrench. They wore the all-too-familiar gray-and-white uniforms and the high, plumed hats of the king's Hielmen. The Hielmen were supposed to have been wiped out. Yet here they were, guarding the residence of the former head of the king's guard. General Westeven was nearly eighty, ancient by all standards, yet it was said he was still sharp and alert. Of all of Adro's commanders, only Westeven had the reputation to match Tamas.

"Is the general in the city?" Taniel asked. Surely Tamas would have dealt with him. A loose end like this couldn't have been left.

"Heard a rumor he was back," the driver said. "He was supposed to be on holiday in Novi. He cut it short and returned just yesterday."

Taniel glanced at Ka-poel. "You sure she's here?"

Ka-poel nodded.

"Pit."

The Hielmen halted five paces from Taniel. Their captain was an older man with a sour face. He was taller than Taniel by half a hand, and when his eyes fell on Taniel's powder keg pin, his lip curled into a sneer.

"You've a woman inside your house," Taniel said, fingering his pistol. "A Privileged. I'm here to arrest her in the name of Field Marshal Tamas."

"We don't recognize the authority of traitors here, boy."

"So you admit you're protecting her?"

"She's the general's guest," the captain said.

A guest. Hielmen under the command of General Westeven and now they had a Privileged? This was dangerous territory. He could see rifles in windows on the floors above and on the parapets. The Hielman captain wore a sword and a pistol. Two of his guards carried long, slender rifles with fist-sized cartridges attached underneath—air canisters on air rifles. Weapons specifically designed to be unaffected by a powder mage's power. No doubt some of the marksmen above carried the same weapons.

With Julene and the magebreaker he could probably fight his way into the manor. Soldiers were one thing to deal with, the Privileged another.

He could feel when Julene touched the Else. He held up a hand. "No," he said. "Back down."

"Like pit I will," Julene said. "I'll burn through this lot and—"

"Gothen," Taniel said. "Rein her in." He had to get away from here. Warn Tamas. If General Westeven was in the city, he wouldn't take too long to marshal his forces. He'd attack quickly and go straight for the heart. Taniel moistened dry lips. "We're going."

"Sir," one of the Hielmen said. "That's Taniel Two-Shot."

The captain's eyes narrowed. "You're not going anywhere, Two-Shot."

"In the carriage," Taniel said. "We're leaving. Driver!"

The soldiers lowered their muskets. Taniel leapt onto the footboard of the carriage. He drew his pistol, swung around. He shot one of the Hielmen in the chest before the man could bring his weapon to bear. He tossed his pistol through the carriage window and looked toward the Hielmen, reaching out with his senses for their powder. Two of them carried standard muskets and the captain had a pistol. They'd all have powder reserves.

He found their powder horns easily. He touched the powder with a thought, causing a single spark.

The explosion nearly knocked him off the carriage. The horses screamed, and Taniel held on for dear life as the animals fled in terror. He took one look back. The Hielman captain had been blown clear in two. One of his companions struggled to sit up. The rest were in bloody pieces in the road. No one bothered to fire at the fleeing carriage.

When the driver finally got control of his animals, Taniel stuck his head into the carriage.

"I could have torn through them," Julene said.

"And gotten us all killed. They had at least two dozen soldiers with air rifles watching us, not to mention the Privileged inside. I want you two to get out. Keep an eye on that townhouse. If the Privileged leaves, follow her but *do not* try to fight your way in."

"Where are you going?" Gothen asked.

"To warn my father."

Taniel climbed up beside the driver and told him to slow down for a moment. Gothen and Julene exited out the other side, jumping to the ground and heading into an alley. Taniel half hoped they'd try the manor against his orders, just so he didn't have to deal with them again. But he needed that magebreaker.

"You'll be paid well," Taniel said to the driver.

The driver nodded, his mouth in a firm line.

"Take us to the House of Nobles," Taniel said. "As quick as you can."

CHAPTER

8

Olem," Tamas said, "did you know someone wrote a biography about me?"

Olem perked up from his at-ease position beside the door. "No, sir, I didn't."

"Not many do." Tamas pressed his fingers together and watched the door. "The royal cabal had them all bought up and burned—well, most of them anyway. The author, Lord Samurset, fell out of favor with the crown and was banished from Adro."

"The royal cabal didn't like his portrayal?"

"Oh, not at all. He was very favorable toward powder mages. Said they were a fantastically modern weapon that would one day replace Privileged altogether."

"Dangerous conjecture."

Tamas nodded. "I'm just vain enough to have rather enjoyed the book."

"What did he say about you?"

"Samurset claims that my marriage made me conservative, that my son's birth gave me mercy, and that my wife's death hardened both qualities with an objectiveness to make them useful. He said that my climb to the rank of field marshal while on the Gurla campaign was the best thing to happen to the Adran military in a thousand years." Tamas waved his hand dismissively. "Rubbish, most of it, but I do have a confession."

"Sir?"

"There are times when I don't feel a sense of mercy or justice or anything but pure rage. Times that I feel I'm twenty again and the solution to every problem is pistols at twenty paces. Olem, that is the most dangerous feeling a commander can have. Which is why, if I look like I'm about to lose my temper, I want you to tell me. No fidgeting, no polite coughs. Just plain out tell me. Can you do that?"

"I can," Olem said.

"Good. Then send in Vlora."

Tamas watched his son's former fiancée enter the room with no small bit of trepidation. Many thought of Tamas as cold. He encouraged the notion. Perhaps his son had suffered for that. But Tamas knew that beneath his calculating nature he had a temper, and for the first time in his life he wanted to shoot a woman.

Tamas interlocked his fingers on the desk in front of him. He fixed his mouth into that ambiguous place between smile and frown.

Vlora was a dark-haired beauty with a classic figure, wide hips and a small chest outlined by the tight blue uniform of an Adran soldier. Her father had been a na-baron who had lost his fortune speculating in all the wrong things. The last of their family wealth had gone to a gold mine in Fatrasta—one that pinched out two months after mining began. He had died a year after that last failure, when Vlora was only ten. Sabon had found her months later, placed in a boarding school by her few remaining relatives; an abandoned child with a unique talent: the ability to ignite powder from not just a dozen paces, as most Marked could, but at a distance of several hundred yards. Tamas had taken her in, provided for her upbringing, and given her a career in the army. What had gone wrong?

"Sir," she said, snapping to attention before him. Tamas found himself looking at an invisible point above her head as he struggled to restrain his anger. "Powder Mage Vlora reporting, sir."

Tamas flinched. She'd called him Tamas since she was fourteen. Not one soul had ever commented on that brazen familiarity. She'd treated him more like a father than Taniel ever had.

"Sit," Tamas ordered.

Vlora sat.

"Sabon apprised you of the situation?" He could feel her studying his face. He kept his own gaze in the air above her head.

"We've lost a lot of men, sir," she said. "A lot of friends."

"A serious blow to the powder cabal. I need mages now. I'd have liked to leave you..." *At Jileman University*, he finished in his head. Where she could continue her studies and continue betraying his son. Tamas cleared his throat. "I need you here."

"I'm here," she said.

"Good," Tamas said. "I'm going to put you with the seventy-fifth regiment on the north end of the city. There's rioters up there to mop up and..." Tamas paused at a low knock on the door. Olem opened the door just a little. A communiqué was passed through, and there was a moment of whispering between the bodyguard and someone on the other side.

"Tamas," Vlora said suddenly. "I'd like to be put with Taniel, if that is possible."

Tamas felt his body jerk and pulled back on the reins of his rage. "That's 'sir' if you please, soldier," he snapped. "And no, it's not possible. This city needs to be cleaned up and I'll have you with the seventy-fifth regiment." He would not put Taniel through that. He was cold, not cruel.

Olem waved the communiqué. "Sir," he said.

"What is it?"

"Problems."

"Of what sort?"

"The boys have run into barricades."

"And?"

"Big ones, sir, though hastily built. Very well organized. Not average looters."

"Where?"

"Centestershire."

"That's less than a mile from here. Have they made contact with the barricade?"

"Yes," Olem said. He didn't look happy. "Royalists, sir."

"They had to come out of the woodwork eventually," Tamas said. "Damned king's men without a king. Numbers?"

"Not a clue. They appear to have gone up overnight."

"What's the extent of their holdings?"

"I said, sir. Centestershire."

"What, the whole center of the city?"

Olem nodded.

"Bloody pit." Tamas leaned back in his chair. He let his eyes fall to Vlora, his anger at her betrayal warring with the stupidity of men who'd throw their lives away over a dead monarch. He felt his hands shaking. "Why?" The word wrenched out against his will. He scolded himself immediately. He had better control than that. He forced himself to meet Vlora's eyes. *Why did you betray my son?*

He saw sorrow in those eyes. A lonely, sad girl. The eyes of a child who'd made a horrible mistake. It made him furious. He stood, his chair thrown to the ground behind him.

"Sir!" Olem barked.

"What?" Tamas practically yelled at the man.

"Not the time or place, sir!"

Tamas felt his jaw working soundlessly. *I did tell him to stop me.*

The door to the office burst open. Taniel stumbled in, breathing hard as if he'd run up all five flights of stairs. He stopped in the doorway, frozen in place at the sight of Vlora.

Vlora stood. "Taniel."

"What is it?" Tamas said, the calm in his voice forced.

"General Westeven is in league with the Privileged."

"Westeven is in Novi on holiday. I made sure of it before the coup."

"He returned yesterday. I've just come from his home. It's guarded by at least two dozen Hielmen. We tracked the Privileged there but couldn't force our way inside. She is a guest of his."

"He has to be out of the city. They may just be using his house as a base of operations."

Taniel strode into the room, stopped beside Vlora, his eyes on his father. "If Westeven is in the city, he'll move quickly. He could strike at any time."

Tamas leaned back, taking in the information. General Westeven, the longtime retired captain of the Hielmen, was a legend. The man commanded respect from noble and commoner alike and had won battles across half the world. He was one of the few military men, foreign or domestic, that Tamas truly saw as an equal. And he was a king's man through and through.

Tamas slid his dueling-pistols case across the desk to rest in front of him and began to load one. "Olem, eject anyone from this building that isn't a member of the seventh brigade. Once the House of Nobles is secure, we'll see about those barricades. General Westeven may be behind them."

Olem left the room at a run.

The rest followed Tamas out into the hallway and down the stairs. Olem met them again on the second floor. The place was packed with people—city folk, peasants, poor merchants. It seemed like half the city filled the hallways. Olem had to push his way through to get to Tamas.

"Sir," Olem said, "There are too many people in the building. It'll take us hours to clear all the rooms."

Tamas scowled. "Who are all these people?" A line had formed, and Tamas couldn't see the front of it. He grabbed the closest man, an ironworker, by his thick overalls with the hammer stitched to one pocket. "What are you here for?"

The man trembled slightly. "Um, sorry, sir, I'm here to debate my new taxes." He spread his hand toward the line. "We all are."

"New taxes haven't been issued," Tamas said.

"For the king!"

A gunshot went off near Tamas's ear and the man slumped to the ground before he'd been able to draw his dagger halfway. Vlora immediately began reloading her pistol. On Tamas's other side, Taniel had drawn both of his.

The entire hall burst into motion. Cloaks and coats were discarded, and from beneath them weapons were drawn—swords, daggers, pistols—a few even had muskets. What had a moment before been an aimless line of city folk and commoners became an armed mob.

They fell on Tamas's soldiers with the same shout: "For the king!"

Olem flung himself between the greater part of the crowd and Tamas. He fired a pistol and then drew his sword, cutting down three of the royalists in as many blinks of the eye. Tamas yanked his sword out and bellowed, "To me! Men of the seventh brigade, to me!"

Soldiers caught unawares were cut down. The hall was too crowded with the royalists, their trap sprung. But they weren't expecting three powder mages or Olem's trained ferocity.

"Back to the stairs, sir," Olem yelled. "Up to the next floor!"

They cut their way toward the stairs in a fighting retreat. The royalists attacked en masse, trying to gain the advantage through numbers. Tamas stepped up beside Olem to hold them back while Vlora and Taniel fired their pistols from behind them. The staircase was soon full of the thick smoke from spent powder. Tamas breathed it in and savored it.

Gray-and-white uniforms emerged from the hall. Hielmen—what was left of Manhouch's personal guard. There were twelve of them. They carried the best air rifles with bayonets fixed and charged forward without hesitation. These were not simple royalists. They were trained killers, notches even above Tamas's best soldiers. They would not waver or retreat until they were dead.

The Hielmen carried air rifles, but the rest of the rabble did not. Tamas felt Vlora ignite a powder horn, and a man nearest the Hielmen exploded, showering the lot of them with gore and knocking two flat. Tamas reached out with his senses and ignited the powder in a man's unshot musket. The unexpected blast blew the face off the woman next to him.

They made it up the stairs to the third floor, the Hielmen dogging their heels. They started up for the fourth floor when the popping sound of air rifles filled the air. It was a sound to chill a Marked's blood, for a Marked knew that shot was meant for him.

Vlora stumbled on the stairs and fell. Taniel, farther up the stairs, leapt to her in an instant, sliding the ring bayonet over the end of his rifle and meeting the Hielmen's charge with a silent snarl. His bayonet sliced a Hielman's neck with the quick, easy motion of a trained butcher. He dodged to one side of a bayonet thrust and grappled with another Hielman. The man was a hand taller than him and at least three stone more. Taniel brought up the butt of his rifle in a blow savage enough to put the Hielman's nose into his brain. The soldier dropped without a sound. Tamas felt a thrill watching his son fight. Taniel Two-Shot he might be, but he had the brutal hand-to-hand skills of an infantryman.

Taniel swung toward the four remaining Hielmen, ready to charge.

"Taniel!" Tamas barked, "Fall back!" He picked Vlora up. Deep in a powder trance, her body seemed to weigh nothing at all. She gritted her teeth against the pain. "Did it hit a bone?" Tamas asked.

She shook her head.

Tamas heard a pop and felt the bullet graze his left shoulder, missing Vlora's head by inches. Tamas turned around only to look down the length of an air rifle, the bayonet coming toward his gut fast.

He transferred Vlora's weight to one arm and drew his pistol and shot from the hip, dropping the Hielman dead from a bullet through the eye.

By the time Tamas reached the fifth floor, the last few Hielmen lay dead on the stairs. Tamas and his men assessed their wounds. Olem had a number of new cuts—they'd need stitching, but nothing more. Vlora's shot had glanced off her thigh. She could handle pressure on it, so the bullet had not shattered the bone, and she'd be fine. Taniel had not been touched. His face was twisted in a savage grimace as he wiped gore from the end of his bayoneted rifle. At some point Ka-peol had joined them. The red-haired girl smelled of sulfur, and her hands were black. She wiped her hands on her buckskins and smiled at Tamas when she saw him looking.

Pistol shots and the sound of steel on steel faded on the floor below. Tamas took a few deep breaths, listening to Vlora's heart beat. They both leaned against the wall, her head on his shoulder. He stepped away from her.

Footsteps echoed on the stairs below them. A moment later Sabon appeared. He had powder marks on the cuff of his jacket and a shallow sword gash along one arm. He breathed a quick sigh of relief on seeing them all together.

"Anyone hurt?" Sabon asked.

“Minor wounds,” Tamas said. “Where were you?”

“The officers’ mess. They came out of nowhere.”

“Casualties?” Tamas asked. *Anyone important?*

“A few,” Sabon said. He gave a slight shake of his head at the silent question. “From the looks of things it was mostly rabble. Took us by surprise, but once we’d rallied the men, it was barely a fight. All the Hielmen came straight for you.”

“Is the House secure?”

“Working on it.”

“Enemies captured?” Tamas asked.

“We’ve taken at least two dozen without a fight. Probably another forty wounded. They’re General Westeven’s men.”

“I know.” Tamas stepped over to his son and laid a hand on his shoulder. “Well done, Taniel.”

Taniel unfixed his bayonet and put it in its case. He shouldered his rifle. One glance to Vlora and then a stiff nod to Tamas. “Back to work, sir.”

Tamas watched his son descend the stairs, followed closely by the savage girl. He felt like he should say something else. He wasn’t sure what.

“Sabon.”

“Sir?”

“Alert Lady Winceslav. Tell her we need her soldiers in the city. General Westeven holds the barricades and I’ll be damned if I send my own men to their deaths against them. The mercenaries will need to start earning their pay. Prepare me a command base near the barricades. We take the fight to him. Vlora.” He paused, considering his decision for a moment. “Go with Sabon. I want you on my staff.”

“Taniel!”

Taniel stopped on the landing and glanced back up the stairs, trying to decide whether to wait or not. He knew that voice. He didn't want to hear anything it had to say. He nudged a body with his toe. One of the Hielmen he'd gutted with his bayonet. The man's eyes fluttered. Still alive. He glared up at Taniel. He gritted his teeth, not making a sound, but he must have been in immense pain. Taniel debated whether to call a surgeon or to kill him. The wound was mortal. Taniel squatted next to him.

"You'll not live out the week," Taniel said.

"Traitor," the Hielman whispered.

"Do you want to live another day or two, kept alive so that you can answer to Tamas's questioners?" Taniel asked. "Or end it now?"

The man's eyes betrayed his suffering. He remained silent.

Taniel undid his belt and folded it over, offering the end to the man. "Bite on this."

The Hielman bit down.

It was over in a handful of heartbeats. Taniel wiped his knife on the Hielman's trousers and jerked out his belt from between the man's teeth. He stood up, buckling the belt back on. Why did he do this? He should be off at the university, chasing girls. He tried to think back to the last time he'd chased a girl. His first night in Fatrasta, before the war began, he'd met a girl at a dockside bar. They'd flirted all night. A little drunker and he might have slept with her, but he'd kept his head about him and remembered Vlora. He wondered if that girl was still there. He had a sketch of her in his book.

The Hielman lay at his feet, at peace despite the scrambled gash in his stomach and the fresh crimson line dripping from his throat. Ka-poel stood a few feet away, silent as always. She watched the dead Hielman as if fascinated.

"We should go," Taniel said to Ka-poel.

"Taniel, wait."

Vlora hurried down the stairs. She stumbled, caught herself on the railing, and sank down to sit on the steps halfway down. She held one hand over the wound on her thigh.

They stared at each other for a moment. Vlora was the first to look away, down at the body at Taniel's feet.

"How are you?"

"Alive," Taniel said.

Several more moments of silence followed. Taniel could hear his father upstairs, yelling orders. Tamas hadn't even been fazed by the sudden attack. A warrior through and through.

A few soldiers passed them, two going up, one going down. There was a commotion in the main hall downstairs as Tamas's soldiers rounded up wounded prisoners.

"Forgive me," Vlora said.

Tears streaked down her face. Taniel fought the impulse to rush to her side, to see to her wound and comfort her. He could sense her pain, emotional and physical, but it could not touch him in his powder trance. He refused to let it touch him. He hooked his thumb through his belt and squared his jaw.

"Let's go," he said to Ka-poel.

Adamat ground his teeth in frustration. Seven days since the coup. Seven days since he'd visited Uskan and gotten only more questions for his time. Who'd been burning pages from books on religious and sorcerous history? Who'd taken the other books? And what the pit was Kresimir's Promise?

Adamat stopped his hackney cab in Bakerstown long enough to grab a meat pie, then continued on past Hrusch Avenue, where the dusty smell of oil, wood, furnaces, and gunpowder whirled between the gunsmith shops and foundries. Here the noise was louder than usual, the crowds thicker. A boy sat on the step of every shop with a bundle of papers, taking orders and reporting numbers as well-dressed gentlemen rubbed shoulders with the lowliest infantryman. A hawker stood on the street corner and yelled that the new

Hrusch rifle would protect a man's home. The gunsmiths were selling the rifles as fast as they could make them.

Adamat flipped through the day's paper. It said that Taniel Two-Shot was in the city, returned a hero from the Fatrastan War for Independence. Now he was chasing after a rogue Privileged. Some said the Privileged was a surviving member of the royal cabal. Others said it was a Kez spy, keeping an eye on Tamas's powder cabal. Either way, an entire block had been leveled already, and dozens had been killed or wounded. Adamat hoped the Privileged would either be caught or would leave the city altogether before more blood could be shed. There was going to be enough of that in the coming face-off between Westeven and Tamas.

The royalists had barricaded off Centestershire, nearly the whole middle of Adopest. They'd launched a preemptive attack against Tamas's forces, only to be driven back. Now it seemed the population was holding its breath. General Westeven, nearly eighty years old, had rallied the entire royalist population of the city, gathered them in one spot, and made enough barricades to stop a damned army. All in one night, or so it seemed. Field Marshal Tamas had responded by bringing in two whole legions of the Wings of Adom mercenary company and surrounding Centestershire with field guns and artillery. Not a shot had been fired yet. Both men were experienced enough not to want to turn the middle of Adopest into a battlefield.

It was a damned nightmare, Adamat decided. Two of the Nine's most celebrated commanders facing off in a city of a million people. No one could come out a winner from that.

Yet life went on. People still needed to work, to eat. Those not involved directly in this new conflict stayed well away from it. Tamas had done an admirable job at keeping the peace in the rest of the city.

To complicate matters, the Public Archives, where Adamat was most likely to find copies of the damaged books at the university, were behind the royalist barricades. It was not a place he was prepared to go alone.

The carriage came to a stop in front of a three-story building off a side street at the far end of High Talian, the slums of Adopest. There was but a single entrance on this street, with a faded olive-green double door. Half of it was closed, blocked from inside, the paint peeling and the masonry crumbling around the doorpost. The other half was open, and a man of small stature leaned against the opposite post.

Adamat fetched his hat and cane from the carriage and held them in one hand, the other seeking a handkerchief from his pocket, which he used to cover his mouth as he stepped out. He paid the driver and approached the doorway, listening absently to the clatter of hoofbeats behind him as the carriage pulled away.

"Where in Kresimir's name did you find an apple this time of year, Jeram?" Adamat wiped his nose and stuffed the handkerchief in a pocket.

The doorman gave him a slant-toothed smile. "G'evening, sir. Haven't seen you for a month or two." He took a crunching bite of his apple. "My cousin in the south of Bakerstown gets fresh fruit all year-round."

"They say we might go to war with the Kez if negotiations don't go well," Adamat said. "You'll have to wait until next fall for another apple."

Jeram made a sour face. "Just my luck."

"How go the fights today?"

Jeram pulled a worn piece of paper from the brim of a threadbare hat and studied it to make out the most recent markings. "SouSmith's done three in a row, Formichael has won twice today. The two of them look ready to drop, but it's the foreman has a death bug in his britches, says the two of them are gonna fight it out this hour."

"Five fights between the two of them already?" Adamat snorted. "It'll be piss poor, they'll barely be able to stand."

"Aye, that's what the tables are saying, and there's not much wagers yet. Everybody that's betting has put it on Formichael."

"SouSmith hits hard."

Jeram gave him a sly glance. "If he can land a punch. Formichael's better rested, younger, and half SouSmith's weight."

"Bah," Adamat said, "you young ones always think the old have nothing left in them."

Jeram chuckled. "Right, then, what'll it be, governor?" He removed a folded paper from his back pocket, covered in smudges and long-erased lines. He set it against the doorframe and poised a piece of charcoal over it.

"What are the odds?"

Jeram scratched his cheek, leaving a bit of charcoal there. "I'll give you nine to one."

Adamat raised his eyebrows. "Give me twenty-five on SouSmith."

"Risky," Jeram grunted. "Figures." He scratched down the numbers and folded the piece of paper, then jammed it back in his pocket. Adamat knew the paper was just for show. Jeram had a memory almost as good as Adamat's, and without a Knack—he never forgot a face, never forgot a number, and had not once delivered wrongly on a bet, though many times was accused of such. That didn't happen often nowadays, not since the Proprietor took over this boxing ring. He didn't take kindly to anyone accusing his bookies.

Inside, the only light came from rectangular slat windows high up under the eaves. Adamat pushed past a series of curtains that muffled sound and hid the inside from prying eyes. The whole building was one big room, long since gutted, with a few stalls and cordoned-off rooms to give the fighters some privacy to recover from fights. In the middle was the building's namesake: the Arena, a round pit twelve paces across, four paces below floor level.

A latticework of haphazard seating surrounded the pit, going back to either side of the building and nearly to the roof. Adamat ducked beneath the rear seating, crossed to the other side, and elbowed his way in among the men crowding the edge of the pit. The stands were full, men shoulder to shoulder in all the seats, enough for a few hundred gentlemen with their canes and hats, street workers with frayed jackets, and even a pair of city police officers, their black capes and top hats hard to miss among the crowd.

A fight had finished perhaps ten minutes ago, and the Arena workers were throwing down sawdust to soak up the blood, readying for the next one. A quiet murmur filled the room as men talked among themselves, resting their voices to cheer the violence ahead. Adamat breathed in sweat and grime and the smell of anger. He let his breath out slowly, shuddering. Bareknuckle boxing was a barbaric, feral sport. He grinned to himself. *How fun.* He took another breath, catching a whiff of pig. Not long ago the Arena had been a sty, and before that? A series of shops, maybe, back when High Talian was supposed to be the newest, richest, most fashionable part of the city.

A pair of shirtless men left the fighters' stalls at the end of the room. They entered the Arena side by side and without ceremony. The workers cleared out, and the fighters faced each other. The man on the left was smaller, leaner, his muscles corded and defined like a warhorse. His curly brown hair bobbed into his face now and then, and he blew it away each time. Formichael. The Proprietor's favorite fighter—or he had been when Adamat had last come by the fights. He was a warehouse worker, young and handsome, and it was whispered the Proprietor was grooming him to be something more than a simple thug.

The man on the right looked twice Formichael's size. His hair had a touch of gray at the sides, his face bore a poorly shaved beard. His eyes were piggish, set deep in his face, and they examined

Formichael with the singular intensity of a killer. His arms looked big enough to win a wrestling match with a mountain bear. Pits marred his knuckles where they'd broken—and been broken by—men's jaws, and his face was covered in the puckered scars of bad stitching jobs. He flashed a set of broken teeth at Formichael.

Despite SouSmith's advantage in size and experience, he was obviously tired. His chin sagged from a long day of hard-won fights, the corners of his eyes betraying exhaustion, and his shoulders drooped ever so slightly. What's more, experience had long worn out its welcome. SouSmith was getting old, and his chest and stomach had given way to flab from excess drinking.

The foreman descended to the second step of the ring and conferred with the two fighters. After a moment he stepped back. He held up his hand, and then dropped it, leaping back.

Three hundred men yelled as the two fighters lashed out at each other. Fists met flesh with dull slaps that were drowned out by the surge of voices.

"Kill 'em!"

"Make him bleed!"

"The gut! Flush him in the gut!"

Adamat's voice was drowned out in the cacophony of wordless cries. He didn't even know what he said, but his heart poured all his frustration with Palagyi, his anger that his wife and children were away, into his shouts. He leaned forward, fists flailing in mockery of the two men, screaming at the top of his lungs with the rest of the rabble.

Formichael connected with a vicious jab to SouSmith's ribs. SouSmith stumbled to the side, and the younger man surged forward and pounded on the same spot, perhaps on an old broken rib, fists flashing in the dim light. SouSmith reeled, trembling, toward the side of the pit until he was up against the wooden slats that separated him from the crowd. Fingers reached out from the onlookers, nails gouged at his bare head, spittle splattered on his cheek. Adamat watched, the fighter's head just beyond his reach. "Go on," he shouted. "Don't let him back you into a corner!"

Something audibly cracked, and SouSmith fell to one knee, hand up in front to ward off Formichael's blows.

Adamat's voice fell to a whisper. "Get up, you bastard," he growled through his teeth.

Formichael punched SouSmith's hands and arms, beat them down until the older man was on both knees, suffering under the onslaught. Formichael's face flushed with the promise of victory and he slowly let up until the punches were mere taps, then altogether. He stood, chest heaving, examining the man at his feet. SouSmith didn't look up.

Bah, Adamat thought. *Finish him already.*

But there was nothing of that in Formichael's plans. Grinning, he bent over and grabbed one of SouSmith's arms, pulling him up into a single, brutal punch. SouSmith went back to his knees, his whole body shuddering. Formichael would string this out, letting SouSmith's exhaustion keep him down and continuing the beating until SouSmith was nothing but a pulp.

Formichael delivered several more single punches before letting SouSmith fall back down to his hands and knees. SouSmith's face was a mess of blood and pulped flesh. He spit into the sawdust. Formichael turned, raised his arms to the crowd, bathed himself in the roar of voices. He faced SouSmith once again.

The big man rose to his feet in less than a heartbeat, all twenty-five stone following his fist into Formichael's pretty young face. The impact lifted Formichael off the ground. His body flattened out in midair and then bounced like some child's toy off the wooden slats before tumbling to the ground. He shuddered once before falling still. SouSmith spit on Formichael's back and turned away, plodding up the stairs and toward the fighters' stalls. Hands reached out to slap him on the back in congratulations; curses lashed out for bets lost.

Adamat collected his winnings and then waited until enough of the crowd was milling about to slip unnoticed back to the stalls. He entered SouSmith's room and closed the curtain behind him. "That was quite the fight."

SouSmith paused, a bucket lifted over his head, and gave Adamat a single glance. He tipped the bucket, letting the water wash away a layer of sweat and blood, then scrubbed his body with a soiled towel. He tilted his head at Adamat, the skin around his eyes puffy and bruised, his lips and brows split. "Aye. Make the right bet?"

"Of course."

"Bastard's trying to kill me."

"Who?"

"Proprietor."

Adamat chuckled, then realized SouSmith wasn't joking. "Why do you say that?"

SouSmith shook his head, twisted the red-brown water out of his towel, and dunked it in a clean bucket. "Wants me to sink." SouSmith was far from stupid, but he'd always spoken in short sentences. A man had trouble collecting his thoughts after years of being punched in the head.

"Why? You're a good fighter. People come to see you."

"People come to see young whips." SouSmith spat into one of the buckets. "I'm old."

"Formichael will think twice next time he's told to fight you." Adamat remembered the still body on the Arena floor. They'd had to carry him out. "If he's still alive."

"He'll live." SouSmith tapped the side of his head. "He'll be afraid."

"Or maybe he'll just be sure to finish it quick," Adamat said.

SouSmith took a deep breath, then let out a chuckle that turned into a grunting cough. "Not bad either way."

Adamat watched his old friend for a moment. SouSmith was a

different man than his appearance suggested. He was no average thug, not like the other boxers. Behind his beady eyes was a sharp intelligence; behind his gnarled fists the soft hands of brother and uncle. Many read him wrong, one of the reasons for his winning record. One thing no one read wrong, though: Behind it all, even deeper than his loyalty to his family or his cleverness, he was a killer.

"I have a question for you," Adamat said.

"Thought you missed me."

"You once told me you were part of the street gang Kresimir's Broken."

SouSmith froze with the corner of the towel still in one ear. He lowered it slowly. "I did?"

"You were very drunk."

SouSmith's movements were suddenly cautious. He glanced toward the stall's single desk, to a drawer where he no doubt had hidden a pistol. Yet a man his size didn't need a pistol.

Adamat made a reassuring gesture. "You were very drunk," Adamat said again. "I didn't believe you at the time. I was there when they pulled those boys out of the gutter. I didn't think anyone had escaped what went after them."

SouSmith examined him for a few moments. "Maybe one didn't," he said. "Maybe one did."

"How?"

SouSmith countered with his own question. "Why?"

"I'm doing an investigation." Adamat had already decided to tell SouSmith the whole story. "For Field Marshal Tamas. He wants to know what Kresimir's Promise is."

SouSmith looked impressed. "One man I'd not cross," he said.

"Agreed. You have any idea what it means?"

SouSmith returned to cleaning himself up. "Our leader was a royal cabal washout." SouSmith opened the desk drawer. He removed a grimy old pipe and a tobacco pouch. SouSmith lit up his pipe before he went on. "A loudmouth. A jackass. Wanted attention. Said our name was supposed to remind the royal cabal of their mortality."

It was the longest sentence Adamat had heard SouSmith utter in years. "Did he tell you what it meant?"

"Break Kresimir's Promise," SouSmith said, puffing on his pipe. The smell of pistachio-flavored tobacco filled the tiny room. "And end the world."

"What's the promise?" Adamat asked.

SouSmith shrugged.

Adamat tapped the side of his jaw with one finger as SouSmith leaned back. He wasn't going to say any more. Not about this. Adamat let his thoughts slip toward Palagyi. The twerp of a banker still had men lurking about. He was unpredictable. A man with SouSmith's size and reputation could keep the idiot in line. At least until Adamat's loan was due and Palagyi had the law on his side. Besides, SouSmith could be very useful in tight places—such as the Public Archives, behind the royalist barricades.

"Any chance you're in need of a job?" Adamat asked.

SouSmith examined him through those small eyes. "What kind of a job?"

CHAPTER

9

Taniel found his father's command post just out of range of the royalist barricades. The empty streets were full of rubbish, the paving stones damp from a brief rain the night before. The city smells threatened to overcome his senses, enhanced from the near-constant powder trance he'd been in for two weeks. The world smelled of shit and fear, of empty piss pots and distrust.

Ka-poel was at his side. Even after all this, she was still mystified by the sight of the city—so many buildings, each one so tall on every side. She didn't like it. Too many people, she had indicated with a series of gestures. Too many buildings. Taniel sympathized. His real talent as a powder mage was being able to float a bullet for miles—to make long shots across the widest battlefield. What good was that when his view was obstructed on all sides?

Gothen stood on Taniel's other side. The magebreaker scratched the back of his head where he still had hair. He watched the barricades with a hand on the grip of one of his three pistols.

"Coming in with me?" Taniel asked.

Gothen shook his head. "Your father makes me nervous."

"You're not the only one," Taniel muttered.

Tamas had set up his headquarters in one of the hundreds of abandoned homes near the center of the city. Soldiers milled about outside. They didn't wear the familiar dark blue of Adran infantry. Their uniforms were red and gold and white, their standard a saint's halo with gold wings. These were the Wings of Adom. The majority of them were Adran, as it was an Adran-based mercenary company, but one could see all kinds in their ranks. Taniel crossed the street and paused just long enough for one of the guards to get a look at his powder keg pin before heading inside, Ka-poel on his heels.

The salon of the house had the look of a command tent. There were maps on every available surface, gear stacked in the corners, even rifles and ammunition crates. Tamas stood behind a table, examining a map of the city while two of the Wings' brigadiers—brigade commanders—stood off to one side. Tamas's bodyguard lounged on a sofa in the corner, smoking.

Tamas didn't look up when Taniel entered. Taniel cleared his throat. No response. The brigadiers gave him a curious look.

"I want Bo," Taniel said.

Tamas finally looked up. He had the tense air of someone whose deep thoughts had been interrupted.

"Bo?"

Taniel rolled his eyes. "Borbador. I need his help."

Tamas scowled. "I don't want a Privileged anywhere near the city right now."

"What about that mercenary you saddled me with? Julene?"

"That's different," Tamas said. "Privileged Borbador was a member of the king's royal cabal."

"Exiled," Taniel said. "And Bo has no love for the late king. He joined the royal cabal for the money and the brothel girls."

"And he was exiled because he slept with the royal cabal head's favorite mistress," Tamas said. He stepped away from the table and sank into a chair. He rubbed his eyes, as if trying to will away exhaustion. "They almost reinstated him just a few months ago. I arranged for his transfer to the Mountainwatch so that when I slaughtered the royal cabal, he wouldn't be there. I do pay attention to these things."

Taniel felt a flicker of gratitude and hated himself for it.

Tamas changed the subject. "How goes the hunt?"

Taniel remained standing to give his report, even when his father gestured to a chair. "The Westeven townhouse has been abandoned. The Privileged is gone, too. She's covering her tracks well, and Ka-poel's methods, though accurate, aren't fast enough to keep up with someone on the move."

"Julene should be able to track her."

"Julene is more trouble than she's worth."

Tamas sat up straight. "Julene's well worth the money I pay her. She's taken care of problems for me in the past. She's discreet and measured."

"Problems, eh?" Taniel said. "Like those three Adran Privileged last year that disappeared? That was in the newspapers in Fatrasta. They were getting too vocal in their opposition to your powder cabal, if I remember right."

"Yes," Tamas said.

"And you trust her?"

"As long as I keep paying her."

"Tamas, she's a powder keg with a short fuse. She went after the Privileged—she and her magebreaker, alone, against my orders. She's either got a death wish or there's something personal in all of this."

"When did I put *you* in command?" Tamas stood up, crossed to his desk, and poured himself a glass of water.

Taniel stiffened. "That was the implication when you paired me with those two. I am a Marked."

"Hmm." Tamas swirled the water in his glass. "Let that Privileged slip through your fingers again and I will put Julene in charge. She's efficient—brutal when she needs to be, but efficient."

"Do that and you'll explain to your council why half the city was destroyed in a full-on melee between two Privileged." Taniel couldn't keep the venom out of his voice. Was Tamas being willfully stupid?

"I'll give you one more chance," Tamas said.

Taniel ground his teeth together. "You don't trust me to do my job? You can't, can you? What will it take for you to put any faith in me? Fifty Privileged notches on my rifle stock? A hundred?"

"I know what you're capable of, but you're still young. You have a hot temper."

"And you have room to speak?"

"Watch your mouth. You're going to follow orders or I'll put someone else on this. Vlora would jump at the chance to get back into my good graces right now."

"I can do this." Taniel spoke between clenched teeth.

"Then prove it. Listen to Julene's advice. She's a veteran Privileged hunter and a skilled sorceress herself."

Taniel snorted. "Kresimir above, it's like you slept with the woman." There was a brief pause, a flicker of danger in Tamas's eyes. Taniel felt the grin sprout on his face. He threw his head back and laughed. "You did! You bedded the mercenary!"

"That's enough, soldier." That came from Tamas's new bodyguard. The man sat on the sofa, watching them both through a swirl of cigarette smoke. Taniel glanced at him once, then back at his father. He could see the veins standing out on Tamas's neck.

Tamas's fists were clenched, his teeth grinding together. Taniel felt his pride warring with the sudden sense of danger in the room. The two brigadiers had their heads together over a map of the Nine, pretending not to hear the conversation between father and son.

Taniel cleared his throat. "Julene can't track her. She admitted so herself. The Privileged is spreading auras using the rain. I've tried my third eye and gotten nowhere. Our only chance is Ka-poel and she's moving slow. Even then, once we catch her—well, this woman is powerful. Not just magically. I've shot her three times. I put my bayonet through her stomach and she destroyed two buildings and disappeared. She's still on the move after a wound that should have killed her. That's why I want Bo."

Tamas seemed to gain control of himself. "Absolutely not. I will not risk a cabal Privileged in the city. Maybe in a few months. You'll have to make do with the help you have. Ryze," he said to the older of the two brigadiers in the corner, a veteran with a patch over one eye, "I need a company at the ready for whenever Taniel needs it. Give him an experienced tracker, too. One that's good in the city." The old brigadier nodded, and Tamas turned back to Taniel. "Dismissed, soldier."

Taniel gave a mock salute and spun around, leaving the room. He paused outside the command post to snort another line of powder. The powder trance intensified instantly. He shivered, the world so clear in his vision it caused his eyes to water.

"Stop looking at me like that," he said to Ka-poel.

The girl mimed his taking a snort of powder and shook her head. *Too much powder.*

"I'm fine."

She shook her head again.

"What do you know?"

Ka-poel glared.

Taniel looked away from her. Gothen was still across the street, fiddling with his private armory so that he'd be able to sit down comfortably on a stoop.

"I think one of them is reporting to Tamas," Taniel said to Ka-poel. "Behind my back. Wouldn't put it past Tamas. He's never trusted me." He rubbed his nose. "Thinks I'm still a kid."

Ka-poel touched a fist to her heart and pointed at him.

"He loves me? Huh. Maybe he does," Taniel said. "He's my father, he's supposed to—and Tamas always does the right thing. It'd just be nice if he *liked* me too." He jerked his head toward Gothen. "I've never much liked mercenaries." He gave a quick glance around to be sure none of the Wings of Adom were within earshot and continued. "They don't work half as hard for the money you're paying them and in the end they'd rather save their own skins than finish a job."

Ka-poel seemed to think on this for a moment. She understood him well enough—when it was convenient for her—but it took her a few moments to catch up when he spoke too quickly.

She made the shape of a woman with her hands.

"Julene?"

She nodded and bared her teeth.

"I don't like her either. She could have gotten us all killed against that Privileged. Even a Privileged—especially a Privileged—should know you don't just walk up to one of them and think you're going to get the drop. She acts like she knows she's going to win every fight."

Ka-poel pointed a finger at him.

Taniel chuckled. "Me? I *do know* I'm going to win every fight."

He headed across the street and joined Gothen on the stoop.

"Where's Julene?" he asked.

Gothen shrugged. "She comes and goes. She won't be gone more than a couple hours, though, with us on a job."

"Have you worked with her long?"

"Two years."

"For Tamas?"

"A little over a year."

"Where were you before that?"

"Kez."

"Hunting powder mages?"

Gothen shifted uncomfortably. "A Warden that went mad. An ex-cabal Privileged. Mostly that kind of thing."

"I'd imagine the money is good in Kez." Taniel decided not to press him on the powder mages.

"Very," Gothen said. "Things went bad for us working for a duke, though, and we were forced to get out of the country quick."

Taniel made a mental note that Julene might have a grudge against the Kez. It certainly explained why Tamas liked her. "How does that work out?" he asked. "A magebreaker and a Privileged being partners. She can't do sorcery anywhere close to you."

Gothen gave a lopsided smile. "Not as bad as you'd think. I have to touch the Else"—he lifted his hands, though he wasn't wearing his gloves—"to truly cut off a Privileged's sorcery. Even then, I have to be within about ten feet of them."

"Which is quite a task in itself," Taniel said.

"Yeah."

Taniel leaned back. "Magebreakers are very rare. I don't think my father even knows how you work."

"We *are* quite rare," Gothen agreed. "I've met only one besides myself. Magebreakers aren't born this way, not like Privileged or powder mages or Knacked."

"Then how?"

"A conscious decision," Gothen said. He had a faraway look in his eyes.

"Simple as that?"

"Simple as that. I reached out, I touched the Else, and I willed away all auras." He pulled his Privileged gloves out of his pockets and showed them to Taniel. They were dark blue with gold runes—

not the usual colored runes on white gloves of a Privileged. "My gloves turned this color instantly. A kind of polarizing, as I understand it. Now, when I touch the Else, the area around me becomes devoid of sorcery. Auras can't be summoned, created, or manipulated. Even when I'm not touching the Else, auras will not come within about six inches of me."

"Can it be reversed? If you wanted to be a Privileged again?"

"No." Gothen returned the gloves to his pocket.

Privileged were the most powerful beings on earth. They threw lightning the way a child might a ball. They commanded the sea and the earth. Taniel couldn't imagine giving up such power.

"Why?" he asked.

Gothen kicked at a paving stone beneath his boot. "I was a very weak Privileged. Barely strong enough to touch the Else, much less command auras. I failed the test to join the royal cabal. I was angry. I thought, if they wouldn't take me off the street and share with me their wealth and power, then I would become what they feared most: untouchable by their sorcery."

"I can respect that."

Gothen returned the grin. "And now I make a lot of money tracking them down and killing them."

"Have you killed many?"

Gothen held up five fingers.

Probably powder mages too, if he worked for the Kez. Gothen didn't carry an air rifle, but a pistol would work if the powder mage was caught unawares. Taniel had heard of bounty hunters who used bullets with gold dust melted into them. Gold in a powder mage's bloodstream prevented a Marked from sparking powder or entering a powder trance. Luckily, that particular technique was both expensive and unreliable.

"How do you feel about the Privileged we're after?" Taniel asked.

A cloud touched Gothen's face. "She's very strong," he said. "Stronger than any I've tracked. Julene says I'm just imagining it."

"I don't think so," Taniel said. "I was there when she wrecked those buildings. Only you standing between us kept me from getting killed. I thank you for that."

Gothen nodded uncertainly. "I think there's something you should know."

"What?"

"When I leapt in front of you, I was touching the Else. I was easily close enough to cut her off. She shouldn't have been able to reach through. But she did. That's never happened before."

Taniel wiped away a bit of sweat beading on his brow. "You'd better warn your partner not to be too confident."

"As if she'll listen," Gothen said. "There's something almost... personal in this. As if she doesn't want your help—pit, as if she doesn't even want my help."

Taniel snorted. "She's welcome to go it alone."

"To go what alone?"

Taniel started. Julene stood over them, a hand on one hip, a frown tugging at the scar on her face. She'd come upon them silently. Only Ka-poel seemed unsurprised by her arrival.

They sat in silence for a moment, Gothen trying to avoid Julene's glare. He seemed to wither beneath her. Taniel climbed to his feet.

He was thrown down again almost instantly as the ground pitched beneath him.

"Earthquake!" someone shouted.

Tamas was leaning on the edge of his map table when the ground began to buck. He reeled backward, thrown against the wall and then tossed to the floor like he'd been hit by a cavalry charge. Plaster fell from the ceiling, obscuring the room in a haze of dust. Tamas clutched at the floor with both hands, stomach churning as he watched the table thump from side to side until a leg broke. It tumbled askew, jumping like a leaf in the wind. Decorations fell from shelves and furniture upended. Tamas heard panicked shouting out in the streets.

As quickly as it began, the earthquake was over. Tamas climbed to his feet, waving a cloud of plaster dust from his face. The room seemed intact, though most of the furniture was dashed to pieces. He breathed a sigh of relief that the whole house hadn't caved in on them. Many of the buildings in this part of the city were old and unreliable, and he imagined plenty of people hadn't been so lucky.

Olem had been thrown to the floor and a bookshelf had crashed down over him. Tamas's legs wobbled unsteadily as if he'd been at sea for months. He crossed to the bookshelf and lifted it up.

Olem lay on his back, rubbing at his forehead with one hand, using the other to clear away the books that had fallen on him. He took Tamas's proffered hand.

"You've blood on you, sir," Olem said.

Tamas touched his forehead. His fingers came away crimson. "Don't even feel it," he said.

"Must have caught a piece of plaster," Olem said.

Tamas looked up. There were several good-sized holes in the ceiling, one right above the command table. "Just a bump," Tamas said. "I'm fine." He surveyed the room, feeling dizzy. It would take hours to get things returned to order. His maps had been scattered. He swayed.

"You sure you're all right, sir?" Olem asked. He put out one hand to steady Tamas.

Tamas waved him away. "Fine, fine. Let's have a look at the damage outside."

The street was in chaos. People emerged from their houses, yelling for help. Mercenaries tried to right field guns that had been tossed on their sides like they weighed nothing. Cobbles had popped from the street as if the ground had flexed beneath them. Whole rows of tightly packed apartment housing had crumbled, spilling bricks out into the road.

One of the Wings of Adom mercenaries paused before Tamas.

"There's been an earthquake, sir," the man said.

"Thank you, soldier. I gathered as much."

The man rushed off, his eyes looking a little dazed. Tamas exchanged a glance with Olem. "We don't get a lot of earthquakes here," Tamas said.

Olem shook his head. "Not in my lifetime."

Tamas turned around, assessing the damage. There would be parts of the city where things were worse, and parts where they were better. Tamas didn't even want to think of the chaos this had caused at the docks.

"Does Sablethorn look like it's leaning, sir?" Olem asked.

Tamas looked. The black spire, rising over the buildings to the west, did indeed look a little off. "At least it didn't fall outright. Olem."

"Sir?"

"Find some runners. I want damage assessment from the entire city. I want to know about the barricades. If some holes have opened up, it may be our chance to punch through them."

"Now?"

"Definitely. General Westeven will take advantage of the chaos to move up his barricades and reinforce them with rubble from the quake. We need to take advantage as well."

"You sure you're unhurt, sir?"

"Positive. Go."

Olem hurried off. Tamas waited until he was out of sight before he sagged against the wall behind him. His head throbbed from where he'd been hit. He could see figures scurrying over the barricade down the street, rushing out beyond them to snatch up bricks and masonry and throwing them back over.

"Ryze!" Tamas said.

The mercenary brigadier picked his way through the rubble to Tamas.

"Any of those guns operational?" Tamas asked.

"Axles are bent, wheels broken. We'll need to call in some smiths to fix them."

Tamas indicated the barricades. "Pass word among your boys to move up within firing distance. Don't let Westeven reinforce his barricades."

Ryze snapped a salute and spun off, barking orders to his men.

Tamas went back inside. He found a chair and righted it, and then rummaged through the mess until he found a spare coat. He wadded it up and pressed it against his head. He sank into the chair.

"You'll have a nasty bump on your forehead."

A man stood in the doorway, hands on his hips, surveying the damage within. He had long black hair, pulled back in a braided ponytail that hung over one shoulder, and a thin mustache. He was a big man, twenty stone or more, and a head and a half taller than Tamas. His skin had a slight yellow tint, hinting at some Rosvelean ancestry, but he spoke with the accent of a native Adran. He wore the brown pants and long, dirty white shirt of a city worker underneath a frayed jacket.

"Yes," Tamas said, tenderly pressing his fingers to his temple. "I think I will. Are you a surgeon?"

The man looked down at his hands, surprised. "No, I think not. These pudgy hands have only one calling: the kitchens."

"A cook?" He sent Olem away for just a minute and now any kind of riffraff just wandered in to his command center. "If you need help, I'm sure the soldiers outside are setting up a field hospital."

The man narrowed his eyes. "Cook?" he snapped. "Do I look like a cheap purveyor of watery soup and half-cooked meat? I'm a chef, damn it, and you watch who you call a cook in the future. Feelings are liable to get hurt."

Tamas lowered his hand from his injured head and stared at the man. Who the pit did he think he was? Amusement turned to annoyance as the man entered the room and set a chair back on its legs near Tamas, taking a seat.

"Do you know who I am?" Tamas demanded.

The man waved a hand, using the other to adjust his big belly comfortably into his lap. "Field Marshal Tamas, unless I'm mistaken."

The gall. "And you are?"

The man removed a handkerchief from his pocket and dabbed his forehead. "It's bloody hot in here. Where are my manners? I'm Mihali, son of Moaka, lord of the Golden Chefs."

The Golden Chefs sounded familiar, but Tamas couldn't quite put his finger on it.

"Moaka?" Tamas asked. "The na-baron?"

"My father preferred to think of himself as a culinary expert above all else, Kresimir rest his soul."

"Yes," Tamas said. He touched his head gingerly. It seemed to have stopped bleeding, but his headache was getting worse. "I attended one of his galas once. The food was unparalleled. He passed on last year, didn't he?" Even the son of a na-baron didn't belong here. Where the blazes was Olem?

"He always cooked it all himself." Mihali hung his head. "A pity. His heart gave out when he tasted my lamb soufflé. He was so proud of me, finally besting him." Mihali stared off across the room, exploring memories.

"Pardon me," Tamas said. The pounding inside his head began to increase. "Why the pit are you here?"

"Oh," Mihali said. "Many apologies. I'm the god Adom reincarnated."

Tamas couldn't help it. He began to chuckle, then to laugh. He slapped his knee. "Saint Adom, eh? That's a good one. Ow." He clutched at his head. Laughing had not been a good idea.

"Saint," Mihali grumbled. "I give order to chaos alongside Kresimir and these people relegate me to sainthood. Oh well, can't win them all, can you?"

Tamas managed to stifle his chuckles. "By Kresimir, you're serious?"

"Of course," Mihali said. He put one hand over his heart. "I swear by my mother's squash soup."

Tamas stood up. Was this some kind of joke? Was it Sabon? Maybe Olem. Olem was far cheekier than he should be. "Olem," he called. There was no answer. Tamas swore under his breath. He'd told Olem to send runners, not inspect the whole city himself. "Olem!" He stuck his head out into the hallway. There was no one around.

He turned about, face-to-face with Mihali. Mihali glanced out the door. "I don't really want to meet anyone yet, thank you," he said. "I don't want to cause a fuss. Meeting a god is an awfully big thing. I think."

"What are you, an actor?" Tamas said. He poked the man in the belly, checking for a stuffed shirt. It was all fat. "A mighty good show, but I'm not in the mood."

Mihali pointed at Tamas's forehead. "You were hit quite hard," he said. "I know it's a lot to take in. Maybe you should sit down for a moment. My memories are imperfect in this body, but I will do my best." He cleared his throat. "Did the dying Privileged warn you as they were supposed to?"

Tamas froze in the act of feeling his head wound. He grabbed Mihali by the lapels of his jacket. "Warn me about what?"

Mihali looked truly puzzled. He gave an apologetic shrug. "As I said, my memories are not what they should be." He seemed to perk up. "They will improve over time, though. I think."

"No more jokes now," he said. "Who the pit are you?"

Tamas flew against the doorjamb, hitting his shoulder hard, then was tossed to the floor. For a moment he thought Mihali had hit him, but then realized it was another earthquake. His heart in his mouth, he gripped the doorframe, watching more plaster fall to the floor and praying the whole building wouldn't come down this time. It was over in seconds.

He climbed up and dusted himself off, searching the room. The man was gone. Tamas gritted his teeth and looked out into the hallway. Olem was there, steadying himself up against the wall.

"Where the pit have you been?" Tamas asked.

"Finding runners," Olem said. "Everything good, sir?"

Tamas eyed him suspiciously. Not even a smirk. No one could play a joke that well.

"Fine. You see someone pass by here?"

Olem glanced at him, looking back and forth down the hallway. He reached down into the rubble at his feet and fished out a still-smoking cigarette. "No, sir."

Tamas stepped back into the command post. There was a back door to the house, he was sure, but no one could have crossed the room with the ground shaking like that.

How hard did I hit my head?

CHAPTER 10

Adamat stopped by his home for his pistols. Five days since he'd hired SouSmith, and the cordon around the center of the city had left no opportunities for them to sneak into the Public Archives. That had changed with the quake. The whole city was a mess. Buildings were down, roads filled with the homeless. Adamat had taken the opportunity to scout the royalist positions for a way to get to the Archives. He'd had no such luck.

There had been rumors Tamas would bring his entire army into the city and push through the barricades, but it seemed he'd turned his soldiers and mercenaries alike to helping the citizens rather than taking the barricades. Once the fighting began in earnest, it would be very dangerous in Centestershire. Then there was the rumor that Tamas's powder mages were still hunting a rogue Privileged through the streets of Adopest. Being out and about in the city was not for the faint of heart.

Every three days, Adamat received a messenger from Tamas. Every three days, he was forced to report he'd made no headway. It was frustrating having the field marshal breathing down his neck and not being able to report any kind of success.

Adamat stooped just inside the front door to pick up the post. At least Tamas kept that running. It was hard not to admire him for that. Adamat waited for SouSmith to come inside, then pushed the door closed with his foot. SouSmith tapped his shoulder.

The back door through the hallway and past the kitchen was ajar. He dropped the post on a side table and removed a cane from the holder near the door. SouSmith headed to the sitting room. Adamat came around the corner behind him, cane held high. He lowered it slowly.

"You saved me a trip," he said.

Palagyi sat in Adamat's favorite chair, next to the fireplace, hands folded in his lap. He had the same two goons with him as last time. The lockpick lounged on the sofa, boots on, and the big one with the coal-stained arms studied his family portrait above the mantle. A fourth man sat behind Adamat's desk, hands folded serenely in his lap.

Palagyi's eyes grew wide at the sight of SouSmith. "You were coming to see me?" he said.

"Yes, I just was."

"I can't imagine why. There's no way you have the money you owe me." Again, he eyed SouSmith nervously.

Adamat took a deep breath, gathered his composure. "No, but I have some of it. You said you'd leave me be until my time was up."

"And I have," Palagyi said.

Adamat looked around the room. "I've got well over a month left."

"You gave me the wrong address for your family," Palagyi said.

"I gave you my cousins' address," Adamat said.

"Your cousins are a family of brawlers?"

"Seven sons, all take after their father," Adamat said. "Very successful prizefighters."

"Yes," Palagyi said, "Well, that may be, your family wasn't there."

"Really?"

"And when my boys pressed the question, they were forcibly removed from the town," Palagyi said. "In tar and feathers."

"I can't imagine why," Adamat said. He smiled inwardly but kept his expression flat.

Palagyi worked to control himself. "I'm willing to let this go."

Adamat froze. Palagyi was up to something. "Why?" he said.

Palagyi examined his fingernails. "I want to introduce you to my new friend," he said. He gestured to the man sitting at Adamat's desk. "This is Lord Vetas. He's a man of various talents. And he has powerful friends."

"Pleased to meet you." Adamat gave the man a curt nod and a quick inspection. He had the dusty, yellow skin of a full-blooded Rosvelean. He wore all-black clothes but for a scarlet vest and the gold chain of a pocket watch visible at his breast pocket. He sat in Adamat's chair like a schoolboy with perfect posture and his eyes traveled around the room with the steady inspection of someone who sees everything.

"You knew about the coup," Palagyi said, bringing Adamat's attention back to him. "Even before the papers. The night before, you were gone half the night. Summoned somewhere. My man saw you leave. You returned and immediately put your family in a carriage to—"

"Somewhere safe," Adamat finished.

"Somewhere safe," Palagyi continued. "And then you wrote a lot of letters. Sent them who knows where? You practically ran up to the university, skipping the execution—which seems strange, because not another soul in Adopest did. Since then you've been prowling around Adopest, hiring carriages to the north and east, writing more letters. You've been to every library in southern Adro."

"I see you've hired better people to follow me," Adamat said.

"Yes, I did." Palagyi polished his fingernails on his waistcoat.

"Even so, it took you this long to add things up?"

"I won't let you spoil my mood," Palagyi said. "You're working for Tamas. I know you are. And Lord Vetas knows as well. Along with his master."

Adamat studied the man behind his desk. "And who might that be?"

"Someone with a vested interest in the affairs of Adro and the rest of the Nine." It was the first time Lord Vetas had spoken. His voice was quiet, measured with the enunciation of a man educated at the best schools.

"A criminal?" Adamat said. "Palagyi rarely deals with people who aren't. The Proprietor, perhaps?"

Lord Vetas gave a dry chuckle. "No," he said.

"Stop trying to change the subject," Palagyi snarled. He stood up. "You work for Tamas now, don't you?"

"Sit down," Lord Vetas said. Palagyi sat.

"And if I do?" Adamat said.

Palagyi opened his mouth.

"Quiet," Lord Vetas said. He spoke the word softly. Palagyi's mouth snapped shut. "You may go now, Palagyi. You've made the introductions."

Palagyi glared at Lord Vetas. "Don't think you'll take the credit for this yourself. I discovered this. I told Lord—"

The garrote came up around Palagyi's throat and snapped tight from behind. Adamat drew his cane sword, SouSmith his pistol. Lord Vetas held up a single hand. Adamat froze. He watched in morbid fascination as Palagyi struggled against the strong hands of his own goon, the coal worker with the quick reflexes. Palagyi's face turned purple, and the goon kept his garrote tight around Palagyi's throat until long after the life was gone from him. Adamat lowered his cane sword.

Lord Vetas folded his hands back into his lap. "I've just taken over your loan from the late Palagyi. It's in your interest to work for me now."

"Doing what?" Adamat's mind raced. Palagyi had been a predictable thug. Adamat could deal with him. This Lord Vetas, however... he was a dangerous man. Dangerous like the Proprietor: the kind that made policemen retire early.

"I want to know everything about Tamas. Everything he does, everything he says to you. What he has you looking for."

"My loyalties are not for sale," Adamat said.

"You'll have to change your loyalties, then."

"I don't know who you are, or who your master is," Adamat said. "I'm loyal to Adro and I will not change that."

"My master has the Nine's best interests at heart, I assure you," Lord Vetas said. His quiet, sibilant voice was beginning to irritate Adamat. He almost had to strain to hear the man.

Adamat said, "The Nine is not the same as Adro. For all I know, you work for the Kez. The newspaper says they're sending ambassadors and that they still want Tamas to sign the Accords."

"I don't work for the Kez."

"Then who?"

"That is of little consequence to you."

"You aren't endearing yourself," Adamat said. "You come into my home, kill a man in my very living room, and threaten me? How do you know I won't send for the police this instant?"

A shallow smile flitted across Lord Vetas's face. "I am not the sort of man one summons the police on," he warned. "You of all people should know that."

"Yes. I'd already realized that." Adamat gritted his teeth. "You're the type of man who gives face to evil."

Lord Vetas seemed taken aback. "Evil? No, good sir. Just pragmatism."

"I know your kind," Adamat said. "And you seem to know me. Or you think you do. Now, get out of my home."

He glanced at SouSmith. Palagyi had been strangled by his own man. Would the same thing happen to Adamat? Was SouSmith really a friend? The boxer looked troubled. He watched both the goons and Lord Vetas all at once and cracked his knuckles like he did when he was ready for a fight. "I will pay you your money," Adamat said, "if you have indeed taken over the loan. Or I will face the streets when you kick me out. I will not betray a client or my country."

Lord Vetas examined his hands thoughtfully. He stood up and took his hat off the desk. "I'll return when I have leverage." The statement was matter-of-fact, yet the word "leverage" sent a chill down Adamat's spine. "Meanwhile, as a show of my master's good faith, we'll suspend your loan." He passed by Adamat and tipped his hat. "Consider our employment offer." He gave Adamat a small card with an address printed on the back.

It was not until Lord Vetas and his thugs were gone that Adamat remembered the body in his favorite chair. He regarded SouSmith grimly. "Find us some lunch in the pantry. I'm going to figure out something to do with that."

"Jakob has a great attachment to you," the woman said.

Nila sat across from the woman at a cafe table and sipped from a warm cup of tea. The sun shone overhead, a stiff breeze moving through the streets, and she could almost forget about the barricades just around the other side of the building, where royalist partisans held a wary standoff with Tamas's more numerous and better-trained soldiers.

"I can't stay," Nila said.

The woman examined her over a cup of tea. Her name was Rozalia and she was a Privileged. The Hielmen said she was the last Privileged left in all of Adro, but no one knew where she'd come from. She wasn't a member of Manhouch's royal cabal. Why she had any interest in Nila was impossible to say. Nila had no idea how to act in the presence of a Privileged. It was impossible to curtsy sitting down. She kept her eyes on her tea and tried to be as polite as possible.

"Why not, child?"

Nila sat up straighter. She didn't consider herself a child. At eighteen, she was a woman. She could wash and press and mend clothes and she might have one day married Yewen, the butler's son, if the whole world hadn't gone to the pit with Tamas's coup. Yewen was gone now, maybe fled, maybe killed in the streets.

When Nila didn't answer, Rozalia went on. "We have a parley with Field Marshal Tamas in the morning. If he comes to his senses, if General Westeven can make him see reason, you may find yourself nursemaid to the new king of Adro."

"I'm not a nurse," Nila said. "I wash clothes."

"That doesn't have to define you, child. I've been many things in my life. A Privileged is neither the greatest nor the least of them."

What was greater than a Privileged? "I'm sorry," Nila said.

Rozalia gave a sigh. "Speak up, child. Look me in the eye. You aren't a duke's washerwoman anymore."

"I'm lowborn, ma'am... my lady." Nila tried to remember how to address a Privileged. She'd never even met one before today.

"You've saved the life of the closest heir to the throne," Rozalia said. "Baronies have been gifted to the common folk for less."

Nila swallowed and tried not to imagine herself baroness of some barony in northern Adro. This kind of thing didn't happen to her. She could feel the Privileged's eyes studying her.

"You think we're going to lose," Rozalia said. She waited a moment for Nila's response, and then somewhat impatiently added, "Speak up, you can talk to me."

Nila did look up then. "Field Marshal Tamas has every advantage," she said. "He won't execute half the nobility only to put Jakob on the throne. Within a few weeks he'll have torn down the barricades and sent Jakob and all the nobles that backed him to the guillotine. I would like to be gone before that happens. I don't want to see it." She wondered, not for the first time, if it had been a mistake to bring Jakob to General Westeven. She could have fled with him to Kez. The silver she took from the townhouse would have more than paid for the trip.

"Smart girl," Rozalia said, placing a finger on her chin.

Nila folded her arms across her chest.

"What will you do?" Rozalia asked. "Once you've gotten past Tamas's blockade and made your way out of the city?"

What interest could a Privileged possibly have in that? Nila realized that she didn't know what she'd do. She had the silver. Most of it, anyway. She had needed new clothes and some medicine for Jakob, and a place to hide during the riots. "I can join up with the army. They always need laundresses, and the pay is good," she said.

"At best you'll wind up a soldier's wife," Rozalia said. "What a waste."

"It's better that," Nila said quietly, "than to die here for a lost cause."

"What did you think Tamas's soldiers would have done if they'd have caught you smuggling Jakob out of the duke's residence? You have courage, child, and don't try to pretend that you don't love that little boy. If you cared only for yourself, you'd be halfway to Brudania by now.

"Stay here," Rozalia continued. "Watch over Jakob. If the parley tomorrow goes well, you'll wind up a rich woman. If it doesn't... you may need to save his life again."

If she stayed by Jakob's side, she could, like Rozalia said, become a wealthy woman. Or follow him to the guillotine block. She remembered the soldier's hands holding her down, the feelings of helplessness and horror. No bearded sergeant would save her the next time Tamas's soldiers came through a door. She had silver buried in the corner of a graveyard just outside of the city. She would never have to feel that fear again.

Nila couldn't help but wonder if Rozalia had other motives for wanting her to stay. A Privileged used the common folk. She didn't help them. There had to be a reason she was showing such interest in Nila.

Jakob came into sight over Rozalia's shoulder. His pallor had improved despite the stress of the last two weeks. Rozalia had done something for his cough. He smiled and waved to Nila, then was distracted by a butterfly flitting through the rubble of a building knocked over by the earthquake. She watched him dance off after the insect, followed by a pair of vigilant Hielmen.

"I'll stay," she said. "For now."

"You can end this quickly," Julene said.

Tamas examined the woman lounging in the chair on the other side of his desk. She'd come alone on her own initiative, leaving Taniel and the magebreaker who knew where. She wore a low-cut shirt that revealed enough cleavage to get the imagination going but that was tight enough for her to move quickly when she wanted. Tamas knew the effect was not accidental. Yet he was not a man to make the same mistake twice. Julene was a dangerous woman. She was the type to use any weapon available to her in order to get ahead. He looked away from her chest and at the scar running from the corner of her mouth to her brow.

He wondered at that scar. There were Privileged who dealt in healing sorcery. It was a tricky art, and they were rare, but with the amount Julene charged for her mercenary services, she could easily afford it. Perhaps she just liked looking deadly.

"How?"

"Assassins," she said. "Send men behind the barricades. Wipe out all their leadership and the rest will surrender easily."

Tamas snorted. "I've been trying my best to scrape together Manhouch's old spy network with little success and you want me to find enough assassins to bring down those barricades? You're mad."

"Use the Black Street Barbers," Julene said.

"The street gang?"

Julene nodded. "They will be expensive, but they're the best at what they do. They'll end this civil war."

"Gangs can't be controlled."

"They can with the right amount of money," Julene said. "The Barbers are different. More organized. They report to Ricard Tumblar. He uses them to police the docks."

"Assassination is risky. It could turn the people against me."

"You're being a fool."

"Careful."

"If you won't consider that, then you need me at the parley."

"Why?" Tamas checked his watch. The parley was set for ten o'clock. Two hours from now.

"Because General Westeven is in league with this Privileged we're hunting. She'll be there. It wouldn't surprise me if she makes a move against you."

"I have my powder mages for that," Tamas said.

"Your boy has shot her three times and put an arm's length of steel through her stomach. Do your other Marked have anything new to bring to the table?"

This confirmed Taniel's reports. This Privileged was something else. Something more.

"You know her, don't you?" he said. "This is personal. I can tell by the way you talk. You want this woman dead."

"Don't be absurd."

"I've had you kill seven Privileged in the last two years. Each time you've been cold, mechanical."

"And each time I've been able to kill them within a day or two," Julene said. "This *is* getting personal. I want the bitch dead."

"So you don't know her?"

"Of course not."

She was lying. Tamas could tell by the way her eyes hardened when she spoke. It was a small tell, and he'd only recently figured it out, but Julene put a little extra fire into her lies when she wanted to be believed. Now, why wouldn't she tell the truth?

"You think you can handle her if she tries something?" Tamas said.

"Of course. Every time we've begun to fight, she's run. At the very least I will scare her off."

"Be there," Tamas said. "In an hour. Bring Gothen and Taniel and his pet savage. And don't do anything stupid."

"I'll only be there to protect you," Julene said.

Tamas stood next to a repaired field gun and watched a line of men make their way over the barricade under a white flag. Olem was on the other side of the gun, leaning against the barrel, speaking quietly to Sabon. Vlora stood somewhere behind him with Brigadiers Ryze and Sabastenien, the only two mercenary commanders posted in the city. From a building across the street Taniel trained his rifle on the barricades. Julene tugged idly at her gloves, her magebreaker partner beside her. A whole company of Adran soldiers stood at attention twenty paces back. Tamas wanted General Westeven to know exactly how bad his odds were.

This would be a crucial meeting. Tamas felt he held most of the cards, but General Westeven was an incredibly capable commander. He could ruin Tamas's plans simply by protracting the civil war.

"A sorry lot, sir," Olem said, motioning toward the approaching royalists.

Tamas withheld judgment. The royalists had been crouching behind their barricades for eight days. They were dirty and disheveled, but they showed no signs of imminent starvation or even fatigue. Behind ramshackle barricades they may be, but General Westeven would see that every man and woman at his disposal slept on a good bed and had plenty to eat—not hard, when they had captured the city's main granaries. The royalists were eating better than most of the city right now.

Tamas floated in a light powder trance, allowing him to examine faces at a distance with ease. He knew General Westeven, a tall, bald man with bloodspots on his scalp. Age had reduced the general to little more than skin stretched over bones, his whole body moving slowly from advanced rheumatism. Still, that was no reason to underestimate him. His mind was sharp as a fine dagger.

Tamas didn't recognize a single one of the men with the general. They were nobles, judging by their bedraggled finery. Men who'd slipped through his soldiers' nets the night of the coup, or were too minor to warrant attention.

He did recognize the woman with them. It was the Privileged who'd killed Lajos and the rest. She looked none the worse for the wear despite the wounds Taniel had supposedly given her. Perhaps Taniel was wrong. Maybe he'd missed. Tamas locked eyes with her for a moment. She returned his gaze unflinchingly.

Taniel wasn't known to miss.

There was a pause among the royalist group and a brief argument before they finished their trek down the street and formed up opposite Tamas and his mercenaries. There were twenty of them, and Westeven was the only soldier of the whole lot. This wasn't opposition, Tamas realized with disgust. This was a committee.

"Field Marshal Tamas," said a fat noble with a stained cummerbund. "Order your men to stand down! We've come beneath a flag of truce."

Tamas glanced at the soldiers behind him. They were at attention, their rifles shouldered. "Westie," he said. "Good to see you."

Westeven returned his nod. "Would it were under different circumstances, my friend."

"There'd be no hard feelings if you stepped away from this lot right now. You'd be a formidable ally in rebuilding the country."

"The way I see it," Westeven said, "is that you are the one destroying it."

"Surely you can see the corruption?" Tamas said. "Nothing short of the destruction of the nobility would have saved Adro."

Westeven's eyes were tired, his face strained. He seemed as if he desperately wanted to say yes. "There is more at stake here than you know. And you killed my king, Tamas. I can't forgive you for that."

"Your king was about to give the whole country to the Kez!" Tamas's voice rose sharply. Westeven was a smart man. No, a brilliant man. How could he not see what Tamas was trying to do? How could he stand in the way? "I could not allow the Accords to be signed and this country sold into servitude. What more important is at stake than the people?"

The general glanced at the members of Tamas's guard. "I won't speak of it here." His eyes hardened. "We're here to negotiate," he said.

"From what grounds," Tamas asked. "You're completely surrounded. I have more men—"

"I have twenty thousand behind those barricades."

"—including women and children, maybe," Tamas snapped. "You might have a few dangerous Knacked at best, and this." He gestured to the Privileged. "Yet I have a dozen powder mages and enough field guns to destroy half the city."

"You mean the half that wasn't destroyed by the quake?" Westeven's calm was infuriating. Tamas gritted his teeth.

"I have time," Westeven continued. "I hold the main city granaries and armory—food and weapons you need, because the Kez ambassadors will arrive any day now, and if they see that we are at war among ourselves, then they will smell blood, and a Kez army will be knocking on our door within weeks. Even if they don't, the people will begin to tire of this civil war. They will see your soldiers and mercenaries as a burden. They will turn on you when you can't feed them, when you can't rebuild their city."

The bastard could read his problems like a book. Tamas sized up the collection of noblemen. "What do you propose?"

The man with the soiled cummerbund stepped forward. "I am Viscount Maxil," he said. He lifted a length of paper and looked it over. "We have a list of demands."

Tamas snatched the paper before Maxil could object. He ran his eyes down the list.

"You expect me to step down? To arrest myself?" He gave the nobles a look of disbelief.

"You committed high treason!" one of them said. "You killed our king!"

Tamas stared them down until another man said quietly, "We're willing to negotiate on that point."

Tamas went back to reading. Before he'd gone another paragraph, he was shaking his head. "You want all the king's land and that of the executed nobility divided up among yourselves? What do you take me for, a fool?"

"These are points of negotiation," Maxil said.

"A moment ago you said they were demands."

"More like negotiation," Maxil said, looking away.

Tamas gave the list back. "Westie, surely you can talk some sense into them?"

Westeven shrugged. "Negotiate, Tamas. I beg of you."

"Give me a moment."

Tamas stepped back behind the cannons and beckoned over the brigadiers. He was joined by Olem, Vlora, Sabon, Brigadier Ryze, and Brigadier Sabastenien. Julene still stood off to the side, staring at the other Privileged with the intensity of a cat.

Brigadier Sabastenien spoke first. "They have no grounds to negotiate from." The man was young, barely older than Taniel, and Tamas had a hard time taking him seriously. Yet one did not become a brigadier of the Wings of Adom at that age for nothing.

"I'm afraid they do," Sabon said. "Westeven is right. We don't have time. If the Kez ambassadors arrive and see us in this state..."

"Not to mention the granaries," Tamas said. "We've reduced rations by a third for the army just to have a bare minimum for the city breadwagons. The people are starving. They won't put up with this for long."

"Your council will be angry if you make any decisions without them," Vlora pointed out. "Sir," she added.

"This is a matter of war, Captain," Tamas said, "and in that they have given me full power. I'll negotiate as I see fit." He turned to Ryze. "Can we take those barricades without losing a few thousand men?"

Ryze considered a moment. "Only if we give them a good shelling first. Even then... it will be costly."

Tamas rolled his eyes. Ryze had been an artillery commander before joining the Wings of Adom. He saw shelling as a solution to everything.

"If we don't shell them?"

"It will be a bloodbath," Ryze said. "On both sides."

"Shit."

Tamas returned to the royalists. "Give me an offer," Tamas said. He motioned to the paper in Maxil's hand. "A serious offer. Not that list of pig shit. And it will include her"—he pointed at the Privileged—"giving herself up to await execution for the murder of my men."

The Privileged gazed back at Tamas with the severity only old women are capable of. To her, they were all children playing at children's games.

"That won't happen," General Westeven said. "Be realistic, Tamas. This is war. Casualties are a fact of that war."

Tamas gritted his teeth. "Give me an offer."

Maxil launched into it immediately, and Tamas realized it was what he'd expected all along.

"We have a cousin of the king's within our barricades," Maxil said.

"His name?" Tamas interrupted.

"Jakob the Just."

Tamas blinked, trying to remember the royal line. "More like Jakob the Child, he's a fourth cousin, at best, and he's barely five."

"He's the closest living relative to Manhouch." Maxil went on. "We propose that we put him on the throne as Manhouch the Thirteenth. You and General Westeven will remain in control of the army, and we along with your council will combine to form the core of the king's new advisory board. Your powder mages will be the new royal cabal."

"And the king?" Tamas asked.

"We will advise him until he comes of age."

Tamas looked to Westeven. There was a levelheadedness to this proposal that spoke of his influence. The nobility would leave most of the control in his hands. Yet it could not stand.

"I will never allow a king to have power over Adro again," Tamas said. "I simply won't have it. If you want a king, he will be that in name only."

Maxil scowled. "A puppet monarchy?"

"At the very best, and I'm stretching my patience to offer that."

"No," Maxil said. "Adro must have a proper king."

"Never again," Tamas said.

"You're refusing us? That's it? No negotiation? We've left the army in your hands. We've made you the next royal cabal head. You'd be the second most powerful man in Adro. Are you that greedy that you must keep it all to yourself?"

Tamas chuckled. "You poor sods. I didn't do this for power. I did it to destroy the monarchy. I did it to free the people. I'm not going to turn around and put a boy king on the throne so that you can go back to your country villas and continue to bleed the country dry." He looked at Westeven. "I'm sorry, my friend. No king, no foreign country must ever have power in Adro again."

"I will fight you to the end," Westeven said.

Tamas bowed to his old friend. "I know." Tamas felt someone touch his shoulder. Julene was there, her face serious.

"There's something wrong," she said.

"What?" Tamas said. He exchanged a frown with General Westeven.

The familiar popping sound of fired air rifles erupted from the barricades. Julene leapt between Tamas and General Westeven, shoving Tamas back. Bullets crackled against an invisible barricade. Julene fell back, throwing fireballs as quickly as she could summon them. They smashed into the barricade, causing blooms of fire.

The other Privileged launched herself into action just a moment after Julene. Hardened shields of air stopped the crack of bullets from Tamas's quickest soldiers, covering the sudden retreat of the royalist delegation. The ground rumbled, the air seemed to shake, and the cannon closest to Tamas suddenly cracked, the wheels falling off, the broken metal hitting the ground with a thud.

Tamas leapt to his feet. They'd attacked him. They'd attacked him under a flag of truce! Westeven knew better than that. Westeven... Tamas's eyes found his old friend. Westeven's body was being dragged toward the barricades. He was missing an arm, his whole chest blackened. Was he already dead? He'd been hit by one of Julene's fireballs. Tamas felt sick.

"Senseless," he spat. "Brigadier Ryze! Prime the artillery. We attack at once!"

CHAPTER 11

The Public Archives are just above us," Adamat said. Somewhere behind him, SouSmith's lantern wobbled to a stop, and the sound of sloshing stilled.

"You sure this time?"

Adamat held his own lantern up to the rusted iron ladder rungs in front of him. There was a plaque on the bricks between the rungs, supposedly to say which building this accessed, but the letters had been worn away long ago. The storm drains beneath Adro were not kept in the best of shape. It was a miracle most of them had survived the earthquake—and a testament to Adran engineering.

"I may have a perfect memory," Adamat said, his voice echoing in the long, shoulder-height tunnel, "but all these damned drains look alike."

"Heh. I liked the women's bathhouse."

"I bet you did," Adamat said. "Wonder anyone's using it, what with Tamas lobbing shells all over this section of town." He rubbed his finger over the plaque, trying to make out any kind of letters. "This has got to be it."

SouSmith sloshed up beside him. The big boxer was bent almost double. Adamat's knees and thighs ached from trying to move around in the storm drains, but SouSmith had to be hurting far worse.

"I'll check," SouSmith said. He handed Adamat his lantern and pulled himself up the iron rungs. The ladder squeaked in protest of his weight. "Lantern," SouSmith said, reaching down a hand.

Adamat heard a grate move to one side, and SouSmith disappeared. Somewhere above them, closer than Adamat would have liked, he heard the deep thump of artillery.

"Come," SouSmith said, his voice muffled.

Adamat followed him up the ladder and found himself in a high-arched basement. The walls were made of cement, damp and moldy, and a half inch of stagnant water covered the floor. No one had been in this room for a decade.

"This is it," Adamat said.

"Really?" SouSmith looked doubtful.

"I used to play in these drains as a boy," Adamat said. "Mother'd get furious. I must have explored half the basements in Adro." He grinned at SouSmith. "I knew we were close when we found the bathhouse."

"Spent a lot of time under there, eh?"

"For certain. I was once an adolescent boy, after all."

They passed through a series of identical arched storage rooms before they found a narrow flight of stairs leading up. The door rattled when Adamat tried it.

"SouSmith," he said. He stepped back, letting the boxer squeeze past him. SouSmith braced his hands on either wall and kicked the door. The lock snapped and the door crashed inward, then fell off its hinges. They glanced at each other as the sound echoed through the building.

They left their lanterns beside the basement door and carried on cautiously. Adamat had his cane, SouSmith a pair of short-barreled pistols. They came out of a long corridor into the main floor of the Archives.

The building was as large as a parade ground and stacked four stories high. Shelving stretched from one wall to the next. Adamat headed down an aisle. Outside the brick walls, he could hear the sound of rifle and musket shots. The air was dusty, the smell of the books almost overwhelming—the scent of glue, paper, and old vellum, of age and mustiness.

"No one here," SouSmith said.

Adamat glanced back. SouSmith was inspecting the shelves of books with something akin to suspicion. When a man solved his problems by punching them, books were often a foreign thing. "Not surprised," Adamat said. "General Westeven has given large grants to at least a dozen libraries throughout the Nine, including this one. He won't let it be touched."

They came out of an aisle and found themselves in the middle of the library. A wide space, free of shelves, was filled with tables for the patrons. Light came from a skylight that went up all four stories directly through the center of the Archives. The tables were all clear.

Except for one. Adamat placed a finger to his lips and signaled for SouSmith to follow. A number of books had been laid out on a table in one corner. They were open, as if left there only moments ago. His frown deepened as they approached. The books were obviously missing pages, and whole paragraphs had been blotted from them. He flipped one of the books to the cover. *In Service of the King.*

Adamat drew his cane sword in one swift motion and spun around. He heard the click of SouSmith's pistols.

A woman had stepped out between them. She wore a wool riding dress and jacket and had gray in her shoulder-length hair, and wise, dark eyes that reminded Adamat of a raven. She wore Privileged's gloves and had a hand pointed at both himself and SouSmith. An artillery blast made the building tremble, kicking up dust from the shelves of books.

Adamat licked his lips. SouSmith's eyes were wide, and his finger brushed at the trigger.

"You'll get us both killed," Adamat said to SouSmith.

"Don't like this," was the response.

"Neither do I. Who are you?" he asked the Privileged, though he already had some idea.

"My name is Rozalia," she said.

"You're the Privileged that Tamas is hunting."

Her silence was enough of an answer for Adamat. His eyes darted to the books on the table.

"Are you going to kill us?"

"Only if I have to."

Adamat slowly lowered his cane sword. He gestured to SouSmith to put away his pistols.

"You're a Knacked," Rozalia said.

"Yes."

"Are you looking for me?"

"No."

The Privileged looked confused. "Then why are you here?"

Adamat jerked his head toward the books. The Privileged still hadn't lowered her gloved hands. It was making him nervous. He said, "Have you been removing those pages? Blotting those books? And taking the ones at the university?"

Rozalia slowly lowered her hands. "No," she said.

"You didn't take the books at the university?"

"I did take those. But I never ripped the pages out. *She* did."

"Who?"

The Privileged did not answer.

"What are you doing with the ones you took?"

"The same as you, it seems," she said. "Looking for answers."

"Kresimir's Promise," Adamat breathed.

Rozalia scoffed. "Simple things," she said. "There are more questions than you know."

"All I care about is Kresimir's Promise," Adamat said. "What is it?"

She tilted her head to one side and regarded Adamat as a cat would a mouse. The sharp crack of rifles filled the silence, and a canon roared outside.

"I need a message delivered," she said.

"What?"

"A message. One that needs to be delivered in person."

"I'll deliver your damned message. Tell me what the Promise is. Give me evidence."

"I don't trust you," Rozalia said. "If you deliver my message, then I will tell you." Her eyes darted suddenly as the thump of rifle butts on a door reached them. The Privileged made a hissing sound in the back of her throat. "Field Marshal Tamas is here. I must go. You won't find the answer in any of these books. Only from me."

Adamat calculated the chance he'd have of catching her unawares. A signal to SouSmith, a blow to the back of the head. They could hand her over to Tamas and let *him* get the answer out of her. Adamat saw that path ending with his death by Privileged sorcery.

"Who's the message for?"

"Privileged Borbador," Rozalia said. "The last remaining member of Manhouch's royal cabal. He's at Shouldercrown Fortress. Tell him that *she* will try to summon Kresimir."

"That's it?" Adamat said.

Rozalia gave a curt nod.

"And Kresimir's Promise?"

She laughed. It was a sharp noise. "Ask Borbador. He'll know."

There were boots on the marble in the Archives' main foyer. Rozalia turned and ran, vaulting a table like a woman half her age. She had just disappeared down a far aisle when soldiers appeared from the shelving aisles on the opposite side. They wore the colors of the Wings mercenaries and they pointed their rifles at Adamat and SouSmith.

Adamat raised his hands and sighed. "Tell Field Marshal Tamas that Inspector Adamat is here to see him."

The mercenaries glanced at one another.

"Well?" Adamat said. "He's nearby, isn't he?"

One of the mercenaries headed back down an aisle. SouSmith glowered at Adamat.

"Not a word," Adamat whispered. "If I'd known Tamas was going to take the Archives today, we wouldn't have spent the last two days mucking through storm drains."

"Bastard," SouSmith said, glancing down at his sodden shoes.

"Inspector?" Field Marshal Tamas emerged from one of the shelving aisles. He carried a saw-handled dueling pistol, the powder on the barrel suggesting it had been used recently. "What the pit are you doing here?"

"Inspecting, sir," Adamat said.

"Of course," Tamas said distractedly, looking Adamat and SouSmith up and down, and sniffed. "Have you been in the sewer?"

"The storm drains."

"Very resourceful." Tamas glanced at the mercenaries behind him. "Stand down. Inspector Adamat is under my employ. Check the rest of the library." The mercenaries headed off, and Tamas turned back to Adamat. "Have you solved my riddle, Inspector?"

"I have a lead, sir. Nothing definite yet. The books I'm looking for have come up defaced or entirely missing."

"I expect you to do more than spend your days leafing through books."

"That's often exactly what investigating entails, sir," Adamat huffed. "One follows any lead one can."

"Very well. Carry on. Wait."

Adamat paused.

"What do you know about the Black Street Barbers?"

Adamat summoned up his knowledge of them, thinking it over for a moment. "Their leader is a man named Teef. Among Adro's underworld they're considered the top assassins. They'll take any job, is the rumor, as long as it pays well. At least a dozen Barbers have tried killing Adran kings over the last few hundred years, when the price has been right. None have succeeded, not with the royal cabal there to protect them. I've met Teef. He's the...least mentally unbalanced of the crew. Frankly, the entire gang belongs in an insane asylum. I hope you're not thinking of..."

Tamas nodded briskly. "Thank you." He strode away.

"...employing them," Adamat finished quietly.

Adamat retrieved his cane from where he'd dropped it when the mercenaries arrived. He glanced the way Rozalia had gone and pondered her cryptic message. "Time to go to Shouldercrown," he said to SouSmith.

"Jakob!" Nila pushed past a royalist soldier and tripped over brick rubble that had spilled out into the street from the latest artillery blast. She lifted her skirt and was back on her feet, stumbling along as she shouted the boy's name.

There was blood on her dress. The cannonball had whistled over her shoulder and taken the head off a man named Penn as they'd sat over a meager breakfast. She could still hear the sound in her head like a horrible kettle, instantaneous death passing inches from her ear. The cannonball had knocked a hole in the wall behind

Penn, straight through Jakob's room in one of the more intact buildings behind the barricades. Penn's body still sat in his chair, shoulders slumped, one hand clutching a spoon. Jakob should have been in bed. He wasn't.

Nila found one of Jakob's Hielmen guards picking grit out of his uniform. His name was Bystre, and he was about thirty-five. A steadiness about him reminded her of the bearded sergeant back at Duke Eldaminse's townhouse.

"Where's Jakob?" she asked.

"He's not in bed?" Bystre said.

"No."

"Pit, he must have wandered again."

A canister shot exploded overhead, sending everyone diving for cover. Nila found herself on the ground, beneath Bystre.

"Are you all right?" he asked.

"I'll be fine. Find Jakob."

He helped her to her feet and they ran through the street, calling Jakob's name. Nila heard the crack of muskets and was struck by the choking smell of spent powder. Down the street was one of the barricades. Royalist soldiers and volunteers crouched behind it, shooting at unseen Adran soldiers on the other side.

The parley had been five days ago. Every day since, Field Marshal Tamas's soldiers had pressed the attack. Cannon and musket fire resounded day and night. The air reeked of sulfurous black powder.

Someone shouted a warning. A moment later, blue uniforms swarmed over the top of the barricade like water bursting through a dam.

"Run," Bystre instructed. "Fall back to the next barricade!" he shouted at nearby volunteers.

Bystre grabbed Nila by the arm. "We have to find Jakob," he said. He spun suddenly, his plumed hat falling from his head as an Adran soldier appeared from a nearby alleyway. Bystre drew his sword, parrying the thrust of a bayonet. The soldier cracked him across the jaw with a rifle butt. Bystre fell to the ground. The soldier stood over him, bayonet ready.

Nila could barely lift the paving brick she grabbed. She swung it up over her head and brought it down on the back of the Adran soldier's neck. The man collapsed to the ground without a sound. Bystre held his jaw and tried to shake off the blow.

She pulled him to his feet.

"There!" she said. She caught sight of Jakob running across the street, closer to the barricade. A bullet kicked up dirt in front of the boy, startling him, and he fell with tears in his eyes.

Adran soldiers had taken the barricade. They were barely a hundred feet from Jakob. Nila was half that distance. She lifted her skirts and ran. She could hear Bystre right behind her. The soldiers on the barricade were more interested in securing their victory than they were in a stray child in the street. Nila fell to her knees beside Jakob and swept him up in her arms. Bystre helped her to her feet, and they both ran toward safety.

Nila stopped short when she realized Bystre was not beside her anywhere. She turned to see him staring back toward the fallen barricade.

"It's lost," she said.

"Him!" Bystre drew his sword.

"What are you . . ." She saw it. Field Marshal Tamas stood on the barricade with his men, surveying the street beyond. Beside him, she saw someone familiar. The bearded sergeant who had saved her that night in the townhouse kitchen.

"Bystre, we have to get Jakob to safety."

"Nothing is safe from that treacherous bastard."

"General Westeven . . ."

"The General is dead."

Nila didn't know what to say. She knew General Westeven had been wounded at the parley, but the royalists had been told he'd survived. Only he could match someone like Field Marshal Tamas in strategic maneuvering. Now their cause was truly lost.

Nila looked toward the next barricade. Royalists waved her forward to the relative safety. She clutched Jakob to her chest. He held his hands over his ears, and she could feel his shoulders heave as he sobbed.

"Bystre," she said, pleading. Where was Rozalia? She was their only hope now. She could bring down her Privileged sorceries on Tamas and his army and drive them from the streets.

Bystre snatched up a spent rifle from a dead soldier and checked the bayonet. He dusted the powder from the pan and, clutching the rifle with both hands, charged alone toward the fallen barricade.

The bearded sergeant pointed toward Bystre and lifted his rifle. Field Marshal Tamas turned. He tilted his head, as if bemused by the enraged Hielman rushing toward him. He drew a pistol and pulled the trigger. Bystre jerked and fell, his body rolling once with forward momentum before twitching and falling still. The bullet had pierced his eye at more than one hundred paces. Field Marshal Tamas waved the smoke from the barrel of his pistol.

Nila screamed.

She saw the field marshal gesture toward her and waited for another bullet to come and pierce her brain. It never came. Instead, Adran soldiers ran down the barricade and toward her. She stared at them, in shock, until she remembered Jakob in her arms.

Nila turned to run to the next barricade. She had a lead on the Adran soldiers, but they were far faster. She tripped and struggled on the hem of her dress. Forty feet away, the royalists fired from behind the next barricade to give her cover. Bullets ricocheted off the paving stones around her, the scent of gunpowder making her choke. Thirty feet to go.

Someone hit her from behind. She fell, turning to see Adran soldiers upon her. She screamed and struggled, but Jakob was pulled from her arms. One of the soldiers turned to her, bayonet ready to shove through her belly. He twisted the rifle at the last second and pushed her away with the stock and the soldiers retreated, taking a screaming Jakob with them.

Nila struggled to her feet and staggered after them. They couldn't take him. Not now, not after she'd protected him this long. She stopped beside Bystre's body. He lay on his belly, his one remaining eye staring sightlessly across the street. Flies had already started to buzz around the bloody hole in his skull. She fell to her knees and vomited.

Someone pulled her out of the street and into a rubble-strewn alley before the shooting resumed.

Nila sagged against the partially intact wall of a tenement. "You let them take him," she spat at her rescuer.

Rozalia glanced out into the street, her gloved fingers poised at the ready until some unapparent danger had passed. She let her hands fall.

"This is no longer my fight," Rozalia said.

"You could have stopped them," Nila accused. "You could have killed Tamas right then. You could have protected Bystre." She heard her voice crack and felt the tears on her cheeks. She wiped them away with a grimy sleeve.

"General Westeven is dead," Rozalia said. "There is no reason to prolong this fight any longer." She paused for a moment, staring back into Nila's accusing eyes. "Yes, I could have killed Tamas, but damage has been done on a scope you cannot imagine. At this point, killing Tamas would only multiply that damage."

"Bystre," Nila said.

"I don't expect you to understand," Rozalia said. Her voice softened suddenly. "You are a brave girl. A smart girl. I only expect you to move on. Tamas has the boy. Westeven is dead. The other royalists will drag this out for as long as they can, but Tamas will win eventually. Get out while you still can. There is a path through the rubble in the southwestern corner of the barricades. Neither side knows about it. Take that way out. Gather what money you can and live a full life far from here." Something wistful entered Rozalia's eyes. "Fatrasta is nice this time of year."

"What will he do to Jakob?" Nila asked.

Rozalia held out a hand. Nila accepted and got to her feet.

"Jakob," she said again when Rozalia did not answer. "What will Tamas do with him?"

"Tamas is pragmatic," Rozalia said. "If he were to allow a monarchal heir to survive, he could have this situation all over again. He'll do away with the boy quietly."

Nila dried the tears in her eyes. She felt something harden in her heart at the thought of Jakob's blond head dropping into a basket.

"Leave Adro," Rozalia said. "That's what I'll do, when my work here is done. Here." She dug something from a pocket sewn into her jacket and pressed it into Nila's hand. A hundred-krana coin.

"Thank you," Nila said. Rozalia waved dismissively and picked her way down the alley, away from the barricades. Nila waited a few moments, thinking of the coin in her hand and the silver hidden outside the city. She could still see Bystre from the alley. His body lay unmoving beneath the constant exchange of gunfire between royalists and Adran soldiers. Nila made a fist around the coin. It was enough for new clothes and a coach all the way to Brudania. Along with her silver, it was enough for a new life.

She saw Field Marshal Tamas in her mind as he coolly gunned down Bystre.

She couldn't start a new life, not with memories of what had happened.

CHAPTER 12

Shouldercrown Fortress rested on the jagged ridgeline of South Pike Mountain. Its bastion walls were sloped and smooth despite the harsh weather at this altitude, a testament to the powerful sorceries that had built and warded them five hundred years ago. To the southeast, the amber plains of Kez rolled out in the distance. To the northwest, the far mountains that ringed Adro could be seen past the hills and forests. Adopest nestled like a diamond on the teardrop tip of the Adsea. To the north, South Pike's peak smoked ominously.

Adamat turned away from the edge of the bastion. Seeing the whole world laid out like that made his head spin, and he wanted to head back into the town—a whole town inside the bastion, that's how large it was!—yet the Mountainwatch soldier had told him to wait here for Privileged Borbador. They could have offered him a room. It was far below freezing at this height. Seemed they wanted to see him shiver.

Adamat was exhausted physically and mentally. Even with modern roads the trip was five days by coach, and they had barely stopped to rest. His body hurt from sitting on an uncomfortable, constantly jostling seat. His head pounded from too little rest. Rozalia's cryptic warning about a woman trying to summon Kresimir had given him nightmares the few times he caught any sleep. What was wrong with him? He was a modern man. An educated man. Kresimir was a myth, an embodiment of monastic power that kept the peasants in line.

"What are you doing?"

SouSmith paused in the middle of loading one of his short-barrel pistols. The weapon looked like a toy in his big hands. "What does it look like?"

"You think he's going to kill us?" Adamat asked. "Just for asking a question?"

"Last Privileged almost did us in."

"And?"

"And what?"

"This is a Privileged, SouSmith. If he doesn't want to talk to us, he waves a hand and sweeps us from this bastiontop."

SouSmith shrugged. "You paid me to be a bodyguard, eh?"

"Yes." Adamat sighed. SouSmith didn't seem to understand. This was a Privileged. There was no guarding anybody against one of these.

"Even a Privileged has to come through me to get ya." SouSmith resumed loading the weapon.

Adamat stifled a smile and realized the words had banished some of his nervousness. He was up here on the roof of the world, a five-day journey from Adopest. He was at a Mountainwatch. Everyone knew the Mountainwatch was filled with convicts and cutthroats and the very hardest men in the Nine. They tended the high passes, manned the mines and the timber yards, and they were Adro's first defense against a foreign invasion. Adamat trusted his country with the Mountainwatch far more than he trusted them with his life.

"What's a Privileged doin' out here anyway?" SouSmith finished loading his pistols and stuck them in his belt. He leaned against one of the fixed guns that faced toward Kez.

"Exiled." Adamat watched his breath come out white.

"What for?"

"Officially? There was a shift in power within the royal cabal, and Borbador was on the wrong side. Unofficially, rumor has it he slept with Privileged Khen's favorite concubine."

SouSmith grunted a laugh. "And he kept his skin?"

"Of course I did."

The Privileged approached them from the town within the bastion. He was far enough away that he shouldn't have heard any of that. He wore a long reindeer-skin jacket that went to his knees, and boots, pants, and a hat to match. He was shorter than Adamat had expected. Under a ruddy beard, loose skin hung from what once had been jowls. The Mountainwatch was kind to no one—not even a Privileged.

The Privileged stopped a few feet from them. His hands were tucked into his sleeves, but Adamat thought he caught sight of the white of Privileged's gloves.

"It wasn't hard, really," the Privileged said. "I told Magus Khen that my best friend would come after him if he killed me."

"And who's that?"

"Taniel Two-Shot. I'm Privileged Borbador. Call me Bo."

Adamat extended a hand. Bo took it in his gloved hand with surprising strength. "Inspector Adamat. This is my associate, SouSmith."

Bo squinted at SouSmith. "The boxer?"

"That's right," SouSmith said, surprised.

"Used to go see you fight when I was a kid," Bo said. "Taniel and I would sneak off and watch you. He lost a lot of money betting against you."

"And you?"

"Made me wealthy—for a kid."

Adamat examined the man. He knew little about this Privileged beyond city rumor. It was never wise to know too much about any members of the royal cabal. "Seems strange, a Privileged and a powder mage being friends."

"Met long before either of us knew what we were," Bo said. "I was an orphan when Taniel befriended me. Tamas let me live in the basement. Even paid for a governess. Said that if Taniel was going to have friends, they'd be educated. It was a shock to all of us when the magus seekers dowsed me out. I haven't seen Taniel since he went to Fatrasta."

"Aren't Privileged allergic to powder?"

"My eyes puff up whenever I'm around him," Bo acknowledged. "Always wondered about that as a kid. So. What brings a gentleman like you to the Mountainwatch? You don't look like Tamas's assassins."

"We're not assassins," Adamat said quickly. "Though I don't blame you for wondering. I am working for Field Marshal Tamas. I doubt you'd still be alive if he wanted you otherwise."

Bo swayed backward on his feet. "He doesn't know," he murmured.

"Doesn't know what?"

"Nothing. Why did you seek me out?" His conversational tone disappeared, his smile fading.

"What is Kresimir's Promise?"

Bo watched him for a few moments. "You're serious?"

"Quite."

"Tamas sent you all the way up here to ask me that?"

"I came on my own," Adamat said. "But I'm searching for the answer on behalf of Field Marshal Tamas." Half disbelief, half mockery, Bo's reaction stirred some disquiet in him.

It seemed as if relief washed over Bo. He cracked a smile, then began to chuckle. "Let me guess," he said. "When Tamas slaughtered the royal cabal, their dying words were something along the lines of 'Don't break Kresimir's Promise'?"

Adamat gritted his teeth. This Privileged was beginning to irk him. He seemed to find great mirth in knowing what Adamat did not. "Yes," he said. "You laugh at the dying words of sorcerers? Was it some kind of morbid joke? A spell woven to baffle anyone who killed them?"

Bo's chuckle tapered off. "Not at all. Those Privileged were in deadly earnest. A spell can be woven, a ward of sorts, that will speak itself upon a sorcerer's death. A joke? No. That's the kind of thing I might do. But not those men. They believed every bit of it."

"And what does it mean?"

"Kresimir's Promise." Bo rolled the words around in his mouth like a bite of something sour. "Legend has it when Kresimir formed the Nine, he chose nine kings to govern the nations he'd created. To each king he assigned a royal cabal of sorcerers to protect and advise him. He called them the Privileged. The kings, seeing that the Privileged were men of great power, told Kresimir that they were worried that the royal cabals might turn against them and take power for themselves. So Kresimir gave them a promise.

"He promised them that their lines would rule the Nine forever—that their seed would never bring forth barren fruit, as it were. Kresimir told his newly appointed Privileged that if anyone were to end one of those lines through violence, he would return personally and destroy the entire nation." He leaned back when he'd finished speaking, like a schoolboy who had remembered his lesson. "What do you think of that?"

"I'm a man of reason..." Adamat said. Yet he couldn't help the shiver that went up his spine.

"Of course you are," Bo said. "Most men these days are. It's a stupid legend. One of many stories to keep the royal cabals in their place. Kresimir's reign was almost fourteen hundred years ago—at a guess. It could have been longer. Not even the kings really believe it, and only the very oldest members of the royal cabal do." Bo reached up and touched something beneath his coat. "No, there are far more effective ways to keep tabs on the royal cabal."

"What should I tell Tamas?" Adamat asked.

Bo shrugged. "Tell Tamas what you like. Tell Tamas to worry about important things, like feeding the people or"—he pointed out over the bastion wall toward Kez—"them."

Adamat took a deep breath. He let it come out slowly. "So that's it, then," he said.

"That's it. Though," Bo added, "I don't know why you couldn't find that in the library. There are a dozen books that mention it."

"Burned," Adamat said. "Pages missing and passages snubbed out. By a Privileged, in all likelihood."

Bo scowled. "Privileged should know better. Books are important. They link us to the past, to the future. Every written word gives us another hint about how to control the Else."

"Bo!" a voice called from the bastion town.

He turned around.

"We're going to the quarry!"

"Five minutes!" Bo yelled back. He removed his hands from his sleeves and flexed his gloved fingers. "Bastards are getting lazy," he said. "They think just because they have a Privileged, they can get me to cut stone, fell trees, and clear avalanches. Cleaning up after that quake nearly wrung me out last week. Well, I'm sorry my answer wasn't very dramatic. If you see Taniel Two-Shot, give him my hello."

Bo was halfway back to the town when Adamat remembered the message he'd promised to give. He jogged to catch up with the Privileged.

"There was a message," he said.

"From Taniel?"

"No, from a Privileged named Rozalia."

Bo shrugged. "Don't know anyone by that name."

"Well, she told me to give you a message."

"And?"

"These were her words: '*She* is going to summon Kresimir.' I don't know which 'she' the woman was talking about. I don't think she meant herself. I..."

Bo had frozen in place. All color drained from his face. He stumbled to one side. Adamat caught him. "What does it mean?"

Bo pushed him away. The man's teeth were chattering. "Pit and damnation. Get away! Go on, get back to Adopest. Tell Tamas to mobilize his army! Tell Taniel to get out of the country. Tell him... Shit!" The last word was a snarl, and Bo went sprinting across the bastion back toward the town.

Adamat stood in place, stunned.

SouSmith walked up beside him, tapping old tobacco out of his pipe. "He's an odd one," he mused.

"I don't like this," Tamas said.

"I don't think anyone does, my friend."

Tamas glanced back at Sabon. The Deliv stood beneath a large parasol, eyes on the distant barricades. Sweat beaded on his clean-shaved head like water on a cold glass. The day was unseasonably hot for this early in the spring. The sun shone overhead, drying up the last of a few weeks' worth of damp weather.

"Will the men understand?" Tamas said.

"Ours, or the mercenaries?"

"Mercenaries are pragmatic. They'll be paid either way. My own soldiers—will they lose faith in me after an act like this?"

Olem stood a few feet away. He turned to regard Tamas, though the question had not been directed at him.

"I think not," Sabon said. "They may not like the feel of it. War is supposed to be a gentleman's game, after all. They'll understand, though. They will respect that you won't throw lives away in a needless battle. They will respect that you don't want to shell your own city."

Tamas nodded slowly. "I've never resorted to assassination before. Not in twenty-five years of command."

"I can remember a few times you should have," Sabon said. "Remember that shah we fought in southeastern Gurla?"

"I try not to." Tamas leaned over and spit. He lifted his canteen to his lips, still watching the barricades. He could hear musket shots and the occasional report of artillery from about two miles away, where Brigadier Ryze was commanding an assault on the armory. "I've met some bad men in my day," Tamas said, thinking of the shah. "But that man was a monster. He'd have a man's entire extended family buried alive if he questioned a command."

"You had him gelded," Sabon said.

Olem choked. He tossed his cigarette on the ground and began coughing smoke.

"War is most definitely not a gentleman's game, my friend," Tamas said. "Else I wouldn't play." He glanced at Olem. "Give us a minute."

Olem moved out of earshot, still coughing. Tamas joined Sabon beneath the parasol. He produced a letter from his pocket and gave it to Sabon.

"Your new commission," Tamas said.

Sabon took the letter. "What?"

"I've put Andriya and Vadalslav to sniffing out more powder mages. With the royal cabal dead, I think the mages will be more likely to come forward. Not to mention the pay we're offering," he said. "They've set up shop outside of town, near the university, and will soon be heading to Deliv and Novi and Unice to recruit. I want you with them."

"No," Sabon said, trying to give the letter back.

"I'm your commanding officer," Tamas said. "You can't say no."

"I can say no to my old friend," Sabon said.

"Why won't you do it?"

Sabon grunted. "Andriya and Vadalslav are more than enough to take care of recruits. You've sent the others to the Gates of Wasal. Taniel is chasing a ghost around the city, and despite the fact that you assigned Vlora to your staff, you're still too angry to even speak to her. I won't leave you without another mage." He gestured toward the barricades. "The Kez ambassador will be here within a week, and you've still got this mess to clean up. Do we even know if the Barbers were successful?"

"You're worried about me?" Tamas said. "That's your excuse?"

"Worried that you'll bugger it all up and need someone to clean up things after you." Sabon paused. They could both hear shouting from beyond the barricade. "Perhaps we should help them," he said.

"Damned Barbers can do it themselves," Tamas said. "I won't fret if they all get themselves killed. Don't try to change the subject. Vadalslav said they've already found seven candidates with a little talent. They say three of them have potential."

"It takes years to fully train a powder mage," Sabon said. "They need to be taught to control their powers and how to be a soldier all at the same time."

"That's why I want you there," Tamas said. "You trained Taniel and Vlora practically single-handed. Now Taniel is the best marksman in the world, and Vlora can detonate a keg of powder from half a mile."

"That's not the same, and you know it." Sabon was angry now, his dark eyes glinting dangerously. "Taniel has been shooting since he could hold a gun. Vlora... well, she's just a prodigy."

"You don't have to go recruiting," Tamas said. "But I want you to start a school. You'll have a line of credit and will have say over all happenings. You'll never be more than a few hours away from me. If I need help, I'll summon you immediately."

"I have your word?" Sabon said.

"You have my word."

Sabon stuffed the envelope in his pocket. "I want to be here when the Kez ambassador arrives."

"Certainly."

"And don't look so pleased."

Tamas stifled a smile.

"Sir!" Olem returned. He pointed toward the barricades.

A figure was slowly picking his way over the barricades and then down into the street, where he maneuvered among the untouched earthquake rubble. He wore a long white apron over a white shirt and black trousers. The apron front was covered in red.

The man headed straight toward them. He snapped open a razor, the blade glinting in the sunlight. Tamas saw Olem tense. The razor was touched to the man's forehead in a mock salute.

"Teef, sir, of the Black Street Barbers," the man said. "The barricades are yours."

"The royalist leaders?"

"Dead or captured," Teef said. "But mostly dead."

Tamas snorted. "Women and children?"

The man snapped his razor shut and opened it again. He nervously ran the flat of the blade gently along his own throat. "Uh, there were a few bad occasions. Some of my boys have problems, sir. I, uh, dealt with it permanently."

Tamas squeezed his hands into fists. This has been a mistake. "And General Westeven?"

"He was dead, sir. As you said he'd be."

Tamas had hoped that the wound Westeven had taken in the brief melee after the parley had been just that: a wound. But his whole arm had been gone, and Westeven was old and no powder mage. "Olem, see that the Black Street Barbers are rounded up and kept safe until we have a chance to pay them."

"Now, look here," Teef said, taking a step toward Tamas. Olem was between them in a second, his bayonet a hair from Teef's bloody apron. Teef swallowed.

Tamas gestured for the closest mercenary captain. "Don't worry, Teef," Tamas said. "If you kept your side of the bargain, I will keep mine. I'd love to throw you into Sabletooth, but I'm a man of my word. And... you may prove useful in the future."

Tamas left Teef behind and approached the barricades with Sabon, Olem, and an entire company of the Wings of Adom. Tamas reached out with his senses, looking for powder charges. He sensed a small munitions dump near the barricade and a scattering of discarded powder.

Tamas climbed to the top of the barricade and looked around. From the few barricades they'd captured he knew what to expect: the semblance of a soldier's camp, the street clear of debris, make-shift flags hung above the doors of homes and shops that'd been turned into barracks.

The streets were filled with people. Far more of them than Tamas had expected. Hundreds of women and children. Far fewer men. Their faces were painted with fear, with dejection, with loss. The faces of people who awoke to find their husbands, their friends, and their fathers and leaders with throats cut in their beds. People had little fight in them after an experience like that.

Each huddled group of people had a Barber watching over them, armed with a pistol or a club, sometimes with nothing more than a bared razor. It seemed to be enough.

"Brigadier Sabastenien," Tamas said.

The young brigadier climbed the barricade to stand beside him. "Sir?"

"Have your men relieve the Barbers. Begin filing these people out of the barricades."

"To Sabletooth, sir?"

"No," Tamas said. He surveyed those faces once more. "I suspect that those most responsible for the royalist uprising have already met their fates. I want all survivors taken to the old bailey. Disarm them, but then feed them. Have them checked by doctors and given beds. They're no longer royalists. They are citizens. They are our countrymen."

"My men aren't nursemaids, sir."

"They are now. Dismissed."

Tamas watched as mercenary soldiers went down among the royalists. Voices were subdued, quiet, and for the most part everyone went willingly. Soldiers began the work of dismantling the barricades. Every so often, heads would turn when cannon fire echoed from the south.

"Sabon, send word to Brigadier Ryze. Tell him we've taken the main barricade. Tell him to offer parley. Every royalist not of noble blood will be pardoned. If the Barbers have done their work through the whole royalist camp, I suspect the offer will be taken."

"You intend to pardon them all, sir?" Olem asked.

"If I treat them like animals, like criminals, then I will have a second royalist uprising on my hands. If I treat them like citizens, if I restore them to their places in this city, if I make them belong, that is the best solution. I will not perform another round of executions."

"Probably wise, sir," Olem said.

Tamas gave the man a long look. "I'm glad you approve."

"Well, sir, even with you offering a month's wages, no one will clean the blood out of Elections Square. Stained the stones rust.

They say the dried blood is a half-foot deep in some places. Wouldn't want to add to that."

"Elections Square?"

"Formerly the King's Garden, sir. It's been renamed."

"I hadn't heard that."

"Well, you've been awfully busy, what with the barricades and all."

"Why Elections Square?"

Olem chuckled. "Well, kind of a dark joke, that. See, the people see those executions as a kind of election."

"There was no voting."

"I think the vote was cast when the people tore those Hielmen to shreds."

A mercenary soldier came jogging toward them through the now orderly lines of royalists leaving the barricades. The man snapped a salute. "Sir, Brigadier Sabastenien said you'd want to know. We found General Westeven."

The general was in a small room behind what had once been a flea market. His quarters were damp, cold. They seemed too small for such a great man. Tamas had to duck to enter the room.

Westeven lay faceup on a cot. A few meager possessions were scattered on the dresser—aside from the bed, the only piece of furniture. They included a pocket-sized portrait of Westeven's late wife; a Gurlan hunting knife, the handle well worn; a beaded native's fetish; a pair of spectacles; and a neatly folded handkerchief.

Tamas frowned down at the body. Westeven lay beneath a thin blanket, far too short for his long body, stockinged feet sticking out the bottom. They'd cleaned up his body, but burns were still visible. His eyes were closed. Even in death his one good hand still clutched at an old leather-bound book. He'd survived losing an arm, it seemed—if only for an hour or so. The man's aged fingers were bent from rheumatism.

Tamas turned his head to read the title of the book in Westeven's hand: *The Age of Kresimir.* He hadn't known Westeven to be religious.

Tamas picked up the Gurlan hunting knife and the native's fetish. "Brigadier," he said softly.

Sabastenien ducked beneath the entrance and joined him. There was barely enough space in the dark room for them both.

"Have the general's body sent to his next of kin."

Sabastenien took off his hat. "I don't believe the general has any living relatives."

Tamas felt a lump in his throat and swallowed. When he'd regained his composure, he said, "I will claim the body. Send word to the city reeve. I want full honors for the general's burial—a state burial. No expense is to be spared. I'll pay for it from my own pocket if need be."

Sabastenien didn't answer. When Tamas turned, he saw that unshed tears glistened in the young brigadier's eyes.

"Sir," Sabastenien said. "I formally request that General Westeven be buried in the Wings of Adom cemetery. I'm sure Lady Winceslav would agree."

Tamas lay a hand on Sabastenien's shoulder. "Thank you," he said. Such a thing was the greatest honor. The Wings of Adom were tough ranks to join living, harder to join dead.

Sabastenien left Tamas alone with the body. Tamas lay his hat on Westeven's chest and took a deep breath.

"A poor scrap to go out in," Tamas said. "I'm sorry, my friend. Yet you went out fighting for what you believed. I've got the Kez to deal with next, and how I wish I had you by my side for that."

CHAPTER 13

She's here," Julene said.

Taniel frowned at the Privileged mercenary. She wore a wicked small smile, tugged up farther on one side by the scar on her face, and her eyes were unnaturally wide. It reminded Taniel of a cougar he'd once seen at a circus. They stood at the front gates of Adopest University. The walls surrounding the collegiate town were little more than crumbling relics beyond which flags waved in the brisk breeze on the towers of the university buildings. Taniel could hear the sound of students laughing. This was not a good place to confront a Privileged.

Yet far better than the crowded city.

"You sure?" Taniel asked. He'd not opened his third eye in days. The last time, he'd nearly collapsed. He told himself it wasn't because he'd been in a powder trance for four weeks running. He wasn't powder blind. He wasn't addicted.

He snorted a line of powder off the back of his hand and shivered.

Julene ignored his question. "Well?" Taniel asked Gothen.

The magebreaker nodded. "She's here," he confirmed.

Taniel looked around for Ka-poel. She was studying the gargoyles above the gate. A group of male students were studying her. Taniel glared at them, setting a hand on the butt of his pistol.

"Is that a real savage?" one of them asked.

"You have to have a permit to carry a weapon on university grounds," another informed him.

"Sod off," Taniel said. "Wait. Where can I find a map of the university?"

The boy—Taniel thought of him as a boy, though he might have been the same age—sniffed. "Sod off yourself."

Taniel turned toward the group until they could see his powder keg pin.

"That supposed to impress us?" the boy asked.

Taniel grinned. "It will when I beat your teeth in." He snatched his pistol from his belt and flipped it around until he held it by the barrel. He flipped it again, then spun it around his middle finger until he held it the right way.

"Fancy," one of the boys said with a laugh. "Administrator's office. Head through the gate, take a right. You'll run into it eventually."

"Thanks," Taniel said. "And yes, she's a savage. *My* savage." His grin disappeared when he turned to find Ka-poel glaring at him.

He cleared his throat. "Let's find a map of the university. Julene, how close can you get to her without her sensing you?"

"I don't care if she knows I'm coming."

"I do," Taniel snapped. "Don't be a damned fool."

Ka-poel tapped herself on the chest, then walked a pair of fingers through the air.

"You can get close?" Taniel said.

Ka-poel rolled her eyes.

Of course she could. Ka-poel could practically walk up and poke a Privileged without being noticed. Taniel wondered where his mind was at. It was the damned powder, he decided. When this was over, he'd go a month without touching the stuff.

"All right. Pole, find the Privileged. I want to know exactly where she is, down to the building and the room. You two," he said, pointing at the mercenaries. "Wait for Captain Ajucare." The captain had been trailing them for a week at Tamas's orders. Far enough to stay out of the way, and close enough to be there if he was needed.

A quick glance down the road gave Taniel a glimpse of men on horseback in the distance. "Tell him to begin evacuating the university. We're going to take this Privileged here, now. Gothen, will you be able to cut off her access to the Else?"

"Of course."

"No problems this time?"

"None," Gothen said. "I won't make the same mistake I made last time."

All that was needed was for Gothen to be able to get close enough to cut off her sorcery. If bullets and blades weren't enough to kill her, it would give Julene the chance she needed to use her own sorcery.

"An evacuation will tip our hand," Julene said.

"I'm not going to let a bunch of students get killed in the crossfire if we mess up and the two of you begin to throw around sorcery."

Julene sneered at him.

"I'll be back," Taniel said.

Taniel headed through the gates and toward the administration building. A series of signposts gave him better directions. The place was practically a town in and of itself. The buildings were huge, built of somber gray stone with towering spires and wide arches.

They were separated by open spaces where students lounged on the grass. Taniel walked through a large quad and past the library. His rifle was getting looks.

"Can I help you, sir?"

A man of perhaps forty intercepted him as he headed up the stairs of the administration building.

"Powder Mage Taniel," Taniel said. "Who are you?"

The man drew himself up. "Assistant to the vice-chancellor. Professor Uskan, at your service."

"Professor," Taniel said. "Is the vice-chancellor here?"

"He's in Adopest on business. Pardon me, are you Taniel Two-Shot? The field marshal's son?"

"Look, I've got a company of soldiers about to come pouring through your front gate. There's a rogue Privileged on your university grounds. We're hunting her on orders of my fa— on orders of Field Marshal Tamas."

Uskan's eyes grew wide. "Wha... No, you can't fight here. This is a university."

"We'll do our best not to. Do you have an evacuation plan?"

"What? No..."

"Well, you should come up with one. Now. The soldiers are from the Wings of Adom. Send word for the students to get out."

"Get out? We have almost five thousand students here! The campus is nearly a mile across! What do you expect me to do?"

"Think of something."

"What about the Privileged?"

"We'll deal with her."

The man wrung his hands. "Privileged! There could be wholesale destruction! The repairs..."

"I'm sure it won't come to—" Taniel froze. There she was, coming out of the library not a hundred yards away. Taniel began to breathe quickly. She wasn't wearing her Privileged gloves. That gave him an advantage.

"Go on," Taniel said. "You should evacuate the premises."

"But what do I say?"

"I don't know," Taniel growled. He slowly reached for his pistol, trying not to look obvious.

Uskan swallowed hard and looked Taniel up and down. He gave him a beseeching look. "Just be careful of the Applied Sciences building," he said. "It's brand-new." Taking a deep breath, he suddenly threw his arms in the air.

"Free lunch!" he yelled. "Free lunch, outside the north gate!" He began to run across the quad.

"Shit," Taniel said.

The woman stared at him. He snatched a pistol from his belt, hesitated. People on the quad were slowly following after Uskan. Taniel gritted his teeth.

The woman began to sprint in the opposite direction.

Taniel aimed his pistol and pulled the trigger. The shot echoed across the quad. Taniel nudged the bullet at the last second to avoid hitting a student, cursing under his breath. The bullet missed the Privileged and lodged in the wall of the library. There was a scream. Students began to run.

Taniel took off after her, jamming the pistol into his belt and drawing his spare. She rounded the edge of the library, and Taniel skidded to a halt. She could be waiting just around the corner. Her sorcery would tear him apart before he could fire a shot. Taniel looked around. His eyes fell on the tower back behind the administration building.

The bell tower was the highest point on the campus. He backtracked, heading through the administration building and across a botanical garden. The garden was enclosed, giant sheets of glass held together in a latticework of iron above. He nearly fell into the pond trying to leap it, regained his footing, and headed for the door to the bell tower.

He took the stairs of the tower two at a time. He paused in a window about halfway up and surveyed the quad. He guessed he was five stories above the ground. No sign of the Privileged. He went up to the next window and looked. There. She was heading across the quad between the museum and a great galleried building with large letters proclaiming it to be Banasher's Hall.

Taniel swung his rifle from his shoulder. He closed his eyes, breathing the calm of a powder trance, and refocused. When he opened them again, he could see her as if she were standing five paces away. She was a handsome woman, with sharp features and a mole above one brow. She walked briskly, still wearing her academic gown. She'd put on her Privileged's gloves. She glanced over her shoulder once.

"Rozalia!" The call echoed across the quad.

Taniel started. The Privileged jumped too, a wild look in her eyes. Taniel settled his finger on the trigger.

Sorcery ripped across his vision. Chunks of sod flew in the air, followed by lines of fire erupting from the ground all around the Privileged. Taniel blinked spots from his eyes.

Dirt rained down, obscuring half the quad. Julene walked toward the area, gloved hands held high. She shrieked laughter.

Taniel caught a glimpse of an academic robe. He lifted his rifle to his shoulder and snapped off a shot. The bullet ricocheted inches from the Privileged's head, cracking against an invisible shield with a sound like a spoon tapping glass. Taniel swore.

A lightning bolt slammed into Julene. She slid backward, her feet dragging turf. She somehow kept upright, hands raised above her head. A crackle of energy, and the lightning bolt returned to the Privileged. The thunder knocked Taniel backward.

Taniel rolled a few steps before arresting his fall. He retrieved his rifle and dropped a bullet down the barrel, then drew a powder charge from his pack and crushed it between his fingers. He returned to the window, leveled his rifle, and fired.

The Privileged spun about, blood spurting from her shoulder.

She caught herself on knees and one hand and looked up toward Taniel's bell tower.

"Oh, pit."

She made an angled chopping motion with one hand.

Taniel squeezed his eyes shut. Nothing. He cracked one eyelid. The world was moving. From beneath him, he heard the terrible grinding sound of stone on stone.

Taniel's heart leapt into his throat. The tower was falling. Clutching his rifle, he leapt from the window.

He opened his mouth, but found he had no breath to scream. The glass panels of the botanical garden rushed to meet him. His feet hit first, legs crumpling beneath him, and then the glass shattered. He fell the last twenty feet and landed on his shoulder. He rolled onto his back and gasped. Shards of glass as big as a man lay everywhere around him. He was lucky none had landed on him.

Powder mages were stronger in a trance. They could withstand far more damage than a regular person, and ignore far more pain. Yet a fall like that should have killed him, or at least broken bones.

The ground rumbled. Taniel felt himself rolled by the shock wave as the entire top half of the bell tower slammed into the building beneath it. Stone ground together, wood splintered. Taniel threw his hands over his head.

When he looked up, the dust was settling. He slowly climbed to his feet.

His rifle lay twenty feet away. He stumbled toward it, stepping over rubble and broken glass. His body ached, but nothing was broken. He checked his kit for his sketchbook. It was still there. He retrieved his rifle. "You and I are surviving far too much these days."

Another thunderclap made him stagger. He limped out of the garden and into an adjoining building, avoiding the debris from the tower. He found a hall where he could look out onto the quad.

The end of the hall had been destroyed—the tower had landed on the administrator's office. He hoped no one had been inside.

He threw his back to the wall just beneath the window and listened. Another thunderclap. Someone was laughing. Julene. He gritted his teeth at the eerie sound, reloaded his rifle, and stood up.

The quad had been destroyed. Ground was torn up everywhere, more dirt than a hundred men could move with shovels in a day, piled up as if scooped from the ground by a god's hand and then patted into hills. As he watched, a thin line of fire sprayed from beyond one of the mounds and tore through Banasher's Hall across the way. Taniel saw faces watching the battle from windows. They were gone in an instant, their final looks of horror frozen in Taniel's mind as the entire façade of the building crumbled.

Taniel dropped back down behind the wall and took a deep breath. This was no normal fight. No, he'd seen Privileged fight before, on the battlefields in Fatrasta. They tossed fireballs and ice and lightning. But nothing like this. Both Julene and this other Privileged were using forces far beyond Taniel's comprehension. By the power they showed, they both should have been heads of a royal cabal.

Taniel wondered where Ka-poel was. His head rang after another thunderclap, and his thoughts seemed distant. Hadn't he sent her off after the Privileged? He hoped she hadn't done anything stupid. He hoped she was safe.

He peeked out once more. He could see the Privileged. She stood on the top steps of a building kitty-corner to his own. *The museum*, he thought. He slowly lifted his rifle.

The Privileged's fingers danced. She thrust one hand outward, fingers splayed, toward the center of the quad. That thin fire erupted from her palm. Julene was lifted up from behind the newly formed hills and thrown bodily into the remnants of Banasher's Hall. Stone folded around her as she hit, the rest of the building crumpling like a house of paper.

The Privileged wiped her hands on her academic gown and went inside the museum.

Taniel leapt to his feet. He was halfway down the hall before he bothered to question himself. What was he doing? These were forces above his ability to fight. No sense in going after her. What could he possibly do?

He thought of the destruction on the quad. Privileged got tired. Privileged couldn't go on forever. She couldn't have much left in her.

The building he had taken shelter in was attached to the museum by a narrow, raised stone walkway. Taniel stole a glance, then dashed down the walkway and leapt through a door. He was in a short hall, practically a custodian's closet with mops and brooms. Another door, this one open, led to the main hall. He caught sight of galleries filled with ancient relics: mummified corpses, the bones of ancient beasts, pottery from some prehistoric civilization, and stones sparkling with gems. He heard the brisk sound of footsteps on marble.

The Privileged marched through the main gallery. Her shoulder still bled from Taniel's only solid shot. She glanced to either side. She didn't seem to see Taniel. She definitely didn't see the movement of the magebreaker above her.

Gothen leapt the banister of a gallery above and landed on the marble not five feet from her. He came up, face alight with victory, a small sword in his hand.

Taniel gave a yell. *Yes!* He jumped from cover. They had her now. She couldn't . . .

The Privileged threw her arms wide. The academic gown fluttered, then began to glow. Gothen's eyes grew wide.

Taniel halted. He took one step back as Gothen began to shimmer. Taniel tried to yell for the man to finish the job.

The magebreaker fell to his knees. He opened his mouth in a scream. No sound came out, and his mouth kept opening farther.

His jaw fell, and then the rest of him began to drop like a wax figure melting before a blazing fire. His clothes burned off, his sword dripping to the floor as molten steel. His body dissolved into a puddle at the Privileged's feet.

Taniel leapt behind a pillar. He wondered what good he could possibly do, even as he felt for more powder. He spilled powder all over his hand, brought it up to his nose and snorted. He looked down. There was blood on his hand. It was dripping from his nose. He felt the calm of the powder trance steady his hands.

He gritted his teeth and slid the ring bayonet from his belt. He fitted it over the end of his rifle. His hands began to shake again almost immediately. He double-checked his pistols to be sure they were loaded, and prepared to leap to his feet.

Taniel felt something brush his head.

The Privileged stood beside him. She had one finger pressed against his head.

He let out a trembling sigh. "Do it," he said.

This close, he saw that she was tired. Her hair was soaked with perspiration. The crow's-feet in the corners of her bloodshot eyes were deep, lines of exhaustion tugging at her face.

"I want you to stop following me," she said.

"You killed my friends."

"The powder mages at Skyline? That was a mistake. No. Not a mistake. I'd have killed them all if I'd have arrived in time to stop Tamas and his foolish coup. I was only there to warn the royal cabal, but I was too late. When I saw that it was finished, I just wanted to be gone."

"Who the pit are you?"

"My name is Rozalia."

"*What* are you?"

She let out a long sigh. "I'm one of the few remaining Predeii. Or I used to be. I'm not in very good shape these days."

"That means nothing to me."

"You're just a foolish boy. You're all just foolish boys. Privileged and powder mages. None of you know a thing."

"Then kill me."

"If I do that, your father will turn out every one of his powder mages. I'll never be able to rest again."

Taniel snorted. So she knew who he was.

Rozalia said, "Tell your savage sorceress to stand down. I don't want to fight her."

"Pole?" Taniel looked around. No sign of her. "Get out of here," he called. He thought he caught a glimpse of red hair behind one of the display cases.

"Let me leave in peace," Rozalia said, "and I'll leave the country tonight. I swear it. I'm done here."

"As easy as that?" Taniel's mind raced. Julene had to be dead after being thrown through an entire building. Gothen was a puddle on the floor. What threat could he possibly be to her? Was she that scared of his father?

Taniel caught Rozalia's nervous glance toward Ka-poel.

She was scared of Ka-poel? Pole was only a girl.

"Simple as that," Rozalia said. "I'm leaving this place. Your father has kicked a hornet's nest and I intend to be gone before the hornets arrive."

"What do you mean?"

Rozalia shook her head. "You really don't know, do you? You're playing with something dangerous—no, more than dangerous. Reckless. But it's too late now. There's no chance to restore the monarchy, to undo the damage. Westeven understood, but you others are blind."

"You're mad."

"Ask Privileged Borbador, if you don't believe me. He's the last of the royal cabal. He'll tell you the truth."

"I will."

Rozalia lowered her hand. Taniel got to his feet.

"I can't guarantee that Tamas won't send someone else after you. But to the pit with this. I'm done."

"I'll be on a ship to somewhere far from the Nine within a week," Rozalia said. "Beyond his reach. Besides, I'll be the least of his worries." She turned away.

Taniel kept a wary eye on her as she headed toward the front door of the museum.

"Wait!" He hurried to her side and opened the door. He tried to avoid looking at what was left of Gothen as he passed it.

There were a dozen soldiers within sight. Their rifles were bayoneted and aimed.

"Stand down," Taniel said. They stared at him. "Stand down, damn it, or we're all dead men!"

Rifles slowly lowered. Rozalia walked down the steps as if she were a queen with an honor guard. She passed them all and headed toward the front gate of the university. She paused twenty or thirty feet from Taniel and turned back toward him. "Beware Julene," she said before continuing on.

It was at least an hour later when Taniel caught sight of Julene heading toward him across the quad. This was a different quad, undisturbed, in a quiet corner of the campus. Ka-poel sat cross-legged beside him. He rested with his head against the wall, his hand on his sketchbook. He'd begun drawing Gothen. The man had been brave, and mercenary or not, he deserved to be remembered by someone. Taniel's head hurt. His body hurt. And the person coming toward him shouldn't be alive.

Julene looked like she's been trampled by a herd of warhorses. Her clothing was burned and torn, indecent parts of her bared to the world, though she didn't seem to care a wit. She strode up to Taniel and paused above him, hands on her hips.

"Where is Gothen?"

"Melted."

She blanched at this, but recovered quickly enough. "Captain Ajucare said you let her go."

Taniel nodded. "She's leaving the country."

Julene bent over, her face not a hand's distance from Taniel's. "You let that bitch go!" She raised one gloved hand.

Taniel didn't even remember drawing his pistol. One second his hands were in his lap, folded, the next he held a pistol, the end of the barrel pressing into the soft spot where Julene's jaw and neck met. Her eyes went wide.

"Go away," he said.

CHAPTER 14

The Lighthouse of Gostaun had been dated by most historians back to the Time of Kresimir. Some claimed that it was older still, and Tamas wouldn't have been surprised. It was certainly the oldest building in Adopest. The stone was carved by the wind, its granite blocks pitted and scored by centuries of exposure to the elements, mercilessly whipped by every type of foul weather to come off the Adsea.

Tamas stood on the balcony of the lantern room, his hands clutching the stone railing. Something was wrong. The royalists were scattered, the granaries opened to the public. Already they had begun reconstruction efforts in the city, employing thousands to clear rubble from the streets and rebuild tenements. He should be concentrating completely on the approaching Kez ambassadors, yet he could not keep from looking to the southwest.

South Pike Mountain smoked. It began as a black sliver on the horizon the day of the earthquake two weeks ago. Since then it had grown tenfold. Great billowing clouds of gray and ebony rose from the mountaintop, spreading as they gained height and blowing off over the Adsea. Historians said that the last time South Pike had erupted had been when Kresimir first set foot upon the holy mountain. They said that all of Kez had been covered in ash, that lava had destroyed hundreds of villages in Adro.

Words like "omen" and "bad tidings" were being spoken by men far too educated to take such things seriously.

He turned away from the distant mountain and looked south. The lighthouse itself was no more than four stories, but it stood on a bluff that put it well above most other buildings in Adopest. A side of the hill had given way during the earthquake, revealing the foundation of the lighthouse but sparing the structure itself. Beneath him, artillery batteries flanked the docks. Tamas didn't think those cannons had ever been fired. They were mostly for show, a remnant of older traditions, not unlike the Mountainwatch itself. In its long history, the Nine had come close to war countless times, but not since the Bleakening had there been actual bloodshed. Off in the distance a Kez galley floated at anchor, flags flying high.

"Have those batteries tested tomorrow," Tamas said. "We might have need of them soon."

"Yes, sir," Olem said. Olem and Sabon stood at his shoulders, bearing his quiet reflection with patience. A full honor guard waited down on the beach for the Kez delegation. Servants rushed around the beach, making last-minute preparations to a welcoming repast for the visiting dignitaries. Food was brought out, parasols and open tents staked in the sand, liveried men trying to keep them from blowing away with the wind coming in off the Adsea.

Andriya and Vlora were hidden at either end of the beach, eyes sharp for Privileged, rifles loaded. Tamas was taking no chances with this delegation, and the wrenching feeling deep in his gut told him he was right. There *were* Privileged with them, his third eye had revealed as much—though at this distance it was impossible to sense how many or how strong.

A longboat was making its way from the galley to the shore. Tamas put a looking glass to his eye and counted two dozen men. There were Wardens among them, easy to pick out for their size and their hunched, misshaped shoulders and arms.

"Ipille dares to send Wardens," Tamas growled. "I'm tempted to blow that boat out of the water right now."

"Of course he dares," Sabon said. "He's bloody king of the Kez." Sabon coughed into his hand. "The Privileged with them likely feels the same way about you as you do of him. He knows you'll have powder mages on the beach."

"My Marked aren't godless, sorcery-spawned killers." Only the Kez had figured out how to break a man's spirit and twist his body to create a Warden. Every other royal cabal in the Nine blanched at experimenting with human beings.

Sabon seemed amused by this. "What scares you more: a man who's next to impossible to kill, or a man who can kill you at a league's distance with a rifle?"

"A Warden or a powder mage? I'm not frightened of either. Wardens disgust me." He spit on the lighthouse stones. "What's gotten into you today? You've been philosophical enough lately to drive a man to tears."

Olem gave a strangled laugh. "Breakfast," he said.

Tamas turned on the soldier. "Breakfast?"

"He ate six bowls of porridge this morning," Olem said. He tapped the ash from his cigarette and watched it blow off with the wind. "I've never seen the colonel put down so much so fast."

The Deliv gave an embarrassed shrug. "That new cook is really something. It was like drinking milk straight from the teats of the saint herself. Where'd you get him?"

Tamas swallowed. He felt a cold sweat on his brow. "What do you mean, 'Where'd I get him?' I've not hired a new cook."

"He said you appointed him head chef yourself," Olem said. He put a hand out in front, miming a large belly, and took on an air of self-importance. "'...to fill the hearts, minds, and souls of the soldiers and give them strength for the coming years.' Or so he says."

"A fat man, this tall?" Tamas gestured above his head.

Olem nodded.

"Long black hair, looks like a Rosvelean?"

"I thought he was a quarter Deliv," Olem said. "But yes."

"You're mad," Sabon said. "He's not got a drop of Deliv in him."

"Mihali," Tamas said.

"Yes, that was him," Sabon confirmed. "A devil of a cook."

"Chef," Tamas said distractedly. "And devil he may be. Find out who he is. Everything about him. He said his father was Moaka, the na-baron of...oh, something or another. Find out." He would not have strange men infiltrating his headquarters with nothing more than a lamb soufflé.

"I'll get right on that, sir," Olem said.

"Now!"

Olem jumped. "Right away, sir." He flicked his cigarette away and went for the stairs. Tamas watched him go, then turned back to the slowly approaching longboat. He felt Sabon's eyes on his back.

"What?" he asked, more annoyance in his voice than he'd intended.

"What the pit was that about?" Sabon said. "A lot of fuss for just a damned cook."

"Chef," Tamas said.

"You think he's a spy?"

"I don't know. That's why I'm having Olem find out."

"What's the good in having a bodyguard if you send him off when the Kez show up?"

Tamas ignored the question. So Mihali hadn't been a figment of his imagination. But what about what he had said? He'd warned

Tamas to investigate the Privilegeds' dying admonition—something he should have no knowledge about.

Tamas wasn't a religious man. If he were to ascribe to any one belief, it would probably be one most popular with upper society and philosophers these days—that Kresimir had been a timepiece god. He'd come and set the Nine in motion and had moved on, never to return.

Yet now the holy mountain itself rumbled in anger. What could this mean?

Superstitions. He couldn't let them get the best of him. He'd have Mihali arrested this very night, and that would be the end of it.

They watched the approaching longboat for a few minutes before Sabon pointed down to the beach. "The rabble-rousers are here."

"About damn time."

They headed down to the docks to join Tamas's council. With aides, assistants, bodyguards, and footmen, it seemed like all of Adopest had turned out. Tamas missed the days when secrecy demanded that they meet in person: just seven men and a woman plotting to overthrow their king.

The members of his council gathered at the front of the group to meet him on the boardwalk.

"Tamas, my dear," Lady Winceslav said as he approached. "Be so kind as to ask His Eminence and the other gentleman"—she gestured disdainfully at the arch-diocel and the eunuch—"not to smoke so heavily around a lady."

"You could ask them yourself," Tamas said.

"She has," Ricard said. "Seems His Holiness doesn't know how to act around the ladies."

Lady Winceslav harrumphed. "Sir, I don't think you do either."

Ricard removed his hat and gave her a bow. "I'm just a poor workin' man, marm. Excuse me."

The arch-diocel and the eunuch both seemed to enjoy Lady Winceslav's discomfort. Charlemund turned to Tamas, blowing smoke rings. "Did you know this fellow had his manhood removed at birth? I didn't know they still practiced such a thing, not for a thousand years."

"The Church favored castrati for their choirs up until fifty years ago," Ondraus said, looking over his book at the arch-diocel. He smirked. "There are still a few famous singers like Kirkham and Noubenhaus who are castrati. They're popular in cathedrals all about the Nine. I'm surprised you didn't know that."

The arch-diocel puffed hard on his pipe.

"It's a common practice," the eunuch said softly, his high-pitched voice nearly drowned out by the crash of the surf on the beach. "In my native land there's a whole caste of eunuchs, created at birth, who serve the Gurlan magistrates. They serve in the harems and the magistrates' courts and see to their every whim." He eyed Lady Winceslav. "Every whim imaginable."

"Disgusting," Lady Winceslav said, turning away.

Tamas watched the whole exchange without a word. Sometimes the council seemed to amount to nothing more than children thrust together at a boarding school that has no thought for class or upbringing. They were a motley assortment. "This is all quite interesting," he said, "but the ambassador is here. I'll greet him myself. Alone. No doubt he'll bring up the Accords before he's even off the boat. I'm going to tell him to stuff them up his ass."

"I think he'd respond better to a lady's charm," Lady Winceslav said.

"I bet you do," the arch-diocel grunted. "I have nothing to say here. The Church is neutral on matters of war in the Nine."

"Your unwavering support brings tears to my eyes," Tamas said. "The Kez will have demands. I prefer peace, if possible. The only question is how hard we sue for it. The Accords are out completely. I'll not have them take this country from us. Ricard?"

"War will bring trade on the Adsea to a crawl," Ricard Tumblar said. "The union doesn't like the idea. Then again, the factories will grind into full use, employing thousands for munitions, clothes, and canned foods. It'll be a great boon to industry in Adopest. Between that and rebuilding the city, we may completely solve unemployment in Adopest."

"Start a war to improve the economy," Tamas murmured. "If only it were so simple. Lady?"

"My mercenaries are at your disposal."

Until Adro ran out of land for her officers, Tamas supposed.

The eunuch shrugged. "My master has no opinion on war."

"Will he hold the gangs in check?" Tamas asked. "If Adopest goes to war only to tear itself apart, things will be over before they start."

The eunuch took a draw at his pipe. "The Proprietor will keep things... under control."

"Vice-Chancellor?" Tamas said.

The old man looked wistfully off over the sea and trailed a finger across the spiderlike birthmark on his face. "There hasn't been a real war among the Nine since the Bleakening. I hope for peace but..." He wiped a hand across his brow wearily. "Ipille is a greedy man. Do what must be done."

The reeve was the last to speak. Ondraus pocketed his ledger and removed the spectacles from his nose, folding them and putting them inside his coat. "It'll cost us more to pay the Kez back what Manhouch borrowed than it will to run a war for two years. They can go to the pit."

Sabon burst out laughing. Ricard and the eunuch grinned. Tamas swallowed a chuckle himself and nodded at the reeve. "Thank you for your educated opinion, sir."

Tamas headed down the dock to greet the ambassador. He removed a powder charge from his pocket, gently unwrapped it, and sprinkled a bit on his tongue. He felt the sizzle of power, the surge of awareness that came with a powder trance, closing his eyes as he walked, one foot in front of the other, the dock boards creaking underneath him. He opened his eyes twenty paces from the boat.

A small delegation disembarked. Wardens scrambled up to the dock and then turned to help noblemen up, their sorcery-warped muscles moving like thick snakes beneath their coats. The Wardens were all big men, some nearly two heads taller than Tamas and each one worth ten soldiers in a battle. Tamas shuddered.

He wouldn't let himself be threatened. Whatever the Kez said in the coming negotiations, he needed to keep a level head. They would menace and insult and he would take it in stride. War was not the best course here. He would sue for peace, but not at the cost of his country.

One by one the delegation climbed onto the dock. There were a number of them, all dressed in the finery of the nobility. He caught sight of a white Privileged's glove as it reached up and took the hand of a Warden. Only one sorcerer, his third eye told him. Tamas took a deep breath, reaching out with his senses. This Privileged was not a powerful one, though such a thing was relative when speaking of men who could destroy buildings with a gesture.

The Privileged stepped up onto the dock and straightened his jacket. He laughed at something one of his delegation said and headed toward Tamas, alone.

Tamas gripped his hands behind his back to keep them from shaking. He felt his heart thunder in his ears, his vision grow red in the corner of his eyes. He shrugged Sabon's hand from his shoulder.

Nikslaus.

Duke Nikslaus was a small man, with the delicate hands of a Privileged and an overly large head that looked to wobble on his small frame. He wore a short, furred cap and a black, buttonless coat. His stopped a foot from Tamas and extended one hand, a smirk at the corners of his mouth.

"It's been so long, Tamas," he said.

Tamas's fingers tightened around the duke's throat before he could even think. Nikslaus's eyes bulged, his mouth opening silently. Tamas lifted him, one-handed, from the dock planks. Nikslaus raised his hands, plucking at the air. Tamas slapped them away before sorcery could be unleashed. He was vaguely aware of Wardens running toward him, of his own bodyguard approaching hastily from behind, and of the cocking sound of Sabon's pistol. He shook Nikslaus hard.

"Is this what Ipille sends to negotiate?" Tamas demanded. "Is this their white flag? I told you if you ever stepped foot in my country again, I would nail you to the spire of Sabletooth by your hands."

"War," Nikslaus wheezed.

Tamas lightened his grip.

Nikslaus gasped. "You risk war!"

"You dare come here?" Tamas said. "Ipille *has* declared war. He sent his snake." He threw Nikslaus to the dock. The duke squirmed along the planks, crawling backward, his hands working silently. Tamas pointed at him. "You try one thing and my Marked will gun you down."

"How dare you?" Nikslaus said. "This was in good faith!"

"Eat your good faith, worm! Get out of my country. Tell Ipille to wipe his ass with the Accords."

"This is war!" Nikslaus shrieked.

"War!" Tamas pulled a handful of powder charges from his pocket, crushing them in his hand. He ignited the powder as it fell, directed the energy. The dock boards beneath Nikslaus exploded upward, throwing the duke into the air and head over heels into the water. The Wardens leapt in after him, and Tamas spun around, ignoring Nikslaus's sputtering cries for help.

"What the pit was that?" the arch-diocel demanded.

Tamas stiff-armed him, throwing him to the ground. The rest of the council stood aghast. He felt their stares on his back as he made his way up the beach to the lighthouse. His ears, tuned from the powder trance, picked up Sabon's voice.

"Go easy on him," Sabon told the council. "That was the man who beheaded his wife."

Adamat pounded on the front doors of the Public Archives for twenty minutes until he heard the sound of bolts being drawn back. One of the big doors opened and the lantern-lit face of a young woman stared back at him.

"Library's closed." The door began to shut.

Adamat put his foot in the door.

"It's three o'clock in the morning," the woman said.

"I need access to the Archives."

"Too bad. We're closed." She pushed the door open a little farther and then jerked back until it crunched on Adamat's foot.

"Ow. SouSmith, if you please."

SouSmith leaned against the door. The woman stumbled backward, lantern swinging.

"I'll call the guards!" she said as Adamat stepped inside. He motioned SouSmith in and closed the door.

"Don't bother," Adamat said. "I've got a writ from Field Marshal Tamas." He didn't, but she didn't know that. "I only need to do some research and I'll be gone before you open in the morning."

"A writ? Let me see it."

Not for the first time in his investigation, Adamat felt a keen sense of loss that he'd had to send Faye away. She had many friends and would have gotten him into the Archives no matter the hour. Instead he was reduced to bullying his way in.

Adamat peered at the woman. She was not what most people expected in a librarian. Her hair was down, curly and gold, and she was very young. Almost too young. She couldn't have been more than sixteen. "Who are you?" he asked.

She drew herself up like one who was used to having to justify her authority. "The night librarian! I tend the shelves and carry out research."

"Yes, well, miss, do you understand where the funding comes from for the Public Archives?"

"The king... oh. Grants from the nobili—oh."

"And do you think Field Marshal Tamas will be pleased about one of his agents being turned away from research on which may rest the safety of the state? Do you think he'll stand up for funding for the Public Archives when his agent was so poorly treated? Funding that may end up going to another library, say, to the Adopest University Library, which I know for a fact I'd have access to right now except that it's very far out of my way."

Employees given the night shift were often easily talked around. They tended not to be too bright. This one followed Adamat's every word. He could tell by her eyes. He was just lucky the argument made some sense.

"All right," she said. "But only for a few minutes."

Adamat followed her into the archives. A few lanterns hung from the walls—but only enough to just light the way. Fire hazards were taken very seriously in libraries. He paused when they reached the tables.

"You said you tend the shelves?"

"That is one of the functions of a librarian."

"So you put away the books?"

"Of course."

"Do you remember a pile of books on that table that was here about ten days ago? The books would have been left out after Tamas retook the library from the royalists."

She rounded on him fast enough to make him take a step back.

"Those books were vandalized," she said, waving a finger under his nose. "Did you do that?"

He heard a snort of laughter from SouSmith. "No," Adamat said with a sigh. "This is very important. Where are they?"

She didn't drop her glare for a good thirty seconds. "This way," she said primly. "They've been taken to repair."

He followed her into the back rooms of the library where a repair bench had been set up in one corner. The bench was well worn, the wood polished from countless hours under a librarian's behind. Stacks of broken and old books lay all around the bench ready to have covers or spines mended. Adamat recognized the books that Rozalia had been reading, all stacked neatly near the end of the piles. Adamat sat on the bench and picked the first one up.

When it became clear he wouldn't actually be "only a moment," the librarian reluctantly left him to his own devices. He sped through the paragraphs, though even with a perfect memory, reading was more than just glancing at the page. It was only when the room was just beginning to receive light that wasn't from the lantern, and he was on the fifth book, that he was satisfied. He gathered three of them into his arms and woke SouSmith.

"We've got to see Tamas," Adamat said.

The Public Archives were only a twenty-minute walk from the House of Nobles. Adamat was amazed as he went through the center of the city. Rubble had been cleared from the main thoroughfares, buildings damaged by the quake had been pulled down, and preparations for rebuilding were under way. The newspaper said that the Noble Warriors of Labor had employed fifty thousand men and women to help with the reconstruction efforts.

Adamat was ushered in to see the field marshal almost immediately. When they reached the top floor, Adamat was almost bowled over at the door. A young woman with dark hair and a powder mage's keg pin on her breast shoved past him. Her mouth was set in a hard line, her face red from yelling. Inside, the room was filled with people who looked like they wanted to be elsewhere. Adamat recognized two of Tamas's councillors—the city reeve and the vice-chancellor. Two men and a woman were brigadiers of the Wings of Adom. A half-dozen Adran soldiers sat around a table to one side, their ranks denoting captain or above.

Field Marshal Tamas sat behind the desk, his head in his hands. He looked up when Adamat entered. He looked like he'd just been shouting at someone.

"You have a report for me?" he asked in a surprisingly calm voice.

"Yes." He hefted the books in his arms. "And more."

Tamas jerked his head toward the balcony. "Forgive me a moment," he told his officers.

Outside, the sun was shining. The breeze made Adamat wish he'd worn a thicker jacket. It was windier up here than at street level.

"What do you have for me?"

Adamat set the books aside. "Kresimir's Promise."

"And?"

"I've just returned from the South Pike Mountainwatch. There I interviewed Privileged Borbador, the last remaining Privileged of Manhouch's royal cabal."

"*Formerly* of the royal cabal," Tamas said. "He was exiled. Otherwise he'd be buried in an unmarked grave with the rest."

Adamat grimaced. "We'll get to that in a moment. When I mentioned the Promise, Bo laughed at me. It's an old legend, passed down among members of the royal cabal. It says that Kresimir promised the original kings of the Nine that their progeny would rule forever. If their lines were cut off, he would return himself and take vengeance."

"A fairy story meant to scare children," Tamas said.

"Bo said the same thing. The legend was perpetuated by the kings in order to keep the royal cabals in line. Their fear was that as soon as Kresimir left, the Privileged would seize power themselves."

"I don't see how it could be true. What educated man would take that seriously?"

"Apparently the older members of the royal cabal."

Tamas grunted at this.

"It did get me thinking," Adamat said. "Bo made a vague reference to the notion that the kings had other ways to keep the royal cabals in line—something that would make Kresimir's Promise unnecessary."

This piqued Tamas's interest. "Go on."

Adamat picked up one of the books. He found a page he'd marked, and handed it to Tamas. When Tamas had finished reading, Adamat had another passage in a different book for him, then another in the third.

Tamas handed the last book back, his face troubled.

"A gaes," he said.

"A compelling, of sorts. Every Royal Privileged has it. If the king is killed, they are compelled to avenge him. It gets stronger and stronger over time until they either succeed or it kills them outright. The gaes is manifested by a demon's carbuncle—a large gem worn on the Privileged's person that they cannot take off. When I spoke with Bo, I saw him fiddling at a necklace repeatedly. And this." He flipped to a different page in the third book and handed it to Tamas.

Tamas scowled as he read. When he'd finished, he flipped the book shut and handed it back to Adamat. "So the gaes is permanent. Nothing can remove it, not even being exiled or removed from the royal cabal."

"Indeed. One other thing," Adamat said. He quickly explained his run-in with Rozalia and the message she'd sent to Bo. "As soon as he heard that message, he bolted back into the Mountainwatch. When I went to find him to ask him what it meant, he refused to see me. I saw him head out of the north gate of South Pike an hour later."

"The north gate...?" Tamas said.

"The mountain gate. The one pilgrims use to reach the South Pike's peak, where Kresimir first set foot on the mountain. It's the only route up there."

Tamas leaned against the balcony railing and looked up toward the sun. "What do you think of all this?"

Adamat had thought hard on this question the entire five-day journey back from South Pike. "I'm a reasonable man, sir. A modern man. While the last words of sorcerers give me the chills, there's no going around it. The whole thing is rubbish. It smacks of religion. There's a reason the royal cabals distanced themselves from the Kresim Church five hundred years ago."

"I agree," Tamas said. "And this thing with the gaes?"

"There's religion and then there's sorcery. I confirmed this with secondary sources," Adamat said, gesturing to the stack of books. "Sorcery is deadly serious."

"Looks like I can't spare Borbador after all." Pain crossed Tamas's face quickly enough that Adamat thought he'd imagined it. Tamas gave him a look up and down. "You've done a commendable job," he said, offering his hand. "You went above and beyond what I asked."

"I'm sorry it came to nothing," Adamat said, shaking the field marshal's hand.

"No need to be sorry about it. Better to know it's nothing than to *not* know it's something. See the reeve about payment. I'll make sure he's not stingy. Good day."

Taniel jerked awake, a pistol in his hand. He struggled to focus on the figure looming above him.

"You're going to blow a foot off sleeping with that."

Taniel sagged back to his bed and dropped the pistol on the floor.

"What do you want?"

Tamas pulled the only chair over and sat down, kicking his boots up on the edge of Taniel's bed. "That's no way to talk to your father."

"Go to the pit."

There were a few moments of silence. Taniel could barely think. He'd tried not taking powder last night. He'd lasted until about two in the morning before he went looking for his powder horn. Ka-poel had hidden it, along with his snuffbox full of powder and all his spare charges. His pistol wasn't even loaded. Savage bitch. He'd just barely fallen asleep.

"Vlora was looking for you."

"I don't care."

"I wouldn't tell her where you were."

"I don't care."

"I threw Duke Nikslaus into the Adsea."

Taniel opened his eyes and sat up. His father was cleaning his nails. He looked pleased with himself.

"I think I've started a war," Tamas said.

"Should have blown his head off. The Adsea's too good for him."

Tamas took a deep breath. "No, a bullet is too good for him. I want that man to suffer. I want that man to feel humiliation. But I want it to last."

Taniel grunted his agreement.

"It was calculated," Tamas said.

"What was?"

"King Ipille sending Nikslaus. He wanted me angry. He wanted me to beat him or kill him. He wanted an excuse to start a war."

"So did you. From the very beginning you wanted to go at them."

"I've been thinking," Tamas said. "Over the last few months. I've been thinking that we should avoid war. Especially after the earthquake. We need to rebuild our country, feed our people. Too late now."

"Can we take them?" Taniel's head was starting to clear. That wasn't a good thing. It pounded harder than a smith's hammer.

"Maybe," Tamas said. "The Church is threatening to take sides. The Kez side, more specifically. They didn't like me throwing Nikslaus in the Adsea. That pompous bag Charlemund says he's trying to convince them otherwise. I believe him. I have to believe him. He was Adran before he became an arch-diocel, after all."

Taniel swung his legs out of bed and groaned. His body hurt. His head hurt. Whatever luck or sorcery or what-have-you that saved his life at the university had not spared him the aches of the aftermath.

"I have a new chef," Tamas said.

Taniel gave his father a long look. Why should he care? His whole body ached. He just wanted powder, and Pole had hidden it all.

"He says he's Adom reborn," Tamas went on. "I should have had him arrested, but his cooking is too damned good. Rumor has it he's been making food for half the regiments. Don't know how he does it, but the men like him. I've got a war about to start and a mad cook quickly becoming the most popular man in the army. And..."

"Out with it," Taniel said.

"Out with what?"

"You're rambling. You only ramble when you're about to ask me to do something I won't want to do."

Tamas fell quiet. Taniel watched him struggle internally, emotion barely touching his face. This was the first time he'd been alone with his father in what, four years? He noticed that Tamas was wearing the saw-handled dueling pistols he'd brought him from Fatrasta. They looked well used.

Tamas took a deep breath, his chuckle dying out, and stared at the ceiling.

"I need you to kill Bo."

"What?"

Tamas explained about the gaes. It was a long explanation, with a great deal of technical detail. Taniel barely listened. There was something about an inspector and a promise. He could tell by his father's tone that Tamas didn't want to say it. That it was duty alone that forced his hand.

"Why me?" he asked when his father finally fell silent.

"If Sabon had to die, I'd give him the courtesy of doing it myself. I'd feel like a coward if I had someone else do it."

"And you think I can kill my best friend?"

"Bo's very strong, I know. I'll send help with you."

"That's not what I meant. I know I can shoot him. I can probably get close enough without him expecting a thing to do it with a pistol. But do you really think I can bring myself to do it?"

"Can you?"

Taniel looked at his hands. He'd last seen Bo over two years ago, the day he'd gotten on the ship for Fatrasta. Bo had been there to see him off. Yet what was another friend? The world was different now. He'd killed dozens of men. His fiancée had bedded another man. His country no longer had a king. Who was to say Bo had remained the same?

Taniel squeezed his hands into fists. How dare he? How dare Tamas come here and ask him this. Taniel was a soldier, but he was also Tamas's son. Did that even matter? "I won't do it if you ask me," Taniel said. "Not if you ask me as a son. If you give me an order as a powder mage—then I'll do it."

Tamas's face hardened. This was a challenge, and he knew it. Taniel's father didn't take well to challenges. Tamas stood up.

"Captain, I want you to kill Privileged Borbador at the South

Pike Mountainwatch. Bring me back the jewel he has on his person as evidence."

Taniel closed his eyes. "Yes, sir." That son of a bitch. He was really going to make Taniel kill his best friend. Taniel wondered if he should come back and put a bullet in Tamas's head once he'd finished with Bo.

"I'm sending Julene with you."

His eyes snapped open. "No. I won't work with her."

"Why not?"

"She's reckless. She got her partner killed, and nearly me too."

"She said the same thing about you."

"And you'd believe her over me?"

"She had the courtesy to report to me after you so freely let the enemy go."

"That Privileged would have killed us all," Taniel said.

"I've given the order." Tamas turned around, headed for the door. "Marked Taniel, carry out your orders. Then you'll need some time off to deal with your... personal problems." He left.

Personal problems? Taniel sneered. He felt something on his arm, looked down. His nose was practically pouring blood. He swore, looking around for a towel. What would help this? Oh yes, some black powder...

CHAPTER 15

There was a room beneath the House of Nobles, deeper underground than even the sewer systems, that had seen its heyday during the reign of the Iron King. Privileged sorceries held back the musky scent and the darkness and kept the walls from leaking even after the deaths of the men who cast the spells. The room was fifty paces wide, ten paces high, white plaster walls covered in wall hangings long thought lost by those who care about such things. There were tables and chairs, lounges that could be used as beds, crates of canned food, and barrels of water hidden behind silk curtains.

Not even Manhouch had known about his father's emergency shelter; only a few of the Iron King's closest advisers, Tamas included, knew about the place, or how to reach it beneath the House of Nobles. The Iron King had been paranoid that the people would rise up against him, or that his spies would turn their knives to his throat. Tamas thought it fitting, then, when it was clear that the place had been in complete disuse since Manhouch XII took the throne, that it should be used to plot the king's fall.

Since the coup, Tamas's council of coconspirators had moved their meetings to a less wayward place, far above on the third floor of the House of Nobles, as befitting a government, but Tamas still used the room as a place to find quiet and solitude. None of his staff knew where to find him here, not even Olem and Sabon. He would head back up soon enough.

Tamas sat in the most comfortable of the chairs, his stockinged feet up on a hassock, a bowl of squash soup in his lap—the only thing Mihali would let him have from the kitchens when he passed through—and a miniature map of Surkov's Alley in his hand. The other hand gently scratched the head of one of his hounds, receiving a periodic lick of affection for his troubles.

He examined the map closely. It had been three days since he'd thrown Duke Nikslaus into the Adsea. It was a three-day ride, trading horses and without sleep, from Surkov Alley—the thin valley through the mountains connecting Adro and Kez—to Adopest. Tamas had received word not an hour ago that the Kez army was gathering outside of Budwiel, the city on the border of Kez at the entrance to Surkov Alley.

Nikslaus and the delegation was a feint, an excuse for a war Ipille had banked on. Preparations had already begun. The Kez meant to invade. Yet it would take them a hundred thousand men to break through Surkov's Alley. The whole corridor was staggered with troops and artillery placements. Unless Surkov's wasn't their target.

He set the map down and repositioned his bowl of soup to a nearby table. Pitlaugh crept away with a light growl. "Hush," he told the hound. Tamas fetched a bigger map, this one of all south Adro, and looked it over.

South Pike was the only mountain pass big enough for the Kez to bring a whole army through without it taking all summer. Could they be trying for that? Would their commanders decide that the smaller choke point with fewer men was a better target than Surkov's Alley? He glanced at the bottom of the Adsea on the map, where one small corner of it touched the only Adsea harbor in Kez beside the river delta. They might try coming over water, but the Kez had hardly any navy to speak of in the Adsea. Tamas sighed, folding the map, and sat back in his chair. He looked down at Hrusch. The hound gazed back up at him, head tilted to the side, panting jowls forming a smile.

What could Ipille possibly be thinking? Kez outnumbered Adro five to one in soldiers, yet Adro had so many advantages: industry, more capable military commanders, the Mountainwatch. Adro held all the choke points.

"I should bring Olem down here," Tamas said to the dog. "I think better when I have someone to muse to." Then the place would smell of his cigarettes. Tamas leaned over for a spoonful of Mihali's soup. He'd never tasted anything like it, milky sweet with a hint of dark sugar.

Tamas heard a click on the other side of the room, near the door. The hallways leading to the room formed a series of dead-end corridors and false walls, switchbacks and trap doors, enough to confound and discourage even a determined individual, so it was with some surprise that Tamas sat up and pulled on his boots. He stood up and turned toward the door, straightening his shirt, a hand out to silence Hrusch's whines.

Tamas's heart beat faster at the sight of the creature that stepped through the door. It was a man, or had been at one time. He wore a long, dark jacket and a stovepipe top hat, though those were hardly enough to conceal his deformities. He was a hunchback with thick, powerful arms and legs. His face was almost handsome, but for an overlarge, misshapen brow. He had no facial hair, and lank blond hair fell down either side of his head.

"Warden," Tamas said, surprised at the evenness in his own voice. Wardens were often used as errand boys for Kez Privileged, but their creation so many hundreds of years ago by the Kez royal cabal had a single purpose: to kill powder mages.

Tamas had no pistol or rifle with him. His sword remained, but he knew what little good those did against a Warden. He was a fool for going anywhere without a guard, even in the most secure place in all of Adro. He checked his pockets. No powder charges, not even his fine cigar box with false, powder-filled cigars. Those were in his jacket. Across the room, hanging on a coatrack next to the Warden.

The Warden perused the room carefully, sure that they were alone, before he removed his hat and hung it from the coatrack. His jacket and then his shirt and bow tie followed, leaving him in a pair of black pants. He took off his shoes, a grin spreading across his face as he did so.

Muscles moved on their own accord under his skin, tightening and loosening, sometimes jumping in spasms. They writhed in tight balls in some places, while they seemed hardly present in others, the skin tight against the bone, and then it would all shift and change again. It was like watching a mass of snakes inside a bag of silk.

The Warden flexed his shifting muscles and stretched. "Mage," he said. His voice was deep, vibrant.

"That's quite the shit-eating grin," Tamas said. He took his sword belt from where he'd hung it on the back of his chair and drew the sword, tossing the sheath aside. Pitlaugh stood beside him, and the old wolfhound had teeth bared, growling dangerously. Hrusch retreated behind a sofa, growling at the Warden from perceived safety.

"It's not often I'm given a powder mage so cleanly," the Warden said. "Nor one with such a reputation. I usually have to eat the dregs the sorcerers can comb from the Kez countryside."

Eat? Tamas felt vaguely sick.

The Warden smiled. He stretched out his arms as if to embrace Tamas from across the room, the warped limbs long enough to wrap around a mortar barrel.

"How did you find me?" Tamas asked. He stepped away from his chair and held his sword out to the side. Pitlaugh moved between Tamas and the Warden, and a vision went through Tamas's mind of the Warden tearing apart his hounds. "Pitlaugh," he said. "Back."

The wolfhound backed down reluctantly, giving Tamas and the Warden a wide berth.

The Warden shook his head, the grin still on his face. "I won't risk you surviving this." He cracked the knuckles of one enormous, malformed hand. "But I will let you die with the knowledge that every one of your precious mages will be hunted down and devoured, body and soul."

The Warden bent his head like a fighting bull and charged. Thirty paces separated them, yet the creature covered that space in hardly any time at all, one big hand reaching out to grab a hassock as he came, flinging the furniture at Tamas as if it were a toy.

Tamas ducked the hassock and sidestepped the Warden. He aimed for the heart with his blade, striking hard. A meaty fist pounded into the side of his head, sending him stumbling across the room.

The Warden didn't give him a chance to recover. He changed directions in a split second and flung himself toward Tamas, ignoring the sword aimed at his chest. Tamas jabbed with all his might, then threw himself out of the way of the Warden's bulk. He ducked, rolling on one shoulder and to his feet.

Blood oozed from the two punctures on the Warden's chest. Tamas must have hit a lung and the stomach, but the creature smiled at him hungrily with no regard for the wounds. Wardens' hearts were protected by a shell of sorcerously grown bones, and Privileged sorceries could keep a Warden's other organs working when they should have long been dead.

The Warden charged once more. Tamas danced to the side for a slashing blow, but one big hand reached out for him. He ducked under the arm and struck from behind, thrusting his sword into the Warden's armpit until the hilt touched skin.

The Warden howled and jerked away, ripping the sword from Tamas's grip. Tamas's heart thumped in his ears and his hands shook.

The Warden thrashed about for several moments before suddenly falling still. His dark gaze was hooded by his overlarge brow, blue eyes beady and bloodshot. His right arm hung loosely at his side, muscles nearly concealing the hilt. The blade of the sword stuck out of his chest, three handspan's worth of steel. The Warden looked down on it disdainfully. He reached across with his left hand and tried to pull out the sword. The angle made it impossible for him.

"You've something in your chest," Tamas said, though he didn't have much energy behind the jibe. His lungs burned from the effort he'd just exerted, his muscles ached. He eyed his coat on the other side of the room. He could sense the powder charges in the pocket.

The Warden leapt toward him suddenly, throwing his body like a flopping fish. Tamas reeled back, trying to get out of his range, but felt the Warden's fingers catch the front of his shirt. He was pulled into an embrace, his neck a mere finger from his own sword blade where it stuck from the Warden's chest. He felt hot, angry breath on his cheek and smelled the scent of bile reeking from the creature.

Tamas struck the Warden in the eyes with one hand. The creature bellowed like an injured bear, wrestling one-armed with Tamas, dragging Tamas's chest across his own blade before tossing him across the room.

Tamas caught himself on a sofa and pulled himself up. He spotted the coatrack nearby and ran for it. "Pitlaugh! Kill!"

The wolfhound darted toward the Warden, ten stone of angry teeth and muscle. Pitlaugh snaked around to the Warden's wounded arm and lunged for the throat. The Warden managed to turn away, and Pitlaugh's teeth sank into the Warden's arm.

Tamas reached the coatrack and threw the Warden's clothes to the floor, snatching at his own jacket. He brought out his cigar case and flung it open, revealing the six carefully wrapped cigars within. He bit the end off one, emptying the secret stash of powder into his mouth. He felt the bitter burn of sulfur on his tongue, then the nausea that came with taking so much powder so quickly. He staggered.

Tamas's head whipped around at a sharp whine. Pitlaugh had been thrown to the floor. Something was wrong with his back legs and he tried to crawl away from the Warden, whimpering loudly. The sound broke Tamas's heart, and something inside him snapped. The powder trance took him over completely.

Tamas crossed the room in a few long strides, barely registering the distance. The Warden threw a punch with his good arm. Tamas grabbed the fist out of the air and ignited one of his false cigars, channeling the power. A bone in the Warden's arm snapped.

Tamas, still holding the Warden's now-limp hand, twisted. The Warden was lifted onto his toes. His eyes were big, his mouth warped in a silent scream. Tamas grabbed the sword hilt with one hand and yanked, sliding it in and out, feeling it scrape against bone inside the creature's body. He ripped the sword from the wound and dropped it, letting it clatter to the stone floor.

The Warden bared his teeth in a mad smile and threw himself headfirst toward Tamas. Even in such agony, the creature would not back down. Tamas caught the big head with both hands. He lifted the creature easily with the strength provided by the powder trance. He twisted the head and slammed it into the marble floor, hearing stones crack beneath. He ignited one of the fake cigars in his pocket and shot the energy into the Warden's brain.

The body slumped beneath him, dead.

Tamas staggered away from the creature. His head was light, his energy spent. His body was soaked in blood and he wasn't even sure how much of it was his. The cuts on his chest were deep enough to need stitches and somewhere outside the powder trance, distantly, he could feel them burning. His wrists and arms hurt, old bones not used to the power he'd unleashed. He took a deep breath, his eyes falling on Pitlaugh.

The old wolfhound lay on the corner of a rug. Hrusch emerged from his hiding place behind a divan and approached Pitlaugh, whining lightly, nuzzling him. Pitlaugh's back was twisted sharply, his rear legs sticking off at an odd angle. He opened his eyes as Tamas gazed upon him, looking up pitifully.

"You did well, boy," Tamas said softly. He stepped toward the door, then stopped when Pitlaugh tried to follow, dragging his legs behind him, whining loudly. Tamas felt his eyes burn.

It took him some time to reach the upper levels of the House of Nobles carrying Pitlaugh. Tamas found Dr. Petrik playing cards with some officers on the second floor. They stared at him as he entered the room, covered in blood, the wolfhound in his arms, Hrusch close on his heels.

Some time later Pitlaugh lay stretched out on a sofa. Petrik examined him while dozens of soldiers crowded the doorway, trying to see inside the room. A few loud curses made them move out of the way, then Olem appeared. He froze when he saw Tamas. Olem's face was red, his eyes wide.

"Sir," Olem said. His hands shook as he reached out to touch Tamas, as if making sure he was still alive. He wouldn't look into Tamas's eyes. "I've failed you," he said.

"It's not your fault," Tamas said. "You couldn't have known. I slipped off."

"I should have been there." Olem's gaze fell on Pitlaugh. "I'm sorry, sir. By Kresimir, I..."

"You never failed," Tamas said firmly. "You weren't even there. Now I need you close by. Get messengers. I want every member of the council here within the hour. I don't give a damn if they have to sprout wings to do it. Go. I want them to meet me in the room beneath the House of Nobles."

Dr. Petrik approached. "There's nothing I can do for him. Not even a skilled veterinarian could help him now."

"Of course. Thank you, Doctor."

Tamas took a pistol from Olem and went to the dog's side. He ran his fingers gently between Pitlaugh's eyes. "It's all right, boy. Have peace."

He felt something jolt inside him when the shot rang through the room. He knelt by Pitlaugh's side for a few minutes, ignoring the commotion of guards checking on the pistol shot.

Tamas got to his feet and picked out a soldier at random. "Find me a hammer and spikes. Now."

In the room below the House of Nobles, Tamas waited. He stared at the Warden's broken body. These things were strong and difficult to kill, but the Kez had to know that Tamas could deal with one. It was only bad luck he'd not had powder on him when he was attacked. What was the purpose? To sow distrust? To bring chaos into Tamas's inner circle?

If that was their aim, they'd succeeded.

His council came in, one by one, and he directed them to chairs on one side of the room, ignoring protests and questions until every one of them had arrived. He stood before them, hands folded, still in his blood-covered shirt. The Warden hung from the wall behind him by a spike in one wrist, crimson drops falling from his body to splatter on the stones below.

"One of you has betrayed me," Tamas said. "I *will* find out who."

He left them there to contemplate the Warden's corpse.

Adamat felt a shadow fall across his shoulders and sensed a man standing over him. He touched the cane leaning against his knee and set his tea on the iron café table. He watched the shadow for a moment, remembered the sound the fall of approaching boots had made on the cobbles, and moved his hand away from the cane.

"Field Marshal," Adamat said without looking up.

Tamas tossed a newspaper down next to Adamat's tea and took the seat opposite. He held up his hand for a waiter.

"How'd you know it was me?"

"Military boots, military step," Adamat said, taking a sip of his tea. "I've not done work for anyone else in the military in ten years."

"It could have been an aide, sent to find you."

Adamat shrugged. "Each person has a particular cadence to their step. Yours is well defined."

"Fascinating. I trust Ondraus gave you enough money to help with your debts?"

Adamat wasn't surprised that Tamas knew he had debt problems. Adamat made a quick study of the field marshal; there were bruises on his face, a few cuts. It looked like he'd been in a fistfight. He looked tired, spent.

"Certainly," Adamat said. *Though not enough,* he thought. If he received a dozen good jobs by the end of the month, he might be able to pay Lord Vetas. "I appreciate your generosity."

"Well worth it." Tamas spoke quietly, his neck craned to watch people passing in the street. He turned away from the street after a few moments of silence and drew an envelope from his jacket. He set it on the table, on top of the newspaper.

"I have another job for you," he said.

Adamat did his best to conceal his eagerness. "Not the dying words of a sorcerer again, I hope?"

"Not yet." Tamas thanked the waiter who brought him his tea. He drank it in one long sip, not seeming to notice the heat of it. When he finished, he removed a handful of coins from his pocket. He grunted in disgust at what he saw, then tossed a coin on the table.

"Find out who's trying to kill me."

He stood and left. Adamat looked down at the coin. It had a likeness of Tamas's silhouette on the front.

Adamat took the envelope, tapping it against the tabletop. He flipped over the newspaper. *The Adopest Daily.* "THE ATTEMPT ON THE LIFE OF FIELD MARSHAL TAMAS."

He gazed at the envelope. He needed the work. Yet this was dangerous. It gave Lord Vetas every reason to come back, looking to blackmail Adamat into telling him about Tamas's inner circle. It also put Adamat—and his family—in danger from the traitor. He'd planned on summoning Faye back to Adopest. That wouldn't do now... not yet.

He opened the envelope. Within was a check for ten thousand krana. A small, folded bit of paper fell on the tabletop. He snatched it up before a breeze could blow it away.

" 'Six people other than me knew the location of the room in which the attempt was made on my life.' " A list of names followed, the names of Tamas's council. Adamat wiped sweat from his brow as he read over the names a second time and wondered if ten thousand krana was enough. At the end of the note, there were simply two words: "Acquire protection."

Adamat pushed the check and the note into his pocket and decided he'd released SouSmith from his employ a little too early.

CHAPTER 16

Sir, we've found out who Mihali is."

Tamas looked up from his desk. For once, things were quiet. Not a Wings brigadier or a councillor or officer or secretary in sight. Olem was the first person Tamas had seen all morning, though he'd been stationed just outside the door.

"Mihali?"

Olem paused to light a cigarette. "The new chef."

Tamas remembered the bowl of squash soup in the corner of his desk. It was regrettably empty. The stuff was as addictive as black powder. "Yes . . . Mihali," Tamas said. "It took you long enough."

"It's been a distracting week."

"That's fair."

"Mihali is the na-baron of Moaka," Olem said. "He's more commonly known by his professional title: Lord of the Golden Chefs."

"And what does that mean?"

"The Golden Chefs is a culinary institute. The finest in the Nine. Graduates of their schools are coveted by the wealthiest families on four continents as private chefs. They cook for kings."

"And their lord?"

"A man considered the greatest among peers each generation."

"He's in our kitchens, making lunch for three regiments?"

"Quite right, sir."

"Why?" Tamas asked.

"It seems he's hiding."

Tamas stared at Olem. "Hiding?"

"He's only recently escaped from Hassenbur Asylum."

Tamas leaned back in his chair.

"What's so funny, sir?" Olem asked.

Tamas chewed on the inside of his cheek. "Has he told anyone that he's the god Adom reincarnated?"

"Yes, sir," Olem said. "That's why he was committed."

"That explains a lot," Tamas said. He glanced down at his work. There were requests on his desk from the Adopest Kennel Society, writs to be signed for Ricard Tumblar's union, and a proposed tax on the Kresim Church. He shook his head. Nothing he wanted to deal with now. "Let's go have a chat with our chef, then, shall we?"

Olem followed him out into the hall. "Do you think that's wise, sir?"

"Is he dangerous?" Tamas asked.

"Not as far as I can tell. The men love him. They've never had someone cook like this for them before. Makes all the other army rations taste like shit."

"What's he making? Squash soup?"

Olem laughed. "Remember what you had for lunch yesterday?"

"Of course I do," Tamas said. "It was a bloody nine-course meal. Candied eel, stuffed dormouse, braised beef, a salad big enough to feed an ox… I've eaten that well only once before in my life and it was at one of Manhouch's parties."

"That was normal ration, sir."

Olem bumped into him when Tamas came to a complete stop. "You mean everyone is eating that well?"

"Yes, sir."

"You?"

"Yes, sir."

"The whole damned brigade?"

Olem nodded.

"He must be blowing through the entire year's ration budget." Tamas resumed walking, feeling some urgency in his step. "Ondraus is going to shit a paving stone."

Olem caught up. "On the contrary, sir. I asked a secretary. It seems he's not even touched the main fund."

"Then how is he paying for all that food?"

Olem shrugged.

One kitchen served the entirety of the House of Nobles. It was located just beneath the main floor so that windows high up one of the walls could provide light during the day, and was nearly as long as the House was wide. Along one side of the kitchen ran dozens of ovens with flues that disappeared into the ceiling and enough cooking space to prepare food for the thousands of secretaries and nobles that would normally have filled the building. The middle of the floor contained broad, low tables to prepare recipes and to ready ingredients, and the other side contained hutches and cupboards by the score with measuring instruments, spices, and other ingredients. Sausages, herbs, vegetables, and more hung from the ceiling.

Tamas patted his forehead with a handkerchief the moment he entered the room. The heat nearly sent him retreating out into the hall. He blinked a few times and held his ground, partially urged on by the myriad of smells: scents of cocoa and cinnamon and of breads and meats. His mouth began to water.

"Are you all right, sir?" Olem asked.

Tamas shot him a look.

The room bustled with dozens of assistants. They all wore a variation of the same uniform: a white apron over black pants, and some kind of hat upon their head. Some of them seemed to be able to afford to acquire better quality, while others looked to have scrounged their outfits from the street. Tamas did notice that no matter how frayed, all the clothing was clean. He noticed another thing: Every one of the assistants was a woman. They varied in age and beauty and all worked with utmost concentration. None seemed to notice Tamas's presence.

The chef himself paced among his assistants. Tamas recognized him immediately as the man who'd appeared at his headquarters the day of the earthquake. As Tamas watched, Mihali stopped to say something to one of his assistants and then immediately moved on to the next, adding a dash of this spice to that dish and gently grabbing the arm of an assistant before too much flour could be added to a dough. He had set the women up in workstations, and he danced between them with the skill of a line commander, issuing orders and making changes to the recipes as he went, always seeming to have an eye on everything at once.

Mihali caught sight of Tamas and smiled. He headed toward the door, only to stop halfway there at a counter of meats and help a hefty-sized woman with her aim at the cleaver. He lopped off a dozen ribs of beef with the precision of a headsman and then nodded to the woman, handing back the cleaver. He whispered something reassuring and made his way over to Tamas.

"Good afternoon, Field Marshal," Mihali said. "Been a busy couple of weeks since we met."

Olem gave Tamas a curious look at this.

Mihali went on, "I'll tell you, I'd work twice as fast if I wasn't training a whole batch of new assistants." He removed his hat and dragged a sleeve across his forehead, staining the cloth with sweat, before wiping his hands on his apron. A look of worry crossed his face. "Lunch will be a few minutes late, I'm afraid."

Tamas glanced across the room. So much was going on that it was impossible to tell what was actually being prepared. He'd been ready to come down here asking questions. He wanted to get to the bottom of this "mad chef" business. Yet his words died on his tongue.

"I doubt anyone will complain," Tamas managed. His stomach rumbled suddenly. "What's for lunch?"

"Blackened salamander with curry and a light vegetable pie," Mihali said. "We're having wine-glazed beef back for dinner tonight, and I thought I'd serve a spiced wine with it. Main courses only. There will be plenty of other things to choose from."

"To everyone in the House?"

"Of course." Mihali's eyes went wide, as if Tamas had suggested something idiotic. "Do you think a secretary deserves to eat any less well than a field marshal, or a soldier than an accountant?"

"My apologies," Tamas said. He shared a glance with Olem, trying to remember why he came down.

"Please, Field Marshal, walk with me." Mihali hurried away without waiting for an answer. When Tamas caught up, Mihali was adjusting the heat beneath a vat of soup by changing the airflow in the stove beneath it. He dipped one finger in the soup and popped it in his mouth, before producing a knife and a clove of garlic from his apron, deftly slicing a measure into the vat.

"I heard about the attempt on your life," Mihali said.

Tamas stopped. He realized the pain of his wounds, the ache of the stitches on his chest, had faded to nothing when he entered the kitchen. They were a distant throb, as if from outside a powder trance.

Mihali had a note of sadness to his voice. "I do not agree with what the sorcerers do to those Wardens. It's unnatural. I'm glad you survived."

"Thank you," Tamas said slowly. His suspicions that Mihali was a spy were slowly fading. His reputation and skills as a chef couldn't be faked.

"Mihali," Tamas said, "I came to ask you about the asylum."

Mihali froze, a forkful of vegetable pie halfway to his mouth. He finished the bite off quickly. "More pepper," he told an assistant, "and add a dozen more potatoes to the next batch." He hurried on to the next station, forcing Tamas to catch up.

"Yes," he said when Tamas was alongside him again, "I escaped from Hassenbur. It was a vile place."

"How did you escape?"

They had reached a portion of the kitchens where there weren't any assistants. In fact, it was as if an invisible curtain had been drawn across it. The heat and steam had lessened, and the noise had become muffled. Tamas glanced over his shoulder to be sure that they were still in the same room. Behind him, the flurry of activity continued.

"They gave me access to the kitchens when I wasn't being treated." Mihali shivered at a memory. "And though they said I was cooking for the asylum, I soon found out they were sending my meals to the manor homes of nearby nobles and selling my services for quite a bit of money. I baked myself into a cake and had my assistants send me to the next manor over."

"You're joking," Olem said. He rolled an unlit cigarette around between his lips and eyed a stove.

Mihali shrugged. "It was a very big cake."

Tamas waited for him to say something else, perhaps his real method of escape, but Mihali remained quiet. This section of the kitchen, nearly half of the space of the whole, contained just as many cookpots and fired ovens as the other, but as Mihali moved from one dish to the next, it was clear he was the only one attending these. Mihali reached above his head and pulled down an enormous pot from its hook. It looked to weigh as much as Tamas, but Mihali handled it with ease, maneuvering it down onto a stove. He opened the fire chamber beneath the stove, checking the heat, before moving on to an open spit in the corner.

Tamas followed him across the room. He paused beside the pot Mihali had just pulled down—steam rose from it. He stepped forward and blinked. The pot was full to the brim with a thick stew of potatoes, carrots, corn, and beef.

"Wasn't that empty a moment ago?" Tamas asked Olem quietly.

Olem frowned. "It was."

They both looked about for the pot Mihali had just pulled down, but all the pots on this side of the kitchen were full and cooking. Tamas felt less hungry somehow, and more uneasy. Mihali was still at the spit. A whole side of beef roasted above the flames. Mihali lifted a small bowl and began pouring some kind of dressing over the meat. Tamas found his stomach growling again, his uneasiness gone with the advent of new smells.

"Mihali, have you told other people that you are the god Adom reincarnated?" Tamas examined Mihali's face intently, looking for signs of madness. There was no question that Mihali was a maestro of the kitchens. Tamas had heard that every genius was equal parts madness. He tried to remember his childhood theology lessons. Adom was the patron saint of Adro. The church called him Kresimir's brother, but not a god like Kresimir.

Mihali poked the side of beef with the tip of his knife and watched grease bubble to the surface and run down the meat, sizzling on the coals below. His frown slowly returned. "My relatives had me committed," he said quietly. "My brothers and cousins. I'm a bastard son—my mother was a Rosvelean beauty whom my father loved more than his wife, and my brothers have therefore hated me since I was a boy. Father protected me and fostered my talents. Against custom, he made me his heir." He prodded the side of beef once more. "My brothers sent me to the asylum the day he died. I wasn't allowed to attend the funeral. My claims to be the god Adom were only an excuse."

Mihali stood up straight suddenly, as if stirred from slumber.

"Bread, bread," he muttered. "Another fifty loaves at least. These girls don't work fast enough."

He moved to the counters in the middle of the room. There were lumps of dough beneath damp towels. He whisked away the towels with one hand and plunged the other hand into the great mounds of dough. "Risen perfectly," he said to himself, a distracted smile on his face. He divided the dough into perfect portions, his hands working so quickly Tamas could barely follow. Two loaves at a time were loaded onto the bread paddle and scooped into a waiting oven, until all the dough was gone.

When the last loaf was loaded in the oven, he immediately removed the first. It was golden brown, the crust crisp and flaky, though it had only been a minute or two since it went in. Tamas narrowed his eyes and began to count.

"That's not my imagination," Tamas said, leaning toward Olem.

"No," Olem confirmed. "He put a quarter that many loaves into the oven." Olem made the sign of the Rope, touching two fingers together and then to his forehead and his chest. "Kresimir above. Have you ever heard of sorcery that can create something out of nothing?"

"Never. But I'm seeing a lot of new things these days."

Mihali finished removing the last of the loaves from the oven. He turned to Tamas and Olem. "Hassenbur has sent men for me," Mihali said. "I would sooner flee to the far side of Fatrasta and cook for the savages than return to Hassenbur Asylum."

Tamas pulled his eyes off the loaves. He looked at the cooked side of beef and the pot of stew that had been empty not ten minutes before. He nodded at Mihali's words and moved away slowly, Olem at his side.

"A Knack," Olem said. "That's the only explanation. I've heard of Knacks stronger than any Privileged sorcery. His must have to do with food."

"Third eye?" Tamas asked.

Olem nodded. "Just did. He has the glow of a Knacked."

"Well, he's no god," Tamas said. "But he thinks he is. And that's a powerful Knack. His food alone is responsible for half the army's morale. Now what do I do with him?"

CHAPTER 17

I'm looking for Privileged Borbador."

Taniel stood in the entrance to a tavern. It was a big place, though very old. Half the roof had caved in and long since been badly repaired. It was called the Howling Wendigo. Its name came from the low whine of wind in the eaves, which now drowned out everything else, as conversation in the place had stopped.

Fifty or more sets of eyes stared at him. He was alone; he'd left Julene and Ka-poel outside to wait. He wore his buckskins and his cap and he was glad of it. Spring or not down in the valley, Shouldercrown Fortress was still locked in winter.

"What business does a powder mage have with our Privileged?"

Our Privileged. Taniel didn't like the sound of that. Bo had made friends with these thugs. Convicts and malcontents, the poor and the wretched—these were the members of the Mountainwatch.

They didn't trust easily, and they welcomed strangers like a crowded city welcomes a plague. They were easily the toughest of the Nine.

Taniel took a deep breath. He wasn't in the mood for this. *I'm here to kill him*, he wanted to say. *Get in my way and I'll put a bullet in your head.* Instead he said, "That business is mine."

A man stood up. He was younger than Taniel by a year or two at most. Scrawny, bearded, he wore a sleeveless shirt despite the cold, his arms corded with the muscles of a man who hauled timber and worked the mines. He scowled at Taniel.

"That business is ours," the man said.

"Fesnik, don't mess with a powder mage," someone else said. "You want Tamas breathing down our necks?"

"Shut up," Fesnik called over his shoulder. "What if we don't tell you?"

"You the toughest one here?"

"Huh?" Fesnik seemed taken aback by this.

"Simple question," Taniel said. "Are you the toughest, father-stabbing, goat-raping, inbred son of a whore in this place?"

Fesnik turned away from Taniel, a half smile on his face. He came back around quickly, knife drawn. Taniel drew both pistols. One barrel went in Fesnik's mouth, cracking teeth and bringing the man's knife thrust up short. Fesnik's eyes went wide. The other pistol pointed at the first Watcher to climb to his feet.

"My name's Taniel Two-Shot," Taniel said loudly. "And I'm here to see my best friend, Bo. Tell me kindly where he is?"

"Taniel Two-Shot?" a voice asked. "Why didn't you damn well say so? Bo's up the mountain."

"That true?" Taniel asked Fesnik.

The man nodded, eyes crossed from staring at the pistol barrel in his mouth.

Taniel holstered both pistols.

"Sorry," Fesnik said, checking his teeth. "Bo said not to let any powder mages know where he was. Nobody but you, that is. Said you might come looking for him."

Taniel tried to keep the scowl off his face. "Sorry about the teeth," he said. Louder, "Drinks on Field Marshal Tamas!"

A general cheer went up around the room. Taniel gestured Fesnik closer. "You say he's up the mountain?"

"He went up there almost two weeks ago. Right after an inspector fellow came up from Adopest to see him."

"When did he say he'd come back down?"

"He didn't."

Taniel scratched his jaw. He'd not shaved since starting his hunt for the Privileged in Adopest. The thick curls on his neck itched. "Why'd he go up?"

Fesnik shook his head.

Taniel felt a sharp fear run up his spine. Bo knew that Tamas would send someone to kill him.

"And he told you to tell only me?"

"Yeah. He's told us a lot about you. Said you two have been chums for years."

That felt like a knife thrust to Taniel's gut. He clenched his teeth and forced a smile on his face. Psychological warfare on Bo's part? Or just drunken chatter? "That's right. How long does it take to reach the top of the mountain?"

"Well, he won't have gone all the way to the top," Fesnik said. "There's a monastery up there for the pilgrims, a couple miles short of Kresim Kurga. He'll have stopped there."

Kresim Kurga. The Holy City. It was a name out of legends. Taniel hadn't heard the name since his nurse had taken him weekly to Kresimir's chapel when he was a child. Even then, he'd never believed it really existed.

Taniel brought himself back to the present. He couldn't wait here. He would have to go up after Bo and leave him buried in the snow. Taniel would be back in Adopest before they discovered Bo was dead.

"I'll go up and see him," Taniel said.

"This time of year?" Fesnik shook his head. "Not even a seasoned Watcher will guide you up, and believe me, without a guide you'll walk into a snowstorm and never come out. The roads are treacherous well up until early summer."

"My father mentioned a man named Gavril," Taniel said. "Old friend of his. Said he was the best mountain man in the Nine. What?"

Fesnik had started to laugh. "Gavril, he might do it. If he's sober enough to see but drunk enough not to think straight. I'll try to find him for you."

Fesnik went off into the barroom crowd. Taniel returned to the street, where he found Julene glaring at Ka-poel. Ka-poel was staring up at the mountain above them.

"Bo's up there," Taniel said, pointing to the mountain. "We're going up after him."

Julene's eyes narrowed. "It's probably a trap. He must know Tamas would send someone."

"He does. But he told the Watchers to let me know where he was if I came. No one else. That means he trusts me."

"Or he trusts himself to kill you before you can get off a shot."

"I know Bo. It means he trusts me." He took a deep breath. "Worse luck for him."

"We'll need supplies and mountain gear," Julene said. "And winter clothing."

"You're not coming."

"What?" Julene stared at him hard.

"You almost got me killed more than once," Taniel said.

"How dare you."

"Shut up. I'm going up there with Pole; we're going to do in my best friend and come right back down. Carefully, quietly. You start throwing around sorcery up there and not only will the entire Mountainwatch know what we're doing but you'll likely bring an avalanche down on us."

Julene sneered. "I don't trust you. You're weak. You won't be able to pull the trigger."

"Killing Privileged is my specialty," Taniel said. He took a hit of powder. A small one, just to calm his nerves. He took a second hit. "Bo's a danger. I know how to deal with a danger. Now, shut the pit up and go find yourself a room to hole up in. There's another reason I'm leaving you down here. If Bo gets the drop on me or slips by me somehow, I want you watching. Kill him on sight. Can you do that, lady?"

Julene's arms trembled. She looked as if she wanted to leap on Taniel and tear his throat out with her teeth. Without a powder trance Taniel might have been intimidated. With a powder trance, Taniel didn't give a damn.

"Well?" he asked. "Can you damn well do it?"

Julene whirled and stalked away from him, down the street.

"I'll take that as a yes."

The door to the tavern opened and Fesnik stepped out, shrugging into a knee-length deerskin coat. He was followed by one of the biggest men Taniel had ever seen. He wore thick leathers and furs soaked with sweat and beer, and he struggled to focus his eyes on Taniel even as he toppled against the side of the building. He shook his head and slurred, "I'm Gavril."

Taniel looked him up and down. "Fantastic."

Taniel paused to adjust the furs protecting his face as a freezing wind spattered him with snow. He flinched away from the biting cold, turning his face from the wind, even though Gavril had warned him that to do so could mean death—always one foot in front of the other, eyes on the snowbank ahead of you or you might step into a half-hidden fissure or off the edge of a cliff.

Right now, Taniel didn't much care. Ten thousand feet below them, farmers tilled their fields as the spring weather warmed. A few more weeks and it would be warm enough to go swimming in the Adsea. Yet here he was, nearing the top of the highest mountain in all the Nine—some said the world—with snowshoes strapped to his feet, armed with rifle and pistols that were probably too frozen to work, on his way to kill his best friend, with a drunk as a guide.

He was tied to Gavril by a sturdy rope, though the wind had died enough that he could see the big mountaineer through the eddy, some ten paces up the slope. Their climb was steep, but bearable. After all, there was a road under there somewhere. This pass was well used in the summer—or so Gavril claimed. The wind swirling around them brought no fresh snow; it only kicked up the top layer from the recent storm. Taniel could have sworn he heard a child's laughter every time more snow slapped him in the face. The mountain was a cruel place, he decided.

Another rope led off behind Taniel, where Ka-poel struggled slowly with her snowshoes, and behind her a small man named Darden trekked along in her wake. He was an old Deliv who had insisted on coming along. He said he had a cousin at the monastery who had been dying last fall, and he wanted to know if he had survived the winter. Taniel didn't trust him. Was he one of Bo's friends?

Gavril was a jovial drunk, and had been surprisingly interested in the trip up the mountain. They'd set off within hours, and though Gavril had wobbled on his snowshoes the first half day, Taniel was certain he'd gotten dead sober by the end of the second.

Taniel paused briefly to check the pistol at his hip. The flintlock was frozen, jammed with snow and ice. The powder still seemed to be dry, though, and the bullet was wedged firmly in place. That was all that mattered for a Marked. He could make his own spark to fire the bullet. Yet... Taniel examined Gavril. Would the man give him trouble when Taniel put a bullet through Bo's eye? Or would any of the monks? Taniel checked his second pistol. Would he be able to make it back down the mountain without Gavril if it came to that?

By the time they finally rose above the worst of the wind, Taniel had long since ceased being able to feel his legs. The swirls of snow died down, and the sun came through the eddy, nearly blinding him. The trail leveled out, and suddenly he saw ground; not just hard-packed trails of snow but real earth notched with shovel marks. This had been cleared recently. He blinked in surprise and tried to smile. His face was too numb.

"How are you?" Gavril's voice cut through Taniel's thoughts. The words were a welcome change to the howling wind and the mountain's mocking laughter after three and a half days of climbing. Taniel realized that they'd not said a word in that time, not even during their camps at night, when the four of them huddled together for warmth in Gavril's small tent.

"Hine." Taniel came to a stop beside the big mountaineer, and they waited for Ka-poel and Darden. Taniel closed his eyes and worked at his mouth, trying to form words.

"Fine," he said. "How much harther? Farther?"

"There," Gavril said. He pointed upward.

Taniel shaded his eyes and squinted into the sun. "It's so bright up here. I can't see. How can you?"

"Years on the mountain. You don't need eyes after as long as I've been here. Novi's Perch. We're just beneath it."

Darden grinned at Taniel through cracked lips, his dark-skinned face split with the size of the smile. He was a small man, and easily as old as Tamas. "Almost there," he said. He was barely breathing hard, Taniel noticed with annoyance, though Taniel himself gasped for breath.

Taniel held his snuffbox of powder up to his nose and snorted straight out of the box. He carefully returned it to his pocket—he didn't trust his numb fingers. The rush of the powder trance made him dizzy for a brief moment, then his breathing came easier and his muscles relaxed.

They removed their snowshoes and finished the climb to the monastery. It was only a few hundred more feet. The trail narrowed as they went. To the left, the mountain rose above them in a sheer rock face. To the right, only white sky was visible—the cliff seemed to have no bottom. They moved into the shade of the monastery, and Taniel was able to look up and really see it for the first time.

Novi's Perch seemed to be part of the mountain. It had been built of the same dusty gray rock, and parts of it had even been hewn into the bones of Pike itself. It blocked the trail—that is, the trail ended at the doors to the monastery, and the building rose up above them for a hundred feet or more. It overhung the cliffside to their right by a dozen feet, and Taniel wondered how the monks could sleep, knowing they were suspended above thousands of feet of nothing.

The monastery was plain and unadorned. The stones were chiseled flat, the arches of the doors and windows rounded at the top. There were no spires or grand façades. Only the location of the place gave it grandeur, and the daring of its construction hanging out over the abyss.

Taniel stepped off the road and onto the stone doorstep. He gazed upward, unaware that he'd been wandering, until Gavril reached out and grabbed the front of his coat. He jumped. He'd been not two feet from the edge of the cliff and its perilous drop.

The double doors of the monastery opened with the whine of unoiled hinges. Taniel's pistol was half drawn before he realized it wasn't Bo. A man and woman, both about Taniel's height, bowed their heads in greeting. They were tall for Novi, and their skin was olive—just a shade lighter than Darden's.

"It's very early in the year for pilgrims," the Novi man commented when they'd all come inside.

Taniel glanced at his weapons, at his thick furs and leathers, and at his companions with their climbing gear. They were obviously not pilgrims.

"I'm here to see Privileged Borbador," Taniel said quietly. The words echoed in the long, stone hallway, and Taniel felt like he was whispering inside of Pike's own old bones. "Where can I find him?" Taniel needed to get this over with as quickly as possible. If Bo had an inkling Taniel was after him…

The woman nodded solemnly. "I see. I'm afraid your journey has not quite ended."

"Pit." Taniel glanced at the monks apologetically. "Sorry, sister."

"He's a few miles up the trail past the monastery. A cave."

"I know that cave," Gavril said.

"Did Bo tell you why he came up here?"

Both monks shook their heads. "He said someone might come looking for him," the man said. "He asked us not to stop him from coming."

Bo was definitely expecting someone. No getting around it.

"How do I get up?" Taniel asked.

"Through the monastery," the woman said. "This is the only true path up the mountain, even in the summer. We are the gatekeepers to Kresim Kurga."

Taniel felt his heart jump. "It really exists?"

Both monks raised an eyebrow at Taniel.

"The Holy City?" Taniel said. "It's really up there?"

"The ruins, yes," the man said. "Long ago, Novi chose his people to guard the high places of the Nine. Kresim Kurga may have been long abandoned, Kresimir's protection dissipated, but we have not shirked the duty placed upon us by our saint."

Gavril stepped up beside Taniel as Darden went to the man and woman and spoke in a low voice. Taniel tried to listen to them. He caught the words "ill" and "cousin" before Darden was led down the corridor by the man.

"What is Kresimir's protection?" Taniel asked.

Gavril was large enough that his head nearly scraped the monastery ceiling. "The God wove powerful sorceries, back during his reign, so that no one, sick or in health, young or old, would be bothered by the elements or the altitude sickness."

"Altitude sickness?" Taniel said.

"Comes from being so high up," Gavril said. "Darden and I, we're acclimatized. Others get thirsty, and bloody noses, headaches, sickness in their stomach. Of course, you'll be fine."

"I'll be fine? Why?"

Gavril didn't answer. The Novi woman approached them. "Would you like to rest before heading up?" she asked.

Taniel knew he should, but he couldn't risk Bo getting wind of his arrival. "No thank you."

"It should be an easy climb," she said as she led them through the monastery. "We've started clearing the road up to the summit."

They passed by many adjoining corridors that seemed to stretch deep into the mountain, and by dozens of smaller rooms, doors open, monks within. There were both men and women. Taniel paused just outside one bedroom. A monk sat cross-legged on the floor, leaning over a box of colored sand, making patterns with a long, curved stick. Taniel did not see many monks outside their rooms, though he did hear voices down from the deeper corridors. He'd never imagined that Novi's Perch was this big, or that so many people lived this high up the mountain all winter long.

Ka-poel paused at every room and hallway, the smile on her face like that of a child who wants to explore. Taniel dragged her along impatiently.

After many flights of stone stairs they reached a sudden end. It looked identical to the entrance on the other side, down to the same double doors.

"The doors will be barred after you have gone through," the Novi woman said. "There are... others... on this side of the mountain."

Taniel paused at this. He opened his mouth to ask her, but she retreated down the hallway. Taniel was left alone with Gavril and Ka-poel. The big mountaineer shrugged.

"The monks have strange stories," he said. "About what kinds of creatures come out during the winter months, up in Kresim Kurga. They've been waiting longer each year before letting the pilgrims up." He shrugged again. "I've never seen anything strange up there, myself, aside from the odd cave lion. Ready?"

Taniel put a hand on Gavril's chest. "I'm heading up alone," he said. Then, to Ka-poel. "I want you to stay here too."

She scowled at him.

"I need to have a private talk with Bo. It shouldn't take too long, and the monks said the road is clear."

Ka-poel held up a finger, then jerked her thumb at herself.

"No," Taniel said. "You're staying here. With Gavril."

Gavril chewed on the inside of his cheek. "I really should . . . ," he rumbled.

"No," Taniel said firmly. He hefted his rifle. "I've got this for cave lions."

Taniel heard Gavril bar the door after he'd gone out and wondered whether the big mountain man was getting any ideas about Taniel's visit. He might suspect something. But then, the man was a drunk. Taniel'd get a few drinks in him back at Shouldercrown before he headed off.

The trail widened enough that there was comfortable space between Taniel and the cliff edge. Eventually the sheer rock face on his left softened, until it became a rocky, snow-covered hillside. The trail was not steep here, and he didn't need his snowshoes.

Taniel spotted the cave from quite a ways down the road. It was easy to see—the entrance was as big as a house. He found a good knoll not long after. It was a small hill, perched just higher than the trail, between the trail and the cliff edge. He climbed it carefully and settled down in the snow. It was perfect for a marksman. He could see the cave entrance completely and he was hidden by snowbanks.

The only downside was that it sat on the edge of the cliff. It might have been ten thousand feet to the bottom, for all Taniel knew. He dug his fingers into the snow. If Bo got wind of Taniel, he'd be swept off the knoll with the flick of Bo's fingers.

Taniel watched from his vantage for several minutes. His powder trance allowed him to see details of the cave even though it was far off. The entrance pointed just slightly off center from him. It appeared bored into the side of the mountain, with a thin footpath leading up to it and a steep hill of ice and snow on the left. It was perched right on the edge of the cliff.

The cave was occupied. A thin trail of smoke curled from within, rising straight into the windless sky, and the footpath was heavily trodden. Taniel opened his third eye to confirm it—Bo was there, his pastel glow wavering beside a fire inside the cave. Taniel crawled back off the knoll and opened his gear.

Taniel began getting ready. He moved methodically, double-checking everything, cleaning the flintlock and pan of snow and checking the barrel before he began. He bit the cartridge and primed the pan, and then poured the powder and ball into the muzzle. A little powder on his tongue to deepen the powder trance, and then he rammed down the cotton. Lastly, he brought out his sketchbook and flipped open to one of the first pages—Bo. A sketch Taniel had done on the voyage to Fatrasta. Bo was clean-shaven with short hair and wide cheeks, a smirk on his lips. Taniel tapped the likeness with one finger and climbed back up onto the knoll to wait.

He remained there as the sun passed its noon height and began to descend to the west. The air cleared, and from his knoll he could look out to his right and see all of Kez, distant plains and cities shimmering on the horizon beneath the setting sun.

The passing time gave Taniel's mind the chance to wander. He couldn't help but think of Vlora. As young lovers they'd spent afternoons shirking their training to take to bed in cheap inns. He smiled at those memories and felt his heart beating faster. No, that wouldn't do. He had to keep calm as he waited for his quarry. He remembered one of those times, returning to find Tamas waiting. Tamas had informed him that Taniel and Vlora would marry when they were old enough, and that had been the start of their engagement.

Unbidden, images of Vlora in bed with another man came to his mind. His hands trembled until he pushed those images away. He forced himself to seek the calm of his powder trance. Think objectively. Did he love her? Perhaps. He'd always enjoyed her company. But did he really love her?

Taniel often wondered about love. It sometimes seemed a foreign concept—something out of poems. Vlora was the first woman he'd grown truly close to since his mother's death, when he was six. He had few memories of his mother. Most of what he knew of her had been told to him afterward: that she was a powder mage and a member of the Adran nobility, though her mother had been Kez. She'd been a hard woman on the outside, as hard as Tamas, but he distinctly remembered a gentle nature that emerged when they were at home. Even when Taniel had a governess to watch him, his mother had always been present.

That had changed after her death. Taniel had gone through a string of governesses, whom he strongly suspected Tamas had been sleeping with. And then the governesses stopped, as if Tamas had had enough. The next woman to enter their lives was Vlora. He remembered competing with Bo to try to impress her. It was the only time in his life he'd been able to best Bo for a woman's affections. Did that mean she was the only one for him? No. It was too big a world for that.

It was surprising to him how little he thought of her now, so many weeks after ending their engagement. He touched his pocket, where he kept the rumpled likeness of her he'd torn from his sketchbook. No, he did not love her. He'd been hurt by her betrayal, but mostly in his pride. Their marriage had been a foregone conclusion for so long that it seemed strange not to have it looming in the future anymore.

He wondered what her assignment was now. Was she still attached to Tamas's staff? Tamas wasn't overly sentimental, not by any stretch of the imagination. He'd be angry that the wedding was called off, but he'd not want a talented powder mage like Vlora far off.

Taniel found himself grinding his teeth together. Not sentimental. Ha. Sent his own son up here to kill his best friend. Why would he do that? Was it punishment for letting Rozalia live? Was this some kind of test, to see if Taniel was still loyal?

No, it wasn't any of those things. It was pure expedience for the old bastard. Taniel was the best shot in the army. He could shoot a man's hat off at three miles on a windy day. If that wasn't an option, Taniel could get close to Bo without raising suspicions, and put a knife in his gut. When would Tamas learn that expedience was not always right? He'd certainly had a dose of it when he threw Nikslaus into the Adsea. Taniel couldn't help but feel proud of his father for that. The pride was short-lived.

"You're going to have to take a shit eventually," Taniel muttered to himself as the day wore on. He remembered a time, crouching on a knoll in the king's forest outside of Adopest. He'd been fourteen. Bo had figured out where the queen and her handmaidens liked to bathe in the river. They'd concealed themselves on a knoll for almost twenty-four hours before the women had come down to the river. Bo had been armed with a looking glass; Taniel had a horn of powder and the eyesight of a powder trance. It was risky, and they both knew the beatings they'd get if caught. Yet the queen was said to be one of the most beautiful women in the Nine.

And she was. The wait—and the risk—had been well worth it.

There was movement in the cave. Bo emerged. He stood in the entrance to the cave and rubbed his hands together, looking out over Kez not a foot from the edge of the cliff. Taniel wondered how Bo could do that without quaking at the fall. He took a deep breath and steadied himself for the shot.

Bo turned to examine the hillside. He removed a thick fur hood, and Taniel examined his childhood friend down the barrel of his rifle. Bo's hair had grown long in the Mountainwatch, and he sported a thin, unruly beard. He'd lost a lot of weight since Taniel had last seen him. Bo studied the hillside and then looked down the road toward Taniel.

Taniel resisted the urge to duck. Bo was looking right at him. Bo shielded his eyes from the sun and tugged absently at his Privileged's gloves. The arcane symbols on the back of the gloves caught the sunlight, and Taniel wondered whether Bo had surrounded himself with a shield of hardened air. Bo's strongest elemental aura was air.

Did Bo know he was here? Was Bo waiting, laughing to himself, ready to strike Taniel down when he betrayed his position? Was he watching Taniel with his third eye? Taniel couldn't sense Bo's third eye, or any kind of shield. Taniel's finger tightened on the trigger.

Bo stood there for another minute or two, squinting down the road before he turned to go back inside.

Taniel swore to himself. Why the pit didn't he pull the trigger? He'd had a good shot. He sighed. He knew the answer.

"To the pit with it," he said aloud, and stood up.

He came off his knoll and gathered his gear, then headed up the path toward Bo's cave.

Pit, what was he going to say? '*Hi Bo, how have you been, I came up here to kill you? But don't worry, I've changed my mind. I hope everything is fine between us.*'

Taniel gathered his thoughts and his resolve—or what was left of it, anyway. He shook his head. He'd been forced to choose between duty and his friend. He hoped that made him a good friend, because he was a piss-poor soldier.

Taniel took one step onto the thin trail leading to the cave and froze. Bo had come out of his cave again. Perhaps fifty paces separated them. Bo would clearly see the rifle over Taniel's shoulder. Would Bo recognize him? Taniel pulled the furs away from his face and tried to smile. He raised a hand in greeting.

Bo's eyes narrowed. Taniel swallowed. Bo tugged on his Privileged's gloves. They blended in with the snow, all white, save for the gold symbols on the back.

Taniel opened his mouth to call out a greeting.

"Not another step," Bo shouted. "Stay where you are!" He tugged on his gloves again, and Taniel could see something on Bo's face that he didn't like. He knew why Taniel had come.

Bo raised his hands over his head. The pose was almost comical. Bo was not a big man, and his thin cheeks and the wispy beard made him look like a boy. Bo's chest rose and fell, his breathing wild. He was gearing up for something big. Taniel didn't have to open his third eye to know that Bo had touched the Else with his gloved fingers. Sorcery poured into the world. Taniel squeezed his eyes shut.

"Get down, you fool!" Bo screamed.

Taniel's eyes flew open. Something hit him from behind, bowling him over. He flew down against a snowdrift, blood pounding in his ears as something big rushed by. Was that Gavril, all wrapped in his furs?

Taniel felt his heart lurch into his throat. No, that wasn't Gavril. That was a cave lion.

The name was a misnomer. It didn't look much like a lion. Its back feet were padded, like a cat's, but its front feet were clawed like a rooster's with three great talons as long as sickles. It had a head like a tiger's and the deep, broad chest and maned shoulders of a lion. This one was bigger than any Taniel had ever seen or heard about. It made a Fatrastan swamp bear look small by comparison, and it rushed down the trail toward Bo on its hind legs.

Bo's fingers worked in the air as if plucking at the strings of an invisible cello. The air cracked, thunder peeling against the mountainside as lightning burst from the clear sky and connected with the lion's head.

The creature wasn't even stunned. It sprang from two feet onto four, bounding with the speed of a jaguar. Smoke rose from its furry mane.

Bo jerked one arm into the air and then let it fall. Ice on the hillside above the cave lion suddenly surged down, a mini avalanche, hitting the lion with the force of ten carriages. The ice split, sliding around the creature as it ran onward, as if it were a shark's fin cutting through the top of the sea. Wind buffeted it; flames shot from the clear air and sprayed across its face. The lion ignored them all.

The cave lion was fifteen paces from Bo, and Bo was looking tired. Sweat poured from his brow. His fingers twitched, jerked at unseen strings. The lion stopped in its tracks.

It slowed, shook its hoary head, and continued onward.

"Don't just sit there."

Taniel felt himself jerked to his feet. Gavril was there. His face was red from a long, hard run. He held a spear in one hand, like the kind used to hunt boar.

"Shoot the damned thing!"

Taniel flipped his rifle off his shoulder and sighted. The creature shook its head, as if dizzy, and let out a low howl. It slapped its ears with both clawed hands. It jerked about, slamming its head against the ground as if its skull was full of bees.

Taniel pulled the trigger. The beast's head jolted back where Taniel's bullet hit it. He felt his eyes go wide. The bullet had connected and simply slid off the lion's ugly face—just like it had the Privileged in Adopest. It howled again and made a gesture of disgust toward Taniel with a taloned hand. There was sorcery in this creature, the kind gods are made of.

Taniel felt the snow beneath him explode. He was thrown into the air, toward the cliff edge. He landed in the snow and slid, unable to find any purchase. He scrambled for some kind of hold. There was nothing. He'd go over the edge in a second.

His boots hit solid ground. Rock jutted from the side of the mountain, a sheet a man's length across beneath his boots that hadn't been there a moment before. Taniel struggled to climb back up to the trail. He felt hands grab him.

"Come on," Darden said. The old Deliv Watcher was armed with a spear in one hand, just like Gavril was. He dragged Taniel up with the other. Ka-poel was there too, lending her small strength. She gave Taniel a wide-eyed stare and then hurried after the others.

Taniel looked for his rifle. It was on the ground, too far away. Did he have time to reload? One glance toward Bo told him no.

Bo retreated to his cave, his back against the rocky wall of one side. The cave lion surged toward him on two feet. It plowed onward as if against a current, each step a struggle. A struggle it was winning.

Gavril reached the lion first. He thrust his spear up, sinking it into the lion's soft flank. It gave a wail and turned on him. He leapt out of range of the raking claws just in time and rolled back down the trail. Darden jumped over Gavril's rolling form, spear held at the ready, and rushed the cave lion.

Darden exploded. One moment he was there, the next he was gone. Blood and ribbons of tissue spattered the mountainside. The cave lion howled triumphantly. Taniel didn't have time to think, didn't take a moment to consider Darden's blood soaking his coat. He aimed both pistols and fired.

A powder mage can float a bullet for some distance. It gives his shots extra range, and it cost nothing but his own mental exertion and a bit of extra powder. He can also ignite powder, transferring the energy by touch. A good Marked can do it with bullets, giving one the strength and energy to pierce rock or steel.

Taniel ignited his whole powder horn and pushed the blast behind his bullets.

They tore right through the cave lion. It screamed as bubbling green blood sprayed the icy trail. The lion turned from Bo, its howls sounding like the scream of a wounded horse, and instead turned to face Taniel. It raised a taloned hand. Taniel felt the heat of approaching sorcery.

Ka-poel squeezed past Taniel on the narrow trail, throwing herself between him and the beast.

"Dammit! Pole, no!"

Ka-poel lifted both hands defiantly. She held something in one hand—a doll. It was naked and about the size of a hand, shaped from wax. The craftsmanship was superb. Every part was accurate to a person—a woman, to be precise—especially the face. It was Julene.

Ka-poel stabbed the doll with a long needle. The cave lion howled again and clutched its side. She jammed the needle into the doll's head, scrambling the tip about inside the skull. The lion twitched and growled. It scratched at its ears and face, which left long, bloody cuts. Ka-poel bent forward, took a long, deep breath, and then blew on the doll.

The cave lion burst into flame. Bo renewed his attacks, fingers flying, lances of ice bursting from the inside of the cave to smash against the lion. Shakily, Taniel reloaded one of his pistols. He had a few powder charges left, though his horn was empty. What could he do against a creature like this? It was trapped between Bo and Ka-poel's sorcery but it refused to die. How long could they keep it up?

Taniel whirled. "Gavril, your powder horn. Now!"

Gavril, a little ways down the trail, locked eyes with Taniel and tossed him the powder horn.

Taniel caught the horn and hefted it in one hand. Mostly full. Good. He turned. Bo looked like he was about spent, and Ka-poel juggled the burning doll in her hands, needle and fingers thrusting, a look of savage glee on her face.

"Down!" Taniel shouted, tossing the powder horn. He grabbed Ka-poel by the shoulders and threw her against the mountainside. The horn landed between the mountain and the cave lion. With a thought, Taniel ignited it.

His mind warped the blast, guiding it with Marked sorceries to maximize the power of the detonation. The cave lion was thrown into the air, twenty, thirty, fifty paces out from the mountain before it began to curve and plummet. Taniel watched it go, howling, clawing. The howl changed, turning to a scream as the lion's shape warped into the body of a woman. It bounced off the mountainside, far down, and continued to fall, disappearing through the clouds below.

CHAPTER 18

Tamas stopped underneath a streetlamp to check the address he'd scribbled on plain stationery a few hours before. "One seven eight," he muttered to himself, squinting to see the number plaques. Olem walked a few feet behind him, pistols hidden under a long coat, keeping an eye out for trouble.

The Routs was a wealthy part of town, where the banks and the remnants of the old merchant guilds still did business every weekday. It had barely been touched by the earthquake, and not at all by the royalist uprising. Side streets were lined with small but well-kept houses for businessmen, clerks, and merchant liaisons. The lanterns were lit, and there was a common police beat on every street, enough that Tamas wondered if he'd stumbled into the wrong part of town.

Bad place to kill a man, he noted. He paused, correcting himself as he noticed that there was a splash of darkness on the street up ahead. As he drew closer, he saw that a good half-dozen lamps had blown out—or had been put out, as was the case. He counted the street numbers so that he was sure to find the right house and approached it straight on, stepping up from the street and rapping on the front door three times. There were no lights on, or any sign of life at all. The place looked abandoned.

The door opened a crack, and he and Olem were admitted immediately. Olem waited in the sitting room while Tamas was taken by the arm and led down a hall and then into what he guessed to be a back room. A match was struck and a candle lit.

Tamas saw a familiar face over the candle.

"Good to see you, Tamas," Sabon said.

"Likewise. I hope I'm not too late."

"The Barbers aren't here yet."

"Good. I want to see how they operate." Tamas's eyes adjusted to the light and he glanced around. They were in a small kitchen, the floors and cupboards bare. A man sat on one of the counters in the corner, an unlit pipe in the corner of his mouth. He was a small man, demure and of medium build, his face covered with a thick black beard that made his features almost impossible to see in the dim light. He chewed on the stem of his pipe and watched Tamas.

"You are our contact?" Tamas asked.

"Fingers," the man said.

"I take it that's not your real name?" Tamas said, raising an eyebrow.

"A pseudonym," he said. "For my protection." The man was studying Tamas with some intent, his eyes working up and down slowly—judging, weighing. Tamas felt there was something peculiar about the man.

"You have the Knack," Tamas said.

Fingers adjusted his long black coat and brushed something off the front. "Ah, yes," he said. "A lot of spies do. It makes it easier to get things done when you have talents that others can't judge."

"It also makes it damn hard for me to put together a spy network, since Manhouch's whole system went to ground when I killed the royal cabal."

"Fearing for one's life gives one an incentive to disappear." Fingers's eyes darted between Sabon and Tamas. It was clear he didn't like being in the same room with two powder mages.

"Yet here you are," Tamas said.

"I have mouths to feed." He paused, then added, "I'm a very minor Knacked. I can pick locks without a set, open latches from the outside."

Tamas had heard scholars talk about this kind of thing. Minor telekinesis, they called it. "Nothing that would be a threat to me," Tamas said. "Yes, I get your meaning, but I have no quarrel with anyone outside the royal cabals—unless they have a quarrel with me. I need Manhouch's spies. You let it be known that we're paying twice what Manhouch did."

Fingers removed the pipe from his mouth and coughed into his hand.

"Are you laughing at me?" Tamas said. He glanced at Sabon. The Deliv just shrugged.

"What the pit is so funny?" Tamas said.

"That stuff about paying us more," Fingers said, "It doesn't really work that way."

Tamas narrowed his eyes. "How *does* it work?"

"Spies aren't like soldiers, Field Marshal. A soldier has loyalty, yes, but at the end of the day he does what he does for a full belly and a month's wages. Spies do it because they love the game. They love their country, or their king."

"Are you saying I won't be able to use Manhouch's old spy network?"

Fingers pointed the stem of his pipe at Tamas. "Not at all, Field Marshal. Some of us were loyal to Manhouch himself. Those have already left the country, or are working for the Kez outright. The rest of us love Adro and will drift back. I suspect the longer I stay alive, being a Knacked and all, the more spies will come out of the woodwork."

Tamas rubbed his eyes. When they came out of the woodwork, he'd have to worry about whether they were double agents and whom to trust. It was all a great big headache. "I thought you said you did this because you have a family to feed," Tamas said.

Fingers nodded. "Right, well, I may have lied about them."

Sabon snickered. Tamas threw him a look. Spies. He'd rather let the whole lot of them rot in the pit. Unfortunately, he needed them.

"Are the Barbers here yet?" Tamas asked.

"I don't know," Fingers said.

Tamas jerked a thumb at the door. "Go find out."

"Someone will let us know."

"Now."

The spy scurried from the room, and Tamas went over to the counter, hoisting himself up. He rubbed at the stitches on his chest, resisting the urge to pick at them.

"I need some advice," Tamas said.

"Of course you do. You're like a newborn babe, without me by your side."

The silence dragged on for several moments. Tamas could read Sabon's eyes. *If I'd been there*, they said, *that Warden wouldn't have come close to killing you.*

"Mihali," Tamas said. "The mad chef."

"Is this really worthy of your attention?"

"He's cooking for the whole army. Morale is higher than ever, mostly thanks to him."

"So what more do you know about him?"

"He escaped from the Hassenbur Asylum," he said.

"Ah. A madman."

"They certainly think so. They've sent some men to retrieve him. He claims he was committed because his relatives and competitors were jealous of him."

"Paranoid?"

Tamas shrugged. "Possibly."

"Send him back," Sabon said. "His cooking is good, but it's not worth making enemies of the asylum's patrons. Do you know who they are?"

"A man named Claremonte."

Sabon was silent for a moment. "The new head of the Brudania-Gurla Trading Company?"

"Yes."

"I think that settles it. We can't risk our supply of saltpeter."

"I'm not so sure," Tamas said.

"That rubbish in the newspapers?" Sabon snorted. "Mihali claiming to be Adom reborn? Evidence of his madness, I would think. Not many educated men believe such myths."

"You haven't met him."

Sabon ran a hand over his smooth head. "You believe him?"

"Don't look at me like that. Of course not. But the man's harmless."

"Then what reason could you have to keep him?"

"Sorcery," Tamas said.

"He's a Privileged?"

"He has the Knack," Tamas said. "Something to do with food. He can create the stuff out of thin air."

Sabon said, "That doesn't sound like much."

"Have you ever heard of anyone who could create matter out of thin air? Even a Knacked?"

"Huh," Sabon grunted. "He'd be the richest man in the world."

"We can use him to feed all of Adro if we need to. Even during a famine. We may need him badly the longer the war lasts."

"Parlor tricks?"

Tamas said, "I think not. Olem and I both watched him carefully. He pulled an empty pot down from its hook and set it on the stove, only to have it full of stew and boiling the next time I looked at it. He put ten loaves of bread into the oven and pulled out a hundred."

Sabon frowned. "It could still be sorcery and tricks. He could be a powerful Privileged, hiding his true strength. There's no telling what Privileged are capable of. Not even the royal cabals know everything that aura manipulation can do."

"Yes, that crossed my mind as well. Rumors are spreading, however, and I fear that a cult might form. Among my ranks, no less, for Olem says he's become very popular with the seventh brigade. They love his food."

"What will you do?"

"I can't just dismiss him and send him back to the asylum," Tamas said, "not after what I've seen. At the very least he's a powerful Knacked—if an odd one—and we'll want him as our ally. As I said. The worth of food during wartime is immeasurable."

They were interrupted by the door opening again. It was Fingers.

"Everything is ready," the spy said. "Come with me."

They followed him in the dark up to a small room on the second story, at the front of the house, with a good view of the street. The curtains were drawn back, but the room was completely dark so as to hide them from any prying eyes. Fingers directed them to a pair of chairs set a pace back from the window. They sat and waited.

"So this is him?" Tamas asked quietly, nodding to the house across the street before realizing they couldn't see his movement.

"It is," Fingers responded. "A long-term spy for the Kez. He owns a small shipping company on the Adsea. The Warden that tried to kill you: He was smuggled into the country on one of this man's cargo ships."

"And you're certain he's involved?"

"The man's in deep. He's a banker here in the Routs and has friends among the city council. He's been talking a lot at the local town hall, spouting about how the powder mages are going to get us all killed and we should pull down your council and surrender to the Kez."

"That's awfully bold," Tamas said.

Fingers said, "Yes, and I would have thought too bold for a spy, if we hadn't been watching him since he immigrated to the country fifteen years ago. There's no doubt that he was involved getting the Warden here."

"I want to make something clear," Tamas said, his voice dropping to barely a whisper. "I don't want a wholesale slaughter of Adro citizens. I don't want a police state. We're only doing this to rid ourselves of Kez spies, so unless you have evidence that a dissenter is indeed a spy, simply pass him on to the local precinct that he needs to be watched. I'm not ready to wage war on our own people *and* the Kez."

There was a moment of silence. "Understood."

"Good. Is everything working out?" Tamas said. "Working with the Barbers? I must admit I have reservations about using them."

"They're a wonder," Fingers said. "I've not seen anything like it, even among our own killers. I'm surprised we've never used them before."

"That good?" Sabon asked.

"That thorough," Fingers said. "They kill quietly and they clean up their messes to perfection. Not a single drop of blood left behind, and the bodies just gone. It's flawless."

Tamas remembered the barricades and the bodies of nobles and royalist leaders lying in their blood-soaked beds, throats slit wide. "So they have some restraint, then?"

Fingers gave a low chuckle. "Yes, well, when they want the bodies found, it's quite messy. It keeps their street reputations intact and keeps the larger gangs from messing with them. We asked them to do it quietly, though, and I'll be damned, they are." There was a wince in his voice that Tamas barely caught.

"And the problem?" Tamas said.

"Sometimes no sign at all is worse than a body. It starts rumors when there's not a book out of place in the whole house and a family was there yesterday and gone tomorrow. Bad kinds of rumors, like ghosts and demons and gods."

Tamas thought of South Pike Mountain, smoking in the distance, and of Adamat's explanation of Kresimir's Promise and of Mihali's cryptic warnings. Rubbish. The common folk would believe anything. "I don't want any more of these rumors. See if you can make things a little more organic."

"We'll do our best."

Tamas caught sight of a dark shape in the street. He tapped Sabon and guided his gaze in that direction. Several more shapes joined the first.

"I'll be back in a while," Fingers said. The spy left the room without a sound, and a moment later joined the dark shapes in the street. Tamas thought he could make out the familiar apron uniforms of barbers. He shook his head.

"I think I'm going to shave myself from now on," he said quietly.

"You and me alike," Sabon said.

"The local police?" Tamas asked.

"They've been warned off tonight. They'll leave us be, because they know they'll have one less problem to deal with in the morning."

Tamas opened his third eye. In that vision, Fingers was a dim glow of color, standing out even through the walls of the house. He followed Fingers as he made his way into the front door of the house across the street and then up the stairs to the bedrooms.

"Wait," Tamas said. "That other spy, the one they're going after. He's a sorcerer. Stronger than a Knacked. A Privileged."

Sabon was silent for a moment. "Shit. Here, watch the windows." He moved from his chair, feeling around for a moment, then pushed a rifle into Tamas's hands.

Tamas adjusted the rifle by feel alone. "Loaded and primed?"

"Yes," Sabon said.

"It'll make a hell of a racket," Tamas said. "There won't be any question of what happened here, not for anyone on these streets."

"Just in case," Sabon said.

Tamas sighted down his rifle, watching the windows of the front bedroom. He could see the glow of the Kez Privileged, lying there in bed, and he could sense Fingers standing in the door to the room. He thought he caught a glimpse of shadows moving in the darkness.

Tamas ducked instinctively as a flash of sorcery lit up the window in his sights. The flash was followed by a muffled thump, barely audible, and then there was silence. Tamas peered out the window, rifle at the ready. He could see the Knacked and the Privileged by their glows. Fingers was in the staircase, flat on his belly, while the Kez Privileged knelt on the ground in the bedroom. Tamas could only guess there had been a razor to his throat—otherwise more sorcery would have followed. Fingers slowly climbed to his feet and entered the bedroom. Tamas lowered his rifle.

A few minutes passed before dark figures emerged from the other house: the Barbers and their prisoners. They crossed the street, and Tamas heard the door downstairs open. He remained in his seat, watching the street for any sign of interested neighbors or overly curious passersby, while Sabon went to check on things. There were no such signs.

Fingers returned a moment later. He held a candle in one hand. He didn't look happy. "You didn't warn us he was a Privileged."

"You should have seen for yourself," Tamas said. "If you really have the Knack, you'd have the third sight as well. Damned sloppy."

"I can't open it," Fingers mumbled. "Leaves me with the runs for a week."

"That Privileged could have left you without a head," Tamas said.

Fingers harrumphed. "It was all show. Light and sound. Nothing real, though for a moment I thought the flesh was going to melt from my bones."

"Fright keeps you honest." Tamas uncocked his rifle and leaned it against the wall. "You brought over the wife," he said.

"She woke up when he made the flash. He must have warded the room. Was awake the moment the Barbers were at his bedside." He shook his head. "I've seen these fellows kill a man with his wife in his arms and take away his body, leaving her sleeping like a babe. If it wasn't for the wards, it would have gone more smoothly."

Fingers was nervous that Tamas thought he'd botched the job, Tamas realized. "Well done," Tamas said. "Let me know what your interrogation finds."

"You're not coming?" Fingers looked surprised.

"Despite what you may have heard, I don't have a bloodlust for Privileged," Tamas said.

Fingers sniffed, as if disappointed. "I don't think he's going to say much. He looks like a tough one."

"Tell him he loses a hand in five minutes if he doesn't talk. Tell him the other one in ten."

Fingers's eyes grew wide. "That's..."

Tamas gave him a shallow smile. "OK, so maybe I have a slight bloodlust for sorcerers. I also know how to deal with them."

Fingers left the room. Tamas listened for screams, yet there were none. Wherever they were, they'd muffled the room well. Sabon came up after a minute.

"Fingers looks ill," he said.

"I told him to take the hands of the Privileged if need be."

Sabon snorted. "That's a dangerous precedent. Is that the policy we're going to take with noncabal Privileged in Adro?"

"Pit, no," Tamas said. "This bastard is a Kez spy, though, and we need to work quickly."

Fingers came into the room not long after. His face was pale in the candlelight, his hands shaking a little. "He's given up three names already."

Tamas felt a bit of trepidation. "Anyone on my council?"

"No. He claims he never had direct dealings with anyone higher than himself. Just coded messages and intermediaries. He did give up the name of his wife." He paused. "Push a man too hard, Field Marshal, and he'll give up his own mother. There's a reason we keep a limit on torture. They'll say anything for the pain to end."

"It's purely psychological," Tamas said. "You didn't actually cut off a hand, did you?" He smothered his disappointment at not having any clue to the traitor on his council.

"No..."

"Interrogate the wife. Find out what she knows. Hand them both over to my soldiers when you're finished and they'll deal with the executions. Any children?"

"One," Fingers said. "She's at a girls' boarding school in Novi."

"A neutral country," Tamas mused. "They were prepared for this eventuality. Send a missive to her school mistress. Tell her to keep her at the school, indefinitely."

Fingers nodded shakily.

"What word do we have about these spies?" Tamas asked. "These plants, like this one. How many do you think they are?"

Fingers chewed on his pipe stem furiously. "You won't like it."

"I don't have to like it," Tamas said. "I just need to know."

"Hundreds," Fingers said. "Just from our first handful of encounters we've gotten dozens of names—good names, too, and not just ones spouted off under torture. People who check out as Kez spies, and hundreds more with a big question with their names. The Kez are in here deep. They've been planning this for decades."

Tamas closed his eyes. Not what he wanted to hear. There could be spies in his army, spies in the city and the countryside, in every building in Adopest. He already knew one of his council had betrayed him. How many more would? "Well done, Fingers," Tamas said quietly. The spy waited a moment before he left, one eye fixed on Tamas the whole time.

"I'll have to double what I'm paying the Barbers," Tamas said. "They have the manpower, if I have the money."

Sabon said, "It's dangerous, depending too much on them."

"A risk I have to take. These spies. They could bring down everything we've worked for. We'll double patrols and give the local police more authority. Kresimir, we might have to push back plans for the new government."

"We've always known it was a dodgy road we would have to walk. Just don't forget about the people."

"Of course not. How goes the training?" he asked Sabon. "Pray, tell me some good news."

A weary smile crossed Sabon's face. "Better than I expected. Andriya may be crazy, but the younger recruits like him. Vidaslav, as it turns out, has some talent for teaching. We've shown the ones with the least amount of talent how to find a powder mage and turned them around, sending them out recruiting. There are already more candidates than I thought possible."

"How many?"

"Thirteen so far with a decent amount of talent. Two of those with the capabilities to rival me. Unfortunately none on your level, or Taniel's."

"Thirteen?" Tamas said. "You're joking. It took me years to gather the powder cabal we have now."

"I wouldn't believe it unless I saw it myself," Sabon said.

"Remember, there was a powder-mage cull less than a hundred and fifty years ago in Adro. Every man, woman, and child checked for any strength with powder and executed if discovered. Nowadays people hide it if they find themselves with the affinity. At least, they did. We're trying to work out a system to seek out powder mages directly."

"You mean like the Privileged Dowsers?"

Sabon nodded. "The royal cabal had more potent sorcery at their call than we do. And greater numbers. I'm sure we'll work out something, though."

Tamas slapped him on the shoulder. "Good work, my friend. Keep me informed. I know you're not happy about the assignment."

"There is one other thing I should ask you." Sabon seemed to hesitate for a moment.

"What is it?"

Sabon spoke slowly, choosing his words carefully. "Until recently, Taniel and Vlora were meant to wed. I must ask you, did you put them together purposefully?"

"What do you mean?" Tamas asked, though he had a pretty good idea where Sabon was heading.

"Did you pair them in order for their children to be powder mages?"

Tamas considered his response. It was opportune, certainly, and his encouraging them to be together was definitely not without ulterior motive. "The thought had crossed my mind."

"Not even the royal cabals resorted to such breeding," Sabon said. It was obvious he disapproved.

"They didn't? Why do you think the king provided each male sorcerer with his own harem? Benevolence? No, Sabon, they most definitely bred for Privileged. It's not common knowledge, but the Beadle alone had over a thousand children."

"Any Privileged?"

"One," Tamas said. "A younger member of the royal cabal. Didn't even know who his father was."

Sabon's mouth hung open in horror. "What happened to all those other children?"

"Work camps, orphanages, the Mountainwatch." Tamas shrugged. "Some were even slaughtered as babes. The royal cabal has never been a pleasant place. I will not let my powder cabal become like that, but yes, I intended for their children to be Marked. In my own studies, powder mages inherit hereditarily far more often than Privileged."

"How long have you been studying this?" Sabon asked.

"Since long before we met."

Sabon regarded him with dark eyes. "Erika was a powder mage."

Tamas fought the snarl that crept onto his face. It was a fair enough assumption on Sabon's part. "Don't even think it," Tamas said. His voice came out an angry growl despite his effort. "I loved my wife. I'd give anything to have her back." His voice cracked. He cleared his throat. "Taniel *was not* an experiment."

"Good." He seemed satisfied with the answer. After a brief pause, "I was hoping after your recent adventure you'd recall me."

Tamas shook his head. "I'm sorry. I need you teaching new powder mages. I can take care of myself."

Tamas could hear Sabon grinding his teeth. "You're a stubborn bastard, and it's going to get you killed," Sabon said. "They'll send more than one Warden next time."

"Likely, but not yet. I'm going to get some sleep. Before you head back to your school, let someone know I want that spy beheaded and his hands sent back to Kez with his widow. I want Ipille to know his spies will start coming back in progressively smaller boxes unless he recalls them."

CHAPTER 19

They buried what they could gather of Darden beneath a small barrow of rock and ice. There were more buried, Gavril told them, farther up the trail: pilgrims who did not survive the journey to the summit, and monks who had fallen prey to winter or to sickness or to predators upon the mountain. He assured them Darden would be in good company.

Taniel clenched a nub of charcoal between his fingers and began sketching Darden's face in his book. The memory of how the man looked was already beginning to fade. Taniel just hadn't known him long enough. He closed his eyes, trying to remember.

The vision of Julene—Taniel knew for certain it was her now—bouncing and screaming her way down the rock face and out of sight haunted Taniel throughout the night. He couldn't sleep, for each time he managed to fall asleep, he saw Julene's body, or that of the cave lion, thrashing and angry before his mind's eye, mocking him. How could he not have seen it? Her anger, her recklessness. At the very least he should have been watching for a double cross. He ended up sitting in the cave entrance, watching the sky above begin to lighten as the sun rose in the east, on the other side of the mountain.

He'd disobeyed a direct order. What would Tamas do about it? What good could come of it? Tamas would just send another powder mage. Maybe he'd even come himself. He'd have Taniel court-martialed. Could Tamas have him executed? Taniel didn't think even a man like Tamas could execute his own son. He hoped not, anyway.

How would Taniel explain this to Tamas? What would they do when another powder mage came for them? Taniel kicked a piece of ice over the ledge. They'd deal with those problems when they came up.

He heard ice crunch underfoot as Bo joined him. Taniel gave his friend a long look. Bo seemed as if he hadn't slept well for weeks. His eyes were red, his face sunburned. He seemed to be constantly sweating, and he fingered the lapel of his coat nervously as he took a seat next to Taniel.

Bo watched the stars fade as Taniel sketched a likeness of Darden, until Taniel heard the first cries of birds looking for a morning meal.

"You're getting quite good," Bo said. "Looks just like him."

"I'm glad you think so," Taniel said. "I was having trouble picturing him." He tucked the bit of charcoal into a pouch and folded his sketchbook.

"Tamas has a lot of gall sending you up here to kill me," Bo said. His voice was pleasant, quiet. A feature many of his women found soothing, no doubt. "Don't get me wrong," he added. "I'm glad he did. Somebody else may have taken that shot. You could have chosen a better time, though."

"You were expecting me," Taniel said. He found he wasn't

surprised. Bo tended to know a lot of things, even when he shouldn't. Taniel blew on his hands to warm them.

"A powder mage, eventually," Bo said. "Actually, I expected Julene first. She's the one I was preparing for." He pointed down the trail, along the ledge of the mountain and the monastery far below. "I've been warding this whole trail for two weeks now. Ever since that inspector visited and gave me the message that *she* would try to summon Kresimir." He fingered his lapel again, running a finger along the collar.

"'She'?"

"Julene. That Predeii bitch."

"Predeii," Taniel said. "That Privileged I tracked in Adopest said she was a Predeii."

Bo swallowed hard. "Two of 'em? Pit."

"What's a Predeii?" Taniel said.

"You don't know?"

"Would I ask if I did?"

Bo frowned. "There's a lot you find out in a royal cabal. Things only scholars remember. Secrets a thousand years old or more. I, uh... you said Tamas slaughtered the royal cabal, right?"

"Yeah."

Bo looked up at the fading stars. "I suppose no one will come after me for spilling secrets, then." He took a deep breath. "Kresimir didn't come here on his own."

Taniel gave his friend a skeptical look. "I haven't attended a sermon since I was a boy. Only peasants listen to that stuff these days."

"Peasants aren't as dim as you think," Bo said. "All superstition has basis in fact."

"And you believe this superstition?" Taniel asked, looking down his nose at Bo.

Bo took a deep breath. "There's a difference between having faith in something you've never seen or experienced and knowing firsthand that it's true."

"You're saying you met Kresimir?"

"No, I didn't meet..." Bo sighed. "Just shut up and listen. They show you things in the royal cabal that have been passed on through the minds of sorcerers for millennia."

Taniel snorted. "Kresimir. All right. Assuming he is real, that was thousands of years ago."

"Oh, Kresimir was real. Whether you call him a god or a mighty sorcerer, every history from that time agrees that he was real. And it was fourteen hundred years ago, give or take. The exact timeline was lost in the Bleakening," Bo said. "He was summoned. Brought here, maybe even forced into this world by the Predeii. Some think that he was even bent to their will."

"God or sorcerer, how could anyone force him to come to this world?"

Bo fiddled with his collar. "Predeii are the predecessors of the Privileged. Powerful sorcerers that make today's Privileged look like schoolchildren playing with fire. They were rulers in the days before Kresimir, and they sought a way to expand their power. They summoned Kresimir from"—he made a mystical gesture with one hand and shrugged—"and they bid him use his power to bring order to the Nine."

"The saints?" Taniel said.

Bo gave a shake of his head. "No. Good thought, though. The saints—Adom, Novi, and the rest—they came later, when Kresimir was not up to the task anymore and needed to summon brothers and sisters to help him. Their shared his power and his wisdom, and when he left, so did they."

"But the Predeii remained?" Taniel asked. "They'd be thousands of years old."

"Or more," Bo said. He shrugged again. "They discovered a way to keep from dying from age or disease, even before they summoned Kresimir. Sorcery was more potent back then. I don't even know if anyone has the power to kill a Predeii now."

Taniel swallowed. He looked over the edge of the cliff, into the swirling clouds of nothingness below. "You mean she's not dead?"

Bo's face was grim. "I don't know. Probably not, though I'm trying to remain optimistic. Either way, we have to go find out. If she survived, then Adro is in great danger."

"How?"

"She wants to annihilate our armies, our sorcerers, and our powder mages. Half the work is already done with the royal cabal dead. If she summons Kresimir back, then he'll do the rest of the work for her and Adro will be under her thumb. Kresimir made it clear once that he had no interest in ruling the Nine for very long. If Julene proves to him that the kings and their royal cabals are not up to the task, she thinks he'll leave her in charge. She's been waiting a long time to rule."

Taniel scoffed. "Kresimir. Who thinks of things like that? Kresimir is long gone."

"Julene doesn't think so. Neither do the Kez nobility, and certain factions within the Kresim Church."

"Why would she want a god here? It sounds like she's nigh unto a god herself." It explained the battle at Adopest University—how Rozalia and Julene seemed so powerful, and how Julene survived Rozalia's assault.

"Power. That's all Julene cares about. Power over others. The history books refer to the Bleakening, a time when knowledge of Kresimir was lost. Only the royal cabals remember what happened *during* the Bleakening. It was a war between the Predeii and the new kings of the Nine and their royal cabals. Julene claims, quite proudly, to have started the war. Millions died. In the end, the Predeii were vastly outnumbered and lost. Some died, some fled. Others hid. Julene was one that survived."

"You seem to know a lot about her."

"We were . . . together . . . once." Bo grimaced.

Taniel couldn't help but bark a laugh.

"I'm not proud of it," Bo said.

"What in the Nine did you see in her?"

Bo sniffed. "She's very good in bed."

"She's—apparently—fifty times your age!"

"That gives her a lot of experience." Bo examined his nails. "And she doesn't have the best judgment when it comes to her emotions. She fell for me and taught me things she shouldn't have."

"And now she's trying to kill you? Why?"

Bo tossed a rock over the cliff and watched it until it disappeared. "You say she was employed by Tamas?"

"As a mercenary, yes. To hunt down the Privileged."

"Likely she saw an opportunity she couldn't ignore. She doesn't like the other Predeii, and she certainly doesn't like me. You saw how hard she came after me. A woman scorned, and all that. I barely even slowed her down, and I had enough sorcerous traps on this trail to kill an army." He gave Taniel an annoyed look. "Too bad you sprang half of them."

Taniel frowned.

"You don't know?" Bo rubbed his temples. "God, how much do I have to explain? You're layered in protective sorcery tighter than your own skin. Not even the strongest Privileged can create that kind of protection on a person. The human body is just too complex. I wove spells on this mountainside strong enough to disable a god—I thought, anyway—and you walked through them without even noticing. I've not seen sorcery like that before. Wards are weaker around a Marked, and some of the strongest Marked, like Tamas, can unravel wards completely, but it takes time and practice."

"That's why you yelled at me not to come any farther."

"Yeah."

"Well..." Taniel flicked snow off his coat. There was so much he didn't know. Bo seemed to have a lot of answers, but even he couldn't provide them all. There was something going on in Adro, beyond the war and the coup and everything else, that was much deeper than anyone knew. It made his head hurt. "Who the pit has been weaving spells around me? I don't even...ah." *Her.*

Bo glanced into the cave, toward Ka-poel's sleeping form. "Tell me about the savage," he said.

Ka-poel was bundled tightly in her bedroll, not a finger's breadth of her visible but for a few stray red hairs sticking out from the top. The bedroll rose and fell steadily with her breathing.

"She's a Dynize," Taniel said. "Not from the Dynize Empire, but from the Fatrastan Wilds."

"How'd you come across her?"

Taniel said, "When Fatrasta declared their independence from Kez I joined up in the war. I spent about thirteen months using her village as a base during the war in Fatrasta. Her tribe was allied with the Fatrastans. I ranged all over southern Fatrasta from there, hitting Kez camps with my unit, killing Privileged and officers. Even a couple of Wardens. Her village was deep in the swamp, impossible to find unless a native showed you the way. It was the perfect place.

"Another tribe lived in the same swamp. They stayed neutral through most of the war, but toward the end of my time they were bought by the Kez. They attacked Ka-poel's village. Her people managed to fight them off, but not before they captured twenty or thirty children.

"The village wanted Fatrastan help getting the children back. The Fatrastans were spread too thin. They said no. My unit was ordered out of the village. I stayed behind and went with the natives to recover the children. Well, they'd killed most of them."

Taniel felt his mouth go dry. The memory haunted him, even now. The sight of dozens of children, crucified on barbed crosses, hung to rot from the twisted branches of moss-covered swamp trees.

"Why?" Bo asked.

Taniel snorted. "They wanted to show the Kez how savage they could really be. The Kez had offered barrels of whiskey, spices, rifles, horses. Anything they wanted in return for helping take down my unit. We'd caused them a lot of grief over that year."

"What'd you do in that village?"

Taniel tossed a rock off the edge of the cliff. "Justice," he said. "I'm not proud. But I don't regret it either."

Taniel watched wispy clouds form and roll and disappear with unseen air currents far off their cliff edge. He felt cold suddenly and wrapped his arms about himself. Memories of murder touched his mind, long shoved to the furthest part of his recollection and locked away. Perhaps there were a few things he'd regret.

He shook himself out of his reverie. "Anyway," he said. "Pole was quite a bit older than the others, but they had taken her just the same. Probably because she was a Bone-eye. I didn't know what that meant to them. I still don't. Yesterday was the first time I've seen her use her powers for more than just tracking, though I've long known she was a Privileged of sorts." Taniel scrounged about his person and his pack until he found a spare powder charge. He bit the end, tasting the sulfuric powder on his tongue, and snorted half the charge in one go.

Bo was watching him, a worried expression on his face. He edged away from the powder and scratched absently at his exposed skin.

"Oh, don't look at me like that," Taniel said.

"I've never seen sorcery like what she unleashed yesterday," Bo said. "Nor the protection woven about you. As far as the royal cabals are concerned, there are three different kinds of sorcerers: Privileged, Marked, and Knacked. We've encountered minor sorceries from witches, and shamans, and warlocks in the far places of the world, but nothing with the potency of what she showed. Does she have the third eye?"

"Yes, I'm certain," Taniel said. "She helps me track Privileged."

Bo reached out and pressed a palm against Taniel's forehead. He closed his eyes, muttering, and then jerked back. He dusted his palm off with snow. "God, you reek of powder. It's gonna make my eyes swell up and the space between my fingers itch. As for your protection. Ugh. I have no idea. It shrugged off my wards well enough. I don't know if it'll stop a bullet or a knife. It could just be against sorcery. Either way, don't risk it."

Taniel thought back to the fight with the cave lion—with Julene. He'd nearly slid off the mountainside, taking a long plummet to his death. Then rock had sprouted from the very earth, jutting out to catch him. He wondered if that had been Ka-poel or Bo. He didn't ask. He didn't want to grow to depend on someone else's protection. Bo might take credit even if it wasn't his. Or even the opposite. He'd always been unpredictable.

"Tamas sent me to kill you," Taniel said.

"Yeah."

They didn't look at each other.

"I didn't."

"Yeah." Bo's voice was wry. He gave Taniel a sidelong look, then a quick grin.

"Should I have?"

Bo's grin disappeared. "He knows about the gaes, then?"

"It's true?"

"Yes." Bo grunted. "Part of becoming a member of the royal cabal." He touched his collar gently. "I'll have to avenge the king someday. I'll have to kill Tamas." He pulled a pendant from beneath his shirt. It was a simple thing, braided silver around a single gemstone. Taniel vaguely remembered seeing similar necklaces upon dead Kez Privileged. Not even the savages had looted those.

"Is... is that it?" Taniel asked.

"A demon's carbuncle," Bo said. "Very dark stuff. You don't want to know. The gaes to protect—or avenge—the king is tied to this.

Even now I can feel a pull, tugging me toward Adopest. It's not very strong. It will grow stronger as time passes. I'm not sure how quickly. If I resist for too long, though, it will kill me."

"The only way to break it is to avenge the king?"

Bo remained silent.

"So you have to kill my father."

Bo picked up a rock and threw it off the cliff. He didn't look happy about it.

"We should start looking for a way to break it," Taniel said. He hoped he sounded confident. "Privileged wouldn't attach themselves to something they can't get out of. It's just another secret. Maybe one of the Predeii knows."

Taniel examined his friend, realizing just how much the fight yesterday had taken out of him. His cheeks were gaunt. His skin looked saggy, wrinkled, as if he were forty years older than he was.

"We'll find out together," Taniel said. "We'll break it. I swear."

Bo gave a tired chuckle. "My eyes are going to itch every day I'm with you, you optimistic bastard. Come on." He stood up, stretching. "We have to go find out if we killed that bitch."

CHAPTER 20

The parlor of Winceslav House was a spacious affair with ornate brick walls and a granite fireplace big enough to drive a pair of oxen through. Adamat had politely refused a seat from the butler and made his way slowly around the room as he waited for the lady of the house. There were a number of paintings of Lady Winceslav and her late husband, Henri Winceslav, as well as a single painting of the two of them with their four children. The painting was perhaps five years old, done just before the old duke passed away and each of the children had since been sent to boarding schools or resided in the country with their governesses, according to Adamat's research.

Adamat examined the floor, the walls, and the doors. A lot could be discovered about the waxing or waning fortunes of an Adran noble family by observing the state of their manor. When money was tight, upkeep and repairs often fell behind as housing staff were let go and materials became scarce.

Everything was pristine. The wood furniture and brass hangings were polished, the floor recently replaced, and the brickwork dusted. Her mercenaries had done quite well, even without Lord Winceslav to direct them. They fought in Fatrasta against the Kez, against the Gurlish on behalf of the Brudanians, and just about everywhere else colonists from the Nine had the coin to pay them.

Adamat had to remind himself that it wasn't Lord Winceslav alone who was responsible for the Wings. It was said Lady Winceslav had a mind sharp enough to match most field generals and that Lord Winceslav had relied heavily on her advice in all matters before his death. The lord had been clever; a man skilled with words and people. The lady was astute and practical; a forward-thinking planner.

Adamat faced the door when he heard voices in the hall outside. He smoothed the front of his waistcoat. A small group filed into the parlor: three men and a woman, all of them in white uniforms, military sashes of gold across their chests. Four brigadiers of the Wings of Adom. They were followed by Lady Winceslav. She wore a riding gown of fine purple wool, the collar pulled tight despite unseasonal warmth, and a matching shawl draped around her shoulders. Her heeled boots clicked on the wooden floor.

The commanders regarded Adamat with some wariness. He recognized two of them from paintings in the great hall outside: Brigadier Ryze was an older man, older even than Field Marshal Tamas, his hair as white as his uniform. He bore a number of visible scars on his hands and face and wore a white sash of linen across one eye to conceal a wound received in battle half a decade ago.

Brigadier Abrax was a woman, and her appearance could not have been more opposite Lady Winceslav's. Short blonde hair was cropped above her ears. Her face was tanned and weather-beaten from too many campaigns in Gurla. Her uniform matched the others' completely, apart from the slight bulge of small breasts. She regarded Adamat with a coldness he rarely felt from another person.

Introductions were short and brisk. The younger two were Brigadier Sabastenien and Brigadier Barat. Compared with their elders they were barely weathered, and looked almost like a pair of boys playing in their father's uniforms. They couldn't have been past their midtwenties. Brigadier Barat approached Adamat.

"I'd like to see your credentials, please," he said briskly.

Adamat narrowed his eyes at the impertinence. "I showed them to the butler when I arrived. They are in order."

"Even so..."

Adamat produced an envelope and handed it to the young brigadier. He forced himself to check his indignation. Unlike many modern armies, a commission in the Wings could not be bought. Everyone climbed the ranks. To be a brigadier at that age was remarkable.

Brigadier Barat read over Adamat's papers. He crossed the room to his elders and handed them one of the papers—the note from Tamas that granted him freedom in the investigation.

"Why," Brigadier Ryze said slowly, "does Tamas feel the need to imply threats to his closest advisers?"

"It's just a precaution," Adamat said. "An assurance that my investigation will proceed quickly, without any...hitches." But there would be plenty, he was sure. Tamas's note promised that anyone attempting to hamper Adamat's investigation in any way would be presumed guilty, yet a hundred of those notes wouldn't prevent nobles from trying to keep their secrets to themselves. Adamat wondered if Tamas would actually back up the threat if he were found facedown in the ditch outside the manor.

Brigadier Ryze handed the papers back to Brigadier Barat, who returned them to Adamat. Adamat took the papers from the younger brigadier without acknowledging him and returned the papers to his pocket. He could almost feel Barat seethe as he returned to his superiors. Barat had been plucked from the nobility, Adamat would wager. The type to look down on anyone beneath him and bend knee to anyone above him.

"Get on with it," Brigadier Ryze said. "Lady Winceslav has nothing to hide."

Adamat ran his gaze over the four brigadiers and turned pointedly to Lady Winceslav. She sat in one corner of the parlor, to the left and behind her brigadiers, as if she expected to be but a witness to an exchange of words. She seemed surprised when Adamat addressed her directly.

"Did you inform the Kez of the location of your meeting with Field Marshal Tamas?" he said.

"How dare you!" Brigadier Barat stood, hand going to the small sword at his side.

Adamat waited for a moment, giving the other brigadiers a chance to reprimand their younger comrade. They did not. Adamat pointed to Barat's chair with the tip of his cane. "Sit."

The brigadier blinked at him for a moment, jaw tightening, before he returned to his seat.

"Do I need to ask again, my lady?" Adamat said.

"I did not," Lady Winceslav said.

Adamat allowed himself a small smile. "Let us pray you are all as forthright and honest."

"That is unnecessary," Brigadier Abrax said. Her tone was like a schoolteacher's, the words said quickly, clipped off at the end.

Adamat paused for a moment. The brigadiers sat as if to form a shield around the Lady. He wondered if she was a fool to be prevented from speaking, of if they were really that protective of her.

"I am here to interview *you*, my lady," Adamat said. "I'm not here to receive condescension from your brigadiers. I'm sure you have servants for that." Adamat cringed inside. He was letting his annoyance do the talking. He could hear his old commanding officer from his young days in the force. The old man had been clear how you treat the nobility: *Never* antagonize them.

Lady Winceslav examined Adamat from beneath the brim of her riding hat for a moment. Her eyes were cool, her hands composed in her lap. She stood and crossed the room, taking a seat just opposite Adamat.

"Ask your questions, Inspector," she said. Despite her polite tone, there was an air of superiority to her words, and her nose was turned up slightly.

Adamat sighed inwardly. It was the best he was going to get. "Why did you support Tamas's coup?"

"I had many reasons," the Lady said. "For one, the Wings of Adom would have been disbanded if Manhouch had signed the Accords with the Kez."

"Why? The Wings of Adom are only *based* in Adro. They are not subservient to the king."

"It was a stipulation in the negotiations," she said. She leaned forward. "Do you know why Ipille wants Adro under his rule?"

"We have an abundance of natural resources," Adamat said.

"That is a reason, yes. But Ipille and his royal cabal fear Adro. In Kez, the nation is run by the court. Nothing happens without their say. Adro is different. Despite his flaws, Manhouch was an open-minded king. He allowed the union, the powder mages, and my mercenaries to all operate independently of the court. This made Adro stronger. The Kez royal cabal fear the powder mages will make them obsolete. They fear the Mountainwatch for their control of the major trade routes through the heart of the Nine. And they fear the Wings of Adom, for Henri gathered the greatest military minds and men of courage from throughout the Nine and bought—and earned—their loyalty. The Accords stipulated that the powder mages would be disbanded, that the Mountainwatch would be reduced, and that the Wings of Adom could no longer function from within Adro's borders." She shook her head. "I could not have that—I would not have that."

"You could have moved your headquarters to another country—even Fatrasta, far out of Ipille's influence."

"No," Lady Winceslav said. "My husband chose Adro because it was his land and his pride. The Wings of Adom are not just any mercenary army. They are a secondary defense of Adro—and that is how Tamas will be using them in the coming war. I will honor Henri's vision."

Adamat examined the Lady. Her cheeks were flushed, her tone raised. She felt strongly about her husband's mercenaries, and about Adro. If this was an act, it was a good one.

"Are the Wings being paid for their service to Adro?"

"They will receive a portion of the land confiscated from the nobility," the Lady said.

"And if the Kez offer payment greater than what Adro can muster?"

Lady Winceslav drew herself up. "The Wings of Adom have never once switched sides after taking a contract. I'm offended that you suggest we would."

"My apologies," he said. "Why else did you go along with the coup?"

Lady Winceslav composed herself. "I agreed with Tamas's opinion of the monarchy. It is an aged and corrupt institution."

"You yourself are a prominent member of the nobility."

Lady Winceslav removed an embroidered pocket fan from her sleeve and spread it out with the flick of her wrist. She began to fan herself. "Despite appearances, I was not born to such a position, nor was my husband. Henri was a soldier of fortune in Gurla, and I was the youngest daughter of a merchant. After Henri made his first fortune in textile manufacturing, he formed the Wings of Adom and purchased a duchy from an ailing old man without wife or children."

Adamat blinked. "Duke Winceslav was not his father?"

She read his expression and gave a light laugh. "Kresimir, no. This is not common knowledge, of course. In fact, few people outside this room know about it. Tamas is one of them. I tell you only in the hope that it helps remove me as a suspect in your mind. Tamas and I are kindred spirits. I would never want him dead."

Adamat let his eyes travel over the four mercenary commanders. They stared back at him, unblinking, sharp as hawks.

"Did you tell anyone, even the closest of confidants, about the meeting of the council?"

"No," Lady Winceslav said, her chin raised. "Tamas forbade it. Not even my brigadiers knew." She shot them a glance. "Much to their chagrin."

Adamat asked a few more basic questions before he sat back and folded his hands in his lap. He struggled to hide a grimace. Nothing. Winceslav was a lady through and through. Polite and charming, and her cards held close to her chest. That bit about her husband buying the duchy . . . Adamat was sure that any of her enemies who could have used that against her were taken to the guillotine last month.

"Thank you for being so forthright," Adamat said, careful to inject the proper amount of sincerity into his tone. "I do appreciate it." He turned to the butler, who had just entered the room. "Is the manor's staff gathered?"

The aged man gave a curt nod.

Adamat stood as Lady Winceslav did. The brigadiers followed suit. Adamat took her offered hand and touched his forehead to it. "I will finish with your staff as quickly as possible."

"My staff and manor grounds are yours for the day, Inspector," she said.

"One last thing, my lady." Adamat paused in the doorway. "Do you have reason to suspect any of the other members of the council?"

Lady Winceslav paused halfway to her chair. She sat back down. "None that come immediately to mind. Charlemund is a man of Kresimir. I would never suspect the vice-chancellor; Prime is an old family friend—a scholar. The Proprietor must be at the top of your list. He is a criminal, after all, despite his connections. I'd heard that Ondraus and Tamas have been arguing about the city ledgers for weeks, though I'm sure there's nothing more to that." She frowned. "I did hear that Ricard Tumblar sent a delegation from his union to Kez just after the coup. Seems he wants to start a chapter there."

Lady Winceslav rose and bid him good day. The brigadiers filed out behind her, leaving him alone with the butler.

Adamat interviewed the house staff and groundskeepers for hours before he moved outside and began to walk around the manor grounds. SouSmith joined him outside, looking almost as if he'd burst through the chest of his new suit of clothes.

"Well?" SouSmith asked.

"She is a capable old vixen," Adamat said. "Despite what her brigadiers want us to think." He glanced over his shoulder. Brigadier Barat and Brigadier Abrax had appeared from a side door after he exited the house. They made no effort to conceal that they were following him and SouSmith. Adamat spied an outbuilding some ways off and veered into a field toward it, just to see how far the brigadiers would follow them.

"The brigadiers are very protective of her. I think it is more likely one of *them* betrayed Tamas, rather than that she did—though she claims none of them knew the location of the meeting. Of course, that doesn't rule out that she was spied upon, or even . . ." He mulled over the idea before speaking it out loud. "Or even spoke in her sleep."

SouSmith gave him a look.

"I cannot rule out the idea," Adamat said, "however improper, that she's sleeping with one or more of her brigadiers. I don't see her as the type to bed a woman, so that rules out Abrax. Sabastenien and Barat are both handsome young men, while Ryze has a particular grizzled quality that women of all ages find attractive."

They followed an old track as it looped toward the horse stables and out of sight of the manor house through a thick forest. The two brigadiers remained a comfortable distance behind them.

"Not one of the staff has seen anything suspicious in the previous two months. They remember Tamas visiting a number of times over the last year, but not once since the coup. There have been no strangers about the place, no one to suggest a Kez agent." Adamat shook his head. "She will start low on my list of suspects. One thing did bother me, however. She mentioned that Ricard Tumblar sent a delegation to King Ipille of Kez. I had not heard that from any other source. It makes me wonder..." He tapped his cane on the ground. "We're done here."

They reached their waiting carriage a dozen paces ahead of brigadiers Abrax and Barat. Adamat turned at the door of the carriage and leaned against it, waiting for the pair. They approached him without hesitation.

Brigadier Abrax spoke. She was distant, cold, as if she was thinking of a battle far away and barely had the time—or interest—in Adamat. "I hope your investigation has been concluded in regard to our mistress, Investigator," she said.

"My investigation is ongoing," Adamat replied. "I'll be sure to inform Lady Winceslav if she is needed further."

"She *will not* be bothered," Barat said. Abrax gave him an unreadable look, and he fell quiet.

Adamat pretended to ignore Barat, focusing his eyes on Abrax. Inwardly, he examined the young brigadier. Why was he so protective? Son-like affection for the widow, or something deeper. Aloud, he said, "I'm conducting an investigation. I'm not some salesman, harrying your mistress without cause. Now then." He opened the carriage door. "I have other suspects to *bother*."

Brigadier Barat stepped forward as the carriage door shut and put his hand on the windowsill. "Brigadiers of the Wings of Adom are not to be trifled with, Inspector. Do not push the limits of your authority."

Adamat pushed the brigadier's fingers from the carriage window with the end of his cane. "Don't try my patience, young man. I've dealt with worse than you." Adamat rapped twice on the ceiling and the carriage began to move. That one would be a problem sooner or later.

"Bo says you've wrapped me in protective sorcery."

Taniel fell into step beside Ka-poel. She gave him a sidelong glance, her green eyes unreadable. She'd avoided him as they made their way off the mountain, by walking either far behind or far ahead. It could have been coincidence that she was always bundled to the ears, unable to talk whenever they passed close by. He thought not. She knew he wanted to ask questions.

Another long glance. They kept trudging through the snow, snowshoes making the going slow and awkward, but saving them from falling through the soft middle layer and having to wade through the stuff.

"Thank you," Taniel said.

Her next look was surprise. He resisted a smile.

"He says you're very powerful," Taniel said.

She paused for a moment and turned toward him.

"I wonder what I did to deserve your protection."

Ka-poel reached out a bare hand and touched his face.

Taniel had an image of Ka-poel in the back of a muddy hut, naked and afraid, crying. They'd blinded her with some herb to keep her from trying to escape, and, unseeing, she had flailed about with a sharp stick, trying to kill one of her captors, when Taniel had entered the hut. She'd recognized his voice, and he'd been able to calm her. He remembered the cuts on her stomach and thighs, and the blood on her face.

The vision left Taniel gasping. He slowed down to steady himself, suddenly weak in the knees. Had she done that? The vision had been from his own eyes. How could she…? He shook his head. He'd ceased trying to guess what she could or couldn't do.

They reached a lip of the trail overlooking the Mountainwatch. Bo was a few paces ahead of them, and when Taniel heard a sharp inhalation of breath from Bo, Taniel rushed up beside him.

It seemed the whole world spread out beneath them. Not far below, Shouldercrown sat on the mountain ridge separating Kez and Adro, like a cork in the center of a dam. Below that, tiny from this height, Taniel saw men.

They filled the basin just below Shouldercrown on the Kez side. There was a sea of tents, and roads that looked like serpents leading back to the center of Kez, each one of them writhing like lines of ants.

"An army," Bo breathed.

"The whole damned Grand Army." Taniel took a snort of black powder.

Gavril grunted. "Or well near it."

"Where the pit did they come from?" Taniel asked. "We've been on the mountain, what, six days?"

"Seven," Gavril said.

"They weren't there when we left," Taniel said.

Gavril just shrugged. "I was too drunk to know."

"They weren't there," Taniel said with certainty. "War was declared"—he did some math in his head—"less than three weeks ago. How could they possibly gather the entire army in that time? And why are they here, when Surkov's Alley is an easier target?"

Taniel found they were all looking at Bo.

"Julene," Bo said with a sniff.

"No," Taniel said. "No way she knew about the army. She's been with me for five weeks."

"It's not *her* army," Bo said. "But I'd be willing to bet she's going to use it."

"How?"

"Plans within plans," Bo said. He avoided Taniel's gaze. "She let slip once that she's well known in the Kez court."

"We're not going to find her body, are we?"

Bo shook his head. "She fell on the Kez side anyway."

"Then what now?" Taniel asked.

Gavril took a deep breath. "We take our places at the Mountainwatch. We do what the Mountainwatch has done for a thousand years." He drew himself up. "We defend Adro."

They reached the fortress by the middle of the afternoon. A small group of men and women waited at the northeast gate. Closer, a group of three women were rushing up the path. Taniel didn't even need to guess who they were.

Privileged were magnetic to the opposite sex. Most agreed it was their bearing and power. It was common knowledge that their constant interactions with the Else gave them incredible sex drives, so few Privileged, especially the males, went without a harem. Bo was no exception.

Bo pushed them and their questions away with a brusque wave of his hand and instead went with Fesnik and another Watcher named Mozes, who took him away without a word. Ka-poel disappeared at some point, leaving Taniel alone with Gavril.

"I want to get a better look at that army," Gavril said.

Taniel followed him across the bastion. He'd need to get a good look at this army to report to Tamas.

Workers were everywhere. Taniel had not imagined so many people could fit in the Mountainwatch bastion and he wondered if reinforcements had been sent from Adopest. Watchers rushed around in a frenzy, most of them carrying muskets or rifles. Despite the hurry, no one seemed to actually be *doing* anything. The Watch was in top shape and they'd done their preparations. Now they awaited the attack.

The southern wall of the fortress was an ancient bastion, designed with the contours of the mountain in mind. The reality of artillery fire meant that the town could be bombarded quite easily from falling munitions, while the wall itself would remain almost undisturbed. The points of the bastion were filled with fixed gun emplacements—as many as could be crammed into the space. It fairly bristled.

Taniel and Gavril went out to the tip of the bastion. They could see the whole mountainside from here and Taniel couldn't help but wonder how suicidal the Kez troops would have to be to attempt to take the Mountainwatch. There were miles of switchbacks within clear sight of artillery and small arms, and only one flat approach to the main fortress—straight up the road. Anywhere else, they'd have to scale the mountainside and then the wall, all while under fire from above.

Taniel held up his thumb, trying to gauge distance.

"There's a town halfway down the mountain," Gavril said. "Called Mopenhague. They've set their advance camp there."

"How far?"

"In a straight line?" Gavril said. "Three miles. Just out of range of artillery."

"Not too far for me." Taniel would crease a few heads when the fighting started, and they'd have to move their camp back another mile.

"Novi's toes!" Gavril was frowning down the mountain. "Those idiots." He grabbed a young Watcher by the shoulder and pointed down the slope. "Who's letting them get this close? They're within musket range, no problem. Almost to our redoubts!"

The boy shrugged. "Sorry. They've just been coming up. No one's given the order to fire. We sent a runner to Adopest when the army arrived, but we haven't gotten orders yet."

Taniel searched the slope for where Gavril had been pointing. There was a thin ribbon of men moving up and down the switchbacks. Their uniforms were sand-colored with green trim. Kez infantry. They carried timber and tools, and they were coming up just below the redoubts. Adran soldiers in the redoubts simply watched as the men worked.

"Pit," Gavril said. He stormed down to the gate and out into the road. Taniel snatched up his rifle and a spare powder horn and followed.

The redoubts were a series of six small forts jutting out from the corners of the first few switchbacks down the mountainside. They contained one small fixed gun each and enough men to staff them with a few riflemen beside. The snow had been shoveled from them recently, the big guns moved out from the fortress. Taniel guessed no one had staffed those redoubts for a hundred years.

Taniel and Gavril descended to the last redoubt on the mountainside. Gavril crossed the walk over the switchback below.

"Who's the corporal of this redoubt?" Gavril asked.

A man raised his hand. He was regular army, wearing the blue of Tamas's forces, sent up from Adopest to reinforce the Mountainwatch. He gave Gavril a skeptical look. "Me. Who are you?"

"A Watcher," he said. "Why are you letting the Kez set up artillery stations and"—he glanced over the wall—"sapper tunnels?"

Taniel frowned. Why would the Kez be working on sapper tunnels? They were too far out to undermine the bastion, and the redoubts could be rushed with enough men—certainly the preferred choice for most generals. They were simply a point at which to give advance fire. As soon as the enemy got past the switchback below, the men would retreat to the fortress.

"Look, I don't have to take this from you," the corporal said, interrupting Gavril's berating. "I may not be a Watcher, but I still outrank you... whoever you are."

Taniel wasn't sure of Gavril's rank. The Mountainwatch had their own system. He pointed to his powder keg pin. "And I outrank you. Listen to him," he said.

The corporal scowled at Gavril, though Gavril was two heads taller and twice his weight. "Well, what are we supposed to do?" the corporal asked.

Taniel could hear the big mountaineer's teeth grinding.

"Your rifle loaded?" Gavril asked.

Taniel handed him the rifle. Gavril gave it a once-over, running a finger down the length of the barrel with an admiring whistle. "This," he said.

He leaned out over the bulwark and fired. A sapper not fifty yards away pitched to the ground. Kez workers scrambled for cover.

Gavril handed Taniel his rifle. "The war's started," he said to the corporal. "Rake those bastards with shot until they're all running scared, or until they get Privileged up here to slap you down."

The corporal looked to Taniel for affirmation. "Go at it," Taniel said.

Taniel walked beside Gavril as they headed back to the fortress. Behind them, intermittent musket fire began to pop, followed by the shouts of Kez soldiers.

"Won't a Privileged just stamp out these redoubts without a thought?" Taniel asked.

The light artillery thumped behind them. "Go at it!" Gavril shouted to the next redoubt. "Anyone that comes in range!" To Taniel, he said, "This whole mountainside is warded. Every brick of those redoubts, and of the bastion, was slathered in protective sorcery when it was built."

"That was hundreds of years ago," Taniel said, glancing back uncertainly. The Kez royal cabal would come soon, he had no doubt of it. He wondered how long Bo could hold them off. Not long. He was just one Privileged.

"They had stronger stuff back then," Gavril said. "They say the power of the Privileged has waned over the centuries since gunpowder. They used to be able to make wards to last a thousand years. Now it's not often that wards will last past a Privileged's death."

Gavril seemed to know a lot about sorcerers and the like. Taniel studied Gavril for a few moments. He barely resembled the drunk who'd guided Taniel up the side of the mountain a week ago.

Mozes, Bo, and Fesnik were waiting for them on the bastion when they reached the fortress.

"I see you started the shooting," Bo said. He held a cloth over his nose and mouth. Taniel sniffed the air. Clouds from the black powder were already blowing up toward them. It would soon get far worse. Bo was not going to have a good time once the artillery lit up.

"Someone needed to," Gavril said. Watchers had come running at the sound of gunfire and now watched as the sappers began to retreat down the mountain. "Ho there," Gavril said to a nearby group. "Prime the batteries. Give them some support. We don't lack ammunition. I don't want those sappers getting to the bottom of the mountain."

Bo and Mozes exchanged a long look. "You're taking charge, then?" Mozes said.

"Pit, no," Gavril said. "Just prepping the men for Jaro. Where is he?"

Mozes shook his head. "Something's taken him. He's far sicker than we imagined. Can barely move. Doctor says he might not live out the night."

Gavril's eyes looked sad for a moment, and then it was gone behind a stony façade. "So be it." He whirled on one foot and marched down along the bulwarks. "You there! Bring those balls.

More powder kegs!" He was off, giving orders, throwing about his ham-sized fists.

"Wait," Taniel said. Jaro must have been the Watchmaster. "*He's* second in command?"

"Used to be Watchmaster, before he started drinking," Bo said. Mozes had gone off after Gavril, and Fesnik went to fetch a rifle.

"Sure, he was a competent guide, but... *him*?"

"Yes. Him." Bo shook his head. "He, uh... well, it's not my place to tell you. Gavril's our man, don't worry. Ah," he added, glancing over the bulwark. "I see they're getting ready to hit back."

A company of men had left Mopenhague. Another company was lining up behind them, and then another. It looked like they were going to try an early rush. It would be close to dark before they got close enough to take a shot. But the war had started.

"Next!" a man called.

Nila shuffled to the head of the line. She stood on the front step of the House of Nobles, at the heart of the Adran army in their new headquarters. Somewhere behind her, the guillotines that had taken the nobility were long gone, but the stains from the blood they'd shed still remained. The sun beat down on her shoulders, the wind mussing her auburn curls. She smoothed her hair against her head. In her new dress she looked a hundred times richer than anyone else in the unemployment line.

The man behind the table looked her up and down. "You don't look like you need a job," he said. He wore a blue Adran army uniform with the staff emblem of a quartermaster on his breast beneath three service stripes.

"I'm a laundress," Nila said, holding her head high. "I keep my clothes pristine."

"Laundress, heh? Dole, the Noble Warriors of Labor need any laundresses?"

A man sitting behind the next table over looked up at Nila. "No," he said. "Boss says we have too many already."

Nila shifted her skirt around. "I heard the army was looking for laundresses."

"Lass, a girl with your looks should not join the army." The quartermaster leaned back. "It's just a bad idea."

"I heard they pay well. Provide a tent and everything. I could make ten times what a soldier does."

"That's true," the quartermaster said. "But I wouldn't brag about it if I were you. We pay better than the union for someone with skills. Are you sure?"

"I need the money," Nila said. She jerked her head toward the empty spot the guillotines had once held. "My last employer wound up losing his head, and no one else pays as well."

"Hear that story a lot these days," the quartermaster said. "You're not one of those royalists, are ya?"

Nila leaned forward and spoke in a low voice. "My lord took me to bed twice a day since I was eleven," she said, injecting as much venom as she could into her voice. "I spit on his head when it dropped."

"I see." The quartermaster chewed on the end of his pen. "You've got fire. Something tells me you can handle yourself. Still, I'll put you working for the officers. Safer with them. Usually. Can you sew? I think the field marshal needs a seamstress."

"That would be perfect," Nila said, smiling the first real smile she'd had in weeks.

CHAPTER

21

Tamas awoke to the sound of his own labored gasps. He sat up, leaning on his elbows, struggling to breathe. It felt like a millstone sat upon his chest. He kicked away the blankets that were wrapped around his feet and sat up, leaning over the edge of his bed.

He slept in his office on the top floor of the House of Nobles these days, forsaking the thick cushions of the royal sofa for a simple but comfortable soldier's cot set up in the corner of the room. The cot, heavy-duty canvas, was soaked through with his sweat, as were his bedclothes and hair. He wrapped his arms about himself, suddenly shivering as his sweat began to cool. The clock, visible by bright moonlight, said it was half past three in the morning.

His dreams came back to him, like memories of long years ago, broken and blurry. His hands shook when he thought of them, and it wasn't from the cold. Men died in his dreams—soldiers he'd known his whole life, friends and acquaintances, even enemies. Everyone he'd ever known. They lined the rim of South Pike Mountain and one by one they leapt into a fiery cauldron. Taniel was there too, though his fate was obscured. He shuddered. Where was Vlora in those dreams? He'd seen Sabon leap into that volcano, but where was Olem?

Tamas took a shaky breath. He made his way to the balcony window and stood for a moment, watching the full moon. The night sky was empty except for a single ribbon of cloud that formed a perfect circle around the moon. God's eye. Tamas began to shiver again, violently, until the shivers turned to shudders. He gripped the wall with both hands until it passed.

He heard a familiar whine and looked down. "Hrusch," he said to the hound. "I'm all right. Where's Pitlau—" He stopped, the name disappearing in an involuntary cough. "Right. Sorry, boy." He bent, offering the hound his hand. "I'll take you on a hunt soon. Get your mind off things."

Tamas found his slippers and ran fingers through his hair. He donned his dressing gown and opened the door to the hallway, blinking against the light. Olem stirred in a chair beside the door. Across from him, Vlora slept in another chair, leaning on her rifle, snoring softly. Farther down the hall a pair of guards waited beneath the lamplight. His commanders had doubled the guard after the Warden's assassination attempt.

"Sir," Olem said. He stubbed out a cigarette on the arm of his chair.

"Don't you ever sleep?"

"No, sir. That's why you hired me."

"It was a joke, Olem."

"I gathered."

"Things quiet?" Tamas asked.

"Very, sir. Not a peep in the place." Olem's voice was quiet, subdued.

Tamas nodded at Vlora. "What's she doing here?"

"Worried about you, sir."

Tamas sighed.

"Are you OK, sir?"

Tamas gave a nod. "Bad dreams."

"My grandmammie used to say bad dreams were bad omens," Olem said.

Tamas glared at the soldier. "Thanks, that makes me feel much better. I'm going to get something to eat." He shuffled down the hall.

Olem gave him some space, trailing along at ten paces all the way down the stairs. The trip six floors down to the kitchens seemed much longer in dark corridors, and Tamas had to admit that Olem was some comfort when shadows in doorways played upon his imagination, reaching for him from the darkness. He jumped once, thinking he saw the hunkering figure of a Warden waiting in a corner. Closer inspection revealed a coal-burning stove.

Tamas had hoped to find in the kitchens some scraps from last night's dinner and be back up in his room in minutes, yet when he approached the kitchen, he saw the low glow of ovens and smelled fresh bread. His mouth began to water—a sure sign he was near Mihali's cooking. He stepped into the room, pausing at a sight he didn't expect.

Two women stood at one of the stoves. They worked over an enormous pan, as big as a wagon wheel, cracking eggs and tossing the shells to the side. Mihali stood just behind them—*just* behind them, his body pressed close to theirs, an arm on either side of the two women, hands moving nimbly above the pan. He added a dash of salt, then one hand dipped down, eliciting a startled giggle from one of the women before appearing again with his knife and a whole green pepper, nimbly slicing it into the pot.

Tamas cleared his throat. The two girls jumped, eyes growing wide at the sight of Tamas. Mihali stepped away from them, moving smoothly despite his girth, and grinned.

"Field Marshal!" he said. He wiped his hands on his apron and patted each girl on the cheek, then headed over to Tamas. "You look like you haven't had a good night."

"You look like you have," Tamas said. "I've seen it all now: seduction by way of omelet."

It was hard to tell in such poor light, but Mihali seemed to turn red in the face. "Simply early-morning lessons, Field Marshal," he said. "Bellony and Tasha are the most promising of my pupils. They deserve extra attention."

"Pupils?" Tamas asked. "I thought they were assistants."

"Every assistant is a pupil. If they don't learn, what good are they? Every master must be prepared to be bettered, as my father was before me. Someone will create more amazing dishes than I someday. Perhaps it will be one of these two."

"I have doubts about that," Tamas said. He glanced toward the two women. One was older, perhaps in her thirties, a handsome-faced woman with a body rounded in all the right places. The other was young and slightly plump with dimples on her cheeks. They watched Mihali more than they watched their pan, with expressions Tamas only saw on two types of people: young lovers and religious sycophants. Tamas wondered which they were.

"You are not sleeping well?" Mihali asked.

Tamas shrugged. "Bad dreams."

"Bad omens, more like."

Olem's soft voice came from the doorway. "I told him."

Mihali gave Tamas a critical look-over. "Warm milk."

"That's never worked for me," Tamas said. "Do you ever sleep? It's three in the morning."

"Three forty-five," Mihali said, though there were no clocks in the kitchen. "I've needed little sleep since I was a boy. Papa told me it was because of the god's touch in me."

"Your father believed you?" Tamas asked. "I don't mean to be rude. You'd said before that he told you to keep quiet about being Adom reborn."

"No offense taken." Mihali edged over to an empty table and began to produce a number of small, clay spice bottles from his apron pockets. There were no labels, but he set them down in a very specific order on the table. "He believed me. He just knew of the problems I'd face if it became public knowledge."

"And now?" Tamas said. "You've told me, and I think word is spreading about your claims." He glanced at the two women. Which was it? Religious adoration, or love? Or both? They still watched Mihali, until one of them noticed that the omelet was smoking and turned around with a cry of dismay.

A smile played upon Mihali's lips. He produced a mortar and pestle and began to grind herbs together. "My claims?" Mihali said. "You don't believe me, do you?"

"I... don't know," Tamas said. "It's a lot to swallow. I've seen what you do with food—how you can make it appear. I've never heard of any sorcery like that. And I've seen the glow of the Knack around you."

Mihali seemed startled by this. "You noticed?"

"Yes, well, you did it right in front of Olem and me."

"Oh. No one is supposed to notice that. I usually pay better attention. Papa told me to hide it when I was a boy. Said the royal cabals or the Church would come for me if they found out."

Tamas examined Mihali's face for any sign of a lie. Mihali was concentrating on his work, combining herbs until he was satisfied with the result. He produced a dark powder and added it to the mixture. "Tasha," he said. "Warm some goat's milk, please."

"I thought you were doing it on purpose," Tamas said slowly. "Perhaps to convince us of your... godhood."

Mihali gave him a shy smile. "I've never been a flashy god," he said. "I leave that to Kresimir."

"You've also been serving dishes very foreign to Adro," Tamas said. "We don't have eels in the Adsea, for instance. You use expensive spices like they were simply flour or water. I served in Gurla for a time. I know what these things can cost, and I know Ondraus doesn't approve this kind of money for food. Is that your Knack? Producing food from thin air?"

Mihali scratched his thin mustache. "Yes, I've been kind of obvious, haven't I? Should I... hide myself?"

"Maybe," Tamas said. Mihali had the Knack, no doubt. Tamas might need his powers someday. Did he humor the madman chef? "Remain quiet, I think. As a precaution."

"May I ask you what your dreams were about?"

"I remembered them when I first awoke," Tamas said. "But now they're fleeting. I think everyone I knew—no, not everyone, but most of the people I knew stood on the rim of South Pike and jumped into the mountain. My son was there too, though I don't know what happened to him and..." He stopped, a memory coming back to him. "Someone stood on the rim with us. Someone I'd never seen before. His eyes were like fire, his hair like gold tinsel. He was urging everyone to jump in, and he held a knife to Taniel's throat."

"Can I tell you something?" Mihali said softly.

Tamas took a step closer to hear him better. "Certainly."

Mihali took a cup from one of the women. "Thank you, Tasha," he said. "I've been listening to the city." Mihali added his mixture of herbs to the warm milk and stirred it with one thick finger. He handed it to Tamas. Almost absently, Tamas took a sip. His eyes widened. He'd had Fatrastan chocolate once or twice. It was too bitter. This had a similar taste, but sweeter, and with a hot, peppery bite. Spice burned his tongue and herbs soothed it, and it rushed warmly down his throat like the finest of brandy. He tilted the cup back, draining the last drop.

Mihali said, "There is danger and betrayal everywhere. Adopest is a bubbling cauldron, and the temperature must be lowered or it will boil over. Before Kresimir comes. I think…I think I need to prepare a welcome for my brother. Good night, Field Marshal."

Tamas glanced down as Mihali took the mug from him. He heard Mihali say, as if from a distance, "You'll need to carry him up to bed. He shouldn't have any problem sleeping now."

"Adamat, my old friend!"

Ricard Tumblar stood in the doorway to a small office, arms spread wide. The years had changed Ricard since Adamat had last seen him. His full head of curly brown hair had retreated halfway across his scalp and was touched with wisps of gray. He wore his beard long in the fashion of Fatrastan settlers. His expensive suit of camel hair was rumpled as if it had been slept in, and his cravat was askew. Adamat embraced his old friend.

"It's good to see you, Ricard," Adamat said.

Ricard grinned ear to ear. He took Adamat by the shoulders, looking him in the face like a long-lost brother. "How have you been?"

"Well enough," Adamat said. "Yourself?"

"I certainly can't complain. Please, sit." He led Adamat into the office. It was a jumbled mess of books, half-empty bottles of brandy, and dirty plates of food. Ricard swept a pile of newspapers off a chair and went around behind his desk. He slid open a window with a grunt.

"Coel!" he shouted out the window. "Coel, bring us some wine. A bottle of the Pinny! Two glasses—no, better make it two bottles."

He slid the window shut behind him, but not before the small room filled with the smell of dead fish and the brackish water of the Adsea. Ricard wrinkled his nose and produced a match from his breast pocket, lighting the half-burned butt of incense on a shelf above his desk. "I can't abide that smell," he said. "It's everywhere down here, and we're a half mile from the docks. But"—he shrugged—"what can I do? I have to be near where the action is."

"I've heard great things about your progress with the union," Adamat said. Not long after they graduated school, Ricard had started his first trade union. It had failed, as well as half a dozen others, perhaps because of the lack of manpower or because the police had been called in to shut him down. Ricard had been jailed five times. But persistence paid off, and five years ago Manhouch legalized the first trade union in the Nine.

Ricard's smile grew wider, if possible. "The Noble Warriors of Labor. We've opened three chapter houses since the Elections, and we're in talks with city councils to open six more by the end of the year. We've over a hundred thousand members, and my number crunchers tell me that is just the beginning. We could have a million members in another few years, maybe more. We've unionized metallurgy, coal coking, mining—all of Adro's biggest industries."

"Not all of them," Adamat said. "I hear Hrusch Avenue is giving you problems."

Ricard snorted. "Damned gunsmiths don't want to unionize."

"Can't blame them," Adamat said. "They already produce half the weapons used in all the Nine. They're not worried about competition."

"And it'd be the whole world if they unionized! Organization is key. Bah," Ricard said. "What we're really excited about is the canal going over the Charwood Pile and through Deliv. When that's finished, we'll have a direct route to the ocean from Adro, and there will be no limit on our production capabilities. Adro will finally have a shipping lane to the ocean." He suddenly made a face. "But dear me, it's rude to talk about my fortunes like this..." Ricard trailed off awkwardly.

Adamat waved dismissively. "You speak of my failed business?

Think nothing of it. It was a gamble to begin with, and I bet the wrong way. I could blame it on the price of paper, or the stalwart competition…"

"Or the exploding printing press."

"Or that," Adamat said. "But I've still got my family and my friends, so I'm a rich man."

"How is Faye?" Ricard asked.

"Quite well," Adamat said. "She's staying out in the country until things have stabilized a little more here in the capital. I've been thinking of having her remain until the war's over, in fact."

Ricard nodded. "War is the pit."

A young man with scrawny arms and old, cast-off clothing entered the room with a bottle of wine and a pair of crystal wineglasses.

"I said two, damn you!" Ricard said.

The young man seemed unperturbed by Ricard's shouting. "There was only one left." He let the platter drop on Ricard's desk with a clang and beat a hasty retreat, dodging a cuff from Ricard's fist.

"Impossible to find good help," Ricard said, steadying the wobbling bottle of wine.

"Indeed."

Ricard poured the wine. The goblets were dirty, but the wine was chilled. They drank two glasses each before exchanging another word.

"You know why I'm here?" Adamat asked.

"Yes," Ricard said. "Ask your questions; I'm no fop to take offense. You've got a job to do."

This would be a relief, Adamat decided. He leaned forward. "Do you have any reason to see Field Marshal Tamas dead?"

Ricard scratched his beard. "I suppose. He's been grumbling lately that he wants to see a reduction in the size of the union. Says we're gaining too much power, too fast." He spread his hands. "If he decides to put a cap on our manpower, or to tax our earnings heavily, it could cause a big problem for the Warriors."

"Big enough to have him killed?"

"Certainly. But one has to weigh the benefits and risks. Tamas is tolerant of the unions—he supports their existence, despite our being outlawed for almost a thousand years now. Manhouch only allowed me to set up the Warriors because of the exorbitant taxes he planned on getting from us. We were able to dodge enough of them to make it cost-effective for us to exist."

"If you could exist under Manhouch, why did you support the coup?"

"A number of Manhouch's accountants were taking a closer look at our books. They realized they weren't getting nearly as much in taxes as they'd planned, and his advisers were encouraging him to have us disbanded entirely. The nobility hated us. They hate having to pay workers more, even if it means higher production. Even if Manhouch hadn't had us disbanded, the Accords put Adro under Kez colonial law—which would have found me and the rest of the union bosses in prison or worse, and the Warriors disbanded anyways, our property confiscated."

"You said there would be risks for you, in having Tamas killed?" Adamat said.

"Mostly questions. I don't have a lot of friends in the council. Lady Winceslav tolerates me. The reeve hates me because my accountants are almost as good as his and the Diocel has excommunicated me twice. Prime Lektor thinks I'm a fool, and the Proprietor—well, the Proprietor enjoys the bribes the union pays him. If Tamas were killed, that would leave me with only two supporters on the council, both of whom could turn on me."

Adamat took a sip of his wine. *It may be that one already has*, he thought, remembering what Lady Winceslav had said.

"Word has it you sent a delegation to Ipille."

Ricard sat back. "Who told you that?"

"You know better than to ask me that."

"Bah. You and your sources. I forget sometimes that you seem to know everything. Even things done in the deepest of secrecy."

"So you did?"

Ricard shrugged. "Of course. Not even Tamas knows. Not that I'm hiding anything," he said quickly, throwing up a hand.

"Why the secrecy if you aren't hiding anything?" Adamat found himself on edge. Old friend or not, if Ricard was dealing behind Tamas's back, friendship was cheap currency.

"I told you we might make a million members?"

"Yes."

"Well, imagine if that could be ten million. Or a hundred million?"

"You're talking every working man in all the Nine."

Ricard nodded solemnly. "The Warriors sent a small delegation to Ipille. Nothing so underhanded as trying to sell out Adro, mind you. Simply a letter of intent that the Warriors want to spread outside Adro throughout the whole Nine. It's well known the Kez outnumber us, but they don't have anything to match our industry. We offered a number of small incentives if they let us start a chapter house in one of their cities."

"I see," Adamat said. He examined the inside of his wineglass. He understood perfectly why Ricard had done it in secrecy. With the war on, Tamas would not want even an inkling of anyone helping the Kez. And the Kez would have much to gain from the unions. Kez was primarily an agricultural country. They had yet to embrace industry, not the way Adro did, so they were behind in technology and production despite their immense population. If the Warriors spread to Kez, their knowledge of Adran manufacturing would spread with them. As Ricard said, the Kez could not match Adran industry. Yet.

"Have you received an answer?"

Ricard made a face. He looked around his desk, then on the

shelves, and finally found what he was looking for underneath a crust of half-eaten bread. He tossed a paper into Adamat's lap.

It bore the royal seal of King Ipille of Kez. Adamat ran his eyes across the contents.

"They rejected you."

"With venom," Ricard said. "My men were thrown from the palace by their belts. The Kez are fools. Idiots. They remain in the last century, while the rest of the world already looks to the next. Damned nobles."

Adamat considered this. This lead was gone, anyway. Unless there were further negotiations going on beneath the surface—such a thing wasn't unheard of. Adamat would dig deeper if need be. Ricard was not such a good friend that Adamat wouldn't see whether his story held water.

Ricard drained the last of the wine straight from the bottle. He set it down on the desk on its side and spun it. "Maies left me last month, right after the coup."

Maies was his sixth wife in twenty years. Adamat couldn't help but wonder what he'd done this time.

"Are you all right?"

Ricard's eyes were on the spinning bottle. "Doing fine. An office near the dockyards has its perks. I found a pair of twins..." He held his hands out in front of his chest. "I could introduce you—"

Adamat cut him off. "I'm a happily married man—and I want it to stay that way." Ricard wasn't the type of man to share. Adamat couldn't even be sure what kind of an offer that was. "What do you think of the other councillors?" Adamat asked, changing the subject.

"Personally?"

"I don't care if you like them. I care if you think one of them would plot against Tamas."

"Charlemund," Ricard said without hesitation. "That man's a cave lion in the henhouse." He shook his head. "You've heard stories about his villa, right? A pleasure villa for the high and mighty just outside of the city."

"Rumors," Adamat said. "Nothing more."

"Oh, they're true," Ricard said. "Makes me blush, and I'm no innocent virgin. Any man with appetites like that has designs for the country. Mark my words."

"Do you have any proof? Any solid suspicions?"

"No. Of course not. He's a dangerous man. The Church already speaks out against the Warriors. Says we're going against Kresimir's will by not rolling over and letting the nobility work us to death for nothing. I'm not putting my nose in that."

"What about Ondraus?" Adamat said.

Ricard became very still. "Watch that one," he said. "He's more than he seems."

An odd warning from Ricard.

"Well, let me know if you get any evidence to convict the archdiocel," Adamat said, picking up his hat.

Ricard put his finger in the air. "Wait," he said. "I just remembered something. There were rumors a few years back that Charlemund was involved in some kind of a cult." He put his hand to his head. "I can't for the life of me think of the name."

"A cult," Adamat said good-naturedly. Ricard was reaching. He obviously didn't like the man. "Let me know if you remember. I'll need access to your books, and to any property the union owns down by the docks."

"Hmph," Ricard said. "You'll need an army to wade through all of that."

"Still..."

"Oh, you're welcome to it. I'll spread the word around with my boys that you're not to be bothered and that your questions are to be answered."

Adamat and SouSmith spent the rest of the day and much of the next walking the docks and warehouses. Nearly everyone in that district belonged to the Warriors of Labor, so Adamat asked a lot of questions. As he suspected, though, they took him nowhere. He wound up speaking to well over three hundred people. There had been suspicions and half-truths and lies and fingers pointed, but it all turned in on itself in a great big circle. Ricard had been right—it would take an army to sort through all of it.

The only thing he *could* confirm was that Kez agents had been coming into the country through these docks, over the Adsea. He dropped by Tamas's military headquarters at the end of the second day and left a list of names and ships for Tamas's soldiers to check out, but went home with nothing further in the search for Tamas's traitor.

He knew his work may have helped avert another assassination attempt, but he couldn't help but feel he was putting his hands into murky, shark-filled waters. He was but one man, and Tamas's enemies could strike from anywhere and at any time.

CHAPTER 22

The pealing of the Watch bell brought Taniel out of a restless sleep and had him on his feet in moments. He snatched his rifle from beside his bed and sprinted for the door. Ka-poel began to stir from her cot in the corner of the room, and then Taniel was out and down the stairs.

The officers' mess was empty. Taniel ran past the rows of tables, their chairs set upside down on top of them, and came out into the street.

He only paused there to pull on his shirt and adjust his rifle kit. Boots came on next, and by the time he was up, men and women poured from the rest of the buildings on the street. Taniel joined the flow of those heading toward the southern wall of the bastion.

"You heard the alarm?" Fesnik asked, dropping in beside Taniel. He'd taken a liking to Taniel in the two weeks since he'd come down off the mountain with Bo. Taniel couldn't imagine why.

He'd cracked one of the man's teeth when he put a pistol in his mouth all those weeks ago.

Taniel rolled his eyes. Of course he heard it. Half of Adro heard it, and the damned bells were still going. "Yeah," he said.

"Think it's the big push?"

"Don't know."

The young Watcher looked far too excited for the prospect. They'd had nothing but potshots at the Kez soldiers since fire was first exchanged. The Kez army had simply lain out on the fields, readying itself for...something...out of range of artillery. Their Privileged had stayed completely out of sight—a fact that irked Taniel—though he'd had his share of shots at Wardens. Killing one of them in a single shot, though, took more luck than skill.

Taniel fell into a spot on the bulwark and got comfortable. He snorted a pinch of powder to sweep away the last of his sleep and squinted into the morning sun.

"They've got the sun with them," Taniel said.

"Bastards," Fesnik grunted.

Taniel said, "We've always known they'd attack in the morning. Their advantage will turn against them in the afternoon, when they're looking up the mountain to make a shot."

The sun had barely begun peeking out from the distant hills. The morning air was chilly despite summer's onset. The snow had disappeared from the lower parts of Pike's skirt and the road up the southern side would be soggy—it'd be trampled to a mud-covered slide when Kez troops began their ascent. Taniel wondered at the Kez strategy.

The bells fell away from the town behind them. Quiet came, save for a few nervous whispers and the rattle of gear. Cannons were loaded, muskets readied. Men and heavy guns lined the entire bulwark with just enough room between them to work. Taniel did not envy the enemy.

"By Kresimir," Fesnik said, squinting. "They've got enough troops to throw men and bullets at us until the end of times."

"They're welcome to try," said a Watcher woman on Taniel's right. He thought he recognized the voice and took a glance. It was Katerine, one of Bo's women. She was a serious woman, not Bo's type at all, tall and thin with raven hair and a severe voice. He gave her a nod. She responded in kind.

Taniel took a little more powder and tried to search the plains below for some kind of movement. Being a powder mage didn't reduce the glare of the morning sun. He felt a tug on his sleeve. Ka-poel stood beside him and pointed down the slope.

Taniel tried to follow her finger, searching the hillside and the plains below. Then he saw it. Down near Mopenhague. The town had long been abandoned in favor of a headquarters farther back. Not anymore. A tower had been erected during the night. It stood three stories high, made of wooden beams and sitting upon a sled, with a full team of oxen ready to pull it.

Taniel felt his heart jump. "A Privileged Tower," he said. He opened his third eye to find out for certain. A glow surrounded the tower in the Else, thick enough to blot out individual auras.

"It's just a pile of sticks," Fesnik said. "One good shot from a big gun and it's splinters."

Ka-poel snorted. Taniel didn't think she'd ever seen a Privileged Tower, but she could definitely sense the sorcery around the thing.

Katerine seemed worried. She gave Taniel an uncertain look.

"Don't get your hopes up on that," Taniel said. "Privileged Towers are more a bundle of sorcery than sticks." He gave the thing a once-over. His third eye found a field of colors below, a thousand pastels all smeared together and mixed up. The tower glowed like a thousand torches. Looking at it gave him a headache. He closed his third eye. "They've been weaving wards into that thing for the last few weeks. I don't think one of these has been built for a long time. It takes an entire royal cabal, and when it's finished..."

"OK, but what the pit does it do?" Fesnik asked. Taniel gave the young Watcher a glance. Fesnik's musket barrel wavered.

"It'll protect the soldiers as they come up the hill," Taniel said. "And the Privileged riding it."

"I still can't see the thing," Fesnik said, shielding his eyes.

"You will soon enough." Taniel lifted his rifle and spun about. "Any idea where Bo is?"

Fesnik shook his head.

"With Gavril," Katerine said. "Above the gate."

The largest of the bulwarks was above the southeast gate. It stuck out from the main wall, looming over the side of the mountain with twenty cannon and artillery pieces. Taniel found Gavril right out on the point of the bulwark, his eyes shaded against the sun, leaning out as if waiting for a bullet to strike him. Bo stood a few paces back, frowning at the hillside below.

"Privileged Tower," Taniel said.

"I know. I've been wondering what they're up to. Thought they were waiting for more men." He grunted and tugged at his collar. "I wasn't expecting this."

"I've never seen one before," Taniel said. "Just heard stories."

"I'd be surprised if you had. The last one made was oh, two hundred and fifteen years ago. A siege of a shah's palace in Gurla by Kez forces. Allied with Adro, no less." He snorted. "The Adran and Kez royal cabals worked together to build three Privileged Towers. Won them the battle, and the war."

"Why'd they need them?" Taniel asked.

Bo gave him a long look. "Because the shah's palace was guarded by a Gurlish god."

Taniel felt a chill in his chest. It wasn't caused by the wind. "You're joking. A god?"

"Royal cabal secrets, my friend," Bo said, tapping the side of his nose. "A young god. Young and naïve." Bo's voice was wistful.

"Not a story you'll hear in the history books," Gavril added. He climbed down from the bulwark and faced them, placing a looking glass back in his pocket. He wore the assorted furs of a mountain man with brown leather boots and a matching vest that barely fit across his chest. The vest was old and faded, and Taniel could practically smell the dust from it, as if it had been sitting in the back of a closet or bottom of a chest. On the left breast it had an emblem of the Mountainwatch—three triangles, a bigger one with a halo flanked by two smaller ones. A Watchmaster's vest.

Gavril, the town drunk, was the Watchmaster. It still boggled Taniel's mind.

"What do you think?" Bo said, nodding over the edge of the bulwark.

"I don't like it." Gavril rubbed at the stubble on his chin. He'd shaved off his beard since he took over as Watchmaster. It grew back in quickly, and he only bothered to shave every few days. "A Privileged Tower means they've got the whole cabal down there."

"Or something worse," Bo said.

"Julene," Taniel said.

They exchanged unhappy glances.

"I've seen her unleash sorceries," Taniel said. "Powerful stuff."

"Bah," Bo said. "She held back. You don't know the half of it."

"Then she'll sweep this fortress aside."

"Don't care who she is," Gavril said. "She'll not get rid of us so easily. Sorceries as old as she is anchor this fortress to the mountain. They've been woven into every brick and every handful of dirt and rock. This is the Mountainwatch."

Bo gave Gavril an annoyed look. "She's not to be underestimated either," he said. "She may be weakened by our fight. She took a beating up on that mountaintop that would have killed half a royal cabal. Not to mention the fall. She probably left a crater in the ground where she hit."

A murmur went through the troops lining the bulwark. Taniel went to the edge to look over. He was joined by Gavril and Bo.

Squinting through the glare, Taniel could see the foot of the mountain writhing with motion. The whole army had moved up during the night, just out of bombardment range. It seemed like one giant, unorganized mass, but as Taniel watched, it began to form into ranks. He saw them then, the banners of the Kez Cabal. They were huge as bedsheets beside a shirt compared with the banners of the nobility and the royal house. They rose, aided by sorcery, above the Kez ranks, untouched by wind, their broad sides pointed toward the Watch. They displayed a white snake in a field of grain that was the Kez symbol of power. The snake writhed and moved as Taniel watched. Sorcery again. The snake's mouth opened, and it spit venom toward the mountain fortress.

Taniel glanced at Bo.

"Tricks," Bo said. "Illusions. Nothing dangerous. Yet."

"Right."

The Privileged Tower began to creep up the road. Soldiers poured past it on either side, marching in step, the steady snare of the drummer boys reverberating up the mountain, the creak of harnesses as a thousand horses began to pull cannons. A trumpet sounded. The ascent began.

Up until now there had been feints and prods, a few companies of soldiers rushing the bulwark and then falling back to the relative safety of the natural breastworks created by the roads cut into the side of the mountain. Adran soldiers in the outer redoubts had retreated several times, but retaken their redoubts without a fight each time when the enemy fell back.

Taniel could tell this was no feint. The real attack had begun. There would be no rest until one side was destroyed.

He felt a tug at his sleeve. Ka-poel pulled him to the side and offered him a satchel. It was the size of a cannonball and felt as heavy as one.

"What the pit, Pole? Ugh, what is this?" He set the bag on the ground and looked inside. It was full of bullets, enough for half a unit. He frowned at Ka-poel. "Thanks?"

Ka-poel rolled her eyes. She struck her fist to her chest—a symbol she used for Privileged, and then mimed shooting a rifle. Taniel felt a smile slowly spread on his face as he began to understand.

"What's that?" Bo asked, looking over Ka-poel's shoulder.

"Bullets," Taniel said. He pulled one out and held it up to the light. It was a standard lead musket ball about the width of a man's thumb. Upon closer inspection one could see a dark red band of color across the middle of the bullet. Bo reached for the ball, which Taniel snatched back. "You don't want to touch this," he said. "It's a redstripe."

Bo gave the bullet a skeptical look. "A what?"

"These have been charmed by a Bone-eye—the Dynize sorcerers," Taniel said. "We used these in the Fatrastan war. Killed a number of Privileged with them."

"How's it charmed?" Bo said. He peered at the bullet, keeping his distance.

Taniel jerked his thumb at Ka-poel. "To cut through Privileged shields. Ask *her* if you want details. From what I understand, they take a lot of energy to make." Taniel gave Ka-poel a look-over. He'd not known she could make these. They looked like the real article, and Ka-poel had bags under her eyes that indicated many nights spent working. Taniel realized he hadn't seen her much the entire week. He'd been on the wall from sunup to sundown, eyes on the Kez.

Bo had the look of concentration he always had when he was using his third eye. "You said not to touch it," he murmured, looking closer. "Do they do damage beyond, you know, the hole they make in a man's head?"

"Yeah," Taniel said. "One Fatrastan Privileged told me they burn at the touch. I can't imagine that inside of you."

"So it doesn't need a direct hit," Bo said thoughtfully. He straightened. "Why have I never heard of these before?"

"If you were the Kez, would you want it widely known that enchanted bullets could cut through your best defenses? If you were the Fatrastans, would you want to tip your hand at having an advantage?"

"Fatrastans could sell one bullet for a lot of money," Bo said.

Taniel could practically hear the gears turning in Bo's head. "Yeah, and then you'd find one coming for you one day."

Bo smiled. "Probably would at that, wouldn't I?" He still looked thoughtful. "I wouldn't tell anyone else about those, if I were you."

Gavril moved up beside them. "Taniel. The Privileged have begun to show themselves. Time to go to work. And you, Bo." The big man snorted. "I want you slinging whatever you can at them the whole way up. The battle's about to begin."

A cannon blast punctuated his words and left Taniel's ears ringing. Another followed in less than a few heartbeats, and then another.

"Get used to the sound," Gavril shouted above the racket. "The only thing we're not short of is ammunition. They'll pound away day and night, till either we crack the barrels or the Kez send us to the pit."

Taniel spent the rest of the morning sending Kez Privileged scrambling for cover. The redstripes cut through the protection offered by the Privileged Tower everywhere but nearest the tower itself. The sorcery was just too strong there, and the redstripes pinged off an invisible shield just as the conventional artillery did. Kez Privileged huddled around the tower, matching its ponderous progress. Some even rode on it, sending halfhearted shots of sorcery up the mountainside in the form of fire and lightning. Not once did a shot make it past the redoubts. The wards protecting the Mountainwatch were too powerful.

The Privileged Tower reached a point three-quarters of the way to the fortress from Mopenhague around noontime. It rolled to a stop on a relatively flat part of the road near a level area of ground big enough for a squat house and a latrine—a resting point for travelers on the switchbacks. Blocks were put behind the wheels and the oxen were corralled. Tents were set up in the shadow of the Privileged Tower.

The Kez Cabal had found their staging ground.

The Kez worked all day beneath the torrent of artillery fire. The air above them shimmered where cannonballs and canister shot rained down upon the sorcery-woven shield. Late in the day Taniel found himself near Bo.

Bo wore his gloves but had yet to make any response to the Kez Cabal. He scowled while he examined the royal cabal's new position through a looking glass.

"Pit," Bo said to himself. He stowed the looking glass, when he sensed Taniel's presence and turned. "She's down there," he said.

"Julene?" Taniel asked. "How can you be sure?"

Bo rubbed his temples. "I've had my third eye open all day. She's hiding herself well, and pit, it's tough to pick out individuals beneath that shield. I've seen her well of power manifest twice now. Each time when the Tower got stuck." He snorted. "Bitch is driving cattle now. I just saw it again, right now. It's her, all right. Only a Predeii has that flare to them in the Else. She's barely bothering to hide."

"What if there's another one down there?" Taniel asked.

Bo turned white as a cloud. He swallowed and turned around, staring through the looking glass again. After a moment he took it away from his eye. He spit at Taniel's feet. "You're a bastard for suggesting that," he said. He rubbed his eyes. "I'll be up all night now, looking for a second one. Damn it."

"So she survived that beating we gave her on the mountain?"

"It seems so."

"How the pit do we kill her, then? Can it even be done?"

"I don't know."

"You inspire a lot of confidence, you know that?" Taniel ignored Bo's glare. "She's really trying to come up here to summon Kresimir?"

"Yes."

Taniel had asked the question fifty times now. He hoped Bo's answer would change. It hadn't. He felt like he couldn't give up trying.

"Why didn't she do it weeks ago? She could have snuck past us and gone up there."

"Last time it took thirteen of the most powerful Privileged in the world," Bo said. "She'll need an entire royal cabal this time."

"Hence, the Kez."

"Yes."

"Why would they help her?"

"Who knows what she's promised them," Bo said. "Immortality? Power? Ruling the Nine at Kresimir's side?"

"We have to tell my father."

"I sent a warning to him over a month ago," Bo said. "The answer I got was that he sent you to kill me."

"I believe you," Taniel said.

"Very reassuring. Have you written him about Julene?"

"I did." He had yet to hear a word from his father. What did that mean? Last news from Adopest was a week ago. A Warden had tried to kill Tamas. They'd not succeeded. Taniel had no idea whether his father had been wounded or incapacitated—or whether he was simply too busy to write back. Or maybe he was still planning on sending someone to kill Bo. Taniel was looking over his shoulder every day for another powder mage. None had come.

"I can already tell you he won't believe all that stuff about summoning Kresimir," Taniel said. "He's too practical."

"You did tell him, though, right?"

"Of course I told him. I told him I couldn't kill you because I needed your help on the mountain. I told him I saw the Kez army and knew we'd need a Privileged to hold them off."

"You didn't see the Kez army until we were on our way back, though," Bo said.

"But it's a plausible lie."

"The only kind that works."

"I requested reinforcements, too," Taniel said. "At the very least Tamas will send those."

"Good. Only problem with a choke point like this is that only so many men can hold it. More soldiers might just muddle things up. I'll talk to Gavril. Having a few companies camped just down the mountain on the Adran side would allow us to cycle men. Give us more rest."

Taniel and Bo stared down at the Kez army for a few minutes of silence.

Bo turned to him. "Tamas is really playing with fire, isn't he?"

"Seems so."

"I have a question," Bo said. He sounded hesitant.

Taniel frowned. When had Bo ever held back from asking him anything? "Yeah?"

"What happened to your mother? I've heard the official stories. On a diplomatic mission to Kez. Accused of spying and treachery, and then beheaded quickly. There's more to it than that."

Bo wanted to know why Tamas had started the war. "I haven't told you?"

"I've never asked," Bo said. "It seemed a topic you were… reluctant to discuss."

Taniel opened his mouth to speak and found he had no words. He choked, then coughed into his hand and tried to blink back the tears. No, he had never talked about it. Not even with his closest friend. He worked to find his voice.

"My mother's mother was Kez. Mother used it as an excuse to visit once, sometimes twice a year. Her status as a noblewoman made her impossible for the Kez to touch, despite their habit of imprisoning powder mages. Each visit, she tried to find a powder mage and smuggle him or her into Adro and under Tamas's wing, or out of the Nine entirely. Duke Nikslaus found out. The Kez arrested her and my grandparents, and they were all put to death by the time word reached Adro."

Taniel cleared his throat. "Tamas demanded that Manhouch declare war. Manhouch refused. The crown buried the entire affair so deep that no one asked questions. My father disappeared for more than a year. When he returned, there was rumor that he'd tried, and failed, to assassinate Ipille. That rumor was squashed just as quickly as the one that my mother was put to death without a trial."

"Your father," Bo said, his voice flat, "tried to kill the king of Kez and got away with it?"

"He's never spoken about it. My mother had two brothers. They both disappeared around the same time. I think they were caught, and Tamas got away, and claimed he had nothing to do with it." Taniel sprinkled powder on the back of his wrist and took a sniff. His uncles were a vague memory. He couldn't even remember their names.

"Should I watch my back for another powder mage?" Bo asked.

Taniel was glad he'd changed the subject. "I don't think so," he said. "With the whole Grand Army here and the better part of the Kez Cabal, Tamas knows he needs you. At least until the army retreats."

"Fantastic." Bo managed a smile and slapped Taniel on the shoulder. He turned to head back toward the town. Taniel fingered the rifle in his hands and watched his friend's back. Bo's shoulders were slumped, his walk hardly more than a shuffle. He was tired, Taniel realized.

Bo was their best weapon against the Kez, and he was getting dull. Their second best weapon? Taniel felt his mouth go dry. That was a lot of pressure on him. Tamas could thrive on this kind of pressure. He'd throw a hundred bullets into the air and kill every Kez Privileged on the mountainside. It should be *his* ass up there.

Taniel shouldered his rifle and headed back to the bulwark. He had to do it the old-fashioned way. One bullet at a time. No, he realized. He was Taniel Two-Shot. He'd take two at once.

CHAPTER 23

Tamas stepped out of his carriage and took a deep breath of country air. Olem already stood in the drive, one hand on the butt of a pistol at his belt, the other tucked into the pocket of his scarlet hunting coat. His nose was in the air like a guard dog as he examined their surroundings. He wore an outfit matching Tamas's with black laceless boots and dark pants in addition to the scarlet coat and hunting cap, a rifle over one shoulder.

The baying of hounds echoed out across the pastures. The hunting lodge rested between two hills beside a stony creek on the edge of the King's Wood. It was a vast affair with hundreds of rooms in the traditional bad taste of the Adran monarchy. It had originally been built of local stone and immense oaks the likes of which hadn't grown in this area for a hundred years. Recent renovations had given it a brick façade. The kennels, a two-story building as big as the king's stables, were visible across the southern pasture.

"Come on, Hrusch," Tamas said. The hound dog leapt from the carriage and immediately put his nose to the ground, floppy ears dusting the gravel. Tamas felt a twinge when Pitlaugh didn't follow Hrusch out of the carriage as he had so many years in the past. A great many things were different about the hunt this year.

Tamas entered the farmhouse and was hit by the nervous titter of uncertain conversation. He was among the last to arrive, yet there were fewer than a dozen people in the main foyer.

"Not many here, sir," Olem said. A butler gave Olem's cigarette a disapproving look. Olem ignored him.

"I killed ninety percent of the people who usually come," Tamas murmured.

Tamas nodded to each of the men and women in the foyer. A couple of merchants of means, and a pair of noblemen with low enough rank to spare them the Elections. Last year they would have worn the pale breeches and dark waistcoats of those not included directly in the hunt. This year, they would wear hunt colors along with everyone else simply to fill out the numbers. Brigadiers Ryze and Abrax chatted idly with the merchants. Tamas exchanged a few words with them and thanked them for their service against the royalists. Conversations died as he passed by the minor nobility.

Lady Winceslav, dressed in colors with a dark riding habit and a black coat with a scarlet collar, swept down the stairs.

"Tamas, I'm glad you made it," she said. Brigadier Barat, a sullen, impetuous young man that Tamas continually wanted to smack, lurked on the stairs behind her.

"I wouldn't miss it for the world," Tamas said. "Hrusch needs something to take his mind off things." The hound looked up from his olfactory inspection of the floor at the sound of his name. "As do I, perhaps," he added.

"Or course," Lady Winceslav said. "Is he in the running, then?"

Tamas scoffed. "He'll win it. Pitlaugh was the only one to beat him last year. With the king's kennels out of contention, it'll be no contest." He felt his smile begin to slide off his face and gestured for Lady Winceslav to step to the side. When they were alone in a hallway, he said, "This is a farce, Lady."

She glared at him. "It is not, and it's insulting of you to say so."

"The king is dead. This hunt was *his* tradition. Most of the people who used to come are dead too."

"So we should let it die with them?" she said. "Don't deny that you enjoy these hunts."

Tamas took a deep breath. The Orchard Valley Hunt was an annual tradition going back six hundred years and marked the beginning of St. Adom's Festival. Tamas struggled within himself. He loved the hunt, however...

"It sends the wrong message," he said. "We want to show the people that we're not replacing Manhouch and his nobility with more nobles. The hunt is a noble's sport."

"I think not," Lady Winceslav said. "It's an Adran sport. Would you outlaw tennis, or polo? This is simply entertainment." She shook her head. "Next you'll want to outlaw masquerades, and then we'll see how popular you are come winter, when there's nothing else to do."

"I wouldn't do that. I met my wife at a ball," Tamas said.

She gave him a sympathetic look. "I know. Look around, Tamas. Some of the finest merchant families of Adro are here. Even Ricard and Ondraus came. I made the invitation open to everyone in Adopest."

"Everyone?" Tamas asked. "If that was the case, there'd be more people here, if only for the free food."

Lady Winceslav sniffed. "You know what I mean. There are even some amateur kennelmasters here from North Johal. Freed peasants. They're rough men, but they seem to know their hounds." She poked Tamas in the chest with one slender, slightly wrinkled finger. "Saint Adom's Festival cannot begin without the Orchard Valley Hunt. I simply won't let it happen. Now, the draggers have already begun laying the scent. The hunt will begin in twenty minutes. Get Hrusch to the starting line. The stable master will have a hunter ready for you to ride."

Tamas and Olem found their mounts and headed out to the kennels, where the official hunt would begin. A chalk line had been dusted on the trimmed grass spanning an entire field. Hundreds of men and women sat atop their hunters. Some held their hounds on leashes, others by command alone, while a number of the wealthier participants had kennelmasters on foot beside them.

Tamas took a place at one end of the line. There were more people out here than he expected, and a far greater number of hounds. "She really meant it when she said she had invited everyone. Half these people aren't even wearing hunt colors." He bit back a comment. It was a damned time to complain. It would still be fine colors and nobility if it weren't for him.

"Aye," Olem said. "I'm glad there's anyone here at all. Would be a sad start to the festival without a hunt."

"Did Lady Winceslav pay you to say that?" Tamas said. Olem was a soldier, risen from the peasantry to his current position. He had no attachment to the hunt.

Olem looked surprised. "No, sir." He flicked the end of his cigarette into the grass and immediately began rolling another.

"I'm joking, Olem." Tamas glanced about, grimacing at the sight of a peasant on a mangy-looking mare with two hounds and an off-red coat that didn't come close to hunt colors.

In a few minutes' time the horn was blown and the hounds were off. Tamas began at a slow canter, watching Hrusch fly off ahead of the rest of the animals in the direction of the scent. It wasn't long before the dogs disappeared into the woods. Tamas urged himself ahead of the rest of the riders until he reached the woods, then slacked off and let himself be passed. He closed his eyes, listening to the softening bays of the hounds, the sound soothing to his ears.

He opened his eyes after some time to find himself alone with Olem. The bodyguard's hunter trotted along beside Tamas's. Olem's eyes scanned the surrounding brush with the vigil of a hawk.

"Do you ever relax?" Tamas asked.

"Not since the Warden, sir."

Tamas could see horses up ahead, and hear others behind them. The huntsmen had begun to spread out in order to enjoy themselves while the hounds ran themselves to exhaustion. The sport would last all day, either until one of the hounds caught up with the volunteer dragging the scent or until they reached the end point of the race. Last year, Pitlaugh had found the volunteer halfway through the day, earning the ire of Adro's nobility for cutting short their hunt, and earning himself a flank of steer from Tamas.

Tamas brushed off memories of past hunts and turned to Olem. "It wasn't your fault. They'll send more Wardens at me. You'll do little against one of them."

Olem rested one hand lightly on his pistol. "Don't write me off so quickly, sir. I can cause more damage than you'd guess."

"Of course," Tamas said gently. He felt more relaxed than he had in, well, it seemed like years. He let his mind wander, enjoying the cool breeze through the trees and the periodic splash of warm sun on his face. It was a perfect, blue-sky day for the Orchard Valley Hunt.

"A question, sir." Olem's voice cut through his thoughts.

"If it has to do with the Kez, I don't want to hear it."

"I was wondering what you'll do with Mihali, sir?"

Tamas stirred himself out of his reverie and gave Olem's back an annoyed glance as the soldier searched the woods with his eyes. "I think I'm sending him back to Hassenbur," Tamas said.

Olem gave Tamas a sharp look.

Tamas said, "Not you, too? I'd expect the common soldiers to grow attached, but not you."

"I *am* a common soldier, sir. But you stated his worth yourself," Olem said. "Creating food from thin air."

"I risk angering Claremonte. The asylum's patron is not a man to be trifled with, not with his position with the Brudania-Gurla Trading Company. I risk our entire supply of saltpeter. At this point in the war, gunpowder is more important than food."

"And later?" Olem asked.

"Mihali is a madman, Olem. He belongs in an asylum." He chose his words carefully. "It would be a cruelty to let him live like a normal man." He knew the words made sense in his head, but when he spoke them out loud, they seemed wrong. He frowned. "They can help him at the asylum.

"Have you checked on those names that Adamat gave us?" Tamas said, unwilling to continue the conversation.

Olem was clearly uncomfortable with the abrupt end to the topic of Mihali's future. "Yes, sir," he said stiffly. "Our people are looking into it. Slowly. We don't have enough men, to be honest, but Adamat's hunches are proving accurate enough."

"He said he gathered that list of names and ships in just two days of investigation," Tamas said. "The entire police force on the docks has only given us half a dozen Kez smugglers since the war started. How can he work so fast?"

Olem shrugged. "He's got a gift. Also, he doesn't have the restrictions of the police. He's not wearing a uniform. He can't be bribed or intimidated."

"You think he can find my traitor?" Tamas asked.

"Perhaps." Olem didn't look so sure. "I wish you'd put more men on it. You shouldn't leave the fate of Adro in the hands of one retired investigator."

Tamas shook his head. "As you said, he can go where the police cannot. I can't trust it to anyone else. Everyone I truly trust—you, Sabon, the rest of the powder cabal—they're doing tasks of utmost importance, and none of them has the set of talents and skills that Adamat does. If he can't track down my traitor, no one else can."

Olem gave him a dark stare. The corner of his mouth twitched, and Tamas felt a thrill of fear through his chest. "Give me a writ of purpose," Olem said quietly. "And fifty men. I'll find out who the traitor is."

Tamas rolled his eyes. "I'm not going to let you hack apart my council with a meat cleaver and a hot iron. You'll leave nothing left of them, and I'll have made enemies of the most powerful people in Adro. I'm sorry, Olem, but I need you watching my back and I need the other five of the council—the ones that aren't traitors—fully intact."

Tamas turned as he heard horses galloping up from behind. "Pit, I was hoping for a pleasant day."

"Ho there, Field Marshal," Charlemund said. The arch-diocel looked nothing like a man of the Rope. He wore his hunt colors proudly on a hunter easily ten stone bigger than Tamas's. He was followed by three young women; probably priestesses, though it was impossible to tell with them wearing hunt colors. Just behind the women was Ondraus the Reeve. The old man wore a black hunt coat and pale breeches to indicate that he wasn't part of the hunt proper, yet he rode his hunter with far more poise and confidence than Tamas would have expected from a glorified accountant.

"How many hounds do you have competing today, Charlemund?" Tamas asked.

The arch-diocel gave him a sour look that always accompanied his response when someone failed to use his title. "Ten," he said. "Though to be fair, three of them are running for the ladies here." He gestured to his companions. "Priestesses Kola, Narum, and Ule, this is Field Marshal Tamas."

Tamas gave the three women a curt nod. Not one of them looked above twenty years old, even though they bore the rank of priestess. They were far too young. And pretty. Women that attractive did not enter into service to the Church.

The reeve rode up next to Tamas.

"Ondraus," Tamas said. "You're the last person I'd expect to see at a hunt."

Ondraus turned in his saddle and pointed behind them. "No, *that's* the last person you'd expect to see at a hunt."

A horse struggled through a patch of briars not far off, urged on with an incessant stream of curses by Ricard Tumblar. The union boss caught his cheek on a thorn and let out a yell, kicking the horse. Hunter and rider surged from the patch, galloping to catch up with the rest. Tamas reached out and grabbed the bridle as the horse came by. He leaned over, placing a hand between its eyes. "Shh. Quiet," he said, soothing the animal. "Lord above, Ricard, stop urging it on. You'll get yourself thrown."

Ricard's heels had been dug into the creature's side. He let up immediately and gave a great sigh. "Son of a bitch," he said. "I was made to ride in a carriage, not on a horse."

Charlemund grinned at him. "I can see that," he said. "We all can. I've seen children who ride better than you."

"And I've seen pimps with fewer whores," Ricard snapped.

The three priestesses gasped. The arch-diocel spun his mount to face Ricard, laying a hand on the grip of his sword. "Take it back or I'll have your hide."

Ricard drew a pistol from his belt. "I'll blow your face off if you come a step closer."

Tamas groaned. He grabbed Ricard's pistol by the barrel and shoved it away. "Put them away, both of you," he said. He urged his mount up beside Ricard's. "Where do you get off threatening an arch-diocel?" he growled. "Are you mad?"

Ricard wiped the blood from his cheek, a scratch from the briars. He looked at his fingers. "Bloody hunt."

"Why are you here?" Tamas said.

"Lady Winceslav insisted," Ricard said. "She said I was gentry now, being a member of the council, and that it was expected of me. I've had more fun in the bottom of a fishing boat."

"You've never ridden before?" Olem asked.

Ricard returned his pistol to his belt and took the reins in both hands. "Not once. When I was a boy, my father had no money for lessons, and by the time I thought of it, I was rich enough to afford to take a carriage. Now, where the pit is that whipper-in? Lady Winceslav said that fool would stay with me and keep me from making an ass of myself."

"He was unsuccessful," Charlemund said.

Ricard glared. Tamas elbowed him hard in the ribs. Ricard turned to the three priestesses. "My apologies, ladies. My comments weren't directed at you." One and all, the three turned their noses up at him. Ricard sighed.

"I came here for a pleasant afternoon," Tamas said, glancing around at the group. "Now, can I have that, or do I need to ride on my own?"

Ricard and Charlemund grumbled to themselves. Tamas resumed riding, leading Ricard's horse. "Let him do the steering," he said after a moment, letting go of the bridle. "He knows the trail, he knows the other horses. He'll follow on his own. He knows you don't know what you're doing. You try to take control and he'll fight you the whole way."

Ricard gave a silent nod and avoided looking at Charlemund and his priestesses.

They were soon joined by the whipper-in.

Tamas was surprised to find he knew the man. "Gaben!" he called.

"Sir." Gaben rode up beside him, all smiles. He was a spry young man who looked well at ease on a horse. Whippers-in usually kept the dogs on the trail, but this one was obviously meant to keep the *people* on the trail.

"Olem, this is Gaben," Tamas said. "Captain Ajucare's youngest son."

"Pleased to meet you," Olem said. "I've known the captain for many years."

Gaben extended a hand. "You're the Knacked that doesn't sleep?"

"Right."

"It's a pleasure."

"So the Lady attached you to Ricard, here, did she?" Tamas said.

Gaben nodded. "Said he might need some help."

"You lost him for a while, it seems."

"He went through a bramblebush, sir. I decided to go around."

"Smart man. I've heard from your father you have a singular skill for horses."

"He overtells it," Gaben said modestly.

"No, I'm sure he does not." Tamas saw him eyeing the young ladies. "Please, don't let me keep you."

Gaben rode up beside the priestesses and answered their questions about the hunt. Soon after, Brigadier Sabastenien came up quietly from behind. He joined the whipper-in and the priestesses, listening quietly to their talk.

Tamas leaned over to Olem. "Brigadier Sabastenien impressed me during the racket with the royalists. We'll keep an eye on him over the years. Mark my words, he'll be senior brigadier by the time he's forty."

Silence fell in the wood, the only sound that of horses and the quiet conversation of the young people a few dozen yards ahead of them. Tamas was just beginning to enjoy the relative quiet when Ondraus spoke up.

"I want to know about this cook," the reeve said.

Tamas turned in the saddle toward Ondraus. The path here was wide enough for the four of them to ride abreast. Tamas was on one end, with Ricard on his right, lagging slightly behind, and Ondraus between Ricard and Charlemund. Olem stayed just behind them, his eyes on the forest.

"What cook?" Tamas said.

"The one who is providing for all the clerks and workers in the House of Nobles, in addition to your garrison," Ondraus said. The bent old accountant looked alert in the afternoon sun and rode his horse like a man much younger. His gaze matched Tamas's.

"The one who creates dishes that have never been seen in Adopest and receives shipments of raw goods that are well out of season in this part of the world, without ever having made an order in the first place. The one feeding five thousand people on a few hundred kranas' worth of flour and beef a day." Ondraus gave Tamas a shallow smile. "The one that claims he's a god. Or had this all gone beneath your notice?"

Tamas slowed his mount slightly and waited for the others to do the same. The priestesses, brigadier, and whipper-in went on ahead, unaware. When they were well out of earshot, Tamas said, "He's a Knacked. Not a god."

Charlemund snorted. "I'm certainly glad. It's blasphemy."

"So you know of him?" Tamas said, resigned. He'd hoped that Charlemund's gaze had swept over Mihali without noticing. A vain hope indeed.

"Of course," Charlemund said. "My colleagues in the Church have been apprised of the situation. I received their communiqués just this morning."

"And?"

"They wish me to take him into Church custody immediately. Before any more of his lies can be spread."

"He's harmless," Tamas said. "He escaped from Hassenbur Asylum. I'm sending him back any day now." The Church's involvement was the last thing he needed.

"Who is he?" Ondraus asked.

"Lord of the Golden Chefs," Tamas said.

"Don't mock me," Ondraus said, taken aback.

"He's not," Ricard suddenly said. "Lord of the Golden Chefs is a title among culinary experts. It means he's the best damned cook in all the Nine. I can't believe he's really in the city."

"You know him?" Tamas asked.

"Know *of* him, more like," Ricard said. "I paid a king's ransom to have him cook for Manhouch five years ago. It was that dinner that convinced the king to let me start a union. I've never tasted such food." He gave a low whistle. "His squash soup is to die for. I'd love to see him."

Tamas stifled a smile at the very thought of Mihali's squash soup. His mouth watered a little, and for just a moment he could smell it, as if Mihali was making it in a pot in the middle of the next clearing.

"Well," Charlemund said, "you won't meet him. I'm bringing him under Church custody tonight. I only held off giving the order this morning in deference to Tamas."

"And if I don't let him go?" Tamas said lightly.

Charlemund gave a laugh, as if Tamas had made some kind of joke. "That isn't an option. The man is a heathen and a blasphemer. We all know there is only one God, Kresimir."

"Aren't Adom, Unice, Rosvel, and the rest all supposed to be Kresimir's brothers and sisters?" Tamas asked. "I'm not up on my church lore as much as I should be..."

"Doctrine, not lore," Charlemund said. "Semantics. They helped him create the Nine, yes, that is why they are saints. Kresimir is the only God among them. To claim otherwise goes against Church doctrine. It was decided so at the Council of Kezlea in five-oh-seven."

Ricard's eyes grew wide. "You *do* know something about the Church. Incredible! I thought all you needed to be an arch-diocel was a nice hat and a harem."

Charlemund ignored Ricard as one might ignore an irritating rug seller in the market. "The Council also established that heretics and blasphemers would fall under the jurisdiction of the Church. Every king of the Nine signed the accord."

"Interesting," Tamas said, "that Adro has no king anymore."

Charlemund looked startled by this. "What...?"

"Has it occurred to any of the arch-diocels," Tamas said, "that Adro is no longer held by any of the agreements signed by previous kings? Technically, we don't even have to pay tithe anymore."

Charlemund sputtered. "I don't think that's true. I mean, we had an agreement..."

"With Manhouch," Ondraus said. The reeve had a nasty smile on his face, and Tamas wondered if he had just given Ondraus an excuse to do something that would completely alienate the Church. Tamas squeezed his eyes shut. *O Kresimir above. I shouldn't have said anything.*

"I think I'd like to catch up with the rest of the hunt now," Tamas said before Charlemund could respond. "I can barely hear the hounds." He urged his hunter on, reaching the whipper-in in a few moments.

Gaben turned. "Sir," he said, "We've fallen significantly behind the rest of the group."

"Yes," Tamas said, "I gathered."

"If you'd permit, sir," Gaben said, "I'd like to lead us on a shortcut through the forest. I know where they're planning on being in, oh"—he glanced up at the sun, which was showing through the trees—"two hours. I think we can catch them there. Otherwise we might not reach them until after the hunt has finished."

"Sir," Olem said in a low voice, "it's dangerous to leave the hunt trail. These forests were the king's own, bigger than Adopest and all the suburbs. I used to play in them as a boy. We get lost here and we could be gone for days."

"The going will be slow," the whipper-in said, "through the brush, but we should have no problem cutting them off. I know these woods well."

"I don't like it, sir," Olem said.

Tamas pushed away his own uneasiness and gave Olem a smile. "Calm yourself. I've known Gaben since he was a boy. The worst things in these woods are deer. Lead on."

They trotted along the deer trail, single file, making their way through the woods. The priestesses bantered loudly behind Tamas. He let his mind wander, considering battle plans and strategies. Battle had yet to be joined at the Gates of Wasal. Only at South Pike had shots been fired, and the unique positioning of the fortress town required very little strategy. They'd been shrugging off Kez advances for a month, with minimal loss and despite powerful sorceries on the Kez side. The very thought of Julene's betrayal made Tamas's blood boil.

And Taniel. What could he do? Bo was still alive and the two were working together to push back the Kez. That pleased Tamas. Yet Bo was still under the gaes. Could Tamas trust them? Taniel had disobeyed his orders. There would have to be redress for that, though Taniel claimed he had a good reason to keep Bo alive—they needed the Privileged to help hold Shouldercrown.

Tamas knew the real reason. Taniel hadn't been able to do it. He'd not been able to kill his best friend, even when it was necessary; even on the order of his superior. Taniel had to know that Tamas would see through the excuses. Tamas pushed the thought aside, unwilling to let it ruin his day.

The terrain slowly changed as they rode. They descended into a valley where moss-covered boulders hemmed them in and the forest floor was thick with fallen branches and rotted pine needles. The place seemed to deaden all sound. An icy hand climbed Tamas's spine. The forest felt old and deep, and the clop of their horses' hooves an intrusion here.

Their deer trail ran out, and they followed a small brook. The boulders grew bigger, the tree canopy overhead thicker. It seemed they had not even reached the bottom of the valley. Tamas had no memory of this place from other hunts.

Tamas found himself staring at the back of Ondraus's head. Wisps of silver hair clung to his skull, along with a pair of moles as big as a two-krana coin. Was he the traitor? Tamas became acutely aware that he rode with four of his council, any one of whom was just as likely the traitor as any of the others.

Olem suddenly spurred his horse forward. He passed the other riders and reined in before the whipper-in. "Where are we?" he said.

"Almost there," Gaben said. "Not a mile from rejoining the hunt."

"Then why can't we hear hounds?" Olem said.

Tamas rode up to the front of the column, followed closely by Charlemund and Ondraus. Ricard remained at the back of the column, staring up at the boulders around them.

"It's impossible to hear anything in these rocks," Gaben said as Tamas reined in beside him.

"We're not anywhere near the hunt," Olem said. "This is the Giant's Billiard Table. I ran here as a boy."

Tamas scowled at Gaben. "Explain yourself."

A rock fell from one of the boulders above. Tamas jerked around, eyes searching the forest. "Ricard?" he said. Ricard's horse was alone at the back of the column, the reins thrown over a broken tree limb. Ricard was missing. Tamas turned back to Gaben. "Explain yourself. Now!"

Tamas heard leaves rustling in the forest around them. He turned again, searching. He saw nothing. Ricard had been carrying a pistol. Tamas reached out with his senses. Ricard was nearby. Tamas could sense the powder. He'd scrambled up onto one of the boulders and lay flat on it, facing the group. Was Ricard the traitor? Was this some kind of trap? Ricard was carrying a pistol. Surely he knew that Tamas could find him just from the gunpowder.

A man stepped out on a boulder just ahead of their trail. He held a bow, strung, with arrow at the ready, aimed at Tamas. He sighted along one eye, because the other eye was covered by a white patch of cloth. The man was older than Tamas, his face weathered by battles. He wore a brown-and-green patched cloak to blend in with the forest.

"Brigadier Ryze," Tamas said.

Olem tossed Tamas a pistol and brought about his rifle, moving with the speed of a seasoned soldier. Tamas caught the pistol and leveled it at the brigadier, not bothering to cock it. A powder mage didn't need to.

"Lower the weapon," Brigadier Ryze said. His aim with the bow didn't waver. He took a half step forward, his footing sure on the boulder. His cloak rippled, revealing the scarlet colors of the hunt underneath.

"I'll kill you right now," Tamas warned.

"Maybe," Ryze said, "But not all of us."

Tamas kept his eyes locked on Ryze. "Olem?" he said.

"We're surrounded, sir," Olem responded glumly. "All of them are carrying bows. Fifteen. But there may be more in the woods."

"There are," Brigadier Ryze said.

"Do you know who I am?" Charlemund demanded. Tamas didn't have to look to know Charlemund had drawn his smallsword. Little good it would do against yeomen far above them.

"We know, Arch-Diocel," Brigadier Ryze said. "And you won't be harmed as long as Field Marshal Tamas comes with us. None of you will be harmed."

"I will destroy you," Charlemund snarled.

"I'm sure you will," Brigadier Ryze said without emotion. "Field Marshal, if you please?"

Tamas took a mental inventory of his weapons. A dozen bullets. Not nearly enough to kill fifteen men by scattering the shot, even at his best. He considered Ricard up on one of the boulders and wondered if he was up there because he had sensed a trap or because he'd set the trap in the first place.

"I don't seem to have a choice," Tamas said.

"That's right," Ryze said. His lone eye traveled around the group slowly. "Let's go."

Tamas reached out again with his senses. None of the men had a granule of gunpowder on them. They'd been very careful. He pushed his senses farther into the woods, trying to find out if there were any more armed with powder. He froze. There was a Privileged in the forest.

"Why did you sell out to Manhouch?" Tamas said. "Lady Winceslav trusted you."

Ryze gave a slight shake of his head. "This has nothing to do with the Kez. I serve Adro and Lady Winceslav."

"Then why is there a Privileged in the woods over there?" Tamas asked, pointing north.

Brigadier Ryze's eye widened slightly. "This has nothing to do with the Kez," he said again. "Now, come with us, or we'll take you all down and sort it out later." Ryze's fingers twitched on the bow. It was said Ryze was a perfect shot with bow, crossbow, rifle, or pistol. He had a reputation for action and brutality—when necessary. He wasn't stupid, either. There was a reason he'd risen to be a brigadier of the Wings of Adom.

Tamas urged his hunter forward.

"Dismounted," Ryze said, gesturing to the ground with the tip of his arrow. "Hand your extra powder charges to your bodyguard. Same with the pistol. Leave the horse tied up to a tree."

Tamas did as he was told and approached Brigadier Ryze.

"You bastard," Olem said. "You filthy bastard. I'll take out that other eye."

"Quiet your dog," Ryze said.

"Olem, it's all right," Tamas said. He paused next to Gaben and glanced up. The man was expressionless. "I take it this is one of yours," Tamas said to Ryze.

"He is," Ryze said. "He'll guide the rest back to the hunt."

"Go to the pit," Tamas said. "Olem, take everyone back safely. You said you played here as a boy. Can you get out?"

"Yes," Olem said. He sounded miserable.

"That's an order, then," Tamas said. "Don't come back for me until everyone is out of the forest."

"If you follow us," Ryze said, "I'll cut his throat." The brigadier leapt from the boulder, landing on the ground with a hollow-sounding thump.

He edged Tamas into step before him. They were soon flanked by a pair of woodsmen, then two more. Tamas saw that they weren't wearing hunt colors under their cloaks. They'd probably been in place for hours.

"Ryze," someone called suddenly. Tamas turned with the brigadier. It was Brigadier Sabastenien, the quiet commander. His voice was calm, collected. "We'll have your head for this betrayal," he said. "The Lady will not stand for it."

"I know," Brigadier Ryze responded. There was a hint of sadness to his voice. He turned his back on Sabastenien and led Tamas into the woods. As soon as they were out of sight of the other group, Brigadier Ryze broke into a trot, urging Tamas forward with the tip of a dagger. He did it absently, though, as if almost forgetting that Tamas was his prisoner. Tamas glanced over his shoulder, gauging the brigadier.

"Why are you doing this?" Tamas said.

"Quiet," Ryze said, his voice not unkind. "You don't even know what 'this' is. You say there's a Privileged in the forest?"

Tamas stopped suddenly. He spun on Brigadier Ryze, grabbing the wrist with the dagger. Ryze gripped tightly, one hand going to Tamas's shoulder. They struggled silently for a moment, neither man the stronger, until one of Ryze's men stepped up and struck Tamas in the small of the back. Tamas grunted, letting go of Ryze's wrist. He dropped to his knees.

"Back off," Ryze snarled at his man. He grasped Tamas by the forearm and helped him up. "I've been betrayed," he said quietly, only for Tamas to hear.

"So have I." Tamas glared at the brigadier. There was a time Tamas considered Ryze a colleague, though never close enough to be a friend. Decades ago, postings had seen them together overseas.

"Not the way you think." Ryze stepped back and lowered his dagger. "I'm not here to kill you, Field Marshal, nor to hand you over to the Kez."

"Then what is this charade?" Tamas wondered if he should go for Ryze again. He might get the upper hand, but Ryze's men watched from nearby.

"To warn you," Ryze said. "I've brought my most trusted men, but apparently that was not enough. You're sure there's a Privileged in the forest?"

"Yes," Tamas said slowly. He opened his third eye. "He's getting closer. He has Wardens with him." The thought chilled him. Brigadier Ryze seemed in earnest, but Tamas was not ready to trust him. He might only be delaying, waiting for the Privileged to catch up.

Ryze swore. "Kah! Loadio! Take positions there and there." He pointed upward to a pair of boulders. The two men nodded and climbed onto the rocks. "Kill the sorcerer," he said. Ryze turned to Tamas. "Run!"

Tamas wondered whether he should break away, take the opportunity to escape. He hesitated for just a moment before following Ryze into the forest. As they went, Ryze called out the names of his men, pairing them up and placing them between himself and the sorcerer. Tamas glanced over his shoulder now and then, watching for the pastel glow of a Privileged in his third sight. The Privileged was coming on quickly, along with dimmer glows of power. Privileged didn't move that fast unless they were being carried by a Warden.

Ryze turned to bark an order to one of his men and stopped. Tamas nearly ran into him. Ryze drew a dagger and fell into a fighting stance.

Tamas turned. Only two of Ryze's men were left nearby. One of them was a yeoman, bow slung over his arm. He toppled onto a bed of dead leaves, a crimson slash across his throat. The other man was Gaben. He wiped the dagger calmly on the yeoman's cloak and faced Ryze.

"Your father..." Ryze said.

"Is a damned fool who should never have followed this traitor," Gaben said, gesturing at Tamas. He readied himself, squaring with his own dagger against Ryze. "All I have to do is keep you occupied until the duke arrives."

The old brigadier threw himself forward, dagger in hand. He parried, slashed, then leapt upon Gaben, driving his dagger into the man's chest. It hadn't even been a contest. Ryze stood up, his lone eye red with anger, and looked back the way they'd come. Tamas heard the report of sorcery in the forest, and the crash of a falling tree.

"I've left my men to their deaths," Ryze said. He squeezed his eye shut, dropping his dagger. Tamas noticed that there was blood on his yeoman's cloak. Ryze touched the wound. "Lucky jab," he said, gesturing at the dead whipper-in.

Tamas helped Ryze to a clear spot on the forest floor, leaning him up against a log. "Tell me what you have to say," he said, "before all this is for nothing." The sound of sorcery was getting closer.

"I've not been able to get close to you for some time," Ryze said. "This was a foolish plan, but understand me, sir, I was desperate. Brigadier Barat has betrayed us. He holds my youngest son captive. I'd hoped to convince you to leave the hunt and help me rescue him. We'd have had hours of a head start before he knew we were gone." Ryze passed a hand over his face. Sweat rolled down his cheeks, mingled with tears. "I didn't know we'd been betrayed."

"Is he the traitor?" Tamas said. "Does Lady Winceslav know?"

"He's not the only traitor," Ryze said. "He's working with someone inside your council. And no. The Lady has no idea. She's blinded by love. Barat has seduced her. I've done my best to get him sent to the lines or out of the country, but she won't hear of it. He is the only one with her ear right now."

"Do you know who he's working with?"

"No," Ryze said. "Run!" Ryze lurched forward, shoving Tamas to the ground. The forest erupted in flames suddenly, heat searing Tamas's face and hands. He hit the ground and rolled, pushing himself up to his feet and spinning toward Ryze. The old brigadier screamed as his skin peeled from his body and his flesh withered. Tamas dove behind a boulder, eyes wild for any sign of the Privileged and his Wardens. He heard a crack, and the last thing he remembered was the boulder exploding.

CHAPTER 24

What do you want?"

Lord Vetas stood on the front step of Adamat's house. He was dressed sharply in a new black tailcoat with matching boots shiny enough to hurt Adamat's eyes. He wore a scarlet vest beneath, and a black silk shirt. He held his hat in his hand, short black hair styled and flattened against his head. Adamat wiped the sleep from his eyes and adjusted his dressing gown. He glanced at the hall clock.

"It's seven o'clock," Adamat said flatly.

"May I come in?" Lord Vetas asked. His tone was polite.

"No. Why are you here?" He paused, suddenly suspicious. "And where are your goons?"

"I've no need to make threats today," Lord Vetas said. "Last time, my men were only there to take care of Palagyi. I trust you had no problem disposing of the body?"

For all the concern he showed, he might have been asking about Adamat's morning tea.

"Not too much, thank you," Adamat said. "Now, tell me why you're here."

Lord Vetas seemed unruffled by Adamat's brusque tone. "A gift," he said. He held up a small black box. "I've not yet heard from you. I assume you have decided not to take our offer of employment?"

Adamat snatched the box. "Tell your master to stuff it. I dropped by that address on the card, an empty warehouse near the river. It was no good to me. And you," he added. "You don't exist. I haven't had much time to hunt you down, but there is no 'Lord' Vetas."

"Very astute," Lord Vetas said. "But the address is quite valid. I'm surprised my men took no note of your visit. Impressed, in fact." He raised his hands and clapped them together softly. "Your skills as an investigator are impressive. I have no doubt you will discover my identity eventually, and that of my master."

"Why don't you tell me who you are and save us both the time," Adamat said.

Lord Vetas just smiled. "You're conducting an investigation for Field Marshal Tamas into the likely traitor within his council."

"No."

"Don't lie to me, Adamat," Lord Vetas said. "I already know as much."

"Even if I were, I'd not discuss a current investigation," Adamat said.

Lord Vetas said, "What are your conclusions so far?"

"Don't you understand me?" Adamat asked. "I have nothing to discuss with you. Good day." He made to close his door.

Lord Vetas held up his hand politely, like a clerk trying to get a superior's attention.

"What?" Adamat said.

"Won't you open your gift?"

Adamat frowned at the box in his hand. It was plain and black, tied with a silk ribbon in the middle like one might find at a jeweler's. He undid the ribbon. Within was a finger. It had been severed at the knuckle, and experience with this sort of thing told Adamat it had come from a teenage boy. There was a ring on the finger. The ring had belonged to Adamat's father. A ring Adamat had given to...

Adamat trembled as he put the lid back on the box and slipped it into his robe pocket. He snatched Lord Vetas by the front of his suit and yanked him through the door. Lord Vetas made no protest as Adamat kicked the door shut and slammed him against the wall. His breathing was steady as Adamat put his face close.

"It belonged to your son," Lord Vetas said helpfully.

"I know who it belonged to!" Adamat couldn't help but shout. He took hold of Lord Vetas's suit coat with both hands and threw the man down the hall. He drew his cane sword from the cane holder by the door and bared the blade. He thrust it under Lord Vetas's chin. Lord Vetas didn't even tremble.

"If he's dead..."

Lord Vetas looked at the point of the sword like a man examining a harmless peculiarity beneath his nose. "Oh, he's quite alive. That's the thing with using people as leverage. They aren't leverage if they're dead."

"I will kill you."

"Kill me, and my master will simply send another. One who will bring a slightly bigger box. It will contain your daughter's head."

Adamat's blade drew a drop of blood at Lord Vetas's throat. Lord Vetas produced a hanky and dabbed the blood away.

"Why shouldn't I kill you now?" Adamat whispered.

"I just told you." Lord Vetas gave a sympathetic smile. "You're very emotional right now. I understand. Take a moment to calm down and think things over."

Adamat wanted nothing more than to run the man through. He strained to keep himself in check. A slight twitch and the man's life blood would be on the hallway rug.

SouSmith had appeared at the top of the stairs in his nightclothes. Adamat waved him away.

"What does your master want to know?"

"Everything," Lord Vetas said. "Whatever Tamas has told you; whatever you discover through your investigation. Starting now."

Adamat sighed, the fight draining out of him. Fear filled the empty space. "Nothing. I know nothing."

A hint of annoyance betrayed itself on Lord Vetas's face.

"My investigation has yet to draw any conclusions." Adamat struggled to gather his scattered thoughts. Josep was still alive, he kept reminding himself. Everything would be fine. As long as he played along with Lord Vetas.

"Let's start at the beginning," Lord Vetas said. "Tell me all about your investigations. Both of them."

Adamat found himself talking. The words tumbled over themselves, as if each one was the brick in a wall of safety he was building around his family. He slumped at some point, returning his cane sword to the cane and leaning upon it heavily.

He told Lord Vetas everything he knew about Kresimir's Promise and his and Tamas's conclusion about the Promise being nothing but rubbish. He told him about the night at the Skyline Palace, and about his meeting with Uskan. He included details he'd not meant to say. He went on, recounting his meetings with Ricard Tumblar and Lady Winceslav. Through it all Lord Vetas remained quiet. Adamat could read nothing on the man's face; he absorbed the information impassively.

Adamat spoke so quickly that it did not even occur to him to fudge the truth or lie outright until afterward. When he finished, he fell to sit on the stairs, his hands shaking, and he felt drained. It seemed his age had caught up to him then, and far surpassed him.

Lord Vetas took a moment to think. "Two months of investigation, and this is all you have?"

Adamat narrowed his eyes. "I've been doing the work of twenty men."

"And these are all the details, you're sure?"

"I'm sure," Adamat said. "I do not forget things."

"Ah, yes. Your Knack. Tell me more about this...pending destruction of Adro," Lord Vetas said.

"I know very little." Adamat was tired. He wanted nothing more than to crawl back into a hole. "It is a prophecy that Kresimir will return. It implies a great deal of violence accompanying his return. An old legend."

Lord Vetas remained thoughtful. He dabbed at his neck one last time to remove the blood there and put on his hat. "I'll be back," he said. "I hope you'll have something of greater interest for me when I do. If not..." His eyes flicked to the box in Adamat's robe pocket.

CHAPTER 25

Taniel wiped the blood from his face and watched a pair of women drag another Watcher away from the bulwark. The man's skull had been creased by a bullet, not a minute after he and Taniel had shared a flagon of wine behind the relative safety of the bastion walls. Taniel closed his eyes and tried to remember the man's face. He'd sketch it later tonight.

Blood was everywhere; new blood, old blood. Fresh splatters of red on the ground and on Taniel's coat; old rusty stains on everything. The whole bastion smelled of salty iron. The sickly, clogging scent of death wafted up from below and warred with the clouds of black powder for Taniel's senses.

The Kez were carrying the wounded down the mountainside at an alarming rate. Men were pushed and passed along like sacks of grain to make room for new soldiers. A week ago they'd constructed a V-shaped slide of lumber that went all the way down to

Mopenhague. The dead were dumped in and prodded down by men with sticks, their faces wrapped in linen scarves. The wood had long since turned a brownish red. Taniel didn't even want to imagine what that slide smelled like. He could see great pits on the plains below where the bodies were being dumped.

Taniel sat with his back against the bulwark, cleaning and reloading his rifle. A regular bullet this time—he was running low on redstripes. Beside him, Ka-poel wore her long black duster and hat. A bullet had taken a piece out of one lapel. She returned his worried look with a cryptic tilt of her head. He got up on one knee and looked over the bastion wall.

The redoubts had fallen weeks ago. No attempt had been made to retake them. Kez soldiers hid on the far side of their walls and waited there for orders. Taniel caught a soldier peeking too far around the wall and took his shot. The man grabbed for his face and yelled. He lost his footing. With a stumble he was rolling down the hill, taking two of his comrades with him as he grabbed blindly to arrest his fall.

If he survived the tumble, he'd be disfigured for life.

Taniel pushed the thought from his mind and turned around to reload. A bullet glanced off the wall near him just a moment after he ducked down. He took a deep breath and began reloading. "Find me a Privileged," he told Ka-poel. She gave a nod and peeked over the top of the wall.

There'd been weeks of this. Kez soldiers held the mountainside just beyond the first redoubt. They piled soil high on the road to give themselves cover and cowered behind rocks and dirt and whatever they could find. Artillery had been moved up. Blasted remains had tumbled down the mountainside not long after, destroyed by the Watch cannons. More artillery moved up, accompanied by shielded Privilegeds. After countless tries, they'd formed a beachhead, and now artillery thumped away at the bulwark from at least fifteen cleared spots on the mountainside.

Every few hours they rushed the bulwark—like clockwork they formed behind their barriers and readied their weapons. A horn would sound. They'd charge up the hill, only to meet with withering fire. Taniel could practically see the promises of glory in their officers' eyes before he gunned them down. It turned his stomach.

Each rush failed, yet each time they inched a little closer to the fortress. The Watch was losing men too. Canister shot pierced Bo's tentative shields of sorcery above them. Bullets took musketmen between the eyes when they lined up to take a shot. Even some sorcery was beginning to make it through. A man had been burned alive by a sliver of Privileged fire yesterday. The bastion still smelled of charred flesh.

Taniel finished loading his rifle with a redstripe and took a few deep breaths. Ka-poel flashed a hand signal. Target found. Eleven o'clock from his position. He pictured it in his mind. One of the gun emplacements.

His rise to take a shot was arrested by the arrival of Gavril. The big Watchmaster scurried toward Taniel, head down, a bottle of wine in one hand and a pewter mug in the other. He fell down beside Taniel, back thumping against the bulwark, and waved the bottle under Taniel's nose.

"How are things on the front, Marked?" he asked.

Ka-poel tapped Taniel's shoulder. Repeated the hand motions. He took a deep breath and stood up at the wall. Less than a second to line up his shot. He pulled the trigger and dropped back down, breathing deep of the powder smoke. Ka-poel watched. She gave him a nod, but moved her hand, horizontally at her waist. He'd hit the Privileged, but not a killing shot.

Taniel gave Gavril his best scowl. "Shot full of holes. Why are you so happy?"

"Saint Adom's Festival wine!" Gavril held up the bottle. "They've sent enough from Adopest to get the whole Kez army drunk. Pity there's a war on. Late spring is the only time of year I can abide

Adopest. The festival wine certainly helps." He paused to fill the pewter cup and offered it to Taniel. Taniel waved him off.

"Already had a lick," he said. "Five minutes ago."

Ka-poel took the wine bottle from Gavril's hand. She upended the bottle, taking deep gulps. Taniel took it from her. "Not too much, girl," he said. She snatched the bottle back, taking another draw from it.

"If they can kill," Gavril said, "they can drink. This girl's plenty grown up, Taniel. Just save enough for me, lass." Gavril took the bottle back and drained the last of it in one long draft. He smacked his lips, thick cheeks flushed, and Taniel wondered how many bottles the Watchmaster had already put away. He felt a little concern—rumor had it that Gavril had started drinking heavily again during the nights. He hoped it wasn't true.

It wasn't the only rumor to concern him. "Wine's all good," Taniel said. "But I'd rather have gunpowder. Any word on the shortage?" They'd gone through their stores at an alarming rate. What should have lasted a year's siege was spent in just a few weeks. The Kez just had too many soldiers.

Gavril shook his head. "Nothing from Adopest. The last courier said the army still has plenty. Even still, they shorted us two whole cartloads last week." He scowled. "I ordered the artillery to go easy the next few days. I have the feeling we'll be seeing hand-to-hand soon."

"You really think they'll make it over the bulwark?"

"Eventually." Gavril suddenly looked very tired. His bulk sagged a little, and his face revealed a man fighting a war of attrition he felt he might lose. "We've killed twenty thousand men already. Wounded as many more, and yet they keep coming. They say there's a million down on that plain below, each one with words of glory and promises of riches in their ears."

"I heard Ipille has offered a whole duchy to the officer who leads the charge that breaks us."

"Heard the same thing," Gavril said. "And they'll make officers of the first thousand soldiers who follow him in."

"That's a lot of incentive."

"Aye. Gives us a lot to shoot at."

"They have more men than we have bullets."

"How many Privileged you think you've killed?"

Taniel ran his fingers along the notches on the butt of his rifle. "Thirteen dead. Wounded twice that many."

"That's a sizable chunk of their royal cabal."

"Not enough," Taniel said.

"Well, I want you to keep an eye on something else."

Taniel frowned. "What's more important than Privileged?"

"Sappers," Gavril said.

Taniel remembered the sappers. They'd tried to start digging their first day on the mountainside, and gunshots had sent them back down the hill with their tails between their legs, not to be seen since. Well, not until the other day. They were back at it again, down below the last redoubt—well behind the Kez front line. They were deep enough already that artillery wasn't bothering them, though a couple of cannons had been blasting away at their position.

"Are you really worried about them?" Taniel asked. "It'll take them years to dig the distance all the way up to us. If they break through, all we do is point a cannon down that hole and fill it with grapeshot."

"Wish it were that easy," Gavril said. "Bo says they've got help. Privileged. And Julene."

Taniel felt his hands begin to shake a little. He stilled them by rubbing them together. "Whatever she feels like helping with can't be good news for us. Still. You want me to shoot at sappers?"

"Not the sappers themselves. Watch for the Privileged helping them."

"Gavril!"

Bo joined them at the bulwark, crossing the yard at a dead run. He dropped down on the other side of Taniel, breathing hard. Taniel could tell he was exhausted. His cheeks were sunken, all traces of fat gone, and his hair dirty and scraggly. There was mud on his face, from Kresimir-knew-what.

"They're planning something big," Bo said.

"The sappers?" Gavril asked. "We know about them."

"No," Bo snapped. "Right now. The..." He stopped as the sound of enemy artillery suddenly fell off. There was a moment of silence before a Watch cannon fired, followed by the cracks of muskets. There was no return from the Kez side. Bo went on. "All their Privileged are gathered just below the last redoubt, near their sappers."

Taniel shrugged.

"Over a hundred!" Bo said. "They don't get together like that for a picnic. There's officers there, too, I wouldn't doubt. They're getting ready for a big push."

Gavril stood up, looking over the bulwark. Taniel closed his eyes and waited.

"Shit," Gavril said, dropping back down. "You might be right. They've got men coming up all quiet on the road. Lots of them. I saw a few black jackets among them."

"Wardens?" Taniel said. "Pit."

Gavril climbed to his feet and was away, barking orders at the Watchers, yelling for every able-bodied man.

"How can you miss that?" Bo said after Gavril was gone. "Aren't you shooting at the bastards?"

Taniel pointed at Ka-poel. "She's my spotter. I'm always behind cover."

Ka-poel flashed a number of hand signals.

"She said they have only gathered in the last few minutes," Taniel said.

"Well, be ready for whatever..."

Bo threw his hand up in a warding gesture. A second later a

canister shot went off right above their heads, the echo of the blast ringing through the bastion. Bo's shields flashed red as the bullets clattered off them, then fell harmlessly to the ground. Canisters exploded over the entire length of the bastion, the sound deafening. The wall at Taniel's back shook with the impact of cannonballs. He glanced at Ka-poel. Her eyes were dark. She hadn't even flinched.

"They must be firing every damned artillery they have!" Taniel said above the din. Bo ignored him. His face was strained, his hands flashing at an incredible speed as he worked sorcery to shield the air above the bastion.

The bombardment was withering. Bo's eyes began to water, veins standing out on his forehead. Fire flashed above them, and Taniel knew that sorcery was backing up the Kez artillery.

Watchers rushed beneath Bo's shields, flinching at the explosions above, carrying sacks and torches. One Watcher set a sack gently beside Taniel and was off for another after a quick glance at Bo and a muttered prayer. Taniel looked inside the sack. It was full of clay balls as large as a man's fist. Grenados. They expected the Kez to get close today indeed.

"Fix bayonets!" Gavril's bellow rose above the concussion of artillery. Taniel felt his heart beat faster. He pulled his ring bayonet from its leather case in his pack and slid it over the end of his rifle. With a twist it locked into place.

"Ready!" Gavril yelled.

Taniel checked his rifle—already loaded. He glanced at Bo. The Privileged was doing all he could do to stay standing while his fingers flashed commands to unseen elements. His shields were beginning to break down. On the other end of the bulwark a canister shot went off within the shield. Men screamed and fell, and a cannon lost its crew.

Taniel peeked over the edge of the bulwark as a trumpet sounded. The mountainside suddenly swarmed with Kez soldiers. They rushed up the road, they climbed the steep rocks. Every inch of mountainside was covered. Where had they been hiding all of these men so close to the fortress?

"Aim!"

Taniel picked out an officer near the front. The man's white feather wriggled in the air as he ran up the road at the head of his men, waving his sword in the air. The Kez troops plowed on behind him, bayonets fixed on their muskets. A black coat among all the red and gold caught his eye and he changed targets. His heart beat loudly in his ears. Wardens. Lots of them, scattered among the troops. They carried big knives in their teeth like sailors as they scrambled over the rocks on the mountainside, heading straight for the slanted walls of the bulwark.

"Fire!"

Taniel pulled the trigger. He burned a little powder, giving extra oomph to the ball. A cloud of spent gunpowder burst into the air, obscuring his vision for a moment. It cleared, and yells of dismay echoed through the bastion.

Only one man fell from the volley: the Warden Taniel had shot right between the eyes with a redstripe. Bullets and grapeshot burst into sparks and fell harmlessly to the ground a few feet in front of the first ranks. The Kez charge didn't even falter.

"They have Privileged in their ranks!" Taniel yelled.

"Fire at will!" came the order.

He snatched for his purse of redstripes and opened his third eye. A wave of nausea came over him, which he pushed away as he reloaded. He didn't have time for powder. He simply dropped a redstripe down his muzzle and rammed cotton swabbing in after it. He sighted down the rifle, opened his third eye.

Pastel colors from the third sight made his head spin. The invisible shield the Kez Privileged were using became a translucent, yellow sheen partially obscuring all behind it. He struggled to pick through the colors beyond. Wardens glowed, and so did Knacked among the Kez troops. Taniel looked for the brightest colors—the

Privileged. He picked one out and pulled the trigger. The man jerked and dropped, and Taniel loaded another redstripe.

He managed two more before the Kez reached the walls. The thunder of artillery suddenly dropped off.

Gavril's voice shouted, "Hold!"

Taniel heard Bo wheeze. He spun in time to catch Bo under one arm and lower him to the ground. Bo shook his head. "Keep going!" he coughed. "You're weakening them." His eyes grew wide and he lurched to his feet. "They're dropping the shield!"

"Fire!" Gavril roared.

Another cloud of powder swirled up around them as the line fired away. A dead silence briefly touched the bulwark, and then men were scrambling to reload as artillery captains barked orders.

The smoke cleared.

The volley of shots had torn through the first few ranks. Men dropped by the score. Wounded tossed themselves to the side, trying not to be trampled by those behind. They could not get out of the way. There were too many soldiers. Adran cannons fired grapeshot, the sound pounding away at Taniel's ears.

Only Wardens remained standing after the grapeshot. They pushed onward, wet stains on their black coats betraying blood loss, yet seemingly no worse for the wear. They bellowed in defiance, shook their knives in the air, and waved to the ranks behind them. The dead were trodden underfoot.

"Grenados!"

The clay balls were lit on torches along the wall and tossed over. Explosions bit into the Kez numbers. A few Wardens were blasted to pieces.

Kez swarmed the base of the bulwark like angry hornets. Ladders were put in place, and grappling hooks thrown. Taniel snatched for a hatchet as a hook landed beside him. He cut the rope with one chop and jumped up, firing at a Privileged at the bottom of the wall.

Wardens scrambled up the slanted walls of the bastion as if they were light inclines. They made it up the wall in moments, and a half dozen jumped down among the Watchers.

"To bayonets!" Gavril yelled. "Keep up the cannon fire!"

One great, ugly head poked over the bulwark right in front of Ka-poel. Taniel swung his rifle toward the Warden, but Ka-poel was faster. Her hand jabbed forward, revealing a long needle that had been hidden in her sleeve. It went through the Warden's eye and into his brain. The creature let go his handholds and fell.

Taniel stabbed a Kez soldier in the shoulder as he scrambled over the wall. He cracked the next man with the butt of his rifle and tried to load another redstripe. The Kez were coming too fast. He took a quick snort of powder and gripped his rifle in both hands, sure he wouldn't get off another shot. He readied himself for the next wave—they'd find a trance-taken powder mage ready for them.

A Warden came over the wall with one hand on the brick, the other clutching a knife big enough to cut Taniel in two. Ka-poel leapt for him, but was batted away like a doll. Taniel yelled, thrusting his bayonet. The Warden reached long arms over the rifle, ignoring fourteen inches of steel through his middle, and backhanded Taniel. Taniel stumbled. The blow had rattled him even in a powder trance.

The Warden spotted Bo on the ground and pushed himself off Taniel's bayonet. Bo raised his hands, trying to manage some defense, but the Warden leapt upon him in a moment, knife raised.

Taniel reached the Warden as he was about to stab Bo. He thrust his bayonet, spitting the creature like a hog. The Warden's head turned, surprised that Taniel had regained his feet so quickly. The Warden tried to use his weight and strength as leverage to throw Taniel's grip on his rifle.

Taniel would have none of it. He could feel the barrel of his rifle strain as he shoved the Warden back against the bastion wall. He set his feet and lifted, dumping the Warden over the edge. He hoped the creature's wounds would prevent it from climbing the bastion again.

He paused for just a moment to help Ka-poel to her feet. She was rattled, but unhurt.

Gavril appeared by his side. "Get back to shooting," he snarled as he grabbed a Kez soldier by the throat. He lifted the man, one-handed, and tossed him over the wall. "Kill the Privileged!"

Suddenly Fesnik was there with Gavril, a small sword in one hand, a long pole in the other, pushing away the ladders. Under their cover, Taniel grabbed his bag of redstripes. He dropped two balls in, rammed down the cotton, and took aim.

Angle floating, powder mages called it—when you fire a bullet and push it in one sharp direction, around a wall or even around a person. Taniel had seen his father do it on many occasions—it was said Tamas was the very best.

Taniel generally had a hard time with angle floating, and often failed to make the angle sharp enough. It took precision timing and a damned huge amount of concentration. Taniel couldn't manage that concentration. A failed angle floater made his head feel like it had been pounded by a hammer. A successful one hurt more.

What Taniel could do was nudge bullets. Nudging a bullet was no more than burning some powder to correct your aim while the bullet was in flight—much like floating itself. It took little more than a sharp eye, yet he'd never seen anyone shoot farther nor more accurately than he could. And he could do it with two bullets.

Ka-poel pointed out a pair of Privileged about ten paces from each other. They stood down beside the easy cover of the redoubts, some hundred paces away and protected by their personal shields. Taniel lined up the shot and pulled the trigger.

Both men dropped, taking the separate bullets to the chest. A third Privileged saw them fall. Taniel ducked behind the wall.

He signaled to Ka-poel to stay down. The Privileged would be watching for him now. He couldn't stop shooting. He took a few deep breaths and loaded one bullet and pictured that third Privileged in his mind's eye. Less than a second to aim and shoot. He crawled, rifle in hand, changing his position on the wall by five paces. A few quick breaths and he sprang up.

The Privileged had his hands up, fingers twitching. An arch of lightning sprang from the air above him as Taniel pulled the trigger. The lightning slammed into the spot Taniel had been a few moments before, the force of the impact powerful enough to knock Taniel, Gavril, Ka-poel, Fesnik, and a dozen Kez soldiers off their feet.

The bullet drifted high and ripped through the Privileged's throat. He went down in a spray of blood.

Taniel breathed a sigh of relief.

A horn resounded across the mountainside. The sound of fighting tapered off as the Kez soldiers retreated back down the mountain.

Gavril pushed away a soldier he'd been grappling with. He held a fist above his head. "Cease fire!" The cannons silenced. Kez soldiers within the bulwark threw down their weapons. Gavril scowled at them. "We're not taking prisoners," he said. "Surrender your weapons and gear, and then down the mountain with you."

Word passed throughout the bastion. Kez climbed back over the walls after being relieved of their muskets and powder, and began the long walk among their dead. Gavril found a Kez officer among the wounded and took him by the shoulder while Taniel watched.

"Tell Field Marshal Tine that he can send some unarmed soldiers up to collect your dead. And I suggest we all take a few days to tend to the wounded." Gavril repeated the order in Kez to be sure he was understood.

The officer nodded wearily and, with the help of a Kez soldier, headed over the wall and down the mountain.

Taniel dropped down beside Bo.

"You OK?"

Bo gave him a long look.

"I'll take that as a no."

"To the pit with all this," Bo managed.

Katerine, Rina, and Alasin appeared as if from nowhere. All three of Bo's women. They surrounded Bo, alternately scolding and fussing, and Bo was carried off toward the town.

Taniel and Gavril watched them go.

"I need to get me one of those," Taniel said.

"What?" Gavril asked. "A harem?"

"Yeah," Taniel said. Ka-poel punched him in the arm.

"I've tried juggling more than one woman at once," Gavril said. "It's a pain in the ass. Don't know how Privileged do it."

"They treat 'em like shit," Taniel said.

"Bo doesn't," Gavril said. "I guess I should say, 'I don't know how *Bo* does it.'"

They turned and watched the retreating Kez in silence for a moment.

"You really saved our asses there," Gavril said.

Taniel gave Gavril a surprised look. "Huh?"

"You didn't know?"

Gavril slapped his knee and gave a loud guffaw. Watchers, tending to the dead and wounded, paused to give Gavril odd looks. "You mean you don't know who you shot?"

"A Privileged?" He bent over, picked up a discarded bottle of St. Adom's Festival wine. Somehow it had gone unbroken through all of this. He took a swig. After a moment's hesitation he handed it to Ka-poel. She drank once and gave it back.

"At a hundred yards even I recognized him," Gavril said. "That last one, the one that hit us with a lightning bolt hard enough to knock through the wards on the bastion. That was Brajon the Callous."

Taniel choked on a mouthful of wine. "The head of the Kez Cabal?"

"The same," Gavril said.

Taniel felt his knees weaken beneath him. He put a hand on the bastion wall for support. "I would never have stood up if I had known it was him. Brajon was in Fatrasta at the beginning of the war. He almost ended it himself. Wiped out an entire Fatrastan army—singlehandedly. The war would have ended there if he hadn't been called back to Kez by Ipille himself."

"Well, I'm glad you didn't know," Gavril said. "They almost had us there. Their Privileged were dressed in infantry colors and hiding their gloves. Blended right in. Bo was too busy tending his shields to notice."

And Taniel hadn't had his third eye open until it was too late. He scolded himself. Stupid. He'd almost gotten them all killed. Taniel watched as Gavril took stock of the damage to the bastion. "You know," Taniel said, "we could have kept firing after they sounded the retreat. Would have wiped out thousands on the mountainside. The Kez did that to us in Fatrasta a few times."

Gavril snorted angrily. "War has to have some decorum. Otherwise it's back to the Bleakening for all of us, and Kresimir be damned."

Gavril left him then. Taniel looked over the edge of the bastion. He thought to open his third eye to track their Privileged, but decided it would just give him a headache.

A thought troubled him. If that was their big push, then where was Julene? He searched the hillside for the entrance to the sapper tunnels. There was some movement there, and he thought he saw a man empty a wheelbarrow of dirt.

Tamas stared up at the ceiling of a small room, his vision blurry. There wasn't much to see even had his eyes been clear. He could make out the slanted logs of a roof, plain wood with mud in the cracks to seal them against the weather. It was light, barely. His body told him it was dawn. The light was gloomy, indicative of a stormy day ahead. He heard the crow of a rooster, and the sound of hoofbeats, followed by a muffled conversation. The men outside spoke Kez.

He couldn't feel his right leg. It wasn't a pleasant sensation, and combined with his blurry vision Tamas had to fight rising panic. Without a leg or good vision, what hope did he have of escape? He breathed deeply, calming himself, and assessed the rest of his body for wounds.

Both of his hands and arms still seemed to work. They moved when prompted. He could feel the stab of a straw mattress beneath him. His chest hurt when he took too deep a breath, but not enough for a broken rib. His side was tender, perhaps from a cut or a bruise. He touched it gently. A bruise, he decided. He was in short undergarments and nothing else, and years of instinct told him he was not alone in the room.

Tamas struggled to push himself into a sitting position. He'd been provided with neither blanket nor pillow, and lay upon a filthy straw mattress on a wooden frame. There was a window on his left, and stairs going down at the end of the bed. He rubbed his eyes, which improved his vision slightly. A Warden sat in the corner, his muscled, malformed body easy to recognize, though Tamas could not make out much more than the outline of the body.

"Where am I?" Tamas said.

The blurry mountain of flesh seemed to regard him for a moment, then mumbled something unintelligible in Kez.

"Where am I?" Tamas repeated.

The Warden left the room.

"Where am I," Tamas shouted after the Warden. He pushed himself up farther. "Monster. Beast!" He lay back down, what little strength he had now gone. His head had begun to throb when he moved. He felt along the wrapping gingerly, grimacing. The slightest touch brought a jolt of pain, and he eventually left it alone. He'd been treated. They'd covered his wounds in strips of dirty linen. His leg was wrapped tight, but there was still circulation. He wouldn't be walking on it any time soon. He heard steps from below, and two pairs of boots upon the stairs. The Warden returned, with him a smaller man.

"Field Marshal," a voice said in accented Adran. Tamas felt his hackles rise at the sound of the voice.

"Nikslaus," he spat. "I thought I threw you in the Adsea."

The duke's voice was genial. "My Wardens fished me out. How is your leg?"

"It's fantastic," Tamas said. "I'm going to dance a jig. Where am I?"

Nikslaus took the Warden's seat in the corner of the room, while the Warden stood at the foot of the bed. "Deep in the King's Wood," he said. "Now, my surgeon said you'd hit your head hard when you fell. Are you having any problems with your vision?"

"No," Tamas lied.

"Of course you are," Nikslaus said. "I can tell that your eyes aren't focusing. I'll have the surgeon take a look at you before we go."

Tamas did his best to glare at Nikslaus, but found it hard when he could barely see him. "Why the pit am I still alive? Where are we going?"

"To Kez," Nikslaus said. "I advised against it, but after that first Warden didn't kill you, Ipille decided that we should send a message. If everything goes as scheduled, you'll face the guillotine beneath my king's gaze on the final day of Saint Adom's Festival."

"You've planned this for a long time," Tamas said.

"One of many contingencies. We need to be rid of you, one way or another, if we're to take Adro. You're the strongest of the powder mages and a tactical genius—I don't mind saying it, it's the truth.

The mercenaries will give us some fight, but you're the backbone of your army. Your soldiers will crumble without you."

"You underestimate them," Tamas said.

"Perhaps." Nikslaus seemed unworried. "The dominoes will fall, Tamas. You're only the first. Adro is outnumbered. With your head in a basket, we will whittle away at the Mountainwatch and hunt down your powder mages. We have every advantage."

Tamas gazed at his hands, trying desperately to focus on them. "What happened to my leg?"

"My fault," Nikslaus said. "The boulder you were hiding behind cracked in a particular way, and then exploded when I applied enough sorcery. A fragment glanced your leg. Shattered it, I'm afraid.

"But I wouldn't worry much about it," Nikslaus continued. "Our surgeon says it might heal, in time. He's quite gifted. Put it back together and stitched the flesh up like no one would know." Nikslaus stood up and approached the bed. He leaned forward, just out of Tamas's reach. "You're a few hundred krana richer, Tamas," he said in a low voice. He tilted his head toward Tamas's leg. "There's a star of gold in there, right up against the bone. You've been cured."

Tamas lurched forward and swung a fist at the blurry image of the duke. His body screamed at him, his leg sending a fiery needle of pain up his body that made his stomach lurch. Nikslaus danced out of the way.

"Cured." That's what Nikslaus thought of it. Gold in the bloodstream of a powder mage was anathema. It removed their ability to sense and touch powder, to enter a trance.

Nikslaus gave a chuckle. "You're cured, Tamas, but it won't help your cause. Your neck will rest beneath the same guillotine blade that took your wife's head all those years ago. You won't go to your death as a powder mage. You'll go as the son of a poor apothecary."

Tamas's blood thumped hard in his ears and his hands shook

violently. He wanted to reach out and take Nikslaus by the throat. He longed to have finished what he started on the docks. Yet he could do nothing. He was powerless.

It was not a familiar feeling. For as long as Tamas could remember, his magery had been there. Even when not in a powder trance, he could sense nearby sorcerers and tell where and how much powder there was within hundreds of paces. He could detonate charges or kegs, he could breathe in the acrid smoke and send his body into a berserk rage.

He had none of that now. Only his hands and a shattered leg, and vision blurred by a concussion. He sank back onto the bed and felt moisture roll down his face. He turned away from Nikslaus as best he could.

The duke left him in silence. Even the Warden was gone. It was plain to see that Tamas could do nothing, and from the growing noise outside the room there was plenty else to be done than watch one broken old man.

Nikslaus's voice was louder than the others. He gave orders with the arrogance of the nobility. Tamas forced his hands to stop shaking. He lifted his good leg and put one foot on the floor. He pushed himself up.

He nearly collapsed there. It took all of his strength to keep from falling flat on his face. He put one hand on the wall, the other on a bedpost. He pushed himself over to the window, hopping on one leg. He stopped only to vomit, the pain finally overcoming his gag suppression, and then he was at the window.

Tamas sank to the floor, careful to avoid the puddle of bile, and put his head against the cool wall. He could hear Nikslaus almost as clearly as if he stood next to him. Nikslaus either didn't count on Tamas eavesdropping or didn't care.

"We'll take the long road to Adopest," Nikslaus said in Kez. "I don't care what the scouts say, I'll not risk encountering those fools from the hunt."

Tamas heard the gallop of approaching hooves. They stopped outside the window.

"Well?" Nikslaus said.

"We tracked down four more, my lord," a deep voice responded. There was a guttural quality to the voice, so Tamas knew it was a Warden.

"Is that the last of them?" Nikslaus said.

"No telling. With our man dead, we don't know how many men Ryze brought with him. I suspect we have them all."

"Don't underestimate that brigadier," Nikslaus snarled. "He was one of Winceslav's best. He'll have had outriders in case anything happened. Leave two Wardens to hunt."

"We had to dodge patrols. They're looking for Tamas."

"We'll be gone before they reach us. Go help the others. We leave within the hour."

With powder mages on his trail, Nikslaus would be in a hurry to get away. Tamas's mood began to rise, only to plummet as logic set in. They had been hours away from the hunt. Half a day from Adopest. Sabon might not even know he was missing yet. And that was all based on the possibility that Nikslaus let the others get away. How many Wardens did he have with him? Did Nikslaus send them after Olem, Charlemund, and the rest?

Tamas gave a weary sigh. Even if they were to find him, what was he? Just an old man now. No more a powder mage.

CHAPTER 26

Adamat spent nearly a week investigating Ondraus the Reeve before making an appointment to interview the man. He almost canceled the appointment due to wild speculation that had reached the city that morning: Tamas disappearing from the Orchard Valley Hunt the day before, a rogue brigadier, sorcery in the King's Forest. None of the rumors could be confirmed, so Adamat went on with the interview, though he had an unsettling feeling that he might no longer be employed.

He arrived at the reeve's home at five past the hour, late for his meeting because he'd passed the house four times without finding it. The house itself was behind a hedgerow, wedged between two manors and easily mistaken for some kind of servants' quarters. There was a small garden between the hedgerow and front step, meticulously cared for, not a blade of grass or flower petal out of place. The house was utilitarian—a simple A-frame made of fine, but not expensive, brick.

The door opened as Adamat lifted his hand to the knocker. An old woman peered up at him. She wore a drab maid's frock, a simple wool shirt that went all the way down to her ankles.

"I'm here to—"

"See the reeve," she cut him off. "You're late."

"I'm sorry, I couldn't find…"

The old woman turned and hobbled away in the middle of his sentence. Adamat trailed off. He swallowed his annoyance and followed her into the house.

The inside was as unremarkable as the outside. The mantelpiece was clear of knickknacks, the shelves freshly dusted and also empty but for two rows of bookkeeper's volumes. A single chair sat before an empty fireplace. There were three doorways. One led to an alcove of a kitchen, where the only sign of use was a fresh loaf of bread on the table. The second door was closed—presumably the bedroom—and the third door was open, showing the reeve sitting at a small desk in the corner, spectacles balanced on the tip of his nose as his finger ran across the page of a book of numbers.

The housekeeper clucked to herself and went into the kitchen, leaving Adamat to show himself in to the reeve. Adamat watched her for a moment, and wondered if the kitchen was used at all—there was no smell of baking, or undue heat from a cooking fire, so she must have bought the bread somewhere else. She turned and caught him watching her and shut the kitchen door.

Adamat turned his attention to the little man sitting at a desk. He's more than he seemed, Ricard had warned. Well, what did he seem? A dusty bookkeeper. An accountant—though admittedly the finest one in Adro. So what more could he be? Anything, Adamat supposed.

"You're late." The reeve didn't bother to look up from his book as Adamat entered.

"My apologies. The streets are awfully full, with the festival and all." Adamat didn't bother adding how unusual it was to hold appointments on a festival evening. Something told him the reeve didn't actually enjoy having fun.

"Save the excuses for someone else. Don't waste my time, Investigator," the reeve said. "I didn't try to have Tamas killed. I have neither the patience nor time to answer your questions. The ledgers still need to be kept in Tamas's absence." He made a face, realizing that he had let something slip.

"So he is missing?" Adamat asked.

The reeve glared at him.

Adamat examined the reeve for a moment. Ondraus was a small man, bent from decades of leaning over a desk, shoulders hunched. His face was long, his cheeks sallow, shoulders narrow. Ondraus was one of the most well known men in Adopest. This was quite the feat, considering that he rarely showed his face in public, he had never sat for a portrait, and he reportedly *tried* to alienate everyone he met. Adamat could see that the last seemed to hold true. He could also see that Ondraus would not be talking about Tamas's disappearance.

Adamat's weeklong investigation had turned up frustratingly little. The reeve handled the nation's treasury—with the exception of the king's purse, though there was a rumor that that had changed with Manhouch's execution—from that little desk in the corner. He had an office on Joon Street, which he never visited, where a team of bookkeepers did most of the labor. Everything they did was double-checked by the reeve. He had no known hobbies, no known friends. His housekeeper had been with him for forty-some years, but no one considered them to be friends. He had one bodyguard, who went with him whenever he left the house, which was rare.

Rumor had it the reeve had ridden at the hunt, that he had been there when Tamas disappeared. Adamat couldn't picture the man on a horse.

"You don't seem the type of man to betray his country," Adamat said. "As the city reeve you could undermine Adro from its very heart without Kez help. It's not a question of money. My research indicates that you're one of the wealthiest men in Adro. You receive two hundred thousand krana a year for services rendered, and you own three million acres of farmland in Fatrasta, half a million acres of Bakashcan coastline that includes a major port, a coal mine in Deliv, and half of a trading company in Kez. I do wonder at all the foreign stock. Do you not have faith in your country?"

"You'd know if you were more thorough," Ondraus said. "I own three gold mines and twelve Mountainwatch toll roads. I own three hundred and twelve thousand acres of vineyards, and I finance a merchants' guild in the north." He waved his hand dismissively. "Ask your friend, Ricard Tumblar, if you want to know more. I personally employ three thousand of his union workers in my ironworks."

"Among other factories," Adamat said.

Ondraus's eyes narrowed. "You knew."

"I was just curious what you'd catalog as the most valuable."

"If you don't suspect me, then why are we having this conversation?"

"I never said I don't suspect you. I'll admit you are low on my list. I want to know, sir, what the books tell you."

"I don't get your meaning."

By the way Ondraus's hand tightened on his ledger Adamat suspected he understood perfectly. "Money. You track everything. Even things a reeve shouldn't know you have cataloged." Adamat pointed at the ledger with his cane. "I've taken a look at your books on Joon Street. Very thorough. Very impressive."

"Those aren't for public eyes," Ondraus snapped.

"I'm not the public. I had to bully my way past your clerks. They're very loyal to you. Now, tell me, what does the flow of money tell you?"

Ondraus watched him through those bespectacled eyes for several moments before he responded. Calculations were being made, thoughts sliding into place.

"If the motive is money," Ondraus said, "which it almost always is, then you have nothing to suspect of either the Proprietor or Lady Winceslav. I've had access to the Winceslav books for months now and there is absolutely nothing irregular about them. The Proprietor—well, criminal or not, he pays his taxes. Every penny of them, even that made on illicit gains. A man who pays his taxes like that is not concerned with the day-to-day of the government. He wants nothing more than a stable world in which to expand his influence slowly, assuredly."

"War can mean a great deal of money for an opportunist."

"Opportunists do not pay their taxes," Ondraus said.

"And the other councillors?"

Ondraus sniffed. "Prime Lektor is a mystery. The man's finances do not exist. Very strange, that. Aside from the occasional grant from the university, it's as if money does not even go through his hands. Ricard Tumblar is a businessman. He cooks the books as well as he can. He's received very large sums of money lately from Brudania and from banks in Fatrasta and Gurla."

"Brudania is a major ally of Kez."

"And the banks in Gurla are owned by the Kez."

"Fatrasta is not an ally," Adamat said. "And I'm not sure if I can trust what you say about Ricard. The unionization of your workers must have infuriated you."

"Did it?" Ondraus raised an eyebrow. "His unions have organized production in a way even I couldn't. Revenue has increased three hundred percent in my ironworks and gold mines since the unions came in. Ask Ricard. I did not bar them. I *welcomed* the unions."

Ondraus made a dismissive gesture, moving on. "Then there's the arch-diocel. As a man of the cloth his movements are completely shrouded in secrecy. No one outside of their order may so much as glance at their books. Yet he spends enough to make a king weep. Far more than his allowance as an arch-diocel. I often wonder at that."

"And yourself?"

"I am to suspect myself?"

"Is there any reason you'd want Tamas killed?"

"Tamas is spending too much on the army and too much on spies. This is wartime, however, so his expenditures are practical. He's increased public rations higher than I would like, but that came about from a previous agreement of ours. A ferret could run this country better than Manhouch did. At least Tamas listens to my advice."

Ondraus went on without prompting. "If Tamas were to die, the military leadership would not be up to the task of holding off the Kez. The Kez would conquer Adro, and Adopest would be taxed. The Kez have a long history of excessive tax on their colonies in Fatrasta and Gurla. We would be no different, and the city coffers would be even worse off than they were under Manhouch."

Adamat considered, not for the first time, Ondraus's singular position of power. If he wanted to thwart Tamas, he could be far more subtle than by having him killed. He could just tell Tamas there was no money to pay the army or feed the people. Tamas would have riots within a month and be completely undone within two.

What he'd said about Ricard bothered Adamat. Ricard may have been the head of the Warriors of Labor and received a great deal of money, but he was not wealthy in the way that people like Ondraus or Charlemund considered wealth. He was no king. The Kez had the money to make him one.

Adamat said, "Thank you for your time. I think I'm done here. I may return if I have further questions."

The reeve turned back to his ledger without another word.

"I'll show myself out," Adamat said.

Nikslaus, whether he feared Tamas or not, was taking no chances. Tamas sat facing backward in the carriage. He wore wrist and ankle irons, both of them bolted to the floor by thick chains in the style of a prison wagon. A Warden sat next to Tamas, his twisted bulk pushing Tamas against the side of the wagon. Tamas's skin crawled being so close to one of the creatures.

Despite the irons, the carriage was fit for a duke. Nikslaus sat opposite Tamas upon a velvet cushion, which left plenty of room for his legs. The wall covering and window hangings matched the cushion and did a little to muffle the sound from outside. The carriage had recently ceased its rocking motion and now moved upon a cobbled thoroughfare. From the sound of increasing traffic they were getting close to the city.

Nikslaus appeared deep in his own thoughts. His fingers danced in his lap, sheathed in white, runed Privileged's gloves. Tamas wondered whether he was doing some sort of unseen sorcery, or simply passing the time. Tamas lifted a finger to the curtains and glanced outside. There was nothing of interest to see. At the sound of his chains jingling, Nikslaus glanced at him. He nodded to the Warden, who reached out and firmly moved Tamas's hand from the window.

Tamas sighed. At least his vision had cleared. They'd left the farmhouse late in the afternoon the day before. Something had calmed Nikslaus and he seemed no longer worried they'd be caught. Tamas sent his senses inward, then probed out. He tried to open his third eye.

Powder mages were the only kind of sorcerer whose power could be disrupted like this. Tamas didn't know how it had been discovered, or when, but gold in the bloodstream could render a powder mage's power completely null. It even blocked their ability to see the Else. Removal of a Privileged's hands at the wrist was said to keep them from manipulating the Else, but not from seeing it.

"I'm not a bad man," Nikslaus said suddenly.

Tamas gave him a glance. The duke stared at him, a troubled look on his face.

"I don't revel in your discomfort, or smile at the thought of your doom," Nikslaus said.

Tamas said, "Such knowledge would not keep me from choking the life out of you, given the chance."

Nikslaus gave him a distracted smile. "I'll be glad not to give you such a chance." He paused. "I was thinking, just now, what it would be like if I couldn't use sorcery. If my hands were struck from me and my ability to touch the other side was gone. It was a harrowing thought."

"You'll not win any goodwill from me," Tamas said.

"I simply want you to know," Nikslaus responded, "that I don't do any of this out of pleasure. I act on the whim of my king. I am but a servant."

"Were you a servant when you delivered the head of my wife in a cedar box?" Tamas said. The sentence began calmly. By the time he finished it, he was snarling, his anger bared. It had come upon him like a rogue wave. His chains jingled and clanked. The Warden gave him a dangerous look.

Nikslaus calmed the Warden with a raised hand. "Yes," he said. "I was a servant."

"You enjoyed it," Tamas said through gritted teeth. "Admit it." Bitterness dripped from his voice. "You enjoyed ordering the headsman's blade, you enjoyed bringing her head to me and seeing my sorrow, and you enjoy seeing me incapacitated now."

Nikslaus seemed to think on this. "You're right," he finally said.

Tamas fell silent, shocked that Nikslaus would admit such a thing. It was beneath a duke.

"When you put it that way... I did enjoy it, and I still do," Nikslaus said. "But not for the reasons you think. This isn't personal. Powder mages are a stain. A black blot on sorcery. I don't take relish in another person's suffering. I take pride in seeing a powder mage struck down, as I did when Ipille ordered the death of your wife."

"It makes you no less a beast," Tamas said. He glanced sideways at the Warden. "No less a beast than the ones who made this."

Nikslaus's eyes narrowed. "Says the powder mage. Your kind are more monstrous than Wardens by far." He looked at the ceiling. "I'll never understand the minds of such as you, Tamas. We've both got our prejudices, I suppose." He snorted. "Had you been born a Privileged, you would have made a formidable ally."

"Or opponent," Tamas said.

"No," Nikslaus said. "Not an opponent. Our antagonism toward one another is based solely upon your being a powder mage."

"I'm Adran," Tamas said quietly. "You're Kez."

"And the Adran Cabal would have been enfolded into the Kez Cabal, had the Accords been signed. As they should have been."

"Does Ipille really expect to rule Adro?"

Nikslaus blinked at Tamas. "Of course."

Tamas could see in Nikslaus's eyes that there was no doubt there. What arrogance.

"I've wondered," Nikslaus said, "ever since news came of your coup, what finally did it? Is it simply revenge? Or do you honestly think you have the best interests of Adro at heart?"

"Do you *honestly* think it is in Adro's best interest to bow to Kez?" Tamas countered. "No, don't answer. I can see it in your face. You're as blind a nobleman and monarchal stooge as any of those that I sent to the guillotine. Do you not read the papers? Do you not hear of uprisings in Gurla? I know you felt the sting of rebellion when Fatrasta rose up and threw your armies out."

"Fools, all of them," Nikslaus said.

Tamas persisted. "The world is changing. People do not exist to serve their governments or their kings. Governments exist to serve the people, so the people should have a say in those governments."

Nikslaus scoffed. "Impossible. Decisions should not be left to the rabble."

"One people should not be ruled by another," Tamas said.

Nikslaus steepled his fingers. The gesture was often one of significance when a Privileged was involved—especially when he wore his gloves. "You're either playing me, or you're a naïve fool. You served in Gurla, in Fatrasta, and half a dozen other savage countries where members of the Nine have claimed land. As did I. The peasants and savages need to be tamed. As Adro and the powder mages need to be tamed."

"We learned two different things from our experiences, you and I," Tamas said.

Nikslaus wore a look that said he wasn't that interested in hearing what Tamas learned.

"Who betrayed me?" Tamas asked. He had answers of his own to find.

Nikslaus gave him a glance. "Do you think I'd risk telling you?" He shook his head. "No. Perhaps when the guillotine blade is about to fall, I'll whisper it in your ear. Not a moment before that."

Tamas opened his mouth, about to taunt Nikslaus with the knowledge that Brigadier Barat was a traitor. He stopped himself. Was Nikslaus really worried he'd escape? Did he really think Tamas had a chance? Tamas was bereft of his abilities, his leg unusable. How could he possibly escape?

Nikslaus shifted in his seat. He moved the curtain enough to look out, then sat back, an annoyed look on his face.

"Are we being followed?" Tamas asked, his voice as casual as he could make it.

"You know," Nikslaus said, ignoring Tamas's question and glancing out the window again, "many in the royal court are happy about your coup."

"I'm sure," Tamas said. "If you take Adro, you'll split the land we confiscated from the nobility."

"Confiscated?" Nikslaus said. "Stole. Land and possessions will return to any living relations of the nobility. Titles will be restored. There will be a tax, but a hand of brotherhood must be extended to the ravished nobility."

"So Ipille is not as big a fool as I thought," Tamas said. "Nor greedy."

Nikslaus looked for a moment as if he'd strike Tamas. He seemed to think better of it, simply raising his nose. "What mistake of breeding gave you such disrespect for your betters? Such disdain for the God-chosen king?"

"A god didn't choose Ipille," Tamas snorted. "Or that god is a fool."

"I draw the line at blasphemy," Nikslaus said. "This conversation is over."

The day drew on, morning giving way to afternoon and the carriage grew very warm. Tamas loosened the collar on his sweat-stained riding shirt. His riding coat had been discarded for an inconspicuous brown overcoat. It was hot and close in the tight quarters, and he wished Nikslaus would open the window. The Privileged and the Warden alike seemed unaffected.

He could tell when they crossed the canal. The bridge was stone on steel over a long, tall span, and the wagon wheels rolled over easily. They were getting close to the harbor. He could smell it.

Nikslaus kept glancing out the window. Tamas wondered what Nikslaus sensed with his sorcery. Was Sabon on their trail? Or was Nikslaus simply nervous about their proximity to the city garrison? Tamas took a deep breath and studied Nikslaus. Nervous? Yes. Near to panic? No, not even close. And panic he would, if he thought any of the powder cabal were getting close.

Tamas listened to the sounds outside the carriage, trying to place their location. Somewhere near the docks and the canal. If they had taken the Roan Bridge, they were very close indeed. They could take a smuggler boat out of any of the pier warehouses. Nikslaus wouldn't wait for anything fancy. He'd want to be off with his prize as quickly as possible.

The carriage rolled to a stop. Nikslaus lifted the curtain and smiled at what he saw. Tamas's heart fell. They were here.

Tamas didn't know which startled him more: the explosion, or the screaming horses that followed it. The whole carriage rocked, slamming Tamas against his chains. He bit his tongue against a scream as his weight—and the weight of the Warden—threw his bad leg against the side of the carriage.

Nikslaus kicked open the door. "Kill him if they take me," he told the Warden as he leapt from the carriage. The echo of sorcery clapped the side of the carriage, shaking it more than the explosion had.

Tamas shared a glance with the Warden. The Warden positioned himself in Nikslaus's seat, drawing a knife.

More explosions followed. People screamed. Women and children's voices were mixed in. Tamas felt ill. People were dying out there. Bystanders, caught out on their weekend errands by a crossfire made in the pit. A volley of gunfire erupted, followed by the nearly inaudible pops of the Wardens returning fire with air rifles. A bullet shattered the window and left a hole in the other side of the carriage, passing right between Tamas and the Warden. The Warden's eyes grew just a little bit wider.

"Clear the way!" Tamas heard the driver yell. "We'll make a run for it."

Tamas gritted his teeth. He wanted to strike, to reach out and wrestle the knife from the Warden's hands. He'd have lost without powder, but at least he'd have *done something*. With both hands and legs chained and his magery gone, he could do nothing but sit and listen, grimacing when sorcery or explosions rocked the carriage.

They began to move suddenly. Whatever obstacle had obstructed the road—probably a burning carriage, one filled with Wardens—was now gone. The driver whipped the horses into a frenzy, galloping down the street to the sound of yells. Gunfire and sorcery fell away behind them. The carriage rocked violently. The Warden held on to the sides with both hands, steadying himself without expression. Tamas jolted back and forth, unable to do the same in his chains, and listened to his own whimpers every time his leg jolted.

The Warden watched out the window. "Almost there," he said. He produced a key, and despite the violent thrashing of the carriage, managed to unlock Tamas's chains. He left the wrist and leg irons on. He brandished the knife, and said in heavily accented Adran, "You give me any trouble and I'll bury this in your chest."

The carriage rolled to a stop. The driver leapt from his post, thumping to the ground outside, and pulled the door open. The Warden turned to get out and froze.

It took just a split second for the Warden to turn on Tamas, knife at the ready. Tamas caught the thrust between his wrists and used the leverage of his irons to twist the blade away. Then he was on his back on the carriage bench, lights swimming before his eyes, his ears ringing. He barely even registered the pain in his leg.

It took him a moment to climb to a sitting position. Every inch was an eternity of agony. His leg screamed. He felt blood on the side of his face; he'd not avoided the knife altogether after all. He braced himself against the side of the carriage, the smell of gunpowder in his nostrils.

The Warden was gone. There was a Warden-sized hole in the carriage, opposite the door. His body was on the ground outside, one leg still up on the edge of the carriage, caught by a splinter of wood.

Tamas looked down as Olem deposited a hand cannon on the floor of the carriage. He grunted from the weight, then looked up at Tamas. There was relief in his eyes. "So I stole the right carriage," he said.

Olem helped Tamas out of the carriage. They were in an alleyway between two brick buildings. The strong smell of the sea and the sound of waves said they were very close to the water. Adran soldiers filed into the alley within seconds. One tried to take Tamas's weight from Olem. Olem waved him off.

"Where's Sabon?" Tamas asked.

"Chasing the Privileged, with Vlora," Olem said. He sounded

tired. Could he get tired? "The bastard cut and run when he saw how many of us there were."

Tamas's eyes grew wide as more soldiers filed into the alley. There were more in the streets. "You brought the whole garrison?"

"As many as were close by," Olem said.

"How the pit did you find me?"

Olem smiled. He glanced down, and for the first time Tamas noticed the hound sitting at his feet, eyes bigger than teacups looking up at him. His tail wagged. Tamas found he couldn't speak. He leaned over, despite the pain, and patted Hrusch on the head.

"That's impossible," he managed after a moment.

"Sabon trained Hrusch to find you under any circumstances. Trained him from birth, the damned pup. Had the help of an old farm witch north of the university, a Knacked who can train animals. Hrusch can pick up your scent anywhere, even if you are in a sealed box in the middle of the sea."

"I never knew," Tamas said.

"It was his little secret. A backup plan," Olem said. "I wish we'd never had to use it."

Tamas felt two days' worth of fear, anger, and anticipation melt under Olem's gaze. The bodyguard looked at him as a parent might at a child who'd gone missing. Anger warred with relief in his eyes. Soldiers crowded around with words of concern. Tamas gave them all a grateful smile. After a moment, he collapsed.

CHAPTER 27

The office on the top floor of the House of Nobles seemed old and familiar to Tamas, though he'd occupied it for only a couple of months. It seemed like home, and he ran his fingers over the braided tassels at the edge of the sofa. His hands shook and he leaned heavily on a crutch. The room smelled of lemons. He wondered if it always had.

Olem watched him from the doorway. Knacked or not, it turned out Olem did need rest. His eyes fluttered like one who longs for sleep, and purple bruises had formed under them. His normally neatly trimmed beard was unruly, his hair a mess. On a regular day, Tamas might have chided him for lax regulation.

This was not a regular day.

I should tell him to get some rest. What was it Father used to tell me? "Rest is for the dead."

"Yes, sir," Olem said.

Tamas glanced at him. "Hmm?"

"You said, 'Rest is for the dead,'" Olem said.

"You look like the dead."

"Don't look so good yourself, sir." Olem struggled to put a smile on his face. Tamas could see worry in his eyes. "You should rest, sir," Olem said. "It almost killed you getting up all those stairs."

Olem had insisted on helping Tamas up every step, half carrying him at times.

"I don't need a nurse," Tamas said. "There's work to be done." He hobbled toward his desk, but halfway there he nearly fell.

Olem was at his side in a moment, a hand under his elbow. "Sit down, sir," he said. "Doctor Petrik will be here any minute." Olem helped Tamas onto the sofa.

"Bah," Tamas said. He motioned to a chair. "Have a seat."

"I think I'll stand, sir."

"Suit yourself." Tamas couldn't let Olem rest yet. He couldn't let himself rest yet. "I need to know how things went in my absence. How many people know of my capture?"

"Word spread quickly," Olem said. "I'm afraid I had other things on my mind. I sent for Sabon as soon as I got back to the hunt, and grabbed Hrusch." He nodded to the hound, fast asleep in the corner. "Charlemund did his best to keep things quiet. I wouldn't be surprised if his priestesses talked. I know Brigadier Sabastenien didn't."

"So everyone made it away from Nikslaus safely?"

Olem nodded. "I almost turned back when I heard the sorcery, sir," he said. He refused to look Tamas in the eye. "If you need my stripes..."

"Shut up," Tamas said. "I won't take your stripes."

"You gave me an order to see the others back to the hunt."

"I thought you had."

"Not quite, sir. I went on ahead, left the others to find their way back. I wouldn't wait."

"Had I been in your position, I wouldn't have followed that order. I can't fault a man for his instincts. Besides, you did your job. You did not turn back. Go on." Tamas swallowed. He wanted nothing more than to lay his head back and fall asleep, but things needed to be done first. He fought back exhaustion, pain, and nausea.

"Word has spread of Ryze's betrayal," Olem said. "Lady Winceslav wants answers. Rumors are flying."

"Put a stop to them," he said.

"What?" Olem looked startled.

"It's not true." Tamas struggled to get to his feet. Ryze was a good man. Tamas wouldn't let him take the blame for this. Olem put a hand on Tamas's shoulder, gently restraining him.

Olem said, "I watched him take you off."

"You found the bodies, didn't you?" Tamas asked.

Olem slowly shook his head. "Blood, yes, but no bodies."

"That sorcery you heard as you left—that wasn't me fighting back. That was Ryze's men holding off Duke Nikslaus so Ryze could warn me. Ryze was cooked alive."

"Are you sure . . . ?"

"Go to the pit," Tamas growled. "Don't patronize me. I haven't gone mad in an afternoon."

"If Ryze wanted to warn you, why did he go to all the trouble?" Olem said. "He could have just sent you a note or come to see you in person."

Tamas rubbed his temples. "I don't remember. I remember he was scared. Angry. Barat had something on him to keep him silent."

"Brigadier Barat? You hit your head pretty hard, from the look of that bump." Olem gave him a weak smile.

"Don't be a fool." Tamas struggled to get up again. His leg burned and he broke into a hot sweat. He gave up. "Send a missive to Lady Winceslav. Tell her Ryze is innocent of all accusations." He paused. "Bring me Brigadiers Barat and Sabastenien."

"I'll send a man," Olem said, heading for the door.

"No," Tamas grunted. "Get them yourself. I don't want either of them slipping away. Take a squad with you. And on second thought, don't tell anyone about Ryze."

"But if he's innocent…"

Tamas closed his eyes. He'd need strength for what lay ahead. "I'll deal with that later. Dismissed."

"Right away, sir."

As soon as Olem was out the door, Tamas let out a gasp of pain. His leg had stiffened up in just a few minutes. It throbbed when it didn't hurt, and when the lances of pain worked their way up his leg each time he moved it, he wished he'd let it throb. He ran a hand through his disheveled hair.

Tamas forced himself to think. Why had Ryze faked his kidnapping just to tell him about Barat? Tamas wished he had Adamat's gift.

His son!

"Olem!" he yelled. He waited a few moments. Olem didn't return. He yelled again. A guard poked his head through the door. "What is it, sir?"

"Kema, is Olem gone?"

The soldier nodded. "Took off just a minute ago. Looked like he was going to give someone the pit of a time."

"Hand me a pen and paper."

Kema fetched a fountain pen and some stationery from Tamas's desk and brought it over. Tamas sketched out a quick note. "Catch up with Olem. Have him do this before the other task."

"Yes, sir."

Kema was gone again in a moment, leaving Tamas alone, when his leg began to throb again. A finger of black powder and he'd feel no pain…if he could use it. He couldn't even enter a powder trance with the gold star in his leg.

"Where's Petrik, damn him?"

"Right here." The doctor closed the door quietly behind him. He carried his medical bag in one hand, his coat over the other. He examined Tamas through a pair of spectacles.

"Pulled me away from a rather good game of bridge," he said. He looked peeved, but he usually did. The man had been drummed out of most of his postings as a public and private doctor because he completely lacked a bedside manner. What he lacked, however, he made up for in brevity and skill.

"My apologies," Tamas said. "I'll just suffer more, if you'd like to return to it."

Dr. Petrik paused. He shrugged, and turned back to the door.

"Have you no concept of sarcasm, you ancient bastard?"

Petrik gave Tamas a long, annoyed look and came to his side. He waddled like a man of twenty-five stone, though he was as thin as a rail. He sat down next to Tamas and removed his glasses. He examined Tamas's face and head through a monocle.

"Some light scratches," he said after a moment. "Nothing to be concerned about. Looks like you had a concussion." He snapped his fingers in front of Tamas's face, looked into each of his eyes. "You're fine." He took Tamas's leg—none too gently—and lifted it into his lap. He removed the linen wrappings and gave it a clinical look.

"You've seen a doctor already," he said. There was an edge to his voice.

"Yes," Tamas said. "It was the physician with my captors. He's the one who put the leg back together."

"What did it look like before?"

"I don't know. I was out for the whole thing."

"Lucky. Looks like you shattered the whole leg. He did a good job, whoever he was," he said grudgingly.

"I want you to take it apart."

Petrik blinked up at him. "Say that again?"

"My leg. You need to take it apart."

Petrik set the leg down gently. "You hit your head harder than I thought."

Was that a hint of concern in Petrik's voice? No, Tamas must have imagined it. "The surgeon inserted a gold sliver before he closed the wound." Tamas paused, swallowed. Even saying it made him nauseous. "I can't use my magery."

Dr. Petrik returned his spectacles to his face. He took them off, then put them on again. He tucked one fist up under his chin, glaring at the leg. "You're mad," he said. "I won't do it. If you leave it, a cyst will form. That should close the gold away from your bloodstream and let you use your powers again."

"Do it," Tamas said. "That's an order."

"You think that'll help? If the shock doesn't kill you, you'll lose your leg. Which might kill you anyway. You're not thinking clearly."

"Nikslaus said the sliver was in the form of a star. Any time I move, it will tear the tissue, letting the gold touch my blood again. I can feel it in there, working its way around."

Petrik hesitated.

"I appreciate your concern," Tamas said.

"Concern?" Petrik said. "Yes, for myself. You *know* what your lackeys will do to me if you die during the procedure? I saw Olem on his way out of here. I'm not an idiot. You sent him away so he couldn't protest, and Sabon isn't back yet. They'd tear me apart."

"Who'd tear you apart?"

Sabon stood in the doorway, paused in the midst of unbuttoning his jacket. The jacket was covered in powder stains, dirt, and burns. It looked like he'd been in a coal mine. He hung it on a peg in the corner. A single cut ran the length of his cheek, the blood already dry, and his hands were dirty and smudged.

"Did you catch him?" Tamas said.

Sabon shook his head. "I'm sorry."

Tamas bit back a rebuke. *Shit.* "How'd he get away?"

"A well-rehearsed route," Sabon said. "Into a warehouse with a false floor, and down into the sewers. Our men are scouring sewer exits, but I'll be surprised if they find him. Vlora is still tracking him, but he could come out anywhere in Adopest. It's as if he expected us to catch up with them." Sabon made a disgusted noise in the back of his throat. He stepped over and gave Tamas's leg a look-over. "You've had better days," he said.

"Right. I have."

"Will he lose the leg?" Sabon asked Dr. Petrik.

The doctor ignored Tamas's look of warning. "He might," he said, "if he has me open it up, like he wants."

"Why?" Sabon looked to Tamas for an explanation.

Tamas took a deep breath. "Nikslaus's physician fixed the leg. Before he did, he inserted a golden sliver right up against the bone. It's star-shaped, to prevent a cyst from forming."

Sabon's eyes widened. "The beast," he snarled. "I'll take off his hands when I catch him."

Tamas couldn't disagree with the sentiment. "*If* we ever catch him," he said. "Petrik, I want the surgery."

The doctor gave Sabon a long look.

"No," Sabon said. "If you die, the whole campaign will be at risk."

The campaign, Sabon had said. Tamas almost smiled. Sabon would never admit to being concerned.

"We just got you back," Sabon said.

"I won't go on without my magery," Tamas said. "Petrik, what are the risks if I don't have you take it out?"

The old doctor frowned. "If what you say is true, you'll be in constant pain. You won't sleep, and the exhaustion will keep your body from healing naturally." He didn't look happy. "We should take it out."

Sabon looked from Tamas to the doctor, then sniffed. "Good luck," he said, leaving the room.

"You wanted to see me?" Adamat shifted from one foot to the other and examined the row of surgical equipment laid out beside Tamas. Surgery had always made him nervous. Too many things could go wrong and it seemed like every year doctors were coming up with a new and painful way to kill you under the guise of medicine. It was an irrational thought and he knew it. The statistics supported the opposite. The ancient practice of bloodletting was becoming more unpopular, while recent ideas about sterilization had begun to spread in the medical field. Survival rates were higher than they'd been since the Time of Kresimir.

The field marshal sat on the edge of an operating table, an impromptu surgery set up in a side room in the House of Nobles. He wore nothing but a towel around his waist and Adamat was amazed at the number of old scars crisscrossing Tamas's chest. Some were from swords, one that looked like a knife wound, and three pink, faded welts from bullet wounds. He had a bump on his head visible even under his graying hair, and his right leg was red and swollen. To one side, a doctor in a white coat examined his instruments with care.

So Tamas was alive, though the worse for wear. The gossip columns would kill to find out what happened over on Palo Street yesterday and where Tamas had been the two days prior. Adamat decided not to ask.

Tamas nodded. "Have you found my traitor?"

"No, sir."

"Why not?"

"Not to offer excuses, but I'm doing the work of twenty men."

"We're paying you well, are we not?"

"Not exactly, and pay doesn't make the work go any faster. I have interviews and research to conduct and a great deal of traveling."

" 'Not exactly'?"

"I'm investigating the reeve, sir. I'm not going to interrogate him and then ask for a check."

Tamas snorted. "Olem, see that the good investigator gets paid."

The bodyguard in the corner paused his pacing long enough to give a brisk nod.

"Surely you have suspicions?"

"Always," Adamat said. "But no hard proof."

"I have here a letter," Tamas said, gesturing to his desk, "from my son Taniel. He is at Shouldercrown with the Mountainwatch, helping fend off the Kez attack. It seems he and Privileged Borbador are in agreement that a powerful sorceress has joined the Kez side and seeks to lead the Kez Cabal through the fortress and up to Kresim Kurga, where they will attempt to summon Kresimir."

Adamat felt his mouth hanging open. "That's absurd."

"Quite," Tamas said. "Men under siege can often lose perspective. What's more, my son is not well." Tamas did not elaborate on this. "Yet I am forced to make contingencies. The Kez may have developed a new weapon or..." He glanced out the window and grimaced. "This business about Kresimir's Promise... did you find out anything else about it in your research? Anything to indicate that Kresimir needed to be summoned, or in what manner he would try to seek revenge for his dead king?"

Adamat said, "No. As I told you, my research came up with nothing. Passages were ripped completely from the books, expunged by someone who didn't want this information known." This alone had troubled Adamat from the beginning. But he was not one to speculate. "My knowledge of Kresimir's Promise comes from Privileged Borbador alone."

"That is unfortunate." Tamas touched a hand to his forehead and swayed slightly. He was not well. "I hesitate to give in to hysteria, but I must guard against the possibility that there is some truth to it. Bah! Summoning gods. Who thinks of such things? I have sent the fourth brigade to Shouldercrown. That should be more than enough to hold the pass against the Kez." He made a dismissive gesture. "I am sorry I interrupted your investigation, Inspector. I did want to tell you one thing before you go."

"Sir?"

"If I do not survive this surgery, or my recovery goes badly, I want you to continue your investigation."

Adamat felt a thrill of fear. "With all due respect, sir, I'd be dead in a ditch within hours. I suspect only fear of suspicion keeps me from falling prey to assassins. Fear of you, to be precise."

"You will have a guard," Tamas said. "If I am dead, justice will be served not from a trial but from cold steel. The seventh brigade will assist you with some glee, I suspect."

Tamas really thought he might die. Adamat's fear deepened. If Tamas died, everything would fall apart. Especially with such contingency. The army would go after the rest of the councillors; every man would be for himself. Chaos would descend upon the country. There would be no winners. And if he lived, Adamat would be forced to continue to betray him, telling all to Lord Vetas. Where had his integrity gone? For the hundredth time, Adamat weighed the risks of telling Tamas all and asking for his help. No, he decided again. His family's safety was more important than integrity or honor.

Adamat's thoughts were interrupted by the arrival of a tall, fat man with long black hair tucked back in a ponytail behind him. He carried himself like a king, though he wore the apron and tall hat of a chef. He held a silver tray above his head and a ladle big enough to brain in a man's head hung from his apron.

Tamas regarded him with some wariness. "Mihali?"

"Field Marshal," Mihali said. "I've brought you a broth to drink before your surgery. It will aid in your recovery, I think."

The doctor scowled at Mihali. "No food or drink," he said.

"I insist!" Mihali held the tray out for Tamas.

"Absolutely not. Food or drink can cause complications during the surgery, I..."

Tamas waved the doctor off. "I think I will manage," Tamas said. "You aren't even giving me ether."

Adamat was about to slip off, leaving Tamas to his broth and surgery, when the door burst open. Adamat recognized the arch-diocel by the robes he wore, if not by his face. Charlemund was a man with a fearsome reputation, and he did not give many public sermons. He was not well liked among the lower classes, as arch-diocels went.

"Tamas," Charlemund said. "I am glad to see you alive and safe, but I've come on business. My men say your soldiers will not give up this blasphemous cook of yours. There was some kind of scuffle yesterday when my guard tried to come for him..."

He paused, a frown crossing his face when he saw Mihali, Adamat, and the rest.

"Surely Mihali is of little import," Tamas said.

"If it were my choice, I would leave him in your hands. What is a mad cook to me? Yet arch-diocels more zealous in the faith than I are demanding his arrest. They are putting pressure on me, Tamas. They are threatening the Church's neutrality."

"You'll have my decision later," Tamas said.

"I must insist that it be now." Charlemund squared his shoulders. His gaze fell on Mihali. "You are he, are you not? The blasphemous cook?"

Mihali set the platter down gently beside Tamas and turned to Charlemund. He took a deep breath, sucking in his enormous gut. "I am a chef, sir, and you will speak to me as such."

"A chef! Ha!" Charlemund threw his head back and laughed. His hand went to the hilt of his smallsword. "Tamas, I arrest this man in the name of the Church."

"Get out."

The words were quiet, yet Adamat felt as if all warmth had been sucked from the room. He turned to Tamas, but it wasn't Tamas who had spoken. It had been the chef.

"How dare you." Charlemund drew a handspan of steel.

"Get out!" Mihali bellowed. His ladle appeared in his hand, for all the world like he was holding a sword. The large end pointed steadily at Charlemund's nose. "I will not have you here. You false priest, you abhorrent fool! Give me a reason and I will strike you down!"

Charlemund's face contorted with rage. "What kind of madness is this? I arrest you in the name of the Church! I don't fear your ladle, you ungodly glutton!"

Mihali advanced suddenly upon Charlemund. The arch-diocel backpedaled a few steps, drew his sword, and lunged. Mihali caught the blade with his ladle, swung it expertly to one side, and backhanded Charlemund hard enough to throw him over the sofa.

The room was silent. Olem rushed to Charlemund's side.

"Did you just kill the arch-diocel?" Adamat asked.

Mihali sniffed. "I should have," he said. "Drink your broth, Field Marshal." He left the room without another word.

"He's alive, sir," Olem said. "Unconscious."

Adamat exchanged a glance with Tamas. He could see his own disbelief reflected in Tamas's eyes. The field marshal held his leg in pain. "Olem, see that the arch-diocel is put in a room downstairs. Let it be known he had a bad fall down the stairs. Find witnesses. Inspector, I'm sure you saw it."

Adamat smoothed the front of his jacket. "It was a very nasty fall. He tumbled two flights before we could catch him."

"I believe that was the case," Tamas said. "Doctor, what could you prescribe for Charlemund?"

The doctor looked down his nose at the unconscious form of the arch-diocel. "Arsenic?"

"Now, really. Something to give him a quality headache and a great deal of memory loss."

"Cyanide."

"Doctor!"

"I'll find something," the doctor mumbled.

"Olem."

Olem paused, his arms beneath Charlemund's shoulders as he dragged him from the room. "Sir?"

"What was that bit about the men scuffling with Charlemund's guards?"

"I was going to tell you sir, after the surgery."

"I'm sure you were. What happened?"

Olem paused with his hands under Charlemund's arms. "Just that, sir. The boys don't want to lose Mihali. Say he's a good-luck charm, cooking or not. I had nothing to do with it. At least, not too much."

"How the pit is he a good-luck charm? What has he done to warrant that?"

"Filled their bellies," Olem said.

"Were there any casualties?"

"There might be next time." A cloud passed across Olem's face.

"And if I give a direct order?"

Olem looked down. "I'm sure the men will follow it, sir."

Tamas closed his eyes and rubbed them. "What do you suggest, Inspector?"

Adamat started. "I'm not sure I know enough details, sir." He felt like a fly on the wall here. This was not an event he was meant to witness. This Mihali character—Adamat would need to find out more about him.

"Pretend you do," Tamas insisted.

"It's a poor commander who gives in to the whims of his troops," Adamat said. "And an even worse one who ignores their wants and needs. Yet there are mitigating factors." He jerked his head toward the arch-diocel, whom Olem had resumed dragging out the door.

"Olem."

The bodyguard paused once more. "He's coming around, sir."

"I'd rather he not yet."

There was a sound like a hammer hitting meat. "He won't."

Tamas put his head in his hands. "Let it be known that Mihali has been conscripted by the seventh brigade of the Adran army. Send a note to Hassenbur, letting them know they may send a doctor to watch over him. We will cover all expenses, and Claremonte will be spared any embarrassment."

"And the Church?"

Tamas sighed. "They can send a priest to talk to him, if they like. To convert him or some such nonsense."

"So Mihali is the legion's official cook now, eh?"

"Chef."

"Right, sir. Thank you, sir."

Tamas waited until the soldier was gone to begin eating his broth. A few moments passed, the only sound that of his satisfied slurping. He looked up. "Inspector?"

"Yes?" Adamat had found his mind wandering again.

"You're dismissed."

As Adamat left the room, he heard Tamas say, "Let's get on with this, Petrik."

He paused in the hallway. Tamas handled that well enough. The field marshal was not a man to tolerate fools questioning his orders. He was not a good man to cross. Adamat wondered again if he should tell Tamas about Lord Vetas. If Tamas discovered Adamat's betrayal on his own, Adamat would lose any chance of rescuing his family. But if Adamat attempted a rescue, even with the help of Tamas's soldiers, his family might die. The risk was just too great.

CHAPTER 28

Come on, you idiot," Tamas said. "Prop me up. Put the pillow there." He paused and gripped the edge of his desk as the room spun around him.

"Sir?" Olem said. He chewed on the end of his cigarette.

"I'm fine. Go on."

Olem wedged a cushion between Tamas and his chair.

"Down farther," Tamas said. "Perfect. Turn the chair a little. I want to look casual."

Tamas gave a few more orders until he was satisfied. He sat behind his desk, pointed toward the office door, his back propped up straight so he looked taller. Olem stepped back.

"Do I look like an invalid?" Tamas asked.

"No."

"You hesitated."

"A little beat up, sir," Olem said. "It'll do."

"Good." Tamas didn't dare lean forward, hardly even to look down, so he felt blindly to a desk drawer and removed a powder cartridge. He broke the end with his thumbnail and poured it out on his tongue. He fought off a bout of dizziness, then darkness as his consciousness tried to retreat before the wave of awareness that flooded his senses. The taste was sulfuric, bitter. To Tamas it tasted of ambrosia.

His exhaustion ebbed. The pain in his leg receded to a steady hum in the back of his mind, a simple reminder that his leg had been cut open, the flesh torn and the bone reset but without the agony that should accompany it.

"Three capsules in an hour, sir?" There was a hint of worry in Olem's voice.

"Save it for someone else," Tamas grunted. "I've no time to worry about going powder blind." Truth be told, he admitted to himself, the euphoria of the powder trance clung to him. He needed it, longed for its strongest embrace like a long-absent lover. He would deal with signs of addiction later. For now, there were more important matters. Despite the powder trance, one of the deepest he'd ever been in, he could barely move. His body still felt the pain, still cried out over his lack of rest—his brain simply did not register it.

"Tell me about Brigadier Sabastenien," Tamas said.

"He was an orphan," Olem said, "adopted into the Wings of Adom as a bullet-boy. The Wings of Adom are his family—Adro his mother, the army his father."

"As I've heard as well."

"He helped me track you," Olem said. "Ryze's betrayal burned him deep."

"Does he know Ryze is dead?" Tamas asked.

Olem shook his head.

"And you didn't say a word of Ryze's innocence?"

"Not one, sir," Olem said.

"Good. Send him in."

Brigadier Sabastenien was one of the youngest commanders of the Wings of Adom, barely twenty-five years old. Tamas knew that brigadiers were not elected at whim. They were quick, they were intelligent, brave, and fanatically loyal to the Winceslav family and to Adro. Or they had been, until Brigadier Barat.

Brigadier Sabastenien was a shorter man, with dark, unruly hair cut just above his eyes. He had grown muttonchops to give him a better appearance of maturity, and wore them better than most men of his age.

"I'm glad to see you back in good health, sir," Sabastenien said.

"Thank you," Tamas said. "I understand you helped Olem track me." Tamas nodded to his bodyguard, and then dismissed him with a jerk of his head. Olem slipped out onto the balcony, while Tamas's head reeled from the sudden movement. *Careful*, he reminded himself.

"I provided what service I could," the brigadier said. "Pray tell me if there is more I can do. I've already begun gathering men to hunt Brigadier Ryze with Lady Winceslav's blessing. He'll not escape."

"There is one thing you can do," Tamas said.

"Anything, sir."

"It's a small thing. You see that screen there?" Tamas pointed toward the corner of the room, where a divider stood of the type a man or woman might change behind. "I'd like you to stand behind it and listen."

"Sir?" Sabastenien said.

"You'll understand soon enough," Tamas said. "Please. For the whim of a beat-up old man."

Brigadier Sabastenien gave him a hesitant nod. "Now?"

Tamas glanced at the clock. "Yes, that would be about right."

Sabastenien positioned himself behind the curtain. A few moments passed, during which Tamas closed his eyes. His mind, though blocked off from the pain and weariness that would have rendered a man unconscious, still spun from the powder trance. Eyes open, he could see Olem out on the balcony, watching the birds fly in the sun over Elections Square. He could see stray fibers on Olem's jacket, and when he concentrated, he thought he could even hear the beat of Sabastenien's heart from where he hid behind the curtain. The young brigadier was calm.

A knock sounded at the door.

"Come in," Tamas said. He straightened in his seat. Now was not a time to appear weak.

The door opened and Tamas caught a glimpse of Vlora waiting in the hall, hands resting on the butts of her pistols, as a pair of soldiers brought in Brigadier Barat. In contrast to Sabastenien, Barat was a tall man, taller than most. His features sharp, his brow severe, though with enough softness in the cheeks and eyes as to remain quite handsome. He was clean-shaven, and Tamas had heard soldiers say the man could not grow a beard if he wanted. Barat was twenty-six, and his father had been a wealthy viscount in the north before his death years before.

Tamas did not miss the look of confidence on Barat's face, nor the sword still buckled to his belt.

"Please, sit," Tamas said, indicating one of the chairs on the other side of his desk.

"I prefer to stand, thank you," Brigadier Barat said. "I hope there's a reason I was escorted here by your soldiers. Perhaps there's been some misunderstanding."

"I'm certain that's the case," Tamas said. "Give me just some of your time." He fell quiet, watching Barat, waiting for him to squirm. A minute or two passed.

"This is quite irregular, sir," Brigadier Barat said.

"Forgive me," Tamas said. "My adventure over the past few days had quite the effect on me. I'm just thinking..."

"About what, sir?"

"You've heard of Ryze's betrayal?" Tamas said.

Brigadier Barat stiffened. "A disgrace for the Wings of Adom. I'm very relieved you're all right, sir," he added, as if an afterthought.

"Thank you." Tamas smiled shallowly. "Do you know why Ryze betrayed us?"

"He was a broken man, sir," Barat said. "Old and brittle."

Tamas feigned surprise. "Really? I can't say that we were ever really friends, but Ryze was a contemporary of mine. He was a few years ahead at the university, and the academy. He never loved anything the way he's loved Adro, and he was a fine commander and father. He handled the campaign against the royalists splendidly."

"That was only *my* impression of him, sir," Barat said. "I mean, I've only known him for a year or so. I meant no offense."

"Why was he 'brittle and broken'?" Tamas asked.

"I don't know. He..."

"Yes?"

"Well, I don't want to start rumors, sir, not without all the facts in."

"It's a bit late for that," Tamas said. "Ryze handed me over to a Kez Privileged. He's a traitor and a villain."

Barat looked slightly shaken by this. He licked his lips. "Well, I think he didn't like me. He was jealous of my favor with Lady Winceslav. He didn't think one so young should have risen the ranks to brigadier so quickly."

"Really?" Tamas once again acted surprised. "I...well, I can't imagine. I know Brigadier Sabastenien rose faster than you. And he wasn't bedding Lady Winceslav."

"Well, yes but..." Brigadier Barat's eyes grew large. "Sir! With respect, sir, I'll have to ask you to take that back."

"We both know it's true," Tamas said. "In fact, it's common knowledge around both my army and the Wings of Adom." It wasn't, but Barat didn't need to know that. Tamas heard Sabastenien shift behind the curtain. Barat glanced that way for a moment. Tamas called back his attention with a cough.

"I will call you out if I have to, sir," Barat said. "To protect my honor, and the Lady's."

"Call out a powder mage?" Tamas said. "You'd really do that?"

A small smile formed at the corners of Barat's mouth. "Yes," he said. "And I'd beg you to choose pistols, even if it meant my death. To prove my honor."

Barat knew about the star in Tamas's leg, or he wouldn't be so cavalier about a duel. He was also grandstanding. He knew he was being watched.

"Where's Ryze's son?" Tamas asked.

Brigadier Barat was taken off guard. "What? How should I know?"

"I'm sorry," Tamas said. "My mind is slipping. I already know. His body was recovered from the canal this afternoon. There were weights on his ankles. He was garroted so cruelly that his head fell off when they brought the body up. Sad, an eighteen-year-old boy with such promise, meeting an end like that. You know, that's another thing both Ryze and I shared. We both married late in life, and were gifted with just one son before our wives passed." Tamas thought of Taniel and wondered briefly how the battle was going at South Pike. He wondered what he'd do if someone took his son hostage. He blinked, his vision blurred for a moment, and fought down his rage. This was best done coldly.

"A tragedy," Brigadier Barat said, his voice on edge.

Tamas said, "A witness at Adopest University saw a man matching your description enter the dormitories late last night. One of his classmates said the boy went with the same man."

"Impossible," Brigadier Barat snarled. "No investigation could go on so quickly..." Barat stopped, sensing the trap. "I hope his killer is caught and brought to justice. That still doesn't excuse what his father did."

"Piano wire is often used as a garrote," Tamas said. "Those with little experience tend to cut their own fingers. May I see your hands?"

Barat clasped his hands behind his back and took a step back from Tamas's desk.

Tamas took a deep breath. Loudly, calmly, he said, "His father warned me of a traitor among the brigadiers. He warned me that his son was a veritable hostage, and begged me to protect him. He didn't care that his own life was forfeit when the sorcerer caught up to us. Ryze was no traitor, Barat. He was a patriot. A hero. And he warned me about you."

"What rubbish is this?" Brigadier Barat hissed. "You've gone mad."

"Sometimes I think that would be simpler," Tamas said. "Who is the traitor in the council? Things will go easier for you if you tell me."

"Go to the pit," Barat scoffed. "You have no evidence, old man. I won't play this game with you." He spun on his heel, heading for the door. The door rattled, but did not open. "Why is this locked?" Barat glanced nervously toward the balcony. Olem watched the scene through the window, a rifle in his hands.

Barat spun on Tamas. "Who the pit do you think you are? Lady Winceslav will not stand for this! What do you think you'll do? Bring me to justice? Send me to court? The Lady will protect me. I'll never see a cell, and you will only disgrace yourself in the process. False accusations from a bitter, broken man," Barat said. His smile grew. "Just like Ryze! Filled with lies and delusions, a traitor to his own country. You're not even a powder mage anymore."

Tamas sniffed. He reached into his breast pocket and removed a bullet. He held it up, rolled it between his fingers. In the other hand he held up a powder cartridge. "Am I not?" He shook his head. "Alas, this is not mine to deal with, no matter how much I'd like to." He lowered his hands. Loudly, he said, "There's a pistol underneath the divan cushion. It's loaded."

"What?" Barat demanded. He drew his sword and stepped toward Tamas.

Brigadier Sabastenien emerged from behind the curtain. He held the pistol up and pulled back the hammer. His hand was firm.

The shot echoed through the room, sending Tamas's head spinning. He gripped the desk until the dizziness was gone, then lifted his head to look at the body as Olem stepped into the room.

Brigadier Barat lay on the floor, his blood and brains scattered across the sofa and the curtain. His body twitched once and was still. Brigadier Sabastenien lowered the pistol.

The brigadier's face was pale. His hands shook a little as he tossed the pistol to the floor, and he stumbled over to the sofa. "I believed Ryze was a traitor," he said after a moment. His voice was agonized, his face contorted by sorrow.

"He was a good man," Tamas said.

"His son..."

"Dead," Tamas said. "Olem, I want Ryze's remains found. He was hit by sorcery, so there won't be much left. Scour the King's Wood if you have to. I want him buried along with his son, next to his wife, with state honors."

"Of course," Olem said quietly.

"What do I tell the Lady?" Sabastenien said. He was stricken. Tamas saw him for the youth he was then, and pitied him.

"You shot him in my defense," Tamas said softly. "I'll not allow a court-martial."

"I killed Lady Winceslav's lover, a fellow brigadier," Sabastenien said. His voice shook. "I'll be drummed out of the Wings with dishonor, no matter the reason." He paused. "May I go?"

"Of course. You'll always have a place in my army," he said. When the young brigadier had left, Tamas said to Olem, "Have someone keep an eye on him."

Olem frowned. "He heard it all. He did the right thing. Why

should he care if they kick him out of the Wings? The army is certainly a pay cut, but..."

"The Wings aren't just mercenaries, Olem," Tamas said. His weariness was breaking through the powder trance, the pain beginning to bleed into his defenses. "The Wings are a life. A brotherhood. To kill one of their own is the worst of crimes. Even for treason, when they handle it among themselves, the executioner is protected, unknown, so that his brothers will not find out and alienate him. Sabastenien's career with the Wings is over."

Olem turned his frown on Tamas. "Then, why...?"

Tamas sighed. He brought out another powder charge, longed to sprinkle the powder on his tongue. He put it back in his shirt pocket. "You'll think me cruel," he said. "I need Sabastenien on the lines. If he survives this war, he'll be a general at thirty." He ignored Olem's look of disapproval. "Have someone ready to offer him a job when he's been drummed out. Full commander."

Tamas leaned over his chair, head light, and vomited on the floor. He dragged his sleeve across his mouth and looked up at Olem's worried gaze. "I think I'll rest for a while now."

Olem went to fetch a janitor. Tamas leaned back in his chair, tasting bile. He'd taken care of the fox in his henhouse. Now he had to find the lion among his cattle.

Nila couldn't take her eyes off the blood on the sofa.

She wondered if Field Marshal Tamas had shot the man whose blood spattered the Royal Offices, or if he'd had one of his underlings do it. She knew he could kill casually. She'd seen him gun down Bystre in the streets without a second look.

"Olem, I..." The field marshal leveraged himself around his dressing screen and stopped when he saw Nila. "I'm sorry," he said. "Didn't realize they'd sent someone up to clean up the mess already."

Mess, he called it. As if the bits of brain and skull and all the blood were nothing more than the leftovers from dinner.

"My apologies, sir," Nila said with a curtsy. "I was just told to come get your uniform."

"Of course. The laundress. Olem! Help me get this uniform off."

Olem came through the front door, rolling a cigarette between his fingers. He smiled at Nila before heading behind the dressing screen.

"Damned blood got everywhere," the field marshal said.

"That's what happens, sir."

"Ow. Son of a... be more careful!"

"So sorry, sir."

"Damn my leg!"

"There's a lady present, sir."

The field marshal's curses lowered to a grumble for a few moments. Olem reappeared a moment later with the field marshal's uniform tucked under his arm and gave it over to Nila. The bearded sergeant looked different from that night when Adran soldiers had stormed the Eldaminse townhouse. A touch of gray had entered his beard; worry lines at the corner of his eyes were etched a little deeper. Nila had seen him around the House of Nobles, but he'd shown no recognition of her.

"Think you could wash the curtains, too?" Olem asked. "Who knows when they'll send up someone to get to the upholstery?"

"Of course," Nila said.

Field Marshal Tamas limped out from behind the dressing screen and over to his desk. He wore a white shirt and blue soldier's pants. His face was white and bloodless from his ordeals. Nila wondered what that face would look like after she'd strangled him in his sleep.

Olem removed the curtains from the windows and gathered them all up in his arms. "Sir," he said, "I'll help her downstairs with these and be right back up."

"Take your time," the field marshal said, waving him off. "Charlemund has sent me some idiotic church decree that must be read by supper."

"I can take them," Nila said when they reached the hallway.

Olem tucked the curtains under one arm. "I don't mind. The field marshal demands time alone now and then."

"Aren't you his bodyguard?"

"His manservant, more like," he said without bitterness. "We've tripled the guard on the top floor. Anything that can get through the rest of the boys watching his back would have no trouble with me. Cigarette?"

Nila studied Olem out of the corner of her eye as they went down the stairs. "Thank you," she said, taking the offered cigarette. He began rolling another one immediately.

"You don't seem the shy type," Olem said. "But the boys say you don't talk much."

Cold fear seized Nila's belly. Why would Field Marshal Tamas's bodyguard be asking after her? "I keep to myself, mostly," she said evenly.

"That's what I heard." He let the conversation lapse for a moment, then, "I didn't think I'd see you again after that night."

Nila's heart jumped. He remembered her? She didn't want to be remembered. She didn't want to be recognized. If he knew who she was, maybe he had figured out it was her who'd smuggled Jakob out of the townhouse.

"Oh?" she said when she'd found her voice.

"You seem better suited here than scrubbing livery for some lord," Olem said. "I like your dress. Better than what you were wearing before."

Nila tried to picture her uniform under Duke Eldaminse. She found she couldn't even remember what it looked like. She needed to turn the conversation away from herself. She didn't need him asking questions.

"You were wearing something different, too," she said.

Olem fingered the captain's pin at his lapel. "The field marshal said his bodyguard couldn't be less than a captain." He shrugged. "I'm not much of an officer. Never liked them much, myself. I'll take the pay that comes with it, though."

Olem removed his cigarette, switched it to his other hand, and put it back in his mouth. He stopped suddenly, forcing her to turn around. "Would you like to see a play tonight?" he asked.

Nila blinked. A play? So he wasn't interested in her in his capacity as Field Marshal Tamas's bodyguard. She couldn't help the relieved grin that spread across her face.

Olem seemed to take that as a yes. "The field marshal insisted I take the night off. Not many better ways to spend it than with a beautiful woman."

"I'd be honored." She gave him a little curtsy and what she hoped was her best shy smile.

They reached the laundry rooms beneath the House of Nobles and Olem left her. She looked through her supplies to find something that would get the blood out of the curtains and the field marshal's uniform. As she scrubbed at the stains, she reminded herself that she was here to kill Tamas. She wouldn't let Olem stop her or distract her. He seemed a good man, but he served an evil master. Tamas had to die before he could get more blood on his uniform. He'd killed men, women. Even innocent children. He had to be stopped.

Olem mentioned he wasn't the field marshal's only guard. If she killed Tamas sometime when Olem was off duty, then he wouldn't be blamed by the failure. Yes, that would be best. She scrubbed harder at the stains.

CHAPTER 29

Taniel listened to the sound of hoofbeats steadily climb the mountainside. He leaned on his rifle and took a sniff of powder. He'd been watching the rider's approach since the sun began to set over the mountains behind him. The rider was coming up from the Kez advance base. He rode under a white flag of truce.

A messenger.

"Go get Gavril," Taniel told Fesnik. The young watcher squinted into the dusk and nodded, heading back into the town. Fesnik had drawn lots for the evening watch. Taniel had given him some company, mostly for an excuse to see the engineers and masons at work as they repaired the bastion.

Fesnik's watch would be over when the last light disappeared from the sky. Taniel would go in then, and was looking forward to a long night's sleep. If fate was kind, this messenger would say the Kez were pulling back.

The mountains were quiet. Only intermittent sounds drifted up from the massive Kez army below. They weren't preparing for a push this night, nor any night for the last week. The battle for the bastion had weakened both sides, and they'd spent a week gathering bodies, restocking ammunition and supplies, and trying to get a little rest.

The quiet of the Kez camp made Taniel nervous.

Taniel turned at the sound of footsteps on stone behind him. It was Mozes, musket on his shoulder.

"I've got the night watch," he said.

Taniel stretched. "You can have it."

Mozes was a quiet man, not often in for a long conversation, but a good drinking companion. They'd spent plenty of hours together at the Howling Wendigo over the last week.

Taniel remained at the bastion wall for a few more minutes. Long enough to watch the rider approach the gates and be admitted and a small group emerge from the town to meet the messenger. The group was led by Gavril, his large silhouette immediately recognizable. The conversation was short, and the rider was soon heading back through the gate.

Taniel nodded farewell to Mozes and headed toward Gavril.

The group was in a quiet conference when Taniel arrived. All heads turned toward him.

"What word from Field Marshal Tine?" Taniel asked.

"He said to consider hostilities resumed," Gavril said. "Any sign of a nighttime attack?"

Shit. "No movement on the mountainside all day long."

"The diggers?"

"No sign of them, either."

The sappers had kept going, even through the week-long truce between the armies. Taniel had wanted to go down and flush them out, but Gavril insisted they keep their side of the truce.

"What are they digging for?" Gavril growled. "They're too far out to undermine us, and Bo said they haven't been using sorcery to dig."

"Have you seen Bo?" Taniel asked. "He's been feet-up in a mug of ale all week and looks like he's been to the pit and back. I don't trust he can tell sorcery from a molehill right now."

"Oh, come now," a quiet voice said. "I'm not that bad."

Taniel turned to see Bo standing a little ways off from the group. Had he been there the whole time? He frowned at his friend. Bo carried a flask, and he was leaning on Katerine. The woman gave Taniel a withering look.

Taniel said, "You need to be sleeping, not drinking."

"There's trickery in this," Bo said, gesturing toward the Kez army. "Who knows what they're planning?"

"What can we do?" Taniel said. "They're well covered from artillery fire. When we bombarded the hill above their cave, there was no sign of having collapsed their tunnels. We have no idea how deep those tunnels are, or where they lead to. They could be trying to undermine the bastion, or come up in the middle of the town, or pit, with the help of sorcerers they could be trying to pass under the whole Mountainwatch and come out in Adro."

"A sobering thought," Bo said. "But you said you've not seen sign of the diggers all day."

"They're still going. No doubt about it."

"That's why I've come to a decision," Gavril said. They both looked to Gavril. "I'm going to lead a sortie to clear the mine."

"When?" Taniel took a sniff of powder.

"Tomorrow," Gavril said. "If I can sober Bo up."

"I'm plenty sober," Bo said. He swayed, and would have fallen if Katerine had not been holding him up.

Gavril appeared not to notice. "I want to say it will be a minimum-risk sortie. Their army is hours away. But if Julene is there—or even a couple of lower-grade Privileged—we'll need more than just Bo." He looked expectantly at Taniel. "The sortie will be . . . volunteer."

Taniel tried to snort. It made his sinuses hurt. He'd done his best to stay off powder for the last week. He'd failed, but at least his nose hadn't bled for a few days. "I'll go, of course."

"Thanks," Gavril said. He looked somewhat relieved. "It's not just you I need, though."

Taniel frowned, and then it dawned on him. "Ka-poel."

Gavril nodded.

"I don't know..." Taniel said. "She's so young."

"She's a sorcerer," Gavril said. "A powerful one. I've had a talk with Bo. He's very interested in her."

"Very," Bo said.

Taniel scowled at them both.

Gavril paused for a moment, then added, "Not *that* way."

"Of course not," Bo said.

Taniel still scowled. "Ka-poel is under my protection," he said. In reality, he was under hers, or so Bo would have him believe. "Sure, she's helped me track Privileged, been in a scrape or two..." He remembered how she'd thrown herself between him and Julene up on the mountain. She was stronger than she looked.

Bo sighed. "Taniel, she makes most of the Kez Cabal look like children. We're going to need her."

Taniel suddenly remembered the day he'd faced off against Rozalia in the museum at Adopest University. She'd been nervous about Ka-poel joining the fight. Had she been able to sense something Taniel hadn't? "I don't think she's that powerful, but let's say she was—I won't put her in danger."

"It's not up to you," Gavril said.

"By pit, it's not."

"I already asked her. She's coming with us."

Taniel leaned back, blinking. "You just went right past me on that?"

Gavril rolled his tongue around in his cheek. He met Taniel's eyes. "I know the risk we're taking going down there, and she's a bigger asset than even Bo at this point. I wanted to know she'd come before I made the decision."

Taniel glared at Gavril. The big Watchmaster ignored him.

"Tomorrow night?" Taniel asked.

"Tomorrow night," Gavril confirmed.

Taniel put his hands in his pockets and headed back into the town alone. The days were hot now, and the nights certainly warmer as summer closed in on Adro. This high in the mountains there'd always be a chill in the air when the sun went down. Taniel pulled his buckskin coat tight and listened to the wind as he got closer to the Howling Wendigo. It was an eerie thing, and it made him shudder.

He paused halfway down the street. The howl picked up as he walked toward the Howling Wendigo, but he thought another sound had joined it, then replaced it. It sounded similar, like a beast's low yowl in the distance. This was... more organic. He shivered and looked around. It came from higher up the mountain, and on a clear night like this, when the stars shone bright overhead, the sound carried. He glanced toward the northeast pass. He rubbed his eyes, looked again. It seemed as if something moved there.

The howl started again, a haunting, feral sound. Taniel remembered reading that there were no wolves on South Pike. Only cave lions. This sounded like no cave lion he'd ever heard. He swallowed and forced himself to look away from the mountain.

A movement in the corner of his eye, someone sneaking up toward him from the side, made him jump. The figure ran. He took off down the road in pursuit. He dashed around a corner, to an alley, and grabbed the side of a building to steady himself.

"Damn you to the pit!" He grabbed Ka-poel by the front of her long duster. His hands were shaking. "Don't scare me like that."

She looked up at him with big green eyes that drank in the moonlight. He let go of her jacket and smoothed the front of his own. "Damn," he said. "You spooked the pit out of me. What are you doing out here?"

Ka-poel pointed to her eyes and then to him.

"Watching me? What in Kresimir's name for?"

She shrugged.

Taniel cuffed her gently on the back of her head. She'd cut her hair even shorter, almost above her ears. Taniel walked back into the street and sat down on a stoop. Ka-poel made to walk off.

"Get over here," Taniel said. He made sure his voice was not unkind. She sidled up beside him like a girl whose father had threatened a lashing, but who knew that an innocent smile would get her out of it. "Why didn't you tell me that Gavril asked you to go on his sortie?"

Ka-poel raised one eyebrow at him. She pointed to her throat.

"Yes, I know you can't talk," Taniel said. He rolled his eyes. "You damn well come up with a way to tell me things when you want."

Ka-poel pursed her lips.

"Don't play coy with me. You do it all the time. I want an answer."

She hugged herself, and then pointed to Taniel. Taniel shook his head. She thumped one hand against her chest, over her heart, and pointed to him again. *You... love me?* No, that can't be right. He shook his head. Ka-poel sighed. She mimed swinging a sword, and then raised the other arm.

"Shield?" Taniel said.

She nodded, and pointed at him.

"Shield me? Protect me? You want to protect me? What the pit? You're what, fifteen years old? You shouldn't be trying to protect me. You're barely past playing with dolls. Well..." Taniel remembered the doll she made of Julene, and what it did. "You still play with dolls. Dangerously. But you shouldn't be protecting me."

Taniel imagined himself at fifteen. A headstrong, lanky boy with straight black hair and just the beginnings of a beard. He had filled out since then, grown stronger, taller, and already bore the scars of a seasoned soldier. He felt old and he was barely twenty-two.

Ka-poel turned her back on him.

"Hey, don't..."

She folded her arms.

Taniel stood up, came up behind her. She flashed her fingers at him rapidly.

"What?"

She did it again.

"Nineteen? Oh, you? You're nineteen." Taniel was taken aback. "I always thought you were a kid. Dynize are married off by sixteen."

She shook her head, still not looking at him, and pointed at herself.

"Not you, eh?"

She nodded.

"Well, damn it, I don't care how old you are, I don't want you protecting me."

She turned around suddenly. Their faces were close enough for him to smell her breath. It was sweet, like honey, and Taniel wondered absently what she'd been eating.

Too bad, she mouthed.

Taniel squared his jaw. Damned girl. "Why are you so worried about me?" he asked slowly.

She leaned in closer to him, their lips almost touching. He searched her dark eyes. They caught the starlight. There was mischief in those eyes and a smirk on her lips. Taniel felt his heart thump. She whirled and was gone, racing down the street.

Taniel inhaled sharply, watching her go. "What was that?" he said quietly. He licked his lips and wondered what she tasted like. He pushed the thought from his mind. She was a servant, an uneducated savage. He shoved his hands in his pocket and headed down the street, hoping that she wouldn't be there when he got back to his room at the officers' barracks.

CHAPTER 30

The streets at the west end of Adopest's dock district were anything but quiet at half past one in the morning. Singing floated into the streets from the bars and bawdy houses, and more than a few groups of drunks had taken their merriment out onto the cobbles, shaking their fists at the wet sky and spitting bad poetry at anyone who'd listen.

Adamat pressed himself into a dark corner, collar drawn up around his neck, wrapped tightly in a long black coat with a bowler hat to keep off the rain and shadow his face. SouSmith waited in another corner, the big boxer surprisingly invisible in a patch of darkness two sizes too small for him. Adamat kept his eyes open and cane handy, ready to fix either of them on anyone sober enough to notice him.

The bawdy house opposite the street was a quiet affair compared with the rest. Its clientele was wealthier than most and its outward appearance was that of a butcher's shed—the place was called Molly's Market, and it didn't accept new customers without a recommendation. A number of hulking men with big fists and small brains crouched under an awning near the door. They were bodyguards and bouncers, whispering quietly to one another as they struggled to stay warm. A couple had noticed Adamat and cast him dark looks, but none had come over to talk to him yet.

The door to the bawdy house opened, giving a brief glimpse of expensive furnishings and black lace. Ricard Tumblar stopped in the doorway and slipped a few coins to the man holding the door open before exiting into the rain.

Ricard walked with the gait of a man who'd drunk a lot but knew his limits. He tipped his hat to the group of bodyguards. Two of them detached themselves from the rest and came to his side. Ricard waved off one that offered him a parasol.

Adamat waited until Ricard was close before stepping out of the shadows. He tipped back his hat to be recognized in the dim lamplight. Ricard's bodyguards stepped forward, reaching for knives, as the bouncers under the canopy stood warily. Muggers were discouraged around Molly's Market.

"Call off your boys," Adamat said. "I just want to talk."

Ricard put up one hand for his guards, another on his heart. "Adamat, by Kresimir you scared me. What is it?"

Adamat twitched his head and took a few steps away from the guards. Ricard followed him.

"You know you can come to me at my office anytime," Ricard said. "My door is always open." Ricard wasn't wearing a hat and he put his hand up to keep the rain out of his eyes.

"I've got a warning for you," Adamat said. "As an old friend."

Ricard had never taken kindly to threats, whether real or implied, and Adamat put a hand on his shoulder to reassure him.

"There are circumstances," Adamat said, "that are forcing me to consider you a prime suspect as Tamas's traitor."

Ricard's mouth formed a hard line, but he remained silent. Now was the gamble. If Ricard was indeed the traitor, he'd set his goons on Adamat.

"You need to clean your house, Ricard," Adamat said. "Kez spies are being smuggled in over the Adsea. Kez Wardens, too. Tamas is not pleased. I think Tamas will hold off for now, because he needs your ships desperately to ferry his men to the Gates."

"What does this have to do with me?" Ricard said. His tone was controlled, but there was anger there.

Adamat poked him in the chest for emphasis. "The docks are your territory, my friend. Tamas knows what's going on down here, and if he feels threatened, he'll shut down everything. All the trade to Novi and Unice, all your factories and mills."

Ricard's eyes went wide. "He can't. That'd tear the heart out of Adopest, and the union would be up in arms."

"He might have to, if he thinks he's got enemies down here."

Ricard seemed to think on this for a moment. "Who else knows you are here?"

Adamat's heart leapt. He gripped his cane a bit tighter, not willing to go down without a fight. If luck held, he might fend the three of them off until SouSmith could cross the street.

"No one," Adamat said.

"No one sent you?"

"I came on my own."

Ricard gazed at him for a moment, his eyes weighing the situation, as if deciding where to put the knife. Adamat considered calling out to SouSmith.

"Thank you," Ricard said. "If you came to these conclusions yourself...I may have some cleaning to do, indeed. Thank you, my friend."

Adamat watched Ricard walk into the night, finally taking that parasol from his bodyguard. His walk was more sober, quicker, as if he now had somewhere to go. SouSmith drew up quietly next to Adamat.

"Take your warning?" SouSmith asked.

"I don't know," Adamat said. "He didn't try to kill me, so that's a start. But he might have known what game I was playing. He's not an idiot. We'll see what he does next."

"What now?"

"I have other suspects. I still have to see the arch-diocel, the Proprietor, and Prime Lektor."

SouSmith gave Adamat a frown. "The Proprietor? Can't get to him."

"I'll think of something." Adamat tried to sound confident. "I suppose that means the arch-diocel is next."

SouSmith made the sign of the Rope. "Don't like that."

Wiser words had rarely been spoken. "He knows I'm coming. We've an appointment with him in the morning."

A young, nervous-looking priest stood on the front step of the arch-diocel's home and watched Adamat's carriage approach with an air of expectation. The home itself was a sprawling affair of a villa, only one story high but with a footprint to rival Skyline Palace. The style of architecture was far-eastern Gurlish with accenting white spires rising above a marble façade. There were satin drapes in onion-shaped windows. Vineyards stretched off to one side of the long cobblestone drive. On the other, grooms trained racing stallions on a horse track.

It was said, Adamat reflected as he stepped from the carriage and stretched his legs, that the arch-diocel was much more a man of pleasures than a man of Kresimir. Yet wasn't that the way of the Church these days? Oh, there were genuine priests; men who loved Kresimir and their fellow man and toiled for peace and brotherhood. But

Charlemund's type was far more common. Their love of women and gold and power burned in them like a fever.

The young priest approached Adamat at a quick shuffle. He wore white robes down to his ankles and sandals on his feet; the clothes of an impoverished monk, despite the obvious wealth of the place.

"I am Siemone," the priest said. He looked at his feet, his hands clasped before him as if praying.

"You serve the arch-diocel?" Adamat asked.

"I have the pleasure of serving Kresimir, sir," Siemone responded, "by attending to his righteous servant Charlemund, arch-diocel of Adro."

"I've an appointment with the arch-diocel," Adamat said. "Are we to wait inside?" He pointed to the front door with his cane.

"Er, no, sir," Siemone said. He wrung his hands as if he were cleaning his laundry. "The house is very full right now. His Lordship's extended family has come to the villa to celebrate the Saint Adom's Day festivities. Children running underfoot, shoulder to shoulder."

Adamat glanced through a window. He could see a very big man watching him from inside the window—probably one of the arch-diocel's bodyguards. No sign, nor sound of children. Admittedly, the villa was huge. Charlemund could put an army in there and one would see no sign of it. The curtain was drawn closed from the inside.

"I see," he said. It was an odd way to treat one's guests, even if Adamat was unwelcome.

Siemone cleared his throat. "Besides, the arch-diocel is a very busy man. We'll have to go find him at the chapel. What with the orgy this morning, he's running late for the afternoon prayer service."

"Excuse me?" Adamat blanched. "The morning orgy?"

"Yes," Siemone said. "Now, if you please, the arch-diocel doesn't like to feel threatened. *He'll* have to stay here." He gestured at SouSmith, who was just climbing out of the carriage, his hair tousled from a long nap.

"This is my associate," Adamat said. "He's aiding me in my investigation. He is no threat to the arch-diocel."

Siemone looked anywhere but directly at Adamat. "You mistake my meaning, sir. Your associate is a very large man, well built, and obviously a fighter of some kind. The arch-diocel doesn't like the eyes of his servants wandering. He, ah, doesn't like the competition, sir. His worship is very particular about which of his guests are allowed on the grounds."

Adamat blinked at the priest. *Doesn't like the competition...?* He shook his head. "You'd better stay in the carriage then," he said to SouSmith.

The boxer grunted and climbed back inside without a word.

"You said your master is running late?" Adamat said.

The corner of Siemone's mouth twitched. "Yes, the orgy. Now, please, come with me. We can catch him right after the prayer service, before the afternoon races start."

Siemone raised a hand. A small buggy emerged from the vineyard, where it had been concealed a moment before, and came up next to them.

Adamat couldn't take his eyes off the driver. She was young, perhaps sixteen, and had long golden hair, down to her waist. She wore a simple driver's uniform, a smock, hat, and gloves to hold the reins—but they were all of translucent silk, and she wasn't wearing anything underneath. The girl gave him a polite smile.

"Sir?" she said. "If you will."

Adamat tore his eyes away and climbed into the back of the buggy. There was only room for one, and he turned to Siemone. Before he could inquire where the priest would ride, the buggy began to move, pulled by a single white pony. The priest jogged alongside.

Adamat clutched his hat as a brisk wind nearly tore it from his head. They moved quickly down a path into the vineyard, passing a number of workers. Despite their pace and Siemone's long robe, the priest kept up with the buggy without seeming bothered. Adamat noted that Siemone kept his eyes on the ground at his feet or straight ahead, and it was clear why.

They passed a number of workers, pruning the grapevines or tending the grounds. All the workers wore basic tunics, but as with the buggy driver, they were all made out of sheer silk. Both men and women worked the vines. They were all young and beautiful.

How could such a place exist? Adamat thought he knew the worst pleasure dens in all of Adopest, but this...These men and women would be prize pieces at a millionaire's brothel, each one worth a thousand krana a night. Yet they worked the fields in such clothes at the arch-diocel's villa.

"You seem...awfully out of place here, Siemone," Adamat said. He realized too late how that must sound and cringed. "Not that you aren't a handsome young man," he added quickly.

A smile flitted across Siemone's lips, but he didn't look up. "I know your meaning, sir," he said. "This is my penance. If I act as the arch-diocel's steward for just another year, my application for a marriage license will be approved." A look of worry furrowed his brow. "If she still wants me, that is."

The Kresim Church allowed the lowest orders of the priesthood to marry, only requiring them to remain celibate if they wished to gain more power within the Church. Even those that married often had to pay some kind of penance.

Charlemund was a cruel man to require this of a priest. "Tell me," Adamat said, "has the villa always been like this? I've heard that it is a magnificent place with vineyards and stables. I didn't realize it was so...unique." He'd heard the rumors, of course. Everyone had. But he'd never believed them. A brothel in one of the outbuildings, perhaps, or a few beautiful women at his beck and call. *This* was beyond debauched.

"Yes, sir," Siemone said. "It's not new. The arch-diocel has a policy. His visitors may pick from anyone they see here—excluding myself—and do as they fancy. Oh, that includes you, sir, as you are a guest."

Adamat felt his face flush. "Oh no. No." He drew the word out long, embarrassed that it turned into a nervous laugh. "I'm a happily married old man. I'm quite fine, thank you."

Siemone continued, "The arch-diocel's policy is that anyone who speaks of his . . . servants . . . isn't invited back."

"There's no way to keep track of that."

"Oh, the arch-diocel knows, sir. He has ears everywhere."

Adamat couldn't help but smile wryly. "If that's the case, then I can see how that would encourage silence. Does every one of the arch-diocel's guests partake of his hospitality?"

"No," Siemone said. "Not all. But those that don't are generally the type with the taste not to speak of what they see."

Or the shame, Adamat realized. No one talked because they didn't want to implicate themselves in whatever sordid misdeeds could be found at the villa. It was the same reason a gentleman never speaks of the bawdy house he frequents.

He removed his hat to scratch his head, and spoke to Siemone in a flat tone. "So, you essentially work at the biggest brothel in all of Adro . . . by the pit, all the Nine . . . so that one day you can marry your beloved and remain a man of the Rope?"

Siemone giggled nervously. "Kresimir works in mysterious ways, sir."

Adamat felt a little ill then. "I think that has more to do with the arch-diocel's sense of humor than with God," he murmured.

The buggy came out of the vineyards and crossed a small field to a chapel. The chapel itself was simple enough, built of small limestone blocks and no bigger than a medium-sized house. It was about two stories tall, with a steep roof and a balcony just above the main door. A gold-braided rope hung from the balcony. Adamat was relieved to see that the area was free of the arch-diocel's servants.

Adamat disembarked the buggy and watched it roll around the corner of the chapel before he approached the door. He reached out just as Siemone touched his shoulder.

"Please, sir, they will be finished with prayer in a moment," Siemone said.

Adamat sighed. "Was I just about to walk in on an orgy?"

For a moment it looked like Siemone would laugh, but he just shook his head. "No, it is the afternoon prayer service. Just wait a moment."

Despite the priest's objections, Adamat pushed the door open just a crack. The inside of the chapel contained several rows of velvet-cushioned benches. The walls were plaster, but half-covered in rich tapestries of gold and red depicting smoking mountains and Kresimir descending from his Rope to the top of South Pike Mountain. There were only a small handful of people attending the sermon, though the chapel could seat at least thirty.

The arch-diocel stood at the front of the chapel, arms raised above him, face tilted toward the sky. His voice drifted through the chapel.

"And mighty Lord Kresimir, protect us from the unjust and the wicked, and deliver us from evil, that we might be taken into your fold..."

Adamat let the door close quietly. He retreated to the old stone wall of the chapel with Siemone and leaned against the cool brick.

"The place seems rather...deserted," Adamat said.

"What do you mean?"

"The arch-diocel is an important man. I expected to see more visitors. Messengers, clerks, all the like."

"Oh," Siemone said, "very few visitors are allowed on the grounds proper. His Eminence sees everyone at the villa itself. It's a very busy house, to be sure."

"And why am I so special?"

"Well, you have the field marshal's writ!"

At least that was something.

"How long have you been here?" Adamat asked.

"Two years, seven days." Siemone still refused to look directly at him, but Adamat thought he understood this now. Siemone was trying to keep himself as pure as possible for his potential marriage—a respectable thing, even if that meant that he rarely made eye contact with anyone. To avoid the lust around him, he had to stare at his own feet.

"You don't get out much, do you?"

"I go into Adopest occasionally. On His Lordship's errands."

My word. "Why don't you leave?" Adamat asked. "You don't need to serve penance to get a normal marriage license."

"I'm a man of the Rope, sir. If I leave now, I'll forfeit my rope." His hand brushed a small rope stitched to his robe above his left breast. "And I'll forfeit my chances to wed."

"She wants to marry a priest, eh?"

"Many priests marry."

"I've never heard of a penance like this. Aren't they usually, what, six months?"

Siemone looked somewhat miserable. "It's the arch-diocel's niece, sir."

Adamat gave Siemone as sympathetic a look as he could muster. "You poor, poor bastard."

"The service is finished, sir."

The front door of the chapel opened even as Siemone spoke. A number of buggies began to roll around from the opposite side of the chapel and waited for their fare. Seven men and women came out and loaded into the buggies. They were dressed in rich silks and leathers and the finest muslin. Adamat recognized a few of them as wealthy merchants. To his surprise, he noted Madame Lourent, a recent client of his. She was from an affluent family, and he was frankly shocked she'd survived Tamas's purge of the nobility. She passed him without acknowledgment.

Adamat imagined Ricard in one of those buggies. He'd fit in perfectly in a place like this, though he wouldn't do much praying. The buggies trotted away, across the field but not toward the front drive. They were heading for the back of the house for whatever tawdry amusements Charlemund had planned next. Adamat shook his head in wonderment.

The arch-diocel came out after everyone else had left and walked slowly toward Adamat.

"Good afternoon," Adamat said.

Charlemund ignored Adamat's greeting. Siemone hurried past the arch-diocel to lock the chapel doors behind him, then quickly turned to take the arch-diocel's robes of office.

"Siemone," the arch-diocel said, "Lady Jarvor fell asleep during the prayer session. This is the third time. Have her barred from the villa grounds."

"Yes, Your Eminence."

"And who is this?"

"Inspector Adamat, Your Eminence."

The arch-diocel squared his shoulders and looked down his nose at Adamat. "Tamas's hound. Right. Why are you here?"

Adamat looked the arch-diocel up and down. Charlemund was an imposing man, standing a full head taller than Adamat, and before he'd become a man of the Rope, he had been the fencing champion of all of Adro. He still moved gracefully enough, his steps long and purposeful, his arms giving him a significant advantage of reach over other men. Adamat still remembered when Charlemund had become a priest, then been appointed arch-diocel of Adro the next day. It had been a scandal, and was talked about for years, though his appointment was never rescinded. Charlemund had powerful friends.

The arch-diocel also had two large bruises on his face, covered up as well as possible with a dusting of white powder.

"Your Eminence," Adamat said, bowing his head. "I hope you are feeling well after your fall last week. I saw it happen. Dreadful accident."

Charlemund snorted. "Get on with it. Why are you here?"

He annoyed easily, Adamat noted. He felt another pang of pity for Siemone. "I'm here to ask you about the assassination attempt on Field Marshal Tamas last month."

"That? Hasn't it been cleared up yet? Bah. The races start soon, so be quick with your questions."

Adamat bit his tongue. Arch-diocel or not, there was common decency to be observed. In a gentle tone, he said, "Your Worship, I'm conducting an investigation into treason, not an inquiry into your favorite strumpet. Now, please, I have a few questions to ask you."

Siemone stood behind the arch-diocel, holding his robes, and the poor priest's eyes looked about to pop from their sockets. He stared fixedly at some point off in the distance and shook his head violently.

The arch-diocel gave Adamat a second look.

"You're perhaps the most powerful man on Tamas's council," Adamat said, "maybe even including the field marshal himself. You have the backing of the entire Kresim Church, an institution that dwarfs Lady Winceslav's mercenaries, Ricard Tumblar's union, and the Proprietor's criminal affairs in size, wealth, and strength. It gives me reason to believe that if you wanted Tamas dead, he would indeed be dead."

Adamat went on, "The only thing that gives me hesitation in removing your name from my list is that I can't for the life of me discover why you supported the coup in the first place. You have motive for neither supporting Tamas nor wanting him dead... that I can discover."

"What gives you authority to question me?" the arch-diocel asked coldly.

Adamat produced Tamas's note from his breast pocket and held it out to the arch-diocel. Siemone stepped forward and took it with an apologetic mumble. He cleared his throat and read it out loud.

The arch-diocel threw back his head and roared with laughter. "Cooperate with you? Answer your questions? What care I if Tamas suspects me? What can he do? He needs me in this war. He needs me to keep the Church out of things."

Adamat took the note back from Siemone and folded it into his pocket.

"I could spit on Tamas," the arch-diocel went on, "and still have him beg for my support. You think I care about this investigation?" He shook his head. "No, not one wit. You are right about one thing, though; if I wanted Tamas dead, he'd be in a pauper's grave right now. Tamas will deal with a higher power one day soon for the things he's done. I have no need to get involved."

A higher power? Adamat wanted to scoff. Charlemund wasn't exactly the model priest. Adamat took a deep breath and leaned forward on his cane, looking the arch-diocel straight in the eye. He knew he was going to pay for this persistence.

"What," Adamat asked, "is your interest in supporting Tamas?"

The arch-diocel met his gaze. He seemed to consider Adamat as one considers a mouse that will not get out of the pantry but is too pathetic to squash underfoot. "The Church deemed it necessary that Manhouch be removed from his position. The monarchy of Adro had pulled too far away from the people."

Adamat bit back a comment about a holy man running a bawdy house out of his villa. "Does the Church still support Tamas?"

"That is a question Tamas may ask me," the arch-diocel said. "Not his dog. Now, if you really want to get somewhere with your investigation you should question Ricard Tumblar, or perhaps Ondraus the Reeve. They are both untrustworthy men—men that should not be on Tamas's council."

"Why is that?" Adamat asked quietly.

"Neither man works for the good of Adro. Ricard is a blasphemer, hidden from justice behind his godless unions. He accepts bribes from any quarter—"

"Excuse me, how do you know that?"

Charlemund stumbled on this. His lip curled in a sneer. "Do not interrupt me."

"I beg your pardon."

"He has accepted bribes from the Kez, from criminals and gangs. He is a corrupt man, evil and beyond Kresimir's love."

"How do you know that he has accepted bribes from the Kez?"

"The Church has its sources. Do not question me."

"And Ondraus?"

"The man tries to levy taxes against the Church," Charlemund said. "His soul is in great peril. He fights me—a man of Kresimir!—on every topic. He does not pay his tithe, and hides his books from Church accountants. Not even the king hid his books from our censure! Look through his books and I guarantee you will find evidence of treachery." The arch-diocel checked his pocket watch. "I will be late for the races. You may leave now, before I lose my patience." Charlemund was off, bellowing for a carriage, before Adamat could get in another word.

Adamat watched him go. Charlemund's opinions on Ondraus seemed to hold little weight. Simply dislike, nothing more. Yet it was the third time Adamat had heard tell that Ricard was receiving large sums of money. It did not bode well.

"I'll have a look around the grounds now," Adamat said to Siemone.

The priest gave a quick shake of his head. "I'm sorry, that's not possible." He wrung his hands.

"I have an investigation to carry out," Adamat said. "I will not be underfoot. The arch-diocel's family will not be bothered."

Siemone licked his lips. "It's not that, sir, I... His Lordship is a very private man. I'm sorry, but you have to go now."

Further arguing got Adamat no closer to even a tour of the grounds. When it became clear he was expected to leave immediately, Adamat brushed off the offer of a buggy from Siemone and strode briskly back to his carriage. He climbed in, more than ready to be gone from the villa, and shook SouSmith awake.

"How do you feel," Adamat asked, "about investigating the arch-diocel's villa grounds under the cover of night?"

SouSmith's eyes widened. "Quick way into a pine box."

"Indeed." Adamat tapped his fingers on the coach window as they pulled away from the villa. "Still... we have work to do."

CHAPTER 31

Tamas woke with a start. His clothes were soaked with sweat, his body almost too hot to breathe. He could see the sun through one of the windows; it was past ten in the morning.

"Sir," Olem greeted him. The bodyguard stood over him. He held a bowl of porridge in one hand, a newspaper in the other. He'd had some rest, apparently, though Tamas didn't know how if the man never slept. Olem's eyes looked more lively, and the wrinkles on his face had smoothed out. He set breakfast down and helped Tamas to a sitting position. "Compliments of Mihali," Olem said, setting the bowl on Tamas's bedside table.

Tamas shook his head to clear the sleep from his brain. He felt foggy-headed and slow. Five days since his surgery, and Brigadier Barat's death. Tamas's damned leg hurt more every hour. It began to throb the moment he moved it.

"Would you like to read on the balcony?" Olem said. "Doctor Petrik said the air would do you good."

Tamas considered the sunny weather through the window. He looked at his leg. Pain, or being stuck inside all day? "Fine."

Olem helped him up and handed him his crutch, and they slowly made their way out onto the balcony. Olem headed back in for a chair while Tamas hobbled over to the railing. "Awfully loud today," he murmured. He glanced over the edge. There were a lot of people in the square. A second look, and he realized the square was close to full. He hadn't seen a crowd like this since the Elections.

"Olem!" He turned, startled when the bodyguard was right there.

"Sir?" Olem wore a self-satisfied smile, a cigarette in the corner of his mouth and a chair in hand. Tamas didn't like it at all.

"What the pit is this?" Tamas gestured down to the square.

Olem craned his neck. "Oh, yes. Mihali's work."

The square below was filled with dozens—no, hundreds—of tables, and chairs around each one. Every table was fully occupied, with countless more people still standing, waiting for their turn at a place to sit. More people stood in line; men, women, children. The line stretched down the Martyrs' Avenue and around the corner. Tamas leaned out, though it hurt to do so, searching for the head of the line.

It was right below them. Long, rectangular tables—Tamas recognized them from the Hall of Lords—stretched the whole length of the building. The tables were covered in food. Mountains of bread. Vats of soup. Meat roasting on spits. More food than one would find at a king's feast.

Tamas turned on Olem. "Wipe that smug look off your face and help me down the stairs."

It took some time, but Tamas was able to hobble down to the front of the House of Nobles with Olem's help. Tamas paused. The crowd had looked overwhelming from the top of the building. It looked twice the size from here. He paused, astonished, on the front step.

"Excuse me, sir."

Tamas shuffled out of the way. A squad of soldiers moved past him, carrying a table from the Hall of Lords. They were followed by clerks bringing chairs and then a cook with a bowl of soup almost too big for her to carry. Everywhere he looked, people were either eating, waiting their turn, or helping. Accountants, soldiers, townsfolk, even sailors and dockworkers. It seemed as if everyone had been pressed into service.

"I trust you're responsible for this?"

Tamas turned to find Ondraus. The reeve was furious. His spectacles perched on the bridge of his nose, an old ledger clutched to his chest. His lip was curled up, and sweat poured from his brow. His face was red with shouting. "I can't get anyone to go back to work! They say that Mihali asked for their help and then they just ignore me!"

Tamas didn't know what to say. He searched the crowd, looking for the tall, fat figure of the master chef.

"Where is this food coming from?" Ondraus said. "Who is paying for it?" He lifted his ledger and smacked it with one hand. "There are no records! No receipts. Not a krana is out of place, yet this! I can't understand it. You said he had a Knack for food, but this is ridiculous! Nothing is free, Tamas. There has to be a price!"

Tamas found himself drifting away from Ondraus, hobbling slowly, and soon the reeve's voice was drowned out by the sound of conversation. He passed his gaze across the people. Merchants sat next to scullery maids, minor nobles shared their plates with sailors and street urchins. Tamas stumbled. A strong hand caught him, helped him right himself. Tamas turned to Olem. "I... I don't understand."

Olem said nothing.

Across the square, the gates of Sabletooth were open, and prison wagons rolled out and joined a long line of breadwagons waiting to be loaded down and sent to the far corners of the city. Tamas caught sight of blue uniforms—soldiers directing the wagons. "Who gave them permission?" Tamas asked, pointing to Sabletooth.

"I'm sorry," a great, booming voice said, "but you did." As if from nowhere, Mihali appeared next to Tamas, his hands stuffed in the pockets of his apron. He wore a grin from ear to ear.

"I did?" Tamas asked.

"Aye," Mihali said. Sheepishly, he added, "At least, that's what I told them. But worry you not, they'll be back when needed. I put one of your powder mages in command of the breadwagons. Vlora, I think her name was."

Tamas said, "Where's Lady Winceslav? She was supposed to be in charge of the festival."

"Sir," Olem said, "the Lady has gone into seclusion. Mihali has taken charge."

Tamas had no reply. He looked around and said to Mihali, "What have you done?"

Mihali's grin stretched even bigger, and Tamas thought he saw tears glisten in the corner of the big chef's eyes. "I am... grateful," he said. "I am grateful that you patched things up with the archdiocel. I am grateful that you have finally welcomed me as one of your own. So in gratitude I have listened to the heart of the city. I've found what Adro needs, Field Marshal."

"What does it need?" Tamas whispered.

"The people are hungry," Mihali said. He lifted his hands, spreading them to encompass the city. "The people need to be fed. They need bread and wine and soup and meat. But not just that. They need friendship." He pointed to a minor noble, some viscount decked out in his finest foppish frills, who poured a bottle of St. Adom's Festival wine into the cups of a half-dozen street urchins.

"They need companionship," Mihali said. "They need love and brotherhood." He turned to Tamas. He reached out with one hand, putting a palm to Tamas's cheek. Instinct told Tamas to step back. He found that he couldn't.

"You gorged them on the blood of the nobility," Mihali said gently. "They drank, but were not filled. They ate of hatred and grew hungrier." He took a deep breath. "Your intentions were... well, not pure, but just. Justice is never enough." He let go of Tamas and turned to the square. "I will put things right," he said. He puffed out his chest and spread his arms. "I will feed all of Adro. It is what they need."

Mihali stopped one of his female assistants as she passed with a basket of bread for the wagons. "Bread is not enough," he said. "Take meat and soup and cakes. Serve the poor on silver. Let the merchants sup from wooden bowls. Take food to every part of the city. The wagons will be protected."

"How?" Tamas managed.

"I am Adom reborn," Mihali said. "Adro must be united. My people will go to battle nourished."

"Adom," Tamas scoffed. He found he could put no strength behind it.

A man in a worker's apron approached Mihali. "Sir," he said slowly. Mihali turned. "Ricard Tumblar sent us over. He told us to help with whatever you need."

" 'Us'?" Mihali asked.

The worker gestured. Behind him, other workers stretched out across the square, intermingled with the tables and the line, their aprons dirty with soot and burns and flour and blood. It looked as if the workers from every dock-front factory and riverside mill were there. The worker smiled. "He shut down the factories, sir. But we'll still get paid as long as we come help."

"The Noble Warriors of Labor, eh?" Mihali asked.

The man nodded. "All of us, sir."

Mihali's eyes grew wide. "Excellent! Come, I'll show you where to help."

Mihali wandered off, giving orders here, offering advice there. Tamas watched him go. "A remarkable man," he said. "Mad or not."

Nila didn't like Mihali's cooking.

It was beginning to destroy her resolve. Every day she could feel her hatred slipping. Every day she paid just a little less attention to Field Marshal Tamas's habits, watched just a little less carefully for her chance to end his bloody campaign. She didn't know how she knew, but it was the food that was doing it.

She tried getting her bread from Bakerstown. It just didn't taste the same, and Mihali was giving away food for free in Elections Square.

Nila couldn't wait any longer. It had to be done tonight. Olem was on duty, but that couldn't be helped. She liked him, she really did. He'd been kinder to her the last few days than any man she'd met in her time under Duke Eldaminse. But Tamas had to be stopped.

She did the lower officers' laundry first, after everyone had gone to bed. She went about her routine as usual, scrubbing and boiling and ironing, and then returning uniforms to their owners' rooms. She waited to fetch the field marshal's clothes till last. She always did. They were given special attention.

The hallway to the field marshal's office had four guards. They recognized her now. Nila even knew a few by name. Since Olem had begun courting her, no one's eyes lingered nor did anyone say anything untoward. They let her pass without comment, but it worried her that Olem wasn't there. What if he was inside?

The field marshal's rooms were dark. She made her way by feel and memory, and by a sliver of moonlight coming in through the balcony windows. She satisfied herself that Olem was not anywhere in the darkness, and came up beside the field marshal. He snored softly, sleeping on his back on his cot. Nila drew a hidden dagger from her sleeve and paused.

Field Marshal Tamas's brow and cheeks were covered in sweat. He muttered something and shifted.

She lifted her knife.

"Erika!" Tamas started in his sleep.

Nila froze. He settled back down to his cot, still deep in sleep. She took several breaths to steady her hand.

"Nila," someone whispered.

Nila closed her eyes. The door to the office opened a crack. "Nila," the voice whispered again. It was Olem.

She returned the knife to her sleeve and took the field marshal's uniform from where it hung over a chair. She slipped out the door. She would find out what Olem wanted and be rid of him. She still had to wash and return the clothing. There'd be another opportunity then.

Olem waited for her in the hallway. The other guards pretended not to notice as he took her hand and gave her a kiss on the cheek. His lips were warm.

"Thought I'd missed you," he said, walking with her down the hall.

"No." She forced a welcoming smile on her face.

He linked arms with her. "I'm glad," he said. "I don't get much time off. With my Knack and all, the field marshal likes me to put in extra hours."

"Of course." She paused. "You should take more time for yourself."

"I would like to. But only to be with you."

That wouldn't do at all.

"Are you sure?"

"Sure about what?"

"That you want to be with me?" She stopped and slipped her arm out of his. "Why do you come to *me*, Olem? I'm not a good prospect. I've no family or connections, and you've not tried to force yourself on me. I don't understand you."

The corner of Olem's mouth lifted. "When the time's right, I won't have to force you."

She smacked his shoulder, her cheeks flushing despite herself.

He laughed. "Come here," he said. "I want to show you something." He took her arm again and led her down a side hallway. "You know," he said, "I wondered about you after you disappeared from the Eldaminse townhouse."

"You did?"

"I wondered especially when we couldn't find the Eldaminse boy."

Nila tripped, and would have fallen if Olem didn't have her arm. Her heart began to hammer in her chest.

Olem continued, "Then I saw you at the barricades. I couldn't get to you. I couldn't leave the field marshal in the chaos of things, but I asked the men not to hurt you when they fetched the boy."

Nila felt her whole body shaking. Olem knew. He'd known all along that she was a royalist. Why had it taken him so long to call her out? Why wasn't she leaning over a headsman's block instead of strolling down the hall with him?

Olem stopped beside a soldier at a door at the end of one hall. The soldier saluted him, and he acknowledged by touching a finger to his forehead. The soldier opened the door for them.

Here it was, Nila thought. She was about to be put under guard. Hidden away until the next round of beheadings. Would they send her straight to Sabletooth? She still had her knife. She could attack Olem... but he'd expect that. She'd wait until he was gone and another guard had taken his place.

The room was dark except for a single lantern on a table by a window. It didn't look like a prison cell. There was a bed, a writing desk, and a divan. An old woman dressed in servant's clothes snoozed in a chair next to the bed.

"Go on," Olem said quietly.

She entered the room. Olem crossed over to the lantern and picked it up. There was something on the table next to the lantern.

A toy horse made of wood. Nila found herself kneeling by the bedside. There was a form there, sleeping soundly, bundled up to the chin beneath blankets.

Jakob looked healthier. His hair had been cut and dyed, his cheeks fuller, and there were now smile lines at the corners of his mouth.

"Tamas is not the heartless man most people think he is," Olem said. "He won't kill an innocent child. He sent no one to the guillotine under the age of seventeen on the day of the Elections. He had a rumor started that all the children of the nobility were strangled quietly in order to explain away their disappearance."

Nila brushed her fingers across Jakob's forehead. "What happened to them? What will happen to him?"

"Sent away," Olem said. "Some to Novi or Rosvel. Some to the countryside."

"Can I see him when he's awake?"

"No. He mustn't know anyone from his former life. He mustn't grow up thinking he's something special. He'll be sent to live on a farm, where his life will be hard but not dangerous or complex. He might marry a laundress someday. But he'll never be king."

Nila knelt beside Jakob's bedside for several minutes before Olem drew her away. The lamp was returned, and the guard locked the door to the nursery behind them. Around the corner, Nila clutched the field marshal's uniform to her chest.

Olem stood, hands clasped behind his back, face serious. "You must hate us," he said. "For destroying your world. I'm sorry for that. But Tamas... all of us... we did it so that the commoners can know a good life someday. So that we are no longer slaves."

"I was happy, I think," Nila said.

"The best kind of slavery," Olem said. "But still slavery." He fell silent for a couple of moments. "I'll understand if you want a transfer away from the field marshal. It must be hard for you, knowing what he did to people you once served. He'll be furious. He says you're the first laundress to starch his collars right since he was in Gurla."

"And you?" Nila said.

Olem struck a match and lit a cigarette, letting out a long sigh. "You can't like someone knowing your secret. The field marshal pardoned the royalists, but there's still no trust of them in the army. I won't tell anyone. And I'll leave you alone."

Nila searched Olem's face for insincerity. She couldn't find any. She had no doubt that if she said the word right now, he'd never speak to her again. His cigarette rolled between his lips. He took a long puff, then took it out, looking away. Giving her time to think it over.

"Are you sure you weren't a gentleman in another life?" she asked.

"Absolutely," Olem said, turning back to her. His face was still uncommonly serious.

Nila tried to tell herself that this changed nothing. That Tamas was still a monster who endangered Adro every moment he remained alive. But Olem had revealed that Tamas was human. That he had compassion. Nila could not look into the eyes of another person and take their life when she knew they still had humanity.

She hated Olem for it.

"I'd prefer," she said, clasping her hands behind her back so that Olem couldn't see them shake, "that we not speak again."

Olem stiffened. His eyes fell, and his serious demeanor dropped long enough for her to see his sadness before he straightened his back. "Of course, ma'am."

Nila watched him walk down the hall and brushed a tear from the corner of her eye. To do what needed to be done, she had to be cruel. No time to cry. There was still laundry to do before the house awoke.

CHAPTER 32

Taniel approached the bastion gate wondering how the St. Adom's Day Festival was progressing in Adro. They'd received a shipment of food that morning: barrels of ale, salted pork, and beef of the highest quality. Much better fare than normally seen on the Mountainwatch.

Mozes was already at the gate, and armed to the teeth with knives, pistols, and a rifle. Rina, the Watch kennelmaster and one of Bo's women, stood opposite of Mozes, crouched among her dogs. The beasts gave a quiet whine when Taniel approached. He squatted a few feet away and examined them in the torchlight.

There were three big, long-haired mastiffs. They wore black spiked collars, and were attached to Rina by nothing more than leather harnesses. Bigger than wolves, they could pull her off the mountain easily if they wished.

"What are the hounds for?" Taniel asked.

Rina didn't look up from her hounds. "The tunnel," she said. Her voice was low, gentle. "I trained these three in the mines. They'll cross forty yards and bring down a Privileged in a second. Musket fire doesn't bother them." She scratched one behind the ears. He turned toward her, massive head cocked, tongue rolling.

"What are their names?"

She pointed to the biggest one. "Kresim." The next, "Lourad." She patted the one who she'd been scratching. "And this is Gael."

Taniel held a hand out to Kresim. The dog sniffed once and turned away.

"They're not trained to be friends," she said.

"They like you enough."

She nodded. "I'm the master."

"I see." Taniel stood up. Bo arrived with Katerine, who gave them all a look of disapproval. Bo squatted beside Rina and slid a hand up around her waist. Lourad growled low in the back of his throat.

"Tst," Rina hissed at the dog. Lourad lay down on the ground.

Bo backed off a step. "Damned big hounds," he said to Taniel. "Things make me nervous."

"You're bedding their master," Taniel said. "That'd make me nervous. I'm surprised you can stand after all the drink you've had."

Bo craned his head toward Katerine. "She has ways of sobering a man up."

"None pleasant, I'd imagine."

Bo cringed.

Ka-poel emerged from the darkness of the town a few moments later dressed in her buckskins. Taniel had not seen them on her since Fatrasta. She normally preferred her long dark duster and wide-brimmed hat. The buckskins clung to her body, reminding Taniel she was a woman and not just a girl. Something he'd not noticed before. He noticed his hands were shaking from lack of powder, and took a sniff from his box. That steadied somewhat. He inhaled deeply and tried to resist taking more until it was needed.

Ka-poel was followed by Fesnik, leading a pair of donkeys laden with powder barrels, and a few steps behind him was Gavril. They all gathered around the Watchmaster.

"We've got enough powder to collapse their tunnel," Gavril said. "We can trust you to set it off when we're at a safe distance?"

"That much powder," Taniel said. "We'd have to be too far away." Vlora could do it from that distance. She'd always been able to detonate powder from farther away than any mage Taniel knew—her unique talent.

"We'll use blasting cord, then," Gavril said. "This will be quick. No one makes any noise until we've checked the tunnel—Rina, that includes your dogs. Who knows what kinds of traps they have waiting for us, or how many workers and soldiers they've got in there. Once that's done we'll set the powder, and then we hightail it out of there. We leave the donkeys if we have to."

"What'd they do to deserve that?" Fesnik said.

Gavril rolled his eyes. "Everyone ready?"

Nods went around, and they left silently by the front gate.

The mountainside below was completely black all the way to Mopenhague, where the Kez army still camped. They proceeded into the darkness, going slow enough to let their eyes adjust. A sniff of black powder made Taniel's brain buzz and brought his senses into sharp focus. The darkness held few secrets for him. For that he was glad—he still remembered the howling from the other night, and the sense he'd gotten of evil creatures prowling the mountainside.

Taniel went on ahead, Ka-poel following twenty paces back. They moved silently down the mountainside, their eyes sharp for Kez guards. Taniel reached the ruins of the first redoubt. It had been taken and retaken, then left for nothing and finally smashed by artillery and sorcery. He expected guards, but when he climbed among the stone rubble it was empty.

He checked each redoubt carefully. Were he the Kez, he would have left a small guard at each of them to raise an alarm of a counterattack—however unlikely. In the fourth redoubt he found a body, head removed by a cannonball and the corpse stinking in the tatters of a Kez uniform: a soldier missed by those who'd scoured the mountain for bodies the last week.

There were still no guards.

The digging started not far past the last redoubt. Taniel scouted the area for some indication of the enemy. There were no lights, no signs of people, nor when he put his ear to the ground could he hear the sharp clicks of shovels and picks beneath him. Taniel frowned. Something was off about this. He sent Ka-poel back to let the others know they could come forward. Nothing moved on the mountainside. Far below, the Kez camp glittered with campfires. Taniel heard the crunch of rock beneath well-worn boots as the others joined him.

They were on the road just above the entrance when one of the donkeys brayed behind them. Taniel felt his heart leap into his throat. He dropped to a sitting position, the barrel of his rifle resting on his foot so he could sight down the mountain. He waited for a Kez head to come into sight, for shouts of warning and then the trumpet of a general alarm.

A few minutes passed. He looked back at Bo and Gavril. Gavril's face was unreadable; Bo looked annoyed.

Bo signaled to Taniel, and then touched a finger to the middle of his forehead. Taniel nodded.

Taniel opened his third eye. The brief dizziness passed and he turned his attention to his surroundings. The chalky, colored residue of sorcery covered the entire mountain like spatters of whitewash on the ground beneath a freshly painted fence. It was all old magic, though, and had begun to fade. He looked toward the tunnel.

What he saw there was not old, and it had certainly not begun to fade. Twin streaks of color passed through the ground, under his feet, and up the mountain. Taniel closed his third eye and scrambled down the rocks to the tunnel, Ka-poel right behind him.

"What...? Taniel!" Gavril whispered. Taniel ignored him. He climbed up above the tunnels, and dropped down to the ground at their entrance. Above him, Ka-poel clicked her tongue. He checked for enemies before gesturing to her. When she jumped down, he caught her and set her on her feet.

Two gaping holes faced him on the mountainside. The darkness was too deep even for a Marked's senses, but he suspected what he might see. A pair of tunnels, each about a foot taller than a man, bored out completely by sorcery as if by a gigantic drill. He sighted along the tunnels, up the mountainside, and guessed at their destination.

Bo and Gavril joined them after a minute.

"There's no one here," Gavril said, bewildered.

"Thanks for pointing that out," Bo snapped.

"Shut up," Taniel told Bo.

"Where are all the sappers? Where's the Privileged?" Gavril said.

Taniel lifted a hand. "Up there."

"You mean they're finished?"

"Yes."

"And they come out...?"

"Above the Mountainwatch," Taniel said. "Up on the ridge. Last night I thought I saw something up there. I dismissed it as a trick of the moonlight. Now I don't think I was seeing things."

Gavril stared up toward the ridgeline far above them. "The sorcery required to carve these..."

"Julene," Bo said. "And probably half the Kez Cabal along with her."

"Then why didn't they attack yet?" Gavril said. "The northeast pass is barely guarded. There's not even a watch on that wall half the time. They could have hit us from up there with a thousand men and there'd have been little we could do about it."

"She doesn't care about the Mountainwatch," Bo said. "Never has. What she cares about is getting to the top of the mountain."

"It still doesn't make sense," Taniel said. "She could have destroyed Shouldercrown and then headed up the mountain. Unless..."

"She's in a hurry," Bo finished. He stared up toward South Pike's peak through the darkness for several moments. "I've heard stories floating around the cabal, as old as Kresimir, that the most powerful Privileged could use the auras of other planets, the moon, the stars, and the sun to amplify their sorcery. She needs the summer solstice."

Taniel felt sick to his stomach. He took a shaky breath. A quick hit of powder helped. "But," he said, "even if she's in a hurry, why didn't she tell Field Marshal Tine about the tunnels? How could she hide them even from him?"

"I think there's more going on in the Kez camp than we know," Bo said. "Julene is using the royal cabal, for certain. Perhaps not Tine, though."

Gavril scratched his chin. "How could she hide this? And if she didn't tell him about it, why two tunnels?"

"She hid it from us," Taniel said. "And I think this is a backup plan. If she can't summon Kresimir, she still wants to be able to take the Mountainwatch. I don't think she banked on us just walking down here to find it."

They stared at the tunnels in silence for a few moments. "Can she really summon Kresimir?" Gavril asked.

"She can try," Bo said. "Whether she'll be successful...that all depends on how many Privileged she has with her."

"I don't like the idea of waiting to find out," Taniel said. He turned to walk back up to the Mountainwatch.

"Where are you going?"

"I'll need some supplies if I'm going to chase her up the mountain."

Bo caught up to Taniel faster than he expected. "That's suicide," he said. "She must have thirty or more Privileged with her. Maybe Wardens and soldiers. Once they get wind of you…" He snapped his fingers. "Gone."

"I'll not let them get wind, then."

They reached the others and told them of the situation.

"I'm going after Julene," Taniel said.

"You mean, the one powerful enough to summon God?" Fesnik said.

Katerine crossed her arms and gave Taniel a look that clearly said he was an idiot. "I suppose you'll tell us next that you're going alone, as it's too dangerous for the rest of us."

Taniel barked a laugh. "Pit, no. Anyone can come that wants. I don't want to die on that cold son-of-a-bitch mountain alone."

Bo nearly choked. "I'll go," he said.

"Like pit you will," Katerine snapped.

"Get off it, woman," Bo said. "Julene's got to be stopped."

"Let the Marked do it."

"I'll go with you too." Rina's quiet voice almost made Taniel jump. She stood off to the side, quietly holding the leashes to her dogs. "Where Bo goes, I go."

"Don't you…" Katerine began.

"I said leave off!" Bo said.

Gavril looked torn. "I should," he started, then fell silent.

Gavril wanted to come with them, Taniel realized, but the Mountainwatch was his responsibility. If Field Marshal Tine resumed the attack, Gavril needed to be there to rally the defenders.

Taniel said, "Your responsibility is here." A thought occurred then. "Will the Novi monks let them pass?"

"I don't know," Bo said. "If they don't, Julene will level the monastery."

"Shit," Gavril spat. "They are good people." He turned to Mozes and Fesnik. "Set the powder."

They pulled back past four of the redoubts before they lit the blasting cord. Taniel watched the spark of flame work its way down the mountainside. It didn't take long for the trail to reach the tunnel. The whole mountain rumbled when the powder went off, and Taniel felt dirt slide beneath his feet. The last redoubt toppled into the remnants of the tunnel. Within minutes there were more lights in the Kez camp, and sounds of commotion rose from below.

They returned to the fortress. Taniel and the others collected more weapons and met back at the northeast gate a half hour later. The group was bigger than he'd wanted: Bo, Rina and her dogs, Fesnik, Mozes, and another eight Watchers—rough-looking men he'd seen around the camp.

"We shouldn't take so many," Taniel said to Gavril.

The big Watchmaster stood by the gate, clearly still torn about whether to accompany them. "You'll need the manpower," he said. "If you get into a fight, spread out across the hill as much as you can. If the worst happens, send someone running to let us know the pit just spewed all over Adro."

"Will do," Taniel said.

"Good luck."

Preparations were finished. Taniel approached Ka-poel. She held her rucksack on one shoulder.

"Any chance of convincing you to stay here?" Taniel said.

Ka-poel planted her feet.

"I thought not." Taniel sighed. "Let's go."

CHAPTER

33

Adamat returned to his home after nightfall, another day of questions without answers, of sifting sand and finding nothing of value. Another day of agonizing over a family he couldn't protect and a blackmailer he had no defense against. His feet hurt and his eyes wanted to close on their own. The buzz of festivity in the city, the growing excitement for a festival that looked to be forgotten amid war and chaos, had bolstered his spirit, but there was only so much excitement a man could take before it wore him down as much as the rest. He paused at the back door, examining the lock for a moment by the light of the moon. He put his finger out, rubbing it over the area just around the keyhole. He caught a hint of some faint smell: sweetbell, a Gurlish spice.

"What is it?" SouSmith asked from behind him.

"Nothing." Adamat unlocked the door. They'd spent the better part of the evening searching the Public Archives for the architectural plans for Charlemund's villa. They'd succeeded, but the plans were old, and even from Adamat's brief visit he knew that Charlemund had made significant changes to the house since it had been built. He wrestled with the decision of trying to enter the villa at night. If caught, the consequences would be severe, but he couldn't conduct a full investigation without a thorough search.

SouSmith went straight to the guest bedroom to change, and Adamat went to his office, feeling his way through the old, familiar home without the lights on. The smell of sweetbell, still very faint, was strongest in his office. He opened the liquor cabinet, removing a bottle of brandy, and poured out three glasses. He took one of them and sat down in his chair, lighting a match and setting it to the end of his pipe. He took a few deep puffs, making sure it was lit, and breathed the smoke out through his nose. He touched the match to his lantern wick.

"I've had a long day," he said. He pressed the cool glass to his forehead and examined the man in the corner through the slits of his eyelids.

The man blinked in the sudden light of the lantern, his mouth slightly open. His skin, hued with an almost reddish tint, marked him from Gurla, while his pudgy face and a body flabby around the middle and soft like a woman's betrayed that he had been castrated sometime before puberty. His head was shaved and he had no facial hair whatsoever.

Adamat gestured to one of the glasses on his desk. "Drink?"

The eunuch had been standing in the corner, hands folded within a long-armed robe. He stepped forward slowly. "How did you know I was here?" he asked. His voice was pitched high, like a child's.

"I've heard about you," Adamat said. "The Proprietor's silent killer. It's said you can appear and vanish without a trace. I've been an investigator for a very long time. Even the very best leave scratches when they pick a lock."

"You are being followed by a number of people," the eunuch said. "Field Marshal Tamas, agents of Lord Claremonte. How did you know it was me?" He sounded genuinely curious.

Agents of Lord Claremonte? Adamat tried not to let surprise show on his face. So that was Lord Vetas's employer? "I've been expecting a visit from you since Tamas set me after his traitor. It had to come sooner or later."

"You didn't answer my question."

Adamat raised his glass in recognition of the question, but did not answer.

The eunuch stepped up to the desk. He examined the glass of brandy but did not drink. SouSmith entered the room in nightclothes and a dressing gown. SouSmith paused. Adamat noticed his fists tighten, but that was the only reaction he gave to the eunuch's presence.

"Hello, SouSmith," the eunuch said. He inclined his bald head toward the boxer. "We haven't seen you in the Arena for some time. We'd wondered when you were going to come back to us."

SouSmith sniffed, as a bear might when it senses a snake. "When the Proprietor stops trying to kill me," he said.

"Have a drink, my friend," Adamat said to SouSmith.

SouSmith took his glass and retreated to the doorway to position himself in the only exit. The eunuch seemed unconcerned.

"I presume you've come because of my investigation," Adamat said.

The eunuch's face took on a businesslike seriousness. "My master instructs me to answer any of your questions, within reason, that will satisfy you that he is not the traitor you seek."

Adamat considered this. He already knew why the Proprietor supported Tamas: Part of the Accords included a Kez police force that would have drastically changed the criminal underworld of Adopest—the Accords specifically mentioned the Proprietor's head in a basket. They knew he was too powerful in the criminal underworld to leave alive. Hidden identity or not, the Kez would have torn Adopest apart until they found him.

With the danger of the Accords passed, the Proprietor might want to promote further chaos by removing Tamas. However, the Proprietor faced the same problems as many of his fellow council members. If Tamas died, then Kez was all the more likely to win the war, and the measures they sought to prevent in the Accords would be imposed anyway, and more besides.

"Why so forthright?" Adamat asked.

"My master has no interest in you putting your nose into his affairs—you have a certain reputation among his colleagues for unswerving doggedness. However, Tamas has made it clear that having you killed will attract his attention in a most unpleasant way. The easiest way to go about this is to get it over with."

"Pragmatic," Adamat muttered. Was the Proprietor being practical, or was he trying to manipulate Adamat's investigation away from him? Adamat rolled the glass of brandy across his brow again. "Does the Proprietor know who tried to have Tamas killed?"

"No," the eunuch said without hesitation. "He has made some inquiries of his own, to little avail. Whoever the traitor is, he is not using Adran intermediaries. My master would have known."

"The traitor is dealing directly with the Kez, then," Adamat said.

"It wasn't the reeve," the eunuch said. "As the funnel through which all money flows in the city, the Proprietor keeps him closely watched. Nor was it Lady Winceslav. We have a few agents in her household to keep an eye on things."

"One of her brigadiers was involved," Adamat said.

"Only one," the eunuch said. "Brigadier Barat did not have the sense of loyalty and justice that the others do."

"The vice-chancellor?"

The eunuch hesitated. "The vice-chancellor—Prime Lektor—is as unpredictable as Brude."

Brude. The two-faced saint of Brudania. A strange reference.

Adamat waited for him to elaborate, but the eunuch said nothing more. The reeve had also mentioned that there was something off about the vice-chancellor.

"You suggest," Adamat said, "that the Prime Lektor is equally capable of treachery as Ricard Tumblar and the arch-diocel? He's a glorified headmaster."

"As I said," the eunuch said quietly, "he is not what he seems."

Adamat took a long pull on his pipe. Assuming the eunuch was telling the truth—a very dangerous assumption—the most likely traitor was Ricard Tumblar. The arch-diocel was corrupt and power mad, but he had little reason to see Tamas dead. Ricard would give anything for his unions. It was perfectly possible he'd made a deal with the Kez in secret.

Adamat wondered again if he should risk a clandestine search of Charlemund's villa. It seemed the only thing standing before an open accusation against Ricard. Of course, Adamat still needed to investigate the vice-chancellor.

"Thank you," Adamat said to the eunuch. "You've been most helpful. Tell your master I will avoid poking into his affairs. If I can."

The eunuch gave Adamat a shallow smile. "He'll be pleased."

"SouSmith, show our guest to the door."

SouSmith returned a moment later and took a seat on the sofa. "My skin crawls," he said.

"Likewise." Adamat took a deep breath, relishing the smell of fine tobacco. It was a cherry blend, pleasant to the nose and throat, that left a light taste upon his tongue. It had a relaxing effect.

"Do you think he's telling the truth?" Adamat asked.

SouSmith grunted. "Reputation for certain honesty."

Adamat gave SouSmith a curious look. "Really? I've heard the eunuch is not to be trusted."

"Not the eunuch," SouSmith said. "When he speaks for the Proprietor, his word is gold."

"I'll have to take your word for it," Adamat said, though he made a mental note to look into the Proprietor's business—though not enough to get himself killed, hopefully.

Adamat spent the next hour at his desk, reading the day's paper while SouSmith dozed on the couch. The night was very still when he decided to head to bed.

Adamat stamped up the stairs, deep in thought, SouSmith following. When he reached the top, Adamat looked down the dark hallway. "Didn't you light the lantern when you came up?"

Some instincts went far deeper than mere reflex. Adamat threw himself backward down the stairs, barely hearing SouSmith's protests as a breeze passed his throat. SouSmith swore aloud, and a pistol shot went off.

Adamat lay flat on the stairs where he fell, his ears ringing from the shot. The shot had come from down the upstairs hallway. Adamat didn't think he'd been hit and he didn't dare ask SouSmith. Adamat pressed his hand to his throat. He felt blood there. Just a breeze of a razor—it had barely broken skin.

Adamat listened carefully. SouSmith had fallen all the way down the stairs and lay at the landing. Either he had the presence of mind to remain quiet or he had been shot and killed outright. Adamat prayed it was the former.

Adamat took a deep breath. Whoever had attacked him waited at the top of the stairs. There'd been no movement in the hallway—those floorboards were awfully creaky. The assailant was waiting there now. He had to know he didn't get both Adamat and SouSmith in one lucky shot. Adamat listened and stared intently into the darkness, trying to determine the number of assassins. They'd entered his house while he was reading the paper, possibly through an upstairs window.

Adamat slowly climbed to his knees, avoiding the center of the steps where they were wont to creak. He moved slowly, on hands and knees, up the next few steps, until he could put his fingers out and touch the floor of the hallway.

He explored farther, brushing his fingers along the floorboards until they came in contact with something. With a feather's touch he outlined the leather sides of a shoe, then another, until he had a good idea of where his attacker stood. He imagined the attacker's stance. The attacker was probably holding his hand up, with a razor or knife. Adamat had no way of knowing which hand. It was a gamble Adamat had to take.

Adamat sprang upward. His left hand caught the attacker's right wrist as his forearm connected with the man's throat. The attacker cried out in surprise. Adamat felt something sharp graze his ear. Wrong hand!

He pulled down on the right hand and twisted the man around, trying to guess how the attacker would flail the razor with his left hand. He brought his right elbow down on the man's shoulder, eliciting a grunt. Another pistol shot rang out, a flash of light temporarily blinding Adamat. Adamat felt his attacker jerk and sag, taking the bullet that was meant for him.

Two of them, at least, maybe more. Adamat threw himself forward. The pistol had gone off up the hall, near his bedroom door. He reached out blindly, grasping a hot pistol barrel. With the other hand he fumbled about his person for the penknife he kept in his pocket. He felt a pair of palms hit his chest. He was pushed backward, toward the stairs. His heel hit something—the body of the first assailant—and he went spinning head over feet down the stairs.

He landed next to the front door. His ears rang, his head spun. Nothing had broken in his tumble.

Footsteps thumped down the stairs after him. Two figures came into the light of the moon shining through the front window. One dropped his pistol with a clatter on the stairs and drew something from his belt. Adamat heard a faint click, and something glinted in the dim light.

Adamat surged to his feet and retreated down the main hallway toward the kitchen so they couldn't come at him from above. The two men followed. One ducked into the study. The other came on fast.

Adamat gripped his penknife. The assailant drifted forward, the only sound the creak of floorboards beneath his feet. Adamat felt a bit of sweat drip down his brow, past his eye.

One of the men lit a lamp in the study. Adamat briefly glimpsed his assailant's outline. The man was of medium height, crouched low, legs spread for good balance. *Pit*, Adamat thought. The other assailant stepped around a corner, hooded lantern in one hand. The light shone toward Adamat, blinding him while giving his assailants a good look at their quarry. Adamat leapt forward, striking sightlessly.

He felt a cold sting across his chest as someone cried out. He jerked back with his penknife. A hand grabbed his knife arm, and he struggled against it, waiting for the familiar weakness of a deadly wound. Pain flared as an elbow struck his chest.

There was a commotion farther on in the hallway. The light spun away from Adamat's eyes. He caught a brief glance of SouSmith, big arms swinging, grabbing ahold of the man with the lantern. A pistol shot rang in Adamat's ears, pounding inside his head.

Adamat managed to free his knife arm. The man with whom he grappled tried to push forward, razor in hand. Adamat's heart leapt and he stabbed with all his strength, praying the strike would fall true. He pulled back and stabbed again, and again, until the man cried out for mercy and slumped to the floor.

Adamat fell against his back door and surveyed the hallway, watching for any movement. He tried to control his ragged breathing, listening for any sign of assassins in the rest of the house.

"All of 'em?" SouSmith mumbled.

Adamat took a few more breaths before he answered. "I think so. One dead on the stairs, two down here. You hurt?"

"Shot," SouSmith said. "Twice. You?"

Adamat grimaced. "I don't know."

He nudged the figure at his feet with his toe. The man gave a low moan. Adamat stumbled into the study, pain blossoming on his chest. He put one hand to it, felt it slick with blood. He bent down, every inch agony, until he got ahold of the hooded lantern where it had fallen. Somehow the candle had remained lit. He removed the hood.

The hallway was a mess. There was broken plaster on the floor in pools of blood. Three bodies. Adamat ignored them all and crossed to SouSmith. The old boxer sat on the bottom step, one hand shoved inside his shirt. His front was covered in blood.

Adamat swallowed a lump in his throat. "Let me get more light."

He lit the hallway lanterns and removed SouSmith's shirt, borrowing a razor for the job from one of the dead attackers. A bullet had grazed SouSmith's left arm, taking a finger-sized chunk of flesh from it. The other had entered his belly, and Adamat nearly choked when he saw the wound.

"It's bad?" SouSmith let his head rest against the wall. Sweat beaded across his brow and cheeks. He'd tried to wipe it away at some point, leaving a smear of blood across his face.

"You were hit in the stomach. No way to tell whether the ball hit any organs. We need a surgeon. Keep your hand here, try to staunch the blood. I'll try to find help."

He didn't have far to go. A number of his neighbors had heard the shots and stood in the street holding lanterns and pistols. They gaped at Adamat and tried to peer past him into his house.

"Someone get a surgeon," he said weakly. "And send a boy to the House of Nobles. A message for Field Marshal Tamas. Make sure he gets it. Tell him… tell him Adamat has been attacked by the Black Street Barbers." No one ran down the street, or went to fetch a coach. Some of them moved back nervously, frightened by the mere mention of a street gang. "Please," Adamat said. He heard the desperation in his voice.

One of his neighbors stepped forward. He was an older gentleman, a veteran of the Gurlish wars, with long gray muttonchops and a black coat pulled on over his nightclothes. He clutched an old blunderbuss in his hands. Adamat recalled his name was Tulward.

"I've some surgery experience. From the field," Tulward said. He turned around, shouted toward his house, "Millie! Send the boy out here. Now!" He turned to the group of onlookers. "Get back to your homes, folks. Go!"

Adamat nodded his thanks as Tulward stepped into his house.

"Are you hurt?" Tulward asked. Adamat pointed to SouSmith. "He's worse. Took a bullet to the stomach."

Tulward grimaced and ran an experienced eye over the bodies. He stepped across them, making his way toward SouSmith.

Adamat sighed, slumping against the wall. He took a moment to look long at the carnage. One of the men was still hanging on to life, lying in the entrance to the study. Adamat ignored the pleading look in his eyes. The second body was at the top of the stairs. He lay on his side, shot by his own comrade in an attempt to get Adamat. The bullet had entered his cheek and killed him instantly, and a pool of blood trickled down the stairs.

The last body still stood upright, his head lodged in the wall. Adamat stumbled over to examine him closer. It was the one who'd been holding the lantern. SouSmith had grabbed him by the face, shoving his entire head through plaster and brick.

Tulward crouched over SouSmith, talking to him quietly, fingers feeling along his belly. Adamat moved over to the surviving assassin. He removed the man's coat, trying not to cause untoward pain. The man moaned.

"I'm trying to help..." Adamat froze. He looked at the man's face again—really looked, for the first time. "Coel," he said. Ricard's scrawny assistant from the docks. Adamat took a shaky breath.

He finished removing Coel's coat. In his panic, he'd stabbed Coel at least ten times in the chest with the penknife. The wounds were not deep, but he would bleed out quickly. He rolled up Coel's shirtsleeve, just to be sure. There it was, as he'd expected: a black tattoo of a barber's razor on his forearm.

Coel was long dead by the time Tamas's soldiers arrived. The house swarmed with men, setting to rest Adamat's fear that more of the Barbers would come to finish the job. A team of surgeons carried SouSmith into the sitting room, and SouSmith's swearing and yelling bore testament to them trying to remove the bullet. Adamat sat on his stairs, watching the front door blankly as people moved in and out.

"You might need stitches for that."

Adamat looked up. Tamas stood at the bottom of the stairs, one hand on the railing, leaning heavily on a crutch. He reeked of gunpowder. He nodded at Adamat's chest.

Adamat looked down. The wound was superficial, but it stung like someone had squeezed a lemon into it, and it still bled.

"When they're done with SouSmith, I'll take my turn." Adamat paused. "You didn't have to come yourself."

Tamas watched him for a few moments. "The Black Street Barbers were not supposed to take other jobs. Things will be very unpleasant for them in the morning. You're a very lucky man. I've seen the Barbers operate." Tamas looked away from Adamat and at the bloodstains on the floor. "It's a pity none of them lived."

"Yes," Adamat said, "I just wasn't thinking right, assailed in the dark by men with razors." He grunted. "I won't be able to shave for months." He ran his hand over his throat, where the skin had barely been broken. There was a line of dried blood there. His hand trembled. A sudden impulse seized him to tell Tamas all: about

Lord Vetas, about his family. Maybe Tamas already knew. He was not a man to be duped. Yet Tamas would not allow Adamat to continue his investigation if he thought Adamat's integrity had been compromised. Adamat felt his face turn red.

Tamas didn't seem to notice. "Who do you think ordered your death?" Tamas said.

It was obvious, wasn't it? "The Black Street Barbers are loyal to Ricard Tumblar." He jerked his head at Coel's body, pushed to one side of the hallway. "And he was bringing Ricard wine when I met with him a month ago."

"Fairly damning evidence," Tamas said. "Any other reasons why Ricard would want you dead?"

"No," Adamat said miserably. He remembered a time when Ricard had been imprisoned for his latest attempt at unionization some fifteen years prior. Adamat, already with a reputation for honesty, had given testimony on behalf of Ricard's character that saw him released the next day.

Two years after that, when Adamat was too poor to buy his children presents for St. Adom's Day, Ricard had shown up at his door with gifts worth half a year of Adamat's salary. They'd leaned on each other a lot over the years. Adamat found it hard to believe such a friendship would end like this.

"I'll send a squad to bring him in right now," Tamas said. He turned to one of his soldiers.

"Wait," Adamat said.

Tamas paused, turned back with a wince.

Adamat closed his eyes. "Give me a little more time. We can't be sure it's Ricard."

Tamas's eyebrows rose. "The Black Street Barbers finish a job, Inspector. This was no feint. They report to Ricard. When I'm finished with them, the Barbers *will not* exist."

"They do jobs for hire," Adamat said. It was a weak argument, even to him. "I gave Ricard a chance to kill me just last week. He didn't take it."

Tamas gave Adamat a level stare. "If we wait even a few more hours, word will get to him that the assassins failed and he'll be on a boat to Kez before sunup."

"Give me until noon," Adamat said.

"I can't afford that." A hint of anger entered Tamas's voice. "If the traitor gets away from me, I'll lose my grip on the council, and they will turn on me."

"Send a squad," Adamat said. "Have them watch Ricard—by all means, arrest him if he tries to flee. It will be a sure sign of guilt. But if you make a mistake now, you'll still have a traitor in your midst, and the Noble Warriors of Labor will turn against you."

Tamas seemed to hesitate.

Adamat said, "Give me until noon. I think I can get to the bottom of this."

"How?"

Adamat swallowed hard. "I'll need to borrow one of your powder mages. I'm going to see the Black Street Barbers."

CHAPTER 34

The Black Street Barbers were one of the oldest street gangs in Adopest. They claimed to be between one hundred fifty and three hundred years old, depending on who was asked and how drunk they were. They operated out of a ramshackle line of apartments only a few blocks from the Jalfast Waterworks. The local police guessed their number at around seventy-five.

Adamat watched the apartments from a safe distance down the street. From the look of things, their fortunes had been better. The building was a dilapidated ruin. It was two stories, all of poorly made mud bricks far too old to be safe. The second story contained dormitories, while the first floor looked to be a large bar. Chairs sat out in the sunshine in front of the building. A number of Barbers skulked nearby, throwing dice on the pavement while they waited for dockworkers in need of a shave.

"Don't like getting involved with the Barbers," SouSmith said.

Adamat glanced at his friend. SouSmith wore a short black coat, the sleeves rolled up. He leaned against the wall of a decommissioned coal coking plant, eyeing the Barbers' headquarters. There was a bead of sweat at his brow and a pain in his eyes, the only indication that he'd been shot twice and operated on last night. They'd removed the lodged bullet safely. A lesser man would be neck deep in opiates to kill the pain.

"I told you not to come."

"You paid me," SouSmith said. "Can't go in alone."

Adamat snorted. He was far from alone. SouSmith just wanted to put another Barber's head through a wall. Adamat rubbed his chest, resisting the urge to pick at the stitches he'd received from Tamas's surgeon.

He watched as three squads of soldiers filled the street, cutting off foot and carriage traffic in both directions. Another two squads fell in behind the Barbers' building, unseen. One of the Barbers throwing dice looked up. He tapped his friend on the shoulder and pointed, then hurried inside.

"Time to go in," Adamat said. He pushed himself away from the wall and strode down the street. Tamas's Deliv lieutenant, Sabon, appeared from one group of soldiers. His blue uniform was immaculately pressed, his ebony skull shaved clean. He wore a pistol on one hip, a smallsword at his other. He greeted Adamat with a nod.

"Don't let them get too close to you," Adamat said. "They're deadly with those razors." He waited a moment for SouSmith to catch up. Just the walk up the street had turned SouSmith's face white, and the old boxer was sweating as if it were midsummer. Adamat opened his mouth to send him off, but thought better of it. If SouSmith wanted to come, he'd come.

Adamat felt for the pistol under his long coat to reassure himself. He took his cane firmly in hand and strode toward the front door, ignoring the pain across his chest.

He kicked open the front door. It fell from the hinges completely, rust spraying the floor. The room inside was well lit, windows open along the east side behind a row of barber's chairs. There were old signs of blood underneath these chairs, rusty stains on the brick floor. On the opposite side of the room was a long bar with bottles of liquor stacked on the wall behind. There was a cask of wine at the end of the bar almost as wide as a man is tall.

A group of men looked at each other and walked toward Adamat from the bar. The type looked contagious: whip-lean, sickly-looking men wearing aprons over white shirts. Adamat addressed the one in front.

"Hello, Teef."

The man was in the process of drawing a razor from his pocket when he locked eyes on Adamat's face. His eyes went wide. He fumbled his razor, nearly dropping it. Adamat's cane flicked out, catching Teef on the wrist. The razor went flying.

His comrades didn't recognize Adamat. Their razors came out true, and pasty-white hands lunged toward Adamat, blades held out front. Adamat flinched.

The three men around Teef all had the same reaction at the crack of gunpowder. Their razors fell from their hands. Surprise crossed their faces, then pain as they clutched at bleeding wrists. Three bullets had gone clean through three wrists without a pistol being drawn. Adamat dealt Teef a glancing blow on the cheek with the tip of his cane, then held it at the Barber's neck. He looked over his shoulder. SouSmith stood just inside the door, eyes closed as he leaned heavily against the wall. Sabon stood silently to the side, eyes traveling around the inside of the barbershop as if he were casually perusing a store. Only the cloud of powder rising from him indicated what he'd done.

"What the pit?" Teef said, his voice cracking. "What are you doing? Cut them down!" He glanced at his comrades, and his mouth fell open. "What happened...?" His mouth worked like a fish out of the water. He stared at Sabon, and realization spread on his face. Adamat pressed the tip of his cane against Teef's throat.

"Cut them down, eh?" Adamat said. "That what you told Coel and the other two you sent to kill me last night?"

"I swear it wasn't personal, Adamat." Teef held his hands out in front of him, glancing nervously at the space between Sabon and Adamat. His eyes stopped over Adamat's shoulder. "Oh shit."

"They didn't tell you SouSmith was my bodyguard, did they?" Adamat said. He smiled at the panic in Teef's eyes. "He put one of your men's head through a brick wall. It'll take me hours to scrub the blood out of my front hall. Now, who hired you, Teef?"

"I swear, I didn't want to, but—"

"It was a lot of money, I know. Must have been a king's ransom. Tell me, how many times did I let you walk, back before you ran the Black Street Barbers? When you were just a stupid kid with talent with a blade and a whole run of bad luck? I don't appreciate favors being paid back like that, Teef." He pressed harder on Teef's throat, and shook his head slightly when Teef tried to step back. The Barber quaked.

"Where the pit are they?" he screamed suddenly. "Help!"

Adamat gave Teef a long-suffering sigh. "Five squads of Tamas's best soldiers are rounding up your boys, Teef. Razors are a pretty thing in a close fight, but not against seasoned riflemen with bayonets fixed." Gunshots went off outside the building as if to punctuate Adamat's words. There was a scramble of feet on the floor above them, then the thud of a body hitting the floor.

Teef clenched his fists, but kept them out in front of him. "We'd give you a run," he said, lip curling, "if all our boys were here, we'd give you a pit-damned run."

"Sure you would," Adamat said. "Who hired you to kill me?"

Teef's jaw clicked shut.

Adamat took a deep breath. He didn't have time for this right now.

Adamat felt himself pushed gently aside. He lowered his cane as SouSmith stepped up to Teef. The boxer was at least a head taller than Teef, and twice as wide. Adamat bit his tongue. SouSmith was covered in a cold sweat, and he clenched his teeth in pain. He reached out and took one of Teef's hands.

"I'll break this one first," SouSmith rumbled.

"Ricard," Teef said. The name came out like a startled curse word.

"Not good enough," Adamat said.

He heard a snap as SouSmith bent Teef's finger back far enough to touch his wrist. Teef screamed in agony. One of the other Barbers stood up and reached out for Teef, only to receive SouSmith's boot on his chest. He was kicked halfway across the floor. Adamat put out a hand, steadying SouSmith when he stumbled. SouSmith regained his balance and twisted Teef's wrist.

The Barber sank to the floor screaming. Adamat tapped SouSmith on the shoulder with his cane. The boxer stepped back.

"Who hired you?" Adamat said.

"The Proprietor!" Teef squealed through a string of curses. "He came in here looking for your head!"

"At least make your lies plausible." Adamat flicked his cane against Teef's wrist. He felt a pang of pity as Teef screamed again, but forced it down. Teef's blades came to Adamat's home, where his wife and children slept, and tried to kill him. His family would have been killed in their beds, every one of them, if they had been there. Adamat knew how the Barbers worked. They were as cold and ruthless as Lord Vetas. Adamat raised his cane to bring it down hard.

"A priest."

Adamat stopped. "A priest? Come now."

"It was a priest," Teef said. He sucked in shaky breaths, chest heaving as he talked, tears running down his face. "He came in here yesterday morning. He was crying the whole time, kept asking Kresimir for forgiveness."

"What did he look like?" Adamat asked.

"A priest. White robes and sandals. Blond hair. A little taller than you. A mole on his right cheek. He wouldn't look me in the eye."

Siemone. Adamat felt his mouth go dry.

"How much?"

"Five hundred thousand krana."

Adamat nearly dropped his cane. "What? For me?"

Teef wheezed a laugh. "Two jobs. Fifteen thousand for you."

"And the rest?" Adamat looked around. He'd trusted it to good fortune that there'd been only a few of the Barbers around. He realized now why there weren't more: They were at a job. The thought made his skin crawl. That made at least forty Barbers unaccounted for, maybe more.

Sabon stepped forward and dragged Teef to his feet by the front of his shirt. "Is it Tamas?" Sabon said. He shook the Barber. "You double-crossing swine! Is it?"

"By the pit, no!" Teef said. "There's not that kind of money in the world."

"Who is it, then?"

"A chef," Teef said. "Some big fat man in charge of the feast. My employer wanted him cut down in public. We don't normally do that, but for the amount he offered..." Teef trailed off.

Sabon dropped him. Teef tried to catch himself, called out in pain. Sabon gave him a look of disgust. "You've made a terrible mistake," he said. He glanced at Adamat. "Take them to Sabletooth. I have to go."

Sabon was gone without another word, and Adamat saw that it was now just he, SouSmith, and the four Barbers. He exchanged a glance with SouSmith. The boxer shrugged. Adamat lifted Teef's chin with the tip of his cane. "What's so important about a chef?" he asked. Mihali, he recalled the chef's name. Had the arch-diocel remembered the beating Mihali gave him in Tamas's presence? It was a lot of money for revenge.

Teef shook his head. Adamat moved his cane threateningly. Teef's head shake was more emphatic. "I don't know, Kresimir damn you! It was just a job."

"And you have no idea where the money came from?" Charlemund. Siemone wouldn't do dirty work for anyone else. Charlemund had been trying to frame Ricard all along.

Teef hesitated just a second too long.

"I suggest you remain ignorant," Adamat said. "Or your fate will be worse than it already is." Tamas would destroy Teef. Adamat almost pitied the Barber. Almost. He stepped away from Teef as a troop of soldiers entered the room. "Get them to Sabletooth," Adamat said. "All of them. I have to go to find the field marshal."

"It'll take hours to get across the city with the festival on," SouSmith shouted after him.

Adamat barely heard as he ran out of the building. He needed to tell Tamas about Charlemund before it was too late.

CHAPTER 35

Taniel's chest heaved, his legs ached. A few short hours of rest just before dawn was all they'd taken in the last two days. Only his powder trance let him keep the pace, but he always found himself outdistancing his companions. Two of the Watchers had collapsed from exhaustion. They left them where they were and continued on. Those men would find their own way back down the mountain.

The going was easier than Taniel's last ascent. Some snow had melted, the rest had been cleared by the Mountainwatch. There'd been some travel between the Mountainwatch and Novi's Perch for resupply since winter. Campfires and old horse droppings remained from resupply caravans sent to the monastery.

Those didn't concern Taniel. What concerned him was the more recent passage. They'd yet to catch sight of the Kez, but they'd found two camps. There was scat and tracks enough for at least a hundred men and pack animals to boot. That many men shouldn't have been able to sneak past the Mountainwatch, yet somehow they had.

They found the third camp midday. It was tucked away off the main trail, down by a waterfall that was still half-frozen despite summer being almost upon them. Taniel checked the ashes of a cook fire. They were still warm.

He took stock of the camp. It brought back memories of camps not so unlike this in faraway Fatrasta when he and the natives tracked Kez patrols and lay ambushes for them. Only that hadn't been in the high mountains, and those patrols weren't filled with Privileged. And Wardens.

His chest went cold as he kicked something with his toe. He picked it up, flipped it around in his hand. It was a metal ball just about the size of a man's fist. An air reservoir from a Warden's air rifle.

"How far behind them?" Bo asked when the rest of the group had caught up to Taniel. Bo looked less well each day. His cheeks were sunken, his eyes underlined by black bags. Their punishing pace had done him ill.

"Hours," Taniel said. He tossed Bo the air reservoir. "I should have expected this."

"Where there are Kez Privileged, there are Wardens," Bo said.

He dropped the metal sphere, only to have Ka-poel swoop in and pluck it from the ground. She examined it closely and tucked it into her rucksack.

"We're gaining on them," Taniel said.

"Close to the top, too," Bo replied. "We're not far from Novi's Perch."

"Everyone rested?" Taniel asked Fesnik. The young Watcher staggered to the waterfall to refill his canteen.

Fesnik groaned. "Pit, no. We supposed to be able to fight after a climb like this?"

"Fight and win," Taniel said. He nudged Fesnik with his toe.

"Right, right," Fesnik said. He climbed to his feet. "Come on," he called to the others. "We're moving again."

Taniel watched them head back to the main trail. These were hard men, Mountainwatchers. Yet none had his advantage with the powder, and even he felt sapped from the climb. What good would they do against Julene and the other Privileged? How could they possibly win a fight?

Taniel fell in beside Ka-poel on the trail. She held a blank-faced wax figurine, pushing and shaping the wax with her fingers.

"What are you doing?" he asked her.

She tucked the doll under one arm. Expecting an explanation of hand signs, Taniel leaned closer. She punched him in the shoulder.

"Ow."

She shooed him away with one hand and returned to her project. He fell back beside Bo.

Bo looked troubled.

"You seem cheery," Taniel said. Bo's expression didn't change. The sarcasm seemed lost on him.

"We might be too late," Bo said.

"We're making better time than I expected."

"We have to be there during the solstice."

"Don't worry," Taniel said. "We will." Taniel spotted smoke in the sky. He grabbed Bo's shoulder and pointed.

"Is that the mountain?" Taniel said. He couldn't remember being able to see the smoking crater from here on his last journey up.

Bo paled. "No," he said. "Too close. That's Novi's Perch."

Word spread and they redoubled their efforts. They reached the Perch within an hour.

The wall of the monastery that effectively ended this portion of the trail had been smashed in. It looked like a giant had stepped up to the side of the mountain and simply slapped it with the flat of his hand. Some of the old rock remained where it met the mountain.

The rest had fallen away into the abyss and was invisible against the stone of the gulch far, far below. The monastery was exposed like the side of a dollhouse, hallways and stairs bare to the elements.

The ruins lay like a smoking animal carcass, splintered timbers jutting out from the rubble like broken ribs. In some places the rock itself had melted away. The invisible fist that had destroyed a great part of the monastery had also destroyed a chunk of the cliff, and the hallway that led from one end of the monastery to the other was now divided by a fissure twenty paces across.

"We can go back, and head down one of the halls," Fesnik said. "There's a warren inside the mountain—that's where the rest of the monastery is. Shouldn't take but a few minutes." His voice was quiet, almost reverent. He gazed about with a look of sadness. Taniel realized that the Watchers must have known these monks.

They found the hallways just as Fesnik had said. Once they were inside the mountain, the smoke got worse. They could barely breathe as they made their way through the crisscross of hallways. Rina's dogs whined despite her rebukes. Taniel paused by one wall, noting a splatter of blood. An odd chip had been made in the stone. He ran his fingers over it. From a bullet, for certain.

"There's no bodies," Taniel said quietly. He spoke mostly to himself, but was surprised to find Ka-poel very close to him. She examined the ruins clinically. Taniel said, "There have to be survivors. The smoke would drive them out. They must be on the other side." He nodded to himself. "That's it." Taniel felt ill.

Ka-poel gave him a look that seemed to say she doubted this.

They came out of the hallway on the other side of the fissure. He could see where the monastery ended, and the broken stairways that led up to the opposite entrance. No one was to be seen.

"Please," a voice said.

Taniel leapt into the air. He spun around, pistol out before he could process a thought. He lowered the pistol.

A monk shied away from him. It was a woman, much younger than he expected.

"I'm sorry," he said. The sight of her made his hands shake. Her face was bruised, battered. Blood stained her robe. "Are there more survivors?"

The woman indicated one of the many hallways. Thirty paces in, as far out of the elements as they could manage, was a ragtag group. The smoke wasn't too bad here. There were seven that Taniel could see still standing, and a large number of linen-wrapped bodies on the floor. His heart fell as he counted those bodies. He stopped at forty, and that couldn't have been half.

Fesnik spoke to one of the monks, an old man, his gown torn and dirty, his eyebrows singed. Taniel approached.

"We gave them the best fight we could," the old man said. He brandished his walking stick. "They came out of nowhere. We should have been better prepared. Had there not been so many..."

Taniel knew the monastery would still have been destroyed. What could a bunch of monks do against half of the Kez Cabal, and Julene on top of that? She stormed through, slaughtering as she went. What could Taniel and Bo hope to do against her?

The man went on, "That was two hours ago. The fight was fast, violent. I've never seen anything like it. Some of the younger ones can't even believe it happened." He gestured to a young monk who sat near the wall, arms wrapped around himself. He was in shock, eyes staring out at nothing. "Del hasn't spoken since it happened. Still, we made a good accounting."

Taniel could barely hold back his bewilderment. "A good accounting?"

The old monk's face was serious but proud. "Well, yes. Half these bodies are theirs."

Taniel looked around. He then saw what he hadn't before—a stack of air rifles in the corner. He realized that many of the bodies were big, bigger than any man should be. Fifteen, twenty. Wardens.

Then there, near a small fire one of the monks was using for warmth, he saw the frayed corner of a Privileged's glove and a Kez uniform. Taniel felt awed. This small group of monks had not only stood their ground against the Kez Cabal, they'd given as good as they got.

There had to be sorcery at play here. Powerful stuff. Not anymore. He wondered if there were more monks farther in the monastery. No, probably not. This looked like it. A meager handful of survivors. Yet they managed to fight Wardens and Privileged.

"Why'd they leave you alive?" Taniel asked as gently as he could.

The old man tightened a bandage around his wrist. "Seemed in a hurry."

"The solstice," Bo said, appearing at Taniel's shoulder.

The monk barely blinked, his face revealing nothing. "There are old magics," he said quietly.

"They were led by a woman?" Taniel asked. "Regal, looks about thirty-five with a great scar on her face."

"A woman?" the monk said. "No, a giant cave lion, slinging sorcery."

"Her chosen form," Bo said glumly.

"We're going after them," Taniel said. "Do you know how many were left?"

The old man gave Taniel an annoyed look. "I didn't pause to count as we collected our dead."

"Sorry," Taniel muttered. There were a lot of bodies here. They may have wiped out a good chunk of the Kez. Mostly Wardens, it seemed. He gave Bo a glance. Bo was examining the wrapped bodies and moving among the survivors. His fingers twitched in his gloved hands. He'd love to know what kinds of sorceries these monks were hiding. Taniel guessed that not even the cabals knew all the old secrets.

Bo returned to the old monk. "This monastery. It was put here to guard against something."

The monk's face remained neutral.

"Against Kresimir's return?"

"Nothing good will come of the god returning," the old man said. "But there are worse things on this mountain." He paused. "Yes, we are the gatekeepers of Kresim Kurga. The Predeii have returned. We were meant to stop them." His proud countenance faltered. "We failed."

"We'll do what we can," Bo said.

Taniel gave what he hoped was a confident nod.

They stepped away from the old monk and put their heads together.

"He knows a lot more than he's letting on," Bo said.

"We don't have time to interrogate him."

Bo rubbed his gloved hands together. "I'd make it quick. It might be valuable." His eyes glowed with curiosity, and his face was more alive than Taniel had seen in weeks.

"No," Taniel said. "Look around. He wants Julene dead. He would have told us anything he knew. God, they really do make you sell your soul to join the cabal, don't they?"

"Expediency."

"We have to go," Taniel said. "The solstice?"

"Today."

"How long will it take to get to the peak?"

"Longer than it is until the solstice."

"We'll have to beat it," Taniel said. "Do we have a plan?"

Bo frowned. "There are plenty of Privileged among these dead," he said. "Maybe enough to ruin her plans. She needs power to summon Kresimir. She needs to bridge great distances to bring him back." Bo seemed to consider his options for a moment. "Take out as many Privileged as we can. Ignore Julene."

"She'll be hard to ignore when we've made her angry."

Bo sighed. "We'll deal with that when we come to it."

Taniel returned to the old monk. The man was kneeling next to the other he'd called Del, and was speaking quietly into his ear. He looked up.

"You'll need a guide in the city," he said. "There are dangerous paths up there. Del knows the way best. I'm trying to coax him up..."

Bo pushed Taniel aside and knelt next to the man. He touched gloved fingers to the man's forehead and held his other hand up. He touched the air gently—a pianist performing a song with one hand.

"Yes," Del suddenly said. The word came out as a hiss. "I'll go." This was a croak. His eyes came awake, like a fire coming to life in a dark hearth.

"Are you all right?" Bo asked.

"Water."

"Get him some water," Taniel told the old monk. He was back in a moment, and they tended to Del before helping him to his feet.

"I'll be all right," Del said. "I'll go. You...you say you can stop them?"

"We'll try," Bo said.

"We have to get to Kresim Kurga before the solstice."

"Do you know where they'll be?" Taniel asked.

Del frowned up at the sky. "There is a coliseum there, built by Kresimir. It helps focus sorcery. I think that is the most likely place."

"Excellent," Taniel said. He pulled Bo to one side. "What did you do to wake him up?"

"Nothing," Bo said. "I was going to touch his mind, see if there was anything there, but he came awake before I did."

"It'll be good to have a guide."

Bo agreed.

Taniel stepped away. A pair of Watchers pulled a body from farther in the smoke-filled hallway—an old woman. She had not a mark on her. She might have died in her bed, killed by the smoke, too deep in the mountain to hear the battle. The Watchers left her body with the monks and turned back to search for more.

"We need to go," Taniel said. He kept his voice gentle, but loud enough for the others to hear. "Fesnik," he said. "Gather the men."

Fesnik had been helping wrap yet another body. He stood up, cast a weary look about him. He seemed to have realized what they were up against. This wasn't an adventure. This was a chase to the death against opponents far more powerful than they.

Bo was arguing with the old monk when Taniel returned to them.

"You can't bury them all," Bo said.

"It's our way," the old monk replied. His face was, as always, neutral.

"Toss the Kez over the cliff. Tend to your own if you can't leave them packed in ice for a few weeks. You need to get down the mountain and tell Gavril what happened."

"We'll send someone," the old monk said.

Bo sneered at the old man. "And your own survival? The monastery is destroyed. The nights are cold enough to freeze anything left outdoors. This is no home for you now!" His voice began to rise, and his gestures were making Taniel nervous.

"Bo," Taniel said.

"What?" Bo whirled on him.

"Time to go."

Bo took a deep breath and collected himself. "Take care," he said to the old monk. There was a hint of sarcasm in his voice. "Stubborn bastard," he muttered as he passed Taniel.

"Your friend is very tired," the old monk said.

"He's had a rough month."

"He has very little left."

Taniel scowled. These monks were a mystery. What kind of sorcery did they have at their call to have been able to fight Julene and the Kez Cabal? He didn't see any Privileged's gloves on any of them. He opened his third eye, fighting the nausea. He closed it again as quickly as he could and tried to blink away the blinding colors of the Else. The sorcery was too thick to make out anything.

"I know," Taniel said. "Find some shelter."

"Good luck," the old monk said. He managed a smile, something for which Taniel found himself more grateful than he expected. "We gave them a good fight," the old monk said. "They are weaker now. Make it count."

If these old men and women could fight Julene, then so could he, Taniel decided. He took a deep breath and clenched his fist. It was time to take the fight after her.

Taniel clasped hands with the old monk and joined the waiting Watchers. They'd done what they could for the surviving monks. Some of the Watchers left their rations and spare blankets—though Taniel hoped the monks would be able to scrounge more from the ruins when the smoke died down.

Taniel did a head count and noticed Rina and her dogs were missing.

They found her at the end of the monastery squatting just outside the broken walls, examining the path up to the peak. She turned to face them as they approached. Her dogs whined and pulled at their harnesses. She silenced them with a hiss, but only for a moment.

"There's something else on this mountain," she said.

Taniel tried not to shiver. "What do you mean?"

"Cave lions." She indicated the ground, pointing to tracks that Taniel could barely see. "We've hunted them before. The dogs know their scent."

Taniel felt relief wash over him. There'd been something so sinister about her statement. He realized his hands were shaking. "Oh," he said. "There's lions on all the mountains. That could even be Julene—the monks said she used that form when she fell among them."

"I don't think that's it."

Taniel felt his heart beat a little faster. "Pole!" he called. "Get back here."

The girl had gone on ahead, some thirty paces, and was squatting on the trail, picking at the ground. She ignored him.

"No?" Taniel asked Rina. "How can you know?"

Rina spread her hands and spoke in her ever-quiet voice. "Because there's at least fifty."

Taniel heard more than one of the Watchers swear. Bo sputtered, making warding signs in the air with his hands.

"What?" Taniel said. The word came out more forceful than he'd intended.

Rina said, "Farther up. Past Ka-poel, where the trail widens. They came down off the slope and fell in behind the Kez."

Taniel glanced at Bo. "Can she summon them?" he asked. "I've heard stories about Privileged who can—"

He was interrupted by Rina's laugh.

"What?"

"They're not with the Kez," she said. "They're *hunting* them." There was a note of hysteria to her quiet voice. "They'll hunt us too when we go up there. Kresimir above, they'll hunt us." She pulled the dogs closer to her and stared at the tracks on the ground.

"Cave lions don't hunt in packs," one of the Watchers said.

They all seemed to turn to Bo at once. He looked back at them, his face tired and haggard. He felt the air tentatively with gloved hands like a doctor feeling for a broken bone under the skin, a warm thread of sorcery touching Taniel's senses.

All he said was, "There's something wrong on this mountain."

Nila acquired a cart for the laundry. One of the many workmen attending the St. Adom's Day Festival helped her build it out of an old washtub and the base of a four-wheeled vendor's wagon. She couldn't bring herself to ask one of the guards, though they'd likely do it without protest. Word had spread that she'd rejected Olem. The soldiers were still courteous, but not like they'd been.

For three days she used her new cart to collect the laundry, so that the guards would get used to the idea. It made sense—she had more work to do than usual, what with half the staff of the House of Nobles skipping out on their duties to attend Mihali's feast. The lack of help left her alone in the basement to do the laundry more often than not, and she was able to amend her usual route to pass down the hallway to Jakob's room.

Nila quickly realized that night would be the hardest time to sneak Jakob out of the building. With the halls deserted, it would be difficult to hide him. During the day, however, the number of people in the House of Nobles was almost overwhelming. The feast going on outside made it impossible to keep track of everyone who came and went, and once out of the building she'd be able to melt into the crowd.

On the morning of the final day of the festival she wheeled her clothing cart down the halls of the House of Nobles. She made her usual stops and collected enough clothes that she'd be able to conceal a child, before turning down the hallway to Jakob's room. She passed men and women, soldiers and clerks, nodding and smiling to everyone.

The guard wasn't at his station. Nila gave a sigh and whispered a prayer of gratitude to Kresimir. Only Jakob's nurse would stand between getting the boy to freedom.

Nila checked to make sure her truncheon was still in her cart. She didn't want to use it, but she would if the nurse gave her trouble.

She came to an abrupt stop. The door to Jakob's room stood open. It was never open. She forced herself to continue on, wheeling her cart past the door, glancing inside as casually as she could.

The room was empty. No nurse. No Jakob. Had she made a mistake? Did they move Jakob to another room this morning, or even out of the country?

She checked the hallway for soldiers and went inside.

The bed was unmade. There were toys on the bedside table, and a child's clothes hanging in the closet. It looked like he'd left only recently. Was he using the washroom? She needed to get out, in case he came back with a guard.

"Who the pit are you?" a male voice asked.

Nila spun around, her heart leaping into her throat. Two men stood in the doorway. The one who spoke looked like a dockworker, with a flat cap and a wool jacket with mended elbows over a grimy brown vest. The other was obviously a gentleman. He wore a black jacket over a velvet vest and white shirt, black pants, and black, polished shoes. He carried a cane and top hat.

"The laundress," Nila said, swallowing hard. Who were these men? Why were they in Jakob's room?

The dockworker frowned at her, then looked back at the clothing cart in the hallway. "Come back later," he said.

"Can I help you with something?" Nila asked. She could tell by the dockworker's accent that he was a local. Probably a member of the Noble Warriors of Labor. The gentleman remained silent, but something about his steady stare put Nila on edge.

"Just came back for the boy's clothes and toys," the dockworker said. "Won't take but a minute."

"I was just about to take them for laundering. I could get them cleaned and then send them after."

"That won't be necessary." The gentleman finally spoke. His voice was quiet, steady. He sounded educated. "Go on," he told the dockworker.

The dockworker pushed past Nila, politely but firmly, and began emptying the closet and the dresser drawers onto the bed. He tossed a wooden train and a pair of tin soldiers on the pile and gathered it all up in one of the sheets, tying it in a knot at the top.

"I'm sure he has a travel bag..." Nila began.

"That won't be necessary," the gentleman said again. "You may take care of the rest of the bedding." He left the room.

The dockworker swung the whole bundle over his shoulder and carried it out into the hallway. Nila followed him, watching him head down the hallway behind the gentleman. When neither turned to look back at her, she began pushing her cart after him.

She followed them at a distance down the main hallway, then down a side corridor before they turned into a room at the end of the hall: one of the many offices in the building. Nila left her cart and slowly approached the door. She peeked around the corner.

A hand grabbed her roughly by the shoulder. She was jerked into the room and slammed hard against the wall. Someone gripped her by the chin, and she found herself staring into the compassionless eyes of the gentleman.

"What does the boy mean to you?" he asked. His voice was still calm, collected, despite the bruising grip he had on Nila.

Nila mumbled in surprise, not certain as to what to say. Who was this man? Why would he treat her like this? How could he know Jakob meant anything to her?

"What," the gentleman said, jerking her face from one side to the other with emphasis on each word, "does the boy mean to you?"

"Nothing. I'm just the laundress."

"I have a Knack for knowing when I'm being lied to," he said. "You have five seconds to tell me. Then I will strangle you."

Nila felt his fingers close around her throat. She stared back into his eyes. She'd seen more life in the eyes of dead men. She counted down in her head. His grip tightened.

"I was..." she started, feeling her throat constrict. He let up slightly. "I was his family's laundress before the purge. I've known him since birth. I wanted to help him escape from Tamas."

The fingers dropped from her throat. "Fortunate," the gentleman said. "We had problems with his nurse. You will take her place and come with us."

"I don't…"

He grabbed her by the back of the neck, half dragging her across the room as one might an unruly child. He opened a closet and forced her to look down.

Nila remembered the nurse who'd been watching Jakob when Olem had taken her to see him. She was an older woman, heavyset. She lay at the bottom of the closet unnaturally, her eyes staring up at nothing. Nila tried to back away. The gentleman's grip on her neck prevented her from doing so.

"This," the gentleman said, "happened because she had qualms. If you decide to have qualms… if you ever disobey me… I will not hesitate to kill you with my bare hands. My name is Lord Vetas, and I am your master now. Follow me."

He closed the closet door and led her out into the hall. The dockworker appeared with the sack of Jakob's clothing over his shoulder. Vetas gestured to Nila. "She will be the boy's new nurse. Take her. I have business to attend to elsewhere."

Vetas left at a brisk pace. Nila couldn't help but watch him go. Her heart hammered in her chest, her legs sagging beneath her. She'd never felt fear like this. Not before Olem had saved her from rape, not when she'd almost drowned as a child in the Adsea. That man was pure malice.

The dockworker shrugged and took Nila by one arm. He led her down the hallway and out a side door, toward a carriage waiting in the street. Even on the back side of the House of Nobles there was a crowd. Nila looked up at the dockworker. His grip was not painfully tight. She could kick him and get away, disappearing into the throng.

They drew closer to the carriage. Some dread in the pit of her stomach told her that if she set foot in that carriage, she would never escape Lord Vetas. She watched for an opportunity, her body tensed, her skirt gathered in one hand so that she could run.

"Miss Nila?" Jakob appeared in the door of the carriage. His hair was mussed, his jacket askew, but he seemed unhurt. "Miss Nila! I didn't know you were here!"

Nila let her skirt fall from her hand. She took Jakob's hand and stepped into the carriage. "Don't worry," Nila said. "I've come to take care of you."

CHAPTER 36

Tamas leaned back in his chair, one leg up on a hassock, and watched Mihali's feast draw what seemed like half the city for a late breakfast. The entire square was full, and the streets beyond overflowing with lines waiting their turn. Some of them watched jugglers while they waited, and thousands crowded around a raised platform near the middle of the square, eating porridge on their feet as a troupe of mummers performed a lewd comedy. This was the last day of the festival, and no expense had been spared for the entertainment of the masses.

A large parasol shaded Tamas from the midmorning sun. He sat on the front step of the House of Nobles, feeling better than he had for months, while he worked his way through a basket of rolls Mihali had left with him an hour ago.

"With your leg, you should be in bed," Lady Winceslav said. "Are you sure you're feeling well enough to be out?"

He looked her over once, noting her pallor, and wondered if he should ask the same.

"Of course, Lady. Never better." Brave words, maybe, but the fact was his leg *did* feel better. He could almost *feel* it healing, his strength returning to him. He knew he had work to do, but damn it, none of it seemed to matter. For the first time since his wife's death, he felt whole again.

Even Lady Winceslav seemed in better spirits. She'd braved the crowds despite her recent scandal with Brigadier Barat. She wasn't directing the festival—that was all in Mihali's hands now—but at least she was here.

"Do you think everyone will come?" she asked.

Tamas eyed the crowd. "I think the whole city is here, Lady."

"I meant of the council." She gave him a playful cuff on the arm.

"Ricard has been here since half past six," Tamas said, "rolling out food and wine with the rest of his workers." And under strict, but discreet, watch, until Adamat returned with evidence for or against his guilt. If the union boss knew anything about the attempt on Adamat's life, he gave no sign.

"Has he?" She seemed surprised by this. "Incredible."

"Ondraus is somewhere out there, yelling at his clerks," Tamas said. "Olem says he saw the eunuch just an hour ago. Of Charlemund I haven't seen hide or hair. And there"—he pointed—"is the vice-chancellor."

Tamas watched Prime Lektor pick his way through the crowd. The birthmark spidering across his face looked darker than usual. The vice-chancellor eyed the food as he passed the serving tables, but he seemed to have something more important on his mind. He paused briefly at a stern look from Tamas's bodyguards and then ducked under the parasol. He tipped his hat to Lady Winceslav.

"Seat?" Tamas asked, gesturing to one of the guards.

"Please," Prime said. He observed the feast while waiting for a chair, and then took a seat next to Tamas. "You seem to be in unusually good spirits."

"I do?" Tamas said. "I haven't said two words."

Prime cleared his throat. "I can sense it about you. It's in the air. Like a first-year student who knows he's going to be every professor's favorite. It's annoying." Prime looked about again. He kept looking toward the serving tables and watching assistants bring out bowls and platters and everything else.

Tamas gave the vice-chancellor a sidelong glance. "Can't you feel it?" he said. "It's not just me. It's the whole city. It's... this." He gestured to the feast, the tens of thousands gorging themselves on Mihali's food without a care in the world. "The wealthy and the poor, the noble and the ignoble rubbing shoulders. I've never seen anything like it."

Prime gave the feast a long-suffering once-over. "You don't believe this rubbish, do you?" he said. "About this chef being a god?" His eyes lingered on a pot of porridge.

Tamas hesitated, trying to read Prime's tone. There was something off about it. Despite the gruff way he spoke, it almost sounded as if Prime wanted Tamas to say yes.

"Ha. A god? No. A powerful Knacked. A little mad, maybe. But harmless," Tamas said. "But then again..." He raised a finger alongside his nose in a secretive gesture. "What does a god look like? What does a god do? Who am I to know one when I see him?" He shook his head with a laugh at Prime's exasperated look. "Mihali is a gifted man. Greatly so. I don't think a god, though. How about you? You're probably the most qualified to know. You've every history of the Nine at your fingertips. Do any talk of Adom?"

"I realized a long time ago Kresimir would never return." Prime fell quiet, and Tamas realized he had no idea how old the vice-chancellor was.

"And Adom..." Tamas prompted.

"He loved his food," Prime admitted. "He's the patron saint of chefs for a reason. He was a big man, strong, powerful, and"—he tracked one of Mihali's female assistants with his eyes as she passed by, a platter of stuffed waterfowl balanced on one hand—"he was very popular with the women. He had over four hundred wives, and loved every one of them. Figuratively and literally."

"Four hundred?" Tamas said. "I could barely handle one." His throat caught on that, and he had to clear it. "You speak as if you knew him yourself."

Prime said nothing.

"Sounds like Mihali is a pretty good candidate."

"There are too many questions," Prime said. "There hasn't been a god on this earth for hundreds and hundreds of years. Kresimir left, off to resume his exploration of the cosmos. Novi and Brude went the same way just days after. The rest followed, or disappeared without fanfare. There was a rumor that one or two of them had remained behind...," he said, trailing off.

Tamas exchanged a curious look with Lady Winceslav.

"Do you feel well?" Tamas asked.

Prime spared him a glance. "Would you believe me," he said, "if I told you Mihali is a gifted sorcerer?"

"Without a doubt. Not a Privileged, though. A Knacked."

Prime snorted. "A Knacked, my ass. What if I were to say, 'the most powerful sorcerer in the world'? Or if I said that that's all the gods ever were: immensely powerful sorcerers?"

"Hypothetically?" Tamas said, revealing his skepticism.

"The most powerful to ever live?"

"You're joking."

"It's just a question," Prime snapped.

"So what if he was?"

"The problem with logic," Prime said, "is that sometimes you are forced to believe your own hypothesis, even if you don't want to. What do you feel when you sense toward Mihali?"

"A Knacked, as I said. He has the soft glow to him. Less power than a Privileged by far."

"Can you be sure?"

Tamas sighed. He opened his third eye and looked toward Mihali. There had to be many Knacked in such a large crowd, but Mihali was easy to find. Something about him stood out above the others. Yet his glow was no stronger.

"Yes," Tamas said. He watched Prime's face. The old man was frowning toward Mihali. "You don't think it's possible, do you? That he's really a god?"

Prime closed his eyes and was quiet for several minutes. Tamas was beginning to wonder whether the old man had nodded off, when his eyes opened.

"Too many questions," he said again.

"You said 'the other gods,'" Tamas said, "I thought Kresimir was the only god."

Prime shifted in his chair and watched a service-pressed clerk roll out a barrel of ale and gingerly move it down the front steps. "That's not precisely true," Prime said.

"It's dogma," Tamas said. "Charlemund reminded me so just the other day."

"Just because something is church dogma does not make it true."

"Well, certainly," Tamas said, "any educated man..." He trailed off at Prime's scowl.

"Educated men," Prime said. "Bah. There were ten gods. Not one god and nine saints. Kresimir came initially, and then requested the help of his brothers and sisters to organize the Nine."

"There's ten gods?" Tamas said. He struggled to remember his history lessons. "I always thought Kez took Kresimir as their patron. Who is the tenth, then?"

Prime shook his head. "That's the wrong question. You should be asking: If Mihali is a god, why is he here now?"

South Pike Mountain was hidden behind the House of Nobles, but they both turned in that direction. Tamas thought back to the warnings he'd received from Bo and Taniel. Ancient sorcerers trying to summon God. It was almost quaint, as if from a storybook. Fears generated from the stress of months of battle. Although, Tamas remembered, those first warnings came before the start of the siege. Tamas scratched at the top of his wounded leg. It began to hurt more, the pain returning like an ache long thought gone.

"Have you ever heard of Kresimir's Promise?" Tamas said suddenly.

"Rubbish," Prime said.

"Rubbish? You know of it? I was told it was a cabal secret, only known to the kings and their Privileged."

"It is." Prime mopped his forehead with a handkerchief.

Tamas was about to press him more when he heard a scream.

Another followed, and then another. A ripple of fear moved through the large crowd as a murmur of yells grew to a roar in moments. People rose from their places, their food forgotten, trying to see the source of the commotion.

"What's going on?" Tamas snatched his crutch and struggled from his chair. "Find out what's going on," he told a guard. "Get inside," he said to Prime. "Guards, take Lady Winceslav inside." Tamas watched Mihali climb up onto a table, nimble despite his girth, and strain to see what was happening.

"Calm down!" Mihali shouted. His voice carried over the crowd with surprising force. "Please, return to your seats." People paused, half-risen, unsure of what to do. Those in line seemed to hesitate, unwilling to lose their places but concerned by what could be happening. Everyone remembered the dragoons on Election Day.

Tamas could still see nothing. The commotion seemed to be coming from the far end of the tables. Some people ran, struggling against those who tried to get closer and see.

"My pistol," Tamas said. He noticed Prime had gotten to his feet and was craning his neck for a better look. Lady Winceslav waited beside the door to the House of Nobles with her bodyguard.

"Get inside," Tamas said again. "I don't want you killed by a fear-stricken mob."

Prime ignored him.

"Suit yourself," Tamas growled, taking one of his dueling pistols from a guard. He checked that it was primed and loaded before scanning the crowd.

"There," Prime said, pointing.

Tamas caught sight of a man several hundred paces away. The crowd had backed away from him. He looked to be holding something in his hand. Tamas bit into a powder charge and swayed as the full force of a powder trance hit him. He took a few shallow breaths and straightened, sharpening his gaze on the man.

The man was dressed as a Barber. He wore a white shirt and dark pants under a white apron. The apron itself was stained with blood. There was a body at his feet, with the long, blond hair of a woman. He wiped the blade of his razor on his apron and sprinted toward the crowd.

"The Black Street Barbers," Tamas said slowly. "What the pit..."

More screams. Tamas swiveled his gaze. There were dozens of them. They dashed into the feast, throwing down platters of food, cutting down men and women and children with impunity, razors flicking the air like a master's brush painting a bloody masterpiece.

"To arms!" Tamas bellowed. His first shot took a Barber between the eyes at a hundred paces. He didn't need his sorcery for that. "Can you reload this?" Tamas said, dropping the pistol into Prime's hands. "Bullets!" One of his guards paused in aiming to give him a handful of round balls and another of powder charges. Tamas flicked one bullet in the air and ignited a powder charge with a thought. Another Barber dropped, then another.

"Why the pit do you even need this?" Prime said, handing him the loaded pistol.

"Better accuracy," Tamas said, surprised that an academic could reload a pistol so quickly. The crowd began to writhe and move, people moving like a panicked herd of cattle at the sound of pistol shots. Tamas steeled himself as he noted some of the crowd looking toward the open doors of the House of Nobles.

"Get those doors closed," he told a guardsman. He raised his pistol. "Make sure Lady Winceslav is inside."

"There!" Prime said. The old man nudged Tamas's pistol toward Mihali. Tamas saw the Barber come out of the crowd near the chef. Tamas pulled the trigger. The man dropped like a stone.

"Novi's frosted toes!" Tamas said. "Sabon was supposed to take care of the Barbers. Mihali! Get out of there!"

The chef did not hear him. He still stood on a table, waving his arms and shouting, seemingly unaware of the dead Barber nearby.

"Another," Prime said, pointing. "They're going for Mihali."

"Why?" Tamas said. He handed the pistol back to Prime and flicked a bullet in the air. The shot glanced off a Barber's shoulder and into the crowd, where a man clutched at his side. Tamas grimaced. "We're too far. I can't help him much without more weaponry." He dug into his pockets for more bullets. He was out. "Shit. God or madman, he may be on his own now. Get me more rounds!"

"No." Prime slowly shook his head. "We can't leave him alone."

"We damn well have to. We won't get through that rabble." The crowd was now on the move. They fled sluggishly, seemingly swayed by Mihali's entreating them to remain calm, but his shouts could not fully quell the boiling fear of a mob.

"We have to try," Prime said. "Come on, bring your guards." He grabbed Tamas's arm.

Lady Winceslav appeared on his other side. Tamas stifled a curse. "Lady, you need to get inside!"

"I won't leave my soldiers out here alone," Lady Winceslav said.

She clenched her fists. "Get me a rifle. We'll fight our way to the chef and—"

Prime's gasp startled Tamas. "It's *him*. Open your third eye!"

"How do you..." Tamas didn't have to open his third eye. He *felt* the sorcery wash over him with the strength of the coming tide.

"Adom," Prime said. "He's dropped his disguise."

"What is he doing?" Tamas felt numb, helpless. He'd never experienced sorcery like this before. If feeling a Privileged do magic was like the heat of a candle, this was as if he stood in a smith's furnace.

"He's channeling a spell!"

"I don't understand."

"Channeling! The few moments it takes a sorcerer to create sorcery, to pluck at the auras of the Else. He's not tearing down a building or destroying a battalion. He's been channeling all week! This food, these people. They are all part of it. He is weaving auras into the very city. If the Barbers reach him, it'll destroy everything he's worked for!"

"How do you know all this?"

"We haven't time!" Prime let go of Tamas's arm as the edge of the crowd moved toward them. One of Tamas's guards was tossed to the ground, nearly trampled underfoot before he was pulled out of harm's way. The crowd began to writhe like an animal. They'd all be swept away, guards or not. This was not something soldiers could tame.

"We need to get inside, sir." Olem was at Tamas's side, rifle in hand. He'd been out among the tables when the whole thing started.

Tamas glanced between Olem and Prime. They needed to retreat, let the panic die down. He would take care of the Barbers later. They were finished. He took a step back, gripping his crutch. What the pit was Prime blathering on about? Channeling spells?

Tamas would have sensed it. "Bar the doors to the House. I don't want this rabble getting in."

"Sir?"

"We're going after Mihali."

"That's suicide, sir."

"Troop, form up!"

His bodyguard fell in around him. Soldiers joined them from the House of Nobles. He had thirty men within a few moments. Thirty men would do nothing against the mad rush of a hundred thousand.

"Lady, you should go inside," Tamas said for the final time.

Someone had given Lady Winceslav a rifle. She looked like she knew how to handle it. Her eyes held no fear. Tamas respected that.

"No bayonets, men," Tamas ordered. "Shove with the stock. Where's Prime?"

"There," Olem said.

Tamas looked over. Prime stood several feet outside his men, the packed rush of the mob only fingers from the front of his coat. "Someone get him!" Tamas snapped. "Old bastard will get himself killed."

A soldier broke off and ran for the vice-chancellor. He grabbed Prime's coat. The old man shrugged him off with surprising force. Beyond him, far into the crowd, Mihali still stood on his table. He'd ceased to yell and now stood gazing down into the mob, a frown on his face. Despite the violence of the rush, no one came within ten paces of his table.

Until a Barber broke through.

"My pistol," Tamas said. "Quickly!"

Another Barber stumbled from the crowd and into Mihali's circle of calm. He shook his head, as if confused, and then exchanged looks with the other. A third joined them, and they began to advance on Mihali.

"Weapon!" Tamas yelled.

The soldier had no luck in dragging Prime toward the building. Tamas caught sight of the old vice-chancellor out of the corner of his eye. Prime's shoulders slumped. Then he reached slowly into his pockets and removed a pair of white gloves with red and gold runes. He pulled them on and raised his hands.

Tamas looked on, astonished. The vice-chancellor, the spectacled old overweight professor of histories, was a Privileged? How had Tamas never known? Prime worked his fingers in the air like an orchestra conductor. An audible *wump* split the air and the crowd was divided in two. A pathway as wide as a carriage opened up. An invisible force pressed people away. Some clawed and thrashed as if at a glass wall, while others were crushed up against it like boats upon the rocks.

"Get your soldiers in there," Prime said over his shoulder.

Tamas hesitated. "Go," he said after a moment. He hobbled toward the vice-chancellor, grabbing his rifle from a soldier and aiming at a Barber. He only had one shot and no spare powder charges. It was too far to make the bullet bounce, and his men wouldn't get there in time. The analysis lasted just a fraction of a second. He aimed at the biggest, most dangerous-looking of the Barbers and pulled the trigger.

The Barber evaporated. The bullet went through a fine red cloud of mist and hit a woman in the shoulder. Tamas felt his eyes widen. He pointed the pistol straight in the air and looked at the barrel. Nothing seemed out of the ordinary. He looked back toward Mihali.

The second Barber paused, eyes on the cloud that had once been his comrade, his mouth slightly open. The red mist disappeared like the smoke from a pipe in a stiff breeze. The third Barber charged toward Mihali, razor in the air. Tamas thought he heard a slight pop, and this one disappeared as well. No clothes, no metal blade remained. Nothing but the red mist, which was gone with the breeze. The second Barber turned to flee, and with a subtle pop—not imagined—he was gone. Tamas shook his head as more pops filled his ears. Someone screamed.

The square began to empty. Mihali was left alone, standing upon his table, arms folded. He looked sternly out across the paving stones as the last of the fleeing crowd took off down the avenues. Food was strewn about the ground; tables and chairs overturned; plates, bowls, and cups abandoned. There a pot had been overturned, porridge slowly spreading along the ground, and here the bodies of bystanders lay unmoving. A woman groaned in pain.

"Help her," Tamas told a soldier, pointing.

Behind him, the doors of the House of Nobles swung open. Soldiers poured out.

"What happened, sir?" Vlora asked, rushing to his side.

"The Black Street Barbers," Tamas spat. "Adamat and Sabon didn't do their job."

"Where the pit are they?"

"I shot a couple. They're..." Tamas stopped. The wounded Barbers were gone. He blinked. Was that a red mist where they'd been? "I saw more. They must have fled with the crowd." He brushed past Olem and hobbled down the stairs. He paused next to the vice-chancellor. Prime stood with his hands in his jacket pockets, surveying the empty square with a firm look of consternation.

"Who the pit are you?" Tamas said. His hands trembled. The sorcery that had washed over him minutes before was gone, hidden again. It had clearly come from Mihali, but then what of the vice-chancellor? A Privileged this whole time? Tamas would have seen it.

Prime removed his hand from his pocket and drummed his fingers on his belly. He'd taken off his Privileged gloves.

"You're one of them," Tamas said when it became clear Prime would not answer his question. "One of the Predeii. Like Julene." It was true. All of it was true. Tamas felt dread settle in his stomach. "Don't go anywhere." Tamas headed out toward Mihali.

The big chef had climbed down from his table and was righting chairs. He paused next to a spilled cauldron of porridge, placing his hand gently on the rim. He frowned.

Tamas paused a dozen paces from Mihali. The porridge faded before his eyes, like rain drying on sun-warmed bricks. Mihali bent over the cauldron and gripped the sides with both arms. He lifted it easily, though it must have weighed twenty stone, and returned it to an iron tripod.

Tamas opened his third eye and fought off the dizziness. The world glowed. The paving stones where the porridge had been were smudged pink to Tamas's inner sight. The colors swirled around Mihali like some kind of festival streamers, though they never once touched the chef himself.

Mihali dropped into a chair and rested his elbow on his knee with his chin in the palm of his hand. He caught sight of Tamas.

"Thank you for looking out for me," Mihali said.

"I was too far to do much good," Tamas said.

Mihali gave him a weak smile. "Still. I am vulnerable in this body."

"They've ruined your feast," Tamas said.

"The people will be back." Mihali brushed a hand across his brow. One of his assistants approached him, put a hand on his back gently. He pulled her close with one big arm and kissed her on the forehead. "And there will be more," he said with a sigh. "My own work was not ruined. Delayed a little, but not ruined."

"Prime says you were channeling a spell," Tamas said.

Mihali looked past Tamas's shoulder toward the vice-chancellor. "Very perceptive." He gripped his assistant's arm for a moment and shooed her away. "I remember you now," he said as Prime approached. "It's been a very long time."

"Fourteen centuries or so," Prime said. "So it really is you? I didn't believe it... I didn't want to believe it." He took a shaky breath. "I believed it had been long enough that Kresimir would never return. I believed it was time for change. I thought all of Rozalia's concerns were foolish, and that Julene was living in the past. I believed we were alone."

"My people have never been alone," Mihali said. "The others may have left. I did not."

"What did you do to those Barbers?" Tamas asked.

Mihali didn't look happy. "They no longer exist," he said. His voice was glum, in the manner of a man who'd done something he didn't want to. "I lost my temper," he said. "I don't like..." He paused, his voice cracked. "They felt no pain. I don't like to harm people."

Tamas watched the chef for a few moments, a thousand questions flooding his mind. Something stilled his tongue.

"Sir," Olem said, coming to his side. "We can't find any of the Barbers. Not one."

Tamas said, "You won't." He took a deep breath. "He's a god, Olem. A real, live god in the flesh." The newfound conviction was not a happy one. His head ached. His stomach reeled. "This is not good."

Olem was staring at Mihali as if trying to make up his own mind. "Why not? I mean, if he's a god, isn't that good?"

Tamas looked up at the sky. It was a beautiful day, warm without being hot, breezy without a strong wind, the sun pleasant on the face. "Because," Tamas said, "Mihali is not the only god. There's Kresimir. And this means Kresimir can be summoned back. It means Kresimir will come for me. It means Bo's warnings were not rubbish. And that's not good." He felt a presence at his side, a big hand on his shoulder. Mihali had joined him.

"It's worse than that," Mihali said. "If it was just you, I'd be sorry, but..."

Tamas felt ill. His leg had begun to throb again. He shifted and felt a stab of pain. He choked back vomit. "What do you mean?"

"He'll destroy the whole country," Mihali said. "Every man, woman, and child. Every plant and animal. He'll raze it to the ground."

"Why?"

"My brother is not a... kind god," Mihali said. "He'll find it easier to start over."

Tamas clenched his fists. Gods. How could he deal with *that*? What could he do? "Why hasn't he done it yet?"

Mihali regarded South Pike Mountain. "He has been on a long journey, my brother. I don't think he actually ever intended to return. But he will be summoned. There are those who seek to accomplish that, those who seek to prevent its happening." Mihali turned to Tamas. "It's too late for you to influence that battle. I will try to protect Adro from his power, but you need to clean your house."

"The traitor," Tamas whispered.

"If there are more interruptions like this"—he gestured around them—"if there are more distractions..."

"But I don't know who it is," Tamas said.

"*He* might," Olem said, pointing across the square. Tamas turned to see Sabon and Adamat rushing toward them.

CHAPTER 37

Elections Square was in shambles. Soldiers wandered about the clutter of fallen chairs and spilled food and overturned tables as if after a battle, dolefully picking among the debris. A few townsfolk were being taken away on stretchers as Adamat arrived, and a knot of men had gathered beneath the steps of the House of Nobles.

Adamat watched Sabon reach the knot ahead of him. He slowed to a walk, casting about for signs of what had happened. Were they too late? People had fled in chaos, that much was clear. But what had happened? Adamat didn't see any of the Barbers or any fallen soldiers. Those on the ground weren't in uniforms of any kind, only townsfolk caught by some kind of crossfire. He saw slashed throats, blood spilled on the cobbles, even a few gunshot wounds. Families gathered around their fallen members. Women wailed.

Adamat reached the knot of soldiers and let out a sigh of relief. Tamas was there, along with the vice-chancellor and Mihali, the master chef. Tamas's bodyguard hovered nearby, a frown on his face as he studied the chef. Lady Winceslav stood nearby, and both Ricard Tumblar and Ondraus the Reeve approached from across the square as Tamas's troops fanned out to help the wounded.

Sabon shook his head to something Tamas asked him. They both turned expectantly to Adamat.

Tamas opened his mouth to speak.

"Charlemund," Adamat said. "The arch-diocel."

Rage danced across Tamas's face. He warred with his emotions a moment before gaining his composure. Through clenched teeth he said, "How do you know?"

Adamat explained quickly about Siemone the priest and Teef's confession. "It has to be Charlemund," Adamat said. "The priest Teef described matched Siemone too well to be coincidence."

"This priest," Tamas said. "It's not possible he's working for someone else?"

"No." Yes, of course it was possible. There was never absolute certainty. But it was very unlikely, and Adamat had to be firm in his decision.

Tamas's bodyguard drew near. "Let's tear him down," Olem said. "We have the name. We have a witness. We can't hesitate."

"Agreed," Sabon said.

Tamas closed his eyes.

"It must be done," Sabon said.

Adamat watched the field marshal. Tamas was scared, he realized. Charlemund was the only member of his council with the power to crush him outright. Tamas could leave him be, and wait for the next assassin, or he could attack and risk the wrath of the Church. Adamat did not envy Tamas that decision.

Tamas slowly studied the faces of those around him. His gaze came to rest on the chef. Mihali gave Tamas a brief nod. There was something here that Adamat had missed. "Why did he come after you?" Tamas asked the chef.

Mihali stared at nothing for a moment, a scowl on his face. "That is cloudy," he said. "Julene is a Predeii. She knows I inhabit a mortal body. Perhaps she warned him. Or perhaps others have entered the fray."

Tamas waited for Ricard Tumblar and Ondraus. When they'd arrived, he said, "Charlemund has betrayed our cause. I will not suffer that. I do not know if his treachery has the blessing of the Church. I do not care. Who stands with me?"

"I," Ricard said, stepping forward.

"I do," Lady Winceslav said.

Prime Lektor nodded.

"Of course," Ondraus said with a snort.

Tamas said, "Prepare the horses and carriages. Get me whatever troops we have on hand. I'm going to arrest the arch-diocel."

"Go to him?" Sabon asked. "Why can't we just call a meeting? When he comes, we will take him."

"We have to force him to play his hand," Tamas said. "His spies will tell him the attack on Mihali failed and that he has been exposed. If he flees, we confirm his guilt. If he stays, we will confront him. Either way, I will not let him escape. Get moving."

Adamat felt himself swept aside as the soldiers rushed into action. Tamas paused beside him, leaning heavily on his cane, and placed a hand on his shoulder. "Good work," he said. "Go home. Pack up." His voice dropped. "Get your family out of the country. If everything goes well, I will have use for you and your skills in the future."

Did he joke? Adamat searched Tamas's face. No. He was serious. Too serious. Tamas moved away, jerking like a marionette as he walked, his crutch clicking against the paving stones.

Signs of cave lions only increased as Taniel's company approached the summit. The dogs pulled at their harnesses despite Rina's rebukes. Half the time they wanted to give chase. Half the time they whimpered, tugging Rina back down the slope.

Taniel felt his own nerves begin to fray. In his mind the cave lions were beyond each slight rise, or waiting to pounce from every boulder. The wild eyes of his companions said they were thinking the same thing. Yet they weren't being tracked. All signs said the creatures were ahead of them, following the Kez in force. By their tracks there were at least seventy of the creatures, and growing more numerous by the mile.

They found the first body partially devoured and dragged to the side of the trail. It was torn and mangled, blood soaking the white snow, but easy enough to tell it had been a cave lion. Ka-poel squatted beside it, her fingers searching through the snow. Taniel thought he saw her put something in her pack. He came up beside her.

"What killed it?" he asked. He already had a pretty good idea.

Ka-poel mimed firing a rifle.

He nodded. "So the Kez know they're being followed. And these creatures. They feast on their own kind. How far from the top?" he asked when saw Bo had joined them.

"Not far, I think," Bo said. "I've only come this high once before." He turned to the monk. "Del?"

Their guide had paled at the sight of the cave lion carcass. Slowly, his hands shaking, he lifted one arm to point ahead. "There," he managed.

Taniel followed his gaze toward an outcropping where the trail disappeared. "That close?" Taniel frowned. "Where's the city?"

"There," Del said again.

"You'll see what he means," Bo said.

It took less than half an hour to reach the height Del had indicated. They climbed a steep knoll in the road. Taniel paused to catch his breath, only to find it whisked from him at the sight below.

He stood on the lip of a vast crater. It had to be tens of miles across and it was hundreds of feet deep. Taniel wobbled, then regained his footing.

There were trees below, species that could never have survived at this altitude. They ringed the inner edge of the crater, towering in the air. He could almost reach out and touch the tops of the closest ones. Yet these trees were long dead. Their sides were scorched black, their branches naked and twisted. Once, they were a mighty grove. Now they looked like the boneyard of someplace long cursed.

Past the trees were the ruins of a vast city. Buildings filled the greater part of the crater—more buildings than there were in all of Adopest, and many taller too. They were little more than stone husks now. Their sides were blackened like the trees, shutterless windows staring out like the empty sockets of thousand-eyed skulls. The sight made Taniel shiver.

"The Kresim Caldera," Del said. His voice quaked.

Bo's face was grim. "Kresimir's protection has faded over the centuries. The volcano's acid and heat have killed the trees and burned out the buildings. Nothing lives up here."

"Except the cave lions," Taniel said. "I don't know how they can."

"Something keeps them alive," Bo said.

Taniel could see a lake in the middle of the caldera. There were plots of trees as well, and ponds, and clear knolls that had once been parks where children played in the Time of Kresimir. Taniel imagined that the waters within the caldera had once run clean and beautiful. From his vantage point he could see that the lake was foul and brown. It bubbled and belched, and a thick cloud of steam and smoke rose from its center.

In the distance Taniel heard the scream of a cave lion.

"Fix bayonets," he said. He heard the clatter of weapons as the Watchers behind him readied themselves.

Spreading out, they proceeded into the crater.

Taniel positioned himself between Del and Bo. "Where is the coliseum?" he asked.

Del didn't respond. Taniel thought he heard a whimper come from the man. Then again, it could have been the dogs. They'd fallen deathly silent since entering the caldera.

"South Pike had a proper peak when Kresimir was summoned," Bo said. His brow furrowed. "It's said that when he touched the ground, the very earth dropped out from beneath him and the mountain erupted, spewing soot and acid into the air, enough to coat all of Adro. The Predeii barely survived. When all had settled, the caldera had formed and Kresimir stood on the shore of Pike Lake." He pointed toward the center of the caldera.

"That's where the coliseum is?"

Del nodded.

"I'll need someplace to line up a shot into the coliseum. The farther away, the better, but it needs a clear view."

Del seemed to consider this for a few moments. "Kresimir's palace. Follow me. I can get us there."

They fell silent as they passed through the deepest part of the dead forest. Their footsteps echoed on the hard-packed cobblestone road, and Taniel realized suddenly that there was no snow. The ground was bare, with even the hardiest forest scrubs and bushes long dead. The air, he also noted, was growing warmer. Some remnant from Kresimir's protection of the Holy City? Or heat from the heart of the volcano? Would they even be able to approach Pike Lake? Unbearable heat and poisonous gases might drive them away. They didn't have the sorcerous protection of Julene and the Kez Cabal. Taniel gave Bo a glance. He was looking less and less well. Taniel doubted he could protect a fly, let alone the rest of them.

They found the next bodies at the edge of the forest on the near side of a small hill. These, Taniel noted as he got closer, were not just cave lions.

A Warden lay torn to shreds among the remains of at least six or seven cave lions. His hand, the flesh stripped from the bones, still remained around the throat of a dead cave lion. Taniel held a handkerchief over his nose against the smell. The bodies hadn't been around long enough to begin to rot, but the lions were putrid, and their stink was far more pronounced here where the cold had begun to fade and the wind did not carry it away.

Ka-poel went on ahead again. She paused just on the other side of the hill, still in sight, and waved her arms at them. Taniel was glad to leave the bodies behind.

Not for long. He came to a stop beside Ka-poel and choked down bile. He heard someone spilling their breakfast noisily behind him. A quick glance told him it was Bo.

There'd been a pitched battle here. Wardens had made their stand in the center of a small park—presumably while Julene and the Kez Privileged escaped into the heart of the city. A dozen of them had died, and three times their number in cave lions. Their remains lay scattered across the onetime park. Nearby, a Warden lay with one arm up on a stone bench, his entrails spread about the ground before him. He'd been feasted upon in great haste.

"These things are hungry," Rina said. Her dogs crouched at her feet, unwilling to leave their master's side. "They run as if they are hunting, as if they have a purpose to attack and kill, yet whenever there is a death, they stop for the meat. They're starving."

Taniel swallowed. "They're hungry? Is that why they're chasing the Kez?" It was much easier to handle, though no less dangerous, than the thought of the lions being guided by some supernatural force or intelligence.

Rina shrugged. "It's possible. But cave lions don't hunt in packs, even in the worst of times. They are solitary creatures."

"How could there be so many on the mountain?" Bo said. "There's nothing to eat up here. I've never heard of more than one or two cave lions on an entire mountainside."

No one seemed to have an answer.

Taniel checked each of his pistols and his rifle to make sure they were loaded, then snorted a pinch of powder. His hands shook. His body told him to take more powder. He'd need it. He fought the impulse. He'd be powder blind with much more. Then again, he'd be dead without the strength. He took another snort.

The trail of carnage led through the park and onto a boulevard that seemed to head into the center of the city. Blood and bits of Warden and cave lion had been dragged along as the cave lions chased the Kez Privileged.

As they entered the city, Taniel kept his eyes on the buildings. Not a sound issued from within any of them, though the wind should have howled, or tiny animals should have moved about. Nothing. The city was completely dead, even the elements, and it chilled Taniel's soul.

A hand on his shoulder made Taniel spin, rifle in hand, and almost gut Del with his bayonet. Taniel stilled his beating heart. "Sorry," he said.

"The palace," Del said, "is that way." He pointed into the heart of the city.

They altered course according to Del's instructions. Though the city spooked the pit out of him, Taniel was grateful to be away from the trail of the cave lions and Privileged. He'd find Kresimir's palace and pick away at the Privilegeds' numbers from a safe distance, and they wouldn't have enough power to summon Kresimir.

Adamat heard rumors all the way home about the massacre in Elections Square. Most traffic headed away from the square. Word was spreading fast and there were signs of the Rope everywhere he went as people warded against bad luck and ill omens. A massacre during the Festival of St. Adom was bad enough to keep many people home.

He hoped he'd be able to hire a carriage immediately for Offendale. He'd get his family and get out of the country and then...

"SouSmith!" Adamat called as he hung his coat on the rack. He stopped. There were three coats too many hanging there. He closed his eyes. *Not again.*

"Can't you let me be...?" Adamat walked into the sitting room and froze.

Lord Vetas and his two goons stood on the far side of the room. Astrit stood between them, Lord Vetas's thin hands on her shoulders. She looked like a helpless fly caught in a spider's web. The sight of his little girl nearly stopped Adamat's heart. It was one thing to know she was in danger. It was another to see her here in Lord Vetas's grip.

SouSmith sat on the sofa. He had returned here immediately after their visit to the Barbers. His face was pale, and sweat ran down his cheeks. His breath labored unsteadily, a hand clutched over his wound.

"Sorry," SouSmith said weakly. "Here before me."

"SouSmith told me of your visit to the Barbers," Lord Vetas said. There was no emotion in his voice, no hint of compassion or pity. "To survive three assassins. Bravo."

"Let her go," Adamat said tiredly. The weight of the last two days suddenly pressed upon him horribly. He wanted nothing more than to drop into his favorite chair and nap the rest of the day. It looked like that wasn't an option anymore.

"Catch me up," Lord Vetas said. "How is Teef?"

"Rotting in Sabletooth," Adamat snapped. "How is Lord Claremonte?"

The look of surprise on Lord Vetas's face vanished so quickly it might not have been there at all.

Adamat said quietly, "Astrit, are you all right?"

The little girl nodded. Her face was smudged with dirt, her sundress rumpled from having been slept in, but she looked unharmed. "I'm OK, Papa," she said.

"Are you scared?"

She clenched her teeth and shook her head.

"That's my girl. Did they hurt you?"

Another head shake.

"Why is Teef in Sabletooth?" Lord Vetas said.

"Because he'd had a deal with Tamas. He broke it trying to kill me."

Lord Vetas frowned. "Why didn't you tell me he'd had a deal with Tamas?"

"I didn't know."

"Really?" Lord Vetas squeezed Astrit's shoulders. She tried to wiggle away, but he had her firmly.

"Yes, damn you. I didn't know, I swear."

Lord Vetas loosened his grip. "I trust you discovered the traitor? Tamas is on his way to arrest Ricard Tumblar?"

Lord Vetas had little reason to think the traitor was Ricard unless he'd been helping frame him all along. "What interest does Lord Claremonte have in all this?" Adamat said. "Why care at all about the politics here? He's not even Adran."

"Lord Claremonte's interests are those of the Brudania-Gurla Trading Company," Lord Vetas said. "And they rest upon the fortunes of the Nine."

"Where does he stand?"

"Neutral," Lord Vetas said. "A nudge here. A push there. That is all you need know. Now, when will Tamas arrest Ricard Tumblar?"

"Never."

"Why not?"

"He's on his way to arrest Charlemund, the real traitor."

Astrit cried out as Lord Vetas twisted her shoulders viciously. "All the evidence points to Ricard," Vetas said. "Why do you think it's Charlemund?"

"He was named in front of Tamas's powder mage. What could I have done?" Adamat stepped forward.

"Back!" Lord Vetas snapped. His goons came alert and shot menacing looks toward Adamat.

"Harm her and you're a dead man."

"Along with the rest of your family," Lord Vetas said.

"Vetas," Adamat said. "I swear on all the Nine that I will destroy you and your house if you harm my daughter. I will bring down Lord Claremonte as if he were a dog for me to kick in the street." He felt something cold quiver in his bowels.

Lord Vetas inhaled sharply. His grip on Astrit's shoulders loosened, and the girl pulled away. Adamat caught her with one hand, pushing her behind him.

The coal-shoveler goon produced a knife, the other goon a pistol. Lord Vetas stayed them with a warning hand. "This can still be salvaged. You're too good to lose, Adamat. We won't kill you... yet. When will the arrest take place?"

"As soon as Tamas gathers his men." Did Vetas mean to warn Charlemund?

"Where?"

"His villa," Adamat said.

"You'd better be telling the truth," Lord Vetas said. "Kale," he said.

The coal shoveler turned his head.

"Go to the villa. Warn the arch-diocel. Tell him you were sent by the Madman. If the good duke is still there, they should be able to construct an easy trap for Tamas."

The coal shoveler nodded his head once. He gave Adamat a warning look and then pushed past him and was out the front door at a run.

"Why is Claremonte working with the arch-diocel?" Adamat asked. "And if he is, why did Charlemund try to kill me? I'm supposed to be working for Claremonte as well."

Vetas regarded him coldly. "One hand does not know what the other is doing—such a strategy has its price, which you almost paid. Charlemund's task was simply to kill the imposter god, Mihali. He became too zealous. And know this: Charlemund is nothing more than a hand. Claremonte uses people like him to his own ends."

"No one uses an arch-diocel."

"Claremonte does."

"To what purpose?"

"Beyond your comprehension," Lord Vetas said. "You've disappointed me, Adamat. The girl was going to be a show of good faith, a gift to you for doing what you're bidden. Now, though, I think she'll come back with me. I've got men who enjoy that sort of thing." He stepped forward, gesturing to his man with the pistol.

Adamat squeezed his hands into fists. "All right!" he said.

Lord Vetas paused.

"They're not going to arrest him at his villa. He's at the cathedral, leading an afternoon prayer service. Please, just leave my daughter here."

Lord Vetas's eyes flashed. "You lied to me?"

"That's the truth of it, I swear it!"

"Pit! You"—he gestured at the other goon—"stay here. If they try to leave, kill Adamat, and then the boxer and the girl."

Lord Vetas swept out of the room, shouldering Adamat hard as he passed. Adamat grunted. Lord Vetas reached the street and broke into a run, coattails flailing behind him. Adamat watched him disappear from view through the window. He let out a long breath.

"Are you OK, Papa?" Astrit said.

"Yes. I'm glad you're safe. How's your mother?"

"Worried. She screamed when they took me away."

"Did they hurt her? Your brother, is he OK?"

"They took Josep's finger. He didn't even cry out."

"He's a very brave boy."

"What happens now, Papa?"

"I don't know," he said.

Adamat couldn't be there when Vetas returned. It would mean

death for them all. SouSmith looked like he could barely walk, and Astrit was just a girl, but Adamat had to warn Tamas.

"Stay here," he whispered to Astrit.

"Hey!" the other goon said as Adamat headed toward the other side of the room.

Adamat stopped, raising his hands. The goon waved his pistol between SouSmith and Adamat. SouSmith's eyes were closed, his hands held over his wounds. He was breathing shallowly. Judging SouSmith to be less of a threat, the goon pointed his pistol at Adamat.

"I just want a drink," Adamat said.

The goon narrowed his eyes.

"Please," Adamat said. He held out his hands to show they were shaking.

"Right," the goon said. "I'll just be watching to make sure you ain't got a weapon stashed here."

"What?" Adamat said. "A loaded pistol in the liquor cabinet? You're mad. If you think I'm going to pull a knife, stand over there." He gestured to the sofa.

The goon shuffled away from Adamat until he was near the sofa. "I'm watching you."

Good. Adamat removed a bottle from the cabinet. "Wine?"

The goon shook his head.

Adamat pulled the cork with a corkscrew and took a moment to unwind the cork, tossing it down on a shelf. He poured two glasses, the neck of the bottle clinking against the rim of the cup as his hands shook. He stepped toward the goon. "You sure you don't want some?"

"I'll let you drink first," the goon said. "I know the tricks."

"No tricks," Adamat said, shaking his head. "You think I'd poison a two-hundred-krana bottle of wine? Besides, poison doesn't work fast enough. You'd still have time to shoot me while you died. SouSmith? Wine?"

The boxer nodded weakly.

"Pardon," Adamat said, lifting the two glasses to show he meant no harm as he stepped by the goon.

He dropped both glasses at the same time. One hand diverted the pistol, the other jabbed the goon's neck with the corkscrew. The pistol went off, deafening Adamat. A window shattered, and Astrit screamed. Adamat grappled with the goon with one hand, shoving with the other. They both landed on top of SouSmith.

The boxer gave a loud grunt. He snaked a ham-sized forearm over the goon's head, holding him in place. Adamat remained on top of the goon until long after he'd stopped struggling. He grabbed the lapels of his jacket and lifted the goon off SouSmith and dropped him on the floor. SouSmith moaned, writhing on the sofa.

"Coulda given me warning," he said, feeling his wound. "I'm bleeding again."

"You big baby," Adamat said. He made sure the goon was dead, and looked up. Astrit was watching from the hallway. He said, "Go to your room."

Astrit stood there, shaking.

Adamat climbed to his feet and stripped his bloody jacket off, tossing it on the floor. He lifted Astrit into his arms. "I'm sorry you had to see that," he said. "Are you all right?"

"Yes, Papa." Her voice quavered.

"Good girl. I need you to be strong, love. I need you to go with SouSmith. You have to hide with him."

SouSmith pulled himself off the sofa slowly, grimacing with pain. "No wet nurse," he said. "Where you going?"

"I have to go warn Tamas."

"Like shit," SouSmith grunted. "I'll go..." He stumbled, catching himself on the sofa arm.

"Take Astrit," Tamas said. He led the little girl over to SouSmith and put her hand in his. "Hide. Protect her. Please." He took a deep breath. "You'll know soon enough if I fail. Just…keep her away from Lord Vetas."

SouSmith considered Adamat a moment, then gave a brief nod.

"Thank you, my friend."

"You don't pay me enough," SouSmith grunted.

"Tales will be told of your sacrifice," Adamat said. He went to his office and opened a long, nondescript chest in the corner. He removed his smallsword from its sheath and checked the blade and hilt. The sword was nothing special—it had been issued to him in the army, before he'd become an inspector. It was undecorated, with an oval shell of a guard over the hilt. It was in good condition. He heard footsteps behind him.

"I haven't touched this for a decade," he said. "It looks to be in good shape."

"Better hope," SouSmith said.

Adamat turned around.

SouSmith held out a pistol, along with extra shot and charges. "Luck to you."

They clasped hands, and Adamat was out the door.

CHAPTER 38

How are you going to explain this to the Church?" Olem asked.

"Easy," Tamas said with a conviction he didn't feel. "The Church doesn't like to be played any more than we do. Charlemund will provide us with what we need to oust him in their eyes. He's pomp and bravado. He'll not stand up to more than a few hours with our questioners."

The carriage rocked heavily as they approached Charlemund's vineyard. Tamas eyed Olem. He was a soldier, through and through. He would carry out Tamas's orders. Yet he was no fool. Olem wanted to be certain he wasn't charging blindly to his death.

"Torture an arch-diocel?" Olem asked. He finished cleaning and loading Tamas's long-barreled pistol. Tamas was grateful he didn't smoke around gunpowder. Olem handed the weapon to Tamas and started on his own. "You really think he'll tell us what we need to know?"

"Yes," Tamas said, hoping that there was enough confidence in his voice. Arresting the arch-diocel was insanely risky. If Adamat didn't really have enough evidence; if the Church decided to ignore the evidence; pit, if the Church didn't care, Tamas's world would come crashing down around him. No one, not even Kez's immense armies of spies and assassins, could destroy someone's life as thoroughly as the Church.

The carriage came to a jolting stop. Tamas glanced out the window. A dragoon rode by, then another. Sabon came to the carriage window.

"We've taken the gatehouse. No sign of movement inside the villa."

"Very good," Tamas said. He lifted his pistol and saluted Sabon with the barrel. "Let's go in."

The carriage rocked forward and through the villa's front gate. A pair of guards in purple-and-gold Church doublets stood between two of Tamas's soldiers, hands on their heads, glaring at the carriages as they went by.

"I hope you'll have the good sense to let us go in first, sir," Olem said.

"And miss the look on Charlemund's face when you tell him the charges? Bloody pit, no. I'll hobble my ass up those front steps with the rest of you."

"He may put up a fight," Olem said.

Tamas fingered his pistol. "I hope so."

"You're willing to risk his bodyguard having a few air rifles?" Olem said. "It only takes one."

"You ruin my fun, Olem. You really do."

The carriage stopped again after a few minutes. Sabon opened the carriage door. "The house and yards are surrounded. Our men checked the chapel and most of the outlying buildings. His carriage is in the carriage house. He is likely inside."

Sabon did not look happy.

"And?" Tamas said.

"No sign of workers anywhere. It's a nice day. They should be in the vineyards working the fields, exercising the horses. The place is like a ghost town. I—"

Sabon's next words were cut off by a bullet as it entered his left temple. He fell without a sound, blood spraying across the inside of the carriage.

The popping sound of air rifles was followed by the shouts of ambushed soldiers. A bullet ripped through the carriage over Tamas's head. A horse screamed. He struggled toward the door.

"Oh no, sir," Olem said, grabbing his coat.

Tamas pushed Olem away and leaned over the edge of the carriage. Sabon lay in the mud, dead eyes staring up blankly.

"Bugger that," Tamas said. He swung out the door, analyzing the villa in a second. It sprawled across his view. The whitewashed stucco front was immaculate and the high, narrow windows and thick brick of the ancient style gave the defenders the advantage. There were at least fifty windows on the front of the building. The air rifles could have been firing from any—or all—of them. Tamas caught sight of the barrel of an air rifle and fired his weapon at that window. He pulled himself in, the sound of bullet impacts and ricochets too loud for comfort. He began to reload. "What the pit . . . ?"

Olem leapt from the carriage. He turned around and grabbed Tamas by the coat, pulling him after, onto his shoulder, and ran toward the vineyards.

"To the pit with you!" Tamas said. He grunted as he was thrown to the ground and felt the pain lance up his leg. Olem dropped down beside him, panting hard, rifle in one hand. They were in a ditch, mud squelching under Tamas's boots. His leg burned horribly, the pain wrecking his mind. Tamas snatched a powder charge from his pocket and tore it open, emptying the contents into his mouth. He crunched down, chewing the grit with rage, ignoring the taste of sulfur and the pain in his teeth.

"What was that?" Tamas demanded.

Olem glanced over the edge of the ditch. "Carriage has taken seven or eight hits since we left," he said.

Tamas didn't reply. The powder trance was coming on quickly. The world spun for a moment and he gripped the grass to keep from falling off. His senses righted themselves. The crack of rifle shots reached him as his men began returning fire. The sound was chased by the smell of black powder. Tamas gasped it in, deepening his powder trance, willing away the pain in his leg.

"They have more than a few air rifles," Olem said. He sneaked a peek over the edge of the ditch, then brought his rifle up, aimed, and fired. "At least twenty. Probably more," he said, dropping down. "And Wardens."

"You sure?"

"Just saw an ugly brute in the window."

Tamas finished reloading his pistol. The pain from his leg had begun to fade to the back of his mind. "Wardens," he said. "I hate Wardens." He looked over the hill. The front of the villa looked normal enough, but the windows were open, rifle barrels sticking through. He could see the grotesque shape of Wardens within, aiming down their rifles, as well as the bright colors of Charlemund's bodyguard. He fired his pistol, burning half a powder charge to nudge the bullet where he wanted. One of the rifles fell inside.

"Who tipped them off?" Tamas snarled. "There's a spy among my own men. Among my elite!"

"We should worry about whether we brought enough men," Olem said. "We have less than a hundred. If he's got any number of Wardens in there along with his own bodyguard, we could be in trouble."

Vlora suddenly dropped down beside him. "Sir," she said. "We need to retreat. We're taking heavy losses. I lost two from my carriage just trying to get to cover."

"Pit," Tamas said. They didn't have enough men to take

Charlemund. If they retreated, however, he'd be gone within an hour. There was no way they could get back quickly enough with more soldiers. "We'll button him up. He can't get out. They don't know whether we have a hundred men or a thousand. Vlora, I want you to get out of here. Get back to the garrison. No, get to Lady Winceslav's estate. It's closer. I want two thousand men from the Wings of Adom here within an hour."

"Sir, I'll send someone."

"No, go yourself." Tamas squeezed his eyes shut and saw Sabon take the bullet to the head all over again. He would not lose another friend this day. He slapped her on the shoulder. "That's an order, soldier. Go!"

Vlora took off running away from the house. Tamas risked another look at the villa.

One of the carriages had overturned when a wounded horse bolted. The animal had been cut free, and four soldiers huddled behind the carriage, reloading desperately. "That's a bad place for them," Tamas said. "We need to get some cover fire, have them pull back to a ditch or the vineyard."

He'd barely finished the sentence when sorcery ripped through the overturned carriage. He turned away, the flash blinding him as men screamed. The carriage was cut in two, the pieces tossed to either side as if discarded by the hand of a god. The soldiers were shredded, thrown through the air like ribbon. One landed near Tamas's ditch.

Tamas dropped his pistol and dragged himself over the bank.

"Sir!"

The powder trance pumping through his veins, Tamas barely noticed the feel of cobbles cracking against his knees. He was next to the soldier in just a second, pulling himself along the ground with his arms. He grabbed the soldier by the leg. A rifle shot went off not far over his head. Olem stood over him, teeth gritted, presenting himself as a better target in order to draw enemy fire. He reached down, snatched Tamas by the back of his jacket, and pulled both Tamas and the soldier back into the ditch.

"What the pit, sir!" Olem said. "Are you trying to die?"

"How is he?" Tamas could see now that the soldier had been cut through directly by the sorcery. His chest was in tatters. It was impossible to tell where the flesh ended and the bloody uniform began. Olem put an ear next to his mouth and shook his head.

Sorcery erupted again. Screams came from the vineyard, where a number of soldiers had found a spot to hide. Tamas gritted his teeth. "It has to be Nikslaus," he said. He reloaded his pistol and looked out of the ditch. "Where are you, you arrogant son of a whore?" He opened his third eye, pushed away the dizziness with anger, and scanned the villa.

"There," he said. A cluster of bright-colored smudges indicated that the sorcerer was hiding in a room not far from the front door, crouched far beneath a window. Tamas gritted his teeth. The brick would stop bullets. But it wouldn't stop a bounce. He fingered a powder charge. He lay a finger on the trigger, when a flash of light caught his eye.

"Mirrors," he said. "Pit. He's using mirrors. He's in a sorcerer's box."

"A what?" Olem said.

"It's an armored box. You stuff a sorcerer inside, with a pinhole and a set of decent mirrors to see what he's aiming at, and he can tear up armies without getting shot by a powder mage. It's hot and cramped, but it keeps them alive in a melee. Charlemund was ready for this."

"Can't you just shoot the mirror?"

Tamas was already lining up the shot. "He'll have extra," he said. His rifle bucked in his hand and the bullet shattered the mirror. "But it might buy us some time."

"Sir," Olem said, tugging on his jacket. "They've stopped firing."

The sound of powder rifles from his own soldiers was few and far between, while the pop of air rifles had stopped completely. He gave a shaky sigh. How many men had he lost already?

"Tamas!" a voice shouted from the villa.

"He might be trying to mark your position, sir," Olem said.

"Tamas, we need to talk!"

"About your execution," Tamas muttered.

"Sir." Olem's voice held a note of warning. "Careful. We don't have many men left. We might want to find out what he wants."

"Tamas!" Charlemund shouted. "I've got Wardens and a sorcerer. We'll tear your men to bits before you have the chance to retreat."

Tamas took a deep breath, trying to still his rage. Sabon's body taunted him from the cobbled drive. "I'll hear him out."

Olem put a hand on Tamas's shoulder when Tamas tried to rise. "Let me, sir." He moved a half dozen feet down the ditch, scooting on his stomach. "Hold your fire!" he shouted. He stood up.

"Where's your master," Charlemund called.

"What do you want?" Olem demanded.

There was a pause. "To talk. We must be able to reach some kind of agreement. Tamas, I'll meet you under a flag of truce."

"Why should he trust you?" Olem said.

"You question me, boy?" the arch-diocel roared.

Olem stared defiantly back at the villa.

"I swear on the holy vestments, no harm will come to him inside my villa."

"Come out here and talk," Olem said.

"And receive a bullet for my troubles? I know Tamas too well. I'm a man of the Rope."

Tamas would hang him from that rope. He signaled to Olem. Olem dropped back down to his belly and moved over to Tamas.

"It's suicide, sir," he said. "I don't trust him."

"We don't have enough men to take him," Tamas said. "He can tear us apart with Nikslaus in there. We can't get a clear shot at the sorcerer."

"What can you do?"

"Send for more men. The rest of my cabal. If I can keep him talking until Andriya, Vidaslav, and Vlora get here..."

"It will take hours for reinforcements," Olem said.

"Regardless..." Tamas watched the villa. Still no sign of Charlemund. The presence of the Wardens and a Kez Privileged was enough for him to know this was no mistake. Charlemund was the traitor. Would he try to talk his way out of this? Did he just want Tamas for a shield? He swore on the Rope. How much did that mean to a man like him?

"Give the order for reinforcements," Tamas said.

Olem scurried off to a nearby group of soldiers. He returned in a few moments. "Done."

"Tamas!" Charlemund called. "I won't wait all day. Do we keep shooting or will you let me explain myself? Be reasonable!"

"Reason," Tamas spat. "This bastard betrays me and talks of reason. What will he say? He was trying to cut some kind of deal with the Kez to save Adro?"

"He'll say anything, sir," Olem said. "Don't trust any man who surrounds himself with beautiful women. Least of all a priest."

"Wise words."

"You're going to go in, aren't you," Olem said.

"Yes."

"I'm going with you."

Tamas opened his mouth.

"Stuff it in your ass, sir. I'm going with you." Olem stood up. He gestured to a nearby soldier. "Don't let them leave this place," he said. "Even if they have the field marshal. Shoot to kill."

Kresimir's palace was immense. Taniel had never seen its equal, not in Adopest or Kez or Fatrasta. He could look down the street and not see the end of it. Unlike the other buildings in Kresim Kurga, the rock had not been stained black by soot. It was volcanic, as if the mountain had spewed it out in one gigantic piece and let it cool, the sides polished enough he could see himself in them. Taniel couldn't find a single crack, or see the marks of a workman's tools.

"It's a complex," Del explained as they searched for an entrance. "Kresimir's home on earth. He and the Predeii lived here for decades."

"Yes," Bo said, feeling along the sheer wall. "I remember reading about this place. But how do we get in? Sorcery?"

"There is an entrance," Del said.

"Lions!"

The call came from the rear of their small group. Del began to shake again, pressing himself up against the wall. Taniel grabbed him, pushed him forward. "Let's go! Run!" he said.

He could see the first one emerge from the street they'd left not long ago. It scrambled around the corner, padded back feet thumping, front claws scrabbling for purchase on the cobbles. It was three times the size of a dog, teeth sharp. There was blood on its jaws.

They fled, looking for an entrance to the building.

"They get bored chasing Julene?" Taniel said to Bo as they ran.

"Or she scared them off," Bo gasped. He was sucking wind. Taniel grabbed him by the shoulder, pulling him on. More lions followed the first. Six in total.

"Pole!" Taniel said. "If you have a trick ready for these things, pull it out!"

Ka-poel sprinted on ahead, putting some distance between her and the others before she came to a stop. She whipped a set of dolls out of her bag. These were not humanlike as they'd been before. These looked like beasts—cave lions. She grabbed a pair by the legs and smashed them against the volcanic building.

One of the lions howled. It skidded to the ground and pawed at its head. Ka-poel dropped one of the dolls and stomped on it. The downed lion erupted, blood spraying from its body as it was crushed by an unseen hand.

Ka-poel returned the other doll to her bag.

The cave lions fell on their crushed companion. Teeth tore, claws flashed. One of them took only a mouthful of flesh and then began to run again, streaming blood behind him as he came at Taniel and the Watchers.

"Wait, that's too loud!" Taniel said.

Too late. Fesnik had pulled the trigger. The shot glanced off the lion's head, bringing it up short in surprise. The sound of the blast echoed through the buildings, interrupting the long silence. A bloom of smoke rose above Fesnik. The other cave lions paused in their feeding and looked toward them. Taniel swallowed hard. So much for the element of surprise.

A low whistle rang through the air in the shocked silence following the gunshot. Taniel looked around for the source.

Rina held a fluted bone to her mouth. The sound rose, and then was gone, as her dogs pricked up their ears.

"Go," she said.

Their harnesses released, the three big dogs tore toward the feasting cave lions. The cave lions barely seemed to notice them, as they'd returned to rip at the flesh of their own kind. One screamed in surprise as Kresim hit it from the side. The mastiffs didn't waste time. They went for throats, and the group of lions and dogs turned into a flying fury of fur.

Despite the cave lions' size and claws, the dogs had taken them by surprise. They gained the upper hand, dispatching three of the lions faster than Taniel would have thought possible. They ganged up on the other two as more cave lions entered the street.

"Run!" Taniel yelled.

"Here." Bo was some distance ahead. He gestured to them furiously. They reached him in a few moments to find a door cut into the solid side of the building. It took two men to push it open, working against the weight of the stone itself and the ages of disuse.

The last man came in and they pushed the door shut behind them. There was neither latch nor lock on the inside of the door.

"Where's Rina?" Bo asked.

They opened the door. Rina stood back in the street, pistol drawn. Her whole body was shaking as the lions leapt onto her dogs.

"Come on!" Taniel shouted.

"I'll not leave them." Her quiet voice carried clearly.

Bo stepped outside. He lifted one gloved hand and twitched a finger, as if tapping on glass.

A sudden gale ripped through the street. Rina grabbed for her hat as it was lifted off into the sky. The fighting animals separated, their flanks covered in blood, the three dogs still miraculously alive. Every animal regarded Bo warily. The wind whipped around them and pushed. The dogs tumbled through the air, leaving the cave lions behind. They slammed into Rina, lifting her up with them. Bo stepped back inside the door. Dogs and woman followed close behind, and the door slammed shut, leaving them in darkness.

Something thumped into the door. Taniel put his back to it. He was joined by others. The muffled growls of cave lions came from outside. Someone lit a match.

Bo lay on the floor in a heap with the dogs and Rina. One of the dogs whined. Bo and Rina were unconscious—or dead, as far as Taniel knew. By the light of the match Taniel regarded his companions. Their faces were coated in sweat, lined with fear, covered in . . . what? Ash? Where had that come from? Taniel examined the floor. There was ash there, ancient, coating the floor a foot thick. At some point a fire must have raged through the building, destroying everything inside. Only the shell remained. He stared into the faces of his companions. They'd come all this way. For what? To be hunted like animals by cave lions in a dead city?

Taniel felt the horrible weight of failure. "Where is Del?" he asked. The monk was nowhere to be seen. Taniel called his name. No answer. A set of footprints in the ash led off toward the center of the building. Taniel heard another thump at the door and the scrabble of claws on wood.

Taniel, his back still against the door, snorted a pinch of powder. His senses grasped at any light—pinpricks, high above—to let him see. They were in a vast, open space. A dark container that seemed more like a mine than a building. He took a deep breath, trying to keep calm. "This doesn't look like a palace," he said.

"Taniel!"

The voice echoed around them.

"Del?" Taniel said.

"Over here, Taniel. Quickly!"

"Bo's hurt," he said.

"No time. You must come."

Another thump against the door. A cave lion outside whined.

"Can you hold it?" Taniel asked.

"Go on," Fesnik answered. "We've got it. Go take the shot."

"Stay here," Taniel said to Ka-poel. "Help them keep the door shut."

He ignored her gesture of defiance and turned to run. The floor was polished, perfectly level. It might have been marble beneath the ash. He distanced himself from the light of the burning match behind him and tried to follow Del's voice. He gave up, keeping his eyes on the footprints in the ash instead. Pinpricks of light from far above gave him just enough light to see in his powder trance.

He found Del standing near an enormous staircase of the type built inside the ballrooms of kings. It had no railings, and must have been made of the same rock as the walls of the palace in order to have survived whatever fire had gutted the building long ago.

"This doesn't look like a palace," Taniel said.

Del was quaking terribly. He barely seemed able to stand. He held out both hands to Taniel as if to plead. "It was once a mighty place," he said. "Thousands upon thousands of rooms filled with gold and the finest woods and carpets. If you had light, you'd see the ashes. Only the husk was created from hardened rock. Kresimir did that. The inside was built by men, with wood and tools. All burned now. All gone." His voice echoed eerily.

"No windows?"

"Come," Del said. He pointed to the staircase. "We've got to get high enough to see the coliseum. The solstice is very soon."

Olem helped Tamas to his feet and out of the ditch. Tamas straightened his jacket, brushed off his knees, adjusted his belt. "My sword," he said. They hobbled to the carriage, where Tamas turned his back on the villa and bent next to Sabon's body. "I'm sorry, my friend," he said. "My arrogance walked us into this trap. It's about to walk me into another one. Forgive me."

"Sir." Olem handed him his sword and slipped him a sack of powder charges. Enough to kill a whole company.

"Bullets?" Tamas said.

Olem patted the breast pocket of his uniform.

Tamas buckled on his sword and turned toward the villa. He took it one step at a time with one hand on his cane and another on Olem's shoulder. Let them think him weak. He was, but they'd think him less than he even was. With each step, Tamas expected to hear the pop of an air rifle or to see the rainbow flash of sorcery. He reached the front door.

"Not dead yet," he said.

Olem gave him a long look. "I'm not reassured."

One of the double doors of the villa opened. A Warden, an air rifle under one arm, stood in the doorway. Olem helped Tamas up the steps and inside. He paused in the doorway, letting his eyes adjust to the dimmer light. He counted four Wardens and three Church guardsmen, air rifles leveled at him.

The foyer was a simple place, white marble covered every inch with built-in benches on the walls to either side. A single marble bust of Charlemund stood on a half column in the center of the room, a testament to his ego. The minimalism of the foyer couldn't be taken at face value. Tamas could see off into well-lit rooms full of vibrant color and art, with gold and velvet trim.

"Leave the door open so that my men can see me safe," Tamas said to the nearest Warden. The Warden sneered.

Charlemund entered the foyer from a side room. "Take him," he said.

Someone shut the door behind Tamas. Tamas reached for his sword, but a Warden grabbed his wrist. Another Warden slammed Olem in the stomach with the butt of his air rifle. Olem grunted, dropping to his knees. Tamas sagged without Olem's support, the pain of his leg flaring through his powder trance.

"You call this good faith?" Tamas snarled.

"I call you a fool," Charlemund said. "Besides, I didn't lie. No harm will come to you in my care. I can't promise the same when you reach South Pike."

"South Pike?"

Charlemund flattened a crease on the front of his duelist's uniform with one hand. "Yes."

"What do you mean, South Pike?" Olem said. He began to climb to his knees.

"Silence that dog," Charlemund said.

A Warden whipped Olem across the face with his air rifle. Olem fell to the floor, blood spilling from his brow.

Tamas clenched his fists and stopped himself from igniting powder. He needed Nikslaus in the room, too. "You had better hope he's all right."

"I'd like to know what you mean, Your Grace." Nikslaus came into the room, patting sweat from his brow. His Kez uniform was dirty and wrinkled from the sorcerer's box. "Tamas isn't going to South Pike. He's going with me, to Kez."

Charlemund turned to Nikslaus. "Not anymore. Kresimir will arrive today. The only hope we have of preventing Adro's complete destruction is to take this low-born swine."

Nikslaus tugged at his Privileged's gloves. "I don't follow your superstitions, Your Excellency, nor do I report to the Church. I report to my king, and he wants Tamas's head on a block."

"There will be no Adro left for us to divide if we don't appease Kresimir," Charlemund said.

Nikslaus squeezed his hands into fists. "You won't get out of this country without me," he said.

"Nor you without me."

Olem stirred beside Tamas's foot. Tamas leaned on his cane and bent over, giving Olem a shoulder to pull himself up by. "Can you stand?"

Olem's brow had been split. He wiped some blood from his eyes and felt his temple tenderly. "Send them to the pit, sir."

Tamas stood up straight and rested both hands on his cane. Nikslaus turned toward him, sensing danger. The sorcerer narrowed his eyes.

Tamas felt Nikslaus open his third eye. "He can use his sorcery!" Nikslaus's hands flashed up, fingers working through the air.

Tamas lit powder. Olem tossed the bag of bullets into the air, and Tamas concentrated on that. The bag ripped apart, shredded pieces falling to the floor. Bodies dropped, air rifles clattering to the pristine marble, blood spraying the walls. Light flashed in front of Nikslaus where bullets hit a hastily erected barrier of air.

"Flee!" Nikslaus screamed. His fingers worked frantically.

Charlemund stared at Tamas for one moment before he turned and ran.

"Don't let him get away," Tamas said. He couldn't take his eyes off Nikslaus. One mistake and Tamas would be dead. He had to keep Nikslaus's hands busy. Tamas lit powder, feeding off it in the smallest amounts, keeping a dozen bullets in the air and spinning. He threw them at Nikslaus. Nikslaus's fingers danced nimbly. Tamas's third eye revealed flashes of color as his bullets struck invisible shields. Tamas lit more powder, throwing the bullets harder.

Olem scrambled to his feet. He raced past Nikslaus, sword in hand, only to stop as five Church guards rushed into the room. They looked toward Nikslaus and Tamas, regarded their silent battle, and turned on Olem.

Tamas gripped the head of his cane. His advances were getting closer to Nikslaus as the sorcerer's defense weakened. He could only deflect the bullets so fast, and Tamas wouldn't give him the time to erect a better barrier with his sorcery. Tamas flicked his gaze toward Olem. The soldier had taken down one enemy, but there were too many. He was being pushed back, almost even with Nikslaus.

Tamas was running out of powder. Charlemund was getting away.

Nikslaus brushed his nose with one of his gloved hands, giving Tamas a moment to whirl a handful of bullets at Olem's assailants. The bullets went through eyes and mouths, dropping the men instantly. Olem lunged forward, leaping the downed bodies, and took off after Charlemund.

Nikslaus brushed his nose again.

Tamas grinned. "Allergies?"

Nikslaus took a step back. Tamas leaned on his cane, hobbled a step forward. Nikslaus gritted his teeth, stepped back. Tamas clicked the tip of his cane on the marble.

Nikslaus's fingers twirled and jumped. Sweat began to trickle down his brow as Tamas sent more bullets at him. Each bullet careened away, deflected. Tamas was running out of powder. He sucked in a raw breath, the smell of spent powder sending his blood pumping. The powder trance was a deep one.

Nikslaus flung his hand in a wild gesture and uttered a hoarse cry.

Tamas yelled out as he tumbled to the floor, his concentration broken. He stared at the two halves of his cane, then up at Nikslaus. The Privileged advanced and stood above him. He held his fingers just so, as if he was about to snap them. His shirt was soaked with sweat, his hair wild. He looked down at Tamas. "You old fool."

"You win," Tamas said, lighting a touch of powder.

Nikslaus screamed. He stumbled back, clutching his left hand. He slammed into the column with Charlemund's bust. The bust clattered to the floor, shattering a marble tile, and Nikslaus tripped over the column and fell to the ground.

Tamas got to his hands and knees, ignoring the pain in his leg. He used the longer piece of his cane to leverage himself onto one foot. He hopped over to Nikslaus. He lit some powder. Nikslaus screamed again as a bullet laced through his right hand, tearing the arcane symbols on his Privileged's glove. Nikslaus stared at his hands, matching bullet holes through the palms of each. The white gloves were covered in blood, obscuring the remaining runes.

"Now you know what it's like to have your power taken from you," Tamas said. He drew his sword and knelt down beside Nikslaus. He took one of the sorcerer's hands in his and pulled off the glove. Nikslaus whimpered.

"Those are some delicate fingers," Tamas said.

CHAPTER 39

Adamat reined in his hired mount at the front gate of the villa. His horse tossed its head, sides lathered from the long gallop. Adamat wiped sweat from his forehead and patted the creature's flank. He could also see the very top of the villa, and the carriages rumbling toward it.

"The arch-diocel isn't taking visitors." These were Tamas's men; soldiers in their dark-blue uniforms, lapels stained silver. One of them gestured to Adamat with his bayoneted rifle. "Go on," he said. "Read your newspaper tomorrow."

Adamat rested just a moment to get his breath, his mount prancing beneath him.

"You don't look like you ride much," the soldier said with a lopsided smile.

"I don't," Adamat snapped. "I have to warn Field Marshal Tamas."

The soldier's easy manner disappeared. He stepped close, while his partner circled around to Adamat's other side.

"Listen," Adamat said as his horse shied away from the soldier. He sawed at the reins. "I'm Adamat, the field marshal's investigator. Tamas is walking into a trap."

The soldier gave Adamat a hard look. "I've heard the name passed around," he said slowly. "Go on. Don't make an idiot of yourself."

Adamat nodded desperately, still breathing hard. He'd not ridden like this since he was at the university.

The gate was pushed open and Adamat urged his mount through. They were on the cobblestone drive, and he kneed the poor animal into a gallop. He bent down next to the creature's neck, white-knuckled grip on the reins. The carriages were to the house now, circled around the fountain in front of the villa.

Rifle shots rang out, startling the horse. It missed a step and stumbled, pitching sidelong into a ditch. Adamat cried out as he was thrown. He cleared the ditch completely, hitting the ground hard, and rolled. A vineyard post arrested his roll. He got to his hands and knees, clutching a pain in his side.

"Rosvel's ass!" There was blood on his hand from some minor cut. He wiped it on his coat, pulling himself up and checking his chest and sides. No broken bones, but some mighty bruises. His mount lay on its side in the ditch, flanks heaving. "You won't be getting me any farther, will you?"

The shots continued. Shouts followed. He was too late. Vetas's man had already warned the arch-diocel. Adamat closed his eyes. What could he do? This was his fault. He had no rifle—just a pistol and a sword. He returned to the drive, eyes cast up toward the house. A carriage had overturned, soldiers had scattered to the vineyard, exchanging fire with unknown assailants. No muzzle flashes or powder smoke from the house. What were Tamas's men shooting at? He shook his head. Air rifles, of course. Damn it.

Adamat went back over the ditch and into the vineyard at a run. He gave the house a wide berth, cutting through the vineyards and then back behind a stable. He glimpsed blue coats here and there, soldiers crouched in cover. The rifle shots were becoming too few and far between. It did not bode well.

He leapt a course of firewood and nearly landed on one of Tamas's soldiers. The man swung his rifle toward Adamat, almost sticking him with the bayonet. He was a young man, unseasoned and more than a little wide-eyed. "Name!" he demanded, voice quavering.

"Get that out of my face." Adamat grabbed the rifle by the barrel, shoving it away. "I'm Adamat. Does Tamas have the whole property covered?"

The soldier regarded him warily. His hands were shaking. He'd probably never seen live fire before, outside of his drills.

Adamat grabbed the soldier by the front of his uniform. "You hear those shots? They've been ambushed in the front. It's got to be a distraction. Charlemund will use that cover to escape."

The soldier hesitated. "I don't trust you," he said slowly.

"Holy pit, look!" Adamat pointed toward the house.

The soldier whirled. Adamat brought his elbow down hard on the boy's neck. "Sorry," he said, taking the rifle. He pushed the boy's unconscious form up against the firewood stack and looked about, trying to spot more of Tamas's soldiers. He caught sight of one near the edge of the house, creeping about toward the front—more concerned about his comrades in the firefight than with anyone escaping out the back.

"Damn it, I'm going to be doing this alone." He ran, half crouching, until he was fully behind the villa. He stopped behind a shed and listened. The shots had stopped. He ducked around the shed for a look. The back of the villa was an open portico, a sun garden with large parasols and awnings for shade. There was a thin gravel maintenance drive. A single-horsed carriage waited in the drive, with a familiar, miserable-looking driver. Tamas checked for guards—there were none. He ran forward.

"Siemone," he said. The driver looked up. The young priest had a stricken look about his face—he was disturbed enough that he forgot to avoid looking Adamat full in the face. For a moment.

"What are you doing here?" Siemone said, averting his eyes. "Get out, before the arch-diocel sees you."

"You're helping him escape," Adamat said. He grabbed the horse by the bridle.

"I have to," Siemone said. He clutched the reins tight.

"No, you don't. He's an evil man, a traitor. Don't help him."

"You don't think I know?" Siemone said. The words came out a sob. "I've known all along. I'm sorry I paid those men to kill you. Please understand, I could do nothing. I can't be free of him. I'm glad you're still alive. Now, get out of here before he comes. He'll cut you down."

Adamat took a deep breath. "Siemone," he said, stepping forward.

"Don't come another step," the priest warned.

Adamat paused. "Please, Siemone." He inched forward.

"Guards!" Siemone called. "Quickly!"

A pair of men rushed from the back of the house. They wore the garb of Church guards, and drew their swords at the sight of Adamat.

Prielight Guards. Elite soldiers in the employ of the Church. They protected the arch-diocels with their lives. If they got close to Adamat, he wouldn't stand a chance. Adamat stepped back and took the rifle in both hands, hoping it was loaded.

He aimed for the first guard and squeezed the trigger. The shot resounded in the yard. The man took a few more steps and stumbled to his knees. The second ran past him, coming fast. Adamat threw down the rifle and drew his pistol. The blast took the guard directly in the chest. He grunted, a look of frustration on his face, and dropped. The first guard had slowly gotten to his feet.

He swayed drunkenly. Adamat drew his sword and stepped forward. The man managed to parry four or five thrusts before Adamat landed a disabling blow.

"Siemone!" someone shouted. "We fly!"

Adamat turned. Charlemund ran from the back of the villa, cape over one arm, sheathed sword in the other.

"Go," Adamat said. "Go without him! You can do it, Siemone!"

The priest squeezed his eyes shut and began to pray. Adamat swore, whirled toward Charlemund.

"You!" the arch-diocel grunted, stopping just inside the garden. He glanced over his fallen guards in disgust.

Adamat stepped forward, between Charlemund and the carriage. The pistol had been his only chance. Charlemund was the best swordsman in the Nine. He'd tear Adamat apart. Adamat raised his sword and swallowed hard.

Charlemund plucked at the string around his neck and tossed his cape aside. He drew his sword and cast away the sheath.

The attack came faster than Adamat could have imagined. Adamat parried by instinct only—he'd been considered a fine fencer long ago, but those years were past and he'd wielded little more than a cane sword since. Adamat fell back beneath the advance. He skipped away, retreating fast. The arch-diocel came on relentlessly, a stab here, a slash there, the tip of his sword mere inches from Adamat's face and chest.

"A fine fencer" was a relative term against someone like Charlemund. Adamat felt worthless, like a child at his first lesson. These were no wooden training swords, though. When Charlemund flicked forward, effortlessly, he drew blood. The initial cuts were merely scratches and pricks. Enough of those would leave a man dead as sure as a plunge through the heart.

Charlemund slapped Adamat's sword away with the tap of his own and stepped forward. He thrust twice. Adamat stumbled backward to avoid the stabs. He recovered his footing and tried to raise his sword. His arm would not obey him. A quick glance down saw the red stains spreading in two dark circles on his coat. One was just over his heart, the other on his shoulder. Adamat felt his body sag, weakened by the sudden anticipation of death.

Charlemund spun away from Adamat, barely parrying a sword thrust. Tamas's bodyguard pressed upon the arch-diocel, attacking with ferocity. Charlemund danced away from Adamat and Olem, into the middle of the gravel walk for clear footing. Olem sprinted after him, sword first, not giving him a moment's respite.

Adamat stumbled to a rock in the garden and sat down. He gripped his sword weakly with one hand, checked his wounds with the other. He shoved his fist into the worst of his two wounds. His head spun, though he couldn't be sure whether it was because of his losing blood that fast or if it was simply from the excitement of the duel and the prospect of death. He watched Olem with a light-headed exhilaration. If Olem fell, Charlemund would kill them both and make his escape.

Olem was clearly a better fighter than Adamat. He went at Charlemund with the reckless bravery of a soldier, a man whose life was dedicated to the sword and the gun. Olem's swordsmanship was less controlled than the arch-diocel's, less clinical, but he made up for that in savagery. His teeth were clenched, his eyes lit with anger, determination, his off hand balanced carefully in the air over his hip. Charlemund took a few more steps back, the onslaught catching him off guard, before he regained his footing and began to press his own attack.

Adamat watched as Charlemund studied Olem's patterns, tracking every movement carefully. His face lacked Olem's sense of determination—it contained the quiet, reserved watchfulness of a student in his favorite class. Olem's thrusts slowly became easier for Charlemund to counter, his parries less effective. Charlemund wasn't just fighting, Adamat realized. He was learning as he went, adapting to Adamat's moves. This was how a master dueled, and

Adamat had never seen anything like it. Olem continued to lose ground.

The duel could have been hours, as Adamat felt it, though he knew that only moments had passed. Olem retreated farther, and the two duelists moved past Adamat and closer to the carriage. Olem held his ground there for several seconds, sweat beading on his brow, eyes desperate for some opening. His face was easy for Adamat to read. He was growing tired, worried. He could not keep up with Charlemund.

He saw one, finally, and lunged. His cut nicked Charlemund's side as the arch-diocel stepped aside. A dagger appeared in Charlemund's off hand, and he stabbed Olem between the ribs. Olem's eyes widened, his sword falling from his hand. Charlemund stepped away and drew his sword back for a finishing thrust.

Adamat looked away. *We're finished.*

Olem coughed out a laugh, drawing Adamat's attention. Charlemund paused.

"You've worse than me to face," Olem said.

Charlemund gave a quick glance toward the villa. He left Olem in the dirt and ran for the carriage. "Go!" he said, leaping onto the sideboard.

"Don't do it!" Adamat called to Siemone.

The priest huddled on the driver's bench, reins in hand. His arms shook. He didn't move.

"Go," Charlemund commanded.

Adamat thought Siemone was about to snap the reins. The priest looked toward the heavens, then at his hands. His lips moved silently.

"Fool," Charlemund said. He swung up the sideboard and into the seat next to Siemone.

The priest cringed away from him. "I can't do it," he wailed.

Charlemund pushed him from the seat. Siemone gave a yell and tumbled from his perch. He hit the ground with the sound of a melon being split open and then lay still.

"Coward."

The word wasn't spoken loudly, yet it drew Charlemund and Adamat's gazes all the same. Tamas stood on the back step of the villa, just above the garden. He leaned heavily on an air rifle, barrel down, in place of his cane. He looked like an old man then, tired and beleaguered. The front of his uniform was soaked in blood. Adamat remembered the mage's quarters in Skyline Palace, and the specks that had covered Tamas then. He shuddered.

Charlemund hesitated. The reins were in his hands, and though he obviously wanted to snap them and make a run for it some kind of morbid curiosity held him back.

Adamat forced himself to his feet. He stumbled, winced at the pain, his head feeling light. He snagged the horse's bridle. "No," he said.

Charlemund barely seemed to notice him. The arch-diocel's eyes were on Tamas.

"I see you've taken care of the good duke," Charlemund said. He stood up, dropping the reins, and jumped from the driver's bench. He landed in a crouch, stood up, and straightened. Adamat felt his heart beat faster.

Tamas seemed unimpressed. "He's still alive," he said. "He wishes he wasn't. I have a lot of plans for him." Tamas took the steps down into the garden slowly, leaning on the air rifle. "For you, too," he said.

Charlemund drew his sword. "You're out of powder," he said. "Otherwise we wouldn't be talking. You're not afraid of my title, of the repercussions. You'd have put a bullet in my head from inside the house. Did Nikslaus use up all your reserves?"

Tamas's face was iron.

"If you had any honor at all," Charlemund said, "you'd be on your way to South Pike right now to sacrifice yourself to Kresimir in hopes of saving this country."

"That's rich," Tamas said. "Coming from a traitor."

"What are you going to do to me, Tamas?" Charlemund said. "On your best day you aren't the swordsman I am." Charlemund broke into a sudden sprint, rushing headlong toward Tamas, arms thrown back like the wings of a bird of prey.

Tamas let the air rifle drop from beneath his arm. He drew his sword, planting his bad leg back, wincing as he did so. Adamat took a sharp breath. That leg had been shattered. Tamas wouldn't be able to maneuver. On a good day, he may have come close to matching Charlemund. As it was, a duel would be laughable.

Charlemund lunged forward, thrusting savagely as he closed with Tamas. Tamas parried, their blades crossed, and Charlemund was behind Tamas, spinning to give a death-dealing blow before Tamas could bring himself around on the bad leg. Charlemund's shout of victory died in his throat, his eyes falling toward his sword.

The black smoke of gunpowder hung in the air by Tamas's off hand. He opened his fist and let the burned wrappings of a powder charge fall to the ground, next to the blade of Charlemund's sword. Charlemund stared at his swordless hilt. His face twisted in fury, eyes alight. He threw the hilt and leapt toward Tamas, who'd turned slowly to face him.

The thrown hilt hit Tamas's forehead, leaving a shallow cut. He blinked, and thrust forward once, his off hand on his hip in a duelist's pose. Charlemund's own momentum carried him a handspan onto the steel. Tamas pulled back, stabbed again, then again. Charlemund stumbled away, clutching at the wounds, the crimson soaking into his pristine uniform. He staggered up against the carriage, one hand reaching, grasping at nothing. He slid down onto the gravel.

Adamat swallowed hard. Charlemund's wounds didn't look fatal, but there were several of them. He'd bleed out slowly, painfully—if Tamas let him. Tamas didn't make any move to help, nor call out for his soldiers. He simply watched as Charlemund tried to stem the blood flow, hands shaking. Tamas wiped the blood from his sword on Charlemund's discarded cape and sheathed it.

Adamat's own wounds were bad, but he judged them survivable if he bound them better. He shrugged the thought off and went to squat down beside Siemone's limp body. The priest's neck had been broken in the fall. His eyes stared sightlessly off into a pasture, mouth open in a cry of despair. Adamat closed the eyes with his fingertips. He stood up and walked around to the other side of the carriage.

Olem and Tamas leaned upon each other, heads together in a conference. Tamas once again held the air rifle as a cane. They both looked to Adamat. "Olem says you delayed Charlemund just long enough for him to catch up." Tamas gave him a slow nod. "You have my thanks."

Adamat licked dry lips. Neither had a look of suspicion, an accusation on their lips. Why not? Adamat's warning to Lord Vetas had just caused the deaths of a number of Tamas's soldiers. They had yet to realize why he was there at all.

"Sir," Adamat said. "I'm sorry. But my family..."

Tamas returned to the inside of the manor. Wardens and Church guards lay about, dead. He marveled at the perfect kills—bullets to the heart or the head, easy hits in the close proximity of a house. Blood pooled thick on the marble floors, making them slick. He found an ivory parasol stand in the corner of the foyer and appropriated a real cane, leaning the air rifle up against the wall.

Nikslaus was gone. Tamas bit the inside of his cheek, fighting against welling frustration. He'd left the Privileged lying on the ground writhing in pain. A blood trail led from that spot off to a side room. Tamas didn't have enough men to tend to the wounded and organize a search. He closed his eyes and limped off after the blood trail.

Adamat. What would Tamas do with the inspector? He'd confessed to betraying Tamas and Adro to this Lord Vetas and his master, Lord Claremonte. How many powerful enemies could Tamas have? Adamat was ultimately responsible for Sabon's death. Or was he? According to Adamat, the warning was sent to Charlemund just ahead of Adamat himself. Charlemund had more than just a few moments to marshal his defenses.

The pain in his leg increased as his powder trance began to fade. It would take a while for the trance to fade completely, and he'd be able to stand for a few hours yet, with the help of a cane. When that time was over, the agony would be so great he'd be lucky to even be able to stand.

Dr. Petrik would be furious. Tamas may have damaged his leg irreparably, fighting on it like he did. Foolishness.

The blood trail led through two rooms, two separate worlds of expensive furnishings rarely seen outside of a king's palace. Ivory-bone chairs from the horns of Fatrastan animals, pelts and taxidermied big cats from the farthest jungles. A squat table chiseled from a single piece of pure obsidian. The skeleton of a long-dead lizard as big as a horse. Artwork from every corner of the world, sculptures from before the Time of Kresimir.

The blood trail led to a servant's door out onto a small patio. Tamas examined the area cautiously. He didn't know if they'd accounted for all the Wardens. He glimpsed movement out across a pasture. A stable door opened, and a pair of horses galloped out, swinging out around the barn and away from the villa. In his powder trance Tamas could see the makeshift bandages on Nikslaus's hands, the writhing muscles of the Warden who led his horse. Nikslaus glanced back toward the villa nervously. Tamas watched until the pair was out of sight.

All of this was for naught if Julene manages to summon Kresimir.

"I can't find Nikslaus," Olem said.

Tamas turned. The soldier had not even attended to his own wounds. He stood straight as he could, trying to meet Tamas's eyes. He did not hide his pain well, which meant there was a lot of it. He fumbled in his shirt jacket for rolling paper and tobacco. They almost slipped out of his blood-slick fingers. Tamas took them from him and rolled Olem a cigarette, then lit it with a match from Olem's breast pocket. Olem took a puff and smiled gratefully.

"Attend to the wounded," Tamas said. "Nikslaus is not a threat anymore. Attend to yourself first. You did well, my friend."

"But Nikslaus..." Olem said.

"My vengeance will be that he continues to live," Tamas said. He smiled, and he knew it was tinted with cruelty. "That will be enough."

CHAPTER 40

Only after climbing stairs for what seemed like hours did Taniel realize the full scope of Kresimir's palace. It was, as Del said, a husk—the giant shell of what must have once been thousands upon thousands of rooms and halls and galleries. Only the volcanic outer crust remained, along with the enormous staircase that spiraled up along the inner wall. The ash thinned as they ascended. Their footfalls began to echo, and Taniel soon realized that the pinpricks of light above were windows. He forced himself to climb hard, fast, not caring if Del kept up or not.

In the near-utter silence Taniel felt as if time were suspended. He thought he saw pale colors flicker in the shadows, like ghostly auras of long-dead magic. Every now and then, puffs of ash rose like phantoms. As they neared the top, he saw windows, yes, but they were too high above the staircase to shoot from, and there was nothing to climb to reach them. He kept going. The walls closed in around them and the staircase narrowed. They reached a platform, bathed in light, blackened by soot, and as wide as a ballroom. Taniel saw the roof arch above them and the slits of windows high up the walls.

Taniel slumped against the wall and waited for Del to catch up.

"Where?" Taniel asked when the monk arrived, panting. He lurched forward and grabbed Del by the hem of his robes. "Where? You said I could shoot from up here. Point me to some damn windows!" He shook the monk hard.

"There!" Del wailed. He closed his eyes and flung a hand over Taniel's shoulder.

Taniel let go of Del and turned around. A chill crept over him as he reevaluated the room. A cold hand seemed to touch his heart.

This was Kresimir's throne room. A dais lay at the end of the hall, thirteen steps up to a place where sat a blackened chair. He saw light behind that chair.

Taniel hurried up the dais steps. He passed the empty throne and found a doorless archway. He gathered his courage and entered.

The room beyond brought him to a sudden stop. He gasped, mind overcome. The room was well lit, fully furnished. Tapestries hung on the walls. There was glass in the windows, and a four-poster bed in the center of the room. Velvet-cushioned chairs and gold-rimmed tables. He'd tracked soot onto a white rug. Taniel might as well have stepped from a cave into Skyline Palace. He stumbled.

"You left Bo behind?" a female voice said.

Taniel felt faint. Julene stepped in from a balcony.

"Yes, ma'am." Del appeared at Taniel's shoulder.

"And the girl?" Julene said, a sneer on her lips.

"Guarding Bo." Del stood straight, his head held high. He no longer shook. He no longer even looked like Del. The youth of his face faded, leaving wrinkles behind, and as Taniel watched, the false monk pulled a pair of Privileged's gloves from his pocket and tugged them on.

Julene strode to Taniel. She put one finger under his chin and lifted up his head to look into his eyes. He felt ill. Dead inside.

"I had a feeling you might chase me up here," she said. "Glad I left Jekel behind. What was his plan?" she asked the Privileged.

"Shoot enough of us to keep you from summoning Kresimir," Jekel said.

"That might have worked," Julene admitted. "It takes a lot of sorcery to pull Kresimir between the Nether that separates worlds."

Taniel felt himself sway. He longed to snatch for a pistol. He might be able to at least kill the false monk. His fingers didn't want to obey. He was defeated. He knew it.

"Why?" Taniel asked. He took a couple of breaths, trying to find the words.

"Summon Kresimir?" Julene rolled her eyes.

"No. Why this dog? Why the ruse? He could have just as easily waited and killed us all. Why not kill me now?"

Julene shrugged. "If your father manages to survive the coming pitfire, I will keep you as some leverage. He's not resourceful, but he is stubborn."

Taniel tried to come to terms with what she was saying. "Just kill me now," he said.

She tapped his neck with long nails. "I will if I need to." She raised one hand. Taniel closed his eyes. After a moment, he opened them, only to receive an open-handed slap. He felt her nails rake at his skin.

"That's for throwing me off a cliff," she said. She turned to go.

Taniel twitched his fingers. They *would* move. Good. What could he do? "Going to summon Kresimir?" he asked.

Julene chuckled. "Already done," she said. "I'm going to watch him descend. Care to come with me? The last time he touched earth, he collapsed half the mountain. You might want to find some protection in my sorcery."

Jekel ducked after Julene with a look of concern. Taniel blinked. He set his fingers on his pistol, then followed after them.

The balcony was full of people. Two dozen Privileged, if not more. They held their eyes to the sky. Taniel was at the peak of the mighty building—or as close as one could get. He nudged his way among the Privileged and looked over the side. He stifled a hysterical laugh as he realized that there *was* a coliseum down by the lake. He could see right into it from this vantage point.

"Enjoy the show," a voice whispered in his ear.

It was Jekel. The false monk gave Taniel a shallow smile.

"You disgust me," Jekel said. "You and your kind. Kresimir will destroy the powder mages once and for all. Damned Marked."

Taniel grabbed Jekel by the front of his robe. Jekel sneered, lifted his gloved hands. Taniel tossed him off the balcony.

The man's scream lasted a long time, even as he bounced and slid down the outside of the giant sheen of volcanic rock that was the building's shell.

"What?" someone asked.

"Who the pit is this?" a Privileged said.

Taniel drew a pistol and then wondered what for. What damage could he possibly do? Out of the corner of his eye he caught sight of a glowing light, up in the clouds. He felt the blood drain from his face. He tightened his grip on his pistol. He could at least take a few of them with him.

A Privileged raised his gloved hands at Taniel. His fingers twitched. Taniel whipped up his pistol, only to hesitate as the Privileged suddenly—and apparently gleefully—threw himself off the balcony.

Another Privileged followed suit. Then a third collapsed to the ground screaming, gouging at his eyes. Taniel whirled toward the balcony entrance.

Ka-poel stood there, legs planted wide, arms spread. Her buckskin vest was loosened sloppily at the neck, and her rucksack lay at her feet. Dolls lay scattered around it. Her fire-red hair was wild. She raised one hand.

The dolls, dozens of them, rose into the air. They spread out before her like cards before a soothsayer, held up by invisible hands. Julene caught sight of Ka-poel, and she screamed.

Everything happened at once. Privileged scrambled for their gloves and made warding gestures. Julene froze, as if in a panic, and Ka-poel began her attack.

Fire spread from her fingertips. It hit several of the dolls, and Privileged burst into flames. A needle appeared in Ka-poel's hand. She jabbed hard, quickly, into different dolls. Screams of agony filled the balcony.

A flash of light raced toward Ka-poel as a Privileged got off a shot. She didn't even waver. The light arced, flashing into a doll. The Privileged to Taniel's right turned to dust and blew away with the wind.

The mongoose had found the serpent's nest, and Taniel was right in the bloody middle. He lifted his pistol and shot a Privileged that wasn't getting any attention from Ka-poel. He tossed the pistol aside and grabbed his second. When that was spent, he rolled his rifle off his shoulder.

Julene regained her faculties as Ka-poel decimated the Privileged. Julene balled her fists and strode toward Ka-poel, face twisted in fury. Taniel felt fear then, and it wasn't for himself. Turn her unfamiliar magics as she might against the Kez Privileged, Ka-poel would not be able to handle Julene.

Taniel rushed Julene, bayonet forward. She waved her hand, and he felt himself sail through the air. Something crunched as he crashed into the balcony railing. He'd barely arrested his own fall, scrambling for some handhold, his rifle clattering away across the balcony. Privileged lay dead and dying around Julene, and she strode on toward Ka-poel.

Ka-poel's dolls melted as Privileged died. Some wavered and dropped, still others drifted away. She twirled her hands, and the remaining dolls rotated. Taniel recognized Julene's doll.

Julene laughed fiercely as Ka-poel massaged the air above the doll. Ka-poel opened her mouth.

"Taniel, run!"

The voice had come from Julene, yet it had not been her voice. It was a girl's voice, a voice tinged by desperation.

"Get out now!"

Julene didn't seem to notice that she'd spoken. She put down her head and charged Ka-poel, fire flinging from her fingertips, setting alight all it touched—stone and flesh alike. It sprayed some of Ka-poel's dolls, and two Privileged wailed in agony.

Taniel found his rifle in the other corner of the balcony. The remaining Privileged didn't even seem to notice him. They had backed away as far as they could from Ka-poel, spread out, and threw their hands up frantically to fend off her magic.

No, he would not run. He'd not leave Ka-poel to fight alone.

Taniel snatched up his rifle. He checked the barrel. The bullet had come out in his fall. He cleared the barrel and loaded one, then another, both redstripes. He rammed cotton batting to hold the bullets in. A Privileged stumbled toward him, hands raised. He rammed his bayonet through the Privileged's eye.

He found a place at the railing to line up his shot. The glow he'd seen earlier was descending from the heavens. It looked like a cloud, falling swiftly as it grew closer.

The cloud flew past, lowering itself into the center of the coliseum below. Taniel licked his lips. He cleared his throat. He tried to steady his hands. A pinch of powder helped to clear his mind and sharpen his eyes.

The coliseum was too far away. Six miles, at least. There was no way he could make a shot that far. He took a deep breath. The cloud touched the ground.

A foot emerged from the cloud, followed by a person. Taniel fought off the darkness of a fainting spell.

The man from the cloud was more beautiful than anyone Taniel had ever seen. His skin was perfect, his golden hair long and lustrous. He wore a tunic, something out of a play depicting the Time of Kresimir. He stepped from the cloud and paused. His perfect face was marred by a frown.

Taniel blinked the sweat out of his eyes and pulled the trigger. The crack echoed in his ears, and he lowered his rifle. He didn't so much see as he *felt* the two bullets speeding toward Kresimir. Long after they should have fallen to the ground, his will kept them in the air. His mind began to hurt from the effort, his hands began to tremble. Pain blossomed in his head as he burned through his powder horn to keep the bullets flying. Still he held on.

One bullet entered Kresimir's right eye. The other hit his chest and pierced his heart. Taniel watched the god's body crumple and fall.

Taniel felt a sob wrench itself from his chest. He'd killed a god.

He dropped to the balcony floor.

He couldn't bring himself to care as Julene's roar of fury tore at his brain. He heard a mighty thump, and then the world began to shake. He cradled his rifle, trying to pull himself into a fetal position. The building was falling. *I killed a god.*

Ka-poel. Was she still alive? He staggered to his feet, casting aside his rifle. Ka-poel was nowhere to be seen. Julene was gone too. The building creaked and swayed beneath him. Another quake? Outside, in the middle of Pike Lake, a great geyser sprayed into the air. Taniel could feel the heat from it. He forced himself inside.

Ka-poel lay near the arched doorway to the throne room. Blood leaked from her mouth and nose and from the corner of one eye. She stared up at Taniel, still gripping one of her dolls. It was Julene, clear as day, and the doll wore a mask of absolute rage.

Taniel fell to his knees beside Ka-poel.

"I can't take you anywhere safe," he said. "There's nowhere safe left. I killed a god."

Ka-poel blinked. Taniel choked on his own sob.

"Pole?"

She smiled, reached up, and grabbed him by the back of the neck and pulled him close to her, stronger than Taniel could have imagined.

That's when he felt the building fall out from under them.

EPILOGUE

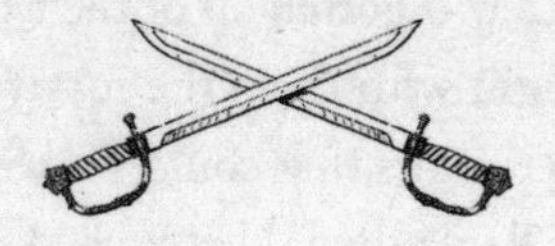

Bloody pit, Olem thought as they brought in the bodies and laid them before Tamas.

Rain beat down and wind whipped at the canvas tent over their heads. The sounds in the air—screams like banshees that came from no mortal throat—and the smell of sulfur that clogged his senses and made him want to spit every few minutes.

He could see South Pike from time to time through the swaying trees. The whole mountain, no, the whole southeastern sky, glowed like the hillside behind a fire. It made him nervous being this close, no matter what the field marshal said. The mountain had changed. Its familiar rimmed top had collapsed on the southern side, spilling out its fiery guts onto the Kez plains.

Olem hoped it swallowed the whole damned Kez army.

Plumes of ash and smoke as big as Adro floated in the air above them, reflecting the harsh flow of the mountain. The ash rained down, requiring every man to wear cloth over his face. A plume of fire spurted from the southern rim and disappeared, heading toward Kez. Olem shuddered. That one plume was probably big enough to cover a city.

Shouldercrown was gone, swept away when the mountain's side gave way. The last of the evacuees had just come into Tamas's camp. It seems that they'd gotten all of the Mountainwatchers out in time. They'd brought with them the survivors of the mountain-top battle along with rumors that could shake a man's soul.

"Are they dead?" Olem asked. He touched a new cigarette to the brazier and brought it to his lips, pulling in the sweet smoke. Dr. Petrik shot Olem a dirty look. Olem grimaced. He should watch himself. This was the field marshal's son he was talking about.

There were three bodies, all bundled head to toe to protect them from the falling ash. One of them was alive for certain. He was a medium-sized man, emaciated and frail-looking. He was carried in on a stretcher, and his hands and feet were very clearly bound. His arms stuck out from his body, propped up by a forked stick so that his bare hands could be seen at all times. Privileged Borbador, Olem guessed. The last of the king's royal cabal. Bo's eyes searched the room. His mouth was not gagged, yet he did not speak.

The two other bodies belonged to a young man and woman. Soldiers unwrapped the coverings so that Dr. Petrik could examine them. The woman—no, girl, from her size—was a savage with freckled skin and hair that might have been fire red had it not been singed to hardly anything. Olem couldn't tell if she was breathing. The boy was Taniel. Olem recognized him well enough. All of Tamas's soldiers did.

Olem sidled up beside the Privileged's stretcher and pulled up a stool.

"Bad up there?" Olem said. He grimaced at the pain from his chest. The wound from Charlemund had been straight and clean, making it possible for Mihali to heal it with sorcery Olem couldn't comprehend. Healed it might be, but it still hurt between his ribs.

Bo gave him a glance.

"Cigarette?" Olem wrapped a new cigarette and put it between Bo's lips. He lit it with a match. Bo breathed in the smoke and coughed. Olem caught the cigarette, put it back in Bo's mouth. Bo gave a slight nod.

"I hear we got all of our boys out," Olem said. "Before the mountain fell. That's lucky."

Bo said nothing.

"Rumors of a great sorceress up there, duking it out with you and Taniel. She survive?"

"Don't know." It was barely a whisper, muttered from between Bo's clenched lips so the cigarette wouldn't fall.

"That's a pity," Olem said. "If she did, let's hope she's on the Kez side of the mountain."

Bo didn't respond.

A man came into the tent then. He might as well have been a bear, for his size and the furs on his shoulders. He wore the emblem of the Watchmaster on his vest. Olem didn't recognize him.

Tamas left his son's side for a moment. "Jakola," Tamas said in greeting to the Watchmaster.

"How's the boy?" Jakola asked.

"Alive. Barely."

"A miracle," Jakola said. "You thank that girl, and give her as much attention as you show Taniel. If he survives, he'll owe her his life. Pit, from what the men are telling me, we all might owe her our lives."

Tamas looked over to the savage girl. "She clings on even weaker than Taniel. I don't know what we can do for her."

"Well, do it," Jakola said. "You've got more surgeons than just this old hoot." He crossed the room to Tamas's cot and sat down, producing a flask from his vest pocket.

Olem frowned. Should he rebuke the man? He looked three times Olem's size. Sabon was the only one Olem had seen speak to the field marshal like that and get away with it.

"Jakola," Olem said. "That name sounds familiar."

Bo gave a slight shake of the head. "I know him as Gavril."

Olem took the cigarette from Bo's lips and tapped the ashes off. He put it back in Bo's mouth. "Jakola," Olem said. "Jakola, Jakola. Hmm. Wait. Jakola of Pensbrook!" He felt his eyes widen. "That's him?"

"Don't ask me," Bo said.

Olem settled back on his stool and smoked his cigarette, trying to remember the rumors passed down through the troops. They said Jakola was one of Tamas's closest friends. Some said it was his dead wife's brother. Olem wondered if there was truth to that. Jakola hadn't been heard from for longer than Olem had been in the army.

Tamas limped over and squatted next to Bo's cot. He had refused to let Mihali heal him until he had Taniel to safety. His leg was bad, getting worse, but his stubbornness remained.

"I have some questions for you," Tamas said.

Olem removed the cigarette from Bo's mouth so he could answer.

"What happened up there?" Tamas said.

Bo stared glumly at the field marshal. He did not look like he'd speak any time soon.

"I'm not going to execute you," Tamas said. "Not yet, anyway. This stuff"—he gestured to the ropes—"is a precaution. I suspect the gaes still holds you?"

Bo nodded.

"Then you and Taniel were not able to find a way to destroy it?"

"We've spent the last few months trying to throw back the Kez," Bo said. His voice was rough. "We haven't had time."

"When will the gaes kill you?" Tamas said.

"I don't know."

Tamas considered this. "For now, you remain as thus. We'll try to make you comfortable. I know your compulsion to kill me is not your fault."

Bo didn't look relieved.

"What happened up there?" Tamas asked again. "Did Taniel really shoot Kresimir?"

"Yes," Bo said.

"Did you see it happen?"

"I *felt* it happen," Bo said. "Every Privileged in the Nine felt it happen. It tore through my soul. Did you feel it?"

Tamas shook his head. "Olem, did you feel anything?"

"No, sir," Olem said. He puffed on Bo's cigarette to keep it lit. "Though I might have. Been having indigestion since eating road rations. I miss Mihali's cooking."

"You'd have felt it," Bo said.

Tamas leaned back, wincing in pain. "So Kresimir is dead," he said. He held on to the edge of the stretcher to stay steady.

Olem frowned. "Where's your crutch, sir?"

Bo began to chuckle. It was a low sound, quiet and unnerving. It slowly grew louder.

"What's so funny?" Olem asked.

Bo shook his head. "Nothing's funny," he said. "You don't understand, Tamas. You can't kill a god."

Tamas sat beside the body of his son. Taniel clung to life. The doctors said he was in a coma. No telling when, or if, he'd ever come out.

Tamas should have insisted that Mihali come. He swallowed a lump in his throat and hoped Taniel would survive the trip back to Adopest. Surely a god could heal him. Once that was taken care of, he'd let Mihali tend to his leg.

"You've done well," Tamas said, laying a hand on Taniel's forehead. It was hot to the touch. "Now, don't die on me. I can't lose you. I lost your mother. I *will not* lose you as well."

The tent flap was pushed back. A large shadow was cast by the fiery mountain outside.

"Your boy is a pit of a fighter."

Tamas regarded his brother-in-law as the big man swept in and took the only other seat in the room. "Do I call you Jakola or Gavril these days?" Tamas asked. He passed a hand over his face, hoping the man did not see the tears he wiped away.

"Gavril will do," the Watchmaster said.

Gavril. The name he'd taken to hide from Ipille's hunters after his and Tamas's attempt to assassinate the Kez king. That had been a long time ago. A lifetime ago, it seemed. And Gavril had been a drunk since. He seemed sober enough now.

"When we left South Pike, we could see the Kez army heading west," Gavril said. "Toward the Gates of Wasal."

"They mean to attack," Tamas said. "In force. No respite."

"They have a god on their side now, if what Bo says is true and Kresimir is alive."

"So do we."

"What?"

"Adom. Kresimir's brother," Tamas said. "Adom is not a violent god. He is not Kresimir. The odds are in favor of the Kez when it comes to war."

Gavril kicked his legs out, leaned back, and then hurriedly adjusted himself when the chair beneath him began to creak. "A god," he breathed. "Two gods! And ancient sorcerers. This is not the world we know, Tamas."

"I can think of nothing beyond this." Tamas gestured to his son.

Gavril gave him a moment of silence before speaking. "I spent fifteen years grieving my sister's death," he said. "If the worst happens, do not make my mistake. I beg of you. And do not grieve him before he has passed."

Tamas nodded. What else could he say?

"I heard about Sabon," Gavril said. "I'm sorry."

"There were traitors among my men," Tamas said.

Gavril scowled.

"The investigator I trusted to root out the traitor in my council." Tamas took a deep breath. "He succeeded, but turned out to be a traitor himself, his family held hostage. It got Sabon killed."

"What will you do with him?"

"Make him answer for his crimes."

"Don't let hate consume you," Gavril warned.

"Not hate," Tamas said. "Justice."

Gavril said, "Justice would have seen Kresimir burn all of Adro."

Tamas pulled himself up and crossed to his traveling case, every step a world of pain. He opened the top and drew out one of the matching Hrusch pistols Taniel had brought him.

"My son lies at death's door," Tamas said. He returned to his seat, laying the pistol across his lap. "My wife is long dead, and many of my friends have joined her." He checked the barrel and drew back the hammer, then aimed the weapon at the tent wall. "I have nothing left to inspire compassion in me. I will meet Ipille's forces at the Gates of Wasal. I will shove them back. I will route them into Kez and burn my way to Ipille's door." Tamas pulled the trigger, heard the hammer click. "I will confront Kresimir and I will teach him about justice."

ACKNOWLEDGMENTS

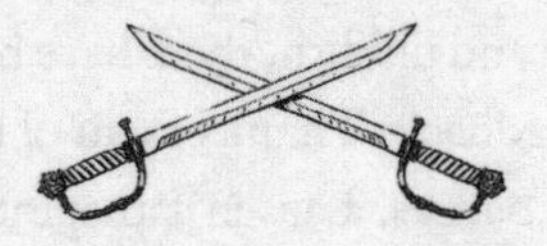

There are so many people without whom this book would not exist.

I will start by thanking my amazing agent, Caitlin Blasdell, for seeing potential and then dragging me kicking and screaming through nitty-gritty edits before she'd even consider letting an editor see the book. Then my editor, Devi Pillai. Her infectious enthusiasm kept me going even when I wanted to cry out, "No... please... don't make me change that character's name!"

Thanks to my brilliant wife, Michele, and the hours we've spent tossing around ideas. So many of the cool things in this book came from her.

I began to realize I wanted to write for a living in high school. Special appreciation goes to Marlene Napalo, who humored me and read my earliest stuff despite really expecting to hate it. She was key to kicking off this whole journey. William Prueter taught me to love history, where even the most fantastical imaginings get their roots. In college, countless people kept me going and gave me advice and encouragement. Foremost among these were Zina Petersen and Grant "Boz" Boswell.

Thanks to Nancy Gould, who acted as my patron in a very transitional time for me, despite having no evidence that I'd ever amount to anything.

Isaac Stewart, Steve Diamond, and Logan Moritz read multiple iterations of this book and others. I cannot express the dedication to friendship this takes. Their feedback was invaluable. Thanks to Charisa Player, the very first stranger who read something of mine and thought I might have a shot at getting published. Throughout my struggles to write and publish, there have been dozens who have read and given me feedback. Thanks to all of them!

Thanks to Susan Barnes, Lauren Panepinto, and everyone else behind the scenes at Orbit. It still flabbergasts me that others can get excited about working on something that came from the depths of my imagination.

My utmost admiration and appreciation goes to Brandon Sanderson, for teaching me more about writing than anyone else and showing me how to navigate an entire industry.

Of course, these all pale in comparison to the gratitude I have for my mother, who made me take interest in things I seldom wanted, and never doubted I'd be bona fide someday; and for my father, for paying for all the things Mom made me do.

Finally, thanks to all of my family for the encouragement they gave me to chase my dreams.

extras

www.orbitbooks.net

about the author

Brian McClellan is an avid reader of fantasy and graduate of Orson Scott Card's Literary Bookcamp. When he is not writing, he loves baking, making jam from fruit grown in northeast Ohio, and playing video games. He currently lives in Cleveland, Ohio with his wife. Find out more about Brian McClellan at www.brianmcclellan.com.

Find out more about Brian McClellan and other Orbit authors by registering for the free monthly newsletter at www.orbitbooks.net.

interview

When did you first start writing?

The first thing I can remember writing was a short adventure story in third grade. It was only about two pages long, but that's quite lengthy for a third grader. I ended up winning a class contest with that story.

I didn't begin writing as a habitual thing until I was about fifteen and I discovered people writing Wheel of Time fan fiction online. I found that I really enjoyed it, and soon I was coming up with whole new worlds.

Who are some of your biggest influences?

I was influenced immensely by some of my favorite books: *Les Miserables*, *The Count of Monte Cristo*, *The Three Musketeers*, Chronicles of Narnia, the Arthurian legends, and Conan the Barbarian. Really there are too many to list. In terms of the classics, I always gravitated toward adventure stories. I loved intrigue and duels and harrowing escapes.

Where did the idea for *Promise of Blood* come from?
I watched *Public Enemies* with Johnny Depp, and was toying with the idea of a short story set in the 1930s with Tommy guns and magic. That had me thinking about how magic would be used alongside (or counter to) advancing technologies.

Not long after, I sat down to watch the first episode of *Sharpe* with my wife. We weren't halfway finished with the episode when I knew that my next project was going to be a second-world Napoleonic epic fantasy. We started hashing out ideas for the magic system that very night.

Why mix magic and gunpowder?
To be honest, it's never been as much about the gunpowder as it's been the time period. The idea of an industrial revolution taking place in a magic world absolutely fascinated me. How would the people adapt? How could magic be used in an industrial world? Better yet, would magic change and begin to develop along with the technology?

The importance and loyalty of family is a huge underlying theme to the book, not only Taniel and Tamas, but also Adamat and his family. How much did that guide the plot of the novel versus the political intrigue and war?
I think the answer is different for each character. For Tamas, the coup and the following war are what guides the plot. He is, after all, the one driving the entire story.

Both Taniel and Adamat are along for the ride and while their narratives are shaped by Tamas's, their actions are very much affected by their familial relationships.

You have bad guys of both regular and supernatural caliber – really they are just being attacked from every side. Which was the most fun to write? The most challenging?
I think the biggest challenge was the fact that *Promise of Blood* doesn't really have a big, bad villain. There are bad people: traitors, enemies, and . . . entities. They are each working toward their own mysterious ends.

However, there isn't a Sauron or Wicked Witch of the West, or someone who embodies all evil, and I think a lot of people expect that in an epic fantasy. So it was a challenge to have several villains working from the shadows and keep the danger to the heroes real and compelling.

Ka-poel is a fascinating, powerful character. What was your inspiration for her?
Ka-poel came out of my desire to have an interesting counterpart to Taniel. I wanted a character that was a little funny and very mysterious, without sending off the obvious "this is a badass" vibes. Taniel is the only one who knows her in all the Nine, and even he doesn't know her all that well. She's a mute as well, which makes her both a challenge and quite a bit of fun to write.

What sort of research, if any, did you have to do to make the war scenes and the army life come to life?
Wikipedia is actually a great tool for this kind of thing. Not only does it tend to give fantastic summations of battles, but you can find the correct terminology and it lists sources for a lot of the information which you can then find and read for yourself.

A few books that helped me out where *The World in 1800* by

Olivier Bernier, *The World of the French Revolution* by R. R. Palmer, and *The Diary of a Napoleonic Foot Soldier* by Jakob Walter.

If you could have one Knack, what would it be?
Adamat's. As it is, I've got a terrible memory for just about anything. I forget names, faces, and facts. I had a terrible time trying to learn foreign languages in college because of it. To keep track of what's going on in my books I have to keep details notes about characters, locations, and timelines. A perfect memory would be pretty awesome.

What's next for Tamas in his quest for justice?
Book two, *The Crimson Campaign*, begins with Field Marshal Tamas facing down a Kez army that outnumbers his own by a staggering margin. Things only get worse when he's cut off behind enemy lines with his two best brigades and no hope of resupply or reinforcements.

We get to explore his relationship with his son's ex-fiancée and with his brother-in-law and find out more about his past.

If you enjoyed

PROMISE OF BLOOD

look out for

THE BLACK PRISM

book one of the Lightbringer trilogy

by

Brent Weeks

CHAPTER 1

Kip crawled toward the battlefield in the darkness, the mist pressing down, blotting out sound, scattering starlight. Though the adults shunned it and the children were forbidden to come here, he'd played on the open field a hundred times – during the day. Tonight, his purpose was grimmer.

Reaching the top of the hill, Kip stood and hiked up his pants. The river behind him was hissing, or maybe that was the warriors beneath its surface, dead these sixteen years. He squared his shoulders, ignoring his imagination. The mists made him seem suspended, outside of time. But even if there was no evidence of it, the sun was coming. By the time it did, he had to get to the far side of the battlefield. Farther than he'd ever gone searching.

Even Ramir wouldn't come out here at night. Everyone knew Sundered Rock was haunted. But Ram didn't have to feed his family; *his* mother didn't smoke her wages.

Gripping his little belt knife tightly, Kip started walking. It wasn't just the unquiet dead that might pull him down to the evernight. A pack of giant javelinas had been seen roaming the night, tusks cruel, hooves sharp. They were good eating if you had a matchlock, iron nerves, and good aim, but since the Prisms' War had wiped out all the town's men, there weren't many people who braved death for a little bacon. Rekton was already a shell of what it had once been. The alcaldesa wasn't eager for any of her townspeople to throw their lives away. Besides, Kip didn't have a matchlock.

Nor were javelinas the only creatures that roamed the night. A mountain lion or a golden bear would also probably enjoy a well-marbled Kip.

A low howl cut the mist and the darkness hundreds of paces deeper into the battlefield. Kip froze. Oh, there were wolves too. How'd he forget wolves?

Another wolf answered, farther out. A haunting sound, the very voice of the wilderness. You couldn't help but freeze when you heard it. It was the kind of beauty that made you shit your pants.

Wetting his lips, Kip got moving. He had the distinct sensation of being followed. Stalked. He looked over his shoulder. There was nothing there. Of course. His mother always said he had too much imagination. Just walk, Kip. Places to be. Animals are more scared of you and all that. Besides, that was one of the tricks about a howl, it always sounded much closer than it really was. Those wolves were probably leagues away.

Before the Prisms' War, this had been excellent farmland. Right next to the Umber River, suitable for figs, grapes, pears, dewberries, asparagus – *everything* grew here. And it had been sixteen years since the final battle – a year before Kip was even born. But the plain was still torn and scarred. A few burnt timbers of old homes and barns poked out of the dirt. Deep furrows and craters remained from cannon shells. Filled now with swirling mist, those craters looked like lakes, tunnels, traps. Bottomless. Unfathomable.

Most of the magic used in the battle had dissolved sooner or later in the years of sun exposure, but here and there broken green luxin spears still glittered. Shards of solid yellow underfoot would cut through the toughest shoe leather.

Scavengers had long since taken all the valuable arms, mail, and luxin from the battlefield, but as the seasons passed and rains fell, more mysteries surfaced each year. That was what Kip was hoping for – and what he was seeking was most visible in the first rays of dawn.

The wolves stopped howling. Nothing was worse than hearing that chilling sound, but at least with the sound he knew where they were. Now . . . Kip swallowed on the hard knot in his throat.

As he walked in the valley of the shadow of two great unnatural hills – the remnant of two of the great funeral pyres where tens of thousands had burned – Kip saw something in the mist. His heart leapt into his throat. The curve of a mail cowl. A glint of eyes searching the darkness.

Then it was swallowed up in the roiling mists.

A ghost. Dear Orholam. Some spirit keeping watch at its grave.

Look on the bright side. Maybe wolves are scared of ghosts.

Kip realized he'd stopped walking, peering into the darkness. Move, fathead.

He moved, keeping low. He might be big, but he prided himself on being light on his feet. He tore his eyes away from the hill – still no sign of the ghost or man or whatever it was. He had that feeling again that he was being stalked. He looked back. Nothing.

A quick click, like someone dropping a small stone. And something at the corner of his eye. Kip shot a look up the hill. A click, a spark, the striking of flint against steel.

The mists illuminated for that briefest moment, Kip saw few details. Not a ghost – a soldier striking a flint, trying to light a slow-match. It caught fire, casting a red glow on the soldier's face, making his eyes seem to glow. He affixed the slow-match to the match-holder of his matchlock and spun, looking for targets in the darkness.

His night vision must have been ruined by staring at the brief flame on his match, now a smoldering red ember, because his eyes passed right over Kip.

The soldier turned again, sharply, paranoid. 'The hell am I supposed to see out here, anyway? Swivin' wolves.'

Very, very carefully, Kip started walking away. He had to get deeper into the mist and darkness before the soldier's night vision recovered, but if he made noise, the man might fire blindly. Kip walked on his toes, silently, his back itching, sure that a lead ball was going to tear through him at any moment.

But he made it. A hundred paces, more, and no one yelled. No shot cracked the night. Farther. Two hundred paces more, and he saw light off to his left, a campfire. It had burned so low it was barely more than coals now. Kip tried not to look directly at it to save his vision. There was no tent, no bedrolls nearby, just the fire.

Kip tried Master Danais trick for seeing in darkness. He let his focus relax and tried to view things from the periphery of his vision. Nothing but an irregularity, perhaps. He moved closer.

Two men lay on the cold ground. One was a soldier. Kip had seen his mother unconscious plenty of times; he knew instantly this man wasn't passed out. He was sprawled unnaturally, there were no blankets, and his mouth hung open, slack-jawed, eyes staring unblinking at the night. Next to the dead soldier lay another man, bound in chains but alive. He lay on his side, hands manacled behind his back, a black bag over his head and cinched tight around his neck.

The prisoner was alive, trembling. No, weeping. Kip looked around; there was no one else in sight.

'Why don't you just finish it, damn you?' the prisoner said.

Kip froze. He thought he'd approached silently.

'Coward,' the prisoner said. 'Just following your orders, I suppose? Orholam will smite you for what you're about to do to that little town.'

Kip had no idea what the man was talking about.

Apparently his silence spoke for him.

'You're not one of them.' A note of hope entered the prisoner's voice. 'Please, help me!'

Kip stepped forward. The man was suffering. Then he stopped. Looked at the dead soldier. The front of the soldier's shirt was soaked with blood. Had this prisoner killed him? How?

'Please, leave me chained if you must. But please, I don't want to die in darkness.'

Kip stayed back, though it felt cruel. 'You killed him?'

'I'm supposed to be executed at first light. I got away. He chased me down and got the bag over my head before he died. If dawn's close, his replacement is coming anytime now.'

Kip still wasn't putting it together. No one in Rekton trusted the soldiers who came through, and the alcaldesa had told the town's young people to give any soldiers a wide berth for a while – apparently the new satrap Garadul had declared himself free of the Chromeria's control. Now he was King Garadul, he said, but he wanted the usual levies from the town's young people. The alcaldesa had told his representative that if he wasn't the satrap anymore, he didn't have the right to raise levies. King or satrap, Garadul couldn't be happy with that, but Rekton was too small to bother with. Still, it would be wise to avoid his soldiers until this all blew over.

On the other hand, just because Rekton wasn't getting along with the satrap right now didn't make this man Kip's friend.

'So you *are* a criminal?' Kip asked.

'Of six shades to Sun Day,' the man said. The hope leaked out of his voice. 'Look, boy – you are a child, aren't you? You sound like one. I'm going to die today. I can't get away. Truth to tell, I don't want to. I've run enough. This time, I fight.'

'I don't understand.'

'You will. Take off my hood.'

Though some vague doubt nagged Kip, he untied the half-knot around the man's neck and pulled off the hood.

At first, Kip had no idea what the prisoner was talking about. The man sat up, arms still bound behind his back. He was perhaps thirty years old, Tyrean like Kip but with a lighter complexion, his hair wavy rather than kinky, his limbs thin and muscular. Then Kip saw his eyes.

Men and women who could harness light and make luxin – drafters – always had unusual eyes. A little residue of whatever color they drafted ended up in their eyes. Over the course of their life, it would stain the entire iris red, or blue, or whatever their color was. The prisoner was a green drafter – or had been. Instead of the green being bound in a halo within the iris, it was shattered like crockery smashed to the floor. Little green fragments glowed even in the whites of his eyes. Kip gasped and shrank back.

'Please!' the man said. 'Please, the madness isn't on me. I won't hurt you.'

'You're a color wight.'

'And now you know why I ran away from the Chromeria,' the man said.

Because the Chromeria put down color wights like a farmer put down a beloved, rabid dog.

Kip was on the verge of bolting, but the man wasn't making any threatening moves. And besides, it was still dark. Even color wights needed light to draft. The mist did seem lighter, though, gray beginning to touch the horizon. It was crazy to talk to a madman, but maybe it wasn't too crazy. At least until dawn.

The color wight was looking at Kip oddly. 'Blue eyes.' He laughed.

Kip scowled. He hated his blue eyes. It was one thing when a foreigner like Master Danavis had blue eyes. They looked fine on him. Kip looked freakish.

'What's your name?' the color wight asked.

Kip swallowed, thinking he should probably run away.

'Oh, for Orsola sake, you think I'm going to hex you with your name? How ignorant is this backwater? That isn't how chromatology works—'

'Kip.'

The color wight grinned. 'Kip. Well, Kip, have you ever wondered why you were stuck in such a small life? Have you ever gotten the feeling, Kip, that you're special?'

Kip said nothing. Yes, and yes.

'Do you know *why* you feel destined for something greater?'

'Why?' Kip asked, quiet, hopeful.

'Because you're an arrogant little shit.' The color wight laughed.

Kip shouldn't have been taken off guard. His mother had said worse. Still, it took him a moment. A small failure. 'Burn in hell, coward,' he said. 'You're not even good at running away. Caught by ironwood soldiers.'

The color wight laughed louder. 'Oh, they didn't *catch* me. They recruited me.'

Who would recruit madmen to join them? 'They didn't know you were a—'

'Oh, they knew.'

Dread like a weight dropped into Kip's stomach. 'You said something about my town. Before. What are they planning to do?'

'You know, Orsola got a sense of humour. Never realized that till now. Orphan, aren't you?'

'No. I've got a mother,' Kip said. He instantly regretted giving the color wight even that much.

'Would you believe me if I told you there's a prophecy about you?'

'It wasn't funny the first time,' Kip said. 'What's going to happen to my town?' Dawn was coming, and Kip wasn't going to stick around. Not only would the guard's replacement come then, but Kip had no idea what the wight would do once he had light.

'You know,' the wight said, 'you're the reason I'm here. Not here here. Not like "Why do I exist?" Not in Tyrea. In chains, I mean.'

'What?' Kip asked.

'There's power in madness, Kip. Of course . . .' He trailed off, laughed at a private thought. Recovered. 'Look, that soldier has a key in his breast pocket. I couldn't get it out, not with—' He shook his hands, bound and manacled behind his back.

'And I would help you why?' Kip asked.

'For a few straight answers before dawn.'

Crazy, and cunning. *Perfect.* 'Give me one first,' Kip said.

'Shoot.'

'What's the plan for Rekton?'

'Fire.'

'What?' Kip asked.

'Sorry, you said one answer.'

'That was no answer!'

'They're going to wipe out your village. Make an example so no one else defies King Garadul. Other villages defied the king too, of course. His rebellion against the Chromeria isn't popular everywhere.

For every town burning to take vengeance on the Prism, there's another that wants nothing to do with war. Your village was chosen specially. Anyway, I had a little spasm of conscience and objected. Words were exchanged. I punched my superior. Not totally my fault. They know us greens don't do rules and hierarchy. Especially not once we've broken the halo.' The color wight shrugged. 'There, straight. I think that deserves the key, don't you?'

It was too much information to soak up at once – broken the halo? – but it *was* a straight answer. Kip walked over to the dead man. His skin was pallid in the rising light. Pull it together, Kip. Ask whatever you need to ask.

Kip could tell that dawn was coming. Eerie shapes were emerging from the night. The great twin looming masses of Sundered Rock itself were visible mostly as a place where stars were blotted out of the sky.

What do I need to ask?

He was hesitating, not wanting to touch the dead man. He knelt. 'Why my town?' He poked through the dead man's pocket, careful not to touch skin. It was there, two keys.

'They think you have something that belongs to the king. I don't know what. I only picked up that much by eavesdropping.'

'What would Rekton have that the king wants?' Kip asked.

'Not Rekton you. You you.'

It took Kip a second. He touched his own chest. 'Me? Me personally? I don't even own anything!'

The color wight gave a crazy grin, but Kip thought it was a pretense. 'Tragic mistake, then. Their mistake, your tragedy.'

'What, you think I'm lying?!' Kip asked. 'You think I'd be out here scavenging luxin if I had any other choice?'

'I don't really care one way or the other. You going to bring that key over here, or do I need to ask real nice?'

It was a mistake to bring the keys over. Kip knew it. The color wight wasn't stable. He was dangerous. He'd admitted as much. But he had kept his word. How could Kip do less?

Kip unlocked the man's manacles, and then the padlock on the chains. He backed away carefully, as one would from a wild animal. The color wight pretended not to notice, simply rubbing his arms and stretching back and forth. He moved over to the guard and poked through his pockets again. His hand emerged with a pair of green spectacles with one cracked lens.

'You could come with me,' Kip said. 'If what you said is true—'

'How close do you think I'd get to your town before someone came running with a musket? Besides, once the sun comes up . . . I'm ready for it to be done.' The color wight took a deep breath, staring at the horizon. 'Tell me, Kip, if you've done bad things your whole life, but you die doing something good, do you think that makes up for all the bad?'

'No,' Kip said, honestly, before he could stop himself.

'Me neither.'

'But it's better than nothing,' Kip said. 'Orholam is merciful.'

'Wonder if you'll say that after they're done with your village.'

There were other questions Kip wanted to ask, but everything had happened in such a rush that he couldn't put his thoughts together.

In the rising light Kip saw what had been hidden in the fog and the darkness. Hundreds of tents were laid out in military precision. Soldiers. Lots of soldiers. And even as Kip stood, not two hundred paces from the nearest tent, the plain began winking. Glimmers sparkled as broken luxin gleamed, like stars scattered on the ground, answering their brethren in the sky.

It was what Kip had come for. Usually when a drafter released luxin, it simply dissolved, no matter what color it was. But in battle, there had been so much chaos, so many drafters, some sealed magic had been buried and protected from the sunlight that would break it down. The recent rain had uncovered more.

But Kip's eyes were pulled from the winking luxin by four soldiers and a man with a stark red cloak and red spectacles walking toward them from the camp.

'My name is Gaspar, by the by. Gaspar Elos.' The color wight didn't look at Kip.

'What?'

'I'm not just some drafter. My father loved me. I had plans. A girl. A life.'

'I don't—'

'You will.' The color wight put the green spectacles on; they fit perfectly, tight to his face, lenses sweeping to either side so that wherever he looked, he would be looking through a green filter. 'Now get out of here.'

As the sun touched the horizon, Gaspar sighed. It was as if Kip had ceased to exist. It was like watching his mother take that first deep breath of haze. Between the sparkling spars of darker green, the whites of Gaspar's eyes swirled like droplets of green blood hitting water, first dispersing, then staining the whole. The emerald green of lupin ballooned through his eyes, thickened until it was solid, and then spread. Through his cheeks, up to his hairline, then down his neck, standing out starkly when it finally filled his lighter fingernails as if they'd been painted in radiant jade.

Gaspar started laughing. It was a low, unreasoning cackle, unrelenting. Mad. Not a preteens this time.

Kip ran.

He reached the funerary hill where the sentry had been, taking care to stay on the far side from the army. He had to get to Master Danais. Master Danais always knew what to do.

There was no sentry on the hill now. Kip turned around in time to see Gaspar change, transform. Green lupin spilled out of his hands onto his body, covering every part of him like a shell, like an enormous suit of armors. Kip couldn't see the soldiers or the red drafter approaching Gaspar, but he did see a Recall the size of his head streak toward the color wight, hit his chest, and burst apart, throwing flames everywhere.

Gaspar rammed through it, flaming red luxin sticking to his green armor. He was magnificent, terrible, powerful. He ran toward the soldiers, screaming defiance, and disappeared from Kip's view.

Kip fled, the vermilion sun setting fire to the mists.

CHAPTER 2

Gavin Guile sleepily eyed the papers that slid under his door and wondered what Karris was punishing him for this time. His rooms occupied half of the top floor of the Chromeria, but the panoramic windows were blackened so that if he slept at all, he could sleep in. The seal on the letter pulsed so gently that Gavin couldn't tell what color had been drafted into it. He propped himself up in bed so he could get a better look and dilated his pupils to gather as much light as possible.

Superviolet. Oh, sonuva—

On every side, the floor-to-ceiling blackened windows dropped into the floor, bathing the room in full-spectrum light as the morning sun was revealed, climbing the horizon over the dual islands. With his eyes dilated so far, magic flooded Gavin. It was too much to hold.

Light exploded from him in every direction, passing through him in successive waves from superviolet down. The sub-red was last, rushing through his skin like a wave of flame. He jumped out of bed, sweating instantly. But with all the windows open, cold summer morning winds blasted through his chambers, chilling him. He yelped, hopping back into bed.

His yelp must have been loud enough for Karris to hear it and know that her rude awakening had been successful, because he heard her unmistakable laugh. She wasn't a super-violet, so she must have had a friend help her with her little prank. A quick shot of superviolet luxin at the room's controls threw the windows closed and set the filters to half. Gavin extended a hand to blast his door open, then stopped. He wasn't going to give Karris the satisfaction. Her assignment to be the White's fetch-and-carry girl had ostensibly been intended to teach her humility and gravitas. So far that much had been a spectacular failure, though the White always played a deeper game. Still, Gavin couldn't help grinning as he rose and swept the folded papers Karris had tucked under the door into his hand.

He walked to his door. On a small service table just outside, he found his breakfast on a platter. It was the same every morning: two squat bricks of bread and a pale wine in a clear glass cup. The bread was made of wheat, barley, beans, lentils, millet, and spelt, unleavened. A man could live on that bread. In fact, a man *was* living on that bread. Just not Gavin. Indeed, the sight of it made his stomach turn. He could order a different breakfast, of course, but he never did.

He brought it inside, setting the papers on the table next to the bread. One was odd, a plain note that didn't look like the White's personal stationery, nor any official hard white stationery the Chromeria used. He turned it over. The Chromeria's message office had marked it as being received from 'ST, Rekton': Satrapy of Tyrea, town of Rekton. It sounded familiar, maybe one of those towns near Sundered Rock? But then, there had once been so many towns there. Probably someone begging an audience, though those letters were supposed to be screened out and dealt with separately.

Still, first things first. He tore open each loaf, checking that nothing had been concealed inside it. Satisfied, he took out a bottle of the blue dye he kept in a drawer and dribbled a bit into the wine. He swirled the wine to mix it, and held the glass up against the granite blue sky of a painting he kept on the wall as his reference.

He'd done it perfectly, of course. He'd been doing this for almost six thousand mornings now. Almost sixteen years. A long time for a man only thirty-three years old. He poured the wine over the broken halves of the bread, staining it blue – and harmless. Once a week, Gavin would prepare a blue cheese or blue fruit, but it took more time. He picked up the note from Tyrea. 'I'm dying, Gavin. It's time you meet your son Kip – Lina'

Son? I don't have a—

Suddenly his throat clamped down, and his chest felt like his heart was seizing up, no matter that the chirurgeons said it wasn't. Just relax, they said. Young and strong as a warhorse, they said. They didn't say, Grow a pair. You've got lots of friends, your enemies fear you, and you have no rivals. You're the Prism. What are you afraid of? No one had talked to him that way in years. Sometimes he wished they would.

Orholam, the note hadn't even been sealed.

Gavin walked out onto his glass balcony, subconsciously checking his drafting as he did every morning. He stared at his hand, splitting sunlight into its component colors as only he could do, filling each finger in turn with a color, from below the visible spectrum to above it: sub-red, red, orange, yellow, green, blue, superviolet. Had he felt a hitch there when he drafted blue? He double-checked it, glancing briefly toward the sun.

No, it was still easy to split light, still flawless. He released the luxin, each color sliding out and dissipating like smoke from beneath his fingernails, releasing the familiar bouquet of resinous scents.

He turned his face to the sun, its warmth like a mother's caress. Gavin opened his eyes and sucked in a warm, soothing red. In and out, in time with his labored breaths, willing them to slow. Then he let the red go and took in a deep icy blue. It felt like it was freezing his eyes. As ever, the blue brought clarity, peace, order. But not a plan, not with so little information. He let go of the colors. He was still fine. He still had at least five of his seven years left. Plenty of time. Five years, five *great* purposes.

Well, maybe not five *great* purposes.

Still, of his predecessors in the last four hundred years, aside from those who'd been assassinated or died of other causes, the rest had served for exactly seven, fourteen, or twenty-one years after becoming Prism. Gavin had made it past fourteen. So, plenty of time. No reason to think he'd be the exception. Not many, anyway.

He picked up the second note. Cracking the White's seal – the old crone sealed everything, though she shared the other half of this floor and Karris hand-delivered her messages. But everything had to be in its proper place, properly done. There was no mistaking that she'd risen from Blue.

The White's note read, 'Unless you would prefer to greet the students arriving late this morning, my dear Lord Prism, please attend me on the roof.'

Looking beyond the Chromeria's buildings and the city, Gavin studied the merchant ships in the bay cupped in the lee of Big Jasper Island. A ragged-looking Atashian sloop was maneuvering in to dock directly at a pier.

Greeting new students. Unbelievable. It wasn't that he was too good to greet new students – well, actually, it *was* that. He, the White, and the Spectrum were supposed to balance each other. But though the

Spectrum feared him the most, the reality was that the crone got her way more often than Gavin and the seven Colors combined. This morning she had to be wanting to experiment on him again, and if he wanted to avoid something more onerous like teaching he'd better get to the top of the tower.

Gavin drafted his red hair into a tight ponytail and dressed in the clothes his room slave had laid out for him: an ivory shirt and a well-cut pair of black wool pants with an oversize gem-studded belt, boots with silverwork, and a black cloak with harsh old Ilytian runic designs embroidered in silver thread. The Prism belonged to all the satrapies, so Gavin did his best to honor the traditions of every land – even one that was mainly pirates and heretics.

He hesitated a moment, then pulled open a drawer and drew out his brace of Ilytian pistols. They were, typical for Ilytian work, the most advanced design Gavin had ever seen. The firing mechanism was far more reliable than a wheellock – they were calling it a flintlock. Each pistol had a long blade beneath the barrel, and even a belt-flange so that when he tucked them into his belt behind his back they were held securely and at an angle so he didn't skewer himself when he sat. The Ilytians thought of everything.

And, of course, the pistols made the White's Blackguards nervous. Gavin grinned.

When he turned for the door and saw the painting again, his grin dropped.

He walked back to the table with the blue bread. Grabbing one use-smoothened edge of the painting, he pulled. It swung open silently, revealing a narrow chute.

Nothing menacing about the chute. Too small for a man to climb up, even if he overcame everything else. It might have been a laundry chute. Yet to Gavin it looked like the mouth of hell, the evernight itself opening wide for him. He tossed one of the bricks of bread into it, then waited. There was a thunk as the hard bread hit the first lock, a small hiss as it opened, then closed, then a smaller thunk as it hit the next lock, and a few moments later one last thunk. Each of the locks was still working. Everything was normal. Safe. There had been mistakes over the years, but no one had to die this time. No need for paranoia. He nearly snarled as he slammed the painting closed.

CHAPTER 3

Three thunks. Three hisses. Three gates between him and freedom. The chute spat a torn brick of bread at the prisoner's face. He caught it, almost without looking. He knew it was blue, the still blue of a deep lake in early morning, when night still hoards the sky and the air dares not caress the water's skin. Unadulterated by any other color, drafting that blue was difficult. Worse, drafting it made the prisoner feel bored, passionless, at peace, in harmony with even this place. And he needed the fire of hatred today. Today, he would escape.

After all his years here, sometimes he couldn't even see the color, like he had awoken to a world painted in grays. The first year had been the worst. His eyes, so accustomed to nuance, so adept at parsing every spectrum of light, had begun deceiving him. He'd hallucinated colors. He tried to draft those colors into the tools to break this prison. But imagination wasn't enough to make magic, one needed light. Real light. He'd been a Prism, so any color would do, from those above violet to the ones below red. He'd gathered the very heat from his own body, soaked his eyes in those sub-reds, and flung that against the tedious blue walls.

Of course, the walls were hardened against such pathetic amounts of heat. He'd drafted a blue dagger and sawn at his wrist. Where the blood dripped onto the stone floor, it was immediately leached of color. The next time, he'd cupped his own blood in his hands to try to draft red, but he couldn't get enough color given that the only light in the cell was blue. Bleeding onto the bread hadn't worked either. Its natural brown was always stained blue, so adding red only yielded a dark, purplish brown. Undraftable. Of course. His brother had thought of everything. But then, he always had.

The prisoner sat next to the drain and began eating. The dungeon was shaped like a flattened ball: the walls and ceiling a perfect sphere, the floor less steep but still sloping toward the middle. The walls were lit from within, every surface emitting the same color light. The only shadow in the dungeon was the prisoner himself. There were only two holes: the chute above, which released his food and one steady rivulet of water that he had to lick for his moisture, and the drain below for his waste.

He had no utensils, no tools except his hands and his will, always his will. With his will, he could draft anything from the blue that he wanted, though it would dissolve as soon as his will released it, leaving only dust and a faint mineral-andresin odor.

But today was going to be the day his vengeance began, his first day of freedom. This attempt wouldn't fail – he refused to even think of it as an 'attempt' – and there was work to be done. Things had to be done in order. He couldn't remember now if he had always been this way or if he'd soaked in blue for so long that the color had changed him fundamentally.

He knelt next to the only feature of the cell that his brother hadn't created. A single, shallow depression in the floor, a bowl. First he rubbed the bowl with his bare hands, grinding the corrosive oils from his fingertips into the stone for as long as he dared. Scar tissue didn't produce oil, so he had to stop before he rubbed his fingers raw. He scraped two fingernails along the crease between his nose and face, two others between his ears and head, gathering more oil. Anywhere he could collect oils from his body, he did, and rubbed it into the bowl. Not that there was any discernible change, but over the years his bowl had become deep enough to cover his finger to the second joint. His jailer had bound the color-leaching hellstones into the floor in a grid. Whatever spread far enough to cross one of those lines lost all color almost instantly. But hellstone was terribly expensive. How deep did they go?

If the grid only extended a few thumbs into the stone, his raw fingers might reach beyond it any day. Freedom wouldn't be far behind. But if his jailer had used enough hellstone that the crosshatching lines ran a foot deep, then he'd been rubbing his fingers raw for almost six thousand days for nothing. He'd die here. Someday, his brother would come down, see the little bowl – his only mark on the world – and laugh. With that laughter echoing in his ears, he felt a small spark of anger in his breast. He blew on that spark, basked in its warmth. It was fire enough to help him move, enough to counter the soothing, debilitating blue down here.

Finished, he urinated into the bowl. And watched.

For a moment, filtered through the yellow of his urine, the cursed blue light was sliced with green. His breath caught. Time stretched as the green stayed green . . . stayed green. By Orholam, he'd done it. He'd gone deep enough. He'd broken through the hellstone!

And then the green disappeared. In exactly the same two seconds it took every day. He screamed in frustration, but even his frustration was weak, his scream more to assure himself he could still hear than real fury.

The next part still drove him crazy. He knelt by the depression. His brother had turned him into an animal. A dog, playing with his own shit. But that emotion was too old, mined too many times to give him any real warmth. Six thousand days on, he was too debased to resent his debasement. Putting both hands into his urine, he scrubbed it around the bowl as he had scrubbed his oils. Even leached of all color, urine was still urine. It should still be acidic. It should corrode the hellstone faster than the skin oils alone would.

Or the urine might neutralize the oils. He might be pushing the day of his escape further and further away. He had no idea. That was what made him crazy, not immersing his fingers in warm urine. Not anymore.

He scooped the urine out of the bowl and dried it with a wad of blue rags: his clothes, his pillow, now stinking of urine. Stinking of urine for so long that the stench didn't offend him anymore. It didn't matter. What mattered was that the bowl had to be dry by tomorrow so he could try again.

Another day, another failure. Tomorrow, he would try sub-red again. It had been a while. He'd recovered enough from his last attempt. He should be strong enough for it. If nothing else, his brother had taught him how strong he really was. And maybe that was what made him hate Gavin more than anything. But it was a hatred as cold as his cell.

orbit